DIMMER

of the

LIGHT

DISAVOWED BIRTHRIGHT BOOK 2

BRITTON BRINKLEY

Dimmer of the Light

BRITTON BRINKLEY

LANDINGHAM STANLEY PRESS

Don't hide your dark side. Embrace it, like the bad bitch you are.

Author's Note

Dimmer of the Light is a continuation through Bryony Guthrie's complicated existence as a Grisym. This story is a wild ride through the pain of separating from the life you've been told to live and choosing the one for yourself. Bryony will find her family, and she will give her heart to her men, but don't take a moment to blink or breathe. They don't get the chance, so neither should you.

These characters put me on the craziest rollercoaster this time and said, 'Good luck surviving without a harness.' I should have known better. I should have expected them to act like fools and for there to be so many skeletons in the closet that none of us would know how to handle them all. As I was writing this book, I legitimately had no idea what was going to happen next.

In a world where it's never clear who is on what side until their actions prove it, I felt for Bryony. For all of them.

Anyway, I hope you enjoy this train wreck of a crazy ride. I sure did.

P.S. You are not allowed to yell at me for the ending.

Trigger/Content Warnings:

The chosen one/most powerful

Why Choose Romance

- Dark Magic

- Divide Between Magical Beings (Similar to discrimination)

- Extreme violence

- Death threats

- Assault between opposite sexes

- Explicit language

- Explicit sexual content

- Sex with non-human creatures

- Sex with multiple partners (individually and in group settings)

- Necromancy (mentioned)

- Student-teacher relationship

- Betrayal by family

- LGBTQ+ side characters

- Murder/violent murder

- Knife play

<u>For the most up-to-date list of trigger and content warnings:</u>

Prelude

I was born of the light and the dark.

A product of the luminescence that guides you through the shadowy claws of the darkness.

I am the one you hunt. The one you fear. The one you will bow to.

Many forced me to hide who I am. Others led the way so I may embrace what lives inside me.

I have been both a coward and brave.

But now I am only one.

I am a Grisym.

I am your worst nightmare and your only hope.

Choose a side.

Just know, if it's not mine, I can only be your destruction.

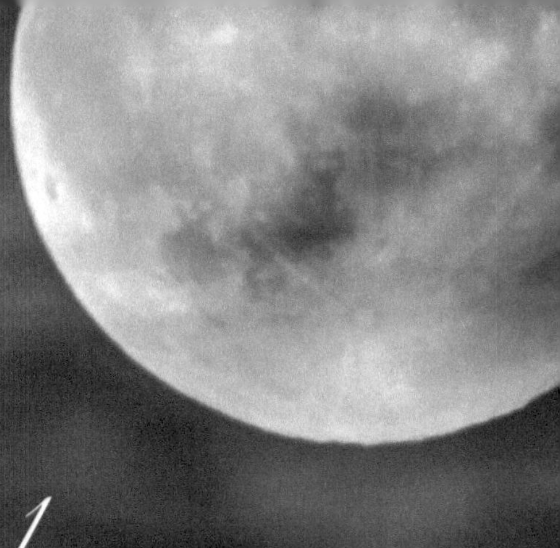

1

BRYONY

It's the endless abyss where calm can find you. It's that freefall off the edge of a cliff, knowing the water below will engulf you as the light dims and the onyx depths engulf you.

In the dark, we can be our true selves. We can let go of the stigma others have burdened us with. We can leave behind the insecurities and embrace the strands of gray we all possess.

Morality no longer sits at the heart of the chaos. The division between right and wrong becomes the blurred eye of the storm.

I am the storm.

The slow wave of my fingers at my side is a reminder of the power that hums beneath the surface. Docile when it chooses to be. Capable of striking the throats of our enemies before wrapping tight and squeezing. Here in the dark, while they choke on their hatred and betrayal, they'll never witness the joy splashed across our faces as we steal lives from them as they are trying to do to us.

That darkness consumes me now. My light side is fading so quickly that there's no holding on to it. The twinkling light pulsing slower and slower as it's shoved out of my consciousness. A shedding of the wielder I've lived as to reveal the one I've become.

That untapped power tingles at my fingertips. Curious. Hungry. Ruthless. Unwilling to be tucked away in a forgotten corner now that I've called on it.

If only we could all live in this judgment-free space.

A body bumps into mine, pulling me out of my villainous thoughts. Still, I don't move. Every detailed movement of the opposing side keeps my eyes shifting to follow them. To watch them continue to fight, scream, and scurry like the scared little mice they are.

Opposition. A concept I once viewed as being solely two-sided. A concept that I thought was always clear in its presentation. Roman Avalon, the man I considered my father for twenty-five years, proved me wrong tonight. He and every wielder he brought to stand with him.

The panic in their voices only makes the corners of my mouth twitch. My lips eager to twist up into a wicked grin as I watch them come to terms with the grave mistake they made tonight. They expected a simple triumph, but the confrontation left them scared and wounded. Overconfidence left many of them dead.

Fear blankets their unfocused eyes. Their chests heaving with their ragged breaths and erratic heart rates. They've witnessed what I can do. A reality that has shredded any desire to remain here.

I'm not supposed to exist.

There's no making out the words of anyone around me. Not from them or the New Order, and with my friends at my back. Voices drifting in and out of focus and muffled as if I'm standing under water, watching the scene play out before my eyes.

But I feel everything.

Their panic. Their rage. The unbridled fear. Even their curiosity.

With a slow, inhaled breath, I call on my focus, zeroing in on their words. Trying to decipher what they say, I still can't move. All I can do is watch and listen.

One word echoes. A name, but not my name.

Valen.

One of mine. One of the men I chose before I pledged my life to my biological father, Jorddan Guthrie.

Valen. Where is he?

As if hearing his name called repeatedly once again wakes me, I jolt out of the trance I'd been in. My body sways, sinking into the chaos surging around me. Screaming, running, bloodied clothes, and thrown curses.

Opening my fist, the ball of light still dances across my palm. Its edges darker than they had been when I first took it. My essence already determined to make this bit of raw power part of us.

I let it roll over my skin, trying to identify its source. Innate, extrinsic, charter. From the living or the inanimate. I can't tell, but allow it to seep beneath my skin anyhow. My insides dance with the new power swirling beneath my skin.

Mine.

My gaze tracks back to the light wielders, once again mobilizing. Their cautious steps edging them further away.

I'm not one of them. Not anymore.

Not since discovering what I am. Who I am.

Grisym.

More dark than light, judging by my particular gift as an Eistiab. A power driven by possession.

My palms raise, clean and unscathed. No dirt or grime, just a mix of power running beneath my skin. The dark and the light combining to form something unique. A product of my father, Jorddan, the most sought-after dark wielder in our world, and my mother, Geneva Avalon, picture-perfect wielder of the light.

The world views my father as the one to fear. He's the name that infiltrates nightmares. If only they knew what my essence would do to them for harming anyone I care for. No one will hurt them. Not anymore. Never again.

Before tonight, I've been slowly coming to terms with the truth of how our world operates. I chose a side. I stood by my convictions, though that seed of doubt continued to grow inside me. Hesitation I could usually stamp down, but it's hard to leave behind the only life you've ever known. At times, it takes a push, and tonight was mine.

For the first time, my chin confidently rises, knowing I'd sworn allegiance to the right side of this war.

"Pierce," I call out.

Warm breaths hit my cheek in harsh puffs. Pierson Flaggstaff's chest is pumping so high from exertion that it seems unnatural. Blood coats the front of his shirt and his hands. Hands that shake, covered in blood that doesn't seem to be his. "Whose blood is that?"

"Valen was hit," he croaks. A deep inhale sucked in before he finger-combs the hair off his forehead.

I swallow hard.

Of all my men, he's the one I'd sacrifice first, but part of me still needs him. Still wants and craves him.

Despite the threats and taunts and cuts and punctures from his precious daggers, if he dies, I won't forgive myself. We've found understanding between us. A bond my body eagerly wants to continue to explore and my brain desires to exploit, siphoning every bit of knowledge I can from him.

Valen has been my key to better understanding the ghouls. Without him, we might not be here. Without him, I don't know what happens after tonight.

If I can help it, he's not dying out here in these damn woods.

"Make them forget," I order Pierce, another of my chosen men.

Shaking fingers grab my arm, spinning me so we're nose to nose. "Bri, we don't have time. We need to get Val—"

"Make. Them. Forget," I growl. "Or I will have to do it myself." My lip quivers as I stare up into those pleading denim-blue eyes. I may hold Pierce's gift now, but I don't know that I'm proficient enough to force dozens of memories away. In truth, I'm not sure his ability to take away someone's choice works that way, but I'm desperate.

I'm grasping at every straw I can to protect us. To protect me and my dad.

Allowing our rivals to keep memories of this evening would be a mistake. It's too risky and puts us at a significant disadvantage.

Roman needs to pay. He needs to be brought down to a level so low he's looking up at the dirt beneath my boot. If only I knew how. Exhaustion and a storm of emotions steal my focus. I've got nothing. There's no grand plan or clear path to revenge. There's just protecting the people who stood at our backs tonight.

Black tendrils swirl around Pierce's fingertips, coiling tight around his ankles before shooting out into the area where Roman and his supporters still stand. Someone else gave them light, their confused and fear-stricken faces clearly visible now.

"Look!" someone screeches, pointing down at Pierce's essence, dark as night, zipping toward them in a single stream before splitting into dozens of streaks. Each one moves like a snake released from its cage, slithering up their bodies and crawling around their necks.

When the tendril wraps around Roman's throat, he fights. He was the first man I loved. A man who pretended to care for me. If nothing else, habit should keep me from enjoying watching him tear at the ropes of magic. The shift of his face from beet red to plum almost making me giggle. A reaction my heart struggles to accept. *It isn't right.*

We share one more look. His eyes filled with hatred and disgust. Pride used to fill those blue eyes when he looked at me.

Maybe it had been something else all along. Perhaps it was the sheen of seeing the key to your prize right in front of you.

My heart breaks a little. Foolishly, I believed he could love me, given my nature, my past. Lesson learned.

We're locked in an endless stare-down, neither one of us willing to care, and then everything seems to stop. They each stand tall, hands at their sides as Pierce's tendrils fade into nothing. He's extrinsic. He doesn't get the magic back once it's used.

As one, they turn, their steps synchronized as they march through the dark.

"Where did you send them?" I ask.

"Back to their lives."

The sound of their steps crunching over the debris of the forest floor slowly fades. "Thank you," I sigh, once again staring at my hands before facing Pierce. "Where's Valen?"

Pierce leads me to a crowd. Every voice tumbles over one another. Their knees pressing into the hard earth, kneeling beside Valen's still body. The pool of blood continuing to spread beneath him, seeping into their pants and coating their hands and clothing.

And the tough-girl facade shatters. "Val. Valen!" I shake him as Graham wraps him in tendrils of his essence, each one working to staunch the bleeding.

"Graham, move." My hand flies out to shove him, but my father holds me back. Strong arms wrap around my middle, keeping me from reaching him. Keeping me from helping keep Valen alive.

"Let him help," my father speaks close to my ear. "He's the closest thing we have to a healer right now."

"What?" I pant.

My father inhales deeply, his hold on me tightening. "Your friend here is what I like to call a mender. He can take the smallest elements of an object and bring them back together." The words are delivered calmly. Matter-of-factly. The tone so even I can slowly relax into it.

"Graham?" I whimper. The sound makes me want to cringe at how weak it sounds, passing my trembling lower lip.

"Bri, I'll explain later. Okay?" Graham Mayer—another of my men—is no stranger to using that exasperated tone with me. It comes out with every acknowledgment of my choices he doesn't agree with.

This isn't the time for a pointless argument. I need him to save Valen. So, I nod, no longer fighting against my father's hold.

Tears burn behind my eyes, each blink meant to keep them from falling as the ground quakes beneath us. Every set of eyes tracks behind me, my ass aching from the ground beneath me. Shifting to my knees and then stumbling to my feet, a crowd of ghouls hovers nearby, staring down at us with those milky white eyes.

Their massive, gnarled bodies are intimidating in the dark, but they are mine. The ghouls answer to me. Tonight proved it, without a doubt.

My Azukeen crouches low. "Bryony, take Valen with me." Though the words are still garbled, its speech seems to get clearer each time it speaks. I didn't have to struggle to understand it for once.

"Where?"

"Hell Gate." It points off into the distance, stretching to its full height. My gaze drifts down to where its massive cock stood the last time we met, but there's nothing.

"Absolutely not," Graham jumps up from his spot beside Valen, his tendrils still encasing his lifeless body. "Light wielders can't go anywhere near the Hell Gates."

"I'm not a light wielder," I grit out. Now that I've told so many, it will be nearly impossible to hide. But I'll have to, won't I? When I return to the Beaux-graton School of Wielding—if I return—I'll still be Bryony Avalon, daughter of Roman and Geneva Avalon, light wielder.

"Take us," I say to the Azukeen.

It steps forward, cradling Valen in its arms, those massive palms like cocoons around his body.

Resting a hand on my father's arm, I hate that worry creases his brow. "Dad, will you be able to track where we end up?"

Jorddan nods. "It will take you to London. To your brother."

My eyes grow wide, but I only nod as I follow my Azukeen and the horde of ghouls. Through the woods. Through the dark. All alone.

2

BRYONY

The wielding world is all I've ever known. I spent my entire existence being told about the wielding world. I took in everything I could, only to realize I knew nothing. Nothing outside of the restricted facts my family wanted to expose me to.

My knowledge of the dark side sprang from the individuals Roman chose to keep around our family. Facts and stories that held their biases in every word. In retrospect, my ignorance is unsurprising. How would I know what a Hell Gate looks like when they brushed the dark aside? I expected beautifully constructed arches or wrought iron designs would signal your entrance into an underworld that only ghouls enter.

But there's nothing—only the trees and dirt, twigs and patches of frozen, trampled grass.

There's nothing but air.

I can't slow my breathing as my gaze scales the towering trees, before squinting into the gloom of the night. The snap of twigs beneath my feet as I involuntarily take cautious steps forward leaves me searching harder through the area before me. My forward movement feels like being tugged by an invisible rope, leading me to a place I belong, though I've never been there before.

It's like a beacon calling me home, beckoning toward a treasure that was always mine.

I was wrong.

It's not just stagnant air in front of us, but a portal. A mirror portal. It appears as smooth as softly rippling glass. A mirror image of your side of the world staring back at you.

My fingers itch to reach out and touch it. To feel its power tingle beneath my skin. I've never seen one in person. Council and Bureau leadership are only authorized to use portals that are sanctioned by the Department of Magical Realms to ensure they are secure and safe for travel.

One by one, the ghouls stomp through. Their knees are forever bent in that slight crouch that makes it appear like they're stalking their prey, ready to pounce at any time. With every cut muscle on display, rolling and flexing with their powerful bodies.

Each one touches their palm to the surface that now seems to shimmer with the same sheen as their leathery skin. Within seconds of contact, they disappear through the wall—a seamless transition from here to there.

But where or what is the other?

"Bryony. Come. Bryony. Mine. I protect Bryony and Valen." The Azukeen raises Valen in his arms as if to remind me that it knows who it is referring to. The both of us bonded together, indebted to the limp man dripping blood in his arms.

A fresh wave of tears burns behind my eyes, my breath stalling in my chest, taking in his ashen skin. Those near-black eyes hosting a glassy sheen, seeing nothing.

With the touch of his palm, the Azukeen disappears through the gate.

A frigid gust of wind hits me from behind. The shiver working through my body so violently that my teeth chatter. A reminder that it's the dead of winter in the mountains. I need to move. Valen's life depends on it. Assuming death hasn't already stolen him from me.

Roughly swiping under my eyes, a shuddering breath fills me before placing my palm against the portal.

At first, nothing seems to change as I become immersed in the shimmering portal. The haze distorting the clean lines of the trees until they disappear, and aged stone cages me in. My insides instantly warm. Not with the scorching heat of one of my men touching me or sinking inside my depths. *No*, it's the warmth that finds me when my Azukeen's power flows through me.

Different from Beauxgraton's stone blocks, this tunnel seems whole. Just a single slab of stone with a carved-out center. A slice of magic was used to cut the precise tunnel we're standing in now. All smooth, edges and floor, with ceilings that still leave the tallest ghoul several feet of room. Their horns, some curled into cues and others in a broader arc, are in no danger of catching.

"Bryony. Come." That growled tone pulls my focus to my Azukeen. It once again adjusts Valen's dead weight in its arms, cocking its head, signaling me to follow.

Apprehension, fear, or skepticism should keep me from following so willingly. Yet it doesn't. The ghouls have never tried to harm anyone. They have only served as my protectors.

I ignore the dank scent and the snarls that seem to reverberate off the walls. The clicks of their claws on the stone floors dictate the pace of my steps, my fingertips trailing along the wall. There is no door, nor a turnoff visible. The endless path leading us somewhere.

London.

My father had said they were taking me to London. To my brother. To my family.

It's well known that these tunnel systems are bursting with earth magic. It's what keeps them standing and allows the ghouls access to any Hell Gate in the world. Right now, this is just an endless tunnel leading us to a destination only the ghouls can find.

I've been looking forward to diving deeper into ghoul studies next semester. Knox and Valen thought it would be smart, given my ability to control them.

Valen.

Gods.

He'd better live through this.

The pinpricks of magic tickle my fingertips. Raw power has boundless ways of presenting itself—methods that I can't even begin to understand. It's now clear to me how sheltered a life my father made me live. *No*, not my father. Merely a man feigning devotion to a child who wasn't his.

A liar. A fraud. My enemy.

When power and your personal desires are all that matter, those you destroy along the way are of no consequence. There are no fucks given regarding the hurt and pain caused. It only matters what it costs them, never you.

There were three things Roman Avalon was determined to never lose: my mother, control over my mother by using me as the leash that kept her in line, and his position in the wielding world. As director of education, he holds almost as much power as the Wielding Council, our policymakers.

Roman controls wielder education globally. He has the power to shape us into whatever twisted vision lives in his warped brain. Our minds are his to mold if we let him, and I'll be damned if I do.

Not anymore.

Never again.

My eyes are open now.

"Azukeen," I call to my beast. "How much further?"

There's a round of grunts as if I've disturbed their contemplative silence with my question. "Bryony, call me hers. Not far," it grumbles.

"Yes, you are my Azukeen, but I don't have a name for you." Somehow, I'd known it wanted me to name it. I'm not sure how or why. A gut feeling. Whispered words in my mind.

But from what I know, ghouls are nameless, even within their own species.

"No name. Bryony choose." My brow furrows. There's nothing to guide me in these interactions with the ghouls. Normally, I would ask Valen these questions, but he's still nothing more than a limp doll in the Azukeen's arms.

"I will call you Aziel."

"A-zeel," it sounds out the name. I realize I may have made a mistake choosing a male name when the ghouls know no true gender, but for me, the Azukeen has always been one. "I keep. You name all of us."

"In time. After Valen is safe." The muscles of Aziel's forearm roll beneath my touch. "After we are all safe. I promise."

The ghoul grunts, his pace quickening as the light shifts into a brighter hue around the bend.

The clap of bare ghoul feet on stone vibrates in my ears, but I can no longer see them. I assume that there are additional portals down here in these tunnels, making my heart race a little faster. The soft trickle of water finds my ears next, but despite the damp air here, I've not seen a single droplet of liquid. Not a single trace as my fingers graze over the walls.

No splash as we've continued forward.

Or footprints to prove a water source flows through here.

Just smooth grayish-brown stone. The texture is grainy beneath my touch, cool, but also perfectly dry.

That same shimmering wall of air appears before us, and Aziel steps through without a second thought; he and Valen disappear seconds before I do.

That soft shimmer comes into view ahead. From this side, there's no visibility of what's beyond.

Following Aziel, a field comes into view. A massive house sits slightly uphill. The distance causing the lights to appear as fireflies in the night. His steps don't pause as he moves toward the house, the other ghouls following behind in silence.

I move beside mine, my gaze continuing to dart to the side, hoping to see Valen quirking that cocky grin at me, but he only looks worse. More lost. More lifeless. Dead.

Tall grass brushes along my legs, somehow allowing me to believe I'm warmer than I actually am. I thought Montana was cold, but, fuck, London is like the tundra.

The ghouls at our back stop when we're about twenty feet from the house—the pale exterior like something I've only seen in movies. Only Aziel moves forward so quickly, I worry he's going to burst through the door when it swings open. He ducks inside, stalking through the house until he comes to a living room.

The style is reminiscent of a bygone era. Victorian pieces mixed with soft, functional modern touches. It's beautiful. The details blurring as I jog to keep behind Aziel. His body continuing to crouch through hallways and doors.

"Aziel, where are we?"

He abruptly stops in what must be the formal dining room. A massive table stretches before us, place settings set as if ready to entertain. With a swipe of his arm, he sends everything flying before softly placing Valen on the dark-stained wood.

"Aziel must go. I find Bryony soon."

Placing a hand on its corded forearm, my ghoul looks down at me. A sea of emotions seems to glow in those milky white eyes. Maybe my connection to the ghouls explains my ability to capture them. My eyes changing into those stark, frosty orbs more often, opening me up to them.

"Thank you."

He grunts, huffing loudly before turning on his heel. The house shakes around me with his retreat until a crack sounds in the next room. The sharp noise pierces my ears. That same sound that accompanies a quickly popped balloon expelling its air. I should check, but I don't, determined to stay at Valen's side.

When the second pop sounds, my body goes rigid. "Hello," I call out into the house.

No one answers, and my heart races. My father insisted they'd meet me here, but never said how they were traveling. I would assume by portal. They should have beaten me here, but I'm all alone.

Or am I?

I at least expected Vincent to be here already. A brother, I'm assuming, I've met but only know through photos. Will he want me here? Will he treat me like Harley or Merrick?

Shutting down the anxiety-driven thoughts about my brother, my eyes rake over Valen's prone body once more. My stare is so intense it's as if I am trying to will his heart to beat for me again. A sound I'd grown fond of listening to in bed at night.

Only an hour has passed since I left everyone behind on the Beauxgraton grounds. Not nearly enough time for them to get here unless they portal. But had they, shouldn't they have beaten us here?

Slumping into a chair at Valen's side, the wooden legs creak under my weight. The antique was likely made for display rather than for use, given its age.

Valen has always had rough palms. Palms I'd grown accustomed to having on my skin.

Wrapping his hand in mine, all that remains is the chill of death.

We've never had a relationship like this. Our connection isn't built on soft emotions or spilling our secrets. Just the same, I couldn't stand it if anything happened to him. As he so eloquently stated, no one gets to kill this asshole except for me. Maybe my dad, too.

"Valen, I need you to hang on." I brush his hair off his pale forehead. There's no sign of life. The blaring neon sign flashing *he's already dead* before my eyes, though I won't fully let myself believe it.

Maybe we waited too long.

Likely, we've already lost him.

In my heart, I know we have. "Valen, I'm sorry," I whisper into the silence.

I wish I knew whose strike did this to him. The fury I would rain down on them would leave nothing but ash behind. Valen may not be my favorite person in the world, but he is someone I care about—someone I value. My days would be dull without him.

A barked curse suddenly sounds behind me. My body twisting to stare down the hallway Aziel had stalked down when he left. "I'll be back," I whisper, kissing Valen's frigid cheek. There was no point in voicing the words aloud. He likely couldn't hear them.

Creeping down the hallway, my lungs burn, holding in my deep breath. Too afraid to release it and alert the intruder to my location. It could be anyone. I assume this is my father's house, but maybe it's not.

Turning the corner into the living area we'd come through, they're all right there. My friends, my father, my men.

My entire support system came.

Headmistress Janelle Milgren.

My boyfriends: Graham Mayer, Pierson Flaggstaff, and Professor Wynston Knox.

My father.

Camilla VanBuren, my roommate and best friend, besides Graham.

Collin Pecket.

Valen and Pierce's friends: Damian Haithwaite, Sean Remington, Kaia, and Kormoran Vue.

Behind them stands Lionel Greer. A man I haven't seen since I was a child. Although his face remains the same, his features have changed. There are more creases at the corners of his eyes. The perfectly blackish-brown waves he'd had are now steel gray and white.

His features seem to droop, heavy with the heartbreak written all over his face. The lines at the corners of his eyes and around his mouth are so pronounced that they could hold water.

There are several others I don't recognize, but they all share the same expression. One that speaks of loss, with eyes full of fury.

With every step I take toward them, they part down the middle. The man at the end with eyes so sinister, I stop in my tracks. Eyes, I know, but should fear. There's no need. Somehow, finally meeting his stare, I know this is a brother I will never have to fear. Vincent Guthrie is my blood.

He takes sure strides toward me before pulling me into his chest in a single, swift motion. The beat of his heart slows as a heavy breath releases.

"Welcome home, Bri."

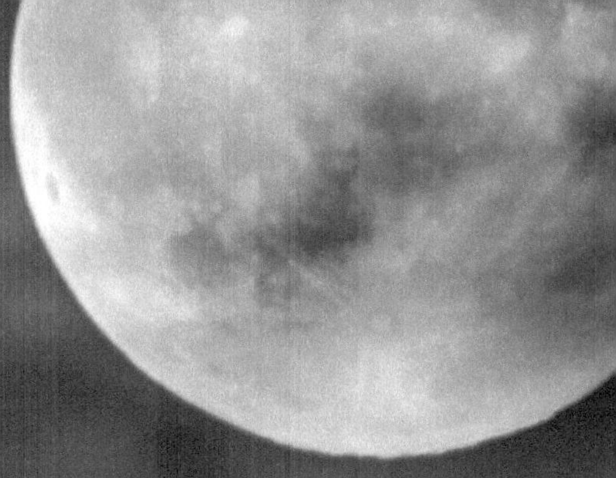

3

BRYONY

I don't remember him at all. There's nothing from the time we spent under the same roof. Everything I know about him is secondhand. Vicious comments in media outlets, Knox, and my father were my only sources.

Shaking my head, as if to clear it, I finally break eye contact. There will be a time and a place to forge that bond. Time to get to know him. But that's not now. Not while Valen's body stretches half the dining room table, either dead or dying.

"I have so many questions," I whisper.

Vincent's heavy palm comes down on my shoulder, squeezing lightly. "Don't worry. You're not leaving here until I get to know my sister." His expression stays vacant. Yet, it's his eyes that give him away. He, too, feels the weight of our separation. Lost years we can never get back. The pain of me never even knowing he was my brother to claim until recently.

"Can you save him?" The words come out sluggish, as if they refused to crawl over my tongue and tumble past my lips.

"That's why you're here instead of anywhere else." This time, a tiny smile tugs at the corner of his mouth. A feature that's a match for mine. With a curt nod, glancing back at the rest of the group, he continues, "I need all of you to stay out here except for Bri and Graham."

"Me?" Graham croaks. His eyes widen, making those greenish-blue and gold irises appear even brighter. So vibrant, it's as if the ocean is racing toward us.

Vincent faces Graham, his arms folding over his chest. "My father said you're a mender."

"Yes, but usually inanimate objects, not people," Graham breathes, backing away with his hands held high.

Vincent grabs hold of his shoulder, his fingers flexing into Graham's flesh. "I can keep Valen alive, but I can't put him back together. I can't fix the hole in him."

Graham swallows, his Adam's apple bobbing wildly before he nods. "Okay. Yeah. Okay."

"Let me see my son," Lionel charges forward. His growled words making Camilla and Collin jump back out of his way.

I'm the one to step in his path, my palms pressing into the large barrel chest of the man before me. "Mr. Greer, please let my brother work on him first. I promise you do not want to see him like this."

"That's my son," he croaks.

"And I will take care of him," Vincent declares with authority. "Dad, keep him here."

Jorddan only nods before extending an arm to Lionel.

From what I've seen, no one tells my father what to do. The scene I just witnessed proving how dire this situation is. There's no time for minor grievances. Vincent had said he could keep him alive. My heart races, clinging to those words, and choosing to believe Valen hasn't yet crossed over.

If that bastard dies on me, I'll have Vincent bring him back long enough just so I can stab him again. I'm not ready for a life without Valen and his threats. We need him.

Graham and I follow Vincent back down the same hallway. This time, my gaze rakes over the paintings lining the walls. All dark and full of gothic images. It's a poetic tribute to this house's origins.

"Vincent, whose house is this?" I ask.

"Ours," he deadpans, keeping his stride even as he leads us toward the dining room.

The hallway seems longer than the two times I've traveled it. As if space and time are trying their hardest to keep us from getting back to Valen. To keep us from saving him.

Ours. The tiny word bounces around my head with all the possible meanings of those four letters. Choosing to settle on this being a family home, I cast it out of my mind. There are more important things to worry about.

Graham hovers at my side, the unease radiating off of him in waves. He's an absolute mess. His clothing was torn from the claws of the ghoul in our battle. Blood stains his cheeks and the front of his shirt. Dirt clinging to every bit of him as if they had become one.

Reaching for his hand, he slips his fingers through mine, his shoulders uncoiling with the release of a massive breath. He hadn't been holding it, but the relief of having me here with him clearly means something. That has to be enough for now.

"Fuck!" Vincent barks as we enter the dining room. "This is worse than you all described."

"But you can help him, right?" I hate that my voice cracks. Hate that I am showing even an ounce of softness toward Valen after the way he treated me. The threats and flying daggers. The constant reminders that he will torment me, how, and when he wants. But what I hate even more is how deeply I care for him. He needs to pull through this.

Vincent grins smugly, as if questioning how we could ever doubt him. Only someone foolish would.

I don't, but I also don't know my brother at all. My only full-blooded sibling. Our features resemble, sure. The nose and the way his hair curls. The cut of his eyes and the shape of his mouth. Even our skin tones are almost a near match.

Where I am full-figured, he has a trim, muscular frame. Our height must come from our father.

None of that matters, though. We are still strangers. Two ships from the same yard sent to different ports a long time ago.

"Graham, get on the other side of the table," Vincent orders, snapping his fingers only for Valen's body to levitate off the table. My jaw drops, eyes roving over the prone, floating body in front of me. "Do you have enough stores or do you need to channel?"

"I have enough," Graham swallows.

"Good. Give Bri a piece of your essence. She's our backup in case you run dry." Every order from Vincent makes my head spin. The authority in his tone somehow comforting instead of reactivating my panic.

Graham nods, his eyes locking with mine as we stand chest to chest. The fight for him to maintain his composure is holding strong enough you'd have to ruthlessly probe to find the lie. Face stoic and posture tall, I'm still a fucking trembling mess. This entire night has become a disaster.

A pointed white swirl exits Graham's mouth as he opens wide. I do the same, letting it enter me. The chill of the tendril caresses the soft tissue of my throat. My swallow is pronounced as I absorb this new gift to combine with my essence.

It's been nearly fifteen years since I've taken in a light essence before tonight. Harley was the last. The half-brother who could never find it in his heart to even tolerate me. I can feel him now, waltzing beneath my skin as if his power is superior to the rest.

It's not.

My body has become so accustomed to the dark flavors that linger beneath my skin. Tastes akin to acrid smoke, dense wintery forests, and licorice.

Graham's is almost sweet, like savoring the rainbow. Seemingly too light to carry the power the dark revels in. Yet, I know it does. I've seen it, felt it. Craved it.

My eyes press shut as I let Graham become part of me. My body absorbing him even quicker than the power I stole hours ago.

The truth of what I am courses through my veins. Light meeting dark with the essence versed in the art of theft. A crude description, but the truth of what I can do. Once my essence grabs hold of another, it holds on. It takes what isn't ours. All it takes is the tiniest sliver.

As I peel my eyes open, the enhanced vision brings the room into focus anew. The icy white of the ghouls has overtaken my irises. Something tells me this will become a new norm. An inconvenience destined to keep me on edge once we return to the classroom. The change isn't something I will, but perhaps an involuntary shift showcasing the foreign power that made me what I am.

"Shit. Dad told me your eyes turned, but it's freaky as hell to witness, and I fuck around with the dead," Vincent mutters, a shiver shaking his shoulders. "Are you both ready?"

Graham and I nod; Vincent begins.

My brother's eyes slide shut. The stark difference between those unnerving mismatched eyes hidden for only seconds before they pop back open. Where mine shines with the frost of winter, his deepens as pits of black—a yin and yang of possibilities.

Vincent's lips part in a quick succession of minimal movements. There's no sound, though, nor can I read the words on his lips. But then I hear it. The voices. So many voices. An invisible crowd, all talking at once. I flinch to cover my ears, but then I hear Valen's voice. His rich tone carrying toward me. Searching for me.

That voice fills my head as if he were speaking to me. "Missed me already?" His body is completely still, but I heard his words. The inflection mixed with sarcasm and humor, clear as day.

Still, his body doesn't move. It just hovers there over the table as Vincent continues his silent recitation.

Then Vincent's essence oozes from his fingertips, his mouth, eyes, and ears. Every surface of skin releases more and more of the steel essence. The shade several hues lighter than mine and void of twinkling stars. A hue only a Grisym could create. Beautiful and uniquely my brother's.

His tendrils roll in a rippling wave as they wrap around Valen, concealing him from view.

"Graham, you need to start mending the moment my essence is absorbed, or it won't matter that I brought him back."

Graham nods, his essence dancing around his fingertips like little snow fairies.

We're ready, but we wait.

And wait.

And wait.

Suddenly, a haze engulfs Valen's hovering body before my brother's essence disappears. As it clears, those tendrils funnel into the massive hole in his stomach and into the sallow skin of his cheeks. As if rushing water flows beneath his skin, the color gradually returns. That first pump of his chest drawing out an audible sob from me.

The clap of my palm draws my brother's gaze up to mine. My fingers pressing harder against my skin as if that would reverse the sound that had just escaped me. There was no holding it back. Not when they saved him.

Leaning in closer, Valen's cracked and dirt-caked lips part as he inhales and then screams!

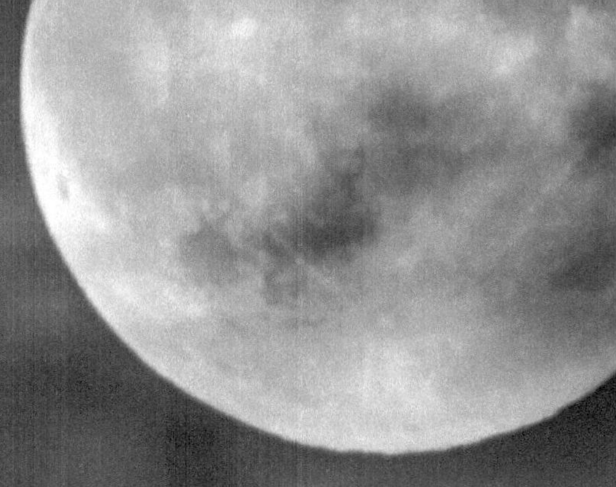

4

GRAHAM

My body vibrates with fear as I witness Valen transition from lifeless to breathing and screaming like he's being split in two. Maybe that's what his wound feels like. A gaping hole large enough to fit a human head through must be agony.

His howling screech reverberates off the walls. But Vincent stays steady, his features stoic, with those pitch-black eyes staring straight ahead. A bead of sweat trickles down his temple, landing on his basic t-shirt that clings to his body like a second skin.

"Now," Vincent growls, and my essence shoots forward, diving into the crater at the center of our classmate's torso.

I close my eyes, focusing on the sensation of weaving threads together. Fitting the pieces where they should go. I've never done this with human flesh before, nor did I think anyone knew I could to begin with. It's not something I wanted to advertise.

Every tendril of my magic weaving through Valen's body seems to send my nerves firing. His prolonged scream assaulting my eardrums and forcing the grit of my teeth. Still, I hold my focus. Not because this asshole is counting on me, but Bri is. If I can help it, I will never let her down. Now that she's my best friend, and possibly more, things have changed.

Valen's body bucks. The movement is so violent that my gaze tracks down to the table. There's no creaking of the crafted wood beneath him. The shake of my head clearing the fog, allowing me to focus on his body still hovering mid-air, held steady by Vincent's magic.

Piece by piece, my essence laces Valen's insides back together. Each cell returned to its proper place. Sliding past each other like a million little fireflies trapped in a jar. They fuse and coil, reforming the structures as they once were. A healing process that's proving to be agony for him.

Good.

Shaking my head again, I clear the thought. This isn't the time to fantasize about Valen suffering. Should this work, I'll curse him myself for *every* bit of torture he put Bri through.

Focus, Graham. You need to focus.

Mending is an art, molded and refined over time. It's not a hobby to dabble with and then use on the living. You get one chance. Just one to get it right without potentially causing lasting damage.

Get it wrong, and the only way to reverse it is with more devastation. Imagine glass shattering into such tiny pieces that it once again resembles the sand from which it came. If I screw this up, we'd have to blow Valen to particles just as microscopic to rebuild. And that I can't mend.

"You're doing great, Graham," Bri whispers in my ear. The comfort of her voice and warmth of her breath on my neck should distract me from my task, but her presence only helps hone my focus. That drive to become the best overwhelms me. I won't fail. I won't screw this up. It's not an option.

Refusing to break my focus with a response, my gaze narrows on the hole, still showcasing Valen's insides. Digging deeper into the well of my power, I push harder. Willing Valen's flesh to mend faster. Willing his tissues to heed my commands.

The quicker he is whole, the faster this ends.

This nightmare of a night. A night that will haunt my dreams indefinitely. This isn't how it should be.

We're supposed to be nothing more than students. Just young wielders tucked away at our boarding schools, learning our power. The only way we'll have a chance of contributing to *our* society.

Pledging ourselves to causes that could get us killed or fighting literal battles against the director of education shouldn't even make our lists. We shouldn't be on the run.

Yet here we are, rebels hiding out in another country.

This semester has been nothing like I planned. It should have been simple. Be the best. Dominate my classes. Forge vital connections that would put me in a position to fulfill my career goals. A foolproof plan that would enable me to graduate with the highest marks and reputation. A reputation every institution would want to be associated with.

Not this. Not death and destruction and lusting after my best friend.

The moment I chose to follow Bri filters to the forefront of my mind. It, too, would have been simple. Grab my research and chase her to the ends of the earth. There was no hesitation in those fretful moments of panic. It was the right thing to do. It was fate or whatever other bullshit you want to define it as.

That was mere hours ago.

And now...

Now I'm realizing this is beyond what I am prepared for. The danger is so much more real. It's more than just my future on the line; it's my life.

Is Bri and her loyalty to a father she has only just met worth all that?

Especially that it's no longer a secret what she is. There was a horde of light wielders out there with her father, Roman—former father. They all know the truth now. Though Pierce said he ordered them to forget, there's no guarantee he got them all equally or that it will hold. He has never used his gift against such a large group all at once.

If they remember, they will come after us. We ran, but the world isn't endless. No matter what happens now, I picked a side when I stood beside her. When I took Jorddan's essence, allowing it to etch his name into my skin.

I chose.

There's no taking it back now.

Should my parents find out what I've done, my problems will only worsen. I'll be the disappointment I've worked so hard never to become. I needed to be their shining star. Yet that may never happen. All because my best friend is a Grisym to the most notorious dark wielder—also a Grisym—in our world. My relationship with the best person I've ever known could ruin everything.

The question is, will I let it?

My parents had always warned me about choosing my company wisely. I thought I was. Befriending the director of education's daughter would have been a strategic move. A smart move. But more importantly, I learned Bri's heart. A heart I love more than I should.

It couldn't be helped, but it also may be the reason they imprison or kill me.

"Concentrate," Vincent warns me. His tone is so low it's as if it vibrates from the center of his being, not his mouth.

He is as terrifying in person as he appears in photos. Those damn eyes are the craziest thing I've ever seen. Just as terrifying as the onyx pits of hell staring back at me now. For light wielders, nothing about our physical form changes when we use our power. Not like the dark and their jet-black orbs. Yet another reason it was easy for us to demonize them for so long.

How he ended up with a mismatched pair, and Bri didn't seems odd. Heterochromia in humans is so familiar that it rarely raises eyebrows when encountered. That's not true for wielders. We're supposed to be one thing. We're conditioned to believe there can only be two sides of the coin. Though Grisyms exist in the thousands, our population lacks accurate knowledge of their characteristics.

It's very rare to have such contrasting features for a Grisym. The grueling research I've conducted has shown photos of several who were apprehended in their youth centuries ago. It's all there is to trust. It doesn't matter what Jorddan knows; I don't.

Yet, I believe this is the largest group of Grisyms I've encountered. Five under one roof seems obscene.

"If you can't hold your focus, move and let Bri take over," Vincent snarls. The bass of his voice resonates as if he's right beside me. As if his mouth is hovering beside my ear, but he's across from me. Right there, cutting me down with the sharp glare of those onyx pits.

Once again, clearing my mind, I concentrate on Valen. The image of him I want in the end filling my thoughts. Whole. Every organ and tissue is properly functioning. Alive. Not a dick.

That last one is wishful thinking; even so, I mend him. Shutting myself in the darkness of my mind, I let my eyelids flutter shut.

Continuing to channel my power into Valen is draining me. Every bit of my power stitching him back together. My eyes peeling open to watch the last bit of skin seal closed, forming the smooth expanse of his stomach once more. The lean muscles settling back into place. The image of him whole causing my molars to grind painfully.

Valen still screams and writhes. I can't imagine this wasn't the most painful thing he's ever gone through.

"Bri, talk to him," Vincent orders.

She steps forward, a hand to his forehead, brushing back his long dark hair. "Valen, you're okay. Calm down. Hear me. Feel me. Open your eyes. You're safe," she whispers the words close to his mouth, but only her palm rests at the center of his chest.

The moment his eyes open, he instantly calms. Valen goes still, his eyes locked on Bri's face. With a snap of his fingers, Vincent lowers Valen back to the table. His body drifting to the surface as if he were nothing but a feather.

"Bryony," Valen breathes, reaching for her. Tears well in her eyes before they spill over, and he pulls her face to his.

I can't watch.

None of us should be able to forget what Valen has done to her. Yet, there she is, crying over him. She kissed him as if she would have lost everything if he hadn't survived.

A throat clears, and I turn back to find Valen on his feet. "Graham, Vincent," he clears his throat again as if something lodged within it. "Thank you."

Vincent only nods, clapping Valen on the shoulder before disappearing down the hall. But it's Valen's arm slung across Bri's shoulders and hers wrapped around his waist that I can't take my eyes off. My brain can't fathom how she's so happy he's alive. She chose all of us, but his death could have freed her.

Until now, I didn't realize what he meant to her, too.

With a forced swallow, I stop in front of them. "Glad you're alive." Reaching for Bri's hand, I can only swallow again when she doesn't immediately take it. My chest pumps faster as a boulder settles in my gut. That creeping doubt swarming me. Torturing me with its cackling laugh that confirms she's choosing Valen over me.

My arm falls, accepting my defeat when she finally grabs hold of my fingers. As if our bodies are attuned, we both turn and shuffle down the hallway back toward the living room we'd originally come from. Valen groaning as he reaches for her other hand, linking their fingers together.

As a trio, we enter the living room. Every pair of eyes focuses on Valen, still in his bloody and torn clothing. Alive. Breathing. Smirking with arrogance, while grimacing against the pain.

Mr. Greer immediately charges toward his son. Bri releases him, but I hold firm to her. We need to talk. I need to know whether everything I am risking is worth it.

Ignoring the reunion, I lead her to a small alcove across the room. The thick brown and tan curtains partially shielding us from view. Damn, I want to kiss her. I want to hold her. The desire to be reminded she's mine too has me releasing my hold on her and balling my fists to keep from caving. My only aid to anchor myself in place. I can't keep chasing a woman who may not want to be caught.

The softness of her palm slides across my cheek. My muscles clenching, attempting to keep from melting into her touch. Worry flooding her gray and green eyes. "What's wrong?"

"What's the plan, Bri?" I grab hold of her hand, removing it from my skin. I can't think straight when she's touching me. Or when she's looking at me, as if her world is shattering, knowing I'm not okay. "We're not supposed to be gone. We need to get back to Beauxgraton."

"I don't know…"

"What? You don't know what?" I question, exasperation coating my words.

"*If* I'm going back. There's a lot to figure out." She knots her hands in front of her, dropping her gaze to her feet before meeting mine again. "My secret is out there now." Overwhelming sadness lives in her eyes—the things I would do to erase it.

I grip her biceps, dropping just enough to look her in the eye. "Bri, we have to go back. I thought I could go on the run with you. But," I swallow hard. "But this is too big now. If my parents find out…" The panic chokes every syllable that exits my mouth. The fight to breathe normally, making my insides burn.

"Then go," she shrugs out of my hold. "If it's too much for you to be here, go back. My dad will help you get back, but don't make it sound like I forced you to be here." There's a watery quality to her words, and I suddenly want to take mine back. But I can't. I need to consider my future. One I'd pictured with my best friend always being in it.

"Are you seriously angry with me right now? I just saved your asshole of a boyfriend! I'm assuming we should call him one alongside the other three of us."

"And I appreciate what you did for Valen," she gestures behind her quickly. "Most of us in this room are." She takes the tiniest step away from me. "But Graham, I never asked you to be part of this. I never said you had to be." She takes another step back from me, her mouth turning down into a frown, eyes glassing over. Her expression revealing how much it hurt her to speak those words—the truth. A truth, maybe I was looking to blame on someone else to absolve myself of the consequences. "If it's better for you to go back to Beauxgraton, then go. I don't know if I am."

"Bri," I breathe. "Do you want me to be here?" There's a niggle at the base of my spine that she doesn't care either way. But I need to hear her say it. My heart hammers, waiting for her to confess she needs me too. Every fiber of my being pulses, needing to know I wasn't just collateral damage. That me knowing her truth was what she wanted. That *I'm* what she wants.

She takes another step back from me. "I want you to do whatever you won't resent me for." Another step in retreat widens the gap she's putting between us. "I need to get back out there." Her thumb points behind her before she turns on her heel, shoving aside the heavy curtain we've found privacy behind.

I have a choice to make, but I have no idea which direction I'll go.

5

BRYONY

MY STOMACH CHURNS, REPLAYING the argument Graham and I just had. He often declares his demands, voicing disapproval of my choices. That's just who he is. Though there was something different this time.

Our endpoint was closing in on us. The finality of our choices threatened to crush us. There are two ways it will end: bliss together or leaving the other in the rearview mirror.

The cruel words that left my mouth were necessary, though. I don't have the time or capacity to be responsible for other people's feelings. Harsh, yes, but I won't let him use me as his excuse for whatever choices he makes.

I just don't know if I can handle the consequences of allowing him to choose either.

Do I want him here? *Yes.*

I need the little school family we created, but I'm also not willing to put anyone in the crosshairs of the war that will surely explode between Roman and my father. It existed long before me. A battle of opposing wills. A reality I may have never become aware of if not for Jorddan. His unhappiness about our lack of a relationship opened my eyes. Just one step from the shadows became our beginning.

Fury boils my blood knowing my mother, of all people, kept it from me. Kept my father from me. My brother. A different existence I should have been allowed to choose years ago.

Now seeing the true colors of Roman, I understand why I never learned it from him. I assume my half-siblings are aware, too. They may know, but aren't part of this family drama. Why would they ever want to be? *No*, this comes down to our mother's heart and their father's insatiable craving for prestige.

A shoulder suddenly bumps mine, my feet tangling beneath me, only for firm hands to keep me steady. "If you're a klutz, we're going to have bigger issues than you not being able to control your essence," Vincent drones.

Our eyes meet, the humor dancing in his dark orb calming me. I hadn't expected playful sarcasm to be a component of his demeanor. Only deranged evil. An image our world wanted us all to believe. Like Jorddan, I wonder how wrong public assumptions have been.

It's odd how little inflection his voice holds. The most he's shown is when he ordered Graham to focus while mending Valen.

"I'm not." Clearing my throat, I stand tall, running my hands down my thighs.

Camilla's narrowed gaze meets mine. Her expression meant to leave me shaking in my boots when all I want to do is laugh. That tiny finger of hers points my way, her long blonde hair a frizzy, matted mess. "You thought you were just going to skedaddle without me?"

Pulling Camilla into a tight hug, she groans against my chest. "I'm sorry. It wasn't intentional. I just needed to keep you safe."

She wiggles out of my hold, that same finger pointing my way, while her other hand cups her hip. "Not your choice to make, missy." She brushes her white-blonde strands from her face with open palms, reminiscent of a toddler. Her lips puckering to blow the stray pieces away, only for them to fall against her cheeks and forehead again.

Camilla has had a feisty, pixie-like side to her since we met. I admit it's what made me enjoy her presence most at first. She may not have led a sheltered life, but she created her own cage. Her own persona. One that has remained, but has also found freedom since we met.

"Sweetheart, I am sorry to interrupt this reunion, but we have things to discuss," my dad grabs my elbow softly.

With a nod, I follow him to the couch, Knox already seated at one end. Wedging between him and my father, expectant faces all watch us. I meet each of their stares, saving Graham for last, where my gaze lingers. Every silent question is thrust into the space between us, only for him to avert his gaze.

A piece of my heart shatters. Graham won't stay.

It's for the best, Bri.

He'll keep my secrets, but he will do exactly what his parents raised him to do. Fall in line. Follow the rules. Be an exemplary student. Be great.

Still, my chest aches.

Forcing myself to look away is one of the hardest things I've ever done. But I turn my focus to Valen. He's the one who needs me now. Graham doesn't; he made that clear.

Somehow, my bad boy looks like himself, except for the slight pinch at the corners of his eyes. A giveaway, the pain must still be enough that he can't ignore it. I'd attempted to use Pierce's gift of persuasion earlier to get him to calm down. That wouldn't erase the pain, though. Mind control can't erase the pain, can it?

"Though most of us survived this evening's events, our fight is not done," my father begins. "Pierson, I thank you for your efforts. They kept my daughter and all of us safer. I suspect it bought us time. Time we must use wisely. I do not like casualties, though they are inevitable." My father's gaze briefly shifts to Lionel and then Valen, but his expression remains blank.

"What did you tell them to do?" I ask, eyeing Pierce.

He'd been vague at first, stating he sent them back to their lives. It was an answer that sufficed in the heat of the moment. Now I wonder. Is there more to it than that?

His fingers run through his hair, gaze averting to the floor. "I told them to go home and to forget everything that happened tonight."

"You have the power to do that?" I gasp. It hadn't occurred to me that when he said he sent them back to their lives, the reason they'd turned and left had been him. I was too distracted to piece it all together while adrenaline soared through my veins and fear strangled my heart.

"And so much more." He lowers his head, his shoulders slumping forward.

Pierce struggles with the burden of his own potential. It always has. A truth he has never tried to hide. A man who wishes he could be different. Removing someone's will through their mind shatters a piece of him each time he invokes that gift.

Though Pierce wishes he could wield from the light, I wonder if he's considered the weight that comes with giving. There are pros and cons to it. There is no true black and white in how light and dark magic can be used. Still, desire often fixates on what is unattainable. We yearn for different, unaware we need not live in another's image.

If only he could understand tonight, he gave. He gave us a chance. He saved us from more bloodshed and from the events of tonight buzzing through the wielding community.

It doesn't change the fact that my former family is still a threat. Roman knows what I am and to whom I belong. Pierce may have willed them to forget tonight, but we didn't wipe the prior twenty-five years. Factoring in my half-siblings, too, Harley, Merrick, and Sicily, the list of those who intimately know what I am grows.

Many others have crossed my path in my lifetime. Others who may or may not know what I am. Roman never told me, and I never asked.

My siblings may be the wildest cards we'll have to work with. Merrick, I trust. He was the only one who showed me what I think was genuine love and respect.

But I also believed Roman loved me as his own. I'd been very wrong. Roman, Harley, and Sicily all fall on my roster of those I have no trust in. My second eldest brother, Harley, has always been against my continued existence, reminding Roman over and over that he shouldn't be hiding me. And Sicily is weak. She is a pushover. My half-sister will cower to Roman and Harley without a fight. Her desire for peace outweighing morality.

"Bri! Bryony!" Vincent's barked tone pulls me out of my thoughts.

"Yes, sorry. What?"

"Is there anyone else who might know about you?" Vincent stands in front of me, his feet spread hip-width apart and arms across his enormous chest. Instinctively, I cower away from him, Knox draping an arm around my shoulder.

"Hey! Back up," Knox snarls at Vincent.

Rage radiates from my brother in waves. His fury burning in his mismatched eyes so bright it's blinding. "She is my sister, Wynston. If you dare to think that thought again, I will slaughter you." My heart races as I witness him come to my defense so intensely. But then I remember, Vincent has always known me, even if I missed out on him.

Knox's brows shoot high. "You don't know what I'm thinking."

Vincent leans closer. "The rumors are true," he whispers before taking a step back. "Bri is the most important person to me in this room. I would never hurt my sister. I've had her watched since I was old enough to understand that bastard Roman forced our mother's hand."

"You what?" I breathe. "Who has been..."

Damian waves two fingers from across the room, chuckling. "Your brother, my best friend."

My eyes dart between the two, trying to determine if it's true. How had I never known? Then Damian cracks his Hollywood smile. I've only seen it on a few occasions when he has tried to have conversations with me. And Vincent follows. The wide grin transforming his face from sinister and menacing to the boy next door, except for the very pronounced canines. So sharp they can't be real.

"Damian wasn't supposed to tell you," Vincent begins. "I chose him once I knew you were also attending Beauxgraton. But make no mistake, Bri, there have been others." An odd sensation settles in my chest hearing my brother use my nickname so easily. Has he always referred to me by it, or did he take note that's what everyone else calls me? "This guy was the only one brave enough to actually interact with you," he huffs as if unsurprised Damian would bother speaking to little old me.

"I didn't have a choice once she involved herself with two of my friends," Damian sighs, leaning back in the armchair and crossing an ankle over his knee. His enormous body dwarfs the chair. The pale green floral woven fabric hidden behind the expanse of his torso and the drape of his arms. The legs groan under his weight. Each ornately carved piece in this house is more for show than function.

My lip curls, pissed that they kept yet another thing from me. "He only watched me have sex with Pierce. Not exactly what you had in mind, I assume." My grin is saccharine, my stare boring into Damian's.

He could have told me.

Pierce coughs loudly, Valen snickering while Camilla fans herself.

"My dear, that will be a conversation for later." My father pats my thigh. "If you could, please answer your brother's question."

"Anyone Roman ever brought in to work with me while I was growing up likely knows. Many of them were there before I could control my essence escaping in a pale enough shade to make them believe I was a light wielder. No doubt they noticed." My fingers knot in my lap, something like shame coursing through me.

"But you're not sure?" Vincent presses.

I drop my head, shaking it. "No. They never said anything, and neither did Roman."

"I want a list of every name first thing in the morning," Vincent snarls. "Dad, Damian, and I will take care of them."

"How?" I ask.

"They can't be allowed to live," my father taps my leg again. "You do understand that, right?"

"I—is that who we are now? Murderers, so we can keep my secret? Isn't there another way to fight back?" Meeting the stares of each person in the room, my eyes draw wider. Each wears a unique expression. Too many to parse through when I'm so focused on my brother. Blind fury still rages behind his eyes, the light-colored one taking on an iridescent glow while the nearly black iris darkens into a bottomless black hole. The veins at his temple and along his throat popping as he fights to contain himself.

"There are plenty of options," Lionel chimes in, clearing his throat. The quick dart of his eyes to my father noted. "We just need to buy ourselves time."

"It will be the safest option once we return to Beauxgraton," Janelle adds.

"Ahh, about that," my father raises a finger. "I am not sure I can allow that. She shouldn't have been there to begin with."

"Jorddan, don't do this to her," Janelle pleads. "She belongs there. With—"

A heavy breath funnels through my father's nostrils, his jaw ticking as he shoots his gaze across the room. "Janelle, I will once again remind you she is *my* daughter, not yours. Roman may have been weak-minded and let you dictate matters to him, but I will not. My daughter, my rules."

"But Dad, wouldn't it look less suspicious if I returned to Beauxgraton, assuming it's safe?" To the public, I am still Roman's daughter. They'll probe and ask questions if his youngest, the female child he's always allowed in the limelight, suddenly leaves such a prestigious institution. Especially in the wake of light wielders joining dark institutions out of necessity. It could cause an uproar that could expose us all.

"My sweet girl, there is no place safer in the world than right here. With Vincent or me, no one can touch you."

"But, Damian..." I begin to protest.

"Graduates this year," Vincent cuts off my argument.

"Janelle, can you find Vincent a place on the staff? Bring him to the school, and then I'll be safe." Turning toward my father, I search his face. A quest for answers in his expression proving to be fruitless. "I want to be safe. I want to keep us all safe," my arm slicing through the air as if including everyone in attendance. "But I have waited ten years for this. Don't take this away from me. Please." A whimper nearly breaks free. They wouldn't understand how lonely and lost I've felt since maturing at fifteen. Looking back, it was a cruel existence.

I honestly can't pinpoint why I am so determined to return to Beauxgraton. Part of me thinks it's the last place they might look for me. Another wants that semblance of normalcy back before shit hits the fan. Beauxgraton is where I finally came into my own. The line between who I was told to be and who I actually am finally blurred.

Roman could strike at any time. It's a reality I am forced to live with, but I won't stop living while I wait.

Time is ticking.

Soon, the world will know Bryony Guthrie. One day, I'll no longer have the advantage of our lies. Until then, why stop progress?

6

VALEN

 through my head. Every bit of inflection resonating inside me, reassuring me that I'm safe. Alive. I'll be fine—eventually.

I wouldn't have found my way out of that hell without her.

She'd used Pierce's gifts to pull me out. A fact I'm equally grateful for and grinds my molars. A reminder of how quickly she took to him. I recognize it as Pierce's gift. Bri may have saved me, but it's not because she cares about me the way she does Pierce, Graham, or Knox.

I fucking hate that it grinds my gears knowing that. Those big gray and green eyes keep finding mine with every wince of pain. Pain that roars through my body, though I am completely calm.

"Valen, you're okay. Calm down. Hear me. Feel me. Open your eyes. You're safe." My eyes screw shut, hearing her voice in my head again—a tone filled with tenderness and desperation.

I was dead. Truly dead, passing on to be with our ancestors.

Vincent brought me back. Surprisingly, Graham helped. None of us, except Jorddan, seemed to know he could mend. Though somewhat unpolished, his hidden talents were appreciated. Now I owe him, too. A debt my asshole side rolls its eyes at paying.

Not once had he ever mentioned or given the impression that he could mend. Our gifts vary, just as they do for every wielder. Usually, those who enter the medical profession or our military forces can mend the living, but are unable to master inanimate objects, and vice versa. Graham's ability to do both should give us all pause. Like Bri, he's a rare find.

Raking my gaze around the room now, it's filled with exceptional wielders. It's beyond mere luck. But that's what it is, right? Graham and Bri became friends by chance. It happened with Camilla, too, thankfully. There's nothing worse than hating your roommate. Though I don't have a clue what her talent could be. We only know that she was successful in constructing her own spells last semester. A skill that normally isn't refined enough to pull off before third year. Collin manipulates the earth—weather, vegetation, and natural disasters. Though unlike Pierce, ghouls, specifically Kirbon's, are his go-to.

Then there are my friends and I. Jorddan chose many of us for his cause, and others he did not. But together, we're equivalent to an unstoppable army.

Vincent brought me back to life. Graham made me whole. But it was Bri who actually saved me. My debt to her can only be paid with blood and life.

"We're not going to get anything more done this evening," Jorddan stands. "Let's all get some rest. We will reconvene here after breakfast. We have a few weeks to plan and execute."

Every eye is on him, but mine are on Bri's. My focus glued to the way she looks at her father like he hung the moon. The curl of her fingers over Knox's knee and his arm around her shoulders. *Fuck*, it drives me insane to know they get to touch her, too. Fuck her, too.

That first night I fucked her in front of Pierce, I thought I would have worked it out of my system. That I wouldn't have to lose myself in her tight cunt again with my dagger at her throat and her nickname on my lips. *Forbidden Fruit.*

I was wrong.

Bri is mine.

I. Need. Her.

Vincent's booming voice pulls me out of my thoughts. A drop back into reality where the pain grounds me. Every throb reminds me that this is as real as the battle we fought tonight. "Follow me. I'll take you to your rooms."

As one, we all push to our feet. The weary groans and sighs fill the quiet. Our shuffling feet and heavy breaths stalking toward the open double doors, crafted with hand-carved wood, a dull roar in my ears.

Only my father, Jorddan, and Milgren stay behind. My last glance back at them, lowering my brow. Their whispered words shielded as I watch their mouths move without a sound. My brain refuses to read their lips, Milgren's hand gestures revealing the gravity of their discussion. One with details I'm sure will be kept from us unless we need to know.

Pulling my gaze away from them, I stomp toward the front of the group. My focus zeroed in on Bri and her gait. Those beautiful curls are more wild than ever, her ass filling out those skin-tight jeans, waving at me with every tired step.

Stopping beside her, Vincent and Damian's conversation fills my ears. We were all aware that Damian and Vincent knew one another. Old family circles or some shit. Yet, Dame never alluded to the closeness of their friendship. A fact that shouldn't give me pause. Damian has always been a part of the friend group, but it ended there. He did what he needed to and kept to himself. He'd already been by Jorddan's side for three years when I met him. However, his friendship with Vincent must stretch back further than that, especially since they are likely six or seven years apart.

My jaw flexes knowing Damian kept something so important from me. Jorddan owes me no explanations, but Damian was supposed to be a friend. It's possible he functioned solely as an ally. "I should gut you for keeping this from me," I growl behind him.

"Go ahead if that'll make you feel better, but I kept your girlfriend safe, didn't I?" That same fucking deadpan tone laced with humor only riles up my anger. Which sends the pain roaring through me.

He doesn't have to say that statement implies safety from me as well. I've been a dick to Bri, and likely that will not change anytime soon. My cock gets hard just thinking about tormenting her, and the fact that she likes my daggers when I fuck her is even better.

Too bad my body is screaming in protest with my every step or breath. At this rate, I won't be back inside my woman anytime soon.

"Fuck you, Damian."

"Love you too, man." He claps me softly on the shoulder. A hand I shake off. I don't take kindly to people keeping shit from me. Secrets are dangerous. Deadly.

"You know we're going to have to talk about that," Vincent mutters.

The group seems to have stopped breathing as they catch on to our three-way confrontation. "You told me to keep an eye on your sister; I did. I don't give a fuck who she was with. Happily married, in case you forgot." He wiggles his fingers in front of Vincent's face, the guy's eyes softening as a grin pulls at the corner of his mouth.

It's the type of happiness you find when everything in life seems to align.

It's weakness, if you ask me. Loving people and caring are dangerous. Deadly, even. I would know. I'd die for the people I'm loyal to.

"You watched my sister fuck one of your best friends," Vincent snarls.

"It's done," Damian retorts, his tone so calm you'd think they were talking about the weather.

Vincent's jaw works hard, the sounds of his molars grinding loud in my ears despite the soft chatter that has resumed behind us. Vincent's gaze tracks to me. My gait is off, back curved to staunch some of the pain radiating through my fucking stomach. "If you need something, I'll get it. Otherwise, it should pass within a week."

How I hadn't realized he and Bri were siblings all this time is beyond me. Now that I've seen them in the same room, they're practically fucking twins. Hell, they resemble more than Kormoran and Kaia do, except for the eyes.

Not a soul possesses eyes with the beauty of Bri's or the unique mix of Vincent's.

"I'll live," I grunt.

"Ha, funny," Sean deadpans behind me, but it's the feel of Bri's hand on my lower back that keeps me from lashing out. Her touch fooling me into believing I'm not seconds from passing out because of the pain.

There's sympathy in her eyes. A softness for me, I hope, lasts. Once I'm fine, we'll be us again. Taunting and tormenting. Teasing and tantalizing one another. That dark glare will fill her stare again. Her agitation is the best foreplay.

Fuck, my dick is swelling just thinking about it. *Not what I need right now.* Shrugging away from her touch, my features pinch. Bri's gaze only darts in a few directions before she takes a step away from me, once again cocking her chin high.

It's a silent trek up the main double stairs at the front of the manor. I've been here countless times, but tonight it's as if I'm viewing the manor with fresh eyes. It has been in the family for centuries. Most of the original art and decor remain. Each piece is like living in a weird-ass time capsule.

Only my groans fill the silence, but Bri doesn't touch me again, and I wish she would. Hope swirls in my chest as Vincent pauses at the first door. "Valen." I nod, recognizing the spot. It's the same room I've always stayed in. Bri follows behind me, only for Knox to keep close behind her.

"Not staying then?" I grunt and groan as I sit on the edge of the bed and attempt to lie back against the expensive comforter, black and woven with gold lace.

"No. I just want to make sure you're okay. If you die on me again, I will have Vincent bring you back just so I can murder you." There's a hint of fear in her words, though they're as sharp as my knives. It's a constant grappling match in my head. A push and pull of wishing I cared less and needing her to want me the way she wants Knox, Pierce, and Graham.

"That's my girl," I quirk a grin, letting my eyes fall shut as my back finally hits the mattress.

I listen to the retreat of their steps as I just lie there, stuck in my position. Even if I wanted to, my body stopped cooperating for the night.

Refusing to linger on who will sleep next to my forbidden fruit tonight, I let my mind wander about what Milgren, my father, and Jorddan stayed behind to discuss. I can only assume it was Milgren who contacted my father. Just the same, I'm surprised he came. There are no true ill feelings between us, but I know I'm not his favorite son either. That's always been Dustin, and it's always been fine.

Normally, I would have pegged such heroics on Pierce. Still, he'd been just as surprised my father was there as I was. He knows our history and my need to pursue justice in my way. My family and I are the same. We want a different wielding world. One based on merit and acceptance. The balance between sides once again restored. They just don't agree with how I've gone about it.

No, Pierce was exhausted like the rest of us. Using your power like that, unbridled and with such relentlessness, takes everything out of an extrinsic. It sucks at our reserves, draining every last drop of stored magic. It defies logic how Pierce could erect that massive, thick barrier, then mind-control forty-plus. Yet, his gifts explode out of him when he channels from the earth, as if any other source muffles his abilities. The purity of earth power melts away those limitations, reforming them like metal in burning, fiery flames.

But Pierce, soft-hearted chump that he is, did it for all of us.

No, who am I fooling? He did it for Bryony.

We're all so anchored in our feelings about her that we act irrationally. We put ourselves aside to protect her. If only it were as simple as just following orders or honoring the oath we swore. That will never be true, though. It's us. It's her. The proverbial spell she has cast over us all makes it impossible to abandon her.

"Fuck!" I roar into the void of my room.

"Does it really hurt that bad?" Pierce's voice cuts through my low groaning. His frame leaning against the doorway casts him in shadows. Illuminated only by the dim lighting from the hallway at his back. A dark prince just casually waiting for answers from his subject.

He looks as horrid as I do. The weight of tonight's events left him covered in dirt, blood, and that ashen complexion I've only ever seen on him the day his parents kicked him out of the house.

If anyone saw what took place on the Beauxgraton grounds, there will be hell to pay. A media field day that Jorddan will use his every connection to keep quiet. It's not part of the plan. But Roman is different, a manipulative psychopath worse than me who will use it to his advantage, whatever his end goal may be.

He might have protected Bri once; that's over now. Roman showed up, guns blazing, in a rage so desperate he kidnapped Graham. If that's not clarity, I don't know what is. Bryony is no longer his daughter, no matter what show he puts on for the public.

Roman will turn the tables in time. Each display, prior to his positive spin, is merely a pretense. His best bet would be throwing his wife, Geneva, under the bus, but I don't foresee that happening either. He covets her too much to let her get away.

He'll never broadcast that his "wife" is a cheater and birthed a Grisym to the wielding world. The fact pertains more to protecting himself than to the love of his life. Not to mention, the truth would free Geneva from his death grip. She'd have the freedom to return to Jorddan. Running straight into the arms of the only man she has ever loved, she could live her truth. It was easy to uncover those skeletons in the Guthrie and Avalon closets once I learned Bri's identity.

Back then, I was proud of my digging. Now, it sends a chill down my spine. If I could find their secrets so easily, anyone else can, too.

But more importantly, Roman won't let that happen because it makes him look like the unworthy piece of shit he is. He was so lackluster that his "wife" preferred a dark wielder. Still prefers one.

"No, and yes. Just a lot on my mind." I'm not sure how delayed my response is, and I don't give a fuck. There is a lot on my mind. Now, I question our direction. A first for me. All I know is our death toll is about to grow, and I'll be damned if I'm part of the tally again.

Pierce comes further into the room, dropping into an armchair in the far corner. He looks out of place against the soft, cream-colored fabric.

"You're filthy," I groan.

"Have you looked in a mirror?" He snorts, leaning further back in his chair. "You're still covered in your own blood." He didn't have to point it out. I'm well aware we look like the walking dead. The feeling of crusted and clotting blood against my skin and clothing is a constant reminder of how much I almost lost tonight.

"Why didn't you go after Bryony?"

Pierce's wry expression only makes me quirk a grin. "She needs rest like we all do. I wanted to come check on my best friend. Sorry, I still care."

There's a snarky remark right on the tip of my tongue, but something tells me to hold it. Pierce has been the one person always in my corner, no matter how awful I have been to him or anyone else. These months, I watched him grow a backbone, owing it only to that fucking woman. My woman.

He stands from the chair with a huff. The silence is uncomfortable for once as he shuffles across the massive room. Stopping with a hand on the doorframe, his back rises and falls with a heavy breath. The single tap of his palm on the doorframe serves as his goodbye, one foot raised, ready to step across the threshold.

"Pierson," I whisper. "Thank you."

7

BRYONY

MOVIES SHOWCASE HISTORICAL HOMES like this. Massive structures with custom rugs lining the hallways and one-of-a-kind original paintings on the walls. Museums full of decorative pieces that either hold unimaginable value or none beyond the attachment of the owner.

The hallways seem endless. Yet another labyrinth for me to learn when I'd only just begun to master Beauxgraton's. New wings and hallways branch off more often than they seem they should. The house had been massive from the outside, but it seems absurd that this much of a maze could exist within it.

Vincent leads me to my bedroom door. Our trek transporting us from the center to the far side of the manor, only for Vincent to weave into a wing you cannot see from the front exterior. My room sits at the end of the hallway, only a few down from his. The door mindlessly pointed out as we passed it. "This was supposed to be your room when you visited and eventually came back to live with us." His palm hovers over the center of the door before he releases a ragged breath, allowing his fingertips to drag down the surface.

"I'm here now," I whisper.

What else is there to say?

Too much.

There are too many confessions and questions ready to spew free. Every word swings on the tip of my tongue, forcing me to press my lips together to keep them in. It isn't the time. Not tonight, at least. We're exhausted, beaten, and bruised.

Vincent pulls me into a tight hug, my cheek resting on his chest as his heartbeat pounds in my ear. "Yes, you are." The release is slow, as if letting me go means I'll disappear again. Now that I've found them, I won't let anyone separate me from my father and brother again. Roman can't stop me. Neither can my mother. I'd like to see them try. "Wynston, don't fuck over my sister."

Knox only grunts at Vincent's warning. The big brother routine is clearly already wearing on him. One day, we'll have to parse through whatever tension of the past still lingers between them. Just not today.

The warmth of Knox's fingers finds mine as he links our hands together. His stare never leaving Vincent's face. Both refusing to yield with their unforgiving grimaces.

"Let's get you cleaned up," Knox whispers, kissing my temple.

The stirring of my mixture of essences churns my stomach. That familiar violent storm building. Knox's fingers squeeze mine, showering me with relief. He knows. He can feel it. That's why he refused to leave me tonight.

"I'll find you in the morning," I nod to my brother before leading Knox and me into the bedroom that was always supposed to be mine.

Every emotion hits me at once. My chest is collapsing from the weight of all that's come to light. It is overwhelming being in this house—my home—among loved ones. This life is everything they deprived me of. For what? So Roman could use me as a weapon? Because my mother didn't fight to keep this family together?

I would never say that her other children are less important. They're not. She should love us all equally. Cherish us all equally, but growing up the way I did, in the dark about my eldest brother and father, she didn't.

My insides continue to riot as I stand in the center of the bedroom. My eyes refusing to take it all in and really absorb it. The truth is more like a dream than my reality.

The strength of Knox's arms circling me from behind only settles my insides a fraction. Our mixture of essences rolling through my body in opposition. The darker nature of my Grisym poking and prodding at this new light power we stole.

As Knox, Vincent, and I took the last turn down my hallway, my brother made it clear he wasn't happy I was sleeping with my professor. He'd made Knox into a predator instead of understanding that Wynston Knox has only been my savior. My safe place since I left home and entered Beauxgraton. It's a connection we'll never be able to explain with words. My brother will have to see it himself. It's the only way others have understood.

"Come on," Knox whispers against my cheek, weaving his fingers through mine and leading me into the adjoining bathroom.

Pausing just inside the entryway, my heart swells with the novelty of the space. A room that has always been mine. Every piece of this house seems to be dipped in wealth. Living as an Avalon, I'd experienced finer things, too. But there's a culture here. There's a story in every minute detail that the modernness of my former house lacked. History and memories exist within these walls. All wrapped up in a legacy I can only hope to be a part of.

A legacy I wish I understood. Maybe there's still time.

Steam fills the bathroom, Knox's touch once again slamming me back into the present. Careful fingers slowly undress me before guiding me into the standalone shower.

Scalding water washes over my skin, my hands running over the top of my head only to knot in my curls. My hair is a tangled mess. I stink, still covered in dirt and blood. Valen's blood.

A whimper escapes me as the memories of Aziel carrying Valen's dead body through those tunnels push to the front of my mind. The images playing like a box office hit horror movie. There's no telling when he took his last breath. Was it before he hit the ground? Or as he lay there, and we continued to fight? Was it as Aziel carried him through those tunnels?

My eyes press shut, shunning the image of my ghoul carrying Valen's limp body. My gut tells me I know the answer to my endless stream of questioning. Valen was dead before his body ever left the ground. He was dead as we carried him through the ghoul tunnels and laid him on the dining room table. He was dead as we waited, and I held his hand, praying to any god who would listen, to keep him with me.

Still, I was hopeful he was alive. Thinking back now, it made no sense. My brother isn't a healer. He's a necromancer specializing in resurrection. My father knew Valen was dead when he told me we were taking him to Vincent.

Yet the surprise had been Graham. Not only his secret ability, but also Vincent's need to include him. Then Graham's willingness to do whatever it took.

The media has painted my brother as many things. Details I am questioning now that I've met him. Those piranhas implied Vincent could revive corpses regardless of their condition. As if no limitations existed, which only made him more dangerous. However, public outlets often have a tendency to twist the story to fit their narrative. Shame on me for not knowing better when that's been my whole life. I hadn't even known Graham would be part of the plan.

What if he hadn't been able to mend Valen correctly? What if I had to step in and do it myself?

Naturally, my essence learns the magic it takes without effort. I'd presume I'd need skill to execute said gift. Right? There's a particular finesse that comes with something like mending living flesh.

The boulder in the pit of my stomach knows otherwise. I've used Pierce's gift without a second thought multiple times. Who knows how many others, too, and I didn't even know.

Tears stream down my cheeks, concealed by the rush of water over my skin. An involuntary flinch whips my body into the tile wall as Knox's hands curve over my shoulders, a tentative kiss pressed to the side of my throat.

"Do you want me to go?" The vibration of his words over my skin further heats my insides. My essence is now responding for a whole different reason. We know Knox can help me control the aftereffects without sex, but our mixed essences now demand it. They refuse to settle for anything less than our bodies connected in every way.

I only shake my head, hoping he won't know I was crying. The weight of everything that has happened and still will threatens to drag me to my knees, no matter how hard I fight to stay on my feet. There were others lost on both sides tonight. I'd seen the bodies lying there, but we saved Valen. Only Valen.

If the rumors are true about my father and Vincent, why hadn't we taken the light wielders that didn't survive? They were corpses that my brother could have easily revived. Their memories stolen and gifted to our father to strengthen his advantage. Nothing more. That's what we've been told he's been doing all these years.

Why didn't Jorddan save any of the men and women who stood with us? There may be more of us all over the world, but that doesn't make us an army. They can't all possibly be part of the New Order, could they?

Why not save any of them?

What made Valen the only one worth saving?

My eyes flutter shut as another whimper escapes me. Realization punching me in the chest. Of all who died tonight, Valen was the only one who meant something to me. I'm the only reason he is alive now. A reality that makes my gut churn with guilt instead of relief.

Knox gently turns me to face him, his dark brow furrowed low, hair drenched and hanging across his forehead and over his eye. "Bri." He crushes me in his hold, my arms trapped between us.

"Tonight could have gone so differently," I whisper. Every tear that falls now breaks another piece of me. It's not the release it should be. There's nothing cathartic about letting it all out.

But something darker lingers beneath the surface with those tears. A darker desire to rectify what transpired tonight, if it's the last thing I do.

The brush of his heavy palm over the back of my head soothes me. Tenderness and uncertainty filling his tone. "I'm just glad it wasn't worse, but whatever comes next might be."

Gazing up into his dark pine eyes, there are so many unspoken words. Each one pounding at each sliver of color, fighting to get out. Reaching up, I comb his wet waves back from his face before pressing up to bring my mouth to his.

The kiss is soft. Just a brief press of our lips before pulling apart. The touch enough for our bodies to come alive. Our essences are eager for what they know will follow, as made evident by the swell of his dick between us. His length hardening faster than should be possible with the exhaustion and horror of today weighing on us.

"Bri, we don't—"

"Just keep kissing me. We need you." Desperation coats my words. We both know what will happen if I don't have him. My body will riot. Destruction finding us in this room that should be our sanctuary. It's happened too many times for us not to be aware of it.

His eyes flare, mouth opening and closing several times before he speaks. "If you are about to lose control, let's clean up first." A soft kiss is placed at the center of my forehead. "Then I'll take care of you."

His eyes search mine. I'm not sure what he's looking for. He knows what I need. Still, my heart warms knowing he cares if I am okay in every way. "You can take care of me while we clean up."

"Bryony," he sighs. Wet fingers tuck a stray curl behind my ear. "I will always take care of you. Protect you. Care for you." He pauses, dropping his lips close to my ear. The fan of his warm breath over my skin sends a shiver down my spine. "Bury myself inside you, so there's no beginning or end to either of us. We're connected now. There's no separating me from you."

A hiss leaves me as Knox's fingers drag over my soft stomach, running over the sensitive flesh between my legs. The press of his thumb against my swollen clit making my body buck in his arms. Although the spray of the water crashes over my body, my pussy is soaked because of him.

Those talented fingers tease me before a single digit slips inside. My calf protesting as I angle my leg up, pressing onto my toes to give him better access. To let him ruin me with his touch. To make me forget the tragedy of tonight and the violent backlash my essence is ready to unleash.

"Knox," I breathe, my fingers clawing at his skin, unable to find any purchase.

"Shower, then we will make sure you don't demolish a four-hundred-year-old manor," he chuckles, pressing his lips to my throat and removing his hand from where I want him most.

The urge to pout over the loss of his talented fingers nearly has me walking out of the shower in search of Pierce or Graham. Knox got me all worked up just to make me wait. Bri can, but my essence can't. Still, I force a slight grin, giving him my back to wash. I'm still filthy. I'm still drained.

Grabbing the sponge and lathering it with half the bottle of soap, it's not enough. The sights, sounds, and smells of tonight once again come alive in my mind without having Knox's touch to distract me. Those that died tonight are on me. That blood is on my hands.

Sure, I never asked to be born. Living as a Grisym was not a fate I pleaded for. That doesn't change the choices I made that led us to this point. I chose one father over the other. I chose not to hide who I am anymore. For that, we all paid tonight.

No matter how hard I scrub my skin, the blood won't wash away. Maybe it never will.

As if in a trance, my movements halt. I can only stand there staring at the wall, my fingers tightening around the dirty, soaped sponge as it hovers over my chest.

That emptiness of feeling lost settles inside me again. It's always been there my whole life. I've always felt a bit off, lost because I knew I was different. Now it consumes me. It's shoving its way to the forefront, and I can't take it anymore.

"Let me," Knox whispers, cupping his hand over mine.

I release the sponge without a fight and simply stand there as my professor-boyfriend cleans my naked body in the bathroom of my family home. If only I could convince myself those facts would sound better on their own. But they can't stand alone. My life, my relationships, my family...they're all complicated. They are all part of me.

It's odd how a moment can feel right and wrong in tandem. That familiar line we attempt to draw between one side and the other is ever-present. In my world, there's only a range of the in-between.

That's life. It's a blurred line between right and wrong, good and bad, life and death.

It's not long before the squirt of shampoo into Knox's palm pulls me out of my trance. His fingertips working over my ends, lightly rolling my bundle of hair through his palms, before the pads of his fingers lightly brush over my scalp. His technique is wrong, but my heart is too heavy to correct the kind gesture. "Gentle," I coach him.

"Bri, I know how to wash hair. These waves aren't easy to maintain."

Usually, Knox isn't vain, so I can only laugh. "Does my professor use the curly girl method?" The soft giggle that follows serving as a sign of how safe I feel with him.

"Yes," he whispers against the shell of my ear. "So, relax. I can wash your hair without making you bald."

He succeeds, gently rinsing the shampoo free before slathering every strand in a vanilla-scented conditioner. Only then does he scrub his own body clean, every ounce of dirt swirling down the drain at our feet. If only my memories of the night would follow.

Knox and I rinse our hair simultaneously before he waves me out of the shower ahead of him. Wrapped in perfectly fitting robes, we wander back into my bedroom. My limbs are heavy. The joints wobbly as if unable to support my weight any longer, just before I drop onto the armless settee at the end of the bed. Yet another item that mirrors the priceless antique furniture prominently placed throughout the manor.

My curls shed fat water droplets onto my thigh. Each one is a blast of cold moisture as it splatters against my bare skin. My head hangs, chin tucked to my chest.

I'm so tired. There's no adrenaline to fuel me anymore. No anger or resentment. The fight to keep my essence contained is sucking every bit of what I have out of me.

What the hell do we do now?

8

BRYONY

 What do I say? How do I atone for what happened? How do I control what I am?

Too many questions swirl through my mind. Questions for which I have no answers.

"How are you feeling?" Knox asks. Not with the soothing tone he'd used in the shower or the flirtatious one that had followed, but one of authority and concern. He can feel it too. The impatience of my essence to break free and mingle with his.

"It won't be long."

He knots his fingers through mine, kissing my knuckles one at a time. "Do you want to try to sleep it off or use me?"

Our eyes meet, the white haze already taking over. My answer is given without words as I grip the side of his neck, quickly pressing my lips to his.

We're slow to move, Knox standing from his seat to tower over me. Heavy palms grip the backs of my thighs, kneading my ample flesh before yanking me forward and twisting me around so my back lies flat along the settee. With each shallow breath, the halves of the robe reveal more of my flushed skin. My full breasts beginning to spill free.

Long fingers curl around my wrist, pinning my arms above my head. With his next blink, the dark green that normally stares back at me is gone. That milky hue is taking over, the same as mine. A change so familiar now, it only brings me comfort.

Lowering his head to my chest, the tip of his tongue runs along the edge of the terry cloth, just along my half-exposed nipple. The skin hungrily sucked between his lips as he releases an animalistic groan. A sharp ache tingles along my sides as my back arches further than should be possible. My body is eager for Knox's mouth, hands, and every bit of pleasure that is sure to follow.

"We've never tried this, but maybe it will help." His voice is a low rumble that vibrates through my chest as he runs his lips over my mostly exposed breasts. Each hardened peak is so taut they throb painfully. An ache only that tongue will ease.

Teeth exposed, he grabs one side of the robe, pulling it to the side, leaving half my body completely bare for him. My men have always appreciated every curve. Their palms trace every inch of skin as if it'll be the last.

The trail of Knox's lips over my torso sears my skin. The flick of his tongue across my flesh just above my pelvis, leaving me writhing beneath him, my hips flexing upward, wanting more. Wanting everything. Shifting both my wrists into one of his hands, those fingers find my core, moving through my soaked flesh in a tantalizing brush. My hips rolling against his long fingers greedily.

"Knox," I groan. "Please."

His touch is light. A tease meant to take me further over the edge. My lower belly fluttering and tightening with the impending orgasm building inside me. One so intense, I'll be left screaming his name when it tears apart my insides, the pitch threatening to shatter the windows.

My hips buck against the vibration of his chuckle against my core. His tongue flicking around the opening, but refusing to enter me.

"Knox," I groan, fighting against his hold on me. I need more. I need him inside me. It doesn't even matter how. I'm desperately so far gone that my body will take whatever he offers.

"I'm listening to your essence, Bri. It's telling me exactly what you want. What you need. Keep quiet so I can listen."

Biting my lower lip between my teeth, I do as he says. A gasp breaks free as his first digit enters me, too, after barely stifling the moan in response to the tip of his tongue sinking inside me. My body reacts as if it's been years without his touch.

If only I could remember the last time we were together. The days are blending into a fast-forwarded scene. Between finals and Roman's bullshit, I can't recall. It seems our entire world was turned on its head, making it impossible to tell up from down or today from yesterday.

My pelvis writhes against his strokes, bucking off the bench when his thumb harshly presses against my sensitive bundle of nerves. The tight circles to follow sending my body into a frenzy. Not once have I ever had to tell Knox what to do. Never have I had to recite what I needed. He simply understood, like we shared one mind, one body. Perhaps it was my essence that was telling him the whole time. Maybe it's our connection. A bond I never want us to lose.

Internally, every essence battles with swords drawn high and their armor locked in place. Their proverbial weapons slashed back and forth while each one fights to sit dominant alongside mine. Crowned my loyal companion. Yet mine only watches as Knox battles the others into submission. Their tendrils whipping at him, wanting his spot on the throne beside me.

They can fight all they want. Knox will win. He's too much a part of me to lose.

His essence refuses to relent, slashing down the strips of light and dark coming for him, only pausing when he comes across my father's. Jorddan's doesn't fight, only moving aside to bear witness to the champion. A spectator in every way.

The individual tendrils move so fast that it's impossible to identify who is who. I can only distinguish the light from the dark. Nothing more. Even with what I know now, it's impossible to decipher how many I've taken.

"Knox, it's coming. This isn't enough."

A frigid cold settles against my skin, chilling my bones as Knox pulls his hands from my body. With a wave of his hand, the robe shreds to pieces, falling away from my body while he pulls me to my feet.

"I'll take care of you," he whispers, shifting us around to take the spot I'd been in only moments ago. His robe, too, is nothing more than a pile of shredded terry cloth at my feet. The moisture between my legs coats my inner thighs. My slick skin hindering my ability to squeeze them tight. Anything to staunch the ache or create the friction my greedy core craves.

Those white eyes find mine, his chest heaving as his body hovers at an angle. Every abdominal muscle flexes in anticipation. Water droplets and sweat coating his tanned skin.

Stepping toward him, I drop a knee on either side of his slightly spread thighs. "Open," I whisper.

His mouth opens wide, a stream of his essence seeping free. Mine following as soon as I position him at my entrance. My entire body pulses, ready to feel him inside me. Eager for the combination of us to tame the rioting magic building within.

"Fuck, Bri," he barks as I slowly lower myself down his shaft. His girth stretches me. A reminder that he hasn't been the one I've been with lately.

Rising until he almost slips free and then sinking a bit more, my head falls back. Sure fingers slide over my belly, between my aching breasts, and over the column of my throat. His grip tightens just enough to crane my head backward, forcing my gaze to meet his. "Look at me." A command, not a choice.

Lifting my hips again, I'm more forceful as I drop this time. Letting him fill me. Taking every inch as if his cock was made just for me. The stretch becomes more delicious with each thrust of him inside me. My pussy refusing to accommodate his size, my walls only squeezing him so tight he grits his teeth, sinking his fingers into my full hips. A grip so tight there will undoubtedly be marks there by morning.

"Harder," I pant. "I need it harder. It's coming..."

My insides vibrate with barely restrained power. Our essences funneling out of our mouths at such a rapid pace, the room is nearly full of the mixture of us. A swirling vortex, cocooning our bodies as I bounce on Knox's rock-hard cock. The repeated slap of our skin competing with the howl of our essences is so deafening that I worry we'll wake the entire house.

Usually, it calms by now, becoming that unique pewter that has become a signature of Knox and me. Usually, coming together is enough for us to settle. But tonight my essence rages as if angry. As if trying to destroy everything in its path. Knox's fights to control me. Fights to find the calm that comes with his fucking us into submission.

"Bri, I don't know what's happening," he breathes, sitting up, his fingers sinking into my damp hair as we continue to move. "Tell me what you both need. Let me fix it."

My eyes press shut. A way to block out the combination of turmoil raging inside me and the orgasm rumbling to the surface. Both are racing to get out, cackling, eager to add to the chaos whipping through the room.

"Knox! Knox!" I shout his name as the combination of essences shoots through me. Nothing but pitch-black darkness surrounds us. Even my stars are hidden. Those beautiful, glowing glimpses of light and hope washed away.

Yet again, I'm flipped, my back crashing to the floor as Knox only drives into me harder and faster. Every flex of his hips only brings me closer to the edge before hurling me off like a rocket. There's no stopping my screams as my orgasm breaks free, a rush of my essence filling every crevice of the room.

So much black I don't even recognize it as my own. So dense, I wonder how there could be anything left inside me.

Knox only moves faster, his length thickening inside me. Every ragged breath filling my ears, competing with the howling whip of tendrils at our skin.

"Knox," I whimper. My insides are still at war. My tissues feeling as though they are being torn apart. Another orgasm is building faster than should be possible. I still haven't come down from the last.

My body is being wrung dry.

What is happening?

How do I stop it?

An earth-shattering pounding startles me. Still, we don't stop dragging out every bit of pleasure from each other's bodies. My name roared over and over again as Knox spills inside me. Every bit of what I do to him fills me to the brim.

A fist slams against the door again, my body trembling as a second release leaves my legs quivering so forcefully I feel it in my teeth. The soft pulse of

Knox's hips into me, keeping every bit of our mixed orgasms inside me. Something he's always done, but nothing I've ever questioned.

His movements are slow as he peppers kisses over my skin. "I need you to calm down, baby. Please."

I nod, still lost in the feel of him driving into my aching pussy, fighting for focus. Fighting to calm the violent essences around us, but I can't. They won't listen. They won't change.

The knocking only intensifies before the last voice I want to hear right now barks through the door. "Bryony, open this damn door!"

9

WYNSTON

THERE AREN'T PROPER WORDS in the English language capable of describing what it's like to feel everything another person does. Every movement, every sensation, every emotion. This connection between Bri and me is so much more than mind-blowing sex. It's deeper than our essences blending into a new entity. It's as if we're becoming one. A possibility unheard of in the wielding world.

Unlike the other magical creatures in books and myths, we don't have mates or soul connections like that. There's no driving force pulling us together or transforming us into a single being, where one heart can't beat without the other. Yet, that's exactly how I would describe this.

Just another jumble of unknowns added to the anomaly of our pairing. Exceptions, we're all continuing to blame on us both being Grisyms.

The pain, the guilt, the turmoil, punish her insides. Their fists beating the soft tissues to a pulp waiting for her to relent. It's all there as if I were experiencing it myself.

Fuck, I'd do anything to take it from her. Neither of us has had an easy life. The Grisym who avoids their death sentence will always struggle. They will live in fear and with incurable doubt. But Bri has it worse than most. Her origins and name have saddled her with more than any of us will ever carry.

Lies, betrayal, and deceit have built her existence. When trusted ones are also those supplying false notions, whom does one believe? How could you not approach every interaction with a certain level of skepticism?

My essence tries to fight against the foreigners. The peaceful balance we've found together refuses to be disturbed. It's our toughest battle yet. Each time she's introduced a new power, my essence has defeated it. But this new light power is different. It's tougher. Yet we snuff out its light, one tiny inch at a time.

"Don't move," I whisper, pressing my lips softly to hers.

Tears stream from the corners of her eyes as I slide free of her wet heat. The chill shooting down my spine serving as a cruel reminder I had to abandon my favorite place in the world.

Another knock cracks against the door. Sharper. More insistent. Impatient.

I scramble in the direction I think I saw the dresser. Typically, I'd at least clean her thighs, careful to keep the mixture of us inside her, while never acknowledging the reasons. I can't. It's not a thought process I can handle on a good day. Toss in everything else imploding around us, and it'll bring me to my knees.

It's a blind fumble through the drawer as her essence continues to wreak havoc on the room. All I have is my touch. Blindly shuffling my hand through the drawer, I grab what I think are sweatpants and t-shirts.

It's an awkward stumble back to the spot where I think I left Bri. My knees crash into the rug beside her, attempting to shimmy the pants up her thighs as she writhes against the battle raging inside her. Giving up, I shove her arms through the shirt, pulling her to sit up enough that I can yank it down her torso.

I could magic the pants onto her body, but I'm too nervous. Too terrified of the consequences should those other essences suspect the worst. They've never enjoyed Bri favoring my essence. And I don't want to give them yet another reason to rebel.

Slipping into the other pair of sweats, I don't bother with the shirt. Somehow, it's no longer next to me where I thought I dropped it. "Hang on, baby." I kiss her mouth, tripping over my own feet in pursuit of the door.

Each pounding fist leads me in the right direction. Reaching for the lock, I go to twist it, realizing we never secured it. It's her essence keeping the door closed.

With a sharp inhale, I clear just enough to crack the door, Vincent charging inside, nearly knocking me to the ground.

"What. The. Fuck?" he breathes. I can just make out his wide eyes. Taking a step closer, the crystalline gray one glows against the dark, making me flinch away from him.

Vincent's glare turns murderous as Bri whimpers my name over and over. "Knox, please."

Her pleas shatter me. I've always been the one to help her. The one who could calm her insides and force them to comply. But tonight I couldn't. I wasn't enough.

"What the hell is wrong with your eyes, and what is this?" Vincent barks in my face, waving his arm through the cloud of essence that has formed a swirling cocoon around us.

"This is what happens to your sister when she takes in new power."

Vincent says nothing, those wicked eyes narrowing on me. The anger rolling off him in threatening waves. The two of us never got along back when we first met, and now that I'm sleeping with his sister, my student, the tension between us may only worsen. He won't see reason. He won't want to understand what Bri means to me.

Just the same, I would rather we keep our shit between us. I've already lied to that woman once. Words that felt like an omission for her own good. When my past felt less like a burden, it's best to avoid slicing open those old wounds. Not just tonight, but ever.

I've wasted enough time engaging in this staring contest. Inhaling deep, I open my mouth as wide as it will go. The corners stretching so much it feels like I've torn the skin. But still I swallow us down in heavy gulps, my eyes never leaving Vincent's. Maybe he'll see the truth.

With every inhale, my insides fill. But no matter how much I consume, it's not enough. The room remains full of Bri's essence storm.

But still, I suck it down. Fight to tame it so it remembers who its leader is. *Bri.* She owns me and will forever. It doesn't matter how hard I fought it when we met. This was inevitable.

Bri leads us all, me included.

It's impossible to know how much I've taken in. I lost track of how long I pulled the cloud of essence into me. Still, our staring contest never broke. Vincent's unwavering gaze only narrowing with each passing second.

Gasping for air, I scramble back to Bri's side, smoothing her curls from her face. My silent plea for her to open her eyes and look at me goes unanswered for several long minutes.

As she peels her eyelids open, the stark white they were is now completely black. "Bri, baby. You're going to have to help me. There's too much. Stop releasing and take it back inside you." It's all I can think of doing.

She shakes her head, sobbing, those tears now soaking into my palm as I cup her cheek.

"I can't do this on my own," I plead.

When she nods, I know she understands, so we fight. Both of us funnel the essences into ourselves until our lungs burn from lack of respiration.

Slowly, the fog seems to clear. The edges and furniture fading back into focus.

I'm on the verge of collapsing when suddenly every ounce of essence just disappears.

When I tear my eyes from Bri's scrunched features, I find Vincent kneeling. One knee drives into the rug, his back curved unnaturally as he drags in ragged breaths. But it's the vessel in hand that holds my attention. Black with a gold-etched design. The symbols from an ancient time and language that few can interpret.

"What have you done to my sister?" he growls.

Bri still whimpers, cradled to my chest, her fingers clenched in my thick strands. The pain of her grip makes me wince, but I ignore it. She's more important right now.

"Let me help her into bed and then we'll talk."

Those mismatched eyes narrow on me before Vincent steps back, cradling the urn to his stomach. But his eyes never leave us as I lift Bri under her arms, her feet somehow finding purchase on the floor. Wrapping an arm around my middle, her cheek still rests against my chest. His full retreat only noted by the click of the door closing.

She may be standing, but my other half isn't steady. Her grip on me tightens as her legs wobble beneath her. My only assumption is she's putting on a brave front for her brother. An attempt at convincing him this isn't as bad as it seems. A lie. It is so much worse.

Not once since we started combining our essences has this happened. With a joint effort, control has always been attainable.

Tears still stream down her cheeks as she moans, swaying in my arms. What I would do to take away every bit of turmoil she's feeling. That I'm feeling.

Bri doesn't say a word or glance my way as I guide her toward the bed. Those black orbs still glisten against the soft yellow light of the chandelier above us. Though my eyes have returned to normal, hers have not. Yet another anomaly of the night.

My mind struggles to determine what happened tonight. What went wrong?

Hell, I still don't know what to make of us. Jorddan believes we can do unthinkable things as a duo—spells and curses I would prefer not to think about.

Brushing her curls back from her forehead, I press a kiss to her warm skin. "I'm going to talk to Vincent. If you're too tired, you sleep. I'll explain it all to him."

She nods, her fingers loosely gripping my wrist as I pull away. "You won't leave, right?"

"Never."

She releases me then, curling to her side, facing the door. Those black eyes held wide open, unblinking.

I've barely got the door open before both Vincent and Jorddan barge through it. Her brother still holds that urn, the damn thing quivering as if there's a creature fighting to break free.

"What is in there?" I question my steps, tentatively putting more distance between me and the two men glaring at me.

Jorddan eyes the object with a quirked brow, but doesn't slow his movements toward the edge of the bed. Toward his daughter. The one person he loves most in this world. The frame groans as he sits beside her, leaning low to whisper words only she can hear.

"What the fuck was that?" Vincent snarls.

"Did Jorddan tell you anything about us?" I point between Bri and me, my arm extended behind my body.

"Just that the two of you could share essences. However, I don't think that's what it actually is."

Hope swells in my chest. Maybe we'll finally have some answers. "Have you experienced this before?"

"No, but Bri is an Eistiab. If any of her essence or yours was returned to you, it wasn't to share." Vincent clutches the urn tighter, mumbling a spell I can't quite hear. The vessel becomes motionless, as if it had never moved at all.

"Then what for?"

Vincent's mismatched stare wanders over to his father before he meets my eyes again. The urn rumbling louder suddenly. It sounds like that of a rattlesnake warning you it's near.

"Sit down, Wynston," Vincent nods to an armchair.

"Call me, Knox."

"Your name is Wynston, so that's what I'll call you. Be glad I'm talking to you at all after you preyed on my sister," Vincent snaps, before his lip curls in disgust.

"It's not like that," Bri croaks.

"I can speak for myself." My tone is curt, though it was in response to her words; the clipped delivery was targeted at Vincent.

There was never a friendship between Vincent and me. Acquaintances would be a generous description even. Just two ships passing in the dark. My fascination with the enigma Vincent Guthrie was no different from any other wielder. We all longed to know his secrets. If the rumors about him were true. We wanted to know about the dirty deeds he and his father committed together. That's where it should have ended.

But rivalry is strong in wielding programs. It wasn't the professors who pitted us against one another, but our classmates.

It was a single semester, but the intolerance that grew between us has never faded, and I doubt it ever will. Even our both loving Bri won't melt it away.

"Tell me why you're nearly forty and fucking a child, then? Your goddamned student, no less?" His arm tightens around the urn again. Fingers flexing against its constant movement.

"You know what it's like. We are isolated in this double life. Constantly living in fear that someone may find out what we are. Maybe it's not the same for you because, no matter what, you had a father who was willing to go to the ends of the earth and then some to protect you, but I didn't, and neither did Bri. Roman can pretend he did her some big favor, but he was protecting himself." A deep, angry growl emanates from Vincent. Vicious enough, I flinch away from him, despite the three feet between our chairs. "Whoever he had working with her while she battled her mature powers for ten fucking years did a shit job. She needed me, but I needed her too." I pause as emotion swells in my chest.

Being a Grisym is the loneliest existence. It's easy to feel isolated. You become anyone but who you truly are. It doesn't matter if you're happy with that existence. You're alone in your truth. Meeting Bri allowed me to be my genuine self for the first time in my life. And I believe I was the same for her.

It didn't matter that my family knew what I was. I had to choose a side. I couldn't just be both. The risk was too great. My father reminds me that I am proof that love is not enough. His passion for my mother couldn't outweigh the life that accompanies harboring an illegal being. I wasn't enough.

"This can be a lonely life, Vincent." My head drops, shaking softly, attempting to shove those emotions back into the pits of hell where they belong. I don't feel that way anymore, not since Bri.

"You could have kept her safe without having sex with her," Vincent quips.

"Yeah, I could have. And I would have, had it felt like a choice." A heavy sigh leaves me as I scrub my hands over my face. "Our essences chose this before we did."

"Quiet. My baby girl is sleeping," Jorddan chides us before coming to stand against the wall between Vincent and me. Our chairs nestled in the far corner, putting the most distance between where Bri sleeps and our heated conversation.

"You said that you don't think Bri and I truly share essences," I whisper, leaning forward, my elbows resting on my knees.

"No. Do you feel any of the other essences she's stolen inside you?" Vincent asks.

I open my mouth to say yes, but quickly realize the answer is no. They're inside her. That's where I feel them. I battle them inside her to submit, so they know I am the primary foreign essence that lives within her.

"No, I don't think so. But our essences seem intertwined. Like she is part of me."

Vincent's features soften, that pale eye looking right through me. "Wynston, you are a vessel."

10

Bryony

A SMILE TUGS AT the corners of my mouth as I stretch awake in bed. The ache between my legs and the weight of my limbs against the soft sheets are a reminder of how thoroughly Knox took me last night. My body is coming to life all over again as he snores softly beside me, fists tucked under the pillow, giving me a view of the expanse of his upper back.

Rolling toward him, perched on my side, I study his handsome face. Dark circles smear under his eyes, and the frown lines on his forehead are deeper than I've ever seen. Visible evidence of his lack of sleep. Last night was of no help in rectifying that. His nights after my episodes always prove to be restless.

Whether it's because of what stirs inside him or out of concern, he's never told me.

Running my fingers through his hair, he moans softly but doesn't move otherwise. My palm hovers over his wild waves, ready to feel them again, but guilt sits in my lower belly. He needs rest. I refuse to intentionally wake him.

Slipping into the bathroom, I quickly freshen up, brushing my teeth and washing my face. Mundane tasks we all do every day. Basic routines used to set the tone of your morning. But they don't have that effect on me today. The sharp pinprick of too many emotions pierces my insides, keeping me wound tight.

My hands shake as I stare down at them. Only water beads on my fingertips, but all I see is red. I still feel dirty. Wrong. Covered in blood. Blood that spilled because of me.

Tears burn behind my eyes. Vincent assured me Valen would be fine. *"I promise he'll be okay with rest. Give him time,"* Vincent sighed. I'd absorbed his words. Words Graham has said to me multiple times now.

Time. Give him time.

I can do that, but something about seeing is believing points me toward Valen. I need to see, with my own eyes, that he's alive. Last night feels like a cruel nightmare.

Confirming my favorite tormentor still breathes will put my mind at ease. All while anchoring me to the present. It will make last night that much more real. A reminder of the evil lurking beyond these walls.

I just want to touch him. Hear his heartbeat against my chest. Kiss him.

Yet, Valen will have to wait. First, I need to speak with my father.

Jorddan Guthrie made it clear he didn't want me returning to Beauxgraton last night. A warning my gut tells me to heed, but my heart wants to fight.

I know he's right. It's dangerous, and with Roman's title, the man I'd spent my life calling Dad can get to me whenever he wants.

Yet, that tiny seed of doubt remains. Doubt Roman will look for me there. He won't expect me to return to the site where we battled a day ago, right?

Sure, he has spies everywhere. I was one of them. How else would he know if I returned?

I wonder who else received the same task. How many more eyes and ears were gathering information? And to what end?

The moment I laid in bed, I'd battled myself over the right decision. I lay still as I let my father's words wash over me. His love filling me with hope of a better future, as long as he's in it.

I'd made my decision just as my eyes drifted shut. A choice I will have to review, in detail, with my father to ensure we take every necessary precaution. The guys may not be happy about it either, but it's not their decision to make.

I'd only held out long enough to hear a portion of Knox and Vincent's conversation last night. There's a tension between them. A past Knox clearly lied to me about. Details I'll uncover when there's time. For now, cooperation is a stretch. All they need is enough tolerance for one another so we can move forward.

We'll need to talk about it, just the three of us. I can predict Knox's responses, but not Vincent's. I don't know how he was raised or what type of challenges he faced. Not when he got to live as a dark wielder and proudly in the spotlight beside our father. A platform that promotes owning who you are instead of curating a public image our wielding peers would better receive.

Taking one last glance at Knox as I exit the bathroom, he hasn't moved. He'll flip his shit when he doesn't find me in bed, but it's not like I can leave this house. The ward around the manor has a timer. It permits no one in or out for the next twenty-four hours.

Father's orders. Just the man I want to see.

I exit, giving my quarters one last look. A room designed just for me. A formerly vacant space that was waiting for me to come home.

Wandering through the corridors in daylight is like something out of a movie. As we'd shuffled to our respective rooms last night—early this morning—only the tiniest sliver of sunrise peeked through on the horizon, casting the interior in the soft glow of lights while the midnight sky still lingered outside the massive windows. You see old-money mansions like this on the big screen all the time. It's always fiction, never reality. The hand-painted artwork on the walls, exquisite hand-carved wood trims and furniture, Persian rugs, and ornate wallpaper.

It's everything you would imagine a centuries-old British manor would embody. I suppose an ancestor in the Guthrie bloodline is of British descent. They shaped this place into what it is now. A home passed down through generations, forever bearing our name. History, I hope to learn, eventually.

There were countless days I could forget Roman wasn't my real father. It was easy when he showered me with kindness and held me as I cried at night. There was no question that I was his daughter when he encouraged me and raved about my accomplishments with pride to anyone who would listen.

But curiosity often still won. I was in the dark too. I always knew that. Felt it. Wanted it.

We all only ever want to belong. To a family. To someone. To a cause or our past or future. There was always a part of me that needed to know where I came from. Only the Avalon home wasn't a place where I could ask. There was no room to speak about the half of me that didn't fit with their squeaky-clean image.

Now I can.

The wood railing is cool beneath my palm as I creep down the stairs. The gaze of each portrait follows me with each forward step. Some hold familiarity while most don't. It can only be their features. Eyes, noses, and chins that are similar to Vincent's and mine.

On the platform, I pause, my fingers brushing over the cheek of what must be my grandpa's portrait. The white-haired version of my father.

"You were here for a short time," my father's voice sounds behind me, my arm pulling back, hand tucked into my chest.

Heavy breaths puff past my lips as I jump before spinning to face my dad. "You scared me."

Jorddan only takes a step closer, his hands finding my elbows. The dark hair of his goatee twitches with a hint of a smile, coaxing my heartbeat into finally slowing. With a soft tug, he pulls me into that hug I've already grown accustomed to, kissing my forehead with a tenderness Roman used to show me.

"I apologize. Perhaps you believe you missed all this, which is partly true." Shifting me to the side, we both stare at the painting, my head resting on my dad's shoulder as his arm curls around mine. "After you were born, you and your mother were here with us for a time. We were a family then." His long fingers squeeze my shoulder. "And now we are once again."

"I love it here," I admit. "It feels like home."

My father only gives me a soft squeeze before shaking me softly. "Good. Would you like to join me for breakfast?"

I nod, wrapping an arm around his back.

We move in silence, my eyes still roving over every surface, taking it all in. After I graduate, I want to live here for at least a little while. I want those pieces of my life back. Pieces I don't remember. Years of memories I never had the chance to make.

I'm lost in the ambiance of this place. Every detail speaks to me as if welcoming me home. I wonder if there are spells on it, and I am truly hearing the voices of the magic the manor holds.

"Oh," I gasp as my father pulls out a chair for me. How had I missed that we'd wandered into the dining room?

Jorddan guides me into a chair before sliding into the one next to me. "That's where you always sat. You weren't happy if you couldn't look out those windows there."

Glancing out now, I can see why. A massive lake shimmers in the distance. The size is similar to the one I'd grown so fond of at Beauxgraton. One side bordered by what must be beautiful gardens in the warmer months and neatly spaced trees.

"It's beautiful," I breathe.

"You've always loved the water. We used to joke that you were actually a mermaid."

I scrunch a brow at my father, wondering if they actually exist.

"Dad," I pause. My stomach rolls, wondering if I should have asked permission to call him that again. "I can still call you that, right?"

His head tilts, face elongating as he studies me. "And what else might you call me?"

"I—" Shaking my head, I continue with my former speech. "I thought about what you said."

"Which part?" he questions as a cook brings out plates full of food. My stomach rumbles. When was the last time I had a proper meal?

"About returning to Beauxgraton. I don't think it's the right move right now. I want to write you a list of everyone who worked with me when I was younger. But more than that, I want to take down Roman. So I was thinking we could get Janelle to sign off on my doing a study abroad program somewhere, but I can actually study alongside the other Grisyms you've been housing at the closed institutions. That will give us time to act and—"

Jorddan holds up a finger, and my mouth immediately clamps shut. "I appreciate your enthusiasm, but it's not that simple."

"Which part?" I echo his sentiment with a huff as I shove a forkful of potatoes into my mouth.

Fuck. These are amazing!

"Ensuring Roman gets everything that's coming to him. I can tell by the look in your eyes you've been spending too much time with Valen, haven't you?"

"I—"

But he continues. "Anyone who potentially knows what you are will be dealt with. My way. You will not be involved. I refuse to allow you to be burned at the stake for doing the dirty work."

"And I won't let you do it without me," I retort with a low hiss. "He used me to keep you on a leash, Dad. He was molding me into a tool to use against you and who knows who else."

Jorddan runs a thumb over my cheek. "And he will get what is coming to him. I promise you, Roman will no longer be breathing once I am done with him, but not before he pleads for death."

"Okay," I concede. It seems this discussion is closed. For now, all I can do is let it go. For now, I will pretend my father's words are enough to curb my desire for revenge.

Stabbing a piece of sausage, he raises his fork to his mouth before speaking. "However, we can talk about your schooling options."

I perk up at that, chewing my sausage slowly. "Is Willoughby one of the schools you took over?" I ask.

"It is."

Leaning forward, I abandon my food. "And are there Grisyms there?"

"There are," my father crosses his arms over his chest.

"Then I would like to go there. It would keep me close to the manor so I can be near you and Vincent."

A broad grin spreads across my father's face. "We would love to keep you here in the UK," he says.

"Bri!" My name is snapped like a whip from across the dining room. "You've got to be kidding me!"

11

PIERSON

GRAHAM CHARGES PAST ME, ranting under his breath. His face is so red he blends in with our precious red moons.

"Graham—"

"Fuck off, Pierson," he shouts in my direction before yanking open the massive front door and bolting outside.

It's not the first time Graham has thrown one of his temper tantrums. His long legs carrying him off to nowhere, while he mumbles to himself about whatever Bri did to piss him off this time. It's how Valen learned about Bri and Knox.

As if glued in place, my feet refuse to move. My focus on the stairs and grounds outside the manor front door, Graham didn't even bother to close behind him.

He's always been high-strung and overdramatic, but the pit in my stomach tells me this response might hold some actual justification.

Determined to find out, I'm seconds from taking a step toward the door when Jorddan calls out my name with an authoritarian tone he's never addressed me with before. "Sir," I answer him with the same respect I've always shown him. A grace the others often lack.

They may be willing to test Jorddan's patience, but I'm not. Joining his mission was never a goal of mine. Rather it was the peer pressure of Valen shoving me into this shit and my guilt convincing me I owed him. He was the one who stood by my side when my parents kicked me out. I could do this for him.

Valen has never lost his knack for dragging me into his shit, but I also let him. Until this year, I've never pushed back. It felt as if invisible hands had sewn my mouth shut when I should have spoken up.

That was until Bri. I finally had something... *No*, someone of my own.

Funny, I wasn't enough for her either.

"Go after Graham. Bring him back," Jorddan commands with a purposeful rotation of his wrist. "We will all meet in the great room in ten minutes."

With a nod, I put more distance between us. Jorddan has mastered schooling his features, but his emotions sometimes seem to radiate off him. Rolling toward you in a violent wave, it's best not to be in front of it. "Yes, sir."

Before Jorddan speaks again, I bolt into the frigid morning. From the doorway, the sunshine proved to be the greatest deception. The rays beaming down as if inviting you to stand beneath them.

Sunlight provides little warmth when temperatures dip this low. It may stretch the minutes you can tolerate, but it never reverses them. Wrapping my arms around my body, I mentally chastise myself for not grabbing a coat hanging on the rack by the door.

"Graham!"

Scanning the grounds, it's nothing but grass, trees, and gardens. There's no Graham. It's been no more than five minutes. I can't imagine that he ran off that quickly. Graham has reminded me countless times that physical activity isn't his thing.

My head moves from one direction to another, searching. There were no cars left out front. That would have been the only way for a speedy getaway.

That's a Guthrie rule.

Despite knowing this is the Guthrie home, no one expects to find them here. Jorddan's staff runs the manor, and otherwise, Jorddan abandons it to anyone outside the New Order or the small circle Jorddan allows into his private life. At least, that's what our world has been led to believe.

"Graham!" I shout again.

"I told you to fuck off," he grumbles off to my right.

Running my hands over my arms again, I round the cluster of trees. His long frame leans against a massive tree trunk, the thing almost blocking his body from view.

"Jorddan wants us all inside," I point a thumb behind me. The chatter of my teeth draws his gaze up from his feet. The set of his jaw is so hard I wince, waiting for him to crack a tooth.

"Why? So Bri can tell us all she doesn't give a shit?"

It's been a while since he's been this on edge. I wouldn't say the two of us have become friends, but we get along. Our relationship is amicable. We're in love with the same woman. Yet, seconds ago, he spoke about that same woman as if she were shit on his designer shoes.

Though his outburst has nothing to do with her being a Grisym this time, it makes me wonder if he's still more bothered by that fact than he lets on. He'd freaked out when he learned the truth. Wanted nothing to do with our girl for weeks, but he slowly came around. For her, he could see reason and realize she was an amazing person, despite her magical composition.

"You know that isn't true," I try. What else can I say? He's angry and hurt. We've all been there, but Bri is my concern. Her feelings are what I'm worried about, not his.

"Yeah. You sure about that, Pierce?" Graham's features darken, contorting into a sneer that I wouldn't think him capable of.

"Where is this coming from?"

"She's staying here." His head drops. "I just overheard her telling her father."

My heart stutters in my chest. A fist pushing through my hoodie and chest to clutch the beating muscle and crush it.

So much has happened since last night. We lost Valen, only for Vincent to bring him back. I'd been so exhausted after using so much I barely said a word to Bri. I honestly haven't seen her since Vincent dropped us at our rooms one by one.

Heartbreak splashes across Graham's face. My chest aching the same way his must be. We just got her. If she stays here in England, it'll be like losing her. It doesn't matter what claim she made on us.

Dropping a hand to his shoulder, his eyes meet mine. "We have to consider what is best for Bri. She's in more danger than we are."

"And what about us? She just stays here safe while we're sent back out into the real world?" His arm flies past my head, fingers shaking as he points toward the road. "Her father knows we know who and what she is! Do you really think Roman is going to just leave us alone?"

I wish I could tell him yes with confidence. I could, but it would still be a lie. Not a single fiber of my being believes Roman is done with us, whether we remain involved with Bri or not. Roman will kill us for sport. He spent Bri's whole life using her as a pawn to control Jorddan. What's keeping him from using us the same to get to her?

"I don't." Swallowing hard, I stare off into the distance before continuing, "But I think that's all the more reason for us to go listen to Jorddan's plan. There is nothing he cares about more than his children's well-being and happiness. That extends to us now."

"I'm not ready for this," Graham shakes his head. A heavy sigh leaves him as he pushes off the tree, clumsily stalking back toward the manor. Defeat makes his steps heavy, his head hung low as if he's already given up on any fight that was left inside him.

Staying by his side, I hope he feels a little less alone. He's not the only one drowning in the crashing waves of change. Ultimately, Bri is the one he needs to hear from now, not me. So I don't say another word.

He's scared. I imagine we all are to an extent, but we chose this. There's no turning back now.

Graham comes from a solid, light family. A rule-following family who worked hard for their places in the world. He's not used to the shadows that lurk in the dark. His light is slowly dimming the more time he spends with us.

Stepping back inside the manor, a blast of warm air sends a shiver through me. My lips rolling together as I finally let my body relax. We quietly pass through the foyer into the large parlor, where Jorddan prefers our groups to meet.

Damian, Vincent, Bri, and the twins are already seated when Graham and I enter. Knox practically drags Valen right behind us. Camilla then follows, babbling about nothing to Collin. His grin as bright as it's always been since the day he met her. Only now he knows a friendship is the only relationship they'll ever have.

As if waiting to see where everyone else will sit, Graham, surprisingly, chooses the spot next to Valen. They grunt, sizing each other up, before settling in on the loveseat. An unspoken message passes between them. The start of a bond causing me to blink several times. But I'm not dreaming. The two are getting along as if they'd always been friends. Perhaps it's that Valen's loyalty is on display. Graham saved him, so now Val is in his debt.

Headmistress Milgren, Mr. Greer, Jorddan, and Sean are the last to enter. The three elders stand in front of the stone fireplace, our leader just a hair in front of them, before facing us all.

"Last night was necessary," Jorddan begins just as the slam of the front doors stalls his words.

Huffing breaths enter through the doorway at the rear of the room. A head of golden, burnt orange hair billows into view. The brightest, piercing green eyes meet ours just before Damian runs across the room, scooping his wife into his arms. Their reunion is so intimate that I almost want to look away.

When did I last hold Bri like that?

"Tosch. Great of you to join us," Jorddan deadpans.

"Oh, posh. Stop being so doom and gloom. I haven't missed anything in the five hours since you contacted me, have I?"

No one gets away with dismissing Jorddan's usual demeanor the way Tosch does. Perhaps it's because Jorddan has always treated her like his own. A placeholder for the daughter he never had a proper relationship with.

Now that Bri's here, it's clear from the glint in both their eyes that they are not letting go ever again. There's no blood bond stronger than Guthrie love.

Jorddan rolls his eyes at Tosch as she nestles into Damian's lap. "As I said, last night was just a small victory."

"Um, excuse me," Camilla's hand shoots into the air, the twins groaning as if someone just told them they have to scrub toilets with their own toothbrushes.

"Ms. VanBuren, yes." Jorddan slightly angles his body toward hers.

"Camilla, please. Well, I was wonderin' how that was a win? I wasn't out there, but to me it seems nothin' was solved, was it?" Her head cocks to the side, those long blonde strands rubbing along the legs of her chair. "From where I'm standing, all you did was send light wielders back to their lives. Unless Pierce can wipe every memory of Bri and what the news has been sayin' about you, all we did was kill a few people. Right?"

Jorddan quirks a brow, his mouth stretching into a straight line as he takes several steps toward Camilla. To her credit, she doesn't flinch at all.

Her big blue eyes hold our leader's gaze, confident in her line of questioning. You'd think she might cower or avert her stare, but she doesn't, patiently waiting for his response.

"You're a smart one. I see why my daughter is drawn to you. And yes, you are right. Roman still knows about my daughter. If angered enough, I have no doubt he will make it known to others. They will come after her. And me." Jorddan tilts his head as if it means nothing. "He will be dealt with in time."

"You mean give him the good old..." Camilla makes a croaking sound, dragging her thumb across her neck, before her head falls to the side, eyes closing and tongue lolling out of her mouth.

"If it comes to that, Ms. Van Buren. You stand with my daughter, do you not?"

"I'm here, right?" Camilla scrunches her nose as if her presence made it clear enough.

"Answer my question."

"Mr. Guthrie, look around. We're all on your side; otherwise, why would we be here? So stop questionin' if we're gonna go through with whatever crazy plans you have. We will. For her. For you."

Jorddan snorts, pivoting toward our expectant stares. "Well, you've all heard Ms. Van Buren here. Can you confirm what she says is true?"

I'm on my feet without a thought. "If Bri is staying here, then so am I."

In seconds, the room joins me, each of us standing tall, baring our marks for Jorddan.

Only three of us stay seated: Milgren, Camilla, and Lionel. They may not bear his mark now, but before this is over, two of them will.

We will fight for Bri the way we have all done for Jorddan.

12

BRYONY

It's overwhelming as I rake my eyes over the marks on their bodies. Each one bears my father's name. It's their pledge to him. The truth of their loyalty until death. A tangible symbol that transcends spoken words or actions.

"Please sit," Jorddan orders. "We have much to cover."

My father commands the room as he always has. He holds every bit of attention, only pausing to probe with specific questions. His plan for our safety and victory unfolding with each word. No matter how carefully crafted things are, they can go wrong. Others would shy away, abandoning the course. Not us; we lean in.

"If Pierce is staying, so am I," Valen grunts, his arm wrapping across his middle.

"Mr. Greer, you will return to Beauxgraton," Janelle quips. "As will you, Mr. Flaggstaff. Your education is not up for debate."

"No, I'm not. Whether we want to believe it or not, Bri is the target. Not Jorddan. Roman may not remember everything she can do because Pierce ordered him to forget that night, but he knows enough. He will know he is missing something too important when Bri doesn't return next semester. Forget when he learns about everyone who has ever interacted with and trained her, turns up dead."

"Dead?" Graham croaks.

"What did you think was going to happen, Goody Two-Shoes? They can't just go about their lives. They'll talk," Valen snaps, shooting up from his seat, his glare murderous.

Graham follows, his movement sending the floral embroidered loveseat groaning across the rug. "And we have to be like them? Killing because we're scared?"

"It has nothing to do with fear," Damian interjects. "It's smart. If you want your girlfriend to survive to see twenty-six, you'll be quiet and listen."

Graham's mouth presses into a straight line, his glare now focused on Damian. The two have never been amicable. Graham was always fighting to keep Damian away when he would come around. We know the truth now, though. Damian was under orders from my brother. He's the last one who would ever hurt me.

"Look, I appreciate everyone wanting to protect me. I do." Stepping between Graham and Valen, the muscles of their chests flex beneath my palms. Each pushing hard against my resistance. "But I'm not asking for that."

I won't back down. Now isn't the time for them to have a dick measuring contest.

"We're telling you we're staying where you are," Valen shrugs away from me, producing a dagger out of thin air. That sneer curls the corner of his mouth as he tosses it handle over blade, catching it by the tip the way he often does. A threat to anyone brave enough to challenge him.

"Enough, Val. Enough." The last word is nothing more than a sigh on my lips. He slumps back into his seat, his dark eyes narrowed on me, that dagger still flipping through the air like it's nothing. Still, there's no mistaking the grimace of pain with the set of his mouth. His short beard is nowhere near long enough to cover his vulnerability.

A shaky deep breath fills my lungs as I search for the right words to say. Maybe there are none. Maybe they're right. Perhaps I am. Or maybe it's as simple as differing opinions that will never intersect. Pierce and Valen are showing me their devotion, and I don't know what to do about it. "Knox," I turn toward him. "I—you're the only one."

"I'm not leaving either," he declares, knotting his fingers through mine. "What happened with your essence last night was out of this world. You could not have controlled that on your own."

"What happened last night?" Valen, Pierce, and Graham all voice at once. My gaze bounces between the three, all poised on the edges of their seats, demanding an answer. Their unified response sets me on edge. They are never in sync on anything.

Kormoran leans his weight back in the chair; the groan of the wood fighting to hold his monstrous frame pulls my attention toward him. "Oh, this is going to be good." I hate that smug grin on his face. His psycho twin sister is wearing a matching one, ready for the guys to finally lay into me.

"Bri lost control of her essence. It filled the room. I think the other new ones were battling... mine," Knox explains.

"They were." Vincent stands from the arm of the couch he'd been sitting on. Tosch and Damian mimicking his movements, joining my brother in the center of the room as if they had planned it. "Does anyone else here have Bri's essence inside them?"

Everyone shakes their heads except Knox. "You know I do. It's part of me."

"I wasn't talking about you," Vincent grunts. He moves past us, pulling that same urn he'd had last night from the mantle. It rattles a few times before it goes still. Swirls of shapes that resemble marble curl around the surface, forming a pattern that evokes infinite possibilities. A pattern I'm sure I've seen before, but can't place.

"No," Tosch breathes, her delicate fingers covering her full mouth.

"Yes. If Bri's essence ever tries to enter you, don't let it." Vincent makes eye contact with each person in the room. Camilla wears a look of intrigue and our father hosts an expression I can't pinpoint. "Her capabilities extend beyond just taking someone's essence or gifts. Her essence craves it, but her body can't hold it all."

"Meaning what?" Graham questions.

"Knox and Bri's essences are intertwined somehow. I haven't figured that part out, but more importantly, she is using him as a vessel. Whenever she takes in new essences or siphons from a ghoul, she loses control, right?"

My men nod, including me. I hadn't been awake for much of Knox and Vincent's chat last night. My brother hinted he might have an idea about Knox and me. Only now is he revealing his suspicions.

"Get to the point," Valen snaps.

"My point is," Vincent holds up the urn, "I had to use this to help clear out the storm that Bri's essence created in her room last night after she took in those light-wielding essences."

"Is that what I think it is?" Sean swallows.

My brother cradles the urn back against his body as if scared the thing will shatter, rereleasing my storm. "Yes. It's a portal vessel. I couldn't close it, so technically her very rambunctious combo could get out, but we have it warded, so hopefully we're safe."

"What's a portal vessel?" Camilla asks.

"Usually, they have specific destinations per the owner's choosing. A place where they can send stored power that's hidden from anyone but themselves. When they want it, their blood can open and close the portal," Vincent explains, his tone softening while speaking to my best friend.

"That thing uses blood magic?" Camilla's eyes go wide with wonder.

"Yes. This is Bri's. Our mother commissioned it when she was a baby." His eyes find me then. "Even then, she held too much power for her body to handle." Vincent averts his gaze suddenly, only for me to confirm exactly what he said by the sadness coating my father's eyes.

"That's why you struggled to close it?" I whisper.

"Yes." He inhales deep, only to exhale longer than should be possible. "Bri, I need you to understand how dangerous you can be when you take more than your body can handle. When you take essences that aren't yours." Vincent returns the vessel to the mantle, his shoulders rolling forward as if carrying the weight of the world.

"I can't always help it." I feel like a scolded child and somewhat embarrassed as every pair of eyes focuses on me.

Before I came to Beauxgraton, I would feel the urge if someone had their essence on display around me. I could feel my insides reaching, but a simple no was always enough. An intensity that grew while attending school with a horde of wielders. The temptation of dark power overwhelmed me. I had to have it. It became a compulsion I couldn't control or stop.

Maybe if my mother had fought harder to keep me connected with my biological father, we wouldn't be here. Rage bubbles to the surface, boiling the blood roaring through my veins. I don't know what happened between Roman and my parents, but I blame her. "This is her fault," I growl under my breath.

"She is partially to blame," Jorddan agrees. "I will deal with that." My eyes shoot up. "No, I will not kill her. Unfortunately, I refuse to live a day in this world without her." The words were delivered as if his feelings for her were the ultimate inconvenience.

Those words should settle me, but they don't. I am a danger to everyone around me. The new version of the apex predator. Even now, I can feel my essence stir, sniffing out the others in the room. Licking its chops, eager for a taste, sporting a hungry grin. I used to feel it all the time, but never admitted the truth of my urges until Beauxgraton. Until Knox and I discovered what we could do.

"Then what do I do? Lock myself away and never interact with anyone but Knox again?" My wince is automatic as I watch him flinch away from me. I hadn't meant it that way. I've never felt trapped by him, but now it's different. Now he's my only key to some semblance of a normal existence.

"That's why I'm here," Tosch chirps.

"You?" I question. "What are you going to do?"

"Tosch manipulates essences," Damian replies. He spoke the words so slowly, choosing each one carefully. A partial truth about Tosch's capabilities.

With a roll of my eyes, I slouch back in my seat. "So does Knox, and all I've been doing is using him as my free storage facility," I snort.

Tosch smirks, eyeing her husband conspiratorially. "Well, it's a bit more than manipulation. I can force essences to comply." Once again, carefully chosen words.

What aren't they saying?

"Are you aware of how a dominant and submissive relationship works?" she asks.

The room goes silent, my swallow audible. "Sure..."

"Consider me your new dom, Bryony." There's too much pep in her step. Her tone is as chipper as Camilla's, but the glimmer in her eye holds no innocence.

I suspect I won't enjoy this.

13

BRYONY

My temples pound. A heavy bass drum *bang, bang, banging* as Tosch grins at me.

Tosch practically stated her plans for unrelenting torment after hours upon hours spent detailing her most effective techniques. An interlude before my father once again took over command of our gathering. It only left me with a pit in my stomach and bile creeping up my throat.

One scenario after another, we walked through the necessary steps, precautions, and pivoting points as a group. Vincent held a steady stream of my father's memories, so we could later reference any point in the conversation. An ability I thought only worked on the dead or those he resurrected. Come to find out, much like Sean, he can take memories and store them at will. A gift that he described is more closely related to mind-reading than actual theft of those recounts.

A fiery red thread waved through the space between their temples. Little whips crackling every few seconds as if to remind us they were there. My fingers itched to touch the connection. It was like seeing lightning up close for the first time. Mesmerizing. Beautiful.

When it came time to reveal my list, my chest seized. The names lodged in my throat. A pit forming in my belly that seemed to cause me to sink into the floor. A visceral reaction, I told myself. In my mind, I've denounced any loyalty or love for Roman, but that didn't mean my heart wasn't still catching up.

My heart cried that I was betraying the man who raised me as his daughter my entire life. It shouted at me to forgive. Still, my mind fought against the weak organ, warning me betrayal like this wasn't redeemable. There will be no begging for forgiveness if Jorddan's plans fail.

My mind grins wickedly, thrilled with the challenge. If only my heart would follow at a quicker pace.

Hours of reviewing every name from the past twenty-five years were exhausting. I could recite every single one, every title, every interaction, every word they said to me. It wasn't a superpower; it was just how strongly I believed Roman was trying to help me.

The love and appreciation I had for him made me cling to those memories. They served as the chains I never noticed I'd snapped on my wrists, ankles, and throat to keep from ever stepping out of line. With a single question about my dark side, my parents shut it down. There was no room for discussion. For months after one of my many slip-ups, they would not tolerate any further mention of it. Just for the cycle to repeat once more.

I was to live as a gifted light wielder from extraordinary bloodlines. Nothing more. Nothing less.

Thirty-two.

The number of witnesses who saw my abilities developing as I grew up. A minimum guess of the potential list of wielders who may know the truth about me.

Thirty-two wielders who may know what I am. I may hold memories of them, but who knows what they may have witnessed in my youngest years. Occurrences I may fail to recollect.

Not a single wielder on that list mattered to me. They were a means to an end. A chance to live up to the expectations my parents had for me. An opportunity presented to me on a silver platter, so I didn't disappoint Roman, my mother, and my siblings. My only hope for Harley to love me back.

In retrospect, they were a mirage of faces that rotated throughout my youth. Their attempts at helping me harness my power requested by Roman. Tools to mold me into a light wielder who could master control after being forced to mature at fifteen.

Grandma Avalon taught me not to rely on my memory. Even if I forgot our sessions over time, my journals never would. A practice I started at age seven, shortly before she died. I always wondered if she knew. Did she have a vision that told her I would need this information someday?

Janelle had come to see me shortly before I left for Beauxgraton. Unwilling to risk them being discovered, I'd asked her to take them with her. She left with them stored in a trunk Grandma Avalon had gifted to me as a child. Roman was none the wiser about the precious information within.

I still read those pages more frequently than I should. A recap of the details I've clung to because I didn't understand what I was, and Roman and my mother were so eager to sweep it all under the rug. They wouldn't have been much help. Not when they couldn't understand what I was. Hell, we don't have all the answers now. A fact that makes me feel even more alone than I always have. Isolated on my own island for their protection. For mine, too.

Jorddan's presence in my life could have solved so many problems. An alternate timeline that makes me question whether my relationships would be different now. Would Knox and I have bonded or even met? What about the guys? Would I have known them before starting school at Beauxgraton? Or even attended there at all?

Though we don't exactly understand the connection between Knox and me, Vincent says there are others out there we can contact. Tosch has academic connections as well. It's my only hope.

The mixing of essences between us is unheard of.

I'm the first Eistiab on record in centuries. The last a dark wielder from eastern Europe who died shortly after maturing. His body couldn't handle what he was.

For now, it's just me.

The knob of my door twists with a squeak, pulling me out of my thoughts, but doing nothing to alleviate the headache. Groaning, I massage my fingers into my throbbing temples. I wish I could sleep for days or wake from this nightmare.

One by one, my guys enter, Valen bringing up the rear, still wincing with his steps. That usual swagger he moves with is gone. Every motion is calculated. His movements remain labored and slow, as if attempting to minimize the pain. Agony that will follow him for at least the next week.

"Movie night," Pierce suggests, the smile pronounced in his tone. He's always been great at making me laugh when all I wanted to do was drown in my tears. His ability to make me forget my troubles, even for just a moment, is unmatched.

And for a moment, I do. For brief seconds, I can pretend we're not in danger. I can imagine a world where we're not on the run and we're happy.

Sitting up taller against the upholstered headboard, I clutch a pillow to my stomach. The lace embroidery distracts me from meeting their gazes. I'm not ready to see them look at me any differently, which is exactly what I always feared. "You guys probably shouldn't be near me right now."

"Bri, look at me." Pierce's smile drops as he stalks straight over to the massive bed, climbing in beside me. "Bri, listen to me. We're not scared of you. None of us. Tosch is going to help you." Large hands cradle my body and head, the steady beat of Pierce's heart making me breathe a little easier. He's telling the truth—a relief.

"I hope so," I whisper. The words are watery and low, but they heard me. They always do. Trying to pull away, he cups my cheek, forcing my gaze to meet his. Those denim-blue eyes stare into mine. Endless questions flash across the swirls of dark blue. But he stays silent. His words trapped behind his tightly pressed lips. "Did you know Damian and Vincent were such good friends?" I ask, determined to take the focus off me as the others all crowd onto the bed around us.

"No. We all knew they knew each other, but never how close they were," Valen confirms, a hint of annoyance keeping his words clipped.

"Oh..."

I have nothing else to say as Knox clicks on the massive flat-screen TV that rises from behind the dresser. A hidden gem I didn't know was there. A modern touch to a historical place. I like it.

Truthfully, I love everything about the manor. It's as if I can sense the memories around every corner. Their tiny voices whispering to follow them so I could see for myself. As if my body wants me to remember this is my home and where I belong.

"We talked to Milgren," Graham suddenly blurts.

"About?"

"She'll submit the paperwork for us all to do a study abroad program here with you," Pierce says, running a hand down my arm. His fingers brush up and down, soft and mindless.

Shifting out of Pierce's hold, I turn toward my one and only academic rival. "Graham?" He won't look at me. Though silent, his gaze shifts back and forth, focused on the duvet, hunting for the right words.

The bed creaks as I scoot closer, opening my mouth to get him to talk to me. This is precisely what I feared.

As if my hand on his thigh wakes him up, vibrant eyes meet mine. "You told me to make the choice that wouldn't make me resent you, but I made the choice that wouldn't leave me hating myself. If something happens to you, I won't forgive myself."

I lean forward, extending my arms to him, his long frame crawling the few inches to me, knocking me to my back as his body presses into mine. My lips hover beside his ear as I whisper to him. "You can still change your mind. If any of this ever becomes too much for you, you can walk away. You'll still be my best friend."

He nods, pulling back, our eyes meeting for a moment before trailing down to my mouth. Graham and I had only that one night together. An amazing night. Where I'd had the opportunity to explore my physical relationship with the others, we never got that chance. "Do it," I whisper, just before his mouth meets mine.

Graham's tongue immediately invades my mouth, his arms holding his torso off of mine as his hips grind into me, his cock bulging behind the zipper of his jeans. We didn't have sex that night. A choice that felt right for us, but now my insides burn for him. His sacrifice for me means more than I could express in words.

His education means the most to him. To change course now must have him fighting an internal battle; his heart must have won. He wouldn't be staying here in the UK otherwise.

"Enough," Valen snaps. "You're not fucking her right next to me."

"Jealous?" Graham retorts.

Valen snorts, leaning further back into the pillows at my side. "No. I've been inside that tight cunt. You haven't."

"Okay, stop. Valen, you're a dick." My arm raises to swat him, his involuntary flinch followed by the low groan reminding me he's in enough pain.

His icy fingers curl around mine, forcing my hand to run along his lower back. That wicked grin spreads as my fingers trace over the knife tucked away at the base of his spine. "I know, but you love my cock and my daggers."

I only roll my eyes, yanking my hand away. The credits roll on the screen, stealing my attention. The original "Amityville Horror."

Great choice.

Nuzzling deeper into the pillows, I'm ready to enjoy another horror movie marathon when my mind catches up. My body freezes, reality setting in.

"Wait, you said all of you are doing this program?" They nod. "What about you, Knox?"

He runs a hand through his hair, causing his biceps to bulge against his T-shirt. A ragged sigh escaping before scrubbing his hands over his face, averting his eyes from mine. "I resigned."

"Wynston!" I gasp.

"Stop. You want us all to make choices for ourselves, and I did. Jorddan and I talked. I'm needed in more important places than the classroom, and that includes you," Knox whispers. The bed creaks again as he moves closer to me, a hand running over my shin and then up my thigh. "It was the right thing to do, Bryony."

"That was stupid," I grumble.

Bending low, he presses a kiss to my hip. "It wasn't. You made a choice—all of us or none of us. Why don't we get to choose you, too?"

I hate that he's right. His point is solid. I don't get to choose what they want to sacrifice. "Watch the movie," I mumble.

As one, they all turn their focus back to the screen. Pierce curls into my side, Valen resting his palm on my thigh, with Knox nestled between my legs, his back against my front, and Graham horizontal across the end of the bed.

They watch, but I can only stare at them. Memorizing their features and our memories. The trek through the months since I've known them fails to adequately map out how we arrived at this place. How we became us.

How did I become entwined with four men? Who would want this?

Yet, we do. The five of us. A unit. A family.

But mostly I just fight back the tears, thinking about the danger we are all willingly putting ourselves in. There are too many paths of destruction weaving a tangled web at once. In the end, the wounded and the dead will be our sacrifice. Our casualties of war.

But for every action, there's an equal and opposite reaction. The light wielders will retaliate. The Council and the Wielding Bureau will make an example of us if they find out.

They'll die, but so will we.

Losing more lives already weighs heavily on me. Not them—the light wielders. Not anyone who ever sided with Roman. They carry no burden or guilt. Why would they? As wielders, we've allowed them to remain on a pedestal solely to be worshipped but never ridiculed.

Eyeing Valen in my periphery, I study the sharp angles of his face. Features that align so perfectly with the dark nature of his gifts. I hope Valen makes them all rot, while Vincent repeatedly brings them back to life to suffer through it until there's nothing left. Until they're nothing but morsels of tissue.

The thought of harm coming to my friends hurts my heart. My guys and all those who have chosen the image my father sees for the world take my breath away.

Is the world my father has been fighting for worth the loss? A world where my brother, Knox, Jorddan, and Janelle don't have to hide. A place where we can thrive, and the light no longer controls our community.

A reality I've spent my whole life brainwashed to believe wasn't the truth. But it is. The light sits above all else.

My eyes are open now.

The truth is obvious.

We will dim the light, then smother them in the dark.

14

VALEN

Pain radiates through my side as I roll over in bed. A bed that isn't mine, in a room I've never visited. Yet, I know this house. I've spent hours upon hours inside its walls.

If Jorddan trusts you, he'll welcome you here to Guthrie Manor. I proved myself early. I made myself valuable. It was necessary to become indispensable as quickly as possible.

My first invitation to his home was only four months after I joined the New Order. It was confirmation that I'd proved my loyalty. In my mind, I was one step closer to becoming irreplaceable.

Still, other than the bedroom designated as mine and the common areas, I'd never seen this chamber. Nor would I have expected it to belong to a daughter no one knew he had if I had seen it. Where so many parents try to shower their daughters in the girly shit littered with sparkles and frills, Jorddan didn't.

The creams accenting the dark hues of gray are perfect for Bri. She is our ray of light, but grayer than any of us. Our woman is a blend of everything we all aspire to be.

She is the balance between good and evil. Even someone as depraved as I am can desire to be more like her. But no one will ever know that.

Darkness silently drapes over the room. Pitch black nothingness keeps me from seeing my hand in front of my face. The sort that steals your sight and senses. Thicker than the cloud I'd seen Bri produce on multiple occasions.

I knew she was special. Even after her true nature revealed itself, I knew there was more. A latent power simmering just beneath the surface, eager to burst free. It's no fault of her own. Many of us would lose our way without the proper wielding upbringing. Those people stifled her gifts, but she took back her power.

Knowing our true nature isn't enough. That we hold power or can manipulate the world around us means nothing without a steady hand to hold. From a young age, we need guidance that helps mold our gifts, keeping us from destroying ourselves.

Creaking fills the room. Summoning a dagger to my far hand, I reach for her with the other. The spot where Bri should have been is cool under my fingertips. Yet, I can still smell her scent lingering in the room.

I'd fallen asleep watching those fucking horror movies she loves so much, but now it's just me. Reaching further, it's clear the bed is empty.

No Bri. None of the guys.

Where the fuck is everyone?

A groan pulls my focus in the opposite direction. I see nothing, yet sense someone here with me. I'm not alone. If only I could spare the bit of essence left inside me to explore the area, but I can't. Not if I end up having to protect myself. I barely have enough magic inside me to send this dagger flying into anything that moves.

Slipping from the bed as silently as possible, I creep around the edge by touch, each press of my feet into the plush area rug muffling my steps.

This time, a sharp crack sounds from behind me, and I spin, drawing my dagger high, ready to eviscerate whoever is in here with me. The combat training I insisted on after joining Jorddan bursts to the surface. My muscles are firing, ready to execute every maneuver they clearly remember.

Jorddan has always kept the manor heavily warded. Following our Beauxgraton showdown, it would be idiotic not to strengthen them. Even with every spell known to man, wards aren't indestructible. There's always someone stronger.

Someone who possesses rare nuances of their gift, who can break what another has done.

If anyone could break through those wards, it would be Geneva and the Guthrie children. Jorddan's family is a weakness. A fact well-known, and a truth he will never hide.

Another creak sounds from behind me, this one longer. More pronounced. The shift in the pitch is reminiscent of barefoot movement. A predator stalking its prey through the dark.

"Vincent?" I growl into the smog of billowing essence. Who else would be in here trying to kick my ass? The guy has a serious overprotective brother complex with Bri.

Keeping low, ignoring the pain ricocheting through my middle, I charge forward, my forearm hitting a body just as I'm whipped backward by invisible hands.

My back slams into the far wall, the tendrils of an angry essence coiling around me. Each tendril eagerly tightens against my limbs and slithers around my neck.

"Do it. I dare you," I growl and writhe against the restraints.

The darkness remains, snuffing out any hope of seeing the light of day again. The sounds of movement seem to have vanished. Yet, there's a change. A vortex of what I assume is Bri's essence suddenly whips through the room. The branches snapping back and forth, the way I've seen Bri retaliate multiple times. It seems to whisper as its stars twinkle against the dark.

"Bri, what the hell are you doing?" I tug against the restraints of her magic only for it to tighten around me. Pulling me away from the wall like a rag doll before slamming me back into the unforgiving surface with enough force my teeth rattle.

My body riots against the pain, but I refuse to cry out. I refuse to show weakness. I'm not sure how her essence will respond if I do.

Using my last bit of reserves, I will the lights on. Blinking several times, the room finally comes into focus, her essence tightening around my throat, cutting off my air supply. A reminder of how I'd once held her against the wall shortly after we met.

Dark orbs glare from across the room. I've stared into eyes like that my entire life. Many of us dark wielders with more sinister powers often succumb to the color change. Our irises of color and balls of white are overcome by the darkness inside us.

If there's a shade darker than the most opaque onyx, Bri's have achieved that now. Her body remains relaxed, her head cocked to the side as if she were studying a newly discovered creature.

There's no emotion on her face. Nothing gives away what's going on, but her essence flows freely from her fingers in a violent rush. So fast and so dark that I can barely keep up with it.

Where it seemed to fill the space in the dark, now it envelops us. A barren space between where she stands and where I'm pinned feet above the ground to the wall.

"Bryony, look at me! Look at me!"

Her head straightens, eyes shifting from black to white as if they are responding to me. That eerie white of the ghoul shines so bright against her warm brown skin. "Why Valen? You were going to kill me," she drones. "You want to kill me." There's a menacing quality to her words I've never heard before.

The voice doesn't even sound like hers, but it is her.

"Bryony, I do not want to kill you. Not anymore. Fuck you, yes. But if I were going to kill you, you'd be dead."

Her head tilts again as she takes several steps toward me. "Do it. I dare you." It's disarming to have her echo my words with a wolfish grin.

"Knox!" I shout. My lungs burn as I call out to him over and over again. There's virtually no power left within me. I have no defense. No magic nor reason will stop this version of Bri prowling toward me.

I can't fight her with no magic in my veins. The single dagger I had in my hand wasn't enough, either. Not that I could use it right now, as it lies on the carpet five feet below me.

"And what is Professor Knox going to do for you? He hates you as much as we all fucking do. He can't save you from me." Each word is so saccharine, I don't know how to respond. I love my girl embracing the dark, but this is different. This is possession by magic she can't control. No one fucks with that.

"Bryony, listen to me."

She stops inches from me, chin cocked high, staring up at me with the same blank expression. Those white eyes seem to pulse in time with my racing heartbeat, quickening with each passing second.

She opens her mouth wide, a new tendril of essence breaking free just as the door slams open. The sharp crack of the metal handle against the wall pulls Bryony's focus away from me for several seconds. The stretch is just long enough to summon the dagger into my barely open palm.

Knox barrels in with Pierce, Damian, and Vincent on his heels.

"Stop it, Wynston," Vincent orders.

Knox's mouth instantly stretches wide, sucking up every bit of essence in the room. The tendrils happily retreat into their vessel with every heavy pull as he steps deeper into the space.

My body crumbles to the carpet with a deafening thud, the dagger clutched to my chest, pointed outward in case Bri comes for me. There's no catching my breath as I sit there panting, still focused on the wicked grin Bri is wearing once again.

More pain that I can tolerate pounds through my body, slowing my backward crawl from my forbidden fruit. But I never break eye contact.

Show no weakness, a voice whispers in my head.

Knox focuses only on Bri, his palms cupping her cheeks, forcing her to see him. With his loose pajama pants and bare feet, I can only assume he'd been asleep in bed. There's no way he heard me, which means he felt her.

Tension fills this space, thick and sour as we wait. Our breaths caught in our lungs, hoping our Bri returns.

We're all silent as we wait for her to come back to herself.

Idly, I wonder if her power has ever taken hold like this before. If she'd lost so much control, she'd lost herself.

"Are you okay?" Pierce is at my side, checking me over as if Bri physically harmed me. She could have, but didn't. As if a piece of her remembered she cared about me, her essence only restrained me and threatened my life. She could have snapped my neck in a heartbeat, but she didn't.

Something inside her recognized me.

She was still there.

Shaking Pierce off, I scowl at him. "Fuck off. I'm fine."

"Sorry I cared," he snaps, shoving away from me.

Shaky, deep breaths pull my attention away from my best friend. I'm awful to him around others, yet he's the one I care about most in this world. Refocusing on Bri, relief washes through me when her eyes open once more. The flecks of green in her gray eyes are shining brighter than usual, serving as confirmation that she's back.

"Valen, I—" she chokes. "I—"

"What the fuck was that?" I bark. The bite to my words is harsh enough I expect her to flinch away, but she doesn't. That defiant, sassy temptress returns, staring me down.

"I don't know, Valen." Each letter of my name enunciated so crisply, I want to fuck that tone right out of her. My dick swelling just thinking about teaching her that lesson. "That's never happened before."

Groaning to my feet, I sheath my dagger at my back. The added weight putting me at ease. "Seems like a lot of that has happened since we got here."

"Watch it, Greer. I have no problem killing you and leaving you dead," Vincent snarls, every vein popping in his thick neck.

Fuck him. We've never been on great terms. Two assholes in one room either will or won't get along, but he's been unbearable since finding out I've been fucking his baby sister. It doesn't matter who the fuck he is, I will cut down anyone who tries to keep me from her.

Changing my tone, I take a casual stance against the wall. One leg crossed over the other, arms folded over my chest. In truth, I'm fighting against the pain. Using every bit of energy I have left to hide it. "Wake up, Vincent. She could have attacked you, too."

"Bri, do you remember anything?" Knox questions.

"I, uh. I got up to use the bathroom, and then it was like I could sense Valen's dagger. Like my body knew he had it in his hand, and then I felt my essence rage and blacked out."

"So you felt threatened by him?" Vincent growls.

"Fuck. Off. Guthrie. I wouldn't hurt her."

Vincent charges forward, his face contorted with anger and blind rage. "That's why you threatened her all fucking semester until you got into her pants?"

Part of me wants him to know that even after I fucked her, I still threatened her. I still fantasized about murdering her for the greater good. I still do. The difference is now I know I wouldn't.

Thoughts are one thing; actions are another.

There's no controlling myself as my hand clasps around his throat, Damian yanking him back before I get a good hold. My stomach convulses with the sudden movements. A punishment for not remembering I'm still healing.

It's a stare-down between men. Between friends and enemies. Between those who love that woman currently nestled against Knox's chest.

And then the room goes dark.

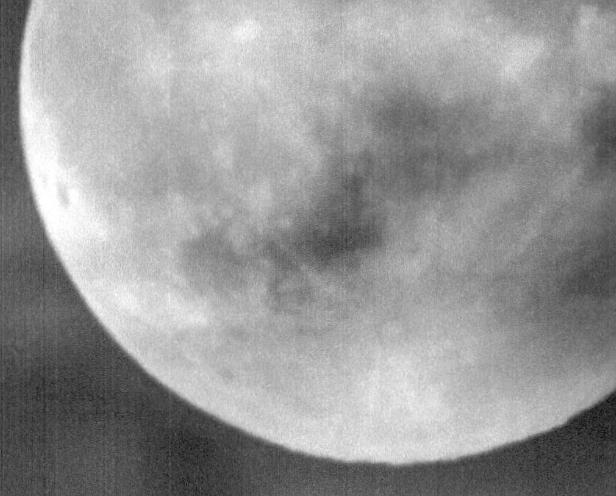

15

BRYONY

DARKNESS PURER THAN THE depths of the Atlantic Ocean at night blankets the room. The clink and whoosh of the curtains being thrown open showers us in the soft light of dawn. An almost complete shift from the midnight hue to a hazy gray. The typical overcast of the UK.

Staring out through the windows, we huddle close together. Our bodies are still, our breathing even as if we've found a tranquil state. There's no sign of anything amiss outside. It appears to be nothing more than another gloomy winter day, but I feel it. The anger and resentment tumbling through me, destroying everything in its wake. But it's not mine. This turmoil belongs to someone else, but who?

Someone is here. Someone who shouldn't be. I can sense them. I can feel their light magic crawling under my skin, as if wanting to tear my insides apart piece by piece.

To my knowledge, I've only ever stolen a few light essences—one from the Beauxgraton fight, Harley as a child, and what Graham gifted me on Valen's deathbed.

Pressing the heels of my palms into my eyes, I fight to identify the feeling. My essence knows it. The magic that runs through my veins has now memorized it. It feels like ancient power, yet that can't be true. I'm only twenty-five.

"Harley is here," I whisper, my eyes bolting open against the dark. It could only be him.

My insides hum as if praising me for making the right choice.

Curling my fingers, a small tendril of my essence releases. A soft glow finds its way to my palm, guiding me through the men gathered in my room, down every hallway, and down the stairs. How he could throw the entire manor into darkness is beyond me. Even the fireplaces and flame-bearing torches no longer glow bright. Only the ball of light in my palm and little splashes of light from outside through the endless windows guide me.

The globe pulses as if it has a heartbeat. My heartbeat, not the one from the wielder I'd stolen this from nights ago. It should be easy enough to produce my own mage luminescence, but this orb is different. A gift from one who manipulates light, born of the purest light bloodlines. It's one of the rawest powers a wielder can have. No wonder she sits on the Council.

Ignoring the men hissing behind me, I jog down the main staircase. With my half-brother present, only trouble seems to loom at our doorstep. He shuns the dark when he is more evil than any dark wielder I've ever come into contact with. A shocking thought, as my days are now filled with Valen's company.

Every creak, groan, and unidentifiable sound that seems to belong to the manor follows me. A euphoric sensation fills me as if the house is once again reminding me I'm home. I am safe here. I belong here. These walls, furniture, rugs, and fixtures are all mine. They have a story to tell. All I must do is listen. Learn. Let their history live within me. The manor and everything in it will stand with me, as if they are my army, poised at my back and ready to attack.

By the time I descend the main staircase, the darkness seems to have lifted. Only it hasn't. We still have no power or fire lighting my home. It's the gray-ish-blue sky outside the massive windows lighting our way. The sky brightens with each passing moment as if it too is pledging allegiance.

The prospect of what lies beyond our front door makes my limbs quiver. My insides rolling as if alerting me to the mood Harley was in. The feeling is unpleasant, but isn't that how my brother has always treated me?

His words and actions were filled with disdain and hatred. With such coldness, you'd think icebergs held more warmth. There's been no affection reciprocated by him. There never will be. Not in this life or the next.

Breathing deeply, I open the front door. As predicted, Harley scowls my way, but Merrick is here too. His features scrunched with too many emotions to parse through.

"You're trespassing." There's no inflection in my tone. I've given too much of myself to Harley over the years. He deserves no more. Yet, my body still shakes in his presence, my fingers curling, tightening around the edge of the door. Held open only wide enough to reveal half my frame, effectively blocking them from entering.

A chorus of footsteps claps against the floor behind me. Their pace slows as they near me. It's more than just my guys and my brother. I can sense it. Our entire household, full of people, is standing behind me. Their presence is enough to reinforce the sliver of bravery I was clinging to. With a hungry breath, I let the door swing wide open, revealing my strength in numbers.

Merrick's gaze tracks over my shoulder for a moment. His eyes search the faces who will surely tear him to pieces should he make a move against me in my home.

But Harley is the one I watch. He's the one I've always had to pay close attention to. Sometimes I wonder if that's the reason fate made me cling to him in my younger years. Why was I so obsessed with having his love and acceptance, but didn't care if I had my sister's?

"Dad said he would bring you here. Predictable," Harley spits the words with more snark than necessary. "You small-minded, filthy Grisyms always are. And those dark wielders at your back," he nods to the bodies behind me. "Are no better."

"Harley, we have no reason to speak or see each other ever again. You go your way and I'll go mine." I say the words with authority, though I don't feel it. Harley is Roman's son in every way. Maybe worse than the man I'd always known as my father. He isn't going to just leave or let me go free. But I'll try to protect the people in this house.

With a snort, he shakes out his hair. Those blue eyes flashing my way with wicked glee. "Make this easy, Bryony. You and everyone else in this shithole can come with us now and..."

"And what? You'll slaughter us?" I step over the threshold, cocking my chin high to meet my brother's gaze. The frigid cold of the stone beneath my bare feet immediately shoots through my body. Its effect is not making me cower away, but become hardened against it. "As I said. You're trespassing. Get off my property."

"Bri, come on, be reasonable," Merrick pleads. My brother reaches for me, but quickly pulls his hand back. Once again, his gaze tracks to the group behind me. The plea in them making me wonder who he is searching for in the crowd.

My eyes narrow on Merrick's face. I don't care how his features pull with emotions he'd do better to hide. "Reasonable? You think that murdering me because my parents love each other is reasonable? I never thought you were like them until..." The words lodge in my throat, emotion balling up in my chest.

I should have known Merrick would eventually turn on me, too, but I'd hoped that he was the last Avalon that actually loved me.

My love for him is a weakness. One I don't have the luxury to wear on my sleeve or sink into. Merrick is one of them.

"Bri..." Merrick pleads.

"Don't call me that. Get off my doorstep. Stay out of my life. I swear, if I see or hear from you again, I will kill you both. I'm sure you've heard all the nasty things an Eistiab can do."

"Bryony, don't do this," Merrick tries once more.

"It's your death," Harley snickers. "Keep defying us, and you'll see just how little our parents care about you."

"Roman isn't my parent. He's not my father. He's nothing to me," I snap, ready to shove Harley down the steps if he says another word.

"Maybe not by blood," Harley leans in close, his breath warm on my chilled cheeks. "But he owns you."

"No one. Owns. Me," I snarl, stepping back into the warmth of my home, my fingers curled around the door ready to shut them out. They shouldn't have been able to pass the wards. Without explicit access given, they shouldn't be on my front step. That fact alone stalls me. My mind is too curious to ignore the one question on the tip of my tongue. "How did you pass the ward?"

A single step brings me closer to my former brothers. Merrick's gaze once again tracking over my shoulder.

What the hell is he looking for?

Harley raises a hand, twisting it through the air, watching his fingers wave past each other as if in awe. "You and Vincent may be what he cherishes most, but our whore of a mother is his weakness, too."

My brow scrunches, mouth pinching tight, not sure what he's getting at, and pissed he would speak about her in such a derogatory way. It doesn't matter that I'm livid with her, too. With a flash of his wrist, the truth settles in. Bright blue veins throb under his pale skin. Bile creeps up my throat. This can't be happening.

Her blood. Our mother's blood. *Jorddan's family is his weakness.* "I will kill you," I snarl. I grew up wanting nothing but Harley's love, but that's no longer the case. Now I want him gone, too.

When this war ends, only one of us will survive. Me or him. Not both. This realm cannot support the both of us.

"Good luck. You're nothing more than a whore, like our mother. The only thing you'll purposely accomplish is spreading your legs—"

Harley barely gets out the last word before Vincent charges him. Football games mark the only occasion I've seen two large men fly through the air like that. The animalistic growl that left Vincent as he collided with Harley left me audibly gasping. Not for fear they got hurt, though they hit the bottom step as one and then loudly rolled across the grass, with Vincent landing on top.

The two grapple and grunt, throwing punches, but never releasing their power. It's an old-school brawl, meant to teach a lesson. A semi-entertaining sight until Vincent and Merrick lock eyes for just a second. Merrick gives a slight nod, panic slicing through my insides.

Something isn't right.

Before I can move forward to urge them to stop, Merrick discharges his essence. The crystalline white swirls appear to glow against the steely gray sky. So bright I want to shield my eyes, but I don't. I stare straight into that stream of magic I worked so hard to emulate my entire life as it turns into thick ropes encasing Harley's writhing body as Vincent smothers him with his weight.

"You motherfucking traitor!" Harley roars. The hurt of betrayal burns brightly in his blue eyes. "You chose them," he snarls, spittle flying past his lips. "You chose these bastards over your family."

Merrick takes a step back as if in fear of Harley breaking free. "I chose peace and what's right. Killing our sister isn't right. What we've done to her kind for centuries isn't right." He takes a deep breath, moving to my side and circling an arm around my shoulder. A reminder of how he often found me alone in tears, nestled in the grass. "And my child is a Grisym. I will protect her with everything I have."

"You're dead to me," Harley snarls as Vincent and Damian yank my brother to his feet. "He knows where I am. He's coming for all of you. You too, baby brother," Harley spits blood at my feet.

Harley fights against Vincent and Damian's hold, but gets nowhere with the magical ropes still holding his body in a straight plank. Still, he spits at me again as they drag him past us. I'll stand tall against his words, but I will not be spat at like I'm nothing.

Grabbing Harley by the chin, I pull his face close to mine. "Good. It'll be easier to kill him if he comes to me. I hope you said goodbye to your father."

Those eyes flare wide again before he's dragged into the house. The moment I hear a door slam in the distance, my hand presses against my stomach, and I suck in sharp breaths. But not a single one provides me any relief.

I can't breathe. I can't...

My head swirls with chaotic thoughts. My brother came here to capture me, or, if that was unsuccessful, then what? He stood there bickering so long it almost seemed as if he were stalling. Patiently drawing out this interaction by arguing with me. The question is why?

Oddly, it's not Harley's intentions that bother me most. His willingness to eliminate me from this earth settled under my skin like a dormant virus years ago. It's that I could feel him. His emotions and intent. His anger and the putrid taste of his hatred.

Stretching back to my full height, I breathe in through my nose. Long and deep, as if the crisp, fresh air will somehow cleanse me and clear my mind so I can search it. Did I experience what others felt before?

Knox, sure. But he makes sense. Our essences are so intertwined that it's as if they are one being.

But Pierce? Valen? Jorddan? Others I've ever stolen from?

Was it Harley's essence or a gift from the other light wielder I stole from on the Beauxgraton grounds? Maybe even the foreign power I absorbed in class numerous times. There's no way for me to know. Not on my own. Not like this.

"Bri," Merrick moves into my line of sight, slightly bending his knees so we're eye to eye. How did all of my siblings end up tall except for me?

"You could have told me," I whisper. That same wound of learning Harley had gotten married, and not a single person from my family bothered to tell me, rips open. Merrick could have trusted me with his secret. What I am is the biggest one I've ever held onto. Surely he would know I would do the same for his child.

"Darryn asked me not to. Not until you knew the truth and chose a side." My brow scrunches low, but I keep listening. "Dad called us all to the house, raving that you revealed your identity in front of the entire council, that you could command ghouls, and that you're the most dangerous one of us all. He kept griping about you being ungrateful for picking Jorddan."

"Merrick, I'm sorry." Regret forms a nasty taste in my mouth. Putrid and heavy. It's not an emotion I'm well acquainted with, but this is Merrick and his family. I never meant to endanger them.

"I'm not. I know Dad's plan, so we need to prepare."

The corner of my mouth twitches, a fight to hold in the question that wants to tumble out. "Why are you helping us?"

Long arms wrap around me, my cheek finding my brother's chest. He smells how he always has. His warmth got me through so many hard days after Grandma Avalon took her own life. "When I found out what our dad—my dad," he corrects. "Was planning. I had to do something. I called Vincent yesterday. Without his help, this could have gone very differently."

My eyes flutter shut, knowing my two brothers worked together to ensure everyone's safety. To buy us time against Roman. This man's failure with his Beauxgraton puzzle piece is a disappointment. He'll pout, butthurt that it hadn't gone as planned. "And what's the plan, Mere?"

He doesn't have to say it. I know the answer, but hearing the words on his lips will make it real. I need it to feel real if I am going to find the energy to fight.

"Extinction of Grisyms and the dark."

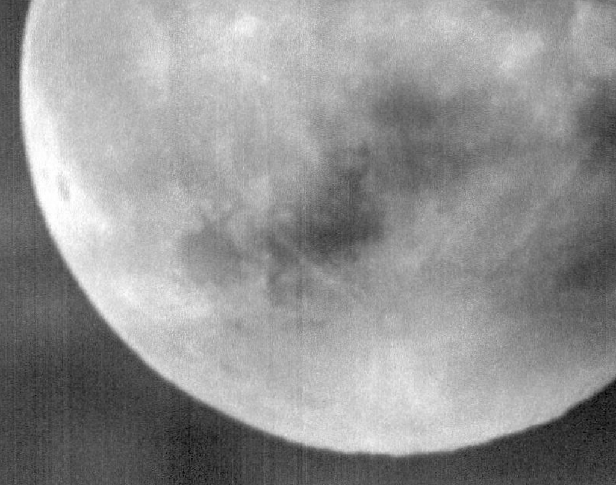

16

WYNSTON

WE SCATTER LIKE A colony of misplaced ants. Our quick steps carrying us to our respective destinations.

Vincent, Damian, and Jorddan were handling Merrick.

Tosch and Camilla ran off together toward the kitchen.

Janelle and Lionel both groaned about returning to bed due to the jet lag.

The twins, Sean and Collin, disappeared as if into thin air.

Graham volunteered to help Valen back to his room. The guy was so pale he looked like he was seconds from passing out. They climbed the steps in unison, arms linked. The sight was odd to witness. Graham and Valen are usually constantly at odds. The shift between them is jarring enough that you couldn't miss it if you tried.

Valen must value Graham's help in saving his life. That's the only explanation that makes any sense. Vincent may have brought him back, but Graham's work ensured he could stay alive.

It's just me lurking in the foyer, watching this moment between Bri and her brother.

I'd only ever seen her interact with Harley. Memories I wish I could wash clean from my mind. He'd been unnecessarily cruel to her. It was gut-wrenching and infuriating to witness.

Had my feelings been this strong then, our meeting would have been different. I would have choked the life out of him right there in Janelle's office. He'd treated her so disgustingly that day, but what could I have done? Their family issues weren't mine.

This is different. The love she fought so hard to claim from Harley shines bright in Merrick's eyes. He cares for her. Wants to protect her.

But more importantly, his family.

A Grisym wife and child?

How did Roman not know? I wonder if Geneva is aware.

It doesn't matter. Roman would hunt them to the ends of the earth. If Merrick truly stands with us, we will protect him as if he were our own.

The two suddenly turn toward me, my eyes wide as if caught with my hand in the cookie jar. "I wasn't—"

Bri chuckles. "It's fine. I'm going to check on Valen." She places a soft kiss on the corner of my mouth. The touch so brief it's almost as if I imagined it. A display likely meant to keep our interaction tame in front of her brother. "And thank you," she whispers before jogging up the stairs.

We stand there awkwardly in the foyer before I wave my fingers, closing the front door and locking it. "Coffee?" I ask.

"Please," Merrick groans. "I am not made for red-eye flights anymore."

I can only laugh at the mundane comment. With the number of ways wielders can travel through space and time, they flew. They took a damn plane just like any human would. It almost relaxes the tension coiling my shoulders tight around my ears.

We enter the kitchen side by side, my mouth pinching tight, surprised that Tosch and Camilla are already gone. Pouring two steaming cups of coffee, we're silent as we reenter the dining room, choosing seats across from one another.

"Why are you really here, Merrick?"

His confession from outside is crawling beneath my skin, and I want to believe it. I wish I could. My heart screams for me to try, but logic overpowers the urge. Too many pretend to be someone other than who they are. It would be foolish of me not to use caution.

I can pretend all I want, but I still live in fear. It doesn't matter that Jorddan is at my back. I am a hunted species. Now and likely forevermore.

"I told you."

"Tell me again," I demand.

With a heavy sigh, Merrick takes a long pull from his mug. "Father called us all to the house the morning after he went to Beauxgraton. He was still in his filthy clothes." He shakes his head as if in disbelief. "There was dirt on his face and under his nails, but we said nothing. He told us he knew someone had wiped his memories. He claimed he could feel it the moment he sat in his car and couldn't remember why he'd come to the school. Instead of coming home, he went to an old friend. They had his memory restored and then called us."

"So he remembers everything?" I breathe.

Merrick nods before continuing. "He was ranting and raving about Bri and Jorddan. I've never seen him like that regarding Bri. Honestly, Sicily and I always thought he loved her best, though we all knew she wasn't his daughter—not like that, anyway." He turns his mug in his hands before drinking again, baring his teeth against the bitter taste. "Then he said he'd been working with the Council. Something about expanding some programs. When I asked, he'd been reluctant to answer, but did with Harley's encouragement."

"What are you talking about?" I question, leaning in closer.

"Not every Grisym is killed at birth. There are a handful of wielders working for the Council who can 'test' a Grisym's abilities. They keep the ones they like. Then, when they find other Grisyms who have slipped through the cracks, like Bri, they conduct similar testing. If the Council deems them useful, it takes ownership of them." Merrick swallows loudly as if attempting to wash away his words.

Merrick takes a deep breath, finishing the contents of his mug.

There's an outburst on the tip of my tongue. A refusal to accept it as truth. The Council and the Wielding Bureau are supposed to be here to protect us. To uphold the laws that govern us and to seek justice when others do not comply. But these same bodies are the ones who snatch newborn babies from mothers' arms and barge into homes ready to slaughter whole families because they have been harboring Grisym children.

They are the same.

So I can't be surprised that they hold Grisyms captive. Capitalizing on the twisted version of our mixed gifts we get from our light and dark sides.

"So he planned on handing over Bryony?" I whisper, staring at the black liquid still in my cup.

"He didn't say it outright, but I think so. Our father would never kill her. Harley, sure, but not him. He can't use a pawn that's dead."

Those words give me no reassurance. Bri is still just a chess piece to him. She's not a person. Not his daughter. Not someone to cherish and love.

"Your father," I mutter.

"Excuse me?" The indignation is thick in Merrick's tone, his gaze narrowed on me.

"I said, *your* father. Roman isn't Bri's father. It doesn't matter that he raised her."

Merrick goes quiet for a few moments, his mouth opening and closing several times, but he says nothing as he rakes his gaze over the room. He seems to study the details. The heavy drapes are embroidered with floral patterns. The walls lined with ornate paintings and portraits. Even the gold china is laid out on the table. A set perfectly assembled in front of each seat, ready for our next meal.

"He loves her in his own way."

"It's not enough." I crack my knuckles against the tabletop, the sound sharp enough that Merrick's gaze tracks back to meet mine. "It's not enough. He came after her. He brought executioners for her."

Merrick stares at his trembling hands before straightening the plates in front of him. The china and silverware clinking as he busies himself. "He wouldn't have let them kill her."

My blood boils listening to him repeat the same shit over and over. He wasn't there. He didn't see it. "So what now? You just showed up here with Harley, pretending to be on his side to save the day?" The bite to my words is harsh, but I refuse just to let my guard down because Merrick told me some story.

He's still Roman's son.

A light wielder.

Even with a Grisym spouse and child, I question where his loyalty lies. He'll have to prove his allegiance. Words aren't enough. All it takes is a split second for allegiances to change. We've seen too many play both sides until the clear winner emerged.

"I called Vincent because I was worried about my sister. You may not want to believe anything I've said, but I've always accepted her. I've always treated her well. I warned Vincent that our father was sending us here this morning."

"What has Bri wanted more than anything in her whole life?" The question is a test. If Merrick knows her and cares the way he claims, he'll know the answer.

"First, for Harley to love her. Second, to learn about her dark side," he releases a heavy sigh. "Third, to have someone look at the real her and love the Grisym."

Hearing the words on someone else's lips gives me pause. Bri and I have shared a great deal with each other. Every hope, fear, and joy lives in our memories of our sessions in the cabin. There, just us, we existed, valued by one another, without judgment.

"I saw the way you looked at her," Merrick whispers. "You're the third thing she wants most in this world."

My mouth opens to respond, just as Vincent and Jorddan come waltzing into the dining room.

"Thank you," Vincent pulls Merrick into a hug. "Thank you for protecting our sister and our kind."

Merrick holds him back, the two embracing longer than I would think necessary. It's almost as if there's a shared bond between them. History none of us would suspect.

"Is there something I should know?" I sniffle, my eyes bouncing between the two.

Vincent only glares at me. "If you weren't sleeping with my sister and exactly what she needs, I wouldn't tell you a damn thing," he grimaces. "But since we're all here for the same reason. Merrick has been giving me updates about my sister for years. When he called me yesterday, I was the one who decided we would take Harley captive. What better way to make Roman beg for his greatest prized possession besides my mother?"

Merrick turns on me then, his eyes narrowing. "You didn't mention you were sleeping with her."

Shit.

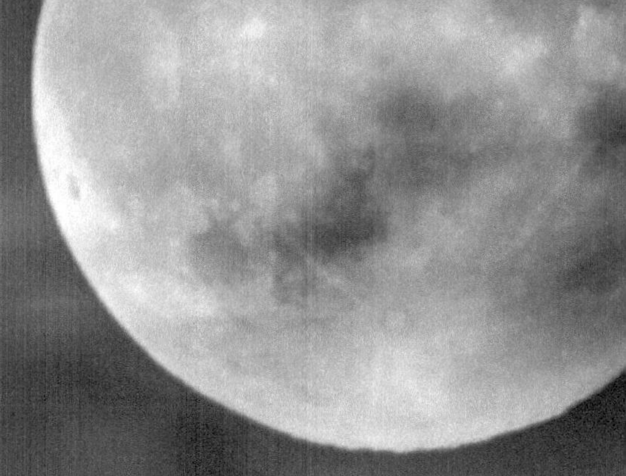

17

BRYONY

A GROAN LEAVES ME as I stretch awake in bed.

Yesterday had been a buzz of activity throughout the house. Both of my brothers were ready to wring Knox's neck. An event, Valen was more than happy to watch once he woke again.

Janelle, my father, and Mr. Greer disappeared for most of the day. The three were barricaded in his office, discussing who knows what.

Tosch cornered me to start our training, but I knew the focus wasn't there. It took convincing between Damian and me, but she finally disappeared with her husband. The two returned to the manor just before we sat down for dinner at eight.

My father also lifted the wards to allow a dozen members of the New Order onto the grounds. Six New Order members stationed themselves outside the manor, and six more guarded checkpoints along the tunnels to Harley's cell.

For hours, I battled myself: go speak with that asshole or hope he rots down there. It burned that I still wanted some kind of acceptance from him. That I wanted him to acknowledge I meant something to him. Instead, I'd sat out on the cold ground by the lake, Graham holding me while I cried.

Stupid, fucking pesky tears. Harley didn't deserve any of them. He never did. Not then. Not now. Still, they fell without abandon. Each fat drop soaked into the wool coat I'd shrugged on.

Dinner had been awkward as hell. My brothers insisted on flanking me. The two teamed up as if they'd been best friends for life. Their barrage of questions was aimed at my men. Knox more than the others. His age was brought up more times than I could count. When my father ordered them to stop, no longer wanting to hear about my sex life, Merrick had asked about my dark side. He'd asked about my experience as a Grisym, telling me things about Darryn.

I'd only met her a few times, and I would never have known. Unlike me, she retained her light features. Soft honey eyes, sandy blonde hair, and an essence she never had to will into a lighter shade.

A smile tugs at the corners of my mouth, knowing she makes Merrick happy. He deserves it. We all do.

Attempting to roll to the side, heavy limbs keep me pressed into the mattress, light snores sneaking past Valen's parted lips, while Knox remains nearly silent.

The pair insisted on staying with me last night. Valen for protection. Knox for my magic. It's already rebelled twice in three days. Who knows if it will again?

I shift to an elbow, attempting to sneak out from between the two men. I need a shower and some food before I allow Tosch to torture me all morning.

"Stop moving," Knox groans.

"I need to get up. Tosch doesn't seem like the type to enjoy tardiness." I shift harder, only for Valen's arm to drape across my middle, one of his spelled daggers in hand.

"No," Knox groans again, flexing his hips into me, his length, a solid rod pushing against the thin cotton of his boxer briefs.

I whimper against another flex of his hips, moisture already pooling between my thighs, knowing he's hard for me. Even after all this bullshit, he still wants me.

A fire burns between my legs. My body wants nothing more than to feel one of them sink into my core and fuck me until I can't breathe. Until I can forget. Forget the unknown. The anxiety and the guilt.

"Knox, you have to let me up," I whine.

"Or," Valen's warm breath fans over my cheek, his lips brushing the shell of my ear. "You could let me and Teach fuck you before Tosch wears you out. First, we'll make you beg for relief, and then she will." The tip of his tongue runs along my jaw, Knox's eyes trailing the slight movement, flexing into me once more.

Turning my head, Valen's lips capture mine in a desperate kiss. It speaks volumes, replacing all the words he can't say out loud. We will never be that romantic couple. But I mean something to him now.

Even if I didn't, I need him.

A moan vibrates up my throat, stretching that wolfish grin across his face. His lengthening beard scratching my skin in the most delicious way. Another escaping me as Knox's long fingers sink into the front of my damp panties.

My body has grown accustomed to having multiple men at once. It craves attention. Their touch. Their pleasure.

"Is she ready for us, Wynston?" Valen croons before sucking the skin above my clavicle between his lips. The heat of his tongue burns me, but I want it. I need it.

My fingers sink into his hair, loosening his disheveled bun. That pleading groan escapes him as my nails scrape over his scalp. The easiest way to turn him into putty at my feet.

"Not quite. I think she needs a warm-up."

Knox slips down the bed, the duvet thrown aside, exposing my naked legs. My thighs press together against the ache building in my core. An ache only their cocks, hands, and tongues can even touch.

"Please," I groan, my fingers tightening in Valen's hair. His hiss drawing out the roll of my hips. "Please."

Wet kisses trail down the length of my leg, each one featherlight. My toes spread and curl in anticipation of Knox slipping those long fingers between my knees and spreading my legs wide. My glistening pussy is exposed to him and Valen to do with as they please.

"Please, what, Forbidden Fruit?" Valen croons, nipping at my hardened nipples through my sleep shirt.

"Fuck me. Now. Hard. Please," I pant.

The soft kiss of Knox and my combined essences curls around my ankles with a caress before yanking them apart so quickly I yelp.

"Shhh," Valen positions his dagger beneath my chin. "We don't want Daddy and your brothers to hear you."

I nod, licking my suddenly dry lips. I'd forgotten my family was in the house with us. Vincent already walked in on Knox and me that first night. No need for a repeat.

"That's a very good girl," Valen smirks, kissing my cheek, before running his dagger down the front of my t-shirt. A shirt that belongs to Knox. The tip of the dagger presses against the cotton, eager to touch my skin. There's virtually no power left in it, but a residue remains.

I can feel it just below the surface. My essence wants it. It calls to that foreign power, desperate to make it part of us.

"Yes," I breathe. My body crackles with electricity as Knox's tongue runs over my soaked panties. The tearing of my shirt from Valen's knife, forcing the arch of my back. I want to feel the blade drag over my skin as it cuts through the bit of clothing covering me.

A hiss slips through my teeth as the cold metal point of the dagger circles my exposed nipple. My breathing, turning ragged, both excited and terrified for him to cut me. "Mmm, my Forbidden Fruit likes my knives."

I nod, my bottom lip caught between my teeth. The teasing is becoming too much. My skin is too sensitive for these games.

The dagger calls to me again.

Take me, Bryony. Take me inside you.

Its voice is a growl. A low roll that rumbles through me. That power wants to be part of me.

"Come to me," I whisper.

My men double their efforts, teasing, kissing, and sucking on my naked flesh. The command hadn't been for them. The mix of their mouths and hands on my body tangles with the tantalizing call of that scrap of power. If I took it, I could make it mine. Learn it. Mold it. Use it.

A dark, dangerous weapon to eliminate our enemies.

"One of you needs to fuck me now. Take turns or take me together. I don't care," I command.

The words are barely free before Knox notches himself at my entrance, burying himself inside me with a single thrust. A guttural sound escapes me, one hand clinging to Valen and the other to Knox. This is what I needed. A distraction more powerful than the magic calling to me.

A scream rips up my throat, my body arching against the intrusion as Knox drives into me again. The pain of the dagger cutting into my skin is welcome while Valen's palm clamps over my mouth. He can stifle my screams, but unless he spells this room, the entire house will hear what they're doing to me.

And I don't care.

My brothers will have to get over it. My father knows more about my sex life than I'd prefer; he'll live, but I might not if they don't keep fucking me. Worshipping me, making me theirs.

Knox moves, a quick rhythm pulling my essence to the surface. For once, it's just me, just my black smoke and twinkling stars. The tendrils wrap around the blade of the dagger, Valen still holding it in place as his mouth clamps around my peaked nipple. Sucking and biting so roughly, I cry out again, the sound muffled behind his large palm.

I focus on my essence, dancing along the blade. The whispers shared between my magic and the remnants that remain in that dagger come to a silent agreement before a greenish cloud bursts free, my hand tearing Valen's away from my mouth to swallow it down.

"Bri! No!" Knox cries, pounding into me harder, one hand holding my leg cocked high to the side, allowing him to sink deeper. His movements don't slow. They become no less punishing as our skin claps together.

I inhale deeply, swallowing down every drop, including my essence. A lazy smile curves the corners of my mouth upward. "Fill my pussy, Knox. Give me more," I moan, my fingers twisting in his hair as his lips meet mine.

He only moves faster. Harder. Deeper. His cock thickens inside me before he spills every bit of his release in my aching core. My walls fluttering around him, but eager for more.

Shoving at his chest, I push him to his back, straddling him before sinking onto his still-hard dick.

"You're not done, are you?" I grin.

He shakes his head, his fingers gripping my hips so tight that pain radiates through me.

"Valen," I call.

It's as if he already knows, his palm at the center of my back pushing me forward as Knox pumps his hips up into me. The clap of our skin reverberates off the walls.

"Yes," I huff out a laugh. "More."

Valen's fingers find their way between us, rubbing tight circles over my clit, lapping up my arousal. His tease was short-lived before those same fingers run down my ass crack, rubbing around the puckered hole before pushing past the resistance.

"Bri, use your magic," Valen coaches me.

I press my eyes closed, my essence slithering past my parted lips this time, those tendrils flirting with my rear entrance along with Valen's fingers.

I've barely had a chance to breathe before he lines himself up and pushes inside.

Stars.

I see nothing but black smoke and stars.

Whether it's my essence or being blinded by ecstasy doesn't matter. I don't care. I'm in heaven.

I ride the wave. The two of them quickly find a joint rhythm as they use me. Own me. Torture my body with the best possible pleasure as both of them fill me completely.

"Fuck!" I bark as my orgasm tears through me. So angry and violent, I know it's because of the new power I took inside me.

I can hear it cackling with excitement.

What have I done?

18

GRAHAM

LOGICALLY, I KNOW THE mountains that host Beauxgraton aren't the only location with miserable weather. The wind, gloom, and chilled air can wear on you. Making you wish for warmer days that seem to never come. But the English countryside is a whole different type of miserable.

It's like dread clings to the air. The rolling gray overcast skies pressing down on you with the weight of a hundred elephants. It's suffocating. It's depressing.

Not that I needed any help in that department. This whole situation has me on edge and trapped in a sandstorm of my emotions. The fresh air was supposed to help. It was supposed to bring peace or clarity to the decision I'd made. A choice I can pretend I made for myself, but I didn't. I made it for her, though I'd told her otherwise.

Valen had cornered me yesterday after he and Pierce came up with the idea.

"You're an ambitious man, Graham. Think about the leg up studying abroad will give you," he'd snickered, his hand resting on my shoulder with a slight squeeze.

"I know that," I'd snapped.

It was only then that he wiped that smug grin off his face and dropped his hand, wincing against the pain still tormenting him. *"Then what's the problem?*

She won't respect you if you take the coward's way and go back. She'll move on. Without. You." The last two words punctuated with his finger jabbing at my chest.

Valen hadn't said anything I didn't already know. My dependence on Bri, her approval, and her friendship made me the most pathetic man on earth. I knew that. If I didn't stay, it would only be proof that I can't handle existing in her world.

"Count me in," I'd whispered.

Then it was only a matter of convincing Headmistress Milgren. A task that proved easier said than done. Only then did we know Knox had quit. A confession that shook our collective. But it was the crease of shame that scrunched her features that confirmed I'd chosen wrong. Agreeing to study abroad here, for her, would be a secret I needed to keep to myself.

Camilla shivers beside me, pulling me out of my thoughts. She and Collin wanted out of the manor. A little fresh air to escape the growing tensions within those walls. Exploring the grounds was our only option. An aimless trek through the frigid cold as my reset.

I wonder if they felt the impending doom, too. Are they trying not to crumble under the pressure closing in on them? Thick, solid walls of steel just waiting to suffocate us. If we were smart, we'd run. Preserve ourselves from whatever we're now mixed up in. But Camilla will never leave Bri's side, and it seems like I won't either. Collin is part of the New Order, so he chose this life well before he ever met us.

I'd been ready to just lie in bed and stare at the ceiling, contemplating my choices, until I went to check on Bri this morning. Valen and Knox laid their claim to her bed last night. It was fine. The quiet solitude of my thoughts felt necessary. Should I have stayed curled up around Bri's curvy body, she'd be my only focus. There wouldn't have been a chance to obsess about a future we may never see.

Her moans assaulted my ears as I neared her door. Valen and Knox's voices carrying from the other side while Bri begged and moaned. But for a solid five minutes, I stood there and listened with my fist raised, ready to tap on her door for entry.

We love to punish ourselves, though, so I'd entered. The quiet twist of the knob and soft push kept the groan of the hinges to a minimum. Their naked bodies moved as one. Valen's hair hung loose down his back as he drove into her from behind, while Knox pumped his hips up into her.

My anatomy didn't get the memo that we weren't joining. We didn't even want to watch. Bri and I's relationship is our own, but she hasn't even mentioned sleeping with me after our one night together. Yet another thing to beat myself up over while I stood there and watched them bring her pleasure.

None of them noticed as I stood there frozen before finally forcing myself to leave. The moment the door clicked shut, my forehead fell to the cool surface. The hand-carved design uncomfortable against the bone, but I didn't move. I am a glutton for punishment. Each sucked in breath was torturing myself for just a few minutes longer.

Camilla and Collin chat animatedly. The topic lost on me, as I hadn't been paying them any mind on our leisurely walk. I don't regret staying here, but I will miss the both of them when they return to Beauxgraton in a week.

We all agreed it was safer for anyone outside the four of us to return to Montana. Valen and Pierce's friends were just as pissed about it as Camilla, but their safety is more important. Too many of us gone would draw negative attention. Put us all in the same study abroad program and sound the sirens. Especially when we're connected through our friendships, it could give Roman ammunition to invoke protocols that will leave us no choice but to turn on one another.

It's already going to look suspicious enough that Headmistress Milgren signed off on four of us doing the same study abroad program in London. Paperwork that will appear unusual as it progresses through the Department of Education. Four students from Beauxgraton with differing course studies and years completed. Wielders of the light and dark.

Beauxgraton ranks atop world institutes. With a well-rounded curriculum, they're not easily matched. There's no need for its students to study elsewhere. Everything they need is under one roof.

We may have made a mistake in staying here, but it's too late to take it back now.

Hopefully, most won't make any connection. Roman would have to supply his spies with that information. Maybe he will. Maybe he won't.

"At least you'll be able to come here whenever you want," Collin huffs. He raises his hand to his brow, forming a visor as he studies the manor in the distance.

"Not sure that matters..." My words trail off. I'm trying not to be this pathetic guy who's upset because the girl he's in love with was fucking two other guys this morning. I'm not as assertive as Valen. There's no one who can match her connection with Knox. And Pierce. *Shit*, he's just as in love with her.

Somehow, the image of the three of them is weighing heavier on me than the fact that I may have fucked up my future because I'm too scared to lose her.

"You all agreed to this. She said she wanted all of you. It's up to you to step up and prove you meant it when you said yes," Collin says.

How he knows exactly where my thoughts wandered is beyond me. Is the guy a secret mind reader?

"He's right. Jump on in that saddle, Graham. Your damsel is waiting," Camilla makes a roping motion before a wide grin breaks out across her face.

"You're so odd."

Camilla giggles loudly. "I know, but that just makes me extra saucy." She winks. Her entire face scrunching and her mouth opening wide.

"Yeah, sure," I chuckle, draping an arm over her shoulders. I'll miss this. Our group of friends has enjoyed the relative ease with which we operated for most of this year.

These people became my new home. They made me feel accepted. Mistakes, for once, were permissible. A trial and error that allowed me to find my way on my own.

The three of us are laughing at Camilla's weird phrases when a figure comes into view in the distance. Squinting, I can make out the perfectly coiffed sandy brown hair of Bri's half-family. They all have the same hair except for her.

Her brother's posture is stiff as he approaches us. His small mouth pinched either in concentration or against the cold. With his broad shoulders hunched high around his ears, I assume the latter. Still, he should be used to harsh winters where they're from. "Merrick, what are you doing out here? Is Bri okay?"

It's the only reason I can think of that he'd be approaching so quickly. She's the only thread we have between him and us. He spent yesterday mostly with Vincent. The two often locked behind closed doors, discussing who knows what. There wasn't much opportunity to get to know the guy. Regardless, he's not Harley. That much is clear.

"Uh, hi." He quickly hangs up the phone, which I hadn't noticed was being held up to his ear. Heavy bags hang under his eyes as he shivers against a powerful gust of wind. "I was on the phone with my wife. Jorddan is having her brought out here today with the baby."

My mouth draws into a straight line. I'm on edge having him here. None of us expected him to come out and say his wife and child were Grisyms yesterday. A convenient confession when he showed up here with Harley. Although it was apparently an act meant to help us, it makes me wonder about his intentions.

Why is this the first anyone is hearing about this? Especially Bri. Wouldn't Merrick trust her above all else?

He and Vincent claim they spoke the day prior. Harley and Roman's scheme helped morph their own. I have no reason to doubt them. Yet, it doesn't ease the knots in my stomach. It's too coincidental. Too convenient.

"We're going to head back," Collin points behind him, dragging Camilla along. She attempts to fight him off, but eventually just huffs in retreat once Collin whispers something in her ear.

"I'm not going to hurt her. I know that's what you're thinking. It's what you're all thinking," Merrick scrubs a hand down his face, his facial hair scruffier than it had been the day before.

The guy appears just as drained as the rest of us. Like he, too, is carrying his own version of the world on his shoulders. Maybe he is, if what he says about his wife and daughter is true, and he kept it from Roman.

"Why are you speaking out now?" I question, removing my hands from my pockets in case I need to defend myself.

Merrick's blue eyes bore into mine. The same blue as Harley. The fight to separate the two grows harder the longer I stare. "Because I should have stood up for Bri more growing up. Because I was a coward and kept the truth about my wife a secret for years. But most importantly, because I know what our father wants to do to her, to all Grisyms, and I won't stand by and watch him and Harley continue to hurt the innocent."

My jaw works as I try to decide whether to believe everything he says, but his voice is sincere; even the best actors could not authentically replicate it.

"Your wife, is she…" I don't know how to ask if she's like Bri. A mix capable of destruction most of us can barely fathom.

"Her father is a Grisym and her mother a light wielder. It was easier for her to hide than it has ever been for Bri or many others, I presume. She told me the night before our wedding. Believe it or not, I lost it. Completely freaked out."

A humorless snort huffs free. "I did the same when I found out about Bri." My chin lowers to my chest as shame fills me. "I was terrified of her."

Merrick averts his gaze, staring off into the distance. "Me too. I'd seen Bri when she lost control in her younger years and listened to the hatred our father and Harley spewed over the years. It was easy to get caught up in the lies. Bri was the only Grisym I knew I interacted with until my wife."

"Same for me. It took me a little time." My gaze casts down to the frozen dirt at my feet. "Eventually, I realized she is who she always was to me. Our friendship was more important than my fear, though…" Merrick takes a step closer to me, his stare forcing my gaze up. "Sometimes she still scares me. I've never heard of a wielder having the ability to share the way she does. Especially the whole ghoul thing. Unheard of."

"I understand." His hand finds my shoulder before quickly dropping back to his side. "But from what I hear, you and Bri are more than friends."

A pang stings the center of my chest. It's true, or at least it's supposed to be, but it's easy to feel like the man on the outside when Bri has such intense physical relationships with the others. It's simpler to think we acted on emotion and impulse. A one-time fling, never to be repeated. The rejection is almost tolerable then.

"We're supposed to be. I mean, we are. It's just weird sharing her with other men."

Merrick nods as if he understands, but how could he? He's with a single woman. "Bryony has always been a free spirit," he chuckles. "I'm not surprised she has several of you on her arm. I don't think just one man could handle her."

"You're not wrong there," I huff out a humorless laugh.

We both turn toward the manor, our focus straight ahead.

"When I was a kid, I was so jealous she got to live here for about a year. That she got to be somewhere else that wasn't with our father."

I look over at Merrick as emotion dances behind his clear blue eyes. "I'm glad you're here to support her, but I swear if you cross us, we will kill you. Bri means too much to lose her." We don't need to specify who.

"You may not believe this, but she is by far my favorite sibling. I want her safe. I want her kind to be safe. You'll see. Whatever it takes, I'll prove it to anyone who doesn't believe those words."

"I hope so."

19

BRYONY

My legs are on fire as my lungs burn with the force of a thousand suns.

Damn Tosch, and this stupid run.

Damn her and her methods of torture.

I thought I would love the woman, but I think I hate her. Every fiber of my being wants her gone. Poof. Disappeared. I'll figure out my shit on my own.

Anything to stop the forward momentum of my feet clapping against this stretch of road. A long, endless path of black pavement with no reprieve in sight. Screw the countryside.

"Go!" Tosch barks, her breaths even and smooth in contrast to my rasping gulps of air.

While discussing the torture she would put me through, she never listed running. It's what I loathe most. She didn't even mention any physical activity. It has nothing to do with my being plus-size or just preferring indoor activities only. The hatred runs deeper than that.

To run means you might escape whatever is behind you. It's a chance to leave it at point A while we disappear to point D. But some of us can't outrun our demons. While understanding they bear no accurate correlation, my body doesn't know the difference. Especially since in my human high school, the gym teacher would literally chase us around the track in a golf cart if we didn't run the mile fast enough.

Nope, running can kiss my big brown ass.

"Can we stop?" I whine. "I've already had a threesome today." The childish quality of my voice makes me cringe, but I literally think I might die.

A chuckle sounds beside me, my eyes cutting to Tosch's face. Other than her cheeks glowing a bright pink, she doesn't even appear winded. Elbows still bent at a perfect ninety-degree angle at her sides, and her fitted athletic jacket with that red ponytail bouncing behind her are all too neat. "You're still able to run. Seems like your men need to work a little harder to tire you out next time."

A scowl pulls at my mouth. This is awful. With every step, I feel like crumbling to the ground, and the guilt knotting my insides is making me nauseous, but I keep my eyes forward. I keep pushing toward an unknown goal. Maybe if I die out here, I'll be able to forgive myself for putting everyone I care about in danger.

"Release," Tosch orders me.

With a grunt, I let a burst of my essence funnel free. The opaque cloud looms darker now than before. As if each additional mile blackened its hue. It's as if it's angry that someone else is trying to tame it. Trying to make it comply with rules it doesn't have for itself.

My body aches, ribs screaming in pain as the stitch in my side continues to torture me worse than this woman. A woman who snorts when she laughs and gets her gorgeous red hair stuck in her obnoxiously long lashes. The same one who hasn't even broken a sweat while my clothing clings to my body with moisture, and my stray curls cling to my forehead.

For an arranged marriage, Damian definitely lucked out. She's stunning, but he's a looker too. Their future kids will grace runways and magazine ads before dominating the wielding hierarchy.

"Focus," she scolds, jogging backward as if to throw in my face how easy this is for her. I long ago lost track of how far we've run. The minutes are ticking by as slowly as years, and it just might be the death of me.

Everything looks the same out here. Only a few cars have passed. Their focus remains straight ahead. A concealment spell keeps us hidden. No one needs the nightmare of a human unaware or opposed to wielders to catch me releasing my essence.

We also don't know who else Roman has sent looking for me. It's best not to take chances.

Shoving every wayward thought to the dark corners of my mind, I call on my essence again.

"Separate them," Tosch orders me, her voice back to that soothing, motherly tone.

All I want to do is close my eyes so I can feel them. The sole way I can parse one from the other. However, face-planting in the street is not on today's agenda. So I stare straight ahead. I let the unique feel of each one run feather-light touches over my insides.

They fight one another. Each eager to break free. The battle for dominance is on the verge of bringing me to my knees. Every shade from frost to onyx writhes and rolls over one another.

Settle. I command you.

As if determined to listen just this once, they settle, allowing me to parse through them. Arms wide, they part, forming a row on either side of me. Their signatures revealing who they are.

Not mine.

Pierce.

Not mine.

Harley.

Not mine.

Not mine.

Mine.

"Stop," Tosch stretches out an arm in front of me.

I immediately double over, my hands on my knees, the stream of essence sinking back beneath my skin. The tall grass at the side of the road billows in the wind. A howl of force reminding us we're outdoors in the middle of winter. Each blade swaying the same way my body seems to as I uncurl back to my full height.

I'm on the verge of collapse. Each sucked-in breath burns. Every wheeze is louder than the last. "That was cruel," I gag.

"It wasn't. I was preparing you."

"For what?" I snap, fighting to keep standing.

Tosch lowers her face close to mine. That drill sergeant stare locks back into place. "You're smart and quite gifted," she pauses, her hands gripping her hips, "and dangerous. You don't know what's out there waiting. Roman won't hold back. He'll send his nastiest supporters after you. If you think you've seen his worst, you can't imagine what else he's capable of. If you can't control your essence and all the others your body is eager to snatch, you're as good as dead."

There's a harsh tone to her words. A glimpse of raw emotion flashes in her eyes. Proof she witnessed unthinkable loss. My mouth opens to ask, but it's not my place. Her story is hers to share only if she chooses to.

I don't know this woman. Not yet.

In time, I will. She's my brother's best friend's wife; it's inevitable.

Still, the little voice that cackles with defiance surfaces. I'm too tired to keep it under control. The words shooting past my lips like daggers through the air. "How would you know?" I groan, attempting to stretch out my burning quads.

"Because I was one of them. I was a weapon the light wielders used to manipulate and control those they wanted to... behave." Devastating sadness fills her green eyes. The kind that lives with you forever. You can never quite carve it out. At some point, you accept that you'll never be without it. No matter how long you refuse to claim it.

"You're a Grisym," I breathe. "Is that why you were..." I can't finish the question. Her arranged marriage to Damian doesn't seem to be a sore topic, but who wants to open old wounds?

"I am. My parents were murdered in front of my eyes. But even at a young age, much like you, my power was boundless. The Council saw that and wanted it for themselves. So they made a deal with my parents: I serve them, and we all get to live. They took the deal, of course. What parents wouldn't?" I bite my tongue, refusing to answer that. "But they made another deal too, with the Haithwaites. Our fortune and access to a particular set of artifacts would be theirs if they married me to their son. My parents were right not to trust the Council. They were murdered a few months after I started... working for them."

A weak smile crests her freckled lips as she stares out at the field of grass to our right. "Tosch, I'm sorry. I don't know what they made you do—"

She turns back to face me so abruptly that I instinctively jump back. The vulnerability she'd shown moments ago has vanished. I've got the commander back. "No, you don't. So instead of acting like this tough woman, listen to me."

"Give me five more minutes to catch my breath, and then you can boss me around some more." It's all I have to offer.

My heart grows heavier the more I think about her past. She was a child forced to do gods knows what. Her past may be our best asset yet.

"No, run." A whip of her essence cracks in my direction. First, a frosty white, she then waves to soft black. The ropes whip at my thighs, making me yelp as I take the first step to propel me forward.

It's a fight against myself. Against the pain and every muscle screaming for me to stop. "When?" I pant, sucking in a sharp breath as I push to keep moving.

"Hold," Tosch orders, her steps keeping pace with mine. A much slower pace than someone in her physical condition would like. But I push with everything I have. I didn't work out before this. Perhaps Tosch is yet another enemy attempting to kill me. "Now!"

I release a breath and reach for the parts of me that remain untouched. The piece of my essence that never leaves her throne, knowing she is the queen of my body. Slowly, I tease out those tendrils. A new one appearing at each fingertip, one by one.

"Good," Tosch deadpans. "More."

I tug a little harder.

Too hard.

The other essences, more than I ever remember taking in, burst to the surface, shooting free. My usual cloud of black smoke is swirling so high it looks like a tornado touched down. Do those exist in rural Britain?

"Okay, stop," Tosch snaps. "Enough for today."

My hands drop to my knees, bending at the waist to suck in precious air. "I'm sorry. I tried."

"I know. I felt your essence. She's a hungry bitch, eh?" Scrunching my features, I twist just enough to glance up at Tosch's humor-filled eyes.

"Seems like it. I never understood what that feeling was. It wasn't until I stole from that light wielder. Every other time I've taken essences, except Knox, has been by accident." Each word comes out as a ragged breath, my chest pumping so far up and down it seems unnatural.

"Yes, your mix with Knox is unique. I don't quite understand it," she exhales, typing away on her phone. I absentmindedly wonder if she takes notes about me. "Knox is as much your vessel as he is your match, I would say. The energies align. They seem to want to work together instead of fighting for dominance."

"And let me guess, no one has ever seen something like that before?" I roll my eyes, hands on my hips.

"No one still living," she grins as an SUV slows next to us.

Damian grins at his wife, rolling down the window. "Mmm," he hums. "Let's get you home."

A blush creeps up her neck and onto her cheeks, those bright green eyes darkening with lust. The desire emanating from their pores is unmistakable. I'd rather miss this. Their intimacy isn't for me to witness.

Tosch jumps into the front seat, just as energetic as ever. You'd think we hadn't just run a million miles. Throwing myself into the back, my breathing still hasn't slowed. The energy to buckle my seatbelt even seems Herculean.

"What did you do?" Damian chuckles, kissing her on the mouth in the most indecent way. Is this what it's like for everyone else with me and the guys?

It's weird seeing him smile so much and hearing the love he has for her in his voice. I thought he was an asshole like the others, but he just saved it for her. His love. His heart. Tosch is everything to him.

My mind wanders to my guys. Are we the same? Do they feel the same about me?

Or are we just a bunch of young people fucking because we can?

"I challenged her. But we have a bigger problem than I thought. She needs to learn control of her own essence first. We can't work on the others until she does."

Their fingers weave together on the center console, Damian's lips pressing to her knuckles before he pulls out onto the road.

"She is right here," I groan, readjusting myself in the seat as Damian speeds down the road. My thumbs kneading into the sore muscles, doing nothing to ease the tightness.

"Her essence wants to consume every bit of power that exists around her. How she made it through a semester at school without worse happening, I don't know," Tosch says, sipping from a water bottle in the cup holder, Damian tossing one at me over his shoulder.

The heavy metal tumbler smacks me in the stomach with an "oof." Drinking heavily from it, I nearly drain the entire thing in seconds. "You're an ass."

"Friends can be asses," he grins in the rearview mirror before returning to his conversation with his wife.

Friends? Is that what we are now?

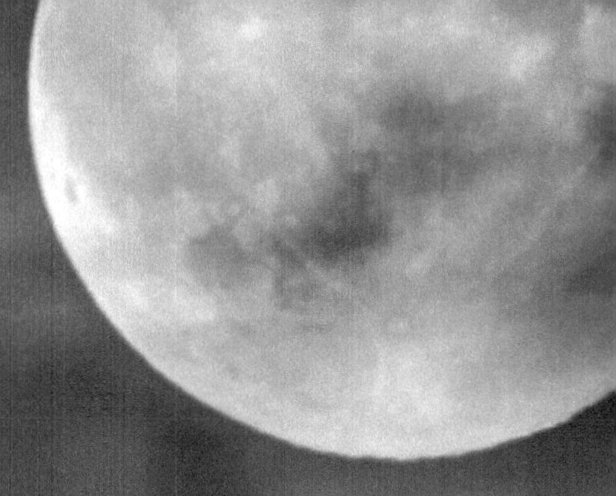

20

PIERSON

EVERY NERVE IS FIRING. My stomach churning with the reality of the un-known. There's a category five storm coming our way. Harley made that clear enough with the information we've been able to extract from him since they locked him away in the basement.

My feet won't stop pacing. Every finger twitches at my sides, repeatedly tapping my thighs in a pattern so erratic I can't even focus on it to slow my racing pulse. Every pounding thump of my heart is slamming against my rib cage with enough force the bone will eventually shatter.

I can't stop moving. Can't sit still. Can't think straight. No matter how many times I wandered through the manor, nothing distracted me.

This is all because of Bri. This war. The turmoil. The impending uproar. Our choices.

But I am in love with her. It's crazy to think that after only four months, I would follow her to the ends of the earth. It doesn't matter if I'm losing my shit, terrified, or confused. I would do anything to keep her safe. I'd been prepared to tell her last night. My lips parted to call her to me when Valen and Knox snatched her away.

We didn't see her again for the remainder of the night. The disappointment crashing through me the second she was out of view. I spent hours in a sitting room staring at the wall before shuffling off to bed.

Graham was kind enough to inform me he walked in on them fucking this morning. A piece of me shattered. Part of me misses the days when it was just me and her. Spending quality time came easily then. Perhaps I took that time for granted now that I'm ready to unload what's on my heart.

Mainly, I crave her touch. To feel her laugh vibrate through my chest as she wiggles in my arms. To feel her lips on my skin from her playful kisses.

Bryony is the commodity here at the manor. It's just us vying for her attention. It's her family, Tosch, the New Order generals, herself. Everyone wants a piece of her, and I wonder if she has any pieces of herself left behind.

Valen later found me on the balcony. His lean frame slumped into the chair beside me as we stared out at the grounds. *"Knox and I fucked our girl this morning,"* he'd chuckled, before recounting Bri's interaction with Tosch afterward. None of it settled me. He got that moment with her.

I already knew. I didn't need a reminder. Pressing my eyes shut, I tried to tune him out. Valen's bullshit is the last thing I needed this morning.

"You don't have anything to say?" he'd pried.

"About what? We're all sleeping with her. It's not a secret," I mumbled, eager for the conversation to end. I had more on my mind than Bri having a threesome with my best friend and our professor.

It has nothing to do with Valen, who made sure Graham and I knew she fucked him and Knox together this morning before Tosch whisked her off to do gods knows what. I know the woman, and whatever it was would bring new meaning to torture.

He'd snickered. *"Not Graham. I'll have to help our boy with his game."* Eyes narrowed, I stared at my best friend.

Graham may have saved him, a gesture Valen will never forget, but *what the actual fuck?* My boy is as loyal as they come. If he owes you a debt, he'll repay it a thousand times over. Yet, I never would have expected this. Valen doesn't share. So, to help a man with the woman he's claimed for himself is out of character.

I tell myself it's because our situation is different. Our woman and us four men are not the norm. We're all in this together, so why not ensure it runs smoothly?

That's all it is, Pierson.

"Later," I waved him off, disappearing back inside. It was a straight path to my room. The only place I might find solitude. Hours of me and my intrusive thoughts to keep me company.

When staring at the ceiling became too much, I went back to my wandering. Muffled voices slither through the cracked door of the front office. The one Jorddan still claims is Geneva's, though she hasn't lived there in twenty-four years. Still, he never touched a thing. It's just as she left it. Artifacts that she had been studying covered the shelves and credenzas. The last pen she wrote with still lies exactly where she left it at the center of the desk, atop the leather-bound journal she'd kept her notes in.

Quiet filled the room a short while ago. Glancing at my watch, only ten minutes have passed. There's been no one in sight or a sound. I've been wandering this main hallway for over an hour now.

Leaning in close, my heart hammers.

"You're in no condition to go," Mr. Greer growls low as if trying to keep his voice down.

With the door cracked and no ward in place, they couldn't possibly be trying to keep this conversation completely private.

"That's not your decision," Valen bites back. Normally, he and his father get along just fine, maybe because he's tossed away the anger that Valen chose to serve Jorddan over something more "legal" like his brother. Lionel's attempts to dictate Valen's actions involving Jorddan's missions never fail to spark an argument, though. Their tempers rise, spewing words slung with every conviction until Lionel finally walks away.

"You can barely stand," Lionel growls.

"Had the energy to fuck his girlfriend this morning just fine," I hear Kaia snarl.

Why the hell is everyone so obsessed with Bri's sex life? I mean, I know we're open about it as dark wielders, but fuck. It's in every damn conversation.

Chancing a look through the crack, I nearly launch myself into the opposite wall. Jorddan's eyes are black as night. His focus pointed across the room, opposite where Valen slumps in his chair. Shooting my gaze back to Valen, my eyes go wide. Valen's features are scrunched tight, as if fighting not to cry out against the pain. The dagger twirling between his fingers, moving with none of the smooth grace it usually does.

Valen is on empty. Neither he nor the dagger holds any power. His father must know that, and that's why he's pushing. Few know how gifted Valen is without his magic. With a simple flick of his wrist, he can send a dagger flying with the same precision as his power does. He never misses.

Pushing the door wide, I step into the room, an immediate scan revealing Kaia in the corner, clawing at a dark essence wrapped around her neck. I'd wondered why Valen had made no smart remarks. He didn't need one. Kaia likely has only seconds more before Jorddan chokes the life out of her for disrespecting his daughter.

Individuals like Kaia harbor venom in their souls. They spew hatred from their tongues. Their shoulders rolled back, balancing massive chips. It was only a matter of time before Jorddan brought her to heel.

Ignoring the display, my gaze rakes around the office. The space is just as I remembered. Geneva's belongings were displayed as if she would return in mere moments. I hope she does, for Jorddan, Bri, and Vincent's sake. They, too, deserve to have their time as an actual family.

Jorddan makes no secret that his heart bleeds for Geneva. He wants her back. Their family reunited once more. He wants what they took from him.

He may deserve that future, but that doesn't mean he'll accept it. Geneva and Roman are equally to blame. They played different roles, sure, but we wouldn't be here if she had behaved differently. She might have avoided this had she allowed Jorddan to know his daughter.

There are too many of us under one roof to support Jorddan's mission. The New Order comes in many varieties. It's what helps keep us anonymous. Our tattoos bearing Jorddan's name are the only giveaway of indoctrination. But should the Council find us here, we're fucked. Concentrating the key players in one place is a risk.

They'd make a spectacle of us. The proverbial gallows is waiting for our bodies to hang. We'd be the example.

"Pierce, get out of here," Valen waves me off, attempting to sit up straighter.

That backbone I'd grown this year hardens a fraction more. "No. What's going on?" My gaze catches on Lionel before tracking back to his son. "What are you planning?" I slam the door behind me, standing my ground.

Before Jorddan's identity as Bri's biological father came to light, this always happened. When it was time for the dirty work or the most dangerous missions, they left me on the outside. I may not have the stomach to take lives the way the New Order soldiers do, but I have worth. Jorddan accepted me, and I expect to be included like anyone else.

The old Pierce was weak. He was too timid to coat his hands in filth. Things are different now. I have more than myself to lose.

"We have a big problem," Knox begins. "Yorgan Dandeluuv undid your mind control on Roman." My brow scrunches, Knox reading my mind before he responds. "He's on the list Bri gave us. He worked with her in her younger teenage years before she matured."

"He did what?" I run my hands through my hair, taking several steps back. Most struggle to undo any orders I've given them. It takes a strong wielder to untangle the new webs of thoughts, memories, and rules my gift allows me to inflict on others. Perhaps the effect had been dulled when I tried to cast it over so many at once. "How?"

"He's a cursebreaker gifted enough to craft his own spells," Jorddan's jaw works. "It's quite...inconvenient, is it not?"

"So, what does that mean?" I practically whine, panicking.

"Roman apparently had an inkling that something was wrong and went straight to him. Yorgan undid your mind control, so now he remembers everything from that night." It takes my mind a moment to process his words. Words delivered so factually and calmly, they seem unreal.

I'm well aware I am no all-powerful wielder. Someone who has mastered counterspell magic could easily undo my planted memories. However, it's rare for someone to notice I've altered their thoughts on their own.

"Does Yorgan know everything?" I press.

"Yep," croaks a broken voice from the corner. I hadn't noticed Merrick sitting there. "My father told Harley and me everything. When he asked Yorgan to craft a stronger spell to bind Grisym magic, I knew I couldn't stand by his side anymore. I have a wife, daughter and sister to think about." Vincent eyes him as if he wishes death on the man who claimed his full-blood sister as his.

"So, what is the plan? We have to kill him, right?" The words tumble out of my mouth as if I never had a chance of keeping them inside. My hands running through my hair for the hundredth time.

Valen snorts, Jorddan eyeing me skeptically while the twins cock their heads to the side almost humorously.

No one says anything for several moments, all eyes on Jorddan, waiting for instruction. Our fearless leader is the one who gives us the go-ahead. Always. Then he inhales a scant breath, folding his hands in front of him. "Valen, Bri has taken essence from you, has she not?"

"Yeah, I think when we were—"

"If you value breathing, do not finish that statement," Vincent snarls.

"Or what? You're her brother, not her keeper. She can sleep with whoever she wants," Valen leans further back in the chair, smirking at Vincent. I hate when he puts on this act like he doesn't give a shit about anything or anyone.

In truth, Bri means a lot to him now, which means by extension, so does Vincent.

"And if I have anything to say about it, you'll be the first piece of shit she ditches." Those words sting, as if he is referring to more than one of us. Casting my gaze around the room, three of us are here; Graham is our sole member missing. No surprise.

"Enough," Jorddan's low tone cracks through the room. "Valen, you will stay behind until completely healed. Bryony, Wynston, Vincent, Kaia, Janelle, and I will leave this evening to handle Yorgan."

"And you think taking Bri to someone who knows exactly who and what she is is smart?" I question. I'm generally good at holding my tongue. At pretending I'm fine with every plan and the Everest-sized mountain of risks we take, but why this one?

"Safe or not, she can wield Valen's power. In addition, yours, Harley's, and mine. Janelle will also give her essence."

My feet move of their own volition, carrying me closer to Vincent. His eyes narrow a fraction, as if assessing my intent. "I thought you said Bri's body can't handle continuing to take in new essences the way she has."

"We did," Lionel nods, my gaze snapping to his. I hate that he's still here. He was never part of anything we've done since working with Jorddan, and I know he's only here now because his son died for the cause. My gut is telling me he'll be around for the long haul.

"That's why we'll have Knox," Janelle says in a placating tone.

"He couldn't even control her," I shout, my arm extended in his direction just as Bri, Tosch, and Damian enter the office. The room is suddenly too small for all of us at once. The temperature is rising, and my chest is burning from the exertion of trying to breathe through this potential death mission.

"Bryony is very special," Tosch begins. "It'll be a process taming her urge to take. It's not something we can change overnight. So instead, we'll willingly give a piece of ourselves to her. If those she has already taken surround her, it should help suppress the urge until I can teach her control."

"I can't believe all of you!" I pant, my eyes pleading with Bri to go against this. Yet, she only stands there.

You knew.

They all knew the plan except for me.

I'm, yet again, the one excluded.

Not this fucking time.

"Bri goes, I go."

"Fine," Jorddan shrugs. "As you wish." The corner of his mouth twitches under his goatee with his concession. "You will be personally responsible for my daughter's safety. Make me proud."

21

BRYONY

Exhaustion weighs me down. My limbs are heavy, my feet achieving no more than a shuffle to move me forward, my eyes drooping a little more with each blink. I need a shower and my bed before tonight's outing. A chance to reset and then center myself. It's all I can think of, so I may control my essence tonight. So I can take my first life.

Gods, when thought of so plainly, it seems almost cruel. How can I consider homicide so dispassionately?

You're tired, Bri. That's all it is. You're still a good person, even if you do this tonight.

The words play through my head, but I can't say that I believe them. Shuffling toward the small couch in the corner, I'm ready to collapse when Pierce's hand catches my elbow.

My eyes will barely focus on his handsome face. The features slightly blurred until I blink a few more times. Too many emotions live in his denim blue eyes. Those deep oceans drowning in everything he must be feeling. My gaze catches his tongue as it swipes along his bottom lip. Not flirtatious, just an expression of the words he wants to say. There's a conversation at the forefront of his mind, and he won't relax until it happens.

This could mark our last moments to share our gentler selves. Once we're in motion, there will be no room for it.

We'll have to be ruthless and swift if we're going to protect the ones we love.

I anchored my self-preservation in obedience and fear when I thought I was alone in the world. Now, I know I am not alone. Each Grisym has a unique gift, and we are all worth fighting for. We're worth protecting and being allowed to live in peace, as any other wielder does.

The office slowly empties, my father, Janelle, and Mr. Greer once again disappearing as a group, but this time with Knox at their side.

Knox is one of them now. One of the "elders," though he has always stood apart, hasn't he? A Grisym in hiding and then a professor fucking his student. The outcast in his family.

The twins shove past me, each shouldering me as if I'm not standing right here. The anger I hold toward them boils hot. They don't have to like me, but if they keep messing with me, I might turn their own gifts on them.

My father demanded they give up their essences. They pledged their allegiance to him. His orders stem from him, not me. I can understand their anger, but I'll be damned if I let them walk all over me. I'm nobody's doormat.

"Next time, walk around," I mutter.

Kaia narrows her gaze at me over her exposed shoulder. "Let's see if you're still that brave when Daddy isn't here to protect you." Then they're gone, the two with their heads ducked low, whispering their demonic secrets.

Merrick exits last, with a backward glance. His eyes conveying an apology he doesn't owe me. For what, I don't know. He's been integral in helping us since his unannounced arrival yesterday, but I also know that until his wife and daughter get here this evening, he will spend his time in the cellar with Harley. Regardless of Harley and my relationship, Merrick will always have his own with his brother.

They don't share the same ill will, though I imagine Harley will see him differently now. His brother will no longer stand on his side of the line. He'll cast aside his blood because of his hatred and ignorance.

My half-brother will never change. Law. Order. Tradition. That is what he lives by. And unless the law states I am free to live, he will never allow me to breathe comfortably.

Even if our laws were to change—and I hope they do in my lifetime—Harley would always hate what I am. His disgust for Grisyms extends well beyond some words on a document forged eons ago. It's ingrained. It's as innate to him as his magic.

If only I knew what made him this way.

My half-brother closes the door behind him, leaving Pierce and me alone for the first time since we got here. I've missed him, his fawning, and his laughter and terrible jokes. He could always make me laugh, even when I didn't think I could.

"Are you okay?" I whisper, pulling Pierce into a hug. His body sinks into mine, arms folding behind my neck to keep me close. His heart pounds next to my ear. A voracious *thump, thump, thump* that's gradually slowing the longer we embrace.

"No, I'm not. This..." he waves his hand, pulling back from me, putting space between us. "It's a lot. I want... No, I need you safe." He takes my hands in his, those sad blue eyes searching mine.

Tilting my head to the side, my chest aches. I wish I could ease his pain. "I've never been safe."

"You know what I mean," he mumbles.

"I do." A tired sigh leaves me. "I also want to live in a world where Grisyms are protected. This is good for someone like you, too," I coo softly, placing a hand on his chest. "Those who want to be someone different from what biology and law dictate."

His fingers skim along my cheek, our eyes locked in a silent understanding that he doesn't get a say in this matter. I am going to do what's necessary to keep all of us safe, even if it means putting myself at risk. "I miss you," he whispers, dropping his forehead to mine.

My eyes close, inhaling his scent, acknowledging how much I miss him, too. Pierce had me first. I was *his,* first.

Since our arrival, every moment has been a chaotic tumble from one minute to the next. I'm a mess, and so is everything else. Pressing up on my toes, my calves screaming against the flexing of the muscles, I press my mouth to his. The touch of my lips, brief but drowning in meaning.

"I just wanted a minute alone to talk to you, but I need a hot bath before my limbs give out," I groan, putting space between us again. But Pierce grabs hold of my wrist, sliding his warm fingers over my skin before linking them through mine.

"Let me take care of you," he all but pleads.

With a nod, I follow. Pierce leads us from the office and through the manor, straight to his room. I'd expected him to take me to mine, but perhaps he didn't in an effort to keep me alone for as long as possible.

The tactic fills my gut with worry for both him and Graham. Worry that they'll think I've forgotten them or cast them aside. I haven't.

I long to return to the night we camped out in my bed, sourcing locations for winter break. A night when life felt simpler. We should have gone. That was our escape. But what would we have come back to?

Our lives had already become a complicated web then, but it also felt so easy.

My guys and I. My friends and lovers. The people I trusted more than anyone else.

It remains true. Only now our circle has grown. My father. Damian. Tosch. Janelle. Camilla. The New Order.

Merrick. *Maybe.*

My train of thought halts on my half-brother as Pierce leads me into his bathroom. The thoughts won't form past his name, my body rigid as I stand there in a trance. I'm aware of Pierce moving around me, gathering bottles, a towel, and turning the knobs on the clawfoot tub. The scent of apples and pears fills my nostrils, but only one name repeats in my head.

Merrick.

Merrick.

Merrick.

Merrick.

I watch him as Pierce adds bubble bath, salts, and some sort of oil he just dug out from beneath the sink. He sits on the edge of the massive tub, his fingers dancing through the water as if testing the temperature.

The calming sight allows me to find my center momentarily before my mind once again dives into the abyss. My thoughts surge through my mind. The images flash one after another, like in fast forward.

I believe Harley was here to do exactly as he said. He always unabashedly expressed his desire for me to leave their lives. I am not an Avalon. I never was. No matter how many years I yearned for his love, it never came. Yet, I was foolish enough to believe that in time he'd see. He'd realize I could be just like them. Then maybe I would earn my half-brother's love.

I realized too late that I never would. There's no changing the core of who I am. With that truth, so comes his. His acceptance was something I could never earn.

But Merrick. I can only wonder if his open betrayal of Harley is part of some diabolical plan against Jorddan and me, or if he truly deceived my family to protect his own. It's impossible to decide whether he chose to keep his wife a secret to protect her or because he didn't trust us.

Merrick and I have always had a solid relationship. He has never given me a reason not to trust him, but for once, I'm unsure. I don't know who or what to trust.

Now is not the time for mistakes.

His wife and baby girl will be here this evening. We'll know then.

"Come here," Pierce stretches a palm toward me.

Moving away from the door frame, I force my muscles to support me just a little longer. I cling tightly to the pain. It's a reminder of everything I have to lose if I can't master my essence. My only way to then master the dark.

Stopping in front of Pierce, he spreads his knees wide, allowing me to stand between them. His hands find the flesh just above my knees. His thumbs work into the knots of my muscles, my hands resting on his shoulders as I groan against the deliciousness of his touch. "Thank you," I whisper.

He doesn't stop, slowly working higher and higher. Inch by inch. His attention lingering longer in certain areas. I groan louder until he grips my hips.

"I'd do anything for you, Bri." Standing, he forces me back a few steps. One hand lifts to caress my cheek. The touch is so gentle, I lean into it. Crave it as much as I have grown to crave him. Pierce is my gentle soul.

"I know you would," I start.

"I'm in love with you," he blurts, dropping back to the edge of the tub, his forehead hitting my stomach.

Those words should have taken me by surprise or made me jump for joy. Somehow, I wasn't prepared to hear them pass his lips, but felt them coming. Pierce fell hard from the beginning. A puppy dog latched onto my heels, eager to please and shower me in affection. Eager to be petted and loved back.

And I do love him, but unlike him, I'm not ready to say those words out loud. I've given my love too freely before. Their affection was never genuinely reciprocated my way, even when I begged for it. Any fondness they did show was nothing more than a facade.

The people I still love disappear or die.

My weird, twisted history with love, both within my family and relationships, doesn't make it easy for me to say those words anymore. I want to love. To be loved. To be cherished and wanted. I refuse to relinquish my heart so freely again. I keep it for myself. Safe. Protected. Unharmed.

A tendril of my essence drifts free, settling beneath his chin, lifting his face so our gazes meet.

"I'm not going to say it back. Not yet. But know that you are the one who saved me. You helped me see what it means to be appreciated. There are no words that can adequately express my gratitude for that."

Sadness coats his eyes, but so does understanding. My swan dive into our relationship was slow from the start. He must have expected this, even if he hoped we would be different now. That he might have misjudged how I might respond.

"I'm still going to," he says, squeezing my hip. "In front of everyone. I won't apologize for that."

"I would never ask you to." I bend to place a quick kiss on his mouth. "Now about that bath." I quirk a slight grin.

He, too, releases a tendril of his essence. The ebony smoke multiplying in volume on its own, covering my body, only to fade away, leaving me naked. I'd felt its soft caress along my skin. A touch so intimate I would have thought it was my lover's. Yet I hadn't felt my clothes evaporate off my body, the pile of sweat-soaked material now lying in a heap on the floor to my right.

Standing, Pierce stays close to me, lifting his shirt over his head and then removing his jeans, briefs, and socks. Taking my hand, he helps guide me into the tub, stepping in right behind me.

He sits first, snapping his fingers so the faucet stops running, before pulling me down to nestle between his legs, my back to his front.

With a sigh, his arms wrap around me, his chin resting on the top of my head. "This feels nice," I grin, sinking lower.

"Good. Just relax. I've got you."

My heart swells with emotion. How did I get so lucky to have so many people care for me?

We're quiet for some time. The warmth of the water soaking into my skin and uncoiling my taut muscles. "Pierce?"

"Yeah," he answers, his voice gravelly as if he'd fallen asleep, though I know he hadn't, as his fingers continue to stroke along my lower belly.

"Please don't come with us tonight."

22

BRYONY

How much guilt can one person carry?

How many wrongs can we bear before we can no longer stand?

My eyes flutter shut, remembering the heartbreak on Pierce's face when I asked him to stay behind. It was meant to keep me from adding to my load, but had the opposite effect. The shape may be different, the density may change, and the material may be finer, but it's still more to lug around with me.

Too many of us are in danger tonight. I couldn't put my sweet guy in harm's way, too. If there were any way I could do this on my own, I would have. Maybe Kaia could join me. I don't care one way or another what happens to her. Not when she sneers at me like she's a hungry beast ready to tear me to shreds and cook me for dinner.

Leaving the others behind was the right thing to do. To merely learn, Jorddan assigned them a separate mission, ground my molars. They weren't supposed to be on my list of worries for the night.

I have limits. My nerves are constantly firing beneath my skin. Each one is fraying. Each one is pushing me closer to a breaking point, even Vincent may not have the ability to bring me back from.

Deafening silence pressed in on us as we sat there in the tub. There was an argument brewing just beneath Pierce's chest. The words huddled in his throat ready to burst free. I could feel it. His essence pushed to the forefront of the others to ensure I was aware of exactly what I had done to him.

I didn't need the reminder.

I knew.

It hurt enough knowing I put him on the back burner, where the New Order has always kept him.

Knowing Pierce, he retreated into his mind. He'll question himself and his abilities. He'll resent his dark magic more than he already does. An outsider with his own kind. The wrong composition to be welcomed into the light.

Contrary to the lies he'll tell himself, this was a selfish decision. It has nothing to do with the type of wielder he is. I cannot stand losing him.

I need the people I care about to be safe.

My body remained tense as Pierce lazily ran his fingers over my naked skin. Conflict warred in his eyes. A rebuttal on the tip of his tongue. Yet, he held back. His silence spoke volumes.

My golden retriever boyfriend fought back without his words, slipping his fingers into my pussy, making me writhe and moan for an ungodly amount of time, before I couldn't take it anymore. Straddling his lap, I'd lazily ridden him, while his eyes pleaded with me. Pleaded for me to stay. To take him with us. To run away. Anything that avoided the trigger tonight would become.

I'd only kissed him, unable to give him the words he wanted.

My father doesn't shy away from the atrocities he's committed in the mission's name. He has taken lives. For decades, he has punished the light. They blamed him and the New Order for every wrongdoing. Yet without proof, the Council and Wielding Bureau can't hold him.

Somehow, tonight feels different. I made a fucking hit list so we can protect me. Murdering light wielders for being a threat to a Grisym will turn the tide. It will shift the precarious balance we were barely clinging to with our nails and fingers worn to the bone.

Only more death and bloodshed will follow.

For the Grisym to rise, the light must dim. Only then may I master the dark.

This war is for all of us. It has to be.

The lake on our property sparkles ahead. The surface eerily calm and sprinkled with frost. A dark pool, the unknown. It only seems fitting that this is where our night would begin.

"Call to it," my father orders.

I press my eyes closed, unsure how to call on Aziel. He always just seems to find me. Father claims I summoned the ghouls at Beauxgraton. However, I have no idea how. I'd only sensed them as they drew near.

Aziel. Aziel. Aziel. Come to me. Aziel.

The chant repeats in my head, something stirring inside me. It's not my essence, but something else. A foreign entity that doesn't belong. Yet, it is part of me, the same as my bones and tissues.

I vaguely recognize it. The rough texture of its power. It's lived within me for some time.

Hours seem to pass before I halt my chant, allowing my eyes to peel open.

There's nothing, just the black of night surrounds us. My father watches my face while Kaia rolls her eyes and smirks as if she knew I would be of no help.

Aziel! I shout his name once more in my head, the ground rumbling beneath us as if in answer. I spin, staring off into the dense area of trees, calling my essence to my fingers to form a small ball of light. A light so dim it couldn't possibly guide our way.

Yet, as if I have night vision, he comes into clear view. A dozen other ghouls are at his back, running toward me. Aziel stops just short of bowling me over, heavy breaths funneling out of his wide nostrils. "Bryony, need me."

"Yes, thank you for coming. We need to use the tunnels to get back to America."

I'm unsure if he understands where I'm asking to go. Since we met, I've always spoken plainly to him. He has always understood. Perhaps this will translate too.

"Ghoul," Janelle comes forward.

He snarls at her, baring those large razor-sharp teeth. That massive clawed hand quickly stretching in front of me as if blocking me from danger.

"His name is Aziel," I hiss.

She furrows her brow. "Ghouls have no gender, Bryony. No names." The urge to roll my eyes is strong. I know all of this. Later, I'll explain our connection to her. With my nod, Janell continues. "The closest Hell Gate is Arrimon. Can you take us there?"

Aziel snorts, but nods. The other ghouls of varying shades all nod after him. "Will you take us?" I ask, looking up at my Azukeen.

"Bryony is mine. Bryony only ask," Aziel grunts, running a claw between my breasts and down my stomach as he squats in front of me.

"Thank you."

"Bryony take power." His cock stretches from his hips, growing until it bobs heavily. The size is making my mouth water and my pussy ache.

Tosch's torture, combined with fucking three men in one day, took its toll. As tempting as the rush of Aziel's power is to my greedy essence, I refuse. We do not have time to take the chance that my essence might rebel. My body has taken enough of a beating lately.

"Not now. I have too much. We have to wait."

Aziel roars, but returns to his full height. That bobbing rod sinks back into his pelvis, then he turns on his heel, marching off into the dark with his comrades following close behind.

The waving wall of air comes into view quicker than I would have thought. When Aziel brought me back here with Valen, we'd entered the manor. I assume there are multiple Hell Gates on the property. A property I don't even know the borders of. It seems excessive, but what do I know? I'm new to the dark.

"We lead," Aziel grumbles before the other ghouls step through the portal.

That same rush hits me as we step through in pairs. The view of being here, but knowing I am being transported elsewhere, seems surreal.

When we return, I hope to ask Mr. Greer about these tunnels. My list of questions stretches miles long. It seems odd that we would just be able to cross their portal barriers. However, perhaps it's a courtesy rather than the norm.

My father is the last to pass through the portal, the waving wall of translucent air falling away to reveal nothing but an endless black tunnel.

It is just as it was a week ago. The same dank air and stone walls, but not a single sign of moisture.

"What the hell is this?" Kaia snarls, her eyes roving over the walls and ceiling, standing several feet taller than a ten-foot ghoul.

"The ghouls live in a different world. This is their tunnel system used to move between their hibernation and mating pits and the Hell Gates," my father supplies. His voice filled with awe, as if he had made the discovery of a lifetime.

He's never been in these tunnels. He's experiencing a first. A special moment I'm privileged to witness.

"Why don't I know about this?" she questions, her glare pointed in my direction.

"You didn't need to," Vincent snaps.

"But that—" her finger waves in my direction, Aziel darting past me, lifting her by the throat and slamming her into the wall. Chunks of rock crash to the floor as she claws at the iron grip holding her in place.

Aziel stares at her with those ghostly white eyes. "You never yell at Bryony. I kill anyone who hurt her."

"Put her down," I grunt begrudgingly. Kaia could fall off the face of this earth for all I care. Just fucking disappear. But not like this. Not tonight, when we need her.

"Let me kill," Aziel snarls, squeezing tighter, gasping breaths barely funneling out of Kaia as she clings tight to his gnarled skin.

No one else steps in. I wait for them to, but they don't move a muscle.

Searching their faces, it's clear they don't care. Not a single one of them wants to. Kaia brought this on herself. Not once but twice today, she tested another's patience. That's on her.

Then it dawns on me. I am the only one the ghouls answer to. A consequence of the power my father transferred to me, forcing me into early maturity. Ghoul magic.

"Now, Aziel," I deepen my voice, the command clear in my words.

With a roar, he tosses her to the ground, the impact of her body colliding with the hard stone making me jump. There's no love lost between us, but I'm in pain just thinking about how that felt.

Janelle is the one to help her to her feet, wrapping an arm around her waist before Aziel moves past us, stalking down the tunnel.

We follow in silence, the clack of our shoes at odds with the huffing breaths of the ghouls leading us.

Our trek seems endless, yet I know magic is at play here. These tunnels don't operate under the laws of man.

Glancing down at my watch, I'm surprised an hour has passed.

"Bryony and friends there soon," Aziel grunts as if he could sense my weary spirit.

"We're fine. Just keep going."

There's no answer, but his pace quickens. Another chunk of untraceable time passes before the ghouls come to an abrupt halt.

"You go," Aziel grumbles. His words are clearer the more he speaks. "We stay outside. We watch over mine."

"Thank you," I say for what seems like the millionth time. My ghoul leans low, allowing me to run my palm over the uneven skin of his cheek. I'm unsure what else to say. Aziel brought us here; what more could we ask for?

The portal shimmers into existence, the outside world hazy and dark beyond. It shouldn't be that way. The time difference should have earned us daylight. An advantage we understood was the need to travel through the mountains in winter.

Stepping through first, the warmth from the tunnels quickly shifts to a cold so startling I check my fingers to see if frostbite has already settled in.

Peering to the left, my eyes narrow against the blizzard raging around us. My vision strains against the onslaught of snow. Each repeated blink fails to clear my field of view enough to know I'm not hallucinating. My gut is telling me I'm not. Our Hell Gate sits at the edge of a massive cliff. The drop-off leading you to nowhere.

It's nearly impossible to make out anything around me with clarity. The wind whips too furiously. The snow falls too heavily. A howling roar threatens to leave me deaf the longer I stand here, shivering.

Squinting, I make out a cabin half a mile up the peak. The flurries clumping in my lashes, only to melt once they brush my cheeks. The dark-stained wood pops against the sheet of white. A pang striking my chest at the familiarity. Memories tapping at the door in my mind someone trapped them behind.

I'm sure I've never been here before. Searching my memories, there's no rec-ollection. Yet my insides stir. My essence is poking at me as if it does. Cowering away with each step I take toward the cabin. A tremor causing the tendrils to shake as they run and hide, burrowing deep inside me.

What happened here?

A hand comes down on my shoulder, pulling my focus away from the cabin. My essence no longer squirming now that I've looked away.

What was that?

"What is it?" Jorddan asks.

"I can't be sure, but I think Roman brought me here."

"Why would he risk taking you out of the home?" Vincent questions the buzz of his lips rolling, drawing our attention.

"I think..." I swallow as the memories come crashing back. "I think he tried to have my dark side stripped."

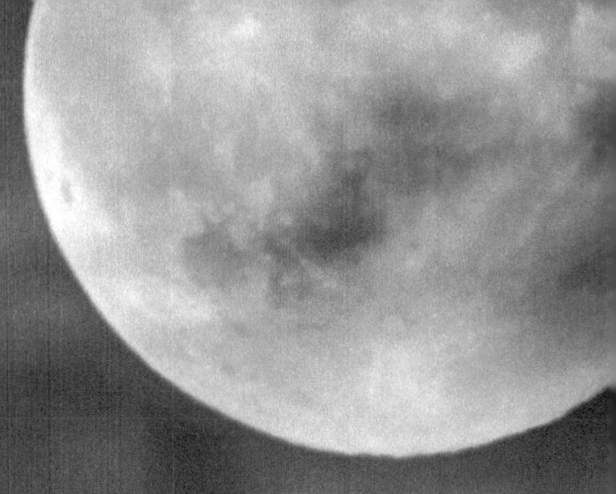

23

WYNSTON

Rage riots inside me. My essence is banging at my wall of skin, eager to get to whoever hurt our woman. Does Roman even understand what he could have done? Bryony might not have survived the damage.

He must have known and not cared. A reality that only further fuels the boundless fury, balling my fists at my side.

Despite the public opinion, Roman was not a well-liked man. He was tolerated. Most complied with the privileges that accompanied being in his good favor. Freedom of curriculum, hiring choices, invitations to elite events, and even changes in student admission criteria.

Roman was an itchy scab throughout my entire career. A man who forced the grit of my teeth with each interaction. My dislike of him turned to the worst kind of hatred after what he did to Bryony. How could someone do that to a child they raised? Theirs or not, it's fucked up.

Few can truly understand the fear of living in hiding. Only a Grisym or their parent knows the iron fist that remains clutched around your heart. The isolation. The constant lies. It's endless days of looking over your shoulder, wondering when. When someone accidentally catches you. When someone who already knows what you are betrays you for their own gain or to spare themselves. How long before hiding no longer suffices? How does one behave if the options are reduced to fighting or acceptance?

Roman could have killed her, the woman he called his daughter. A glittering gem he held high for everyone to see. Roman paraded around Bryony like the prize he always saw her as. Only she wasn't his prize. Our girl was the means to his.

Part of Bri believes there was genuine love between her and Roman for a time. When that switched, she may never know.

As wielders are our essences. Our magic is the core of who we are. It's our heartbeat. It's the blood flowing through our veins. That power is our soul. The same is true for a Grisym. The mixture of what we became is our life force. That is why the tangible smoke we produce is referred to as an essence. It is us.

Stripping that away would be equivalent to erasing a wielder's life force. Their shell-like body would have no reason to continue living. A punishment that has been documented only a few times in modern history.

Yorgan is very good at his spellwork, sure, but why would Roman pick him? Cursebreakers can undo spells, curses, memory locks, and much more, but a wielder's essence seems too far-fetched.

Bri's collection of essences rolls through her. Each one surrounding hers, protecting it from whatever it experienced inside that cabin.

"Bri?" My mouth opens, ready to shout it again, knowing the howling blizzard is making it impossible to hear.

"They're remembering," Jorddan announces, his eyes the pitch black that takes over when he uses his power. Snow clings to his nearly black goatee as he trains his stare ahead, laser-focused on our target's hideaway.

There's no more hiding. Jorddan knows what the man did to his daughter. A simple death won't suffice. Roman will suffer, and Jorddan will enjoy it. Every rumor is true. We know that now.

"Why is it so fucking dark?" Kaia grumbles. Vincent scowls at her. An expression so sharp it could eviscerate.

"Spelled and warded," Jorddan slips out of his trance, his eyes returning to their normal hue. The coloring is so similar to Bri's, it's a wonder anyone could ever mistake her for anyone else.

Pressing her lips into a straight line, Kaia steps forward. Her expression turning blank before her mouth moves. The hand in her pocket clearly fiddling with something. Likely, whatever herbs she traveled with. Though her spellcasting is above average without them, it's exponentially stronger with the proper foliage.

She stares straight ahead, her lips moving faster. The moment her eyes close, Janelle jumps forward, grabbing hold of Kaia's arm. Her concentration is broken as they both nearly tumble into the snow at their feet.

"Stop!" Milgren snaps. "You can't. If we manipulate his security measures, he'll know we're here." Kaia's face goes white as the snow as Janelle holds her arms from behind, the two staring at the same cabin we've all been watching.

"He already does." Bri cocks her head to the side. "I can feel him inside me. His essence. I took from him." One step at a time, she moves closer to the mountain. Her even pace as if some invisible force is pulling her forward. "He's waiting. Let's go."

Without another word, we trek up the snow-covered mountain, Kaia spelling the deep snow away enough that we don't die as we move.

The moment we clear the ridge, Yorgan's yard comes into view. His storm was meant to distract, stopping at the border of his property. The sky, though overcast, showers us with daylight. The change is so stark that we're all left blinking, allowing our vision a chance to adjust.

Short, faint green grass spans ahead of us, the ground squishy beneath our feet. The earth is damp despite being clear of snow. A sign that his property is vulnerable to the natural elements. Magic shields the area. Protection from any uninvited guests. That's to be expected.

The door swings open with a boisterous groan as Yorgan comes into view. I've never met the man, but his body fills the frame. Tall and with considerable girth, blocking out every ounce of light behind him. A replica of the superheroes we see in movies.

Not much has changed from the photos I searched. There's some additional gray spattered throughout his beard and hair; otherwise, he's the same.

"Welcome back, Bryony. It's so good to see you brought company," he bellows. His voice booms louder than it should, as if trying to call out to us through the blizzard raging at our backs.

Jorddan's hand drops from his daughter's shoulder, allowing her to move toward the wielder who tried to break her. My pace quickens to keep time with her, unsure where this interaction might lead.

We took a massive risk with Bri last night. One that seems to have paid off after she absorbed three new essences. Still, my hackles remain high. Just because there was no rebellion last night doesn't guarantee she'll maintain control. That's the only reason I'm here. I am the only one who might be able to calm her if her body rebels. I am Bryony's vessel.

"It's been a long time," Yorgan states plainly as Bryony slips past him and into his house. Her movements are smooth, but I can feel the tension inside her. She's fighting to keep it together.

You can do this.

"Not long enough," she retorts. "Only Jorddan." She holds up a hand, stopping the rest of us from approaching.

Yorgan cocks a brow, as if surprised. It's unclear if he's aware of her relation to Jorddan. That alone is the most unsettling unknown. Without a clear picture of who knows what about Bryony, we're acting on assumptions. It's a guessing game we can't afford to get wrong.

"Absolutely not," Vincent roars. His role was played perfectly. A hot-headed brother ready to defend and protect his little sister at any cost.

"Stay out here," Bri bites in his direction.

Still, Vincent charges forward, only for Kaia and me to wrap our arms around him. He only fights harder, snarling as both eyes shift to black. Yorgan only smirks at the display as he allows Jorddan entrance and slams the door.

"Get off me," Vincent barks, ripping his body from our hold. His chest heaves angrily. The veins popping at his temples and throat a clear sign of how far gone he is.

This isn't just for show. It's there, written on his face. His fists clench, shaking uncontrollably. He's heartbroken and pissed that he can't be in there with his sister. Bri took that choice from him.

It seems we have all been making our choices with the same unforgiving edge, only to leave those we care about most hurt and disappointed.

"Do you think he bought it?" Janelle whispers, waving a hand in front of her.

Kaia's essence spreads, spelling our pathway. A quieting spell that will ensure our silence as we creep to the rear of the cabin.

"It doesn't matter. We have shit to do," Vincent growls, sneering at Kaia. "Stay the fuck away from me."

Kaia flinches, moving to Janelle's other side. Her gaze trails over to Vincent repeatedly, though he doesn't bother giving her another moment of his attention.

None of us is a fan of Kaia, but there's something deeper here. A past none of us knows.

Not my business.

A part of me regrets ever taking Bri out there to fuck a ghoul. I should have known better. Perhaps we wouldn't be in this position had I not. A lie I can tell myself until I believe it.

If not me, someone else. Valen. Pierce. Worse yet, another wielder who was unaware she's a Grisym. A disaster waiting to happen. The mess stretching far beyond those present to witness it.

Bri may not be mine otherwise.

Fuck.

Shaking my head, I work to clear my thoughts as we round the rear of the house. Somehow, Lionel obtained the blueprints. Where he got them from, none of us asked. The how and why weren't important. It was an advantage. A way for us to navigate the property with the same level of knowledge as the owner.

Turning the corner, the cozy alcove comes into view. We agreed it would be a better entry point than windows or the underground cellar. The door sits cracked, an onyx tendril floating around the edge. The tail curling as if beckoning us forward. *Jorddan.*

Kaia hesitates, moving in front of Vincent, his scowl forcing the clench of her jaw as she follows him inside, with me bringing up the rear.

I glance once more over my shoulder at Janelle, our amplifier. The one we brought with us to hide any magic we are doing on this man's property. Janelle appears to be on a walk as she focuses on amplifying every spell and ward Yorgan constructed here. We've identified at least six so far.

Kaia and Vincent creep forward, aiming for the opposite end of the cozy, yet modern, cabin.

My ears perk up, following the cadence of Bri and Jorddan's voices. They sound fine. Her essence remains steady within me.

Their voices sound different as they project from the front of the house. Far enough away, I wonder if they made it past the front entryway. Definitely no further than the living room or the den that sits off the kitchen area, if I'm remembering the floor plans correctly. It was an odd configuration.

I listen closely, trying to capture what they're saying.

It was Bri's idea to make it appear she was coming back to Yorgan for help. Though we were unsure if he knew Jorddan was her biological father, it wouldn't matter. Regardless of parentage, her struggles would be what they are. Harley confirmed Yorgan was aware Bri was a Grisym. That's all we needed to know.

"Roman doesn't know I brought her here. We're aware of your friendship with him, but we do ask that you be discreet," Jorddan relays calmly, the slightest hint of a plea in his tone. His acting fits perfectly into the role he was always meant to play. A concerned father looking to help his daughter in secret.

Creeping down the center hallway, I can flatten my body against the wall just enough to get a partial view of them. It has been interesting watching him interact with Bri. She acts like they were never apart, despite lacking all memories of Jorddan. Maybe in a way it hasn't.

Bri stole from him, too, when she was only five days old. In the blink of an eye, she'd snatched a sliver he'd had floating there. It was a secret he kept from her mother. He knew then what his daughter was. He hoped it would be a gift she could live with. A gift she could learn to control, which proved to be wasted hope. Jorddan still carries the weight of having forced his daughter into maturity at fifteen. She alone bore those lasting effects and secrets.

Geneva should have helped her. Guided her. Protected her. Why she never crafted additional storage vessels is beyond me. Why she kept Bri from the one man who could help her makes no sense.

Jorddan fought for his daughter. He seized his opportunity to support her. A chance that ended in Roman threatening to slit Bri's throat and bleed out every bit of her magic if Jorddan tried to have any relationship with her.

Geneva did what she had to do to protect her daughter. And Jorddan got angry. He plotted and planned. He'd waited for his chance to isolate his daughter from the enemy and succeeded.

Hours of Vincent and Jorddan recounting those horrid years with Bri gutted me. Every ounce of their pain, regrets, and missing her acutely cut into my flesh. I had no choice but to listen to their words. My lone chance to potentially bond with her family alone in the parlor. Why they chose me to spill their thoughts to is beyond me. But I'd listened, sipping scotch alongside Vincent.

"...in it for me?" Yorgan quips. A portion of the conversation was lost to me as I'd been shuffling through my own thoughts.

Jorddan's chin rises a fraction. A sign he is about to offer what no one should refuse. "My protection. Surely, even you understand what that's worth in our society," he responds coolly.

Yorgan grunts in response. "That I do." Keeping my body pressed to the wall, I carefully round the doorframe, finally able to watch them from a small extension off the wall. Yorgan shifts to face Bri, who's curled in on herself, seated on the couch next to her father. "Bryony, do you remember the last time you were here?"

She keeps her head down, shaking it several times before sniffling. "No," she whispers.

"Hmm," Yorgan strokes his chin. "Then come with me. We'll need to do this in my work area."

Jorddan and Bri stand, his hand on her shoulder as if comforting her through her fear. But I feel her. Her essence is fighting and screaming not to go back to that dark dungeon.

Pressing my back against the wall, holding my breath as they move past me, I wish I could touch her. Only Jorddan glances my way out of the corner of his eye. My tattoo of his name is buzzing beneath my skin.

He shielded me.

Thank you.

He nods as if he heard me.

Only when he looks back over his shoulder before turning the corner to a basement stairwell do I know he's released the shield. It's safe for me to follow.

Vincent and Kaia should have grabbed what they needed from the basement, where Yorgan's laboratory is by now. A place where he concocts the most vicious spells and curses from his mind.

"On the bench," I hear Yorgan instruct Bri as I magic the creak of the steps away.

I've just reached the bottom step when a crash seems to shake the house to its very foundation.

A barked curse roars through the basement level. "What the fuck is this?"

24

BRYONY

CRIPPLING PAIN SHOOTS THROUGH my spine. My knees buckle, my already straining muscles screaming as they attempt to keep me on my feet. The crash that followed reverberated off the walls at such a pitch that the heels of my hands clapped over my ears. My balance is once again challenged as I shove off the shelf, digging into the throbbing flesh of my midback.

Movement pulls my focus to the opposite end of the room. Kaia and Vincent are hiding behind their own ceiling-height metal shelving unit. My teeth dig into my lower lip, hoping no one has spotted them but me. Kaia should have been able to use a locator spell for everything we needed.

They were supposed to be done.

They should have been out.

This wasn't the plan.

Fear and fury contort my brother's features as Yorgan spins on me, shouting in my face. "What the fuck is this?" Spittle hits my cheeks; the panic he is witnessing is genuine.

"Now!" Jorddan snaps.

We spent hours mapping out every nuance of tonight. We did not anticipate encountering this particular issue in the plan.

Stupid. It was naive to think we could pull this off without encountering any major issues.

We couldn't have planned for my essence to hold memories of a tortured past here. There is no way my father or I would have known that. I couldn't have predicted the moment that Yorgan told me to get on the bench, my essence would gut punch me so hard I'd fly into one of the shelving units, lining the wall.

And now I'm forced to react without preparation. Adrenaline zips through my veins, causing my thoughts to scatter and my hand to tremble, but at least it blocks the pain. I was supposed to have time to parse through my essences. Time to find Valen and Pierce's gifts so we could eliminate Yorgan as fast as possible.

But there is no time.

There's only now.

Reaching inside me, I call to the essences I want. I pray they are the ones to answer. But my magic is coming too fast. Too unfocused and I can't stop it, so I let it go.

My essence billows out of my mouth while winding in long streams from my fingers.

I can feel them all there. Each dark whip is eager to eliminate the threat lunging for me, but the light is only insistent on protecting me. I am their home now—their host. Without me, they are nothing.

Evolution made me an apex predator. Greedy enough not only to take, but then to learn my new treasure's secrets. The strengths and weaknesses. The dirty little tricks I can employ against anyone I'd like. That's power. That's me.

I became each one of these magical signatures. They became me. Like DNA that was always meant to be part of my genome. We are one, never to be separated again. I'd like to see them try. They'll gasp their last breath before they even come close.

They are the same, but different. They are part of me. Even if I knew how to return those essences to their rightful owners, they would no longer belong.

Yorgan attempts to grab me through the haze of essence rotating in front of me, the tendrils securely wrapping around his body. Each arm tightening around him in a looping rope that squeezes unforgivingly.

"Your eyes," he breathes.

I'd known they were changing. There was no point in stopping it. Yorgan won't survive tonight to tell anyone what he's seen.

My head cocks to the side, a precariously slow tilt that seems to stretch the muscles. Each blink clears the enhanced ghoul vision as I focus on the unbridled fear in Yorgan's beady eyes. Revel in the streak of sweat running down his temple. Cackle at his hands trembling as each essence subdues him and steals his breath. That grimace against the pain fighting to become a snarl.

The corner of my mouth crooks high. Twitching. Threatening to become a full-blown grin.

My dark side wants that.

My light side says I should show mercy.

The Grisym wins.

Don't speak—my first order.

Yorgan's lips press together tightly. His grunts mumbled behind them. His brow furrowing, trying to separate them and spew whatever curses he'd like to continue to sling my way.

That grin spreads wide. My teeth flashing as I watch him struggle.

Sparks of electricity flash through my body. The dark magic racing through my veins, eager to exit my body anywhere I'll allow. A sense of invincibility stretching my lips wide in a grin. This must be what Valen experiences, torturing the victims he forces to rot from the inside out. This power. Twisted and hungry. Its boisterous cackle almost drawing out my own villainous laughter.

It's euphoric.

"Did you tell anyone else the truth about me?" I ask. My voice is deeper, almost distorted, as if it's not mine in my ears.

Searching for my piece of Pierce, I release my following command. *Speak.*

Yorgan fights against his magical restraints, his sneer showcasing his yellowed teeth. "No. I'm not dying for you."

"But you are," my father deadpans from beside me. "Do it, my daughter."

Yorgan writhes against the restraints. The veins at his temples are popping as sweat coats every inch of exposed skin. The hue shifts to a deep cherry before that color too fades. Every droplet of sweat that marred his skin seems to evaporate. The tomato coloring suddenly shifting to an ashen gray. My gaze trailing its first appearance at his hairline, over his distorted facial features, down his thick neck to his limbs. The vivid blue veins beneath his skin are darkening. So dark they appear as black as my essence.

"You tried to take away my dark side, and now I am taking your life," I croon. My voice sounds distant. The timbre is not at all mine, but I felt the vibration of each word in my throat. It was me. This is me.

Yorgan howls and pleads. The Bri I pretended to be my whole life hears him. She hesitates, but right now I'm not here. I'm the Bri I've become. The Grisym. The one who takes and doesn't fear crossing the line of my dark side.

Nobody can reason with her. She won't bend or break. Beauxgraton released this Bri when I almost took my first life. This Bri won't stop this time.

Back then, I didn't have Valen's power.

My dark side could only command her death through actions.

Now I can taste the deliciousness that comes with Valen's power. The temptress who enjoys watching someone's own shell eat them alive until there's nothing left. A death by my command, but not my physical touch.

The evil excitement of it fills me. I breathe it in.

This is me.

Rolling my neck, I revel in the feel of Yorgan dying before me. His essence is leaking out of him and joining with mine.

"It seems I get to take more than your life today," I snicker. That same deep voice filters past my lips.

This is unapologetic, Bri.

A ruthless Bri.

A Bri that will do whatever it takes to protect anyone important to her.

My essence swirls faster, expanding, knocking into beakers and vials lining the far workbench. The glass shatters in a ricochet of sound. With the shards flying through the room at such a high speed, the air shifts as they brush past my face. Items tumble from the shelves. And then the walls begin to crumble. Concrete falling in chunks, crashing to the floor, only to split into a million particles of dust and small rocks.

"Bri! Bri! Bri!"

Who is shouting my name?

Why?

It's a voice I recognize. My essence curls and smiles. It wants him to come and play.

Kill with me. Join me. I beckon to the voice.

"Bri, stop! You need to control it. You'll kill us all."

My head jerks to the side, my essence forming a billowing wall behind me, Knox's face coming into view. My head tilts again. He appears different from his usual appearance when the ghoul vision takes over. His eyes don't match mine.

"Please stop," Knox begs. "Listen to me. You've done enough. You did it." Strong hands wrap around my arms, shaking me. Knox's hands. Knox's voice.

My gaze meets his again. This isn't right.

As if that single look had broken the trance, my body jerks forward. Slowly, my essence slithers back into my fingers, more of it being swallowed down by Knox in front of me.

Scrapes and gashes line his face. A deeper cut oozes down his cheek. There are tears in his coat and dirt smeared across his nose.

"I didn't—" I sob.

I understood our purpose in coming here. Information and elimination. Yet, my hands won't stop shaking. I hadn't meant to lose control the way I did. I hadn't meant to lose myself. No one except Yorgan was supposed to get hurt.

Though the plan was always for Yorgan to die, I'd hoped to subdue him. To make him beg for mercy and convince my father to take him prisoner like Harley. I didn't want bloodshed, just peace and protection.

I failed. As I stare at the prone body on the floor, parts of him literally caving in under his clothing as his body painfully eats itself, too many emotions battle inside me. His flesh waves beneath his clothing as it melts away.

My gods, what have I done?

Another sob escapes me, my hand cupping over my mouth as I double over.

Grief I hadn't prepared for tries to push to the forefront. Its fat tears vying for the spotlight over every other emotion pinging through me.

It's too much. My body convulses as I hyperventilate, unsure of what I feel.

It's unclear whether I need to laugh or cry. To cheer victory or hate myself.

Today I became the bad guy. I ended another wielder's life. Their existence was stolen with the force of my power. A reality I must live with until the day I die or forgive myself. We'll see which comes first.

"I didn't mean—" I try again.

Jorddan folds me into his arms. "Shhh, Bryony. You did nothing wrong."

The urge to argue back—I became the exact danger the light wielders have tried to eliminate from the world—terrifies me. This is why they want my kind dead. People should fear my capabilities.

I fear myself.

A groan sounds from behind me, Yorgan's body reforming and his color returning as if I just imagined it all.

"What is happening?" Kaia pants.

"As long as Bri is still here, all of her essences will continue to inflict their power on him," Vincent says plainly. "I can bring back the dead. Graham can mend. Only I imagine he'll be dead again soon."

My father's threat to Valen comes alive in my mind. The fate he promised of using his own gifts, just so my brother could bring him back to life. A fate of dying repeatedly at someone else's mercy. At least, until they grew bored or decided it was enough.

Awful.

"Make it stop," I plead.

My father hands me to Knox, who gently wraps me in his arms.

With the flick of two fingers from Jorddan, a large shard of glass rises from the concrete floor. It sails smoothly through the air before pressing against the once again graying flesh of Yorgan and slitting his throat wide open.

"There. It's done," my father proclaims, turning on his heel and exiting the room.

This is not how it was meant to be.

25

GRAHAM

LIKE EVERYONE ELSE LEFT behind tonight, they gave me a job. I can better utilize my intelligence and research abilities in the library. A room that happens to be a three-level wonder, sequestered at the rear of the east wing.

I'd hoped Bri wouldn't know I hadn't preferred to be with them tonight. I've accepted there may be a lot of laws broken when I pledged myself to Jorddan, but premeditated murder was a line I didn't want to cross. That cowardly knot had formed in my stomach, only for a sigh of relief to release it once Knox informed me I was to stay behind.

One hour of strolling the Guthrie home library's three floors guided my understanding of the layout. History. Spellbooks. Memoirs. Journals. Fiction. The classics. Archives. Original copies of documents. A treasure trove of inked pages that could rival Beauxgraton's main library. The most extensively stocked I've stepped foot in yet.

Camilla was the key to finding the library. *"Call it intuition, Grammy,"* she'd grinned at me as she practically skipped through the winding hallways. Our adventure abruptly ended before I could set foot inside. Apparently, Tosch and Damian needed her assistance. Their silence when she asked why only answered with a nonchalant shrug, before she followed them around the corner.

I stood there frozen for several long moments. As far as I know, Camilla's gifts haven't materialized yet. They couldn't be recruiting her for a mission. Bri was adamant that her roomie was left out, no matter the circumstances.

Wandering the halls of Guthrie Manor reminds me too much of Beauxgraton. Though months had passed of living there, I would lose myself among the hallways. Often finding surprises at the end, new locations, or differing ones I'd sworn weren't there the day before. If I hadn't known any better, having studied Beauxgraton's history before attending, I would have thought the structure morphed and changed on its own: no rhyme or reason, just chaos.

It happened so frequently that I'd consulted a professor asking if Beauxgraton was its own *Rose Red*, building and reforming itself of its own volition.

"What would make you think such a thing?" He'd guffawed as if the idea were so preposterous only the demented would even consider it.

An idea he'd treated as too far-fetched, though it hadn't originated with me. Yet his tiny black eyes gave him away. The brief passing of shadows over them revealing a hidden piece of the truth before he averted his gaze. Just another secret they meant to keep locked away. Only when the opportune time arose would it be released. Its reveal either wreaking havoc or allowing the light of the heavens to shine down on us.

That's not the truth about Guthrie Manor. With a few aimless trips alongside Camilla and Collin, we eventually figured out the layout.

Once Camilla is done with the happy couple, I suspect she'll be in her room packing. Though she and Collin weren't supposed to leave for another week, Jorddan decided it was best to remove them from the equation sooner. Their absence won't go unnoticed for long. Headmistress Milgren's reach can only extend so far when she's not even currently at Beauxgraton herself.

Jorddan will ship both of them back to Beauxgraton the day after tomorrow. The tears that clouded Camilla's eyes when Jorddan attempted to send them back tonight, while Bri was gone, had nearly shattered me. Camilla never distanced herself from Bri, even after learning her true nature. Not like I did.

I'd let prejudice and fear cloud my judgment. I'd let those negative emotions rule me instead of taking a moment to compose my thoughts. No, I'm the one who wavered in my trust of Bri—I still do at times. Yet, I am the one who has the privilege of staying. A benefit I'm not sure I am worthy of.

The lies we tell ourselves are the ones that can ruin everything. For weeks after Bri and I made up, I told myself my perception of her never changed. But it did. Societal norms overshadowed everything I knew about my best friend, casting a shadow over our memories with doubt.

I do view Bryony differently now. The woman she is has been cast in a fresh light. Learning her secret prompted me to open my mind to possibilities beyond what I had always been taught to believe. It went beyond the image wielders are told to uphold. I've never voiced my gratitude. Perhaps I'll possess the courage to say all of that and more in the future.

I am proud to say she changed me. My heart is hers. The love I have for her is stronger than it ever has been.

With a sigh, I slam shut yet another book.

Not a single tome has gotten me closer to understanding the bond between Bri and Knox.

Mates are common in the fictional worlds we immerse ourselves in. Vampires, werewolves, and any creature of the night often have them. The media tells us this is the norm, not the exception. Creatures fated for one another, bound by an invisible string, always destined to snap into place.

There's no denying the connection between Bri and Knox mimics those features. Their magic acts as if it were destined to become one. It's impossible, unheard of in the wielding world. We don't have fated mates. We wouldn't. Our power is designed to avoid the vulnerability of being tied to another. The ultimate protection mechanism. Evolution at its finest.

"Where the hell are you?" I grumble to no one but the text-filled walls.

This is a puzzle we can't afford not to solve. We need answers. The insecure man in me needs to understand what I'm up against. We've agreed there's no competition between us men for Bri, but it doesn't erase the feelings of never achieving a bond like she has with him.

Tosch divulged everything she knew. Revelations that produced no result. It's unlikely this is because they are both Grisyms. That's all she could tell.

"Talking to yourself now?" Valen quips, leaning against the doorframe, one leg crossed over the other. His stance is so casual you could almost ignore the pain that still leaves his features pinched.

"If it helps me figure this out, sure." I run my hands through my hair, my frustration making me groan aloud.

A person like me can't handle not having the information. It's like a trigger that sends off bells shouting "Failure! Failure!" in your head. The intrusiveness of the negative thoughts makes you question your worth and everything you've ever done.

I am my father's son. He made me this way. He made me such a high achiever that I can't appropriately navigate not having or finding the answers.

"You need a break, and I need a... partner," Valen grimaces at the word.

"Partner?" I question, sitting straight in my chair.

There's certainly no love lost between Valen and me. We weren't friends before, and we aren't now, but the tension between us has shifted. There's less bite to our interactions, and the conversations we've had since I saved his ass haven't been entirely unpleasant. Whether it's what I did or both of us subconsciously doing better for Bri doesn't matter. "For what, exactly?"

"Mayer, shut it. Let's go."

He turns on his booted heel, the clomp of his steps filtering out into the hall.

With a groan, I scoot my wooden chair back, the same type at Beauxgraton that sits around the long wooden library tables. The residence selection is curious. Many of the rooms resemble a museum more than a home, where children once ran through. My home is nothing like the aged extravagance here.

Valen says nothing as I join him in the hall, his steps effortlessly winding us through the manor as if he knows it well. Despite his posture leaning to the side, his typical swagger has returned. That nuance in his gait making those around him stand a little taller.

Sinking my hands in my pockets, I clear my throat. "How often do you come here?"

"Not often," he responds, turning another corner and yanking open a door.

The small space becomes visible as the door swings open. The walls are plain, and the shelves are empty. Spotless! Not a single speck of dust or dirt.

Valen's mumbled words drag my attention back to his face. The spell voiced so quickly I hadn't been able to catch what it was.

A soft rumble shakes the floor, my arms stretched out to the side to right my balance as the wall in front of us fades away to an open doorway.

Peering forward, a steep set of stairs seems to disappear into the black abyss. There's no sign of light or how far down it descends. And suddenly my pulse races, terrified that Valen bought me here to kill me. He'd do something like that. Wouldn't he?

"What is this?" I swallow, stepping down onto the first creaking plank of wood. Wood that looks older than time, but seems to hold our weight as we descend.

"Mayer, shut the fuck up," he snarls. My mouth clamps shut, and I swallow hard, sweat trickling down my temples.

Rubbing my palms down my thighs, the moisture clings to the fabric. My nerves are getting the best of me. Those same lies I like to tell myself are surfacing.

Valen would never hurt me because it would hurt Bri. I'm safe. I'm safe alone with Valen.

According to Pierce, there's no magic left in his veins. It depleted the night of the fight without an opportunity to replenish those stores. His body needed time to settle before siphoning or channeling again, per Vincent.

People like Valen don't need power to slit your throat. They're just as efficient in doing away with their enemies without it. No doubt he's more skilled with those daggers than I've ever seen.

"Let's go." Valen stomps down the stairs. No light. No guidance. His steps are sure once again, revealing he knows the way. So, I follow, my breath coming so quick and loud I can't hide the nerves knotting my stomach.

As we hit the last step, a soft glow illuminates the space. It's barely enough to guide your way. The edges are not nearly bright enough to chase the shadows away from our surroundings. Cold, concrete walls stretch higher than seems plausible. The surfaces are as smooth as the floor beneath our feet. The walls and floor are as dreary as a dank medieval dungeon.

He stops at another door, a hiss sneaking out when he reaches for the handle, twists, and pushes.

"Welcome to the Guthrie artifacts room," Valen announces, as if he's proud to show off this gem.

Artifact rooms are a sign of wealth. Those who can afford them will either acquire pieces to store their magic at exorbitant prices or have gathered them over the generations, comprised of specifically crafted vessels made for those in their bloodline. Though priceless to them, worth a fortune to others.

The room is massive, with shelves, tables, and displays full of magical objects. "This is..." The words won't come to me. Words fail to adequately describe the beauty, wealth, and power that are here.

You can sense it the moment you enter. The various forms of magic are stored away for the wielder who may use them.

I've never seen a room so well stocked as this one. There's such a rich history here. Every artifact is a testament to the genuine appreciation the Guthrie family has for wielders.

"You know how to check if shit's compatible with you?" Valen practically snarls.

My brow furrows, throwing Valen a wry look. It's fine for him not to like me, but to constantly undermine my every ability as a wielder is wearing on my nerves. It's not like I put him back together or anything. My skills withstood scrutiny then.

"Charter. Remember?" The bite in my tone makes Valen cock a brow before a wicked grin spreads. Those dark eyes focus on me. For once, there's no malice. Maybe amusement.

He nods, moving deeper into the room. "I need to recharge. Make sure I don't pass out. Not sure if there are any side effects from coming back to life. You should fill up, too," he calls over his shoulder. "Who knows what nasty shit is coming." I swear there's a wicked grin in his tone. One that beckons the awful shit he just spoke of.

Feet glued to the spot, my gaze rakes over the space, ignoring Valen as he drifts toward the far corner. He knows exactly where he's going. Rarely may have been the answer given for how often he comes here, but it's been enough;

he knows the way. Frequently enough, he could navigate the hidden passageway. A comfort level that spoke volumes with the way he waltzed into this artifact room like he owned the place.

A pang of jealousy sits in my chest, knowing he got to experience this indirect piece of Bri's life when I didn't. Neither did she.

"Why are you helping me?" I question.

Valen circles back to face me, two daggers pulled from inside his leather jacket, before twirling them between his fingers. "I don't have to like you to keep you alive. Bri, does. It's for her."

I say nothing more, disappearing to the opposite end of the room.

This tolerant side of Valen is getting under my skin. So much so that it's distracting me from what's important.

Mending him a few nights ago somehow rejuvenated my charter magic, rather than simply draining it. It's not an ability I use often, only occasionally for minor things. Valen is the first living creature I've ever attempted to fix. It's impossible to say whether this has ever happened before. Yet, my stores aren't full. Unoccupied space fills most of my insides, eager to overflow with power I may or may not need.

I ignore Valen's grunts and the clang of his daggers falling to the concrete floor. Knife after knife after knife. Where the hell does he keep them all?

Sneaking a glance over my shoulder, a towering cloud of black essence filters from a painting hanging on the wall. The horse is up high on its hind legs, so tall its rider's feet hover so far above the ground that a fall would leave his legs shattered. The rider's fingers cling to the horse's mane; the strands of stark white hair vibrate against the ebony smoke seeping out of the canvas.

Raising my palm, I allow the power in the objects filling the room to call to me. To summon me.

Every bit of dark power curls away from me in disgust. The magic pulling away, knowing I'm not compatible. It hisses and snarls so sharply I nearly flinch.

But a soft song filters through. The sound guiding me to a stunning candelabra; the silver finishing so pale it appears like arms of solid ice. Each arm twists in its own intricate vine, like gnarled tree branches following their own crooked paths of growth.

A choir of angelic voices sings to me. They call to me. Beg for me to run my fingers over the surface. My breath catches in my lungs as the cold bite of the metal almost makes me flinch away. But I can't. The pull is too strong. Like opposites drawn together.

With my cathartic exhale through my flared nostrils, its essence breaks free.

The rush is like nothing I've ever felt before. I'm moving and I'm still. Breathing and suffocating all at once.

Concrete is at my back. Frigid. Hard. Unforgiving. Each convulsion causes my teeth to crack and grind against the power filling me. Power so pure and divine it belongs to a god-tier specimen.

There's only crisp white light. The dark washed away by the essence surrounding me.

Then there's nothing.

26

BRYONY

How long can a person shake before they scramble their brains beyond repair? My body won't stop vibrating. The tremor refusing to still as the seconds turn to minutes.

Death isn't a normal occurrence in my life. Outside of the news outlets and Grandma Avalon, I'm not acquainted with it all. To jump from that to murder makes me crumble. My world is imploding around me as I tear myself apart from the inside out. My internal claws are attempting to rip the ruthlessness free. Shame washing over me for caring so little.

Tonight I took a man's life, all to save mine. It was selfish. Cruel. Not me.

At first, it had felt wrong. Perverse. The worst act I could have committed against my fellow wielders, despite the heinous treatment my kind had endured for centuries.

The shift in my mindset was so subtle I almost missed it. Curled up in Aziel's arms while he stalked through the ghoul tunnels, I was once again safe. My mind was free to roam through endless possibilities. Many are more plausible than others. None of which aligned with what actually happened.

Still, I delved deeper, seeking to understand the meaning. Searching for justification from my life's experiences to absolve me of the guilt sitting at the base of my belly. The boulder was so heavy that it was crushing my organs. Stealing my life the same as I'd stolen one. The deeper I dove through my memories, the more I could convince myself that tonight was necessary. Gradually, my wrong became a right.

I'd done the right thing. The necessary thing. Yorgan's death wasn't just to protect me. It was for all of us. Every Grisym out there is creeping through the shadows, hoping for a peaceful existence.

The sacrifice of one life can be worth it if it means thousands of others will go on. I saved lives tonight.

Aziel carefully lowers me to my feet at the front door of Guthrie Manor. "Thank you," I whisper, running my still-trembling fingertips over his rough cheek.

"Aziel. Protect. Bryony. Mine."

A soft smile tugs at the corner of my mouth, though it feels wrong to allow one. "Always."

He turns, the thunder of his pounding steps shaking the ground.

The other ghouls wait in the distance. Their massive bodies spread in a straight line as they hold out for Aziel's return. I wonder if his connection to me now makes him their leader.

"Come on," Knox whispers, wrapping an arm around my shoulders as he guides me into the house. "It's okay, baby." His lips press against the top of my head. Tenderness, I don't feel like I deserve, despite convincing myself we weren't wrong tonight, washes over me.

Bickering draws my attention. Vincent and Kaia are viciously snapping at one another. The heat of their argument seconds from becoming physical as her hands fly in front of my brother's face.

His temper is barely hanging on by a fraying thread. The veins along his thick neck become more pronounced with each word. Still, she pokes at his chest. Her thin finger is digging into the muscle repeatedly as she spews insults his way. Yet Vincent doesn't budge or touch her back.

There's a dynamic that doesn't add up between them. It's off. No one genuinely likes Kaia, except her brother, but the ball of tension between her and my brother is something more significant. A volcano ready to erupt. Or maybe it just did, but I'm too tired to care.

Knox hasn't moved me past the circular table in the foyer when grunts once again draw my gaze up. The sound of clothing dragging over the marble floors isn't right. Shifting to the side, a strained grunt burst from Valen as he drags Graham's limp body around the corner by his collar.

A rumpled shirt and slacks draw my brows low. Clothing, I'm sure he'd meticulously pressed earlier. Graham's button-down shirt is untucked, and one designer pants leg is hiked to the knee. There's a shoe missing, and his hair stands on end.

This isn't right.

"What the hell are you doing?" Knox barks, releasing me. "What did you do to him?"

Valen snorts, but doesn't stop attempting to drag Graham across the floor. Sweat plasters his black hair to his forehead, his breath labored, but he doesn't stop until my best friend's body is in full view. "Idiot touched the Sachre," Valen grunts, falling to his ass at Graham's side. He keeps his knees bent, elbows resting on them as his head falls forward. Every heavy breath draws him back high, but he doesn't look up again.

"What's a Sac—" My brain seems foggy, unable to complete the words I was trying to ask. Not after tonight. Not after I...

"It's your mother's," Jorddan waves me toward him. "I'll explain in a moment, but you need to coax it out of him. You cannot take it. Do you understand me?" My nod is so subtle, I wonder if he saw it before continuing. "Just extract enough so he comes out of his current... coma."

"A...coma?" I croak. "He's in..."

I can't breathe, my feet retreating from where Graham lies stretched on the floor.

A firm hand meets the middle of my back. "We will discuss after. Lure it out of him. You are the only one who can." The soft quality of my father's voice has my wide eyes meeting his. The truth swirls in the steel gray. He believes in me.

Graham needs me.

It's the right thing to do. I let those same memories course through my mind. Running them over and over and over. Anything to put me back in the mindset that tonight was right. Necessary. Unavoidable.

Validation that chases away the negative emotions pounding in my chest. I can't stomach them. It's too much.

Swallowing, two steps carry me back to my best friend's side. My knees slowly bend before tapping the hard marble beneath me. My hand hovers over Graham's chest, the tremble even more noticeable than before. Nothing happens for several long minutes. My heart accepted defeat. I can't do this.

"Call it to you, Bryony."

My throat aches as another hard swallow works its way down my throat. *Come out. Please.*

Only seconds pass before I feel it. Several more before swirls of frost-white essence bleed from Graham's chest. They twirl through the air so gracefully, it's as if watching fairies dance through the air. It's ethereal.

The stream flows upward, forming what looks like a massive icicle above my palm as I flip it toward the three-story ceiling. "That's it. Nice and easy," Jorddan coaches me, the heat of his hand hovering over my shoulder, but he doesn't touch me.

I'm guessing he can't. Any closer and he would disturb the delicate balance. Though this is taking less concentration than I'd thought, any distraction terrifies me. This power terrifies me.

The minutes seem to pass agonizingly slowly as I draw more and more of the essence from him. A shiver works through my body as the temperature drops. With each tug of the foreign power, my insides cool. The power mimicking icicles as they funnel into my waiting palm. I've never felt magic like this. It reminds me of the purity of princesses in fairy tales. Something too clean for someone like me to manipulate and hold.

The first twitch of Graham's eyelids shatters my focus. My subsequent pull proving to be a little more forceful than I meant. "Enough. Stop," Jorddan orders me.

My essence rolls beneath the surface of my skin, eager to take in the purest source it has come into contact with.

Take it, Bryony. Take it all. It belongs to us. My essence hisses inside my head. An invisible being taunting me to do what I know I shouldn't.

Shooting to my feet, the stream of white still floats above my palm, forming a structure I can't begin to put into words. The branches curve, extending tall. Each one waving as if they're as fluid as water. Each limb stretches long and far, towering high above my height.

"Mold it, Bri. Just like we've done in class." Knox is beside me, whispering in my ear. "It's not yours. You must give it back."

My essence riots inside me, all but kicking Knox's off the throne that sits beside her. She's pissed. She wants it. Craves it like a man needs water in the desert.

Pressing my eyes shut, I cast away the other essences, burying them deep within me so I can focus on the one now curling around my open palm as if searching for a way inside.

You will yield, I command. The voice in my head is the harshest version I've ever produced. *You will condense and stay calm so I can put you back where you belong.*

At first, it seems as though the essence will not listen to me. Then I feel it shift, the soft lilt of a song filling my mind as it forms a long staff in my palm. Opening my eyes, it almost appears to be a solid mass before me, but I know it's not. The tendrils intertwine with one another in gentle caresses, keeping the structure in motion with a fluid flow.

"Bring me the candelabra," I whisper. My brow furrows, blinking rapidly. I cannot fathom how I knew that's where this power is kept. Maybe the magic told me. Perhaps I always knew. A quirk of my Eistiab nature I'd yet to uncover.

My father's eyes darken, the black shutting out the white.

Silence falls over the room as I continue to watch the essence shifting in my grasp. My focus is so locked in that only the thunk of the massive relic dropping to the marble at my feet pulls me out.

I cannot explain the sensation of familiarity coursing through me. I'm sure I've never seen it. It's not an artifact from the Avalon home. Nor has it been in a text I've read. That, I would remember. Otherworldly, intricate swirls such as these would be unforgettable.

It's as if I've seen it before, held it. Taken from it.

"My mother made this." Though I speak the words, they are addressed to no one in particular.

My body circles the five-foot-tall work of art, inspecting every branch as if it will tell its story. It's an image straight out of a winter wonderland. Cautiously reaching forward, I brush my fingertips along the freezing cold surface, a hum running through me as if I'm being welcomed home.

Go home. Go back to where you wait.

The white mass leaps from my palm. Every tiny particle swirling like the snowflakes from the spelled blizzard we just endured. Collectively, they gather close around the base before seamlessly flowing into the arms. It remains cold under my touch, with the same song now filling the room.

"What is that?" Kaia grunts, her eyes roving over the space.

"The lullaby our mother used to sing to Bri. It was the only way to calm you when you were fussy." A sad, nostalgic grin pulls at the corner of Vincent's mouth. A fond memory is clearly playing in his mind.

My eyes meet my brother's, his deep hum following along with the tune.

More humming trails down the stairs to join. *Merrick.* My brothers find an odd harmony, as memories shadow their distinctly different shaded eyes.

"I'd almost forgotten it," Merrick whispers before taking in the scene before him. "Do I want to know?"

"No," Vincent grumbles.

My focus returns to the candelabra, a cold front emanating from the surface. "What is it doing?" I whisper, my eyes narrowing as frost creeps over the surface.

"Responding to its keeper." Without Vincent or my father saying anything more, I knew this was yet another object my mother had made for my protection, for me to store magic when I took too much. A place where I could always store the purest light.

Maybe even as a baby, she knew I would favor the dark.

27

BRYONY

LIGHT WIELDERS REFUSE TO siphon from living creatures. The light treats them as sacred beings. Their magic is the purest there is. Despite those traditional views, the deeper reason lies in the darkness. Because the light wielders refuse to behave like "animals" and pull from the living. Unlike siphoning from ghouls, creatures that harbor light magic differ. Regardless, the ghoul is the same.

My mother made this for me, and who knows what else.

Graham's groan pulls my attention back to the floor. The chill that had drilled down to the bone, leaving me shivering violently, vanishes as if it had never been there. The candelabra is once again as it was.

I'd been so lost in the power and this new vessel, I hadn't noticed Valen somehow propped himself and Graham against the wall. Both their heads rest against the coffered wooden frames, their throats exposed, Adam's apples bobbing, still working to catch their breaths.

Side by side and exhausted, you could almost mistake them for friends. *Almost.*

That wicked grin stretches across Valen's mouth when he locks eyes with me.

My focus seems to drop back into place instantly. Worry and frustration are mixing dangerously inside me. "What were you thinking?" Graham's stare immediately meets mine with my harsh tone. His features rearranging under-standing why my outburst was for him, not Valen's heroic gesture.

"V told me to get my stores up. I could feel it. The light magic, I mean, and when I touched it, the whole thing just blasted into me." Graham groans again, sitting up a bit straighter.

"V?" I question.

A humorless huff leaves my best friend as he rolls to his knees, his fists planted against the unforgiving floor. "He's not horrible," Graham grunts, attempting to get to his feet.

My hands won't stop running over his arms, touching and inspecting him as if there's physical damage we missed. "Graham, why would you?"

He shrugs me off, scowling before he sighs heavily. "Bri, just stop. I'm fine."

My body reels back as if he shoved me. The other manor inhabitants slowly disperse around us, as if clearing themselves from the thick tension filling the foyer. It's just me, my friend, and our inevitable spat.

Pain lances through my chest anew as he once again tries to brush me off. His attitude is forcing me to forget my own choices of the night. "So it's okay for you to lecture me on my choices, but I can't have concern for yours?"

Strong hands grip my cheeks, forcing my gaze up to meet those blue eyes fused with green. "Bryony, I promise I'm okay. I don't know the artifacts here. I touched the wrong one. Let it go."

If only I could.

Graham doesn't make mistakes. His logical mind shouldn't have allowed this. A lapse in judgment that could have led to a devastating outcome. He doesn't jump before he investigates. And he'd said Valen wasn't horrible.

Tonight has me reeling, and I don't know what to do. My chest is tightening with each breath when the front door flies open, the other half of our mini army waltzing through into the foyer.

We'd split up tonight. Two groups in the field. Then the others left behind at the manor, tasked with specific pieces of our intricate puzzle.

Kormoran, Pierce, Damian, and Tosch went to retrieve my brother's wife and child from the meet point. He'd insisted on going with them. A mission smothered in less danger if his renowned persona remained unattached to a band of dark wielders.

"Where are they?" Merrick bellows.

His voice booms from behind me. Had he been here the whole time, watching the threads of my relationship slowly unravel? At least that's how it felt.

Tosch is the one to step forward, her hands on his chest, before he charges out the front door. "They're safe. We had the New Order soldiers take them to a hotel. Another set will take you there."

My brother's eyes glaze over with unshed tears. His love for his wife and daughter is so apparent in his eyes. The fear slowly fading away. Every bit of tension melting away the longer he stares into Tosch's eyes.

When he drags her into a tight hug, she gasps. How I wish I could be the one to bring my brother some comfort, but a part of me still isn't convinced we can trust him.

He's slow to release her. The reluctance in his backward steps drawing my brow low. But then he quickly turns away, snatching a coat from the rack and stalking toward the open door. He stops at the entry, one grip on its frame. His fingers curl along the wood as if fighting himself. All while refusing to glance behind him. "I will bring Darryn and Misha here to see you tomorrow."

There's no stopping the single tear that slips down my cheek. That pure soul has only ever stared at me as if I hung the moon. I'd give anything to see her. To hold her and draw out her laughter with goofy faces, but I won't risk it. I won't risk her safety for my desires.

"I love you. You've always been good to me," I nearly whisper. "But if you ever cared for me at all, you won't. You won't bring them here. You won't put them in danger until we can ensure that being around me is safe."

It's my turn to be wrapped in Merrick's arms, his warmth chasing away the last bit of cold from the candelabra. Drawing me close, he breathes me in. His hold is so tight, I wonder if he believes this may be our last embrace. "It might take you some time to believe this, but, Bryony, I've always loved you. You're my sister. It doesn't matter what you are."

We squeeze each other once more, his single sniff filling my ears before he pulls away. Then he's out the door, disappearing into the night.

Another tear slips free.

That felt too much like a goodbye. It's the echo of permanence ringing through the air that turns my stomach. *I'll see you again, Merrick—all of you.*

I hope.

We're doing the right things. I have to believe that.

My moral compass tips. The balance no longer leans toward "right." When you find yourself in the haze of the in-between, there is no concept of right or wrong. A land many of us try to pretend we can't exist in. It means we must acknowledge there is no good or evil, but a constant mix of the two. One cannot exist without the presence of the other.

All minus Kormoran shuffle from the foyer, offering light pats to my shoulder. I'm left staring at the closed front door. My thoughts wander as my insides crumble under the weight of tonight. A trance falls over me. One that paralyzes my muscles, anchoring me in place, time passing at its own pace.

Per Jorddan's command, the New Order will protect Merrick and his family. They will watch him, too. His every word and action will be scrutinized and reported, ensuring he's not a traitor.

My heart screams that he'd never betray us. I'd heard him. Felt his love. Listened to his heartbeat and the unevenness of his breaths. My half-brother is no enemy of ours, but he isn't one of the Avalons either.

My feet barely have any feeling when I finally turn to face the candelabra. My brilliant mother curated the vessel. Fragments of her life live throughout the manor. Evidence that she loved us. Remnants of a life she enjoyed within these walls. Yet, she's not here.

It should be simple. Why women find it so hard to leave marriages they're not happy in is beyond me. According to my mother, they're not even married; they never were. She should be able to leave without a second thought. Yet, she doesn't.

What could Roman possibly have on her to make her stay? Does she value my half-siblings more than earth-shattering love? Are they more valuable than the offspring she birthed alongside the man who still owns her heart?

What holds her back?

Why stay trapped in a life she doesn't enjoy? Willfully standing by a man she has never loved. She can love her children without remaining in that sham of a relationship with him.

My fingers tremble as they reach toward the work of art in front of me. A perfectly constructed piece rich humans would love to have in their homes to boast of their wealth, or in museums, pretending they actually know from which royal line it originated.

"You remembered it?" Vincent whispers beside me.

My hand immediately pulls back, tucked into my side. "No. Not exactly. It was just a feeling."

"You are such an enigma, little sister." He wraps an arm around my shoulders, pulling me to his side. "I'm just glad this time I'm here to help you figure it out. I've missed you."

"You barely got to know me," I sigh.

Vincent runs his hand over my shoulder, pulling me in tighter. "And that should make me miss my sister less?" He presses a kiss to the crown of my head. The affection both he and my father display for me is new. The unrestrained devotion to me surpasses what I'm used to. It's almost uncomfortable, though I don't want them to stop. "I didn't get to know you as you grew up. Not directly. But I've been watching you from afar your whole life. I never missed the big moments, even if I couldn't be there. Not even when that asshole ex of yours told you he was done. I heard every word he said." My eyes press shut in embarrassment. Shame washes through me because I know my brother is aware that limp dick left me for being plus-sized. It's not shame with my body, but giving my heart to someone who didn't deserve it. "I almost killed him for that, especially as I watched you disappear into yourself."

I sniffle, letting my head fall to his shoulder, my gaze never leaving the frosted vessel. "You can say it. Fat. I'm not delusional about being a big girl."

"Call it whatever you want, little sister. You're beautiful. You're smart. Impulsive," he chuckles, "and the strongest person I know."

Those damn tears build behind my eyes again. My emotions tumble over one another tonight, overwhelming me. My attempt to process them all is a failure. I'd gotten good with the normal lineup. Loneliness. Boredom.

Then I stepped foot on the Beauxgraton grounds. That first deep inhale of that crisp mountain air changed my entire world.

And here we are.

I only wrap my arms around my brother's middle, squeezing tight. His words meant more to me than he will ever know. The Avalons, even my mother, made appearance important above all else. I taught myself to love all of Bri after my ex. My men taught me that someone else will love me. But my brother... He just taught me it never mattered in the first place.

The rumor mill can be a cruel pool to draw from. It spoke of every horrible thing my brother had ever done.

I expected cold. I expected short-tempered and indifferent.

He may be those things to everyone else, but not me. I didn't expect him to be so loving toward me. His laid-back personality stands in stark contrast to his menacing, multicolored eyes and perpetual scowl.

"You're different from what I thought you'd be," I whisper as he leads us to the stairs, both of us taking a seat a few up from the bottom. The wood is hard under my ass, but I don't care. I'm not ready for this moment to end. Fear twists in my gut, making me believe that if we part, I'll never see him again. If I turn my back, the dream will be over, and I can't handle that.

Still, our stares stay latched on the candelabra.

"I've always had a soft spot for you, if that's what you're getting at." He drapes that arm around me again, my head falling on his shoulder. "I was so excited to be a big brother. Don't get me wrong, Bri, I have done some nasty shit in my lifetime. If you piss me off, I can become your darkest nightmare. Couple that with my ability to raise the dead and who our father is, and it makes sense that you would have that assumption about me."

There's nothing accusatory in his tone. Just that same matter-of-fact way of speech our father often employs.

I bolt upright, not wanting him to think I harbor negative thoughts about him. I don't. "That's not—"

He's just not what I expected. He pats my shoulder, my head falling back onto his.

"Shhh, I know. To you, I will always be the protective, sarcastic, fun-loving guy. That's all I ever wanted to be for you." He playfully pats my cheek. "Make no mistake, Bri, I have no problem being the dark creature the world believes me to be."

"Okay," I whisper, patting his leg. "I'm just glad I have you now. It was hard growing up with Harley, who hated me, and Sicily, who kept her distance. Merrick was always good to me, but he held back in front of them."

An animalistic growl vibrates through Vincent's chest. One that would make a sane person run in absolute fear. But not me. *No*, his dark side draws me in. "It took everything in me not to tear out Harley's insides when he showed up here."

With a sigh, I look up at my brother, my eyes darting between the light and dark irises. "He has never given me the love I deserve and has been cruel, but if anyone is going to punish him for how he treated me, it's going to be me."

The words leave my tongue like a deadly poison. Each one meant to kill on impact.

A wide grin spreads across Vincent's face, the shadows of the devil draping his features. "Then I'll sit back and watch."

28

VALEN

Three sharp cracks against my bedroom door startle me awake.

Finally getting some fucking decent sleep, and someone has to interrupt it.

With a flick of my fingers, the door flies open. Irritation draws out my growl, spotting Sean and Jorddan on the other side.

"Up," Jorddan orders.

Grumbling to myself, I toss the duvet aside, adjusting my boxer briefs that shifted up my legs in my sleep.

"Give me a minute. I need to piss." Shuffling to the en suite bathroom, I don't even bother closing the door as I relieve myself.

Dark wielders don't have the same qualms about nudity and privacy that light wielders do. One of the many reasons they say we have no decorum. That we are like the animals us extrinsics and charters fuck.

In truth, we have bigger issues to worry about. We're held down at every turn, forced to form our own organizations, and thrive on our separate curricula, which are no longer only ours.

After washing my hands, splashing cold water on my face, and brushing my teeth, I take my time rejoining them in the bedroom.

"Sit," Jorddan commands me for the second time.

It's best not to test him. Who knows where his head is at right now. He's been different since Bri returned to his life. A shift that has left us puzzled. Is it a benefit or a hindrance?

"What's going on?" My eyes dart between Sean and Jorddan, waiting for one of them to say something. It better be a damn good reason.

"I'm going back to Beauxgraton today," Sean relays, rolling a small marble between his fingers. A seemingly mundane object that is, in fact, one of his memory capsules.

"Okay... And? You're all going back," I grunt.

"True, but I'll be making a stop first."

"Okay..." There's something my friend isn't saying.

Turning my focus to Jorddan, that same stoic expression shields his thoughts. The type of poker face I once admired, but this morning only pisses me off because I can't read him.

There's something on the tip of their tongues. The words so close to slipping free, I can nearly taste their meanings. Words that will only leave a foul taste in my mouth.

I wish they would just come out and fucking say it. It's a waste of everyone's time to stand here staring at one another.

My finger twitches, and a single gold dagger whistles through the air, stopping half a centimeter from Sean's throat.

"Valen, stop."

"When you tell me what the fuck this is about," I growl, my scowl deepening.

"I was able to extract some of Harley's memories last night. He has very intricate blocks in place. Whoever taught him to shield is the best of the best," Sean relays, his Adam's apple bobbing, though he doesn't break eye contact with me.

Willing the dagger a fraction closer, Sean's throat bob becomes more exaggerated. A slow, laborious swallow that causes his eyes to drift down to the dagger for a brief moment. His only outward sign of any fear. "Get on with it."

Sean cocks his head back a fraction, lowering his gaze to the dagger, watching for movement, before shakily licking his lips. "There are several council members at his level who have been conducting unlawful questioning of dark wielders."

"Meaning?"

"If someone threatens any light wielders in power, they're taken. Murdered if need be. Taken to executioners more frequently," Sean continues, his gaze briefly shifting to Jorddan's.

The man's expression stays blank. Why did he come if he was just going to sit there?

"Continue, Sean," Jorddan encourages.

There's another swallow, Sean's gaze drifting down to where my dagger holds steady before once again focusing on my face. "Your brother is part of a team. Per the Council, they don't exist at all, but they are hunting us."

"Someone is always hunting dark wielders," I wave him off. Turning on my heel, ready to climb back between the sheets, Sean's hand grips my shoulder, spinning me back around. Another dagger is in my hand before we're even facing each other again, the sharp tip pushing against the soft flesh of his stomach. "Get your hand off me."

He immediately lets me go. "You don't get it. Your brother isn't just going after his own kind; he's coming after us. According to Harley's memory, you're the first he wants to turn or kill."

My jaw works. The muscles growing sore as I search for the right words. There are none. Not a single fucking one. Dustin and I have never been close, but we've also never been distant. We're just two guys who share parents and blood existing beside each other. Our five-year gap made it easier for us to do our thing. He'd barely graduated high school and was already interning with the Council. He knew from a young age that policy was his path. His one true calling to ensure maximum impact. To right the injustices.

But if those memories are genuine. I have to assume they are since Sean extracted them. A reality that serves as the type of gut punch, stealing your breath and will to stay alert.

My brother has switched sides. He's not there advocating for the dark. Dustin chose to silence those of us fighting for better, fighting for more. Those of us desperately craving equality.

It's not about upholding the law. Not anymore.

I turn my back on Sean. Knowing I'm struggling with this news doesn't help anyone. "What are you going to do?"

"We thought I might be able to get close to him since he knows me as your friend. He might believe it if he thinks you sent me to him. You know, make him think I'm interested in the Council. Then extract a few memories," Sean shrugs as if it's the simplest plan. As if it's not bullshit, my brother will see right through it.

My body whirls back around to face my friend and my leader. "That's a bullshit plan. He will never go for it."

Jorddan takes a step closer, cupping his hands in front of his thighs. "Tell us what you suggest."

"You'll need my father. Does he know?"

Sean's gaze drops to his feet. "No. Technically, your brother is following a legitimate path, like your father wanted. We never expected him to be on our side."

"Fuck!" I roar, my fingers sinking into my loose hair. They're right.

Though my father stands for equality, no one is a bigger stickler for the laws than he is.

I'm not sure how long I pace, searching for a solution. Trying to convince myself my brother wouldn't come after me. Not his blood. Not when family means so much to our mother.

"Do nothing. Just go back to school. Assume the memories you got from Harley are accurate. Do the others know the New Order is being targeted?"

"As you said, there is always someone hunting us," Jorddan breathes in deep. "Sean, ensure you all are taking extra precautions this semester."

"Yes, sir."

"Now, Mr. Greer, dress. It's impolite not to bid your friends farewell. They have a flight to catch."

Then Jorddan leaves me there, Sean quick on his heels as they retreat into the hallway, leaving my door wide open.

Shoving my legs through a pair of black jeans and shrugging on a black t-shirt and hoodie, I'm distracted. The emotions roll through me. My teeth are gritting, fighting against getting lost in them. There's no time. Not now. Not ever.

The cold Valen, who deems everyone his enemy until they can prove themselves otherwise, shoves back to the forefront. Bri is living proof that blood doesn't mean shit. So is Pierce. His parents threw him to the curb the moment he said he wished he had been born a light wielder.

Betrayal doesn't care if the person is family, friend, or acquaintance. It still stings the same. A sting I refuse to let settle inside me any longer. There are too many wielders counting on us to let some bullshit like this cloud our judgment or actions.

Feet barely in my boots, laces trailing beside me, I jog downstairs. Thankfully, I'd gotten a good fill before Graham about got himself killed. I swear, as smart as the guy is, he has no self-preservation like our girl. It is not surprising they're obsessed with one another.

Cheerful laughter filters up from the foyer as I round the last leg of the steps.

It's a fucking swarm of hugs, laughter, and "I'll miss you." The type of lovey-shit I don't tolerate. The twins notice me first. Their matching frowns deepening as they linger a distance from the edge of the group. If anyone hates this bullshit more than I do, it's them.

Where they watch with scowls, I only watch Bri. Her arms wrap around Collin's neck, and his wrap around her middle, squeezing her close. I can't hear what he whispers in her ear, but she throws her head back, cackling like a hyena before hugging him close once more.

Camilla is next. The tiny thing is attempting to pull Bri closer, but her arms are too short. Still, tears pool in both of their eyes as they rock back and forth.

"Don't ya forget me now," Camilla warns before finally releasing her friend.

"Cami, baby, how could I ever? We'll talk every day. I'll miss you too much if we don't."

Camilla lets the tears run down her pale cheeks before she hugs Bri again.

Everyone else has finished saying their goodbyes except for those two.

I always see a tough woman. The one who plows forward and doesn't stop because she can't. The woman who proves she cares with her every action. Yet, that guard never quite comes down. She refuses to let the emotions bubble to the surface. It makes her too vulnerable.

Watching Bri with Camilla, I can't help but wonder if this is why she is fighting with us. If the version I'm witnessing now is who she prefers to be, always. Loving. Nurturing. Laughing.

"Sean," I call.

He jogs over, that same marble twirling between his fingers. "What's up?"

"You'll call my brother. Ask him to go for coffee. Tell him I am studying abroad to learn about foreign policy." My molars grind, hating the next words that will pass my lips. "Tell him he was right."

Sean steps in closer, his brow furrowing, voice lowering. "About what?"

The muscles of my jaw flex painfully, my fingers curling into a tight fist before they extend once more. "Tell him I want to be just like him. I always have. Guarantee he'll tell you anything you want to know."

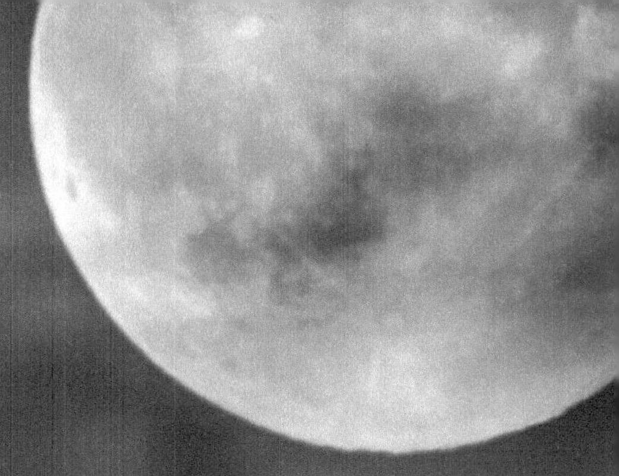

29

BRYONY

Time passes at a funny pace when you ask too many things of it. Slow down. Speed up. Stand still. Turn back.

A week has passed since I killed Yorgan. That night I'd talked myself out of the guilt. I'd convinced myself we'd done the right thing. We saved lives. It was necessary.

Still, that sneaky swarm of guilt crept inside me each night. The moment my head hit the pillow was the beacon it needed to slither through me, knotting my insides and bringing those burning tears to my eyes.

Night after night, I've chased it away. I've told myself that my reason for murder was justified. It wasn't wrong.

Yet, it never finds me during the daytime hours. Not when I'm being tortured by Tosch daily, followed by taking in a new essence. A desperate plan that leaves Knox having to calm me once again. Fucking me and taking more and more of my essence's greed inside him.

It's the same every night.

Snatch.

Revel in the feel of new power.

Lose control to my dark side—an identification I hadn't known I'd made until Damian read my energy before, during, and after one of my episodes. A scarce talent to hone and learn among wielders, but helpful.

Vincent stands outside the door waiting, if needed, while my professor fucks me into submission, ready to barge in with one of the dozens of portal vessels my mother made for me.

I sleep.

I wake early. My mind wanders. It's always back to that kill list. Back to the names of wielders I've met and known my whole life. People I never thought would hurt me. Then I'm reminded I held similar views of Roman once.

When I finally peel myself out of bed, it's for our morning powwow around the dining room table while everyone gives their updates. My father assigned the list to Knox.

I can see the frustration building inside him. The levels are rising so high that they might drown him. Several of the wielders on the list have gone into hiding. William Danvers, being the one he has found no trace of.

Each morning, it's a search for the right words of reassurance, but they won't come. I have none.

Once I've picked over my food, Tosch makes me run. The torturous cycle restarting all over again.

It's a cycle that wears you down piece by piece. The increments are so small that you miss the chunk of you that you lost until the gaping hole is too big to ignore. Until the exhaustion pulls at your limbs with so much force that the effort to keep your eyes open feels like moving mountains.

The more I take in, the more my essence becomes satiated. She's still a hungry bitch, but with those around me who have already given, she calms. Her position on her throne, legs crossed while licking her fingers clean, allows me that precious moment to breathe.

Oddly, the more I take, the less pain finds me, as if each new signature essence is protecting my shell. After my body loses control, it settles faster, each magical party inside me stationed at its post. Posture straight, focus straight ahead, they wait for their queen. They wait to be called on and used at my discretion.

Tosch has helped me tame what I have, but hasn't been able to stop my insatiable thirst for every bit of magic I don't already possess. Wielders. The earth. The Hell Gates. My essence wants it all. Her staff striking the ground with a roar each time I deny her.

The individual signatures may have fallen into line, no longer battling for dominance, but it has not made me any more proficient at calling a specific gift to the forefront. No matter how hard I try, it doesn't always work. Other times, they rush through me all at once. Each one sits back and snickers behind their hands as they overwhelm me. As if overjoyed they'd made me look like a complete fool.

Staring down at my palms, I wish I had a better understanding of what I am. Shame washes through me, wishing I could be the being I'd pretended to be some days. Life would be simpler if I could just be a run-of-the-mill light wielder like anyone else. There was safety in that. The unknown was so minuscule it was negligible.

But it was a lie. I was never that person. I never will be.

Refusing to linger on the losses, I let my thoughts drift over every change. My life. My friends. This newfound power. My family.

Tension still fills the manor, but a fraction of it departed with Mr. Greer when he walked through the front door four days ago. Valen was entirely himself once again. There was no more reason to linger. Learning about ghouls from him, while brief, proved insightful. He'd promised to send me some additional text for me to refer to. Even encouraged me to join the Ghoul Conservation Program once I'd graduated.

Even after learning I could command ghouls, I never looked past the day ahead. How could I when my eyes remained trained over my shoulder with every breath? I had a future when I was nothing more than a light wielder.

Things have changed now. The truth of my abilities and my blood shattered the possibility of a clean future. One free of turmoil or tough decisions. That vision has crumbled. There's nothing to sift through the rubble for. There may never be more than today.

Every day, the possibility of living as a normal wielder melts away. Even if my father succeeds in his mission, can society allow someone as dangerous as me to be a part of it?

So instead of clinging to the seed of hope Mr. Greer planted, I shoved it away. Down into the depths of my being. A location inside me meant to hold the things I've buried and ignored over the years. A place where those malicious thoughts go to die, so I don't have to live with the pain.

But not before telling Merrick. He's followed my ask and stayed away from the manor, though he and his family are still close by in Manchester. Every evening after dinner, he calls wanting a recap of my day. I give it to him. The raw and unfiltered version I don't give to the others. In front of them, I am the same resilient Bri. I refuse to let them see anything else. We're all carrying enough uncertainty as is.

My half-brother listens. There's never any judgment or toxic encouragement. As much as I believe he won't betray us and will help where and how he can, I refuse to classify him as an ally. Merrick straddles two worlds. He's an Avalon after all. His wife and child don't change that.

Fortunately, he doesn't ask about Harley. My elder half-brother was left chained to the walls in the bowels of the manor. From what I've heard, he either remains so silent and still you'd think him dead, or he screams relentlessly.

Everyone remains alert, waiting for Roman to swoop in and save him. Our bodies coiled tight, expecting an attack. A charge we'll be ready for should Roman bring the fight to my front door.

He won't.

A gut feeling I keep to myself. Roman thinks about himself. A truth I knew even when I thought he hung the moon. If he knows we have Harley, he is no longer of use to him. My half-brother is his firstborn. Perhaps that holds more significance than I believe. Even then, Roman would not risk his own ass and failure again.

The thought that plagues me most always draws me back to Yorgan's death. His bond with my former "father" was beyond public knowledge. A point Yorgan made clear when we went to his home a week ago.

Will Roman know we caused his gruesome death?

Exhaling the thought from my mind, my head falls back against the wooden bench I perched on hours ago. Vincent had surprised me this afternoon when he slipped into my room, stating he knew exactly what I needed.

Surprisingly, the manor has a state-of-the-art gym that he had designed for himself. *"It's the best way to work out your... frustrations sometimes,"* he'd said. I'd averted my gaze, hoping that my brother wasn't referring to his sex life. I'm still getting used to how open a topic it is amongst dark wielders. Typical dinner conversation, and no one blinks an eye.

Beside the gym, he'd had a sauna built. A room the size of mine back in Seela. Three walls lined with tiered benches that could provide enough seating for thirty people without them touching.

The steam penetrates my skin, easing my tense muscles as I let my eyes flutter closed. Though I loathe working out, my morning runs with Tosch are growing on me. I'm still out of breath. Each sucked-in gasp burned my throat, lungs, and rib cage. Every joint screamed with every strike of my shoe against the pavement. My lack of activity over the years has become a regret.

Somehow, these runs have become my escape. A place where I can pretend this isn't the life I'm leading.

Tosch has become more than my tormentor. She is a friend. One I hadn't known I needed. A reprieve from the probing eyes of my family and my guys. Like Camilla, she can talk non-stop, an endless stream of words passing her lips without taking a breath. But she, too, knows when to seek the silence. Perhaps she can sense when I need it. Having her there helps me feel less alone and makes it easier to sort through my thoughts.

The grating sound of the sauna door over the wooden planks almost forces my eyelids to peel open as I grin at the thought. *Almost.* Maybe whoever it is will think I'm asleep and allow me to sweat and stew in silence.

One can only hope.

30

BRYONY

"Thought I'd find you here." Graham's voice pulls my focus to him. His naked torso already glistens with sweat. The lean muscles disappearing beneath a white towel wrapped around his waist. The feathered muscles of his abs twitch with his steps as he comes toward me.

I hadn't appreciated him during our one night together. Not the way I have with the other three. As if my eyes are aware, they rake slowly from head to toe, analyzing every bit of hair out of place and the paler hue of his skin. My core tightens as I trail down to the obvious outline of his cock behind the towel.

Dammit, Bri. You've become such a fiend.

I say nothing, pretending not to ogle him as the muscles in his arms flex, lowering himself to the bench beside me. His groan making my muscles clench tight, my pussy throbbing as he stretches his long body out straight.

My heart races knowing he's naked beneath. It's the best way to enjoy the sauna. His skin, already beading with sweat, is just within reach.

Shaking my head, I tuck my hands into my lap. "Running for miles on end is no joke," I snicker, letting my head fall back, the rivulets of sweat weaving their way down my exposed throat.

Focus on the ceiling. Think about anything. Yorgan. School. The shock of electricity that burns your insides when Tosch slams her palm into your chest, somehow reaching inside you with her essence to submit what you've stolen.

The inner dialogue barely settles me, but it closes my eyes, clinging to it like a lifeline.

"You said it's been great for your mental health, though." Hopefulness blossoms in his words. So he has noticed that I'm slowly falling apart, crumbling minute by minute. Soon, nothing may remain.

"It has, but honestly, I am just ready to get back to normalcy." I sit up straight, slightly turning to face Graham. Only he's already switched his position, staring at me. "Sometimes I wish we could go back. I wouldn't change knowing any of you. Having any of you." My eyes shift down to my lap before finding Graham's again. "I just need to feel like me again, but oddly enough, I'm not sure who she is anymore."

A humorless laugh leaves me. I hadn't been this honest with the guys since Yorgan. I smile and pretend I'm mostly fine. It's better if they think I'm handling this like the champ everyone believes me to be. Vincent and my father fawning over me is more than enough to tolerate.

"What even is that anymore?" A soft smile pulls at the corners of his mouth. "Normalcy, I mean."

My mouth twitches to the side. It's a question I have no answer to. How could I?

Graham shifts closer to me. So close that our knees touch. Our matching towels keeping our thighs from being skin to skin. My body wants more of his touch. My insides have been craving him, but there's been no time.

Normalcy.

That's what I'd asked for, right?

As if he can sense what I need, his large palm settles on my bare thigh. My temperature is skyrocketing as more of our skin comes into contact. A single finger moves back and forth with ease. A mindless motion, but one that sends my pulse a fraction higher. "Are you nervous about starting at Integretew next week?" The words are huskier than they should be. His eyes are darker when I glance at him. Those deep pools luring me in.

You're imagining it, Bri.

"No," I answer honestly. "School is school. I wish I could attend with the other Grisyms. I'd give anything to be surrounded by others like me. But I do agree it's too suspicious for me just to drop off the face of the earth. The world knows me whether I want it to or not."

Abandoning my inner thigh, his hand finds mine. Our fingers instantly weave together as if we've held each other like this a million times. We haven't. "Are you ready to hide again?"

My chest seizes. If there were any way I could swap my reality, I would. Even if I couldn't live as a Grisym, it would be easier to be a dark wielder like Knox. "What choice do I have for now?"

His other hand cups my face, his thumb stroking my cheek. The Caribbean Sea stares back at me through his irises. Searching. Asking silent questions, I would rather pretend I can't interpret, so I don't have to answer them. "There isn't a better one." As his face nears mine, my lips part, hoping he'll close his mouth over mine. "I just worry about you. You're my best friend, my—" His words stall, the steam billowing around us in a heavy cloud for a few moments before it dissipates.

Vincent warned me about the timer, but I hadn't noticed the change until now.

"Your what?" My tongue flicks over my lower lip, eyes drifting down to his mouth before meeting his eyes again.

"Girlfriend." The word should make me want to laugh. Such carefree, innocuous things can't exist here. Not in a world that thrives on secrets, sabotage, and death. It's not possible.

"Kiss me, Graham."

There's no hesitation as his mouth presses against mine. This is the first kiss we've had in days. In truth, other than Knox, I have had little alone time with any of my guys since we got here. I miss them and their touches and their mouths and hands roaming over my skin. I miss the fullness of their cocks inside me, pulling out my pleasure while washing away the pain.

Pierce could pull laughter out of me when all I wanted to do was cry. Graham's challenges made me dive outside the constructs of the boxes we're often placed in. Valen's taunts.

Fuck. My pussy pulses just thinking about his venom-coated words and the sharp point of his dagger dragging between my breasts.

Graham and I still haven't made it past fooling around. A choice we feel is right for our relationship. We were friends first. Our foundation was built on different materials than Valen's death threats, Pierce's persistence, and Knox's truths. We really got to know each other, and neither of us wants to lose that.

Deft fingers pull at my towel where it's tucked along my cleavage, the fabric falling open, exposing my upper body to him. Beads of sweat creep over my full breasts, turning to steam as they hit the floor and bench.

My chest heaves, breathing him in and sucking his tongue into my mouth. Our kiss deepening before I tug his lip between my teeth with a salacious grin.

He hums in appreciation, devouring my mouth as if he'll never get enough of the way I taste. Releasing my hand, his palms slide up my soft stomach. The hardened peak of my nipple twirled and pinched between his fingers. A deep ache settles into my back as it arches, further pushing me into his palm. My body is begging for more, begging for everything.

"I like having you to myself," Graham whispers against my lips before dipping his head, taking one hardened peak into his mouth. A hiss snakes past my teeth as he nips at me, then slowly swirls his tongue as if easing the ache he put there.

My fingers sink into his hair, holding him closer, needing all of his skin touching mine. "Graham. That feels so good."

He doesn't respond, continuing his ministrations before tugging me so I swivel on the seat. With a chuckle, his knee wedges between my legs, forcing them apart, the towel falling the rest of the way open, revealing all of me to him. A chill runs down my spine despite my body temperature continuing to climb. Every swipe of his tongue and caress of his palm is driving me crazy.

"Graham," I pant.

A hard kiss slams against my mouth, his tongue demanding entry. My moan allows him just that as I screw my eyes shut, lost in the taste of him. The dance of our tongues is a reminder of how Knox and I's essences move together. In sync. Hungry.

The wooden bench is hard against my back. The planks are digging into my oversensitized skin. An annoyance shoved out of my mind as Graham's mouth works its way over my cheek, softly sucking at my jaw, before lingering at my throat. It's impossible to keep up with the downward descent of his mouth, the mixture of his lips, tongue, and teeth sending me into overdrive.

"We're doing this. Right now," he breathes. "I need you too."

My insides shatter. A trillion particles of dust are splitting apart before coming back together under my best friend's touch.

I'm too lost in the pleasure to process the consequences of crossing that line. We'd promised to talk about it first. To ensure that as friends and a couple, we were solid enough to take us there.

That promise is forgotten as he tears his towel from around his waist, exposing his thick, solid cock standing tall at his hips. *Fuck.* My tongue runs over my swollen lips, remembering the feel of his cock in my mouth. The salty taste of him and the way he seemed to pulse as I took him to the back of my throat, eager to give him as much pleasure as he'd given me.

My fingers cling to the back of his neck, desperate to hang on as he tortures me. An involuntary jolt zaps through my body as his cock touches my slit for the first time. He's impossibly hard, flexing his hips, allowing his shaft to slide between my lips. My arousal coating him with every shift forward and back.

My insides scream to be filled by him. Touched by him, cherished by him.

A single finger slips through my wet pussy, slipping inside my entrance with ease.

"Graham, please," I beg. I'm too wound up for all this foreplay. My insides are burning for him.

The muscles of his back roll beneath my fingertips. My nails are surely leaving marks that will last for days.

His movements halt. The thick mushroom head of his cock poised at my entrance. Each palm plants against the bench on either side of my head. "If I sleep with you, we can't take it back. Bri, I—" The man who had just moved with confidence retreats. My worried best friend is now staring back at me with those beautiful, pleading eyes. "I want this, but I won't lose what we already have. Not for sex."

My fingers apply more pressure to his mid-back before drifting lower. "I know," I breathe. "But, please."

"Promise me something first…"

Pulling my arms up between us, I cup his cheeks, forcing our gazes to stay locked. "Anything." My fingers trail up, combing the hair back from his face.

"No matter what, our friendship sticks." His Adam's apple bobs, droplets of sweat plastering his hair to his temples. "Even if we don't work, we find a way to hold on to—"

I pull his face to mine, kissing him softly. "No matter what. Now, please. I want you inside me."

A grin stretches across his face as he flexes forward just the slightest. My pussy is fluttering in anticipation. Once we've had Graham, we'll be complete. They'll all truly be mine in every way.

With a soft pulse of his hips, Graham enters me the first inch. The stretch is delicious. The feel of him is different from the others. Though Knox is the most endowed aside from Aziel, Graham still forces my body to accommodate him.

Each quick pulse allows him to sink a little deeper. To fill me a little more.

Long fingers trail over my thigh, running over my knee, before dipping behind it. The slight shift of my leg up and out allowing Graham better access. And he sinks deeper. Drives into me harder.

"Graham. Yes," I whimper. "More."

Every controlled, leisurely stroke is driving me crazy. His pace is no faster than when he first slid inside me. I want him to really move. To take me and make me his.

"Please," I whimper again.

That grin once again greets me, his gaze focused on where he slides in and out of me. "I'm almost all the way in. You're tighter than I imagined, Bri."

I can't hold on tight enough. My fingers are clawing at his shoulders and his hair, our skin slick with sweat. "Yes. Yes, I want to take all of you."

"Working on it," he grunts, retreating just to thrust forward harder.

There's a pause. A soft kiss pressed to the corner of my mouth as he retreats. Then he suddenly slams forward, my cry ripping through the room.

"Fuck!" I roar as he really moves. Our bodies meet each other in a frenzy of motion. He's so deep. Too deep. My body is on fire.

"Yes, Bryony," he groans, rolling his hips in a tantalizing rhythm, pushing against my knee to widen the spread for him. "You were made for me. Do you feel that?"

I nod, unable to speak. I'd witnessed a bit of Graham's bedroom talk the first night we messed around, but this is something else entirely. A different man as he thrusts into me, filling me and driving me to the edge.

My muscles clench around him, eager for his throbbing cock. Eager for everything.

"Yes. Like that." I lick my lips. "Make me come," I moan.

A soft chuckle vibrates against my chest before he nips at my painfully hard nipple. "Patience." He bends to place a kiss between my bouncing tits, his soft chuckle vibrating against my skin.

We move together, my lower belly igniting with flames. Our breathing is turning more ragged with each thrust of him inside me.

Two fingers find my clit, making tight circles, driving me to that cliff faster and faster.

"Fuck, Bri," Graham barks, quickening his pace. His movements become less steady as I fly over the edge, crying out his name and every curse in the book.

My walls clench him tight. Fisting him. Eager to pull his release from him.

"Come for me," I whimper.

He loses his rhythm. Each thrust is sloppier than the last as he swells inside me. A heavy growl flies past his lips as he reaches between us, pulling himself free. The first rope of his cum hits my upper pelvis before the rest spills over my stomach and my tits.

Graham hovers over me. His large hand gripping himself tight, milking his cock empty on my skin. My eyes droop, barely able to rise to his heaving chest and beet-red face.

I crook a finger his way, beckoning him forward with a finger once he opens his eyes, his legs unsteady as his feet find the ground.

Pulling him toward me by gripping the back of his thighs, I slowly sit up, grabbing hold of his semi-rigid shaft.

Wrapping my lips around the head, I suck him down, licking him clean. He stares down at me, tucking my curls behind my ears. "Beautiful."

I smile around him before releasing him from my mouth with a pop.

"Have time for a shower?" I wink before taking his hand and leading him out of the sauna.

That was too good not to have more.

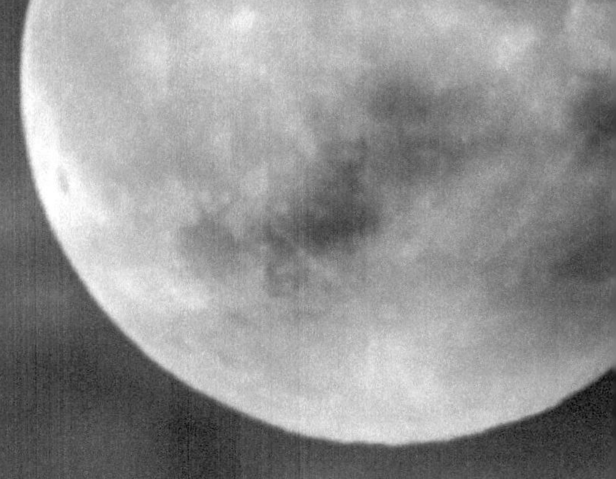

31

BRYONY

I've always been able to walk through the doors of an institution—human or magical—and feel at peace. A feeling like coming home. Like my soul has found tranquility amidst the smell of book pages and the discipline of learning.

Merrick used to say I'd become an educator myself. Someone like me, who loved school above all else, could only want to mold young minds. He was wrong. It has never felt like that for me. I don't have the patience or the trust in myself to lead others down their proper path.

How could I when mine has always been dictated for me? Attending school here in London may have been my choice, but not the institution. Not the students who I get to learn beside. Like Roman, Jorddan gave me no choice.

Before that point, positive emotions toward my father were the only feelings I experienced. But I couldn't tell him that. Not when he just got me back, and he's moving heaven and earth to ensure the safety of a daughter they deprived him of knowing.

Learning institutions have been part of my life since the day I could walk. Roman took me every chance he could. Our travels took us around the world. Growing up, that's how I knew Roman valued me. A concept I now look back and realize I confused with love.

Harley may have been his prized child, but I was more precious to him. I was a chess piece. His bargaining chip to keep my mother and father in line. Who knows who else he used me to manipulate. That may be a question we never get the answer to.

Reliving those moments in my head, I'm a young girl again. Nothing but smiles and bright eyes holding my daddy's hand. It was the most natural thing in the world. I felt so special. It was an honor to stand by his side. A man I idolized for his passion and kindness. Roman's broad smile and the way his eyes shone with excitement with every question I fired past my lips vividly replay in my mind. Emotion that always seemed so genuine.

Maybe for a time it was. When it changed for sure, I'll never know.

I do know that the last time I looked into Roman's eyes, no fondness remained. Only the blackest hatred shone there. Embarrassment and rage mixed with the emotion as I revealed what I had become to him.

With every rejection from those who are supposed to love me, it's easier to act as if I'm fine. The energy spent pretending their actions mean nothing is like a muscle built over time. The endurance and will used to push aside the heartbreak have become mindless work.

Heartbreak, I won't reveal to anyone because who could understand this unbelievable situation I was born into?

No one.

Not even Vincent. My brother got to stay with our father and be himself his entire life. They forced me to live in the shadows. They made me become someone I could never have been.

And now we're here. I don't understand what I am. There's minimal control over my abilities. The worst is that, somehow, though I'm free to embrace what I am now, I still don't feel like I belong. I'm still different. I'm still alone.

No one, living or dead, seems to have ever encountered someone like me.

Bryony Guthrie is still an island unto herself.

A palm slides across my lower back, my messenger bag trapped between mine and Graham's thigh.

"We have most of the same classes," he whispers as the four of us ascend the short flight of steps to the front entrance of the Integretew School of Wielding.

The institution Vincent attended. His countless pointers are already forgotten as I take in the massive entryway.

It hadn't seemed so gigantic when I was a child. But today it looms over me. Imposing and threatening. Those double doors made of thick wood and trimmed in decorative metal molded into swirling shapes dare me to enter.

With a deep breath, I move ahead of my guys, pushing open the door on the right with a grunt. Had we arrived hours ago with the rest of the student body, they'd have been open for us. Welcoming us in as if we belonged here. But I needed a few more minutes. Time with my dad and a walk with my brother.

Stepping across the threshold thrusts me straight into the past while simultaneously landing in the present. The natural stone finishes and decor of historical significance are like stepping inside Beauxgraton. Like we never left.

Nothing has changed. Not the rugs or the thick curtains pulled back from the two-story windows. Not the chandeliers or the armchairs that line the formal entryway.

"Wow," I breathe, taking it all in. The sconces are made of silver, and the gothic-style paintings are done in shades of gray and black, with single accent colors.

I hadn't been here since I was five. It's the same, but the more I rake my eyes over every detail, I realize it's different. It's brighter now. A radiance suited for light institutions, not those cloaked in the shadows of the dark.

Back then, I'd thought of the place as Dracula's castle. A comparison I often brought up to my father. *"I promise it's not, Bryony. Dracula was in Transylvania,"* Roman always chuckled.

"But he could move his castle, right?" I'd always asked, tugging on his hand wrapped around mine.

"No, he can't. There are no vampires here." He'd kiss the crown of my head, drawing out my giggle, and the conversation would be over. Though still scared, I would venture to the next topic, ready to explore the hallways all over again. This was one of the institutions we had returned to dozens of times throughout my youth. I'd never wondered why only a few became regular stops, and now I wish I had asked.

Morsels of regret settle in my gut. My mind is failing to chase them away. Knowing what I do now, any question would have been pointless. Roman would never have been honest with me.

Tears burn behind my eyes, recalling the memories. That same pain lancing through my chest, remembering those moments that were so magical to me. Every detail flashes before my eyes. They move so quickly that it's impossible to analyze each one. Was one instance more genuine than the last? Should I have recognized deceit in Roman's blue irises when his smile failed to curve up to the corners of his eyes?

Vincent warned me not to go down this path. He knew I would dig until I found the truth. A truth that would reveal the things I'm not sure I want to know. *"It will consume you, little Bri. I don't want to see you hurt anymore,"* he'd whispered, holding me in a tight hug.

Shaking my head, working to clear those very memories, my shoulder is bumped hard from behind. As if my limbs have no control, I jerk forward, saved by Pierce's arm snaking around my waist. My knees wobble as I fight for balance. Each breath comes in heavy pants, searching for the rude motherfucker.

"Watch where the fuck you're going," Valen barks at the guy who hit me.

He turns back, glistening green eyes like emeralds staring solely at me. His complexion so pale I wonder if he is a vampire—*those don't exist, Bri*—and his shaggy blond hair shaped around his face almost artfully. A very handsome face.

My essence seems to sniff at him. Tiny whips of her tendrils licking at the stranger who dared touch us. Curious if he has something she wants. Power we don't yet possess.

Light, but dark, it hisses in my head before sitting back on its throne.

I'm unsure what that means. Nor do I have the energy to process it at the moment. I'm more intrigued that my essence didn't immediately want to snatch power from him.

Stepping forward, I reach out my hand to the stranger. His large palm wraps around mine, a brow raised high with a quirk of his full mouth. "Bri Avalon." The last name tastes sour on my tongue. I want to gag as bile rises up my throat, knowing I have to continue using that name.

The day I can rid myself of it can't come soon enough.

The world doesn't know I'm a Guthrie yet. A secret I hope won't follow me to the grave. In time, Roman will out me. He'll find a way to spin the information to his advantage. Then they'll know I'm a Grisym.

"Carter James," he shakes back, giving a soft squeeze. "I heard you were transferring here for a semester." His eyes drift down my body, taking in the leggings molded to me like a second skin and the fitted thermal pulling taut over my full breasts.

"Eyes on her face," Valen snaps.

Carter smirks at me, finally releasing my hand. "Tell your dog to stand down. I'll see you in spellcasting."

I'm shocked into silence as he disappears into the throng of students. There was something so off about him. The whole interaction making the hairs at the back of my neck stand on end.

A hand cups my elbow, bringing the present back into focus. "Let's go." Pierce's voice is soft, his words low next to my ear.

With a nod, the four of us keep moving. It's so similar yet so different from the day of arrival at Beauxgraton. Most of the student body clump together in groups no bigger than five. Their conversations varying from animated recounts of events to family drama to their emotional rollercoasters regarding classes for the upcoming semester.

Like our crew became at Beauxgraton, the groups are mixed. The distinction between light and dark blurs into a gray backdrop. For a moment, it almost feels like we're all Grisyms. All the same. All equal.

"I hate that we're on different floors," Graham mumbles beside me.

It was necessary.

Mr. Greer demanded we separate. A command that left us all on edge. An added layer of security. Though it took a minute to understand why separating us would provide us with more protection than keeping us together.

He'd sighed heavily. *"Perception is everything. It's already going to draw enough attention that you all are from the same institution. Think about it,"* he'd scoffed. *"Four Beauxgraton students transferring to study abroad at the same time. You're going to need to put distance between you all."*

"We're not abandoning our girlfriend," Pierce snapped back.

"Son, I don't care who you date, but for your sake, do as I ask. Do whatever you want behind closed doors. In front of others, you need to act as if you were no more than classmates. Acquaintances at most, not friends."

None of us liked it, but we understood. The more we're associated, the more we all become targets of any sort of retaliation or potential spying Roman might conduct within these walls. He lives for it. I would know.

As if it wasn't enough to have Mr. Greer speak of our relationship, my father did too. Our relationship must remain as protected a secret as my identity.

Jorddan didn't stop there. I am to avoid taking in new essences at all costs. Knox isn't here to save me from myself. Though Vincent sent me with two vessels, there's no guarantee I'll be able to open them for myself if I've lost all control. Now is the time I need to keep my essence on a tight leash.

The pang of knowing Knox won't be here hadn't hit me yet. Dismissing it felt simple, given the manor is only a few hours away. A place I could reach in seconds, but not if I've lost control. I wouldn't risk teleporting in that condition.

The weight of missing him already sits in my stomach. He'd been my rock last semester in so many ways. How will I survive this without him?

It's not only Knox missing, but all our friends, too. We'd formed a close-knit group. It's funny that when you look back at the things you thought you had, you realize they didn't compare to what you've found.

I had friends before Beauxgraton. Our group was small. A circle that began when we were children and stretched through the years. I'd thought that was the pinnacle of friendship until Beauxgraton. Those people became my family. School won't be the same without them.

They've all been gone for over a week now, except Damian. Like us, he returned to Beauxgraton today. Tosch had been the one to tell me about the special provision for married couples during semester breaks. Until Damian graduates, it's most of what they have. Tosch, being older, has no limitations on her schedule.

I miss them.

I miss my home.

Bickering between Valen and Pierce pulls me out of my wandering thoughts. The fog of my immersion in the past *is* slowly clearing. It's their voices that drop me back in the present. My focus once again sharpens. I'd been semi-cautious at Beauxgraton, but I'll need to be more vigilant here. There's no staff or daddy to protect me this time.

Every previous fail-safe I had at Beauxgraton isn't here. Knowing Vincent, my father, and Knox are close eases my worry. Just not close enough if we run into serious trouble.

"Knock it off, you two," I whisper-shout.

"Hell no. That asshole isn't going to—" Valen sneers in my face.

"Back off. Let's go find our rooms." Graham puts a hand on Valen's chest. Valen only gives a soft nod, his hard stare still focused on me before shifting to Pierce.

Valen grunts, pushing Graham's hand away. "Fine. See you at dinner." Then they both turn on their heels, Graham urgently whispering to Valen, while he tucks his dagger back into his jacket.

What the hell did I just witness?

"Did they?" Pierce's thoughts seem to stall on the same hill of confusion as mine.

The two barely tolerated each other before our Beauxgraton battle. It was only trading harsh words, slinging them like deadly arrows. But now... dare I call them friends? I'd noticed them spending more time together at the manor. They often departed as a pair at random. Just a silent exit out of a room or a whispered conversation as they stalked right past you. They never shared their plans or where they went.

I let it go. Told myself it was Valen paying his debt to Graham for saving his life, but from what I saw, their newfound friendship runs deeper.

"They did. I—"

"Yeah..." Pierce says, wrapping an arm around my shoulders. "Guess we should find our rooms too."

Janelle ensured our items were transported via the school portal system here to Integretew. An amazing and intricate network I may never understand. Students at all schools are not permitted to visit institution-sanctioned portal sites. It was a law enacted by my father over a decade ago. No one questioned it.

Pierce and I wander the halls in silence. This place is enormous. A former palace for the royals. The pattern consists of rectangles and hallways that border them. A carved-out atrium at the center overlooks a massive garden. A focus that matches the expansive area at the rear of the building.

Here, regardless of your year, you will have a roommate. The structure may be larger, but so is their student attendance. It's vital, considering it has four times Beauxgraton's count.

Ten other buildings border this main one, outfitted for classrooms, simulation training spaces, staff quarters, and additional amenities, including six libraries. As the school's attendance grew, so too had the space they used. Our new residence was no longer large enough to contain it all.

This main building houses all student dorms, dining halls, the second largest library on campus, study rooms, first-year primary classes, and a movie theater—a more recent addition, added at the request of students. I haven't explored since I was a child, when I was locked out of my father's business meetings. I can only hope time will allow me to while we're here.

Pierce stops at my door, an interior room per my father's request. Instead of a view of London, I'll look down at the atrium. A precaution meant to decrease visibility to me.

Pierce runs his hands over my arms, the thickness of my jacket doing nothing to keep his touch from warming my insides. "You want me to stay with you for a bit?"

"Let's lie low. Go find your room; we'll meet at dinner." I step closer, lowering my voice. My gaze darting left and right, checking for anyone coming our way. "Then Janelle said we're supposed to check in with my Dad."

A frown pulls at the corners of Pierce's mouth, his thumb stroking over my cheek as a profound sadness dances in his eyes. "I don't like this."

There's no controlling how I melt into his touch. "I know." My words are barely above a whisper. I feel for him. This will be hard. We'd been so open since day one, and now we're forced to take a step back. Stealing another glance down the hallway, only a few linger, their backs to us, before I press my mouth to his. This kiss is brief, but full of unspoken words I hope he hears. "Until later."

Then, I place my palm on the door and walk through it.

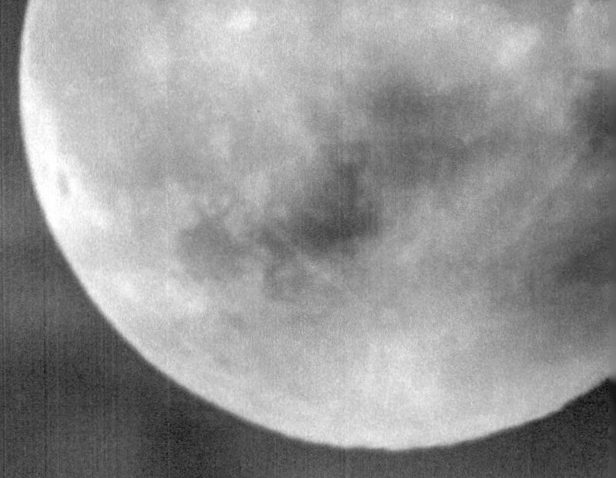

32

PIERSON

Invisible chains anchor my body in place. Their hold serves as a torturous reminder that my girlfriend just rejected me. My chest squeezes against the pain. My mind is trying to convince that lump of muscle that we're not losing her. It's just the stress or being in a new location.

"Bri is still ours," I whisper into the ether.

The moment my girl's palm met the solid surface of her door, it faded. The translucent wave of the spell was visible only to me for seconds after she'd walked through it. The door reformed an instant later, just as it had been—whole—as it blocks me from her.

It should be my analysis of the security feature Integretew uses versus Beaux-graton. A new system I'll have to work to unweave, so my door remains open, the same as I'd done back in the States. At a surface level, the functions are the same—the unique signature of its "owner" is necessary. However, the spell must be different to either form a portal or cause the door to dissipate, allowing a body to walk through before reforming. Either way, the spell weaved into each door needs our essences. Only their soft kiss will allow us entry.

However, it's not unraveling a new security spell that paralyzes me. It's the brush of abandonment. Not only did my best friend walk away without a backward glance, but so did she.

I understand that we need to keep our relationship more discreet here. It would raise too many questions to witness Bri getting cozy with all of us. I won't survive on a few stolen kisses or a quick screw in some closet somewhere, though. It won't be enough to feast on tiny pieces of her when she's given me almost everything now. That is how we began, but I refuse to go back to that. I crave a connection with her. Sex means nothing without it.

A woman with thick dark waves stops beside me. "You lost?" Her eyes are shockingly light blue, like a frost that has washed in. Running a glance over her features, I realize her hair can't be a natural color. Her eyebrows are a much softer brown, possibly a dirty blond, with long, thick lashes coated in makeup.

"Uh, no. Just making sure my friend got to her room."

"Who's your friend?" she asks, cocking her chin my way, while crossing an arm across her upper stomach as if testing me.

"Bryony," I mumble before clearing my throat. "Bryony Avalon."

"Ahh, my new roommate, then. I hear she's quite the powerhouse, is she?" It takes me a minute to parse her thick accent. There's a crude, unpolished edge to it. Malicious intent dancing in her eyes as she stares me down with a wicked one-sided smirk.

"She is. I've gotta run." I spin on my heel, leaving the woman behind. Something about her unnerves me.

Shoving my hands into the pockets of my jacket, I keep my head down, traveling up one floor and to the south wing.

According to historical records, this place was intended to be a palace for the royal family. Weeks before they were to move in, they deemed the space too vulnerable in the heart of London. There are too many windows and entrances, and not enough ways to fortify it, given that the city surrounds it on all sides. It functioned as a museum before transitioning to a wielding school.

To the human public, it is a very exclusive boarding school for those requiring special educational attention. They may see us come and go, but if they hold no knowledge that wielders exist, there's nothing for them to question. It's also why any power use is prohibited outside of institutional walls here, except in the gardens, unless under duress.

We've dodged the truth for decades, to my surprise. In a structure this massive, it is beyond me how the wielding community has managed to uphold the lie. A problem that's not mine to question.

Empty hallways serve as my only company as I follow the mental map to my bedroom. Placing my palm on the door, my magic breaks through the sound barrier.

Music blares through the solid surface, threatening to burst my eardrums. The urge to clap my hands over my ears causes me to flinch as I push forward, the slight bit of resistance from the spell giving the illusion of walking through water.

Stepping through, I wince as the sound amplifies. More than a dozen pairs of expectant eyes stare back at me in confusion and anticipation. Their bodies twist where they're seated, clearly waiting for an introduction I don't feel like giving.

Somehow, I expected the decor to differ from Beauxgraton, but it doesn't. Perhaps it is a standard across all institutions—the beds and desk with hutches. The blue comforter is wrinkled from the bodies seated on my bed. And the impressive wardrobe on the far wall stretches just high enough almost to kiss the ceiling.

"Eh, it's me new roommate!" A redheaded guy cheers in the corner, his beer sloshing over the rim of the massive mug in his hand.

My lip quivers, wanting to curl in annoyance. I'd grown used to having my space. Sure, Valen walked in whenever he wanted, but it was just me.

I give a single awkward wave. "Hi. Pierce."

Those in the group quickly introduce themselves. The guy who said he was my roommate clapping me on the back and pulling me into a one-arm hug. His beer splashes on my jacket, my molars grinding. "Ahh, sorry, man. Nolan Walsh," he claps me on the back again, the force knocking me forward a few steps. "So you're from America?" he questions, taking several large gulps of his drink.

Taking several steps back, my hands forcefully shove into my coat pockets. The need to put space between myself and this guy is making me twitch. My typically friendly nature won't come to the surface today. I'm too on edge. Too hurt. "I am. I've been at Beauxgraton."

"We heard," another woman speaks up, her words accent-free. Having another American present somehow puts me at ease, which is odd since I've been around foreigners for years serving Jorddan. Not once has this anxious pit sat in my stomach, being in a room full of them. "We heard there were four of you coming."

Sweat trickles down my spine. Was it an announcement to the entire school? Had it been a post on social media that someone found and then shared? Why would it matter that four Americans from a US school were coming here?

My stomach knots, unease turning my breath shallow. Pressing my lips tight, I fight to steel my expression. They can't see what that small admission is doing to my insides.

"Uh, yeah," I rub along the back of my head. "We arrived together today."

"You'll have to introduce us," Nolan bellows as he collapses back into the chair he'd been sitting in across the room. "Grab a drink. Relax."

So I do, there's nothing else to do until I meet the group for dinner.

Maybe I'll have taken a normal breath by then.

The dining hall could be a replica of Beauxgraton. I'd wondered how every detail would compare within these walls. Every thought pegging my life at Beauxgraton versus the one I'll have here at Integretew. How many of my comforts will be disturbed?

Chatter and laughter filter into the room. The three-story dining hall is topped with stunning ebony wrought-iron chandeliers, allowing every sound to reverberate off the stone walls. Each candle holder burns bright with their crimson wax sticks, the wax clearly kept from falling by a spell. The same wooden tables, accompanied by a mix of chairs and benches, occupy most of the space.

Spelled conveyor belts and endless amounts of food to feed every person on campus chug along at its center, illuminated by floating orbs in varying colors. The lights changing as new dishes appear as if shifting to match a mood. It's odd, but enticing to watch all the same.

Being surrounded by a crowd of people seems strange after weeks at Guthrie Manor. The place is so massive that it's nearly impossible to hear someone else down the hall, unless they want to be heard. It was a sense of peacefulness and privacy I'm already missing, and it's only been five hours.

There was no guarantee it would be safe enough to return to school. I've never been married to staying. My education was mandated, an obligation rather than a choice.

Then we joined the New Order, becoming an integral part of Jorddan's mission. Students from all around the world have proved to be his greatest asset. We're an overlooked level of infiltration he can't accomplish on his own. At some point, I started to believe the mission would outweigh the obligation. That on any given day, my formal education would cease to be a part of daily life. Funny, with graduation, that would be true anyhow.

"Pierce!" Jerking my head to the right, Bri's gaze meets mine. Those gray and green eyes sparkling as her smile lights up the room. Something inside me loosens. My heart is swelling with hope that we might find some happiness here, too.

Valen and Graham already have our girl bracketed between them, Valen rubbing his thumb along her inner thigh as I approach the table. There was a time when his touch repulsed her. She wouldn't allow it. Didn't want or crave it. Then he fucked her in front of me, and everything changed.

Her body is like a magnet for his hands. His fingers running along her bare skin without a thought. A touch, she now welcomes and melts into.

That used to be me.

Watching my best friend with his hands all over the woman I'm in love with rips me to shreds as much as it turns me on. We only had that one night together, but sometimes I wonder if she would have allowed it to go further.

Now, I know she would. She is what keeps us bound together.

"Hey," I drop onto the bench across from them, Bri sliding a tray to me, biting her lower lip before grinning once more.

Her eyes scrunch with joy as I mouth "thank you" to her. "I already got you food. The lines are insane here," she huffs. My gaze wanders around the packed hall. Bodies fill every seat and even perch along the sills of the windows, stretching from the ceiling to three feet above the stone floors. The longer I stare, the more they seem to multiply.

The dull roar of hundreds of voices grows louder. A disorienting mix of accents making it hard to focus on their words.

The mix of light and dark wielders is similar to what Beauxgraton became. But now I study their features, searching for anomalies, searching for signs of more Grisyms wandering amongst us.

Before her, I never paid attention. Sure, a feature might stand out, but I wasn't concerned about it. You told me you were a light or a dark wielder, and I believed it. I only learned six months back that Jorddan has been mobilizing Grisyms. Yet, it didn't bother me then. There was a barrier between me and them. They lived elsewhere, and I didn't interact with them at first.

Then I met Bri, and it's as if I lost every bit of logic. I was so wrapped up in her. In us. That woman consumed my every thought. Every action became a guiding force in pleasing her. Nothing else mattered. For once, I put myself first in pursuing her. Our blissful bubble blinded me. I missed every obvious sign. Even learning she too was a Grisym barely kept me away.

Until Bri, I may have never known how many Grisyms I'd been living beside. Jorddan. Headmistress Milgren. Knox. Vincent. Tosch. The count just seems to keep growing.

My gaze rakes over each face, studying their features, searching for hidden secrets. Perhaps this is my curse for choosing her.

I will look for those truths, though they no longer scare me. It's quite the opposite; the unpredictability of the Grisym pulls me in.

It reminds me that we can be more than one thing. A truth I'd always wished was a reality for myself. I dreamt of being a dark wielder who gave the same as the light.

Dreams are just that. They're fantasy. Nothing more than our desires flashing before our eyes, always out of reach. No matter how we wish them to be, they aren't reality. At most, they are distant, hazy memories that eventually fade into nothing.

Mouth open, my body shoots forward as a forceful clap lands between my shoulder blades. The sandwich I was set to bite into scatters across the tabletop, carrying my patience with its components. Toppings and half the bun fall to the surface, mustard smearing over the wood.

"You ran off so fast, I couldn't catch you," Nolan bellows, his voice booming in my ear.

Gathering the remnants of my burger and dumping them on the tray, I wipe my hands before spinning to face my roommate. "Went to find my friends here," I smile awkwardly. "Nolan, these are my classmates from Beauxgraton: Bryony Avalon, Valen Greer, and Graham Mayer. Meet my new roommate." I wave a hand back toward Nolan with a tight smile.

"Pleasure," he waves, sliding onto the bench beside me. "Look, we're going on a bit of an adventure tonight. You should join us and bring your mates too."

One of Valen's daggers miraculously appears, the tip dancing between his thumb and pointer finger mindlessly. "We'll think about it," he deadpans.

That tight smile only stretches a fraction further on my face. The fight to make it appear more genuine is exhausting. "Yeah, thanks, Nolan. I'll let you know."

He only shrugs, getting up from his seat and making his way across the hall. The boisterous crack of his words grates on me. His laughter making me cringe as he greets person after person.

"He's interesting," Bri snorts.

"This is going to be a long semester," I grumble.

Reaching across the table, I snatch Bri's burger, immediately taking a massive bite. My jaw aches as I fight to chew before swallowing the huge glob and biting into the sandwich again. Judging by the curious glint in her grayish-green eyes, we'll be on that adventure tonight. I'll need all the energy I can get. So I stay silent, shoveling food into my mouth like my life depends on it.

With our luck, it might.

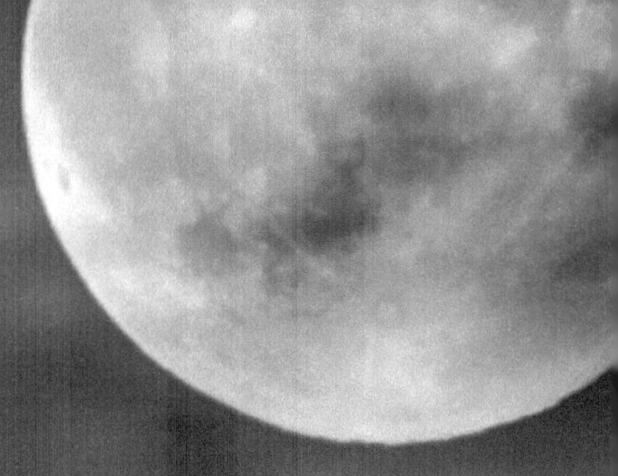

33

BRYONY

THERE'S NOTHING LIKE THE rush of London. A claim that so many broadcast about their favorite cities around the world. They all come with their own rhythms. A heartbeat unique to their own that changes the beat of yours.

I've been around the world, but til this day, London remains one of my favorites. Maybe it's because of how often I came here growing up. A place that was always my home. Perhaps my heart knew that even when I didn't.

Beauxgraton is a place of seclusion. A former private estate, gated and on a mountain surrounded by dense woods. You couldn't see the city lights or the people who inhabited it. It took a thirty-minute car ride down the mountain to hit civilization, then fifteen more to experience small-town life off of the campus grounds. Although I loved that too, this brings my soul to life.

Here I can't be lonely.

Here, an entire city is right at my doorstep. My fingertips itch to touch it. Every taste bud is waiting for the explosion of its flavors on my tongue.

Pierce's roommate promised an adventure, so perhaps it's time we take one by choice.

Every institution has mandates regarding curfews and off-campus policies. Though we begin our studies as adults, for our safety, they treat us like children.

A precaution because of our newly matured magic. I always thought it was over the top, but never spoke the words aloud. I never imagined insulting Roman's work at the time.

Compared to most, Integretew is lax. Our freedom is our own. As long as we are present for our classes and exams, the list of rules remains short.

Pierce drapes an arm over my shoulder as I shiver against the cold, the four of us waiting for his roommate to finally show his face. Several other classmates wait near the front entrance as well. Their bodies huddled into smaller groups, holding their individual conversations.

Butterflies soar through my stomach in anticipation. The excitement is palpable as we wait. Tonight is for fun. Nothing more.

We could use it.

The weight of current circumstances still hangs over our heads. Our eyes weary, remaining trained over our shoulders, waiting for the next strike from behind. Anyone could come for us at any time.

No, Bri. They're coming for you. Your friends will simply be collateral damage.

I'd seen a glint of mischief in Nolan's light blue eyes at dinner. The same hint of the unknown I'd seen in Valen's when he'd tried to talk me into joining him and his friends for the Red Moon Festival months ago. It seems ages since then.

That mysterious glint always seems to be the deciding factor for me. It served me fine prior, so why would tonight be different?

From what I gather, this will be nothing more than a bar crawl. A pastime I've never indulged in due to one of the countless restrictions my mother and Roman put on me. My drunken scene would reflect poorly on the Avalon name, so it was best to never even allow myself to be in a situation where that could be a possibility.

What a shame it would be to embarrass them now.

A chuckle breaks free, imagining the anger contorting Roman's face. I have no reservations about ruining his image, but I hesitate when I think of my mom. I am furious with her. Heartbroken and confused over her decisions, I grapple with my bleeding heart for her.

I always understood and accepted it for what it was. What other choice was there? I was—*am*—the daughter of public figures. My actions not only reflect on me, but on my family. My heart knows I'm not an Avalon. I never was. But Merrick is. My mother is in her way, too. I still want to make them proud, no matter how angry I am. The pathway of betrayal and spectacle has led us to our current destination. There's no changing that.

But I am also a Guthrie. Though I don't publicly associate with them, I am one of them by blood. If someone caught me in a compromising position, the impact would still affect my father and brother. It would weigh on my heart just as heavily as the other bullshit circling us like vultures now. The universe has finally given me a father and brother who love me unconditionally, and I will do anything to protect that. So, bar crawl or not, I'll enjoy myself without making a fool out of the ones I love.

"Where is he? It's freezing." Pierce's teeth chatter, pulling me closer into his side.

Leaning into his vibrating body, looping my arm around his back, I try to warm him. Calling forth the necessary spell, relief spreads over us like a heated blanket. But my focus shifts to Graham and Valen, the two of them carrying on their own conversation without us.

When had they moved further away? The distance is just far enough that I can't reach out and touch them. Their heads are bowed as they'd been earlier, when Graham coached Valen into calm as they'd stalked away from us. Their conversation remains hushed, but animated, as is given away by Graham's ever-changing expressions. His face always reveals every thought, emotion, and desire, even when he tries to hide it.

Valen's dark stare briefly meets mine. His body moves just close enough that he can reach out, running a palm over my ass. Their conversation never stalls, though. The volume is lower now that they are a few feet closer. My frown deepening until Valen's hand finds me again. This time, squeezing softly. A reminder of the fun we'd had after dinner.

The four of us had barely made it out of the dining hall before Valen tugged me into an empty room. My breath came in heavy pants as we tumbled across the threshold. My front still facing away from him as the barrier spell rippled along the walls. The click of an unbreakable lock sealing us in, causing my core to pulse in anticipation.

Our movements were frenzied. Mouths and teeth clashing sloppily as he snapped his fingers, stripping us of our clothing. The chill of the room sent a shiver down my spine. One quickly replaced by Valen's body pressed against my back. *"Bend over,"* he whispered against my ear.

His fingers tangled in my hair as he shoved me face-first into the table beside us because I hadn't moved fast enough. But I didn't fight back. Not when he dragged his dagger down my spine or when he pushed into me with a single thrust, fucking me so hard all I could do was scream out for mercy. His name was a chant on my lips, repeated so many times it could have been a sacred curse. The sting of him pulling my hair and the dagger biting into the flesh of my ass cheek was the most delicious form of pleasure.

We came together. Stars bursting behind my eyes as I fought to breathe. *"I don't give a fuck what our fathers said. You're mine. I'll fuck my forbidden fruit where and when I want."* He'd dressed me then, allowing my unfocused stare to rove over the tattoos covering his body. His story is there for me to study whenever I want.

My essence suddenly pounds against the barrier I've been working to build and hold with Tosch. A layer that will keep it from immediately jumping out of my skin and snatching every new essence around me. But now it's *bang, bang, banging* against the plexiglass, fighting to get out.

Glancing over my shoulder, Carter James comes waltzing through the front door. His hands sweep through that unruly blond hair before he catches my eye.

He moves as if in slow motion. That grin quirking while my essence screams to get to him. A reaction I don't understand. Earlier, it had sniffed him and then settled, but now I can barely contain it.

Pierce's hold on me tightens. "What's wrong?"

"Nothing," I lie.

My lungs burn with the effort to breathe. Fighting to reinforce my wall to keep my essence in. Carter walks right past me, his eyes never leaving my face. And my insides go wild.

Now, all of my essences riot behind my own. They want his. They want everyone's. Jerking forward, I'm gasping for air. Tears burn behind my eyes, unsure how much longer I'll be able to keep my magic from bursting free.

Then Carter looks away, and it all just...settles.

Sucking in a deep breath, I'm lost.

Likely, better preparation would've helped. Tosch warned my essence might react this way. We've been willingly feeding the beast for a week now. She's awake and hungry. The queen of power will not be denied.

Tosch cautioned it might be a constant battle, me against her highness. I either tame her, or she owns me. There's no happy medium.

The desire to consume it all had never been so strong. Those claws sinking into my flesh, urging me to take and take and take until there was nothing left. Yet, I'd held back. I'd remained in control.

There had been a fifteen-year gap between Harley and the essences I took while attending Beauxgraton—that I'm aware of. A decade and a half of that low simmering thirst I could never identify. It was a slow trickle taking them in. A taste that allowed my essence's hunger to grow slowly. It grew stronger with each stolen essence, those waves of fresh power merging with mine to create a new version of me each time.

The floodgates are now open, and I wish Tosch were here with me.

A howl once again pulls my focus behind me. "Alright, let's get smashed!" Nolan cheers, exiting the front doors of the main building with several other guys in tow.

As if Nolan were our missing piece, the group immediately begins its trek down the street. Each person falls into step as one, sauntering off down the block without a care. Our horde of pairs continuing their animated conversations, their laughter drifting out into the night.

Choosing silence, my mind wanders back to the memories I have of this place. There's something to be said for experiencing the world as an adult. Exploring the place you always loved by choice nestles inside you in a different way. The same details, once shining in welcoming pastel, become vibrant before your eyes. The sights, sounds, and aromas are more potent. Now, this city seems mine. I'm no longer the tiny ant clinging to her father's hand, encouraged to love the architecture and culture.

I chose London.

Not much has changed since I came here as a child, but I also can't shake the feeling that I'd witnessed it through a filter previously. Absentmindedly, I have to wonder if it was yet another "gift" Roman gave me. If I didn't see the world in vivid streams of color, why would I ever want to be part of it?

An easy leash to keep his dirty little secret behaved at his side.

Anger boils inside me, Pierce's hand rubbing up and down my arm, likely thinking the quake of my body is due to the cold. I don't even feel it. Not as I linger on the list of things Roman may have stolen from me besides the known.

Years of manipulation have left a scar. Side effects that will linger and attempt to run my life until I can find the strength to let them go. Those memories will haunt me, leading to countless minutes of self-recrimination. I'm smart. I should have seen it. How could I mistake genuine love for puppetry?

"Looks like we're here," Pierce whispers against my temple, before lightly pressing his lips to the same spot. "Hopefully, you'll warm up quicker in there."

I give him a tight smile, Carter once again catching my eye, quirking a grin.

The reaction is the same. My insides churn and riot. A battle cry roaring in my head as my essence claws at the barrier of my skin. Her determination to reach the man only a few feet away, relentless.

And again, once he looks away, my essence goes quiet.

What the hell is happening to me?

Shaking it off, I suck in a deep breath, eager to enjoy the night. The bar is everything I would expect it to be. Dark and filled with drinking patrons. Nothing but wood-finished tables, stools, and benches. The stench of beer clings to the air like bad perfume.

My gaze scans the interior, foam sloshing over my chilled skin as someone shoves a beer into my hand. Only seconds later, a glass clinks against my mug, sending yet another wave of beer soaring, my lower body barely hopping back fast enough to avoid the splash. "Cheers," I mumble, throwing back the first half of the drink. Maybe a few will help me forget what a mess my life has become.

Turns out a ton of drinks, four pubs, and a dance club will make you forget a lot.

My clothes cling to my body, drenched in sweat. The moment Audrey dragged me onto the dance floor, she tore free the ponytail I'd arrived with. Her mahogany bob is nothing more than wet and wild waves. My curls are a match as they stick to my cheeks with each whip of my head back and forth.

This is another first. Dance clubs were on the forbidden list, too. Tonight, I let go of obligation. I forget the ever-growing list of those only I can disappoint. Tonight, for once, I'll allow myself just to live. Allow my body to move to the music, and the smile never to leave my face.

My cheeks are sore from laughter. My mind is free of all my worries. And I couldn't be happier.

The women in our group have proven to be a riot. Their off-the-cuff jokes and boisterous laughter draw out my own. New acquaintances, I wasn't ready for. A pang of guilt striking me in the chest, believing I'm betraying those from Beauxgraton.

My father promised that someone would watch them, but things happen. The Council and Roman are powerful and cowards will switch sides to ensure they win.

Arms slip around me from behind, the brush of soft lips over my earlobe making me grin wider. "Hey, we're leaving," Pierce shouts in my ear.

"Already?" I whine, my movements sloppy from the booze I ingested as I spin in his hold, draping my arms around his neck. His dark blue eyes dip down to my mouth and then back to mine before I tug him to me. Our lips meet in a hurried kiss, his fingers sinking into my hair, pulling me closer.

Our mouths slant, his tongue running along the seam of my lips before pushing inside. His deep moan leaving me vibrating through my entire body, down to my aching core. "I want to get you home," Pierce groans, tugging the shell of my ear between his teeth, before kissing along my jaw.

"Only if you promise to fuck me."

His eyes go wide before narrowing on my face. "That was implied," he smirks.

My teeth sink into my lower lip, our eyes locked on one another. The throb between my legs intensifies as he licks his swollen bottom lip, and I know I won't be able to wait that long.

Moving my hips against him, his body sways to the beat. That laugh I'd grown addicted to only months ago vibrating through my chest.

"Hey, you two. Where have you been?" Graham questions, stopping beside Pierce and me.

"Dancing," I cackle, throwing my head back, before releasing Pierce and pulling Graham into me. He's shocked as I grab the back of his head and kiss him like a hungry woman. I need my men. All of them.

Knox. A pang settles in my chest knowing I'll have to wait until next weekend to see him again.

When I'd claimed them all a month ago, I hadn't meant for this to become some twisted relationship or family unit. I just needed each of them on my side for various reasons. It didn't matter that I'd slept with three of them at the time. But this is better. The four of us are out in the open, just them and me.

"Bri, chill." Graham softly pushes me away, his fingers curling around my upper arms. "We're not supposed to be..." His voice trails off, glancing side to side as if checking for any gawkers. No one is paying us any mind. They're dancing, talking, and drinking. We're the last thing they're concerned about.

A heavy arm falls over my shoulders. "Hey, let's go! One more stop." A male front presses flush against my back as long arms wrap around my neck, and a scent that doesn't belong to my men wafts up my nose. The combination of expensive spicy cologne, beer, and cigarette smoke makes my stomach churn. Yet my body remains stock still, attempting to avoid allowing this stranger to get any closer.

My men only glare at the asshole behind me. Whoever was brave enough to touch me so freely must be either too drunk to realize he's about five seconds from death or simply not care.

Valen seems to appear out of nowhere. His snarl nasty, marching into my space. "Hands off."

Nolan's hold immediately drops, the heat from his body gone in seconds. "Hey, meant nothin' by it. Let's head out."

We're quick to grab our coats, the group once again gathering on the sidewalk before we stumble off to our next destination.

The frigid air quickly cools my overheated skin, a reprieve from the sauna the club had become.

I'm busy chatting with an animated woman, Ingrid—I think—to notice we've moved away from the pubs and nightlife to a quieter, more historical part of the city. As the haze of the booze slowly wears off, my surroundings become clearer, the area funneling into sharp focus quicker than it should have been possible.

A familiar, aged stone looms in front of me, the wrought-iron gates with their menacing skull at the center immediately sobering me.

I know this place. We shouldn't be here.

Marching to the front of the group, I grab Nolan by the shoulder, spinning him to face me.

"Why the hell did you bring us here?

34

WYNSTON

A HEAVY BREATH LEAVES me as I enter the parlor, which is inhabited solely by Jorddan, who is still stationed by the window, his hands clasped behind his back. It's exactly where I knew we'd find him. He hasn't left the spot since Bryony left this morning, to my knowledge.

His frame remains centered in front of the window facing the front drive. If I didn't know better, I'd say he hasn't released a single breath since watching a third of his heart drive away earlier this afternoon. He'd fought himself as they said goodbye. Anyone could see he longed to be the one to deliver his daughter to school, an opportunity he never had as she grew up without him. But he wouldn't risk her safety, so he ordered several New Order soldiers to take the four young folks off to their new institution.

"Jorddan, we found him."

We're down to a house of three. Just me, my girlfriend's dad, and her exasperating brother. It's odd having so few of us here. Coupled with Jorddan's nonchalance and Vincent's death stares, I'm in hell. But for her, I'll endure. For her, I'll focus on what I need to do to keep us all safe.

The New Order soldiers come and go. They stagger their shifts for patrolling the grounds, reporting in, and guarding Harley, who remains locked in the basement. Their presence failing to dissipate the low-level stress choking the air out of every room.

Merrick had come early this morning to see his sister off, though she'd warned him not to. The baby cradled in his arms was sleeping soundly, unaware of the type of future she might lead if we aren't successful in forcing change on the wielding community. I can't remember the last time I saw Bri smile so freely as she'd held that baby girl to her chest. Mine aching, wondering what it would be like to see her hold ours. A thought I quickly shook off, refocusing on Merrick.

Vincent is the only one of us who has handed over his trust to Bri's half-brother. Their long-standing mutual agreement proved to be impenetrable against our skepticism-filled rebuttals. But I still question the limits of Merrick's allegiance, and I know I'm not alone.

He's yet to confirm whether their mother is aware. An omission that leaves unmatched fear spider-walking its way down my spine. If she knows and Roman directs any of his anger toward his "wife", there's no telling what she might reveal.

Now, should he harm Geneva, that's only one more reason for Jorddan to eliminate Roman. His desire to annihilate his rival visibly burns in his eyes. The mixture of gray becoming rolling waves of molten steel.

Fuck. Bri. Just the sight of Gray eyes brings me back to thoughts of my other half. She's only been gone a few hours, but my body knows. My essence is well aware that she is not near. It riots and raves beneath my skin. My focus wavers as I try to will it to calm. What lives inside me now wants its other half, but she isn't here.

It would serve us both well for me to control my emotions and my mind before we both end up dead because of my mistakes.

Vincent stalks into the room behind me, just as I close the distance between Jorddan and me. His presence is like a wintry cold front that sends shivers down my spine.

The memories of every interaction with him in our younger years assault me now. Each one slithers to the forefront of my mind the moment we share space.

At first, I hadn't known exactly why he made the hair at the nape of my neck stand on end. Then I'd caught him in action. I wasn't even supposed to be there, but I needed my textbook that I'd left in class. It was he and another student standing over the dead body of our professor. Paralyzed, I watched him resurrect a man and then extract every memory from him. It was his friend who spotted me standing there like a statue.

The first threat came the next day. And then another and another. When I confronted Vincent about it, the professor who replaced our newly deceased instructor pitted us against each other. It was our punishment for our unbecoming behavior. We were trapped in a time loop for seventy-two hours. A curse that held you in place and time while we battled until death. Only one of us was meant to be left standing. The winner walks free. But I refused to kill someone. I wasn't like him.

We exited bloodied, bruised, and still with Vincent's secret between us. When Bri asked me about our past, I couldn't bear to tell her I could have killed her brother. The thought of mirroring the actions of others in her life gutted me. I couldn't admit to nearly becoming a man who took from her. My cowardice wouldn't let me.

Vincent never forgave me after that. Everyone expected him to emerge victorious from our battle. He was older, stronger, and more experienced than I was. I shouldn't have survived every bit of dark magic he could throw my way. The fact that I refused to kill him and he hadn't succeeded in eliminating me during the time limit bruised his ego. Frankly, it's baffling that he never let the grudge die.

My view of him never changed. He was a murderer lacking respect for the living. The type of monster he could be always shaped my hatred. To an extent, it still does.

Existing in the same space as him after all this time leaves me teetering on edge. There was no predicting our responses before we saw each other again. The possibility of varying outcomes spiked my heart rate. Since the day we've walked through those manor doors, I've wondered how long I have before he strikes.

I'd hoped Bri's brother would no longer harbor ill feelings toward me. Clearly, he still clings to the past. My sexual relationship with his sister only heightened the tension that has remained between us. Not only does our age gap label me as a predator in his eyes, but my position of power over her, as her professor, also raises concerns.

Somehow, despite witnessing what we are capable of together and how much I've helped her, he's only met me with fierce distrust.

Words have never been adequate to describe the connection between Bri and me. It's our cells and souls. A bond that goes far beyond anything physical. He should understand the position we were in. We were two scared and lonely Grisyms. It was our chance to have someone to lean on. Another wielder who understood the death sentence attached to the Grisym identity. Another who values our secrets and the importance of keeping them.

"Where?" Jorddan pulls my focus back to him with his gruff demand.

Clearing my throat, running my hands through my hair, I move a few steps closer. "Integretew," I nearly whisper. It may not be my personal failure that she is now there, possibly unprotected, but it feels like it. My body pummels me from the inside out, shouting that I shouldn't have let her out of my sight. I'd promised to protect her, and now she is in the middle of London with a potential threat lurking around some dark corner.

Jorddan's men were supposed to vet the place. They were supposed to comb it from top to bottom. Their investigation included every student who was supposed to walk through those doors. They claimed none of the threats we were aware of were there. There were no direct ties or connections.

They fucking swore.

Lunging forward, Jorddan's nose is less than an inch from mine. "How did we miss him?" His sharp words cut into me. My hands fumble to staunch the bleeding as my stomach drops, watching his eyes shift. The gray of metal becomes the onyx of the pits of hell. Their dark glimmer locked on my face, burning with unbridled rage.

My insides tighten against the grip of his power. The tattoo bearing his name burns so intensely, I grit my teeth against crying out.

Then it stops, Jorddan backing away, straightening the lapels of his jacket. Those black pits of hell don't leave my face waiting for an explanation, though. The accusation is clear in the set of his features. He wants answers, then he'll demand blood.

Vincent steps close to his side, arms crossed, glaring.

The two men's facial features are so similar that it's unnerving. There's no doubt that they are father and son. Their matching expressions reveal the thinning of their patience as if they were clones.

Clearing my throat, I tug at the collar of my sweater. The fabric seems to tighten as if determined to strangle me, too. The lump sitting in my throat swells, my Adam's apple painfully bobbing against it. "He changed his appearance. This is the man Bri knew him as." Jorddan grimaces at the two photos I slip into his hands. The first is a prior picture, and the second is his current face. "Supposedly, this is what he looks like now. It turns out he's still in touch with the spell master Yorgan also consulted with, and we intercepted correspondence between him and William."

"Do we know who he is posing as?" Vincent questions, studying the pictures. His mismatched eyes shift between the two photos as if cataloging each nuance.

"A student. Though it's technically not posing, he never completed his studies after the deaths of his parents. They gave him time off, and then he just never returned until last year."

Jorddan's stare never leaves the two photos. The black pits in his eyesockets make it impossible to determine if he stares at both or just one. "Do we have any idea if he knows who she is?" he asks, his voice filled with the same eerie calm he often addresses us with during our "meetings."

I can only shake my head. It's been a wild-goose chase hunting down every man and woman on Bri's list. Fortunately, a few are already dead. One less worry on our docket of many. There are many more still to be found. If Roman still has any contact with them, they'll all be after her.

A minor slip. That's all it would take, just a mindless recount of the past in the name of nostalgia. A classmate spotting Bri release her essence at just the right time. Those precious few seconds before she shifts from black to her soft steel betraying her.

My eyes press shut thinking of The Council. There have been accounts of them keeping Grisyms. People said their gifts were too precious to waste. No one can confirm the truth of the rumor. Regardless, I can't stand the thought of them getting their hands on Bri.

There's no telling how they'd view someone like her. She's too unique, too valuable, too dangerous. A threat they couldn't allow to breathe for even another second.

If Bri doesn't learn to control her power and it's unleashed, we could all be dead.

With a simple taste, Bri changes. With each novel essence, she is reborn anew. A wielder with the ability to become anything is unstoppable.

"Allow me to make a call," Jorddan quips before exiting with his son at his heels.

I hadn't noticed that Vincent had given me back the photos. The glossy images stare back at me as if daring me to dig deeper. A challenge to discover the truths none of us may be prepared for.

This altered face stares back at me. His wide, pale lips quirked at the corner. The shadow of a smirk, knotting my stomach. His head of blond hair is vibrant against the darker backdrop. Blue eyes as clear as crystals. At first glance, he appears to be Bri's age. That youthful quality that seems to radiate off newly matured wielders, shining through, which would make him over a decade younger than my thirty-seven years. But he's not. William is nearly twenty years my senior.

Magic has the power to unlock potential. It opens us up to endless possibilities. Proper spellwork is capable of so much. A master could transform one's appearance effortlessly. They'll become only memories of what those who knew them can recall.

"How did you do it, William?" I mumble to the empty room.

Our issues extend beyond his appearance. William Danvers became a ghost after his parents' deaths. There are no records. No clue where he's been.

Looking at my watch, it's late, but I haven't heard from Bri or the guys. They're supposed to check in regularly. A request that I'm sure makes them feel like babies, but is a necessary evil until we can contain this. We must wait until we can ensure her safety. Both Bri and every other Grisyms. A process that could take more time than we have to spare.

Dialing Bri, it just rings until I get her voicemail. The same is true for Valen, Pierce, and Graham. My heart rate immediately skyrockets. Sure, they could be fine just sitting at dinner or getting to know their peers or having a fucking orgy without me. A scenario that burns a hole in my stomach. I miss Bri's bare skin against mine too much already. Or worse. Trouble's nasty fist has already met them.

Me: *One of you needs to answer your phone.*

My text is delivered to our group chat, but there's no response. It doesn't matter how long I stare at the screen; there's nothing.

Those ruthless scenarios buzz through my head again.

Trouble, sex, fun, sex, orgy, trouble. Sleep.

"No!" The word barked into the empty room. Shunning that last possibility aside, I know it's not my answer. It was unusual for any of us to be in bed, knocked out at one in the morning.

My cock twitches in my jeans, missing our girl and imagining what she must look like with all three of them filling her holes at once. My essence stirs, itching to touch her. To further ingratiate itself with her.

That rolling wave of dark magic rushes beneath my skin. Never has my essence reacted so strongly. My mind is at a loss for how to handle my own body's rebellion.

Tosch has been our expert these past few weeks. But she, too, is gone, off in Romania doing more research. The anomaly of Bri and me has stumped too many of us. If anyone might have answers, it would be those elderly Grisyms I hadn't known existed, who serve as archivists for our kind. They lived their whole lives undiscovered. Now they just enjoy their peaceful existence in one of the many light institutions Jorddan commandeered.

Texting Bri separately, I bite the inside of my lip, hoping she answers.

Me: *I miss you. Just making sure you're okay.*

Again, no response.

Anxiety ripples through me. My body is unable to stand still, encouraging my mind to continue raging as it refuses my pleas to settle. Unwilling to wait like a well-behaved puppy, I head to the underground caverns. For whatever reason, Jorddan's ancestors felt the need for cells, bunkers, and tunnels under the manor grounds.

It's also where we're keeping Harley. With this portion of the house spelled and soundproof from the remainder of the manor, it's easy to forget he's here. Reports of his howling all hours of the day are just words. We'll never hear him as he writhes under Jorddan's magic that tortures him twenty hours a day.

Pressing my palm to the first heavy metal door, a tendril of my essence seeps free, slithering across the surface before the latches undo themselves.

Stone walls, ceiling, and floor surround me. The dank air clings to my skin as I continue forward. Though I've yet to visit Harley, tonight I'm itching for a turn with him. He has information I want. I can only hope he'll comply enough to give me something. He likely knows William's activities all these years. Men like him keep company in similar circles. They thrive on controlling the masses. Casting illusions of a world they want them to believe they are meant for.

My magic allows me to clear three more doors. The clap of my leather-soled shoes against the solid floors reverberates off the naked walls, the sound so loud it drowns out my heartbeat pounding in my ears. A jolt pulling me out of my thoughts when the sharp slaps finally stop as I stare at Harley's cell. Grunts force my gaze to the two dark wielders guarding our prisoner before they grant me entrance; the door only cracked wide enough for me to slip sideways through the opening.

My eyes rake over the space. Yes, it's cold, dark, and uninviting, but Harley also has every necessity he might need.

Prisoner or not, he's been taken care of. *Bed. Shower. Clean clothing. Toilet. Food and water.*

Roman once used Jorddan's baby as a bargaining chip. A dangling carrot meant to keep him in line. Now the tables have turned. Yet none of us fault Jorddan for doing the same. Harley has always been Roman's pride and joy, but without him, he will make mistakes. Mistakes we can capitalize on before we eliminate him from this world.

"I was wondering how long it would take you to come find me," Harley snivels, curled up on his basic bed in the corner.

Taking a few steps closer, I glare down at him. "I have only one question."

Light eyes meet mine. Eyes, Bri, and I never acquired. Not being mixed the way we are.

"William Danvers," I begin.

A smirk pulls at the corners of Harley's mouth before he shoves his lengthening soft sandy-brown hair off his face. "What about him?"

My feet carry me two more steps forward, moving of their own volition as my hand trembles at my side. Balling it into a fist, there's no missing Harley's gaze track down, his smirk growing wider. "Did he pose as his uncle to give Roman his position as director of education?"

A barking laugh leaves Harley, his body suddenly lurching to his feet. His laughter continues. Unhinged. Nothing like the cruel, controlled man I met at Beauxgraton only a few months ago. Then he slumps back onto his mattress, his spine meeting the wall with a soft thud. "For such a disgusting excuse of a wielder, I warned my father you were smart."

I fight the urge to charge him. Fight to hold my composure.

"One more question," I state, taking a step closer. "Does he know?"

The smirk falls, replaced with the most demonic grin I've ever seen. "You're smart. Figure it out." A growl vibrates through my chest causing Harley to chuckle. "Hurry, it might already be too late."

35

VALEN

THERE ARE TWO REASONS a wielder finds themselves at the Cavea de Mors.

One: honor those who moved past this existence onto the next.

Our burial process doesn't mimic that of humans. Wielders may not attend the digging of the crypt. It's said to be too dangerous. A time when the soul is passing from our world to the next, and so their power may wander into another instead of back to the earth.

The second is my fault. *Death*.

Globally, three similar gravesites exist. This is the biggest. The oldest. A structure built on the backs of our ancestors. We bury those who are worthy here. The men and women we've spent our lives honoring, and we'll continue to do so in the next life.

Staring at Bri tearing into that Nolan bastard, my skin prickles. The dead are not to be fucked with. Vincent has taught me that more than anyone.

The rumors about him are both true and false.

Yes, Vincent is a necromancer. *Yes,* he can raise the dead. Whether they return to life for minutes or years is his choice. A decision made with intent as he resurrects the body.

I felt it.

His whispered words drifted through me. Each one spoke years back into my shell, reviving my essence. Years I lost as I tumbled through fucking purgatory, clinging to life and... her. At first, I hadn't realized Bri's presence was what I was reaching for most. She wasn't speaking or touching me, but I felt her there. My essence was getting back to her, no matter what it took.

Vincent claims there are limitations to his gift. Immortality or anything close to it is out of the question. Though Vincent can choose how long to keep you amongst the living, he sends you back to the land beyond once he has what he needs. There was a baby he once gave a lifetime to, but that was an exception. A mercy to a New Order soldier who laid his life down for Jorddan.

Only a spell master can come remotely close to what he's capable of. Still, the dead are meant to stay dead. They don't return as they were. Where Vincent quite literally speaks life back into you, a spell master can only reanimate. Like zombies, they are mere shells of their former selves. Hence, banning those spells in most countries.

Goosebumps trail over my skin, imagining it was me here. Visions of my parents and brother walking these tunnels just to view a plaque taunt me. The shell of my body would be bound and hidden behind feet of stone. It would have been worth it to stand for Jorddan's mission with the New Order, but I don't belong here. None of us does.

Even Vincent comes here as little as possible. Just as he can speak life into the dead, they talk back. A million voices in his head, all shouting and moaning at once. They beg for his mercy. For second chances and their previous existences. He hears them. Feels them. Vincent takes on their pain, their anguish, and their pleas.

His ability is miraculous. A talent that the Wielding Bureau sought before he even graduated. To him, it's a curse.

These are not confessions Vincent has ever given me. They were silent admissions passed along as he fought to save my life. Whether it's a side effect that everyone he resurrects experiences, or not, it doesn't matter to me, but knowing that forces me to see him differently.

The wielding world has been conditioned to see him as the most evil anomaly they've ever seen. He is feared. He is hated. The rumors are rampant. They only grasp the surface of his malice. They've never seen the worst. The true darkness that lingers in that man's heart.

A vicious side will surface if harm comes to his baby sister, which is exactly why I stalk over to where she continues to shout at Nolan, her scowl nasty, and his smirk only pissing her off that much more.

I'm steps from Bri when she grabs Nolan's arm, the tiniest sliver of her essence with those twinkling stars leaking free. "Relax. We tinker here all the time," he shrugs her off.

She spins away, angry eyes meeting mine. Eyes that aren't quite right. It's almost as if the whites are smaller. A shadow of black bracketing it. "Let's go." Cold fingers wrap around mine, pulling me behind her, that pouty mouth pressed into an unforgiving line.

Her anger radiates from her in waves. The cold is melting away as the air around us increases by too many degrees.

"Oh no," I stop her, my arm slipping around her neck, her back flush against my front. My dick twitches in my jeans, but now isn't the time. He'll have to wait to have his forbidden fruit again until later.

Nolan and the others eye us, that same blond guy, Carter, stepping in closer with a smirk. "What do you plan on doing with that dagger there?" he taunts.

Bri wiggles against me, my dick swelling, knowing she likes it when I bring my knives out to play. I can see the blood trickling down her throat now, ready to coat my blade as I drive into her. We kept it clean earlier. Pity there are no new wounds to speak of. "Nothing Bri wouldn't like," I croon. My girl partially spins in my hold, her arms wrapping around my middle, the squeeze so tight you'd think she was hanging onto me for dear life. Ignoring it, I turn my focus back to the fucker in front of me. "Seems odd y'all would want to hang out in a wielder graveyard."

"Like I said, mate," Nolan wipes a hand across his mouth as if clearing away the remnants of a drink he's not consuming. "This is our hangout spot. Come in. Or don't. I don't care."

There's another hard squeeze around my body, Bri's breaths quickening until Carter finally snorts and walks away. Then she just lets go, shaking out her hair.

She averts her gaze, only making her behavior stranger. "Fine. Lead the way," she scoffs.

Studying her face, she seems fine. That woman gives away nothing. It can only mean that her curiosity has won out. That impulsive side she fails to ever control, taking hold of the reins. If my forbidden fruit wants to know, then so do I. That reckless side of her benefited me in getting her to the ghoul pit after all.

It seems so long ago. The days flew by and carried with them my overwhelming desire to slit my girl's throat. At least not permanently. My hand still itches to drag my daggers over her skin, watch her bleed, and then come all over my cock, knowing I am the one person who can bring her equal parts pleasure and pain.

The brush of her soft lips over my earlobe pulls me out of my fantasies. "We can play with your daggers later. For now, I need you alert. I don't trust him."

Her words are all I need to get my shit together, my head cocking to call Graham to my side.

Since our mishap with the Sachre, there's been an understanding between us. Graham pretends to be this perfect light wielder. Obedient and filled with the fear of upsetting everyone around him. Equally driven and crippled by not living up to the impossible standards he's set for himself. My new friend is much more. He's ambitious to a fault. A fault that guarantees he will do whatever it takes to get whatever he wants. In a world where many try to live under the cover of darkness or in the glare of light, shades of gray truly govern us all. He's proof of that as much as the rest of us.

Tucking my girl back under my arm, she seems to curl into my side. "Keep close," I whisper to Graham as Pierce passes us, taking the lead.

The heavy groan of the gates creaking open under Carter's magic makes my temples throb. A testament to the spells used to keep this place closed unless you're meant to be here. Had the spell been easy to break, those heavy metal barriers would have opened with silent ease.

The gates remain unlocked during the daytime hours—our time to mourn, visit, and bury the dead.

As the sun sets, the center skull, currently split in two, reforms. The shape transforms from the flat mask to a three-dimensional skull. The spell lock is similar to every gate guarding our burial sites. Legends say that the spirits of lingering souls roam freely in the dark, seeking revenge, love, or peace, but the gates confine them. Every spell woven into the entire area was meant to keep the bodies and souls of the dead right where they are.

When I'd first heard the stories, that's all I believed they were. Tales of ghosts and dumb shit that made human children piss their beds or behave in public. Then the day comes when you learn just who makes things go bump in the night. You either avoid them or become one.

My molars grind as we file in through the man-made cavern entrance. The chatter of a horde of drunken people reverberating off the carved stone walls is the last thing I'm in the mood for.

My gaze rakes over the interior as shivers work their way through my body. It's just as I remember it. But places like this, molded in tradition, never change. They can't.

My tongue sweeps over my teeth, annoyed when Graham pulls me away from our girl. Her fingers link with Pierce's when he reaches back for her. "What?" I growl the single word so low I doubt anyone heard it.

"What did Bri say to you?" Graham snaps. That fucking tone puts me further on edge. My body feels it too. That low-level danger siren is blaring in my head. This whole situation is fucked. For all we know, we walked into a death trap.

My gaze roves over the group ahead, tracking where Nolan's head of red curls bobs above the others. "She doesn't trust Nolan. Neither do I. And something is up with that Carter guy." My fingers sink into my tangled curls, inadvertently loosening my bun. "Bri acted really off when he came around."

"There's something familiar about him. His face..." Graham's voice drifts off.

I'd thought the same, but couldn't quite place it. If I can, I'll get a picture of him and send it back to Knox. He'll be able to look into the guy. While the thought is fresh in my mind, I pull my phone out of my pocket, ready to text him the name so he can get started, only to find missed calls and texts from our former professor. "Come with me," I whisper-growl to Graham. "Pierce," I clap my best friend on the shoulder. "Don't leave Bri's side."

Bri eyes me suspiciously, but she says nothing as Graham and I spin on our heels, returning the way we came. No one tries to stop us. Their eyes bore into the back of my skull. I sense it, but say nothing as we stalk through the entry tunnel. The only light guiding us comes from the outside world, but it's enough.

The phone rings several times before Knox answers, barking his question at me. "Where the hell have you been?"

"Out," I grit my teeth, not appreciating Knox's tone. Fucker isn't my professor anymore. "What's up with all the calls and messages?"

"William Danvers is there." There's a slight pause, my gaze raking over the surrounding courtyard. "At Integretew. His appearance is different now, but he's a student." A sledgehammer wallops me in the chest with the news.

Is that why Carter looks so familiar? They're both blond with those clear blue eyes.

"What else?" I grunt.

Knox releases a ragged breath, not responding right away. "Harley all but just confirmed William impersonated his uncle and is the reason Roman became the director of education."

"Fuck!" I bark.

"What?" Graham hisses beside me, his eyes darting around as if needing to be sure no one heard my outburst.

Waving Graham off, I focus on our phone call. "Knox, I need you to look into two people for me. Nolan, Pierce's new roommate, just took us to the Cavea de Mors. He says it's their normal hangout, but that seems odd to me. Also, look into Carter James. There's something fucked up about him."

"I will. Is she okay?" Knox practically whispers.

"She's fine. You know I will gut anyone who tries to hurt her. The only dagger that touches her skin is mine," I quirk a grin Knox can't see.

Tonight. Later. She's all mine.

"Comforting," he groans. "Let me get to work. I still need to talk to Jorddan about what I learned from Harley. We need to find William. I don't like him being there with Bri. No doubt he knows who she is."

"Wait, how is he here as a student?" Graham questions, his breath white as it bursts past his parted lips. I hadn't thought he could hear any of the conversation. My failure to notice the tendril of white essence floating around his ear quirking my grin. *Amplification spell. Smart.*

Knox's voice pulls me back into focus. "Long story short, he never finished, so he's allowed, though technically mandated, to return." His heavy sigh reveals just how exhausted he is. We're all fighting against an enemy with a reach that may stretch further than any of us are prepared for.

Graham snatches the phone, holding it between our ears. "But he's what? Forty now?"

"Fifty-five," Knox confirms.

"Shit. The rumors are true, then," I snort.

"What rumors?" Knox questions.

"They say his family still has special Amovea abilities. We used to call them body snatchers as kids because they can alter their forms to look like anyone they want. Dad says that ability, much like Bri's, died out centuries ago, though."

It's Knox's turn to bark a curse before he ends the call.

Fuck this, we're getting out of here right fucking now.

Nothing is right.

36

BRYONY

THE CORRIDOR WE'RE LED down seems to stretch on forever. The light tan stone surrounding us is beautiful in its own right, but eerie due to our location.

With another bend, an open area comes into view, the space reminiscent of our Vault arrangement at Beauxgraton. Massive stones serve as chairs, with longer slabs clearly chiseled into benches ages ago. Several tiny fires ignite throughout the chamber. Each burning bright, casting shadows along the walls as the bodies move through the space.

The chatter never stops. Music was suddenly added, giving those of us who had not finished dancing an opportunity to move to the beat. The group continues to pass around more drinks. The cups and bottles of booze appear out of thin air, our comrades clinking them in cheers as they laugh uncontrollably.

I don't know whether to applaud their bravery for partying amongst the dead or gasp at their lack of respect.

Ingrid calls me over with a sloppy wave of her hand. "Have a seat or grab a drink," she smirks, pulling a bottle of liquor out of nowhere before she swivels her hips. "Pretty boy, we're gonna have to teach your girlfriend to let loose more, eh?" she laughs, tossing her head back, taking several hard pulls from the bottle.

Pierce drapes an arm around me, pulling me to his side, and kisses the crown of my head. "We can go if you want."

The cavern is so loud I can barely hear him. Every single sound vibrates off the walls, bouncing back in my direction with more force than expected. How had the club seemed quieter?

Nuzzling my face into Pierce's neck, hoping that it will help conceal our conversation, my gaze rakes over the room. "No. I need to learn more about Carter. I keep..."

It's impossible to find the right words to describe my response to him. That's never happened so intensely before. And the times it has, my essence at least gives me clues as to why she is rebelling.

But not tonight.

Tonight, it's as if all she can do is scream into the void. My essence has become a banshee roaring at his presence. The piercing screech is harder to tolerate the closer he is, and when those dead blue eyes focus on me. My magical army is ready to charge to...

I don't know. Fight. Avenge me. Consume him. There's no simple answer.

Soft lips brush the side of my forehead. The gesture likely appears as an intimate moment to everyone else. "Why?"

"Because there's something familiar about him, but something off, too. I can practically see his secrets slithering beneath his skin. We—sorry, *I* have too many potential enemies out there, Pierce. Plus, he seems to have some sort of fascination with me. What if he knows something?"

I hate that the panic leaks into my tone. It shows vulnerability I wish I didn't have. Weakness we can't afford.

My essence stirs with my fluctuating emotions. Pressing my eyes shut, I whisper to the magic swirling inside me. I beg and plead for calm so that I do not lose control here. A threat that nearly drowns me with each flick of Carter's eyes in my direction.

We've reached a baseline in my tolerance for taking in new essences over the past few days. A midpoint between a simmer and boiling. I refuse to tip that balance, not when I've just found it.

At first, I'd blamed the separation from Knox as the cause of the rebellion I've felt since arriving at ISW.

Deep down, I know it's not true.

Unless... A far-fetched possibility latches on. What if one of our essences recognizes Carter? Does the magic inside me know him? Remember him?

It's not long before Valen and Graham come stalking down the corridor that led us here, their heads ducked together in some sort of intense conversation. The two have been acting so weird. They were never friends before, so I don't understand this sudden closeness between them. I'm ready to ask when Carter suddenly appears at our side.

My insides stir anew, but I keep my eyes on my boys. The lack of seeing his face somehow deters my essence from all-out rioting.

This is so odd.

"Bryony." My name, pronounced with every fucking syllable, is harsh and clipped. "May I show you something?"

My essence's violent swirl changes. She's still battling to get out. To get to Carter, but there's a wicked calm now. Like a predator knowing they're about to catch their prey alone so that they can strike with incredible precision. A shiver runs down my spine, my jaw clenching, ready for my magic to rebel when I face Carter, but it stays level. "Uh, sure," I agree, following him as he leads us across the open cavern and to the mouth of another corridor. "Where are we going?"

"To your grandmother," he smiles against the dark, his blue eyes sparkling with some emotion I can't place.

My breath catches. *Grandma Avalon.* That's the only one he could have meant. My mother's parents were dead long before she ever had me. "Did you know her?"

"Maybe once upon a time, we all knew each other. Come."

I obediently follow, turning his words over in my head. I'm sure the guys, especially Valen, are blowing a gasket right now. My soft hand gesture pleading for them to stay put was likely the last thing they wanted. But they respected it.

Jorddan made them swear to protect me and each other, and once again, here I am putting myself at the mercy of a stranger, leading me down a dark hallway, supposedly to the crypt where my dead grandmother rests.

Will I ever learn?

"Here," he suddenly stops, pointing at a placard on the wall. "She's here."

My fingers itch to trace over the letters of her name. I haven't been here since the first anniversary of her death.

Roman thought it was too hard for me to come back. He saw how much her death hurt me, but what I never told him is that it hurt me more to be away. At least here I could be near her.

I could pretend she was still in our home, brushing my hair and telling me her secrets. She would still be the one to hold me when Harley would cast me away. Yet another thing that man stole from me, I all too easily swept under the rug. "Why did you want to show me this?"

"I thought you'd never been here because this is your first time in London. You were so close to her growing up." That chill of fear shoots down my spine. His words put me on edge. He seems to think he knows all about me and my family.

But he's wrong. I've been to London dozens of times, but here... I've only been here once.

"Did you intern with my father, or did your family know ours?"

His head tilts to the side, a soft glow illuminating it from the essence swirling around his arm. In the dim light, he looks devilish, as if he could swallow me whole and envelop me in a dark so unlike the one I now embrace.

"I'm not as young as I may look. And, as you know, the wielding world is smaller than it seems." He takes a slow, calculated step toward me. Those light eyes never leave mine. "I'll give you a moment alone with your dear nana. I'm sure you have much to talk about."

Then he's gone, sauntering off the way we came and leaving me alone in the dark. Pulling my essence to my fingertips, I call on the power of the light I stole from that wielder in the field at Beauxgraton. There's a different purity to it than just using an illumination spell. It was as if my essence pooled the stars together to give me light.

The tendrils swirl through my fingers, weaving in and out as if exploring me for the first time. Only for a morsel to reach forward, touching the space just below the placard. The wisp jumping back as if burned.

Not here. Not here. Not here.

Something shouts the words in my head over and over again as if in warning. My hands clamp over my ears as I duck down, trying to block them out, but they only ring louder. Each repetition is more forceful and deeper.

"Bri," Pierce's voice sounds right beside me, his arms looping around me, before I finally look up at him. "What happened?"

"Do you hear that?" I can't catch my breath. My eyes are wide and panicked as I search around me, knowing I won't find the voice. It was in my head. It was me—my essence.

"Hear what?" He looks around, his brows knitted, lips turned down into a frown.

The voice is still there. Repeating those exact two words. The chant is growing louder by the second. An even-cadence drum hammering the words in my head.

Breaking out of his hold, I draw my essence back inside me, plunging us into endless darkness. "We need to go. Now!"

As if moving with superhuman speed, my feet carry me down the corridor in record time. I can barely see an inch in front of me, but I run. Away from the voice. Away from the truth. Toward the unknown.

"Bri, wait!"

I don't stop. I can't. "No, we need to get back to the manor."

I'm vibrating with a million different emotions by the time we get back to Integretew.

There were no goodbyes. Just the clap of our swift exit against the stone floors. My essence was itching to leave the Cavea de Mors behind.

Not once did my men ask a single question as we walked back and followed Pierce, who led us to his room. The safest place for now. A relative concept rather than a solid truth.

Nolan reveled in the freedom of booze and music while we crept from the chamber. I've seen the type. Takes nothing seriously. Wants to live life to the fullest. Likely has a wealthy family waiting in the wings to carry him through life with their wallets and name. Wielders like him have nothing to lose. He won't be back until the sun paints the sky in shades of baby blue.

My signature pacing keeps me on my feet. Back and forth. Back and forth, my lip worried between my teeth. "Why hasn't he called us yet?"

"Baby, it's after midnight," Pierce sighs, the plea in his voice giving me pause.

Worry creases his eyes and forehead. That same frown never leaves his face, and it shatters a piece of my heart.

I'm worried too. There have been too many instances since we stepped foot on this campus that have shudders working their way down my spine. Not the type that leaves my toes curling in ecstasy. This is the shudder of dread, the ice-cold finger walk of indiscriminate destruction.

"Then we need to go back to the manor. I'll teleport us." It's all I can think of doing. We don't have hours to waste attempting to get a ride back. I need to talk to my father.

"Bri, we can't," Graham stops me. His hands shake as he curls his fingers around my biceps, forcing my movements to halt.

The urge to shake him free screams inside my head, but I don't. Not when I can stare into his eyes and unleash everything I'm fighting to keep inside.

"Don't tell me what I can and can't do. That Carter guy is weird as hell. The things he said..." my voice trails off as I shake my head aimlessly. "He knew too much, though he didn't outright say it. I felt it." My teeth sink into my bottom lip, fingers cupping my chin. "He knew enough to think it was fun talking in fucking riddles. Then that voice. That voice..." A whimper leaves me, remembering how it had pounded through my head. The further I drew away from my grandmother's resting place, the quieter it became. Only fading once the crisp night air swept over my cheeks. "It said, 'Not here.' What if it meant my grandmother's body isn't there?"

"Of course it is," Graham huffs. "She's a wielder from a prominent bloodline; there's nowhere else they would bury her."

Until tonight, that's exactly what I would have believed. Now I don't know. This year has changed my view of everything. There's no room to trust anything I knew or anyone.

"But what if they didn't?" I press. "What if this is another lie from Roman? What if he never gave her peace?" A sob breaks free. One I'd tried desperately to hold in. Roman took so much from me. I hadn't even known. Had he taken her peace to punish me? "I was so close to her growing up. He knew that." I nod as the threat of tears burns my nose. "Now we know I was just a pawn to him."

Should I find out he had anything to do with this, I'll show no mercy. I'll allow my magic to tear him apart from the inside out. It'll hurt. It'll bring him to his knees as his scream pierces through the night. That woman was my solace during my childhood. She didn't deserve this.

"My little forbidden fruit," Valen steps in front of me, gently pushing Graham aside, his finger trailing down my cheek. "You need to sit the fuck down. You're putting us all on edge. I swear to you, if Roman did, I will let you watch me torture him until his flesh eats him alive, and while he withers and dies, he can watch me worship his daughter." My lips part, core tightening. Why does Valen's dark side do such wicked things to me? "Now. Sit. The fuck. Down." His mouth smacks against mine before his fingers wrap around my throat, forcing me to perch on the edge of the bed. "Better."

My core pulses in response to his hold. A good fuck might help me forget.

I shouldn't be so turned on right now. *What the fuck is wrong with me?*

My panties aren't supposed to be soaked thinking about Valen killing the man I always thought of as my father and then fucking me like he owns me in front of him.

That's demented.

That's Valen.

"Stay," he orders. Placing the tip of a dagger beneath my chin, he levels me with his stare, my ass shifting further back as if to show him I can follow instructions. "You're such a good girl."

"Fuck you," I spit, though there's no bite. This is our game, and we're ready to play.

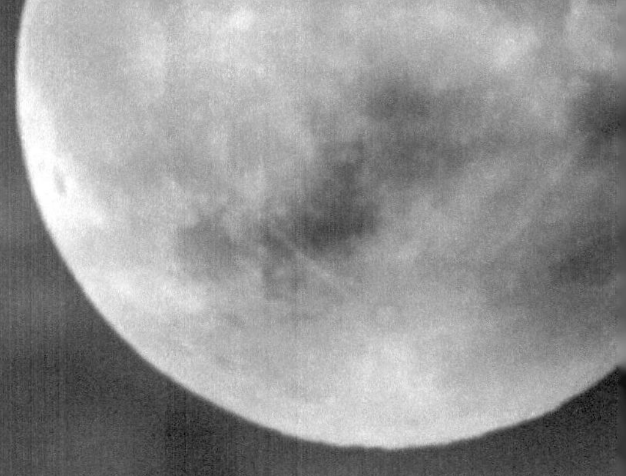

37

BRYONY

THAT FAMILIAR TENSION, WHICH both draws me to Valen and pushes me away, surges to life. A desire I shove back down into the depths of my being. Now is not the time to get my brains fucked out. The secrets and oddities are piling up, crushing my chest, stealing every precious breath. For once, I need to ignore the impulsivity that often guides my choices.

It's been less than twenty-four hours since we left the manor. Less than a whole fucking day, and there are more questions, but no answers. We have no solution or clarity regarding which direction to turn toward. The obvious eludes us, while what we've seen sends our pulses bounding at our throats.

The muscles cinch around my rib cage. My lungs are refusing to inflate. That voice booming in my head, screams that I made a mistake coming here. I was stupid to think I could avoid the issue, hide out until we were ready, and then strike with minimal casualties. It was idiotic to think that surrounding ourselves with strangers would protect us. At least Beauxgraton was familiar, filled with people we knew. It would have been easier to parse the unusual from the norm.

"Bri. Vincent." Graham shoves his phone in my direction, breaking me from my stare down with Valen. A trance that was likely minutes from becoming a fuckfest despite scolding myself to remain focused.

"Vincent." His name is nothing more than clipped syllables on my tongue. "Where is Dad?"

There's a soft rustling in the background. "Both he and Knox are here. We're on speaker." There's a low bass to his voice. One that speaks of barely contained rage.

"Bryony, sweetheart, what's wrong?" My eyes press shut at the soothing cadence of my father's voice. A tone Roman had used with me so many times growing up. It's a struggle to reconcile the Roman of a few weeks ago and the one who raised me. They are two different men who inhabit the same body. One a facade and the other the truth I should have always seen.

But I was blinded. I'd allowed my desire to be loved by my family, knowing I wasn't one by blood, to cloud my judgement. I'd let it provide me a safety blanket that only served as my cage all this time. My half-siblings never cared, and Roman was never my father. I was only his pawn.

"Vincent, is Grandma Avalon buried in the Cavea de Mors?" Silence greets me from the other end of the line. Silence so pronounced it's deafening. Silence that chokes you with the truth you know you're not ready to hear. The type that reminds you that sometimes living in the dark is better. Easier. Safer. Cowardly. "Where is she?" The words are a mix of a sob and unrestrained rage. "Tell me. Vincent, you tell me where my grandmother is!"

Valen's arms wrap around me from behind, his lips brushing over my ear as he hums softly, trying to calm me.

"There are a lot of things we still haven't told you, Bri," Vincent begins, his voice once again settled into its usual even rhythm. A soft haze washes over his features. The kind brother I've grown closer to over the past few weeks is staring back at me.

My patience is wearing thin. A vice is tightening around my heart, wondering where my grandmother is. She was never my blood. I knew that when I realized I couldn't be an Avalon. Still, that woman was mine. She was then, and she still is now, the only grandmother I've ever known. "Then you tell me now!" Another sob breaks free, the command that accompanied my words lost behind it.

"Not over the phone," he replies. No room for debate. No room for my disappointment either.

"Fine. Then we're coming to you. Dad, lower the wards so I can teleport onto the property."

That rustle comes again before Jorddan speaks. No doubt he'd taken the phone from Vincent. "No need. You are my blood. That is enough to earn you unrestricted access."

With a nod, I end the call, snatching my coat from the bed. "Are you coming?"

"Bri, we shouldn't..." Graham stutters.

"Are. You. Coming?" I practically growl, stopping an inch from his chest. Mine heaves, my cleavage pressing against the edge of the bra that's more uncomfortable than I care to admit.

Graham's eyes plead with me, but I don't care. He can do as he pleases. I told him that. "We shouldn't..."

I only nod, taking a step away from him, before stalking toward the door. The heat of Pierce and Valen at my back reinforces my confidence. Neither would ever allow me to venture off into the night alone. It doesn't matter that they likely think I'm insane. They have my back.

Graham does too. In his own way. I may never be his priority, and that's okay. That I can live with if it's his choice.

It's a quiet stomp through the building until we reach the main doors. "Not far that way," Pierce points ahead, "there's a little tree park. We can go from there." Linking his fingers through mine, chilled lips brush over my knuckles. The quiver forcing my eyes to meet his. There's only a slight upward tilt of the corners of his mouth before he leads the way.

The night air seems colder than it had been. Frigid cords of wind lashing at my cheeks as I fight against it. Each whip is a warning. My push against all that moves to oppose us will continue to be a painful one. It will beat me down, but I can't stop. I won't.

Fear seizes my heart, clutching it too tight for me to breathe. I'm terrified. Not just for me, but for my guys and my family. For my friends: Damian, Camilla, Collin, and all the others sequestered at Beauxgraton. There's no telling whether Roman will target them.

He might.

He might not.

Unlike him, we don't have spies on the inside. Merrick would have been our only option. Although he has given me no reason to distrust him, there's no other choice. We've all built up a wall between him and us. One that protects us. Should he prove to be a staunch ally, the wall may crumble.

Until then, he's being kept at arm's length. Even by me.

We can only hope the New Order soldiers hidden within Beauxgraton's walls will be enough. Students, professors, staff, watchers. They're my only hope. The single source I can rely on to protect the people I love when I can't be there. Janelle will do her best, too. She'll sacrifice until there's nothing left. If only she too weren't on the witness protection list.

Like Grandma Avalon, she means the world to me. A woman who has given so much of herself for me over the years. Too much. Her friendship with my grandmother bound her to me. Yet another weakness Roman will use against me if given the chance.

"Over here," Pierce tugs at our clasped fingers, Valen twirling a dagger in each hand, eyes narrowed on our surroundings.

There's no shortage of tourists and locals on the streets. The trees hide us from view at various angles, but not them. Their voices carry over the wind. Carefree laughter causing me to ache for the times when this wasn't my life.

"Be quick," Valen orders, a single dagger spelled away. Hidden somewhere on his person, for only him to see.

I only nod, linking my fingers through his, too. My eyes press shut, allowing my mind to empty of everything but the view of the lake behind the manor—my newest place of sanctuary without Beauxgraton.

The soft rush of the water and the gentle breeze brushing through the grass along its edge fill my mind. My heart swells thinking of home. The vision is born of memories, rather than my imagination, for once. A grin curving my lips just as that first pinch of discomfort hits me. Our molecules separate. Shredding apart as they teleport us from one place to the next.

How had my life been so simple, only to become this?

Simple is not living, Bri.

The thought filters to the forefront of my mind, just as my feet materialize in the frosted, tall grass, with Valen and Pierce at my sides.

My home shines in the distance. Each light is a beacon beckoning me forward. My essence is stirring beneath the surface, knowing Knox is nearby. He's here, and my body calls to him. Our essences clawing for our skin to touch as his tongue tangles with mine. He became my safe place for my words, my heart, and my secrets.

And Roman knows. He's known for months. Whatever plan he has for me is likely to be the same fate as Knox's. And I hate myself for putting him in that position.

He'd done just fine staying hidden before me. He lived a life of contentment. My essence and I ruined that. However, Knox would tell me differently.

He'd tell me we were inevitable. That he loves no longer being alone. That he wouldn't change a thing.

The list of other Grisyms who mean something to me runs through my mind. How many does Roman know about? Darryn and Misha—Merrick's chosen family. Janelle. My father.

How many of us will die for the light to remain on the pedestals, pretending they're untouchable?

Each horrid thought propels me forward at a quicker pace. I quickly make my way across the field toward the manor's rear entrance. A door I've never used, but which was often left open while our meals were being prepared.

Not even two hours ago, I'd felt wasted. Sobriety hit me like a brick once we arrived at the Cavea de Mors. Now I'm just scared, pissed, and tired.

I wish I knew the true nature of the relationship between my mother and Roman. In front of us, they performed as any other married couple who have spent a lifetime together. Those moments were infrequent due to their work schedules, though. A reality that made it easier to pretend they were something they weren't. We only caught glimpses of those moments of sparkling joy.

It was a show. Not for our benefit. It was just another deep-rooted deceit built on secrets and glitter-drenched lies.

But behind closed doors... That's the view I wish I had. Does she hold any hatred or resentment in her heart? She displayed no signs when they arrived at school after I had nearly killed that girl. She'd only expressed her apologies and love for my father, but never denounced Roman. Not once.

Could she possibly love him, too? Enough to choose, play both sides, or pick his?

"Fuck!" I shout into the night, my fingers catching in my knotted curls still hanging loose down my back.

My eyes shift back and forth, focused on the ground beneath my feet, as I search my memories. I never doubted my mother had feelings for Roman; it was just clear he was never the one who owned her heart, and now I know why. I know *who*.

She chose Roman over my father. A truth that brings my blood to a boil. I'd seen the clouds in her amber eyes at the mention of Jorddan. I'd watched her break and yearn for him, only for her to pretend she hadn't. She abandoned him and then kept my biological father away. No matter the threat, she had no right to keep me separated from *my* father and brother.

And if she doesn't have genuine feelings for Roman, why not leave? My half-siblings are now adults. There's no reason for her to stay anymore.

The front door groans as I shove it open, Knox rushing me, scooping me up into his arms. A yelp escapes me as my feet leave the ground before he sets me down again. His palm cups my face, mouth crashing to mine in such a frenzy I don't have time to react. Only when he pulls away does he seem to breathe, his forehead resting against mine. "You're okay." Relief floods through him, my essence stroking his in reassurance. "No one saw you?"

"No." I shake my head against his, our skin rubbing together uncomfortably before he pulls away.

"They're in the parlor," Knox points a thumb behind him, barely acknowledging Valen and Pierce.

My body melts into Knox's, his mouth resting against the crown of my head as we enter our designated meeting area. My father and brother immediately lock eyes with me, their postures tall, as they sit in the high-back wing chairs that border the fireplace.

Neither speaks as we move deeper into the room. Pierce and Valen choose their own seats while I perch on the edge of the table.

My elbows rest on my knees, staring into my father's gray eyes. "What do I need to know?" I'd debated how I was going to approach this as I neared our front steps. Is it better to confront him directly or cautiously circumvent every dark secret? The cavern of burdens inside me is growing heavier by the second. The weight is growing so heavy I might break.

"Who told you Davora wasn't buried in the Cavea de Mors?" Vincent leans forward, something like sadness blossoming behind his dual-colored eyes.

Leaning back, I swallow hard. "There's this guy we met today, Carter James."

"Is that the same guy you asked me to look into?" Knox questions, eyeing Valen. The bastard only grunts in response. They spoke tonight, and no one said anything?

What the hell is going on here?

"Go on," Vincent encourages.

"He said he wanted to show me something, then led me to the placard that had her name. I asked how he knew her. He only gave me some cryptic bullshit about knowing lots of things, and then he left me there alone. When my essence touched the stone, this voice filled my head. It repeated over and over and over again..." My words drift off before I whisper, "'Not here.'"

"That's all?" Vincent presses.

The corners of my mouth pull dangerously low. I'm tired of being kept in the dark. "Someone better tell me what the hell is happening?"

"She's not there," my brother confirms, our gazes locking. An emotion I can only compare to regret lingers in Vincent's distant stare.

Tears well up behind my eyes. "Where the hell is she?" Davora may not have been my biological grandmother, but she treated me as if she were. She showered me with love and cared for me as if I were her greatest treasure.

No matter how much time has passed, the memory of her body, stiff in death, tears me apart. The torrent of grief is ripping through me, leaving a path of destruction in its wake. Damage, I have to sift through and repair every single time. I miss her like I have missed no one in my life. Finding out that she isn't even buried where she should be guts me.

Grandma, you don't deserve this.

When I finally have the strength to look up again, Vincent's expression has changed; hope shines behind his light eye, the dark like a pit of hell. "She's not dead," I all but whisper. It's not a question. It's a feeling.

"No," he admits. "She's not."

"Where is my grandmother?" I snarl.

My father sits forward suddenly, his movement stealing my attention. "She is not your grandmother," Jorddan retorts. "I know you care for her, but it's best you do not know where she is. She is important to our cause."

"Fuck the cause. Where is she?" The first tear slithers down my cheek, hitting my thigh. That single droplet sounds thunderous in the room's silence. "I cried myself to sleep for years, missing her, and she wasn't even dead this whole time?"

"She was dead." Vincent clears his throat. "I brought her back about five years ago. As our father said, we needed her."

My brother's jaw works. In frustration or a silent plea. I don't know, and I don't care.

How could they keep this from me? I'd confessed how miserable I'd been without Davora. He knows how heartbroken I still am.

Still, my curiosity wins. My intestines are knotting; assumptions about what they needed her for come to mind. "For what?"

"Your future."

38

GRAHAM

REGRET SEEMS TO BE my new steady state. Before becoming friends with Bryony, I'd never had any. There was no baseline for me to compare to, and now it seems that's all I do every second of every day.

Every "what if" and "shoulda, woulda, coulda" taunts me. My fingers sink into my hair for the hundredth time, pulling to the point of pain.

I should have gone. I should have been there to support my best friend and girlfriend.

But my father's voice is always there. Every warning about following the rules is broadcast in my head on repeat. *Make the first best impression. Never cross too many boundaries. You can't afford to burn bridges. Prioritize yourself first because no one else will.*

But Bri does for all of us.

She thinks we don't know that she is doing everything in her power to protect us. To keep us from being involved in whatever shitstorm is catapulting our way.

My eyes screw shut as my father's words continue to play on repeat. *"You will abide by every procedure and mandate. You will not associate with anyone who can tarnish your reputation."*

If only he knew. My parents would skin me alive if they knew I bear Jorddan's name. The proud image they hold of me will be shattered once they learn that I pledged allegiance to him because of his daughter.

Those seven letters seem to burn against my skin just thinking of his name. A name I had called out months ago when Roman took me hostage, but he never came.

I try not to think my choice has fucked up my future. That my decisions regarding the company I keep have either signed my death warrant or kept me from fulfilling my purpose. It's already clear my blinders are often on when it comes to Bri.

In a hierarchy such as ours, there are no opportunities for a retry. We don't get second chances to climb the ranks. You get one. Just one chance to excel during your education and prove you have what it takes to hold a position of worth in the wielding world.

My regret outweighs any promises I made to my parents now. Those gigantic eyes had pleaded with me before I let my woman walk out the door.

You should have gone.

What if something happens to them?

Then you'd be in trouble too, dumbass!

I scowl, knowing I am talking to myself.

Fortunately, Pierce's roommate still hasn't returned. Glancing at my watch, it's almost three in the morning. Though Bri didn't think he'd return soon, I'm not sure I want to be here when he does. We don't know these people. I'm not sure I want to.

Checking my phone, there's nothing from Pierce, Valen, or Bri. Knox and Vincent have been equally silent. There's not a single sign confirming they made it safely. Though I suspect Knox or her brother would have reached out if they had never arrived.

"Shit!" Everything about these past few weeks is so fucked.

If anything happens to them, I'll blame myself. It'll be an unforgiving beratement of my cowardice and my need to please my parents. It'll be my fault because I stayed behind.

Finally settling on the edge of Pierce's bed, I let my head fall back, nervous energy coursing through me. I should do something. I have to do something.

I'd barely settled before shooting to my feet, my movements are so quick that a hit of dizziness throws my balance before I shake it off. I exit the room and damn near jog through the residence hallways before letting myself into the first library that catches my attention.

Here I can be helpful. Here, I can prove my worth. If only it were for me.

William Danvers is clearly going to be a thorn in our side. Any additional information we can find about him and his family may be helpful. Valen's mention of rumors comes to mind. It had drawn a response out of Knox. One that makes me believe there's something more just under the surface.

Body snatchers. A reference I never thought I'd hear outside of Hollywood, but here we are, potentially facing the reality of wielders powerful enough to take any shape or form.

Using my mind is the best I can do. Gather what I can and share it with the group. Maybe we'll find an advantage in this war. A war that's sure to end in nothing but bloodshed and heartbreak.

With a groan, the massive double doors swing open on their own, a sharp breath sucked in, eyes wide, taking in the sight before me. Beauxgraton's libraries were amongst the most impressive I'd entered, but this is ethereal. The decor is the perfect Gothic mix of academia and a mad scientist's lab. Walls full of shelves of history and trinkets of the past, mixed in with the endless tomes.

I strain my neck upward, yet it's as if my vision fails me. The steepled ceiling is too far for me to appreciate from where I stand. Not as the five stories of full shelves stare back at me. In a world full of leather, ink, and pages, I could easily lose myself.

"How?" I breathe.

There's no one here to answer my question. No one is present to witness gasp after gasp as I rake my gaze over the space. The chamber must stretch well past where old palace roofs end, yet from outside, nothing mirrors what I'm witnessing.

"It's a cloaking spell," a soft voice sounds next to me.

A woman with long straight black hair and eyes to match stands beside me. Her head tilted up, like mine, limbs crossed over her chest, smiling at the ceiling. Having just arrived, I had never seen her before. A point that gives me no pause. Yet, she seems to have appeared out of nowhere. Her sudden presence as if she wanted to be seen.

"Sorry, I didn't think anyone else would be here," I mumble.

Her head tilts to the side as she studies me, that same close-lipped smile holding steady as if unable to break its position. "This is my favorite place," she whispers. Narrow dark eyes rove over the space as if I should have guessed that.

She reminds me of what I imagine nostalgia would look like. A fondness that remains. Its warm embrace nestled inside you long after the years had come and gone. It's as if your heart settles and the world around you becomes bearable because you have this memory. This moment. This thing in your heart that means everything to you, and likely nothing to the person beside you.

Reaching my hand toward her, I pull my own welcoming grin. "Graham Mayer."

She stares down at my hand. Dark, wild, wavy hair curtains her face as she once again cocks her head to the side. Her expression is strange. Her demeanor suggests that she lacks social interaction. "My name is Raven Heroux, third year."

"I'm a first. I transferred from Beauxgraton this semester to study abroad." Raven only stares at me, those big black eyes appearing like endless wells of nothing. Where Jorddan's black eyes seem to convey so much, there's nothing in hers.

Those are the eyes of the dead. But she can't be. She's here talking to me.

"America?" She says the word as if testing it. Based on the absence of a detectable accent, I guessed she too was from there. Perhaps I assumed wrong. Maybe it's hidden. There are plenty who can mimic another's vocal nuances as easily as they breathe.

"Yes. And you?" I dip my head, trying to refocus her stare on me. The roaming of her eyes over the space causes the hairs at the nape of my neck to tingle. It's as if she's looking for something, or maybe it's someone. Either way, it's unnerving.

"Here. I was born right here." She stomps her foot as if signaling it was this exact spot.

My brow scrunches low. This is weird. She's weird, sending goosebumps skittering over my skin as the hair stands tall at the nape of my neck. Plus, I have work to do. "That's cool. It was nice meeting you." I take a step back, ready to end this odd encounter. "Have a great night."

I turn away from her, meandering toward the rear of the library. My quick pace is likely making me look ridiculous. But I don't care. Not when I am trying to get away.

A sudden rush of air whooshes past my face, then three more, before I spin to face the direction it was traveling in, ragged breaths leaving my chest pumping wildly. Raven stands right where I left her, four books piled in her hands and that same disarming smile on her face. "This is what you're looking for."

She holds her arms forward, the books stacked perfectly, spines facing me. Each one lined up as if someone had taken meticulous effort to do so.

"How did you—"

That smile widens, but she never reveals her teeth. "Here. Take them." Her arms stretch further, but she doesn't move from her spot.

Inching back toward her, I slowly slide the books from her grasp, backing away several steps before I turn away toward the closest table. When I glance back over my shoulder to see if she is following, Raven is gone. The spot is vacant as if she had never been there. But she was. I saw her. I spoke to her. "Raven," I call out into the otherwise empty library, but there's no response.

Tearing my gaze away from the spot she'd been, I sit at the closest table, opening the first book on rare gifts.

The author divided the book into three sections: light, dark, and other.

Other.

It doesn't explicitly state Grisyms, but what "other" would there be? Every other wielder, to my knowledge, neatly falls into dark or light. There's been no debate about that.

Since magical creatures, such as ghouls, do not qualify as wielders, this book does not include them. The law does not consider creatures wielders, no matter their level of advancement. Always destined to exist beneath us on the food chain. They are a source of earthly power, nothing more.

As light wielders, we're taught that siphoning power from magical creatures is disgusting. It's ingrained in us just how disgraceful the extrinsic dark wielders are for doing so. Although the teaching influenced me to think that way, my feelings never quite aligned with it. Sure fucking ghouls is the crudest way in which to siphon power, but there are other animals where you can drain their venom, drink their blood, extract pieces of them like nails or hair to siphon power through potions and spells.

I've only ever siphoned magic from objects. It was the rule in my home and what I have always abided by.

I've never seen Bri with that ghoul, but I can see it so clearly. Her body spread wide, welcoming the beast as it rutted into her. I know she enjoys it. She said as much. Part of me wonders what it would be like. How liberated would I feel in the end?

Flipping to the index, my finger runs down the page looking for Amovea. Those who can shift. Not in the traditional sense of the paranormal, such as animals or werewolves. It references those who can change their features as their gift. Several charms exist with equal effect, but an Amovea's ability is unique, like a fine-tuned fork that vibrates at a very specific frequency.

William would have to be a powerful one if Knox's reaction meant anything. Spells and potions don't last indefinitely. He would need constant access to the wielder who has developed that kind of spellwork skill.

That type of spellcasting is not a common ability that many focus on. Similar paths, such as medicine or human doctorates, require years of training. An endless line of practice to hone your techniques that follows you for a lifetime. A false move could leave a wielder permanently altered.

William Danvers comes from a long line of accomplished wielders. Like Avalons, the Danvers name remains prominent. Though none of them are known active Amovea. They aren't shifters. Like Eistiabs, it's a gift that seems to have died out over time, though both should have remained potent in strong bloodlines, passed down from generation to generation.

William's father had been a powerful telekinetic, and his mother's specialty was extraction. She could remove impurities from the body, as well as from magical objects and animals. She once worked with Bri's mom, though that ended well before Mrs. Danvers died.

William's uncle, Archibald Daniels—his mother's elder brother—still sits on the council. One of the five chairs chosen to be responsible for the final votes that govern our world. Our laws.

There was a time shortly before William's parents tragically died, when Archibald disappeared. The reminder that Knox had mentioned something about William impersonating him suddenly resurfaces in my consciousness.

If he's an Amovea, he would be able to. He could mimic form, structure, speech, and demeanor with ease.

Finally locating the chapter, I swiftly flip through the pages until I find the proper section. How Raven had known this is precisely what I needed is beyond me. I hadn't mentioned anything, and I doubt she can read minds. But it's possible. I felt too nervous with her to recall why I'd come here.

My eyes dart over the words on the page, every single one confirming William could have, in fact, impersonated his uncle and could have changed his appearance so completely now.

Then, the floor seems to drop out from beneath me.

The most historically significant Amovea bloodlines in history have been the Thunnis, Cumberlands, Zepoply, and Danvers. Their bloodlines have proven to stand the test of time.

The air in my lungs refuses to move. We knew his lineage had a history of Amovea, but according to this, these four families are different. There are a handful of gifts considered "timeless" as they date back to the most ancient bloodlines. They are powers that continue to be present in offspring through the generations and are thereby considered the most potent.

Amovea and Eistiabs are two of the gifts that have historically been on that list, though Bri is the first documented one we've seen in centuries. If the Amovea gifts have truly continued down the Danvers line and been kept hidden, there's no telling what William could do or who he might be. Not when he's had a lifetime to refine his talents.

Shit. How do we find someone who could be anyone at any time?

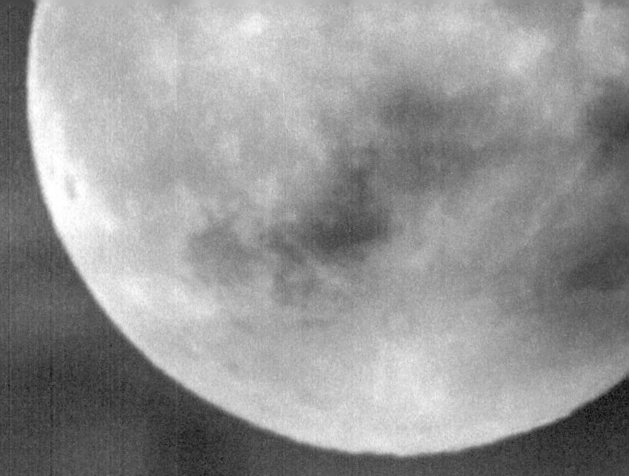

39

BRYONY

MY MOLARS GRIND, FIGHTING to hold back the outburst threatening to break free. But I can't. I won't. Everyone in my life has excelled at keeping secrets from me. I'm kept on the outside for "my protection." *Bullshit!*

I'm not some fragile vase that will shatter if I know the truth. It may take me a moment to process, but I'll handle it. I've always had to handle the burdens that come with what I am.

For once, the pain outweighs the fury. My insides are tearing themselves to ribbons against the sharp points of their lies. No, not lies. Omissions. They let me pour my heart out. The countless tears I shed reminiscing over my time with Grandma Avalon and how the loss of her still sat with me like a festering wound that refused to heal. Wounds that continue to ooze and are relentlessly throbbing with just enough of an ache that you couldn't ignore them.

Still, they. Said. Nothing.

Assholes!

"Five years? Five years! Five. Years." There's no stopping the repetition of those two words. The more times they pass my lips, each inflection different from the last, does nothing to make it seem any more real. It does nothing to absolve the hurt they caused. It does nothing to erase the past.

Sixty months, over 1800 days, and countless hours she has been alive and breathing, yet I never knew. Just one more thing they have stolen from me. Time is the one thing we can never get back. There's no earning more with good deeds or revisiting the past. I lost decades, and they can't even attempt to look remorseful. Do they even care, or is the finish line for the Grisym mission more important than healing my soul?

"She is hidden away and spell-locked. She couldn't have come to see you, sweetheart." My father's voice pulls my watery gaze back up to him.

"She could have... told me." Pain tears through my chest. Was she simply another person in my life who pretended to love me, out of obligation or for their benefit?

How many pretended to care about me all these years, but didn't. I've never questioned my brother or father. They've shown me what I mean to them. Until now. Is this just a cliché revenge plot? Payback for Roman's misdeeds and my mother's disloyalty. Is Davora Avalon their pawn?

My trusted circle seems to be contracting around me. The list of those I can allow complete vulnerability with is shrinking with my every breath. It's wearing on me. Breaking me down to the point I fear I'll never stand again. My patience is wearing thin with the secrets and its-for-your-own-good crap. I get to decide what I can and can't handle. Me. No one else. Not anymore.

We all have a breaking point, and I'm teetering on the edge of mine. One feather-light touch and I'm going over. Maybe I'll save myself, but it's more likely jagged rocks await my fall below.

"I can promise you will see her soon. But not yet. Not now." Jorddan's hand finds my knee, and I want to believe what he says. In my heart, I do. My essence stirs as if reassuring me he speaks the truth, even though I'm unsure if I ought to believe it.

Jorddan has yet to lie to me about anything I've asked. There was never any doubt he omitted plenty. A villainous mastermind set out to restructure an entire world will always have information that only lives with them. Not everyone will know the details. That's how plans fail. That's how dreams and ambition die.

Take a deep breath, Bri. You can trust Jorddan. You can trust Vincent. They care. It's not a lie or manipulation.

Even as I say the words to myself, I throw in some extra bass. Extra conviction, so maybe I can wholeheartedly believe it instead of listening to the whisper of doubt.

"I've met her, Bri. She's a brilliant woman. She misses you," Pierce supplies. Pivoting in my seat, my eyes meet his denim-blue stare. He'd kept this from me, too. Had everyone kept me in the dark? To what end?

"Why wouldn't you have told me upfront about her? You clearly knew what she meant to me," I whimper.

My shoulders sag forward. I'm so tired. So hurt and lost. Grandma Avalon was my safe place growing up, until she wasn't. Until I had to find safety elsewhere. Sometimes Merrick. Always Janelle.

"You are my daughter, and I love you more than life itself, but I had to confirm your allegiance to me, did I not?" Jorddan speaks calmly as if the answer is so plain. When he states it like that, it makes all the sense in the world.

Like any other Grisym, my father needed to assure my devotion to him. Words mean nothing without proof. Without action they are as empty as a used jar tossed into a trash can.

My proof was that night at Beauxgraton. I'd stood tall at his side with no need for embellished bravado. I felt it that night. His love and protection. Our connection and my heart knew without a doubt that I would never leave my biological father's side. Never again. They'll have to kill me to rip us apart. Him too, I'm sure. Jorddan, too, witnessed it that evening.

That night seems eons away now. Just over two weeks, yet it seems like ten lives have passed since. We wish we could forget that night. But we can't. Every action has a consequence. My impulsivity has left us in a very compromising situation. The targets on our backs are glowing brighter because of me.

For a while, I convinced myself that one night changed my whole life, but it didn't. It goes back to my mother's choices when I was a baby, my grandmother's sacrifice and subsequent revival, my attendance at Beauxgraton, and involvement with men I should have steered clear of. The quiet existence I suffered isn't the future I envisioned.

"I understand that, but I think I've made it pretty clear I am with you. With all of you." My arm whips through the air as if presenting every follower behind me. They're not here. Yet, that makes my words no less accurate. "You should have trusted me."

"You're right," my father says, leaning back in his armchair and crossing his legs. "You want the truth, do you not?" I nod. "Then listen closely."

I nod again, settling into my spot, my stomach dropping with every confession from my father. The history, turmoil, and injustice revealed churns my stomach. Thick acrid bile creeps up my throat as I listen to more and more of this horrid story, my hand clapping over my mouth in case my body chooses to expel everything inside me.

When my father finishes, I'm on my feet. "Thank you. That's all I ever wanted. The truth."

"That's all?" he questions.

"And to be loved for me," I confess. Leaning over him, I hug him close. "Thank you, Dad."

Without another word, I exit the parlor. Only my forced deep breaths and the soft tap of my shoes over the foyer floors and up the stairs to the bedroom accompany me. No one follows. No one says a word.

Weights pull at my limbs as numbness fills my body. Even my essence refuses to stir, paralyzed by Jorddan's revelations. Every atrocity is true. Every rumor held not an ounce of fabrication. My father just admitted that to me. He's the morally gray villain, whose every action was in the name of a better tomorrow. Every death, torment, and illegal dealing meant to protect his Grisym children and their future. In his eyes, his actions don't even scratch the surface of the wrongs that people have done against us. He may be right. He *is* right, but it doesn't change what he's done. It doesn't erase the fact that he holds no remorse and will continue on this path until they kill us all or the desired outcome presents itself.

The list I provided is just a continuation of that legacy. Every soul who has witnessed my magic at Roman's request will die because of me. It's not a matter of can I live with it. As with my past, there's no other choice. Instead, it's letting those deaths sit on my conscience and not collapsing under their weight.

Whether I am the one who steals their last breath or not, I will carry them with me until I take mine.

The term narcissist describes Roman perfectly. Even when he was still my dad and I loved him, I would have said the same. One could only describe a man consumed by power, image, and the pursuit of self-promotion as such. But we all have flaws. That was his.

The corner of my mouth twitches, eager to grin at that small bit of fortune. Should Roman expose us, it'll be with self-declared assurance that he'll be immune to the consequences. Protection only the council chairs or the bureau director have the power to grant him.

I'm numb as I reach my bedroom, shoving open the door carelessly while my thoughts scramble in my head.

So much has happened since I started attending Beauxgraton. Wielding school was supposed to be some of the simplest years of our lives. Knowing my origins, hardship was always part of the life agenda. I accepted that. I prepared for every wielder who might come against me, but never did I picture it being the man who raised me. Not when my only crime was being a Grisym, who matured ten years early, and had no other specific gifts than teleporting.

It's one thing to be an anomaly, but I wasn't special—or so I thought. I never imagined I was a rare wielder, one no one had seen in perhaps half a millennium. An Eistiab. Hell, I might as well have been a fucking myth. Yet, my gift had been presenting itself my whole life. It was in plain view, and Jorddan was the only one who realized it. A man forced to keep away from his only daughter, his youngest.

That anger revives alongside the hurt. My body is in constant turmoil, and I'm so tired of it. It's exhausting.

The blinders are off. Now the truth lies bare at my feet, and I'm terrified of what will come.

A sharp knock sounds at the door. An exaggerated sigh leaves me as I slowly spin on my heel, my brows arching high. Knox leans against the doorframe with one ankle crossed over the other. His hair is wavy and disheveled as that sexy smirk pulls at the corner of his mouth. The new, longer length of his beard almost hides it. "Want some company?"

"Come in," I gesture him forward, his strides carrying him straight to me.

Ass resting on the edge of the bed, though I don't remember sitting, I let my head fall to his shoulder as he perches beside me. When his cheek hits the side of my head, we sigh in unison. My insides are calm now that we're reunited with their other half.

"That was... a lot." His voice is lower than usual. A sign he must be feeling what I am. It's an endless swarm of emotions and information to parse through every day. Though I'm not alone, so often it feels like I am.

"It was." I shake my head as if confused about how we got here. Truthfully, I am. "Did your father ever threaten to expose you?" I ask. Knox has told me plenty, but talking about his childhood years with his father and stepmother isn't a topic he broaches often.

"Yes." His head bows between his shoulders, my palm flattening on his back, rubbing tight circles. "Most of them were empty threats. You know, the kinds of things parents say to keep their children in line. But there was one occasion when he meant it. We'd been at a family gathering, and I was hanging out with the other kids in the backyard. The game we were playing required you to battle someone else with your essence. At the time, he was still trying to impress my stepmother. He wanted me to be this perfect child, not the standoffish one I often was out of fear of someone finding out I was different. Long story short, I did the wrong thing, said the wrong thing. I was single-handedly ruining my father's life by being a Grisym. The next day, he took me to Council headquarters, signed me in, and requested that the Council hear us."

A gasp leaves me knowing what that would have meant. Immediate death. Not just for Knox but for his father, too. "Wynston..."

He softly shakes his head. Those waves are shifting across his forehead and into his eyes as if trying to shield him from view. His hair is longer now. I hadn't quite noticed it, too distracted by everything else to appreciate him like I'd done last semester during our stolen moments in the cabin.

"While we sat there and waited, wielder after wielder exited the chamber. He didn't pay attention to any of them until a young mother exited, covered in blood, her stomach still swollen as if she'd recently given birth. She was crying uncontrollably, barely stumbling with each step forward, mourning her now dead baby. The only reason they let her live is because her husband claimed the dark wielder who got her pregnant raped her. He was her lover. Also killed right in front of her alongside their baby."

Knox goes silent for a moment, his eyes shifting side to side as if searching for answers. Truths that shouldn't have been so clear at that age. I keep my hand moving in circles, not to force more out of him, but to let him know I'm here. He's been a rock for me so much this year. My spirit sinks knowing I don't have the energy to be his tonight. But I can be here. I can listen if he wants to talk. "You don't have to keep going."

"Yes, I do," he sucks in an exaggerated breath, moving from my side to crawl to the opposite edge of the bed, patting the spot next to him. "Come here." There's no hesitation in lying beside him, our essences humming beneath the skin at the closeness of our bodies. "He'd told me we went home that day because he would not enter a blood and guts-stained room." A humorless laugh leaves him. "I knew better, though, so I made it my mission to be small. I stayed out of the way. All I had to do was be a great son until I could leave and never look back. Before you, Kellerman was the best thing that ever happened to me." He brushes a stray curl off my face. "You show me I don't have to shrink to protect what I am."

His mouth lowers close to mine, the softest brush lighting up my insides.

My words are whispered against his full lips, "How could I when that's how I lived too?"

The warmth of his forehead pressing to mine causes me to suck in a sharp breath before he responds. "But you didn't. Living a lie isn't the same as trying to make yourself so invisible you cease to exist."

My heart aches with his words. I struggle to picture young Knox forcing himself into the shadows, cowering behind the fear of his father's threats, doing everything in his power not to get dragged back to the council chamber. How could a child survive under that weight throughout the years?

At least it was never a serious threat in my house. Roman told Harley under no circumstances, and he obeyed. Harley has always bowed to Roman's every whim. Pity fills me when thinking of my half-brother's wife. A woman I've only met once. She's stuck with that asshole for life. If Roman won't let my mother walk away, I have no doubt Harley would ever allow his wife to do so either.

Knox's lips brush mine again, pulling me back to the present. "I need you," I whisper.

"How?" he questions, grazing kisses along my jaw.

"Everything," I breathe just as the first stream of essence flows past my lips.

It seems like ages since the two of us have been together, our essences mixing and becoming their own new creation. Apart, we are Grisyms, mixtures of the light and the dark, but together we are something different. Together, we are powerful. Unstoppable. New.

Knox's hands roam over my body as our essences swirl through the room, his onyx and mine ebony with its usual speckling of stars. I worried I would lose the beauty as I continued to absorb new essences. But it hasn't. It is the same, only internally we are different. We are more.

"I've missed you," he breathes against my throat, his cool palms slipping beneath the low-cut collar of my top, eager to squeeze my pliant flesh. A single finger plays along the edge of my bra, dipping beneath the cup to tease my nipple. A hiss slips past my parted lips as he flicks the hardened peak. The pain preceding all the pleasure I know will come with having him inside me.

Knox has always felt like he was made for me. Our bonding was inevitable. *Bonding.*

The word rings through my head like an alarm bell. Paranormal creatures who have fated mates come to mind, it's as if the same has become true for Knox and me. Our magical response to one another is rare. Vincent claims that merging essences should be impossible. Others have used wielders as "vessels," but the power dynamic skewed the relationship—one was weak, the other strong. It doesn't work any other way, not like Knox and me. We both harbor a great deal of power in our veins. Using another like any other curated storage tool shouldn't be possible between us.

It makes me wonder if we have something similar to a mate bond or if we are just two anomalies. Others like us might exist. We lived under the radar, so why couldn't they?

According to my father, there are more Grisyms than the Council could imagine. The degree of our mixture varies. Any mix at all makes you a Grisym, whether it's only a drop of the opposite type of wielder or half of your blood.

"Stay with me," Knox croons as his tongue flicks over my exposed lower stomach. The button on my jeans is already undone, the zipper resting at the bottom of its jagged pathway.

"You can tease me later. I need to feel you," I breathe, yanking him up by the shirt, only to tear it over his head. He chuckles as I toss it aside before flicking his wrist, my door shutting so quietly I can almost pretend I never heard or saw it.

The vibration of his chuckle against my lower stomach makes me squirm. His lips brush my skin, tickling me as he speaks. "Bryony, we're going to have to spend a lot of time apart these next few months. Can't you just let me enjoy worshipping your body before I make you come all over my cock?"

"No, please, Knox. Can't you feel it?" I whine. Our essences are growing impatient with us. They want him buried inside me as much as I do. His hips pumping hard and fast, while I chant his name like a prayer, as our essences dance around us.

Knox doesn't answer me, shucking his pants and dragging mine down my legs. "Keep quiet, he smiles against my lips." That wicked grin is so intoxicating I don't realize our clothes are gone with a snap of his fingers before he enters me in a single thrust and my world goes black.

40

WYNSTON

MY VISION GOES BLACK as I seat myself inside Bri. Instinct tells me to move. Our bodies creating a rhythm that could only belong to soul-connected beings. My flesh knows Bri's as well as my own. Our essences are celebrating the opportunity to blend once again. Our connection goes beyond thought. It's innate. Primal.

I'd remain here every second of every day. For the rest of my life, I would stay buried inside this woman. My cock thrusting in and out of her tight pussy as if she were made for me. Her walls flutter around me as our magic twirls through the room with glee. We're whole again.

Ecstasy roars through my veins as I move inside her. My hips rolling, drawing out each powerful stroke. The bite of her nails against my skin makes me hiss. My teeth clenching more forcefully than before, a mix of pleasure and pain. It's bliss. It's everything.

"Bri," I call her name, though I see nothing but the black of night.

"Knox... I can't—" her voice sounds so far away, but I feel her right here with me. Her thick thighs are stronger after Tosch tortured her for almost a week. They squeeze tight around my hips, keeping my body close to hers. My weight is sure to crush her in time, but she loves it; she always has.

It's as if her words project all around me, but are also blocked by an invisible barrier, muffling the syllables as they pass her pouty lips. My name sounds distant and distorted as she repeats it like a prayer, but she's right here. She's right in front of me, with our sweat-coated chests pressed together. Her warm breath washes over my already heated skin, causing the nerve endings to fire uncontrollably. My teeth sink into her skin as I softly bite the space between her throat and shoulder, drawing out her sultry moan.

Yet, I still see nothing. Every sensation is an all-consuming combination of sound, touch, and scent. Her arousal causes me to inhale deeply as I drive into her harder. Her moans vibrate through me, her demands for more serving as the most glorious music to my ears. "Just listen to my voice. You can feel me, right?" I growl against her sweat-slick throat.

"Yes," she breathes, her torso arching high as I pull out to the tip just to push back in. "Just like that," she moans.

I have no idea what's happening. We're both accustomed to our eyes shifting. It's second nature. Even the eerie onyx she often adopts now has become normal. But not once have we ever lost our vision.

Still, her body responds to me. Sight isn't necessary when I can feel her walls flutter around me and her nails dig into my bare back. "You missed me," I growl.

"We did," she purrs. Her fingers sink into my wild hair, tightening around the strands before she brings my mouth down to hers. Our tongues duel, warring for dominance, taking everything, needing and wanting more. I let her control the moment while I drive into her, my blood racing through my veins as our essences vortex through the room. The once uncontrolled rage it once exhibited is absent. Our magic cocoons us in, protecting the merging of our bodies as if it's promoting our creation of something good and new.

There's no way I could count how many times we've had sex. It's not something I would catalog. Not after I had her the first time. Still, this might very well be a novel experience. This time is different. Life-altering even.

Each instance with Bryony feels fresh, like a new journey through rolling seas. She's ever-changing. Which means the way our essences interact does too. It was a thought I had brushed aside; the differences being so minimal that I chalked them up to distraction. The combination of us is never the same after she's taken in a new essence. I'm as much changed as she is.

A groan leaves her as her hips buck high. My thrusts sync with the movement, driving me impossibly deeper into her greedy pussy. *Fuck*, I will never get enough of her. Every fiber of my being will never stop craving this woman beneath me.

In a single swift motion, I pull free of her, an immediate cold washing through me at no longer being connected to her. Our essences stop, hovering above us, poised as if ready to attack. They wait, the tendrils sniffing out our surroundings. It's as if they whisper to me, questioning why I would stop fucking the woman beneath me.

"On your knees." I can feel the shift of her movement, but still can't see her. Instead, I sense her. And it hits me—we haven't lost our vision. We've gained the advantage of the ghouls. They don't see either, but they sense. They feel and allow the sensors in their eyes to guide them. It's their window to the wielders who come to them, seeking their power.

With each passing day, we take on new characteristics. Tiny glimmers of everything my woman is becoming flash before my eyes. Those traits cycling through me with her stored essence.

Grabbing hold of her hips, the thick head of my cock notches at her entrance. Her warm arousal coating my skin, soaking me in what I do to her. Her muscles pulsing in anticipation of me filling her again. It takes everything in me to hold still for just another moment. To let those senses flare and take her in. The feel of her skin, the pump of her chest, and the way those full lips are parted.

I close my eyes, breathing her in, trying to memorize the feel of this moment and her heated flesh. She connected with parts of herself without even knowing she had them. Jorddan mentioned that what he did to her at fifteen has something to do with ghoul magic, but he refuses to divulge the whole truth to me. It only explains her connection to them. Her ability to command them. And potentially why we are now experiencing "sight" the way they do.

"Harder, Knox," Bri moans. Her ass pushes back into me so forcefully that we shift down the bed.

My fingers dig into her hips. A grip so tight I'm sure there will be bruises tomorrow. "Grab on," I grunt.

"To what?"

Once again, I can sense her movement as if I can see it firsthand. The twist of her torso back toward me with the sultry gray and green eyes peering at me over her shoulder. Running the tip of my nose along her spine, a shudder runs through her body, my cock twitching with excitement. "Are you looking at me?"

"Yes," she breathes.

A grin quirks at the corner of my mouth. The words to adequately describe the sensations flowing through me won't come. "Hang on to the headboard, Bryony."

She leans forward, my dick almost popping free of her slick pussy, only for me to drive into her again. Our pace is frantic. The speed at which our combined essences move through the room matches our ragged breaths and pounding hearts. Furniture and decor topple over, sure to leave a mess that I won't have the energy to clean without my magic.

Despite the shattering glass and wood splinters flying through the room, Bri is my only focus. The feel of her walls squeezing me tight, and the sounds she makes as the clap of our skin reverberates off the walls. I didn't barrier her room, so if her brother is in his, he'll hear. He'll know I don't give a fuck what he thinks about the two of us together.

Bri is mine and Val's, Pierce's, and Graham's. Ours to cherish, fuck and... *No*, I'm not going there. Not right now. Not when she feels this good, and my wayward thoughts will ruin the moment.

Not when she's moaning my name, still looking over her shoulder at me.

"Fuck, Knox. I'm—" Her walls squeeze me tight, her fingers brushing my cock as I slip in again, hard, fast circles pressed against her clit. Her body convulses beneath me. Her breathing is so sharp and shallow I worry she'll pass out, but she doesn't. She only pushes back into me harder.

They say the light gives and the dark takes. With us, that's true. We are both. We give and we take in equal measure. Our contributions building atop one another as we barrel toward the pleasure at the end of the tunnel.

"That's right, take it. Fuck me until you make yourself come." The words tumble out of my mouth. They don't feel like mine, but they are. I've become feral for this woman, and I want all of her, even though I've accepted I have to share her. "That's my girl. Come for me."

Her orgasm barrels through her seconds later. Her walls pulsing so intensely, I can't hold back my release. The truth of what she does to me spills inside her, fills her, and drips out around us. Still, my body refuses to stop moving. My hips flex in a slow, languid rhythm as I draw out the high, stretching out the moment in hopes it never ends.

Ragged breaths fill my lungs as we collapse onto the bed. Our limbs are still partially tangled, and my cum is dripping down her inner thighs. Bri's hand runs along my cheek, her thumbs brushing over the exposed skin, while her palm runs along my short beard. "Close your eyes," she whispers. "I want to see your face."

I'm not sure what she means, but I do as she says, pressing my lids shut for brief seconds before opening them again. When I do, it's her face. I committed every detail to memory long ago. Sage-greenish gray eyes, freckles splattered from cheek to cheek, a straight nose, and that breathtaking smile parting her full lips.

"How did you know I'd be able to see again when I opened my eyes?" I ask, pulling her closer to me. A sigh breezes past my lips as she nuzzles into my chest.

"I willed it."

Her answer is simple. Straightforward.

She willed it?

What the fuck does that even mean? I want to ask, but her eyelids are already fluttering, and I need to get her cleaned up before she falls asleep. "Let's take a quick shower and then you need some rest. I'll take you back to school tomorrow."

She nods before whispering. "What if I didn't go back?"

"Bri," I sigh. "You know exactly why that isn't an option."

She only nods, a slow, resigned motion that breaks my heart. It was a scenario we had once discussed. Was her safety worth her returning to an institution? We decided it was. That it might actually be the next safest way to protect her besides locking her away in this manor or another secure location. No matter her allegiance, the wielding community still believes she is Roman's little girl.

She is still the daughter of the most powerful man in our education system. An abrupt departure from her schooling would draw unwanted attention. There would be questions no one wants to answer publicly. Sadly, Bri cannot vanish into the shadows. That's not an option she'll ever have.

Suspicious wielders dig. They'll probe into every dark crevice, searching for the secrets we've tried to hide. They're relentless in their search for answers. It's in our nature.

The moment they find anything that is even remotely set apart from the norm, they'll draw their own conclusions. Assumptions that could get people killed. They'll talk, sharing information that they likely haven't even confirmed as fact. It'll come back to haunt us. It will ruin everything. Should we get to that point, I'm not sure I can protect her. An internal admission that breaks my heart. The balance is too delicate to be tipped unnecessarily. The risk is too great.

Bri doesn't know I am the one who pushed for her to return to school. Janelle and Jorddan were both in favor of hiding her away. They fought nonstop about it, though, per usual, they were on the same side.

Janell has shown how protective she is of Bri. Protection Jorddan doesn't appreciate, want, or need for his daughter. It's a double-edged sword. It's easy to see Janelle did what she thought was helpful, encouraging Roman to send her to Beauxgraton, where she could watch out for her, but to Jorddan, all she did was work alongside the one person who kept him away from his daughter.

I suspect there is something more involving the tension between the two, but it's not my business. Not unless it endangers Bri. Then I can't have it.

I wish I could say it was solely because of her, but it's me, too. It's being a Grisym. I, too, still live in fear of being captured. They'd cage me only long enough to execute. While my family serves no other role than distant acquaintances, I don't want to see their deaths. It would be blood on my hands, though I am not the one who created me. And as much as my family is just a fixture in my life, I don't want death for them either. The witch hunt wouldn't end there. It would extend to everyone I've ever known, since I'm so much older. They would get the answers they wanted. Determine who knew and who didn't. It would be equivalent to a massacre. I couldn't live with that guilt.

Bri leans against the shower wall as the water washes over her. Those beautiful curls I've become obsessed with are coming to life under the spray. "Are you okay?" I ask, pulling her into my chest.

She wraps her arms around me, releasing a slow, shuddering breath. Her essence stirs beneath our skin, every emotion rolling through us. "I'm scared."

Pulling back, I run my hands along the sides of her head, brushing her wet strands back. "I won't let anything happen to you. We're here to protect you and each other."

"Not about that. I'm not scared of what Roman will do or the Council. I'm scared of what I can do."

My eyes meet hers, waiting for her to continue. I can only assume she means the many ways her essence has gone haywire lately, but assumptions are dangerous. Assumptions will get you locked up or killed. I can't afford to make a mistake with her.

"What do you mean?" I ask softly.

"I keep thinking about Yorgan. About what I did to him. Most days, I can convince myself I did the right thing." She nods absently as if once again attempting to convince herself. "But..." Her pause draws me in closer, my thumb stroking over her bare skin. "It was so easy for me to slip into the dark and kill him." Her gaze casts downward, her eyes darting back and forth beneath her eyelids as if the shower floor will have answers for her. "Then what I did tonight with our eyes... What am I really capable of, Knox?"

I don't know how to answer that question, so I only place a soft kiss on her lips before grabbing a sponge and handing it to her. We wash in silence before towel-drying ourselves and climbing into bed naked. "We should probably put something on," I whisper into her hair.

"No. I need to feel you. I'm calmer when my skin is against yours. You are my muffler."

Those words drape over me like a heavy blanket, a memory of an old text dancing on the outskirts of my brain. If only I could remember exactly what it was.

41

BRYONY

MY BODY JOLTS AWAKE to the roar of shouting. The shriek of a female voice echoes through the manor. At first, confusion clouds my mind, immediately jumping to the conclusion that Camilla is being harmed. Only for the reality of my surroundings to remind me she isn't here. There's only one other female in this house. *Tosch.*

"Fuck!" I bark, launching my body out of bed, quickly glancing back at Knox, hoping I didn't disturb him. Though maybe I should. If Tosch is in trouble, my father and Vincent could also be indisposed. *Valen. Pierce.* "Fuck!" I growl again, racing toward the bathroom, my bare feet clapping over the marble floors.

Frigid water smacks me in the face as I quickly wash away the sleep. My hand flipping through the air, calling clothing to me. A skill I've become proficient with since arriving at the manor. No one cares to knock here, and more often than not, I'm naked in my room.

Swishing mouthwash, I barely get it into the sink before darting back out of the bathroom. My sweatpants are barely over my ass, and the sweatshirt is only half on as I reach my bedroom door. Glancing over my shoulder, my heart rate only races faster as the shouting somewhere in my home grows louder, more agitated. Knox is still sound asleep, his arm draped over the edge of the mattress, face nuzzled into my now-empty pillow.

With a deep breath, I sneak out of my bedroom, hoping Knox will stay asleep until I return. Judging by the dark smudges under his eyes, he needs the rest, and I need him to be okay.

My bare feet clap against the floor as I speed-walk through the manor. The closer I draw to the main staircase, the louder that voice becomes. Every word wraps around me like barbed wire. Digging into my skin and drawing blood as if they're pointed at me, though I am still unsure exactly what this woman is raging about. My breathing only evens out, realizing it's not Tosch.

She's okay.

But I do know this voice. I know it well, and my stomach drops.

The moment I round the last corner of the stairwell, I nearly tumble head-first. My elbow locks painfully as I grip the banister, holding tight enough to keep me on my feet.

She's here.

What is she doing here?

It's two against one. Vincent and my father on one side, and my mother on the other. The three of them locked in a battle of words and accusations.

I struggle to breathe, picturing my family existing in the same room. An entire lifetime flashes before my eyes. Portraits and vacations. All of us together, as Vincent and I matured into our powers. Quiet nights by one of the many fireplaces, as we reminisced or Mom regaled us with stories about her antiques.

But it's not real. It has never been, and it will never be. We're not a family. The choices of my mother and Roman ensured we couldn't exist in that sort of bliss. The Guthrie family will never have a future mirroring the countless images I've drummed up in my head.

"Bryony," my mother breathes when she spots me, running toward me with open arms.

Sluggishly, I descend the steps, briefly holding her back in a hug that is entirely too tight. "What are you doing here?" My voice doesn't sound like my own. It's dead. Detached. Void of every emotion that's currently swirling through me.

"Oh, sweetheart, are you okay? We have been looking everywhere for you," my mother croons, tears pooling behind her honey brown eyes. She's never been affectionate like this with me, and I'm immediately on edge. Stepping out of her hold, she tracks my movements with her eyes. My father's arm drapes over my shoulders when I stop at his side.

Her gaze sweeps left, then flicks right, before gliding back. A ping-pong between my father and me. Each shift gives her new insight into what our relationship has become without her.

"Why are you here?" I ask again.

Her spine straightens, shoulders rolling back at my tone, but tears still glisten in her eyes. "I came for Harley."

Harley. Fucking Harley.

And my stomach drops. The concern she'd just expressed was to butter me up. To make nice so she could demand Roman's son back. Her son.

Crossing my arms over my chest, chin cocked a little higher, I meet her defiance. "How do you know he's here?"

She sighs, reaching for me only for me to step back. The defeat in her stare as her hand drops almost makes me want to hug her again. Jorddan has freely given me hugs since the day we met, but it always seemed like I had to earn them in the Avalon house. Affection only came from my grandmother without question. "Bryony, we don't have time for this. I just need my son."

The words sting like a dagger piercing my heart. So I push against her and the pain. "So you knew he was here, but didn't think I would be? Did you even care where I disappeared to?"

Yet again, she reaches for me, her petite mouth opening and closing as if she were going to deny it. This time, she pulls back on her own, a single blink replacing the emotion drawing on her features. Smoothing her hands down her thighs, she presses her mouth into a hard line. "Listen to me. You need to let Harley go. Roman..."

There are pedestals in the Avalon family. Harley is sitting second tallest beside Roman. His prodigy son is set to follow in his footsteps. Sure, Roman carted me around everywhere, and my mother showed me fondness when she felt like it, but not like Harley.

It should be no surprise that my mother is once again kneeling at Roman's feet, bending over backward to ensure his happiness. All of this for a man I'm convinced she never loved. "You come here and expect us to side with him? He tried to kill me!" I scream.

My temper rages, barely contained as I face the woman who, for once, I wish would pick me over the Avalon name. Growing up, I never resented it. I said nothing because, in the end, they were protecting me. An illegal wielder. That name kept me safe.

"Bryony, there are things you don't understand. He will burn this world down for his children, you included."

Anger boils through me. I was his pawn. How does she not understand that? "I'm not his child. He made that clear."

"Just give me Harley and I can explain."

"No, you can explain now, Mother. Explain to me how you will still stand by a man who tried to kill *your* daughter. What does he have on you that makes you so weak when it comes to him?" Even my father flinches at my words. I hadn't intended the harshness to bleed through in my statement, but perhaps my shell was tired of holding it in. The raw emotion coursing through me causing my voice to crack as I released my vulnerability.

My mother doesn't understand. Roman wasn't threatening her in the dead of night, in the woods on top of a mountain. She didn't look into his eyes and witness his unbridled hatred. My mother can claim he wouldn't have killed me, but he wouldn't have batted an eye had I not made it out of there. I know that without a doubt.

The plea shines in her eyes before it bleeds into her words. "I can't just go against him, Bryony." That same tone she often used when I would ask about my dark side, and she wanted me to stop before anyone heard me, resurfaces.

"Why?" I press.

"Tell her, Geneva." Jorddan flicks a hand her way as if to encourage her.

Too many emotions flash behind his eyes at seeing her mere feet away from him. He loves her fiercely. We all know that, but for whatever reason, my mother is stuck with Roman.

"I am oath-bound to your..." She clears her throat. "To Roman. It doesn't matter what I want anymore."

Something inside me breaks. I never knew. Yet another secret. *Another excuse for her actions.*

Every spell or curse can be broken. There has to be a way. My mind is debating whether she chose not to or hasn't found the answer yet. Would the answer change how I feel about her in this moment?

Yes.

The little girl in me still wants the family she never had. She wants to believe that with this new knowledge, her mother was only trying to survive. "We can find someone to break it." I step toward my mother, my fingers itching to cling to her waist as I did when I was young and hurting.

Tears build behind her eyes. "No, sweetheart. I am spellbound by blood. Mine, Roman's, and the wielder who performed the bonding."

Determination swells in my chest. They are my mother's only hope of breaking free. Maybe then she can make better choices. I can't expect she'll choose this family of four solely, but she can walk away from Roman. That's what's important. Harley, Merrick, and Sicily are still her children, too, and I believe she loves them as well. Possibly, given different circumstances, she could love us all equally.

"Then we find her," I blurt out, my stare met with blank expressions. "Why are you all..." The question dies on my lips as my brother's hand cups my shoulder.

"She's dead," Vincent deadpans.

"Then bring her back," I spin to face him. "You can bring anyone back, can't you?"

He nods. "I can, but first I have to find them."

The world drops out from under me as my fingers sink into my rat's nest of a fro. This is all too much. Too much bad news and not enough good. Too many surprises and not enough upfront truth. Too many brick walls and not enough ways to blast them away.

"Mom," I whisper. "I'm sorry."

"I know." She pulls me into her chest. "I am, too. I would have done so many things differently if I could have." Her gaze drifts to my father and then back to me. "You are in the best hands with your father and Vincent. You two are my world, as is your father. Know that, Bryony. You may not believe this right now, but I made the choices I did to protect the people I love the most. Know that too. And I will continue to protect all of you in the best way I know how. My methods don't need your approval. Give me Harley."

"No," I snap, wiggling out of her hold. She did it again, spewing words meant to get me to cave. I am heartbroken for her, but I won't allow myself to be weak like her. "Do you know about Merrick?"

The abrupt change in topic has my mother dropping her brows. "Yes. His Grisym child and wife are safe from Roman. He doesn't know."

A sigh releases from me. They're still here in Manchester. They approved his request for an extended vacation enthusiastically. Like the other Avalons, he's been a workaholic for years, slaving away behind his desk. From what I've heard, his supervisor commended him for his willingness to take some time away—a perfect cover.

Tosch begged for them to move into the manor once we'd all left for school, but Merrick refused. They wanted their space. At first, it made me suspicious. Why wouldn't he want to stay under my father's roof and receive his protection if he was truly on our side?

Then I saw the look in his eyes the day before I left for school. The same fear Knox and I have lived with our whole lives. A haunted expression I wish I weren't so familiar with. He's protecting his family the best way he knows how.

"Jorddan," my mother turns away from me, moving toward the man she loves with everything she is, taking his hands in hers. "You know the truth. Now, give me back my son. Let me diffuse this in the only way I know how. I've done everything I can for our children, and I will continue to protect them, but Harley is my son, too."

"Genny," my father whispers, releasing her hands, gripping her cheeks. The moment is so intimate between them that I feel awkward being part of it. "You will own my heart until my last breath, but I cannot release a man who showed up on my front doorstep prepared to murder my daughter. You have an allegiance to *your son* and *our daughter*. Mine is only to our daughter. She will always be the priority over the love I hold for you."

My mother rips herself out of my father's grip, tears building behind her eyes before one slips free. "Then I'm sorry for anything that happens. I tried, and I will do what I can to keep Roman at bay. He won't spare anyone to get his children back."

Jorddan moves so swiftly, I'm almost knocked on my ass as he charges my mother. His fingers latch onto her throat, an audible gasp leaving me, before Vincent's arms wrap around my middle from behind, keeping me in place. Even in profile, there's no missing the shift of my father's eyes to those ebony pits of hell. His head tilting to the side, eerily slow, as his fingers tighten ever so slightly. "That bastard is not my daughter's father. Never use that term when you speak of him again. Are we understood?" He delivers each word with such even calm that I stop breathing.

My mother nods twice before he releases her, her hands rubbing along the slender column of her neck. "I love you," she whispers, then spins on her heel and walks right out the front door.

My feet push against the floor as if ready to go after her. My heart and head are torn between what's right and wrong. What's proper and what's unforgivable. Can I fault her for wanting to protect all of her children? Or am I livid she chose him over us, over finding a solution to the oath bond?

"Sweetheart, I am very sorry you had to see that." My father pulls me into him, Vincent finally releasing me.

He has nothing to apologize for. Our lives have become so muddled, I'm unsure of who does now.

I brood about the wielder who bound my mother. A thief. A traitor to me. That single bond stole my mother's life and, consequently, mine too. However, I now understand her allegiance. She, too, has no choice. Yet, that doesn't erase the why. Why would she enter an unbreakable contract? What forced such desperation on her? "Dad, has anyone tried to look for her? The wielder who did the bonding?" My eyes search his, but no answers are waiting for me there. "Are we sure she's dead?"

"Yes," my father looks down at me with something like pity.

Stepping out of his reach, the corners of my mouth dip down into a deep frown. The wheels of my mind spin. Countless facts cycling as I search for the pinprick of information that will free us. "How can you be so sure?"

The black fades, revealing my father's steely gaze once more. His calm, firmly back at its even keel. "Because I killed her," he deadpans. His stare is devoid of all emotion. His body is so still that he could be in a catatonic state. My mind is questioning whether I heard him correctly with such an apathetic response.

"You—What..." I breathe, taking yet another step away from the man who has only ever made me feel safe. "If you... Then you... Where did you leave her?" It's like the full sentence won't make its way past my lips, my frustrations coating every word.

"Sweetheart, I wish I could tell you. I had the memory stripped. The only one who knows where Sable rests is she."

Sable. The name turns over in my mind. There's something so familiar about it, but I can't quite put my finger on it.

It doesn't matter why her name sounds familiar. The ground once again falls out from underneath my feet. That overwhelming helplessness is drowning me in a torrent of violent waves, dragging me through an undertow I'll never escape.

I'm only one more revelation away from losing every bit of my sanity I have left.

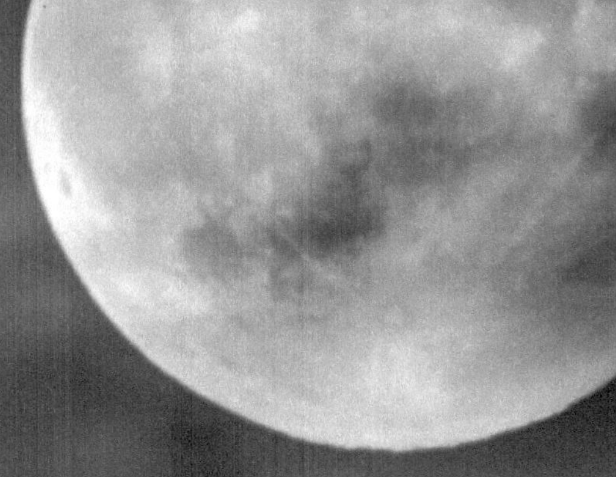

42

BRYONY

When your world implodes around you, it's hard to predict how you'll react.

Breakdown.

Grow brave.

Remain still, drowning in the numbness.

Scream.

Rage.

Fuck and drink until you forget.

I should know my response by now. Since the day I stepped foot on campus at Beauxgraton, my life has been nothing but a constant trek across this endless landmine of potential missteps and unintentional mistakes. With every breath, it's a prayer for reprieve. Just a few moments to collect my thoughts and gather my energy to prepare for the next massive boulder that inevitably rolls my way. It's a constant fight for survival.

With every new world-stopping event, I've behaved differently. I've run. Yelled at the top of my lungs. I let myself fall into the dark place that lives in all our minds. Not the area that houses our intrusive and mischievous thoughts. The place anchored deeper within where pity reigns and hopes wither and die, destined for the pit we allow ourselves to drown in, because it's less painful than fighting.

And now, as I stand here with my father and brother staring at me with mixed emotions, I don't know how to respond. I only know I can't stand here while their pity, apologies, and anger shine bright behind their eyes.

I don't want to be anywhere but alone.

But my feet won't move. My eyes stay latched on their faces. Faces with features so similar. The same ones I've been staring at in the mirror my whole life. How could someone have ever believed I was Roman's daughter?

It doesn't matter that Vincent got the same light fawn skin I did, though none of my other half-siblings got even a lick of color. Hours of summer sun brought them close, but we never matched. As a child, it was my favorite game on our beach vacations. How much of a tan could they achieve so they matched me? So I wasn't the different one. It has been over ten years since one of those family trips. Just another reminder, my half-siblings stopped prioritizing quality time as a family. The time frame aligning too closely with my early maturity for me to ignore it.

Looking back now, my blindness is so apparent, and I hate myself for it. I yearned for acceptance in my home. No matter what I did, the welcome would never truly be an open door. That sting of knowing I was nothing more than a visitor inside those walls nearly burns me alive.

I need to get out of here. I need to think and scream and cry and purge every bit of negative energy from my body. Anything to eliminate the iron grip of being simultaneously suffocated by the past and present, while praying I get to see a future.

Knox only groans when I charge into my room. Articles of clothing are shoved aside as I rifle through my drawers with reckless abandon.

The rumble of his voice sounds behind me. Each word unintelligible as they're mumbled into the pillow.

Stripping, I tug on my sports bra, panties, leggings, and that same sweatshirt.

Tosch may have been the one to have me running to exhaust my body to the point she could tame my essence, but it became therapeutic. Day one was torture worse than death, only for day five to become my reprieve.

I used to run from so many things—figuratively. I shoved the realities under the rug or into a closet, pretending they didn't exist. It was a headfirst drive into the unknown when I could. It dulled the sense of emptiness that often filled me. A release from the resentment of being forced to forget my dark half.

As wielders, pieces of us "die" when we don't act as we should, whether that's by stifling our gifts or pretending we aren't the complex creatures we were born as.

You'll never have to go back to that existence, Bri. Not entirely.

Though so much bad has happened these past few months, I wouldn't trade it. Every obstacle shaped me into this hardened version of myself. A path that has left me with the privilege of embracing who I am.

But that doesn't change the fact that my stomach is churning and I'm overwhelmed with every new secret. Their steel-toed boots drove into my gut harder than the last. As much as I love having my proper family, it's terrifying too. I could still lose them to the lie I've always lived.

And Merrick. I would never wish the existence I lived on anyone. It's lonely and isolating, no matter how many around you love you. I hope Misha won't have the same experience. She'll grow up with a Grisym mother and father who always accepted them. She'll have better than Knox and I did.

Toss in Carter James and the bounty my former father has on my head, and it's a miracle I'm still standing. Amazement courses through me with each smile that pulls at the corners of my mouth. It's a wonder I can still find hope for light at the end of this twisting tunnel.

When Roman decides to collect, it won't just be me. It'll be all of us. Everyone who has ever stood with my father and the New Order. We all sealed our graves with our allegiance.

Society should not sentence a wielder to death for their innate qualities. Grisyms did not choose to be what we are. Yet, we are punished for another's actions—punishment we don't deserve. We don't differ from any other wielder in all the ways that matter. Like a singer, actor, or athlete, we might need fine-tuning. An opportunity to hone our skills and refine them to create a fine piece of art that can be genuinely appreciated. That's all the Grisyms need.

People shouldn't kill us out of fear. Every human and wielder alike begins as a blank canvas. It takes time, patience, and craftsmanship to transform it from nothing into beauty. Grisyms require effort toward understanding, just like anyone else. We need to be embraced.

So many thoughts tumble through my mind. I hadn't noticed I'd already made my way outside under the overcast sky. My feet are pounding against the road beneath them, carrying me down the same path that Tosch had first tortured me on. A road that's nothing more than a stretch of pavement. It couldn't possibly know the nuances of my being. It doesn't know what I am truly capable of. Yet, my feet strike its surface over and over as if the next step will reveal it all.

Logically, I know I won't find the answers by pushing my muscles to the point of failure and sweating through my clothes. They won't come with each ragged intake of precious, crisp air. However, I discovered something even more valuable: my center. A point of clarity that will allow me to decipher which direction to charge in next.

Running has become a way for me to streamline my mind. Tosch thought that might contribute to my internal magical goddess no longer throwing temper tantrums unless I took in new essences.

With no concrete knowledge, everything about how I respond to magic is a matter of trial and error. We suspect that I'll continue to react to taking in new power, especially when they are spaced closely together. Or maybe my tolerance will grow, and my body will stop rebelling against its natural disposition.

My breath comes in heaving pants past my parted lips as I charge forward. My plans are clearer in my head. Plans my guys will not readily agree to, but it's them I am thinking of. It's all of them. If I were the only one in danger, then I might have second thoughts. I'd grown accustomed to living in fear and cowering behind the façade because that's what my parents had told me to do.

Now I embrace that fear. I let it fuel me.

It's not long before I arrive back at the manor. Sweat drips off my chin, absorbing into my damp clothing. It might be winter in the UK, but these fleece-lined sports jackets will make you believe it's the dead of summer after ten minutes.

Stalking through the lower level, my breathing still hasn't slowed. The combination of my run and what I am about to ask my father is spiking a second shot of adrenaline through me. "Dad, where are you?"

Most days, he spent his time between my mother's office and the parlor. I don't recall seeing him on the upper levels other than on the occasions he found me on the stairs. The main level served as his sanctuary. His grounding point. The location he could best protect his family in our home.

More than once, I caught him staring out the window. Hands tucked behind his back, he stood as still as a statue. Never moving. No emotion. Just waiting and watching. Part of me believes this is how he spent many of his years, hoping my mother and I would return to him. That we'd be a family. That the oath she was bound to wouldn't keep her away.

Maybe he was.

Maybe he knew my mother would come.

Maybe he was waiting for Roman. For his chance to strangle the man with his dark magic for how he allowed me to be treated. Jorddan's essence rolls beneath my skin, itching to do the same to Harley. All it takes is a mention of his name, and the tendrils gather at my fingertips, ready to strike. Yet, even with my father's essence inside me, it maintains its control as if he's still pulling the reins instead of me. To our disappointment, Harley is worth more alive than dead—for now.

He served his purpose when Sean stole memories from him. Information was never the primary reason we held him. Harley is a hard lesson for Roman. A bargaining chip. The pawn that might keep Roman in line.

"Dad!" I call again.

"What is it, my dear?" He appears out of nowhere, and absentmindedly, I wonder if that's how I always appear when I teleport. I've watched my father do his version of it back at Beauxgraton in the Vault, but I never considered how alarming it is to watch a person just fade into corporeal form from nothing. An object seems so much less impressive.

"We need to let Harley go." I square my shoulders, faking confidence I don't quite feel. "Then I need to get back to school."

His jaw works. A slow roll beneath his goatee as he watches me with indifference. "No."

"You don't get to tell me no on this," I snap. Stepping closer, my eyes narrow on his face, my mouth set in an unforgiving straight line. "You asked me to trust you. You asked me to prove my loyalty. I am doing that. Let Harley go. Roman will think we're scared. He will think we are weak, but we're not."

"I'm not endangering your life by releasing that lunatic," Jorddan growls.

The corner of my mouth quirks, wanting to laugh at my father's choice of descriptor for Harley. More choice words exist, but now isn't the time to name-call. Clearing my throat, I know I have seconds to make my point. Seconds before he shuts me down. Once that door slams shut, my father will no longer entertain my demands.

Squaring my shoulders, I make my case. "And I'm telling you I am in danger no matter what, but something tells me to believe Mom. Roman wouldn't have killed me. I don't think he would let the Council kill me either. Not right away. Think about it. Catching a Grisym like me would be a prize. Before I came along, wielders believed Eistiabs were extinct. They became this mystical specialty wielder we could no longer rely on or manipulate. But I'm not like my ancestors. We know this." I take his hand, squeezing lightly. "Not a single Eistiab documented in history was Grisym. I assume that's why Roman treated me so well over the years. He always told me he had plans for me after school. He always said that I didn't need to worry about what I studied. I just needed to get in and out as quickly as possible."

My breath comes heavy as I wait for my father's response. I hadn't meant to give an entire speech, but I needed to convince him. I needed him to understand that, for once, I was thinking this through, even if my newly developed plan proves to be a mistake.

His mouth twitches, my eyes tracking the way his perfectly trimmed goatee shifts. "Your point?"

"I think he planned on handing me over." The room seems to close in. My father's gaze darkening.

He will not cave.

He will not listen.

But he needs to.

"You'd better not be suggesting turning yourself over to the Council," Vincent roars from around the corner.

"No. Never. Not unless that was the only way I could protect everyone," I reply, never breaking eye contact with my father. A silent plea for him to do as I ask.

They both stare at me, so many unspoken words passing between us. "You're right. I asked you to trust me. I will trust you this time, but I will not release him until you've left the manor."

"No. Let me teleport him back."

"You can't teleport between countries?" Vincent voices the words as if in question, disbelief dipping his thick brows low.

Heat creeps up over my face. Roman is the only one who knows I have the capability. When I was about seventeen, we missed our flight for an important meeting in South America. We couldn't secure transportation that would allow us to arrive on time.

Hope sparked in Roman's pale blue eyes as he questioned how far I could teleport. An answer a teenager wouldn't have. It's not like I had someone to help me hone that gift.

Sure, short distances never proved to be a problem. Another country must be different, though, I'd assumed. Teleporting us to a foreign place I've never seen sounded dangerous. Nausea swirled in my stomach, worried I'd get it wrong. I swore I couldn't, but he'd pushed and pushed and pushed, and so I made it happen.

I'd been exhausted when we arrived. Three days passed, and I barely had the energy to stumble to the bathroom. I slept most of those hours, the world around me nonexistent. I hardly remembered the trip. Roman brushed back my knotted hair when I finally woke long enough to sit up and speak. *You're my special girl. You did it,* he'd praised with boundless pride in his eyes.

"I did?" The words burned in my throat. My tongue stuck to the roof of my mouth, dry from lack of food and water for days.

"You did. Dropped us right in front of the hotel." He'd hugged me close. *"Now shower, and then we'll grab some dinner."*

That was it. I'd done the unthinkable, and my dad was proud. What more could a girl have wanted?

"I've done it before. Once," I nearly whisper. Averting my gaze, I hope it hides the shame splashed across my features. I'd been useless afterward. An experience better kept to myself. Jorddan will worry if he knows. He'll deny me this act of bravery—or stupidity. I'm different now. Stronger. More proficient.

There's a chance I might need time to recover before I return. I'd be at the mercy of Roman and Harley if I do this. Hopefully, my mother would take pity on me and keep me from their wrath. Hopefully, she would protect me, like she failed to do previously.

Vincent's warmth envelopes me as he hugs me to his chest. Considering his unforgiving coldness toward others, his fondness toward me continues to serve as a shock to my system. His affection is something I missed from my half-siblings. It'll take longer than two weeks to grow accustomed to it, but it only took me one night to crave it. "Bri, we can put him on a plane and get him out of here. We also have access to certain portals. But don't ask us to let you teleport him halfway around the world."

"It wouldn't be halfway around the world," I mutter, squeezing my brother back. My eyes screw shut at the sound of his heart racing in my ear. "It's just a few towns over, technically."

"What are you?" My father doesn't finish his sentence before he realizes what I am suggesting. "You have lost your mind." Jorddan's words drift off, his jaw working and the veins at his temples throbbing beneath his dark hair. "If you think I am permitting my only daughter to escort a man who wants to see our demise stateside via ghoul tunnels and then teleport him from the nearest Hell Gate back to the house you were forced to live in..." He leans closer, his grimace deepening as his glare levels mine. "You. Are. Mistaken."

"I'll go with her." Knox appears behind the two of them, his hair standing on end as he rubs at his eyes. He must have felt our essences stirring, ready for an adventure. Adrenaline surges through me, imagining such a dangerous journey. One, I wholeheartedly think, might buy us some time and grace with Roman.

"You will bring her right back. Do you understand me?" My father snarls in Knox's face.

A heavy sigh leaves Knox's shoulders sagging as he runs his hands through his messy hair. "You don't need to threaten me. I need her back and safe as much as you do."

"I highly doubt that," my father scoffs.

"Doubt it all you want, but I'm in love with your daughter." Knox stands a little straighter, his eyes quickly shifting to my brother before he focuses on my father once more. "I am tied to her, so if she doesn't make it, neither do I."

"You don't mean?" Vincent breathes.

"Yeah, I think I do," Knox sighs. "We're Gemminai Animyrum."

What the hell is that?

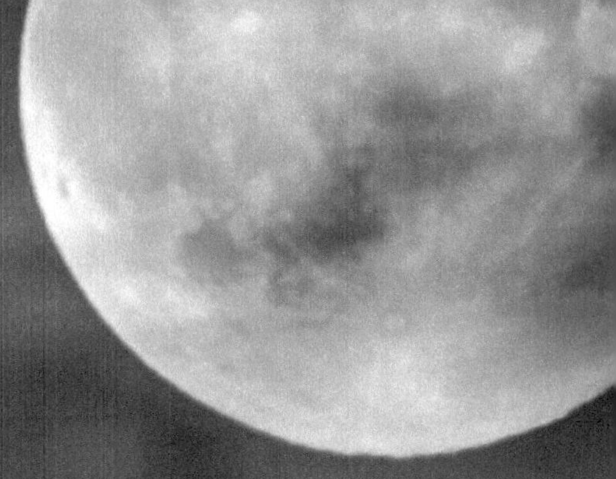

43

PIERSON

THE DEEP SIGH OF exhaustion has barely passed my lips when Graham and Valen come charging into my room. The handle cracks against the wall as the door is shoved open, forcing me to bolt upright.

"What the hell?"

Valen smirks. "Next time, shut your damn door the right way. Stop being so fucking basic, Pierson."

My molars grind. He pulled the same shit at Beauxgraton. The undoing of the spells allowed anyone to enter at any time. I always liked the idea of friends coming and going. It was a fun concept in college, and I guess it just followed me here. But also, unlike Valen, I am a people person. I genuinely like them.

Scrubbing my face with my hands, I don't want to hear whatever shit they are here to divulge. I'm exhausted. Partying was never a pastime I enjoyed like my peers. In neither my "human life" nor since I arrived at Beauxgraton. The Red Moon balls were the only celebrations I went to willingly, too conditioned to ignore tradition for my personal comfort.

Bar hopping and clubbing have drained my energy. Couple our trip back to the manor, and I've got nothing left to power me through the day. In the few times Bri has teleported us, I'm left disoriented after. The nausea is threatening to bring anything left in my stomach up. A raging headache followed, as if my body couldn't tolerate moving from one place to another.

Only for Valen and Vincent to rope me into killing an entire bottle of scotch with them. I would have rather been curled up around my girl, but according to her brother, Knox was handling it for us. Naturally, getting drunk was the only other option besides sleep.

I sat there in silence while they discussed Jorddan's plans for the remaining names on the list, the evil glint in both their eyes a match. Once more, I was reminded that I don't fit in with my fellow dark wielders. My heart doesn't beat the way theirs do. I don't revel in taking from others just to appease a gift I never asked for.

My gaze flicks down to my palms, my essence shifting lazily beneath my skin. All it takes is a single reminder of the wretched things I've done with my powers for bile to creep up my throat. My gag reflex activated as I fight to keep from spewing vomit on my shoes.

The mission transcends our prior struggles. It's more than the petty squabbles we've had over power between the light and the dark. It runs deeper than equality. The biting cuts of injustice sink deep into our flesh, just waiting to heal. Roots that prevent the light from embracing the dark. The Grisyms. Now, it's Bri's safety. Above all else, that's at the center of Jorddan's world—his mission. Vincent might be his son, but Bri is his baby girl. So, I understand the plan. I respect what needs to be done, but that doesn't mean my intestines don't knot at the thought of murder.

Sacrifice is part of any push toward change. They are inevitable and will cause hurt that we all wish we could avoid. I accepted that. Still, the reality doesn't keep me from hoping for a better way. A more peaceful way to coexist, while forging an alternative path that welcomes dimming the light so the shades of gray stretching to the most opaque black can also shine. Our only opportunity to live as the wielders we choose to be, versus what we have been told we must be.

"Get up." Valen shoves at my feet, my legs slipping over the side of the bed.

"I literally just got in bed."

"I don't give a shit. Get your ass up. We have prey to find." He rotates his daggers between his fingers, Graham watching them spin as his hands rest in the pockets of his perfectly pressed slacks. It never much bothered me how put-together he was, but now I just feel inadequate.

Graham is the smart one. He's her best friend. And now he's sleeping with my—*our*—girlfriend, too. A woman who may not make it to twenty-six if I don't find the balls to do what needs to be done. We agreed to "whatever it takes" when we took Jorddan's name on our skin. We agreed to be anything he needed us to be to support the New Order. I never forgot that.

"What the hell are you talking about now? I'm tired. I'd rather wait for Bri to get back." A heavy groan leaves me, reminding me how exhausted I am, down to my bones. My eyes are burning, and my limbs are nothing more than dead weight.

"Check your phone," Valen cocks his chin, flicking his wrist so the dagger flies across the room, burrowing itself in my roommate's desk. With a twitch of his fingers, it breaks free, soaring back toward him in reverse, only for him to repeat the action.

Pulling my phone from my pocket, my screen lights up with notifications from Knox in our group chat.

Knox: *Bri and I are going back to the US for the day.*
Knox: *Don't ask!*
Valen: *Well I'm not asking but you damn sure better tell me what you're up to.*
Knox: *Asshole, I said don't ask.*
Bryony: *We'll be fine. Aziel will be there.*

"What the fuck?" I blurt, my gaze catching on Graham and Valen. "Where the hell are they going?"

"Fuck if we know. You read the messages." Valen rolls his jaw. He's as pissed as I am.

We both stare at the cryptic messages on our phones, my pulse racing, waiting for those three dots to dance along the bottom. Waiting for them to explain what the fuck they're talking about. If Bri is calling on her ghoul, this can't be good. There's no reason she would need him. Not for power or protection. It makes zero sense, and I'm suddenly pissed they forced our return to Integretew while she stayed behind this morning.

"We have other issues," Graham inserts himself, running his hands over his pants as if they're not already wrinkle-free. "The Danvers family is known for being Amovea."

"They're actually skinwalkers?" Valen snickers as if in disbelief when he's the one who originally called it.

"How did you go from calling them body snatchers to skinwalkers?" Graham scrunches his nose before shaking his head.

Though it's not the proper term, it is one of the names we gave them when telling ghost stories as kids. Their bloodline is one of the most prominent. Traits like that aren't lost through the generations. It doesn't matter if human blood becomes part of the mix. There are certain gifts potent enough to withstand dilution. They will travel through the genetic line, no matter how minuscule the blood in their offspring's veins.

Most wielders like to pretend this isn't true. They would rather believe that their family's genealogy didn't disadvantage them to the bottom of the totem pole. Nor do they want to endorse the idea that gifts that strong can continue to exist because it means the rest of us will always be inferior. Unfortunately, this is a topic I know more about than most, as my parents are essentially wielding geneticists for a private company owned and operated by dark wielders.

"William Danvers is here and has changed his appearance. He has to be one," Graham confidently announces.

"He could have had spell work done, too," I retort.

Everything about Graham's expression has the wheels turning in my head. I'd given an argument he clearly doesn't believe; neither do I. For once, I just needed something to be simple, but Graham ruins that with his explanation. "He'd have to have a spell master at his disposal. Spellwork like this requires constant touch-ups. I'm not saying there isn't one here, but it seems more likely he is carrying on the family gift."

"Fine. How do we find him?" Valen snorts.

"Knox sent the picture of what he looks like now," Graham shrugs. "We find him and find out what he knows about Roman becoming director of education."

"Excuse me?" I snap. "What did you say?"

My heart is racing. Those two, who are suddenly up each other's asses, must have gotten this information from Knox. It would explain their odd disappearance while we were at the Cavea de Mors, but they never shared it with us.

Graham holds up a hand, keeping me from saying anything more. "Knox asked Harley about Danvers. He all but confirmed that William impersonated his uncle and put Roman in his current position. But no explanation of why."

Agitation causes me to grind my teeth. "And you think we're just going to walk up and say, 'Hey William, why did you cheat the system?'" I scoff.

"Something like that," Graham whispers, turning on his heel toward the door. "Let's go. Classes start in a few days, and I still have prepping to do."

Valen snorts, shoving Graham in the shoulder. "Fucking book nerd."

"Some of us still need our education," Graham retorts, but I don't miss the quirk of his grin and the playful humor in his eyes. What the fuck. When did my best friend become Graham's?

The two laugh as Valen's arm wraps around Graham's neck from behind. "Yeah, whatever. Just keep using those smarts so we can take over the world."

"Will do," Graham chuckles, shoving Valen's arm away. "Now knock it off. You're wrinkling my shirt."

It's like watching the Twilight Zone play out before my eyes. An alternate universe where the enemies become inseparable. When did tolerance morph into enjoyable companionship? My stomach churns, lacking an understanding of how we got from point A to B. The jealousy over my best friend drifting away, one would expect, never to surface.

We're all wondering when the two had time to bond. When did that pivotal shift happen between them?

Let it go, Pierce. I shake my head, clearing my thoughts. It's not like they're lovers, and it only benefits our unconventional unit if we all get along. Still, this goes beyond Graham saving Valen's life, so I need to know what they're hiding or up to.

And yet, I don't have the mental fortitude to analyze their new friendship while working off no sleep and a hangover. So I push them out of my head, following the two whispering back and forth ahead of me.

It's not quite as disorienting as Beauxgraton's maze of hallways, yet there are just as many interrupted by alcoves showcasing antiques and massive windows. The decor lining the walls speaks of European history. The transformation of the intended palace into the institution it is now has left humans and wielders alike in awe.

While attending Beauxgraton, I'd always loved walking the halls, taking in the surrounding history. A pastime Bri and I loved engaging in together, often in the middle of the night when neither of us could sleep after I'd made love to her.

Made love.

There it is.

I'd been refusing to acknowledge the word in my head because it would mean I would have to admit to myself that I fell in love with Bri so fucking fast it made my head spin. That I'd wanted her so bad, I was willing to share her with my best friend, her best friend, and a professor. Not to mention, I'd have to accept that when I said those three words to her, she refused to say them back.

It isn't easy being so consumed by another that you accept them however they offer themselves to you. Like a hungry dog, you're snapping your teeth and licking your chops for just a tiny taste. You don't get to release those feelings or tell them to stand down. They hold strong, eager to grasp onto the bits and pieces that are free to you, because it's better than not having any of them at all.

Bri may not love me yet. She may never love me, but it's enough that she cares about my safety. Putting herself on the line to protect me reveals more than hearing her voice that four-letter word.

No one has ever made me feel more seen than Bryony Guthrie. No one ever will.

Please be safe tonight, baby.

A deep inhale drags through my nostrils, my eyes pressing shut for a moment. "You good?" Valen snickers.

"Yeah, fine." I clear my throat, putting our girl out of my head. Swallowing hard, I focus on my best friend's face. That wicked glint in his eye tells me there's some bullshit mission he's about to lead us on. I can either come along for the ride or be ridiculed for it now and later.

Just as Valen's loyalty to his loved ones always wins, mine to him does too. With a sigh, I signal for him to lead the way and hope this doesn't go horribly wrong. A scolding by Jorddan, if it does, will send me straight off a damn cliff today.

Although Integretew's structure features endless passageways, the central design remains simple. It all circumvents the atrium, making finding the main lounge effortless. The atrium is full of plant life, creating a calming ambiance that can help ease the stress and tension that school can bring.

Graham comes to a stop, glancing down at his phone for the hundredth time. He has the current photo of William pulled up on his screen. His brow furrowing low each time he stops to glance at it as we continue our wild goose chase.

Scanning the room, not a single wielder is familiar. Scrutinizing every feature, hoping to find a match for William's given face or the one he supposedly wears now is proving fruitless. However, if he's as talented an Amovea as his bloodline suggests, he could look like anyone. His features are shifting just enough that they don't match the ones we're looking for. It would make it nearly impossible to know we're spotting him. But a brilliant tactic for a man clearly determined to hide in plain sight.

Leaning close to Valen, he eyes me with annoyance. "Do we even know when that picture was taken?" I whisper, careful to angle my mouth toward his ear to muffle the sound and keep anyone from reading my lips.

My paranoia is alive and buzzing through my veins, moving through me so quickly my heart might give out. Every face is a potential enemy. Sweat prickles at my temples with each glance in our direction, as if the real William is hiding behind their features, laughing at us.

A tight grip suddenly wraps around my arm. The pain brings me back to the present as my gaze follows Valen and Graham, who focus on the closest TV screen. "What?"

Their eyes are both plastered on the screen, news coverage showing Roman Avalon standing behind a podium with tears in his eyes. "...missing for weeks. My granddaughter is a shining light in my life. If anyone knows the whereabouts of my sons, my granddaughter, or my daughter-in-law, please come forward. No harm will come to you."

My brow scrunches low at his words. *Harm*. Why would helpful citizens expect to be in any danger for offering valuable information? If anything, they would feel nothing, knowing they had no part in it.

"We thank you all for your support during this time," Geneva's voice broadcasts out over the crowd. The cameras suddenly pan over the hundreds gathered in front of the makeshift stage. Tears well in their eyes with palpable sorrow written all over each of their faces. A baby girl is missing after all.

But it's the location that catches my attention. The backdrop gives away just how high we place the light. The Council headquarters, with its limestone and whitewash, casts the two in an angelic light.

They're anything but.

If only the world knew what a sham this whole press conference is. Just more bullshit spewed from the lips of a man who had deceived them for years.

"What the hell is he trying to pull?" Graham sneers.

"Geneva was at the house this morning begging for us to release Harley," Valen grunts in response.

Neither takes their eyes off the screen, continuing their private conversation as if I'm not even there. A back-and-forth volley of events making me question if Graham had actually been at the manor instead of me.

It was heartbreaking to watch Bri run off, realizing her mother was choosing Harley, and she couldn't do a thing to free her from Roman. Our girl fights so hard for the people she loves. Even when they don't deserve everything she is willing to give.

Shortly after, a car pulled up and brought Valen and me back here. A supporter of Jorddan's, though I couldn't tell you the guy's name or even if I've seen him before. But it was as if I could feel his tattoo speaking to mine beneath his clothes. That's how it's always been. It's as if Jorddan embedded a way for us to recognize one another without speaking a word. The magic woven into our skin guiding us toward the loyal.

"Whoever took my family, know that you are cruel. Know that you will not break us. We will find you. In the meantime, we will step back from the spotlight while we work through this difficult time, including pulling our daughter Bryony from wielding school. This world has proven dangerous for those of us who live under the bright lights of notoriety. Thank you." Then Roman bows his head, wraps an arm around Geneva's waist, and leads her through the front doors of the council building.

My friends slowly turn to face me, their movements delayed and calculated. Determination glows in their eyes. "What do we do now?" Graham whispers.

If only I knew.

44

BRYONY

THE WIND TOSSES MY curls as I inhale the freshwater scent floating in off the lake. It was the peace I needed before carrying out this idiotic plan.

Knox has been kind enough to stay silent. His essence is likely the culprit informing him of exactly what I need: his presence, and nothing more.

Defeat and frustration swirl in my chest. The combination is stealing my breath. I've called out to the ghouls on several occasions, but never during daylight. There's no instruction manual or almighty elder to explain to me how I've summoned them before. It's nothing but words in my head and a plea in my heart. My essence whirling through me, eager to remind me, ghoul power made me this way. It tamed me. They are mine.

Inhaling deeply, I let the crisp winter air fill my lungs.

Come to me.

Come to me, Aziel.

Come.

Please.

I need you.

Aziel.

Come to me.

I chant the words so many times in my head that they begin to morph into the tune of a song. A melody of begging for a miracle that my ghouls hear me. That my Azukeen hears me and that he will come. I can only hope that he will help me once again.

We know I command them, but I'm convinced there are limits no one else is ready to accept. But I refused to expose my insecurities. If Jorddan thought I had doubts Aziel wouldn't come, this mission would have been over.

My pleas continue for so long, I don't think he's coming. My plan is already unraveling before it could begin.

Aziel, where are you?

Please come.

"Knox, I—" The words die on my lips as the ground rumbles beneath our feet. Tiny waves quiver across the lake surface, my eyes widening as Knox grabs hold of my waist, keeping me in balance.

The quaking grows stronger, accompanied by a thunderous roar. They charge forward in a synchronized rush of massive bodies. Their bare feet strike the earth, tossing up clumps of dirt and grass behind them. Every muscle of their naked forms flexes with their intentional movement, as their massive razor-sharp teeth flash in the daylight, while those forked tongues swipe over their barely recognizable lips.

They heard me.

Come to me, you beautiful beasts.

Thump. Thump. Thump. Thump.

Their pace quickens as I beckon them forward. The details of their forms fill my vision as they advance toward us. Terrifying, beautiful creatures who are mine to command.

My Azukeen leads the charge, with dozens of other ghouls at his heels. The color of their gnarled skin becomes more vibrant in the daylight. Subtle tint variations present themselves with clarity. Their leathery skin, which appears dull in the red moonlight, almost appears metallic under the grayish-blue sky.

It's a physical reminder of the magic that lives within them.

The edges of each peak along their snaked bodies seem more pronounced. Sharp as knife points, ready to slice through anyone who makes contact.

But I've felt that skin under my palm. I know how unforgiving it is, but pliant too, as it seems to mold to my touch. I've had my Azukeen's cock inside me multiple times. Expanding and contracting to fill me perfectly. A ghoul made for me, just like my men.

"You came," I breathe.

My ghoul's chest heaves, those crystalline white eyes focused on my face. "Aziel always come to Bryony. Bryony, mine."

I reach forward, his body dipping low so my palm can run along his ridged cheek. "Yes. I'm yours, but Aziel, I need your help."

"We will kill for Bryony." As one, they roar. The world is tilting on its axis as if leaning away from the pitch, quivering under the force of it. Waves crash over the lake's surface, my gaze drifting over my shoulder to ensure the manor is still standing. Once satisfied, I return my focus to the mini army of ghouls waiting for my direction.

"No one dies today. I need you to take me through the tunnels again." Aziel's eyes glow before narrowing in my direction. "This time I need to go to the Hell Gate near my hou—" I pause. That house is no longer my home. I renounced it that night with Roman.

The manor is my home. Wherever Vincent, my father, and my guys are is home.

"Where?" Aziel questions.

"The closest gate to Seela. Let me show you."

I move closer to the ghoul, both palms cupping its cheeks, and focus. Another plea sent out into the universe for my eyes to change. For them to become the sensors the ghouls have. As if it happens to all of them at once, their spines snap straight. I can't see it, but I feel it. They're seeing what my memories are showing them. I lack an understanding of our bond, or why my gut assured me this interaction would be a success. Instinct guides much of my present existence. I only wish I understood how I'm meant to operate.

"We take you. Not him."

"Aziel, Knox has to come with me. We're taking a bad man. I need you to take all three of us. Do you understand?"

The Azukeen roars, the others following suit. "Bring him. Aziel choose." His tongue seems to stumble over his name as if still getting used to the taste of it on his tongue. I wonder if the others refer to him by it now, or if it's only when he's with me.

Knox nods, running off to the manor. It's twenty minutes before he returns, practically dragging Harley across the muted green grass. My half-brother's scowl is the nastiest I've ever seen, likely livid, he has the hands of a filthy Grisym on him.

"This is my brother," I say. "I need to take him back to Seela."

Aziel stares into Harley's eyes. My brother's wide as he's shoved face to face with a snarling ghoul. Something like joy bounces through me, knowing Harley finally fears something. Someone. I assume he has never been so close to a ghoul. Most light wielders haven't. We're warned to stay away.

The lies we've told the light wielders about the danger of death, quirk my grin now. Most ghouls ignore light wielders unless they are threatened. The magic isn't compatible, so they are of no use. Should a ghoul choose to fuck a member of the light—an obscenely rare occurrence—one of two things will happen: nothing but the soreness of a good bang, or the power will successfully siphon, but likely kill the wielder shortly after.

"He wants Bryony dead."

"I know, Aziel, but I need to return him so I can live."

The ghoul grunts, dropping his face level with Harley's. He has just enough strength to flinch away, Knox's hold keeping him from gaining even an inch. "You touch mine, you die."

Harley only flinches before a Cupprien steps forward, grabbing him by the shirt and throwing him over its shoulder. Aziel scoops me into his arms, while a Kirbon also tosses Knox over its shoulder. "I can walk," Knox grunts, attempting to adjust himself and failing.

"No walk. We carry. We protect mine."

Knox and Harley are both silent, one realizing he will become a ghoul chew toy if he doesn't, and the other doing what he knows I'll ask of him.

The ghouls carry us along the same path we'd last traveled. We needn't speak, slipping past the spelled barrier, to trek through the stone corridors. We've been here before. The urgency is no less anxiety-inducing than the previous trips, so I melt into it. Allow it to wash over me.

Time passes differently in these tunnels. Minutes are actually hours. Feet are like miles.

Though Mr. Greer had given me great insight into the magic housed in these tunnels, I want to hear it from Valen. Somehow, I know he'll bring the world of ghouls to life in the most intoxicating manner. His passion for ghouls helped me warm up to him. He speaks about them as if they're a sacred treasure versus creatures we fuck for power.

It'll have to wait. For now, we don't have the luxury of breathing or enjoying each other's company worry-free.

Let us all live to see it.

The thought gives me pause. Who could have imagined I would ever enjoy Valen's company?

Memories of the day we met filter to the forefront of my mind. Then the night he wrapped his long fingers around my throat and threw me to the ground. Followed by the dagger, he slung down the hallway that drew blood. Still, I want him around. I crave his touch and his mind and his mouth pressed to mine. I crave his undying loyalty. More than anything, I appreciate the edge he pulled out of me.

I haven't laughed enough with Graham or loved enough on Pierce. I haven't bickered with Valen or explored more with Knox. Developing the budding relationship between me and my four men requires finesse, time, and security. Sex is one thing. It's been amazing. One of the many anchors holding us together. But they mean more to me than a fuck when we're all too overwhelmed by our circumstances. We're so desperate for any connection that helps us forget or feel grounded; often, it seems that the physical is all we have.

I meant what I said when I told them all or none. Together, they make me whole. Aziel too. It's something I couldn't explain even if I wanted to.

"Aziel have Bryony today."

I'm so caught off guard by his garbled words that it takes me a moment to process what he asked.

No, not asked.

Demanded.

It's been over a month since I was last with Aziel. As much as my body and magic have grown to need my ghoul, fear keeps him at arm's distance. The first time I took from him, my body revolted. My magic raged and roared for unrestricted release. I was terrified that night. When I took from Harley, that hadn't happened, nor had it when I accidentally took from Pierce and intentionally from Knox. Yet another reaction I don't understand.

"Let's get to the gate first," I grit through my teeth. My lips roll, contemplating whether Aziel will obey once we exit these tunnels. My being yearns for my ghoul. His cock moving inside me as those claws dig into my skin. But not tonight. That's not why or what I needed from Aziel tonight.

Aziel grunts, adjusting me in his hold. Muscular arms cradle me to his chest as if I weigh nothing, and I am the most precious thing all at once. "All have Bryony," Aziel grumbles. The statement is clearer than his last demand.

My eyes flash wide, staring up at him. Though my vision is normal once again, those milky white orbs stare back down at me. They see everything. Hear everything. Feel everything. I know it because I, too, have experienced it.

I've gotten lost in what your other senses can tell you when you no longer have your sight. When all you have it's what's available to you, those remaining senses sharpen. Brutal points that keep you on your toes, poised for actions only instinct and muscle memory can accomplish for you. The sensations, tastes, and smells are all richer. The experience heightened until it became otherworldly.

It's the sweetest addiction once you've had a taste.

"I only siphon from you." The politest way I can say I'm too chicken shit to fuck a different breed of ghoul. To take in a new type of power that may leave me losing control so horribly we can't contain it this time.

"Bryony needs more."

"More what?" I question.

"More dark," he growls.

45

BRYONY

FOR THE FIRST TIME, my heart beats differently in Seela. It was always the place I knew. The place I called home was secure because no one could touch me there. It never mattered that as I got older, I wasn't always at my happiest. My family taught me happiness was not a luxury meant for a Grisym. I didn't always feel loved, seen, or heard. But it was home.

Now...

Now, part of me wants to burn it to the ground. Set flames to every memory that was less than amazing. Watch the flowers turn to ash and the structure crumble as it's torched away.

That's when the smaller piece of me kicks its way to the front. There are fond memories here. Twenty-five years of my life are here. My stories are woven into those walls and etched into the grooves of the hardwood floors. Good or bad, they are part of me.

Even so, I thought I would miss it more. My room. My old haunts and my balcony. The chaise I often lounged on while watching my mother reconstruct her artifacts. I imagined I would yearn to come back every chance I could. That I would need this place of sanctuary, especially as secret after secret unfolded. But I didn't. I never even thought about coming back. Not once.

I wait for those feelings to steal my breath. To bring me joy. To cause me to feel anything but indifferent or angry, but they never do. Our stroll down my street is nothing more than Knox and me walking Harley back to *his* safety net.

Harley cackles as our house comes into view. That sharp, wicked crack of laughter only a villain could perfect. "You're as good as dead," he snickers. "But you knew that."

My essence shoots from my fingers. The color is so dark that it hides even my stars as the rope wraps around his throat. "One more word, Harley. One more and I won't be the one who saved you tonight, but the one who kills you. I've already done it once. I can do it again." Every word is snarled through gritted teeth.

I spent years fighting for his acceptance and his love, but I'm done. Done playing nice. Done with being the peacemaker. I am doing this for myself and for the people I love. For the first time in my life, I can confidently say I no longer love my half-brother. Once upon a time, I did, and he didn't deserve it then. I know that now.

The sun beats down on us as we reach the edge of the driveway, my steps halting before crossing onto Avalon property. The shadow of that house looms over me. Every bit of betrayal and pain from my years as an Avalon and since repeatedly stabbing me in the gut.

I hate how it taught me to hide. The family who belongs inside those walls kept me from embracing who I am. They're the reason I never learned how to control this. I hate that I suffered so much torment at the hands of this coward I am now returning in good faith.

My hands shake as I look down at them. The blood that already stains my skin stares back at me. That tendril I'd released to put Harley in his place, still waves at the end of my finger. Calling it back, his gasping breaths allow me to move forward. To move into the lion's den.

What I hate most: not a single one of them ever loved me the way I deserved. They lied to me and used me. I hate that I let them, although deep down I knew it was the truth.

Sometimes, when we are so desperate for acceptance, we trick ourselves into believing that the warped version of what we're receiving is all we deserve. That it's all we're meant to have.

Janelle taught me differently—Beauxgraton, Camilla, and my friends, too.

Taking my second step, I'm ready to get this over with. "Let's go."

Harley only grunts against the restraints of Knox's magic. His steps quicken as we climb the soft hill at the base of the driveway.

The feel of Knox slipping his fingers through mine pulls my gaze up to him. Harley snorts, catching the moment.

"We give him back, and then we're gone. I'm not risking you," Knox whispers.

"If we're lucky, you'll both be dead before we leave the front door," Harley snarls.

That black essence leaves my fingers again, this time knitting his lips shut. I've never cast a curse before. With a single thought, my essence acted. It knew precisely what I wanted and made it true. "Enough, Harley," I snap as I punch in the code for our gate.

The groan of the bars parting settles something inside me. A sound I've heard a million times—the sound of returning home.

I hate this.

Knox never releases my hand as I fight to slow my breathing. To find the ruthless calm that took over me when I killed Yorgan. Pulling my essence free of Harley's mouth, I keep it in my palm. Ready to strike. Ready to defend. "You're as good as dead, baby sister," the title spewed like a curse.

Not once, to my recollection, has Harley referred to me as his sister. Not aloud.

The words give me pause now. I know the bastard meant them to hurt, and maybe a tiny piece of me, shoved deep down, weeps at the single word, but the new Bri only laughs. An unhinged cackle that sends my brother's brows up to his forehead.

"I might be as good as dead, but I'm not your sister. You made it clear I never was, and for once I'm so fucking happy about it."

Harley only sneers as we climb the drive, the front door swinging open before we're even halfway.

My mother races outside, her feet bare despite the cold. The oversized sweater and wide-legged pants are too dressy for her to have been lounging at home. She wouldn't have been at work today either. I'm prepared to ask her where she'd been when she wraps her arms around Harley's neck, pulling him into her. Her hands cup the back of his head, a soft sob shattering a piece of my heart. Her hands cup his cheeks, pulling back to look up at him. "You're alright. You're safe."

"Yeah, Mom. I'm okay. Don't cry." He fights against the restraints, Knox finally whispering the counterspell to release him as we stand there and watch.

It's only moments later that my father and Sicily come racing down the drive, too. Roman latches onto them, his arms circling *his* family. His children melt into his hold, welcoming his embrace. Tears stream down my sister's face as Harley sobs so loudly it can only be fake. My half-brother's attempt at garnering sympathy he doesn't deserve.

None of them acknowledge my standing there as if I don't exist at all.

I take the first step away.

This isn't my family. It never was.

Then I take another and another, when Roman's glare finally finds my face. "Where do you think you're going?"

"Home." Defiance bleeding into that single word.

"You're not going anywhere." Roman lunges for me, but Knox and I are just far enough to slip away from his outstretched grasp, his large hands wrapping around nothing but air. The toe of his dress shoe catches, and he almost crashes face-first into the pavement. A sight that would please my darker half. Especially if blood and flesh paint the ground at our feet. He deserves that and so much more.

"Roman, stop!" my mother shouts. "Don't hurt her."

"Geneva, take our children inside. Now."

"Don't hurt her," my mother pleads. Still, she doesn't come to my aid. She holds Sicily and Harley to her sides as if protecting them from danger, but not me.

Never me.

"I'm sorry," I whisper, before grabbing Knox's hand and teleporting.

Too many emotions surge through me as we materialize at the Hell Gate. "Bri," Knox whispers, wrapping his arms around me from behind. "Baby, I'm so sorry."

"She... she didn't even attempt to protect me."

Choked sobs escape me as I relive the sight of my mother holding my half-siblings and pleading with my former dad not to hurt me. Yet, she didn't stop him. She barely even acknowledged me.

"Bri, I—"

"Please don't. If I've learned nothing else these past few months, it's that I can't afford to be weak for the people who won't be there for me. My mother has proven that Harley means more to her than I do twice today. When someone shows you their truth, it's best to believe it."

Though I utter my words with conviction, uncertainty swirls inside me. Shaken and hurt, abandoned and betrayed, Knox will know regardless of how fine I may sound. He will feel it. Tosch and I haven't gotten around to honing my ability to block others out. We were unsure if hosting another's essence would allow them access to me at all. It seems it doesn't. Only Knox. He is the one who can feel me as much as I do myself. For his own good, I'll need to learn to block him out. He deserves that peace.

I spin in Knox's arms, his hands gripping my hips, our bodies flush. "Baby, I am so sorry," he says again, kissing my jaw.

"Don't apologize for them. I'm not alone anymore. I'll get over it."

A roar sounds behind me just as Knox's hand cups my cheek. My body melts into his touch despite the snarls at my back.

Snorted breaths heat the rear of my neck. *Four.* I can sense them. A line standing tall behind me.

Rotating slowly, I come face-to-face with the ghouls staring me down. Their blank frosted eyes remain focused on me, Aziel not revealing why it's now only the four of them.

My ghoul lurks at the forefront. A few steps behind him are the three others, snarling and flashing their yellowed teeth: a Virideist, the shade of forest green; a Diennar, with skin as murky as muddy water; and a Nigeros, with skin the shade of ebony.

My head cocks to the side, studying the lineup. The Nigeros had not joined us previously. I haven't seen one in person, but Valen has talked about them countless times. The single breed that can supply him with everything he needs on its own. A rarity.

Plumes of white air burst from its nostrils, the frigid cold holding each stream steady for long seconds before they disappear. Though they all watch me, there's something more intense about the Nigeros's stare. Something more threatening.

It huffs loudly with each tentative step I take forward. Shaking fingers reach for the beast, unsure how my magic will respond to touching another ghoul. I've only ever been this close to or touched Aziel. "Are there more of you?" I ask.

It only grunts, dropping its face close to mine, its forked tongue slipping past those leathery lips, slithering along my cheek, my mouth, and down the exposed part of my throat. I expect to feel the chill of the outdoors with the removal of its warm, wet tongue from my skin, but my body is on fire.

My gaze tracks down to the thick cock growing at the ghoul's hips. Black and ridged. Long and stiff. Its hips flex forward in invitation until Aziel roars. "Mine."

Looking up into his white eyes, I echo his declaration. "Mine."

The single word seems to calm him, while my magic hammers beneath my skin, eager for a taste of what the Nigeros might offer. Then the Diennar steps forward, sniffing my hair loudly. It's the smallest of the four, nearly the size of a large man.

"Bryony. Name. Bryony, take power," Aziel grumbles.

Chilled fingers wrap around mine, Knox keeping me from taking another step closer. "Bri, I don't think that's a good idea." The words are whispered through gritted teeth as if he believes the ghouls won't hear him through me.

His gaze bounces from beast to beast. Each with rock-solid staffs waiting to take a wielder, waiting for me. I can feel them all beneath my skin, calling out to me. Eager to give me more than my body can likely take.

"My essence wants their dark magic." The words leave my mouth, but sound distant. As if I'm listening to someone else say them from afar.

"Bri." Skepticism is thick in Knox's tone. His tight squeeze of my hand is his final warning against what I am about to do.

I understand his fear, but he's here with me. He will help me should things go wrong.

"Do you want me to name you, too?" I ask the ghouls.

They all grunt in unison, each taking a step closer.

It was easy to name Aziel. I could feel him, so I knew he was the same Azukeen. Not to mention, he could talk and knew my name. Will it be the same for these, too?

Standing a bit taller, I face the small army of ghouls I'm slowly making mine.

Stepping before the Diennar, I place my hand on its chest. "Your name is Tarak." He roars, making a sound that might resemble the name I gave him, but could have been nothing at all.

Then I move to the Virideist. "You will be Warrick." He, too, roars, producing similar noises to his brethren.

Last, I stop in front of the Nigeros, my hand over its chest, the pump of what must be its heart underneath strong. "Keres. I will call you Keres." He, too, roars as if in agreement before snatching me off my feet.

"Keres give you power," he grumbles. The words are just clear enough that my eyes go wide before his claw hooks into my pants, tearing them down my legs.

What have I done?

46

BRYONY

THE HOT BREATH OF the Nigeros fans out over my skin, my bare legs covered in goosebumps from the winter air. The contrasting temperatures overwhelming my oversensitized skin.

As if he can tell I'm close to freezing, Keres carries me through the barrier leading to the tunnels, the other ghouls at our heels. I can only assume Knox is too, as I can't see him around the massive barrel chest blocking my view.

The moment we pass through the barrier, I'm held against the wall, a gnarled hand running over the crotch of my soaked panties. This may be the worst idea, but my body wants this. My essence is calling out to take more inside us. To have more dark power coursing through me. Power my dark side wants to use to eliminate everyone who stands against my true family.

Continuing to pursue me would be a grave mistake. A misjudgment that would leave them dead and buried. Anyone who comes for me or the people I love will receive no mercy from me. The definition of who I must be now. It's the ruthless edge I have to adopt to make amends for the danger I have put everyone in.

I shake my head, trying to clear the violent thoughts. Graphic, brutal and bloody scenes flashing through my mind and drawing out my grin. Surely a consequence of spending too much time with Valen and his merciless behavior.

Pain explodes at my entrance as Keres presses inside me, dropping me back into the present. My fingers claw at his rough skin, trying to find purchase against the intrusion. Aziel stretches me, but it always seems as if he slid in with relative ease and then expanded to fit me.

The hot breath of the Nigeros fans out over my skin, my bare legs covered in goosebumps from the winter air. The contrasting temperatures are overwhelming my oversensitized skin. My body is incapable of managing the stark changes while my nervous system feeds on its adrenaline boost.

As if he can tell I'm close to freezing, Keres carries me through the barrier leading to the tunnels, the other ghouls at our heels. I can only assume Knox is, too, as I can't see him around the massive barrel chest that blocks my view.

The moment we pass through the barrier, I'm held against the wall, a gnarled hand running over the crotch of my soaked panties. This may be the worst idea, but my body wants this. My essence is calling out to take more inside us. It screams to have more dark power coursing through me. Power, my dark side wants to use to eliminate everyone who stands against my true family.

Continuing to pursue me would be a grave mistake. A misjudgment that would leave them dead and buried. Anyone who comes for me or the people I love will receive no mercy from me. It's the definition of who I must be now. It's the ruthless edge I have to adopt to make amends for the danger I have put everyone in.

I shake my head, trying to clear the violent thoughts. Graphic, brutal, and bloody scenes flash through my mind, drawing out my grin. Surely a consequence of spending too much time with Valen and his merciless behavior.

Pain explodes at my entrance as Keres presses inside me, dropping me back into the present. My fingers claw at his rough skin, trying to find purchase against the intrusion. Aziel stretches me, but it always seems as if he slides in with relative ease and then expands to fit me.

But not Keres. His cock is stretching me too far, too fast. My panting breaths wafting into his chest, my eyes shifting as they do with Knox.

My senses sharpen to the ghoul version. The sights, sounds, and feel of Keres working himself inside me, exceeding the limitations of my human shell. Every thrust is more relentless than the last. His cock fills me until my body feels as though it may split in two. One half light and one half dark, crumpling to the ground, still eager to absorb every bit of power that surrounds us.

Ecstasy shoots through my veins with the first spark of power siphoned between us. My fingers claw at his shoulders, taking punishing thrust after thrust. A sharp sting draws out my hiss as my shoulder blades scrape along the stone walls, tipping me more toward pain than pleasure. But I want it. Crave it. Need it.

"Keres," I groan, as another bolt of power shoots through me, his cock expanding inside me and pulsing. A *thrum, thrum, thrum* that only sends me barreling toward my release.

The ghouls all roar in unison as Keres pounds into me. The pressure is building inside me, my body ready to combust. Every sensation overwhelms my senses. My essence is craving more, but my body is on the verge of collapse.

Aziel's power funneling into me is like the darkness snuffing out every bit of light. Like, I am filling my body with the dominant side of my magic. The dark. The heart of who I am. A pool for me to draw from, sharpening my view of the world, my abilities, and my desire to step out of the shadows.

As expected, Keres is nothing like Aziel. Not in the way he fucks me, not in his power. His magic is a raging fire of onyx flames licking at my insides. Hot and searing my flesh, burning it to ash so it may rise anew like a phoenix. The temperature is rising higher and higher with each thrust of his hips, and all I can do is bask in the heat.

Those claws are biting into my full thighs, leaving me with fresh wounds and scars that will follow. Scars that will match the ones Aziel has already left on me. A collection Valen has promised to add to using his prized daggers. The thought makes my walls flutter in anticipation. I want that. I want it all.

My hands grip the back of Keres's neck, his head dipping low, those curved horns tangling in my loose curls. His horns are longer than most ghouls, winding high like a corkscrew from just above his temples, adding to his height.

His forked tongue slips along my lips, a slow glide as if begging for entrance. Fucking a ghoul is one thing, but kissing one might be another. Still, as if his power funneling into me calls for me to open up freely, my lips part, and his tongue slips inside my mouth. That fire consumes me as I taste a ghoul for the first time.

More of his power rushes inside me, so quickly and in such abundance that it's overstimulating. My essence is soaking it all up, cackling as if it's some evil villain who has finally conquered the world.

"More," I groan, yanking my mouth away from Keres's when a new set of claws scrape over my skin.

That deep green palm runs up my thigh, Warrick's forked tongue slithering out past his lips as if ready for a taste. A playful nature to the movement in contrast with the rough drag of those sharp points over my flesh.

That line of pleasure and pain is once again blurring.

And then it occurs to me. These ghouls wanting to fuck me shouldn't be unexpected. They are mine and my three dark wielders. The Virideist primed for the dichotomy that comes with being Grisym, the Nigeros, Valen's preferred, and the Diennar, Pierce's.

Their essences live inside me now, and so the ghouls have come to share that power.

Keres suddenly swings us away from the wall, my legs shoved from around his waist, so my feet hit the damp tunnel floor. It's only seconds before I'm bent over, my palms barely catching the wall before my face does.

"Careful," Knox growls, eliciting roars from the ghouls surrounding me. Aziel previously allowed Knox to play, though not this time. His aggression is punching through my insides as if it were my own. Tonight is for him and the three new ghouls I've now come to know. It's for them to service their queen. Their power is ready to merge with mine, too.

Keres notches his thick cock at my entrance, a garbled version of my name on his lips before driving forward. A scream barrels through me. Pain ricochets through my insides before that fiery essence fills me again. "More. Give me more."

I'm like a moth to those flames. An addict in need of stronger hits of her favorite drug. My groan rumbling up my throat as the wet, warm touch of a tongue flicks over my clit.

Ghouls don't kneel. That's what Knox and Valen both told me. Aziel had been the first to break that norm. My sign that my connection to the ghouls would be something to revel in. The power balance I have with the creatures we siphon from is unlike any other wielder has ever experienced. I wasn't just another dark wielder or Grisym looking to fill an empty tank with power that wasn't rightfully mine.

Commanding them had been a surprise, but it shouldn't have been.

The bite of sharp teeth against my inner thigh pulls me out of my thoughts, the pain and pleasure swirling with the new power coursing through me. Tarak's tongue flicks over my swollen bundle of nerves before he drags those dagger-sharp teeth over me. A back and forth that keeps my body guessing and teetering on the edge.

My head flies forward, forehead tapping the cool stone of the wall. I wait for the pain to explode there too, but a cushion of dark essence floats in my peripheral vision, Knox's eyes meeting mine. Concern shines behind his eyes, a plea for me to stop this on the tip of his tongue, hidden behind his parted lips. My mind cannot focus long enough to give him the reassurance he needs. Not when my core is full and my essence is drinking in Keres's magic like a dehydrated man in a desert.

Not when Tarak is torturing me with that tongue and Keres is pounding into me so hard his claws have pierced my skin. A smile pulls at my mouth as I think of the tender bruises that will mar my skin tonight.

Bruises Graham will obsess over, and Pierce will caudle me for. Only Valen will look at them and smile, that wicked grin revealing just how much he enjoys watching me bleed.

"Enough," Aziel growls, shoving Keres out of the way. They both roar at each other, chests heaving, but I can't move. There's no time to intervene as another cock rams into me from behind. That leathery skin scratches along my bare skin, drawing out my hiss through gritted teeth.

Initially, just the sensation of a new ghoul rushes through me. My essence is eager for novel power to race through my veins and intertwine itself with our DNA. Yet, the ghoul holds its magic at bay while my body learns this new beast. While Warrick drives into me with the same force as Keres had, the roll of his pelvis elicits new sensations. Places inside me that no one has ever explored, his essence entering me like a soft caress.

The slow trickle of his power binds to the core of who I am. His magic kisses along the length of mine, the way Knox's does. "Fuck." My fist slams against the stone wall, the sensations washing over my body overwhelming.

Tarak doesn't stop teasing me. My release is ready to boil over. When the same warm wetness strokes across my bare ass before sneaking between my cheeks, the tip of a forked half slips past the ring of muscle of my back door. Yet, Warrick doesn't stop moving behind me. A languid rut keeps me tumbling off the edge, instead of allowing me a slow creep.

Still, I'm so close. Too close. I'm not ready to be done.

Not as my ghouls play my body like a fiddle.

"Fuck. Aziel! It's—"

The words die on my tongue as my release barrels through me. What had been a simmering storm suddenly rages, Warrick's power finally bursting inside me in heavy waves. The shot of power is too intense for the shell of my body to hold, but he doesn't stop, and I don't block it out. A technique Tosch had been teaching me.

I take it in. Every. Last. Bit.

I'm spent when all three ghouls finally pull away from me, my body slumping against the wall as I fight to catch my breath.

My ghouls only stare as Knox comes forward, my jeans dangling from his fingers. "As good as new," he grins.

"At least something here is."

47

VALEN

The anxious knot of the unknown fills my gut.

I want to know where the fuck my woman is. Neither she nor Knox is answering our calls or messages.

Vincent and Jorddan only stated they had business to tend to. No matter how much I snarled and questioned, they gave nothing else away.

We even reached out to that worthless brother of hers, Merrick. It's undecided whether he's playing both sides or if he's really on ours. My gut tells me that even if he proves he won't betray us, we will never have one hundred percent of his loyalty.

It still doesn't sit well with me that he showed up unannounced with Harley at the manor. Not that his warning call would have been enough for me just to let him waltz through the door. It had been for Vincent, though. The fucker kept their relationship to themselves, the details they've shared remaining vague even now.

Vincent can vouch for him all he wants, but the world is full of skilled actors. Backstabbers who will become whatever is necessary to get under your skin. To force you to lower your guard before slitting your throat.

I've been by Jorddan's side for a while. I've seen the New Order men and women who would die for him. The thousands who would dive off a cliff for the cause and protect everyone sworn to it without question. I'm one of them.

There was no desire or room for me to question my orders. It didn't matter if I knew the why or the details. The tiny nuances bore little weight versus my vow to Jorddan.

There's never been another priority above the mission until Bri. I cannot pinpoint when this started, nor when I decided to brutalize any and every soul who so much as looks at her wrong. That soft shit is for Pierce. He's the one obsessed with her, so attached to her that he can't go five fucking minutes without talking to or about her.

Yet I'm the one sitting here in the dark, in her bedroom, waiting for her to return. She should have only been delayed a few hours. Vincent insisted it was best to let her cool down when Bri had sped from the house like her ass was on fire this morning.

Pierce and I didn't argue with Vincent after Geneva's departure. Their family had shit to work out, and that was understandable. So we climbed into the car with a New Order soldier, who drove us to a portal, which brought us back to Integretew. Vincent swore he'd get her back safely. That was almost twelve fucking hours ago.

We only have a few more days of freedom before our class schedules bog us down. Not that I give a shit. Mandate keeps me here, not the desire to listen to a bunch of old fucks try to teach me something. I don't need them for the future ahead.

I twirl my daggers between my fingers, eager to launch them across the room, but not wanting to waste my power stores in case I need to make someone rot from the inside tonight. Considerations I never paid much attention to before Bri barged into my life and fucked my shit up.

Pierce and Graham insisted on waiting with me, but I couldn't stand either of them and their bleeding hearts tonight. Not when I'm this on edge, a gut feeling settling at the base of my stomach, shouting something is very wrong.

"Where the fuck are you, Bryony?" I growl into the dark, stabbing my favorite dagger into her mattress. Protection I've had with me since I was a boy.

The room is silent, the dark refusing to answer me. Why would it? I am *the* dark—a weapon of death and destruction.

My focus remains on the bed across from me. A twin to Bri's that likely hasn't been touched. Someone smoothed the comforter perfectly over the full-size mattress, fluffing each mint-green pillow to perfection. I'd wanted to gag when I knocked on the door and Ella answered. Her upbeat, yet surprisingly snarky, personality somewhat reminded me of Camilla. At least I'd gotten used to that weird girl. Still, there's only room for one chipper woman in my life, and I choose my girl's best friend.

Although we haven't been here long, Bri hasn't even laid eyes on her new roommate since the day we arrived. Like ships passing in the night, they miss each other every time. A small mercy, as I doubt Bri wants someone new and inviting prying into our lives. Not with the mess we're wading through.

Camilla's mere memory sparks thoughts of our friends at Beauxgraton. My scowl deepens, wondering how I'd let her, Bri, and Graham crawl their way under my skin these past few months. I've barely spoken to them since the New Order soldiers escorted the group back to campus. Damian is the only exception, as he has been reporting back to me on a few that I thought he should keep an eye on.

Worry knotted my insides until I knew our crew was back safely, but never surfaced for Damian. He's used to coming and going on his own, the perks of being a married man in wielding school. Your freedoms are different. The utmost respect is given to quality time with your spouse and the continuation of our magical lines. Though I doubt a baby is on the horizon for him and Tosch anytime soon.

Most of those soldiers returned to their posts after the drop-off, while others remained at Beauxgraton as our version of spies. Our watchdogs are planted in various roles to protect them and us. Our eyes and ears to report back to Jorddan. The intel they've already gathered is funneling back to us in droves. Roman's undercovers have been easy to spot. Almost too easy.

Men like Roman won't hesitate to use whomever they need to get to their target. Our friends are those pawns for him to get to Bri. We know that. It's only a matter of when. The how is irrelevant. We'll strike back with the force of ancient armies, ready to mutilate him and his sympathizers for once again harming the innocent. It wouldn't be the first time.

My personal grudge with the Avalons bubbles to the surface. It was yet another reason that it was so easy to hate Bryony from the moment I first saw her. I made it my mission to punish and torment her for the wrongs of her family name, and that was before it appeared she'd be a problem getting involved with Pierce.

Roman invalidated my father's work long ago. Biological research and study used to be part of the curriculum. My father was a consultant for the Department of Education until about a year after Roman took on the position as director. The man dismissed my dad without a thought, and the program was cut at almost every institution. Integretew is one of the few that refused removal from their curriculum, invoking their privilege to choose.

My father encouraged Bri to enroll in the course if she stayed here longer than this semester. My chest suddenly aches as I contemplate my thoughts on the matter. The heel of my hand only makes the ache worse, as if acknowledging it intensifies those sensations of disapproval, making them harder to tolerate. It's easier to deny that I have genuine feelings for her. Easier to pretend I only enjoy the banter and fucking her until my name is the only one she knows.

It's a lie. I'd lay down my life for Bryony. A truth that only amplifies the risks of her existing at the center of this war. She has always been the key. She and Vincent are both insanely powerful Grisyms who should rise to save the world. But so is Jorddan. A truth he never shared with us until fucking Bri tattled on me to Daddy, and he looped her into the fold as if they'd had a whole life together.

The groan of hinges draws my focus to the door, a dagger tight in my grip, ready to mutilate anyone who isn't supposed to be here.

Bri shuffles into the room alone, a smear of dirt on her cheek and above her eye as she snaps the lights on. The tendril of essence she'd used sinks back into the tip of her finger when our eyes meet, her stare telling me what I need to know.

Exhaustion rolls her shoulders forward, but her eyes look different. They're not as stark white or as black as I've seen before. There's a cloudy quality to them, with stars. Flickering little dots to match her essence.

"Where the fuck have you been?" I snarl.

"Save it, Val. I'm not in the mood for your broody shit. I'm tired and I need a shower," she sighs, not even bothering to slow her progression toward the en suite bathroom. A tight box similar to what we have at Beauxgraton.

I'm on my feet in seconds, following her as she discards layers of clothing, leaving a trail on the floor. Her body is deliciously exposed as she steps behind the curtain into the shower.

Not quick enough, though.

Dried blood clings to her thighs, trailing from scratch marks and deep holes still open and oozing.

Shoving the curtain aside, I ignore the spray of the water soaking the front of my shirt as she tilts her head back, allowing the water to saturate her long, dark curls.

"What the fuck happened?" I attempt to soften my tone, but the edge remains. She looks like she went through a fucking battle when she supposedly hadn't left the manor grounds.

"Valen, can I have five minutes to shower alone? I don't need you hovering, too," she bites, grabbing her shampoo and lathering it through her long strands.

"You're going to talk to me right fucking now," I demand.

Her eyes meet mine, angry and full of disdain. "I. Do not. Answer. To you. Get out of my bathroom. I will talk to you when I'm ready. Take it or leave it."

My fingers grip her chin, her teeth grinding beneath my firm grip. "This is your fault, my little Forbidden Fruit. You let me fuck that sweet pussy, and then you made me give a damn about you. Too late to take it back now."

That defiance fades from her eyes, but the set of her mouth doesn't change as she snatches her face out of my grip. The clouds dulling her irises, shifting with her emotions. I can almost feel it. Feel her beneath my skin.

Fuck, I've never wanted anything so much. Every fiber of my being burns for Bri's attention and her trust.

"Get. Out."

Then she snatches the curtain closed.

Not willing to piss her off and have her magic try to murder me again, I stalk back into her bedroom, strip down to my boxer briefs, and climb into her bed. I'm not leaving until she talks to me. She can just fucking deal with it.

I meant what I said. She made me care, and I won't fucking apologize for how I choose to go about ensuring her safety or determining who I need to kill on any given day. Bri can take it or leave it.

A man like me remains loyal to the people who live in his heart. We will pillage and plunder whomever and whatever we have to for them. I don't know how that witch did it, but Bryony Guthrie somehow became the most important person in my life.

It's nearly thirty minutes later before Bri waltzes out of the bathroom, a towel wrapped around her hair and a robe covering her body. Thick water droplets still trickle down her temples and dot her cheeks and legs.

"You're still here?" she scoffs.

"Dry off and get in bed."

"You piss me off so much sometimes." Her eyes roll, but she does as I told her, meticulously drying her skin, not even bothering to hide her body from me. The marks on her skin are a distraction. I'll force Graham to work on them tomorrow. It's not exactly how his gift works, but he'll be all too happy to try for her.

She's slow to slip on sleep shorts and a tank top that hides none of her ample cleavage from my view. The shorts revealing the lower curve of her ass. Flesh I want to squeeze while she rides my dick.

Running my hands down my stomach, itching to grab hold of my swelling cock, I keep quiet as she braids her hair. A ritual so her curls don't tangle when she sleeps. She'd done the same for me a few days after Vincent brought me back to the land of the living, my body still so riddled with pain I couldn't put my hair up.

The weight of my bun feels heavy now as I adjust myself on the pillows, moving toward the center of the bed instead of to the side to allow her more room. I'm not giving her space. Not tonight.

Bri chose me, and I picked her. We don't need distance, but I'm also smart enough to know that tonight she doesn't need my dagger at her throat while I ruthlessly fuck multiple orgasms out of her before filling her with my release. She needs Pierce or Graham. Their tender shit, not me forcing answers out of her.

Judging by the marks on her body, she's been with a ghoul. Likely that fucking Azukeen, who seems more keen to bow to her than all the others. It's as if she claimed it too.

Bri collapses back onto the bed, her head landing on my outstretched arm, but she just lies straight. Her body stretched into a straight plank beside me. I may not be the cuddly type, but it's rubbing me the wrong way that she won't even face me.

"Ready to tell me why the hell it looks like a wild animal mauled you and where you were?" That same edge of arrogance that usually accompanies my tone is still there, though I try to stamp it down. There's an openness she has with the others, her secrets and desires laid bare. Her trust in them is eons beyond what she might have in me. The hard ass in me loathes how I crave her trust, too. I need her inner thoughts and fears as much as I need her body. Selfishly, I need it, knowing I cannot be the support the others are for her. I'm not built that way.

"Will you shut it if I do?"

"Forbidden Fruit." I place a finger under her chin, forcing her gaze to meet mine in the dark. "That all depends on what you tell me."

"You don't get to say a word until I say so. Do you understand me?" A smirk draws up the corner of my mouth, my fingers gripping her chin hard this time, before pressing a kiss to her pouty lips.

"We'll see. Now talk."

And she does, recounting walking in on her mother pleading for her piece of shit son back. Fury tightens my jaw, the muscles flexing so uncontrollably I can't help but grunt against the pain.

"But thought better of it, and Knox and I returned him. Gods, it was awful. Roman came after me, but my mother didn't do a thing to stop him other than ask him not to hurt me." Sarcasm bleeds into her tone, her head shaking slightly as she mocks her mother's response.

Seconds pass before I process what she'd said, my eyes gaping in her direction, baring my teeth. "Hold the fuck up! You gave Harley back?" I bolt upright. I'd been listening, but somehow the words hadn't registered. Maybe I was too distracted by the way her body shifted under the idle strokes of my thumb on her bare skin. More likely, I didn't want to hear the truth.

"Down," Bri orders, but I don't obey, staring defiantly. "Yes, it was safer for everyone; he doesn't matter. How my mother treated me matters."

I know I should soften toward her, but I can't. I'm too worried about how many wielders I might have to filet open and how pissed I am that her mother once again didn't choose her. Blood oath or not, that choice doesn't change. My parents may not be fans of how I've decided to leave my mark on the world, but they've always been rocks in this tumultuous life.

"Bri," I lean over her, my face hovering so close our mouths brush. "This is not what I'm good at. I'm not showering you with sweet words or compassion, but I can promise you that no one will harm you but me. I will eviscerate anyone who tries. I don't give a fuck who they are. Do you understand?"

She nods, her lips softly pressing to mine, before her hands find my bare back. Her touch is feather-light, tracing over the tattoos that paint my skin.

"I fucked a Nigeros," she whispers. "I named him Keres."

"You... what?"

"That's why I'm so exhausted and... beat up."

Once again, my eyes widen as I search her features for the joke in her admission. "Not the Azukeen?" I question.

"Well, let's just say I had my first foursome. Aziel, Keres, a Virideist I named Warrick, and a Diennar I'm calling Tarak."

I kiss her hard, my tongue sweeping into her mouth, so fucking turned on I'm ready to explode. "Forbidden Fruit, you have no idea what you've done."

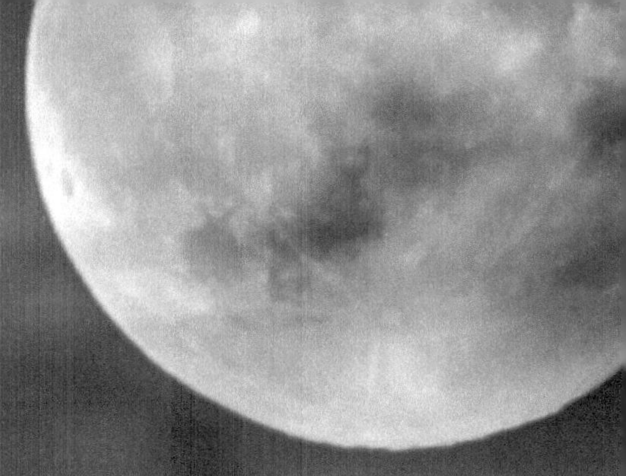

48

GRAHAM

NO MORNING SHOULD START with walking in on your girlfriend fucking another one of her boyfriends.

Valen kept Bri sequestered away all day yesterday. The two of them were trapped in a bubble of my new best friend's making. Even when Pierce and I dropped by, he only allowed us in long enough to view Bri's sleeping form before shoving us back through the door. *"You assholes aren't going to disturb her sleep,"* he'd growled before slamming the door in our faces.

It was seconds later that his text came through, stating she'd fucked with a bunch of ghouls, her essence went wild, and he had to use her urn to store her magic.

We only received one more text after that yesterday. His confirmation that Bri woke up and seemed fine put me at ease. Still, I wasn't going to use Valen's distancing messages as an excuse not to go to her this morning, though now I wish I hadn't.

I'm not disillusioned enough to believe Bri won't continue to dip her toe into the ghoul pool. She commands them. It's only natural that she'd feel the need to siphon from them. Still, his message gave me pause. Where the hell had she encountered multiple ghouls and then been able to screw them without being noticed?

I hadn't thanked her brother for much, but this was all Vincent's doing. He'd insisted she take several storage vessels with her, each requiring her blood to portal the magic elsewhere. The three of us had to learn how the spells worked in case Bri was incapable of activating them on her own—a small blessing, judging by Valen's description.

That eerie dread of helplessness still lingers with me. It has been looming over me since yesterday. Hell, maybe for weeks now. A light wielder doesn't belong in this world I dove headfirst into. My parents didn't teach me to take by force or pledge my soul to a mission that has nothing to do with me. I am the exact type of wielder they were working to dethrone. Someone like me shouldn't be wrapped up in dark matters.

Yet, I'm in now. So deep in the trenches, the sky seems to fade away from view. There would be no chance of pulling out even if I wanted to. My skin burns with Jorddan's tattoo as if he knows my chaotic thoughts.

Bri needs me, and in a way, I need the friendships I've formed with the guys. We contemplate our futures all the time. Trying to determine how the pieces will fit together as we live the journey. The road we're forging will be the past future wielders will read. History has always been the calling I saw for myself. However, with the New Order, I've been given a genuine purpose.

The moment my eyelids flew open this morning, I needed to see her. It wasn't enough to hear it from a man I would trust with my life. My mind was convinced that unless I laid eyes on her, it wasn't real. She wasn't truly okay unless I could see it myself.

It's not that I didn't believe Valen. He has been nothing but brutally honest with me about who he is from day one. Our newly budding friendship was unexpected, but necessary. I hadn't been prepared for us to understand each other as well as we do. We're proof that similarities stretch beyond what the naked eye detects.

Ambition, drive, loyalty, and the willingness to sacrifice comprise the core of our values. We may differ in our approach to expressing these characteristics, but they remain the same. We're just two wielders willing to make tough choices to achieve our desired outcome, and there's nothing regrettable about that.

In truth, getting to know the guy is helping me release myself from the constraints my parents and our community have put on me. Permission I unknowingly willingly granted to others, allowing them to dictate my path ahead. Limitations and hurdles I allowed myself to believe were my ticket to success. It's bullshit.

No matter what avenue we pick to achieve what we deem success, it doesn't matter. Someone will praise you. Another will disagree. One will give advice that propels you forward, while the other waits to watch you fall. Another will criticize you for opposing norms, while they remain trapped in them, complaining about the injustices of the world. I don't give a fuck anymore.

Who could have predicted Valen Greer would be the one to set me free?

It's the first day of classes. It's instinct to start my day with my greatest academic rival. My best friend. My girlfriend. The plan was to lead her down to breakfast and then to class, the way we'd done most mornings at Beauxgraton. Then hold her hand and kiss her before she walks backward into her classroom.

Normal stuff.

But it seemed Valen never left her side, which is how I found my new friend balls deep inside our girl, her body bent over the desk, with her skirt flipped up, showcasing her bare ass. The clap of their skin was silent until I stepped foot in the room.

She never saw me, but he did, smirking before I bolted. I'm not shy about sex like I thought I'd be. It's just a constant uphill battle acclimating to watching her with someone else. Oddly enough, it never even crosses my mind when I'm part of the action. It's only when I'm a spectator, on the outside looking in.

I can't shake the sounds she made as Valen drove into her from my consciousness. My feet carrying me through the hallways at an angry pace, while I mindlessly search for Pierce. Our quad is my only piece of normalcy here. A base I can ground myself on when my anxious thoughts get away from me. We don't know anyone else. There's no desire to make friends or play nice. Not when anyone could be a spy of our enemy.

This is a whole new setting. A reality that equally excites and sets my nerves firing.

That first day stepping onto campus at Beauxgraton was supposed to be the beginning of an epic chapter—a last first day of my education. Yet, here I am in another new place, traversing the halls of an international institution. This was not the plan.

One would think the nausea bubbling in my gut is nothing more than "new kid jitters", but it's not. This is not a situation where it pays to be the fresh-faced transfer. It draws attention from those do-gooders who always want to befriend the outsider, so no one is alone. I don't want that.

But I am another outsider simply trying to fit in. Not because I want friends. I found those, though many are an ocean away. Keeping them here wasn't worth the risk of drawing unwanted attention from our director of education. Instead, they can remain a safe distance away and serve as a level of infiltration Roman wouldn't expect. They can be our eyes and ears, allowing us all to watch our backs without anyone suspecting.

There's no question that Roman is already aware that the four of us are here. Some professor looking to climb their way up the education ladder may have already reached out, beaming about teaching the director of education's "daughter" for a semester. It may be an innocent conversation or one built on their ambitions.

A student may have already informed their parents that they've seen Bryony here.

It's possible Roman finds us himself, actually conducting his own dirty work. Men like him will either find the answers on their own in secret or they'll aim to keep their hands clean of malicious intent. Bri has called her former father selfish, so I suspect it's the latter. The question is, who does he trust enough to do his digging? Once Jorddan finds out, they too will be added to the kill list—*such a shame.*

Either way, we're not hidden as long as we're registered in the school system. That was never the point. Bri wanted to stay close to her father, and he wouldn't allow her to drop out of the publicly mandated system. She was never trying to hide; she was stacking the deck in her favor.

We followed. A path I'm confident we'll continue down until we take our last breaths. It won't matter what our romantic relationship becomes. Bryony is now a fixture in our lives. A precious charm none of us can live without, regardless of how we grow or change with time.

The rich scent of cologne wafts up my nostrils, my nose twitching against the sneeze as a body slides up beside me. I recognize his face, but can't recall his name. "Hey Graham." His British accent gives me pause. I'm not used to all the accents. There are a handful of international students at Beauxgraton. Here, we Americans are the minority.

"Hi," I practically groan, my hands tucked in my pockets as I jog down the staircase.

"Percy," he supplies as if aware I couldn't remember his name. "Percy Carden."

I give him nothing more than a glance in his direction, then hit the next platform of the main staircase. My pace quickens, wanting this interaction to end. "Oh, right? Sorry, I'm kind of in a rush."

He pats the air as if attempting to calm me. A peculiar gesture, but perhaps it's typical of the British. My parents worked hard for everything we had. Their wealth was enough to keep up appearances in society, but not to travel the world. I've never been anywhere until now. "Oh, right, right, of course." His crisp accent oddly stresses each word. "I was actually looking for your friend. Bryony Avalon."

My body jolts to a stop so abruptly that pain shoots through my joints. A silent curse leaves me gritting my teeth as my foot nearly misses the last step, which would have sent me hurtling toward the floor. My abdominals painfully contract, keeping me balanced as I grip the railing for dear life. "Why are you asking about Bryony?"

"I'm her student liaison. They assign them if you're studying abroad from other countries." My brow lowers. I hadn't heard anything about it. No correspondence. No whispers. Nothing. Jorddan would have ensured that they vetted anyone with that sort of required access to his daughter, and we were aware.

Nausea swells in my gut.

Knox, too, was titled her mentor. A "position" Headmistress Milgren created to keep their need to work together under lock and key. Memories of following them in the early hours of the morning and finding out they'd been sleeping together make it hard to swallow. The lump in my throat is forcing me to believe this guy is a threat to what the four of us have built. My mind is convinced that he shouldn't be alone with Bri; they'll end up fucking too.

It's not fair to hold it against Bri and Knox. They're different. We know that, but I can't ignore the overwhelming dread washing over me. A weight heavier than worrying about my girlfriend will add another man to the mix. It's the cold sweat of danger. The pit that lingers at the bottom of your stomach, knowing the worst is lurking just around the corner, waiting to sink sharp talons into your skin, so there's no running away. It's the acrid taste of genuine fear.

I'd known something was off with them then. The spying only confirmed it, and then Bri's reaction when she pushed me away. That same feeling hits me now. Only stronger. More violent and unhinged than before. With Knox, I never felt like his eyes held evil intent.

This Percy guy is different. His grin spreads wide, like a possessed doll, as his eyes lock onto my face, unblinking. "Are you alright?" He ducks his head, forcing my stare to meet his. Every nerve ending is firing in warning. *Get away. Run.*

Narrowing my eyes, studying his face, I roll my shoulders back, stretching my spine a little straighter. Hoping I've schooled my features into an air of indifference, I keep my tone cool. "Fine. But why are you asking me if you're supposed to be her liaison? Shouldn't you have her schedule? Room number?"

"Well, you seemed to be friends last night. I saw…" My mouth presses into a tight line, features steeled into what I hope is an intimidating expression. My trust in everyone around us who wasn't in that manor was non-existent. He clears his throat, that stupid grin finally dropping. "Well, uh, you're from the same school in America. I assumed—"

"I don't know where she is," I cut him off, turning on my heel and storming away.

That guy sets me on edge as much as Carter. Something isn't right about either of them. I need to talk to Pierce. We need to figure out if either of them is an actual threat.

Me: *Where are you?*
Pierce: *Meet you in front of the dining hall in 5*
Me: *Hurry up*
Pierce: *I said I'm coming*

My frown deepens with Pierce's last text. He's not usually short with me. We're not besties or anything, but he's always been amicable. It makes me wonder if he, too, went in search of Bri, only to find Valen plowing into her. His mood always darkens to a scolding black when he doesn't spend enough alone time with her. A point I would never bring up, because I also live with the insecurities of wondering why I alone am not enough.

I hadn't noticed I'd been pacing like a caged animal until Pierce's hand clasps around the curve of my shoulder. My movement stops as if realizing he's there for the first time. "What's wrong?" His brow furrows, wrinkles deepening on his forehead as he stares back at me.

"Nothing." Releasing a deep breath, my head falls back. "Maybe nothing. I don't know."

"Graham, what the hell happened? Where's Bri?"

"Why the fuck does everyone think I'm her keeper?" I hadn't meant for the words to burst free. I have nothing against Pierce. Not anymore. I'm not pissed at him. I'm worried and fucking stressed out of my mind. My inner perfectionist bristles with frazzled energy, leaving me unsure of what to do next or even how to operate like a normal fucking person anymore.

I'd chosen to follow Bri here. She is my best friend and might be the love of my life. I would follow her anywhere, even at the expense of everything I have worked so hard for. It does not void how intense this is. The constant adrenaline dumps might kill me before Roman even gets the chance.

Regardless, the second term starts today. The old me is still ingrained. It's still who I am. The need to make a good impression and ensure I am unforgettable to my professors lengthens my spine as reminders filter through my head in my dad's authoritative voice.

I'm just rattled.

This will pass.

"Calm down," Pierce whispers low. "We don't need to draw attention to ourselves."

"It might be too late for that. Some guy was asking me where Bri is. Said he's Bri's student liaison, and oh, that was after I found her being fucked by Valen over her desk."

Pierce doesn't flinch, but something passes behind his stare. When he and Bri first started hooking up, I'd doubted his intentions, but now I know he'd been just like me, caught up in the spell that is Bryony Avalon—Guthrie. Everything about her pulls you in and then drags you under. Her siren song is a call you can't resist, whether it's from a romantic standpoint or a platonic one.

No, I understand Pierce's obsession now, because I, too, had it from the beginning. Mine was just a detour through academics, friendship, and then a shared connection we could no longer ignore.

"Student liaison?" Pierce questions. "Did you get one?" He scratches the back of his head, his features scrunching as if piecing together a puzzle.

Readjusting my bag on my shoulder, I shake my head. "No. I've never heard of such a thing."

Pierce's hand clasps my shoulder again, angling me toward the dining hall. An attempt at making this look like an everyday conversation between friends. "Me either. We're not letting Bri alone with that guy or anyone. Not until we have some answers."

"Agreed," I nod. We both fall silent as we enter the food hall, gathering our trays and loading them with enough to feed the four of us.

Five minutes pass from the time we sat at a far table in the corner until those two waltz in, Bri's cheeks flushed as she rolls her eyes at Valen's words. Those pouty lips are more swollen than usual, with her wild curly hair loose over her shoulders. A smug grin pulls at Valen's mouth as he twirls his favorite dagger effortlessly, his eyes never leaving her face.

"I'm starving," Bri slides onto the end of the bench, Valen right beside her.

There's no missing his hand moving to her bare thigh, his fingers likely grazing higher than they should be in public under the hem of her uniform black skirt. We agreed to keep our relationship hidden for all our sakes, but, as usual, Valen seems determined to do as he pleases. The more the booze flowed a few nights ago, the less we thought about keeping our hands to ourselves. But this is broad daylight. We can't blame lowered inhibitions this time or forget our promises.

"I heard from Jorddan," Valen whispers across the table. "We'll be heading back to the manor after classes on Friday and then going after Mikhail Sorrhenson."

"Mikhail?" I ask. "As in the famous historian?"

"That's the one," Valen smirks, popping a piece of toast into his mouth.

Bri's list wasn't a public document passed around to everyone at the manor. Jorddan, Vincent, and Knox kept it close to them, only divulging certain names to us along the way. I didn't care to see it.

There was no need. Research was where I contributed. An assistant to Tosch as we rifled through texts attempting to find out more about Eistiabs and the connection between Bri and our professor. Jorddan made it clear my light heritage wouldn't be of use in the field. I wouldn't be out there murdering alongside them, but a bookworm they could use to gather and then decipher information.

Apparently, Bri was perfectly capable on her own.

"She was one of the wielders who spent a lot of time at my home when I was a child," Bri whispers, her eyes casting down to her lap. Her tone sounds distant, as if attempting to separate herself from the memory. "Mikhail was a wealth of knowledge according to Roman," Bri lets out a humorless huff of laughter, chewing on her inner lip. "He'd bring her around anytime my magic did something new. I was an object for her to study and document. She used to keep these journals of our interactions and the things she'd make me do." Bri's brow scrunches, her eyes darting back and forth as she parses through her thoughts. "She always used spelled ink. Only she could activate and then read it. Thinking back on it now, I wonder if she knew what I was."

"How long did this go on?" Pierce presses in, leaning across the table.

"The first time I remember meeting her, I was maybe five. Then she kept coming around until I left for Beauxgraton. As I got older, I got a little wiser and thought it better I didn't show her everything. Regardless, I was an anomaly. I could do things a light wielder shouldn't be able to do. It took me too long to realize I shouldn't have allowed her to see those things. Eventually, I hid them, but it would have already been too late."

Valen stabs his dagger into the tabletop, his essence dancing around the handle as he plays with Bri's hand. "Don't worry, my Little Forbidden Fruit. The second kill is so much easier than the first."

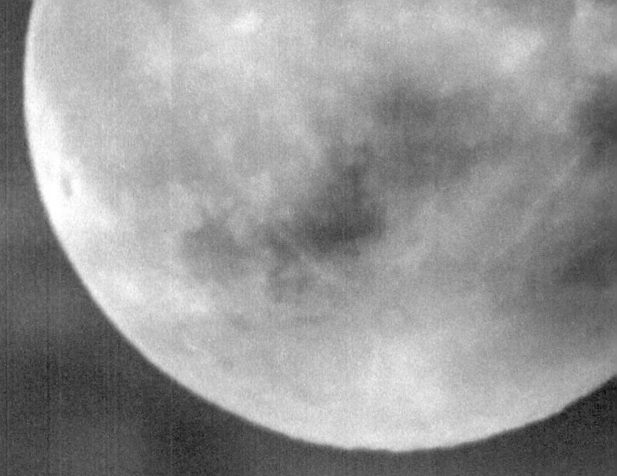

49

BRYONY

It's nearly impossible to ignore the scents that come together in a classroom. The wooden desks, ink, textbooks, plants, and unused magic serve as a novel essence waiting to be explored, mixing to become the most intoxicating aroma.

Inhaling deep, I take it all in. This is my place of peace, the place where I'm happiest, aside from Guthrie Manor, of course.

It's in human and wielder nature alike to yearn to find our place in the world. Our mission is swaddled in the innate need to find others or places where our passions and values can align so we have a place to call home. Institutions of any kind have always been where my puzzle piece fits. It was the one place where being a book nerd was not only acceptable but also often appreciated. The only place I didn't feel so alone. I could just be Bryony the braniac. That's what Merrick used to call me.

My heart races knowing I won't be able to hide as easily here at Integretew. Knox isn't here to purposely overlook me during specific modules. I'll have to hold my own.

Essence manipulation is a class that follows us through our years of study. The levels may change, and the professors may switch, but the class remains every semester until you graduate. The teaching styles differ so much that you're left with whiplash and confused. But the skills acquired from these classes are vital to a wielder's success. Our ability to manipulate our own essence and that of others becomes the foundation of our ability to work in the world of wielding, especially if we plan on taking on positions held in high esteem.

Graham and I slip into two desks, dead center in the front row.

The back of the room would have been my preference. It's easier to hide. Easier to blend in physically, but still stand out verbally. Refusing to sit in the front row is a sacrifice for him. In his mind, that single change ruins his chance to impress on the first day.

It would be stupid to believe Graham followed me here, but has no qualms about it. Every emotion flashes in those Caribbean turquoise eyes. He's never been able to hide them from me.

Fear.

Exhaustion.

Regret.

Worry.

Determination.

Resentment.

The crushing weight of knowing I am responsible for everything he's carrying damn-near guts me. I'd talked to Tosch about it. Her wisdom reminded me that I had given Graham an out. I told him to make a decision that wouldn't leave him hating me in the end. I think he made that choice based on the assumption that our lives wouldn't become more complicated than they already were. That we would find some steady ground and breathe as first-year wielding students.

I tell myself he knew better. That I wasn't unfair. But I was selfish. Even if I never said the words to him, I'd wanted him to pick me. To pick us. The New Order. I wanted my best friend to want to stay.

The chatter of our new student body fills the room. It's so different from what it had been at Beauxgraton. The clear divide between the light and the dark was ever-present, though our friend groups quickly mixed. Here, there is no divide. It's a jumbled mix of the light and the dark, chatting animatedly, laughing, and holding hands. It's everything my father has always wanted for our world.

Leaning in close, my fingers curl around Graham's, his warmth settling my insides. "We're welcome here." The words are barely above a whisper, but I know he heard them when he gives my hand a slight squeeze back.

Graham may be a light wielder, but part of him never felt like he quite fit either. Oddly enough, he fits with us more than I would have thought. He and Pierce were born into a power that should have been reversed. One shines bright in the light, and the other claws its way out of the dark. Perhaps that's why he and Valen have bonded.

"Welcome to a new semester," a raspy female voice carries over the chatter of the room. Her long dress flows out behind her as if she's wearing one of those sheer house gowns from the sixties. A regalness on display in the way she holds her chin high and shoulders back.

I gape awkwardly, my jaw dropping as the features of the face at the front of the room come into focus. A face that shouldn't be here.

Rosaleen Perrue retired decades ago. A light wielder who chose to teach here in Europe at a dark-wielding school. Her life's work revolved around bringing the two sides together to make us whole. How else would we understand one another and coexist? Though many embraced Perrue's argument that collaboration would bring the necessary peace to create a stronger governing framework for wielders, the decision-makers remained unconvinced. None of us should have been surprised to hear that the Council nor the Bureau would ever cave. They are the reason things never change.

She'd fought for this very outcome her whole life. The fine lines marring her forehead and the corners of her eyes reveal all she has given to her cause. To her life. To her love of educating the young.

I met her only once when I was a child. Her extremely long, lithe frame led me to believe someone had stretched her as a baby. An ancient torture practice was the only explanation for my young, impressionable mind. Otherwise, there was nothing to support a woman standing so tall, with nothing but skin and bones to fill her frame. Her stature is breathtaking. Ethereal. Rosaleen's presence was like standing in the glow of a goddess.

Pale canary eyes meet mine before she speaks again. The coloring is so translucent it's hard to call her eyes brown, but it would be odd to think of them as yellow. Wielders don't have yellow, purple, or red eyes; those are the shades of fictional creatures that invade children's nightmares while they sleep.

You don't forget eyes like hers. They appear to be all-seeing, piercing through you, pulsing as they collect every detail. Feeling as though she might learn my darkest secret with nothing more than her stare should have terrified me. Yet it didn't. I felt an inexplicable pull toward her. So preoccupied with loitering at her side, Roman had to drag me away so I wouldn't be a bother to the woman.

Rosaleen fascinated me nearly as much as the ghouls back then. There were so many nights I lay awake remembering how it felt to have her stare at me. Tracks of her spoken words and whimsical lilt would play through my mind, envisioning a world she believed was right there at our fingertips. In a way, her lifelong goals have always aligned with those of my father. A dream that we would all live as wielders and nothing more. In my mind, she wouldn't care what I was, but I doubt Roman ever told her.

"Though this is a second-semester, first-year class, I expect that you all have excelled past being novices. We will study the nuances of another's magic. How it responds and how to work alongside it in a cooperative manner. This class will not be about dominating the opposition, but embracing them."

Her words fill me with hope for a better future. It doesn't matter that ice coats every syllable, and her tone remains detached. It's a match for the harsh set of her mouth and the slight Irish accent poking through from her years living in Ireland since retirement.

"Split yourselves into groups of four. We will start slow today. Release your essences and allow your classmates to explore the nuances. Allow them to learn about you, so they may understand you, and then properly apply this knowledge throughout this course. It will be the key to mastering manipulation without force." Those all-seeing eyes once again meet my stare, the corner of her mouth twitching with a hint of a grin. "Go."

Groups of students crowd together. Graham and I are slow to move when a female plops down on my desk, a wide grin on her face. "Diselle, nice to meet you." Her hand extends to me, held perfectly still while she waits for me to take it.

I do before Graham reaches out moments later giving her a single shake, then settling back into his seat.

Her lack of an accent throws me for a second. *American, like us.* It's no secret that Integretew has one of the most diverse student bodies from around the world. We're not the only students or faculty from the United States here. Still, it's as if life has thrust our unit out of our bubble, launching us back into reality. In our private world, we were the only four who came here.

Waving awkwardly, I introduce myself and my boyfriend. "I'm Bri, and this is Graham."

"Cool. It looks like we're the last three," she hums. There's an upbeat nature to her, but not like Camilla, more like she's excited to attack the day like those motivational speakers.

We get to work, Graham and Diselle sharing first. When it's my turn, I hesitate, a sweat breaking out over my brow, praying my magic obeys me for once. Valen had done well helping me contain it after taking so much from the ghouls, but I can't guarantee it will cooperate.

Willing my essence from my fingertips, I keep my hand beneath the desk until I sense the soft shade of gray hold steady, only then raising my hand into view. The tendrils dance whimsically, as if always well-behaved. Their show is making me want to roll my eyes. It swirls in a calm wave, Diselle's slowly reaching out to touch mine.

Tremors creep their way from my fingertips and up my arm. The tendrils of my essence, which usually lurk just under the skin, are retreating, understanding that harm may come to us if we're exposed. A mix of rational and unfounded thoughts zip through my mind, converging on the conclusion that we're seconds from being discovered. One touch and she'll know. One touch will expose my secret to everyone.

Graham's stare bores holes into the side of my head, drilling long and deep. An imaginary ache building at my temple as if trying to force him away.

My gaze follows the movement of the dark tendrils as they float toward me—each nearing but pulling away at the last moment. My essence calls to hers. A hungry song meant to lure her in, so we can consume what isn't ours.

Stand down. Now.

My order is answered with a hiss, forcing a grimace to tug at the corners of my mouth.

Bryony, it's new. We like new. It should be ours. Take it.

A single sliver nearly touches my curling swirl. The call is growing more urgent. More insistent, only snapping back as Professor Perrue stops beside my desk. My essence immediately seeps back inside me, my heart racing as my queen of magic pouts and pounds at the barrier of my skin. But I hold her back, keeping her locked away.

That was too close.

"How are we doing over here?"

"Great!" Diselle smiles, her onyx essence still swirling in the space between us as if waiting for mine.

A hard lump lodges in my throat, pain radiating through the soft tissues as I force my swallow. The sharp edges are tearing at the fragile flesh as I fight to find words. Words that never pass my lips.

"You and you," Professor Perrue points to Graham and Diselle. "Show me."

Graham releases a string of his nearly white essence, the colors a yin and yang as they circle one another just above the surface of our desks. They softly poke at one another like children who find worms in the mud during the spring months.

"Don't hold them back," Professor Perrue instructs.

Their essences combine, forming a deep, steel-colored hue. A shade that nearly matches my father's eyes. *Beautiful.* "Fabulous. Now, Bryony, add yours."

My eyes won't meet hers as I will my essence to my fingertips, commanding it to release as the faintest color I can muster. My prayers are answered when the soft dove curls to join Graham's and Diselle's. It kisses Graham's like a lover, knowing his power. It's been inside me for weeks, but Diselle's is new. That novel magic is like a carrot being dangled that I have to resist swallowing whole.

The sultry flavor of her power lures me in. Sweet and earthy notes call to me, my essence's mouth watering, eager to swallow it all down. A flavor far too enticing to deny myself. Her magic is dark, but warm, like sitting in front of a cozy fireplace with your favorite fleece blanket. I'm not sure exactly what her gift is, but my essence wants it. Its mouth stretches wide, ready to consume, when Professor Perrue, once again, interrupts. "Great work, you three. I'll have high expectations this semester." Then she moves on to the next set of students, my essence drawing back inside me.

"That was amazing," Diselle beams. Her wrists twirl, palms shifting in a rotating motion as if impressed with the sight she just witnessed. Disbelief widens her doe eyes as she focuses on her waving fingers.

"Have you never touched another essence before?" Graham asks.

She shakes her head. "No, not a light wielder. I was attending the Gochman Institute. They didn't take kindly to integrating light wielders into their school. Most classes that involved actual use of our magic kept us separate." Her nonchalant shrug makes my heart hurt.

That's not how it's supposed to be.

"That's a shame," I say. It truly is.

Leaders of every institution made promises to Roman pledging against that exact thing from happening. I'd been there during the annual summit, a meeting I begged Roman to attend out of curiosity. They argued about the inconvenience of forcing the light wielders to join the dark, but we should have handled our education with the utmost care. It's what the wise uttered throughout their lifetimes. Our years in wielding school are the most important of our lives. Without those years, we cannot mold ourselves into individuals who will contribute to society and truly make a difference, ready to shape the next generation.

As light schools around the world began closing without notice, I watched Roman slowly unravel. Back then, I pitied him. His greatest achievement was unraveling faster than he could grasp the threads. There was no clarity about what was happening, not from his contacts or the Council. For once, Roman knew what it felt like to fumble around through the dark. I'd watched him struggle not to crumble under the pressure. My heart ached for him then. My father didn't deserve to lose everything he'd worked his whole life for.

Now, I want to watch the motherfucker's entire existence go up in flames, obliterating any trace of the life he felt entitled to.

A smile tugs at the corners of my lips, knowing my father was the catalyst for bringing down Roman's precious world. He had been working behind the scenes to ensure every wielder had a chance. Jorddan only wants us all to exist together instead of in opposing institutions. Divergent paths created before our lives began separated us for far too long.

Now there's nothing but rage left for Roman, especially if it's true that he didn't even earn his position. His connection to William Danvers and whatever deal they struck all those years ago has left me stumped. Men in power don't do favors without receiving a reward in return. If we can't determine the why, perhaps we can find the prize. It may prove to be the only doorway we need into the dark underbelly of dealings within the Council.

A question I hope to get the chance to torture out of him. The same brutally vicious way Valen would if we ever actually find him. Thus far, we haven't seen the man Knox stated William appears as now. That excruciating knot always parked in my gut, twisting even tighter, convinced that maybe this man had once again changed his appearance.

If that's true, there's no questioning his role in someone's plan for domination or destruction. Just not ours. Jorddan wouldn't have allowed him to stay on my kill list otherwise.

"That's it for today." Professor Perrue's voice pulls me out of my progressively darkening thoughts. Her gaze briefly locking with mine before refocusing on the class.

It's a race for the three of us to pack our things. The animated, intellectual conversation between Diselle and Graham continues as if I'm not even here. That's fine. Too many distractions keep me from participating in comparing notes on their observations of wielding school thus far.

I trail behind them, ready to exit the room, when my name is called. "Bryony, please stay behind for a moment."

I give Graham a small smile, but then turn back to the professor's desk, where she stands, leaning over the top, her fingertips pressing into the surface. It should be an intimidating pose. But somehow, it invites me in. My gut is telling me I can trust her.

"Yes, Professor."

"You exhibited impressive control today. It will become increasingly challenging as the semester progresses. I will do what I can to keep you from having to interact more than necessary." Her pointed chin rises, staring down her sloped nose at me. "We should meet privately to continue working on it."

I'm at a loss for how to respond. She speaks as if she knows what I am, what I can do. Sweat breaking out over my brow, I'm terrified that yet another person may need to be added to my list to protect us all.

Trust her, my essence hisses.

"I—" My swallow once again lodges in my throat. "Yes, thank you. I am always open to extra instruction."

"Your brother said you would be. He was one of my favorite students, you know." She smiles fondly, as if remembering a past life only she can see.

My brow furrows. I can't remember Harley or Merrick ever speaking of attending any of her classes. Rosaleen has only ever taught at dark institutions, so they wouldn't have. I am the only "Avalon" to study abroad. Perhaps it was a post-school seminar.

"I'm sorry. I didn't know you taught..." I pause, not wanting to speak my half-brother's name. Bile burns my throat like corrosive acid, just fathoming those two syllables leaping off my tongue. Licking my lips, I force a scant breath. "Was it Harley or Merrick?"

A wolfish grin spreads on Professor Perrue's face, her eyes glinting with amusement. "It seems I need to give your father a talking to. I taught Vincent."

And my heart stops.

50

WYNSTON

THE *TICK, TICK, TICK* of the small hand on the grandfather clock in the corner of the parlor taunts me. It's a reminder of time slipping away, causing my molars to grind painfully as the seconds turn into minutes of nothing.

Bri was supposed to call after her day ended. Her nature poses too many points of uncertainty, a troubling reality for us. It's why we set parameters and rules she was told to abide by. One of which was daily check-ins, especially on days she must physically use her essence in class. Glancing up at that spiteful clock once more, my frustration flips to worry knowing she'd finished her classes for the day over two hours ago.

There's been no communication from her or the guys. Nothing from our soldiers stationed at the school or any other students of the New Order. Every single member was briefed on the protocol involving Bri. They sent those who fumbled the details to stations elsewhere, especially if they didn't directly connect to Bryony's safety.

The radio silence is the cruelest torture. The sting of daggers pierces my skin with each brutal thought about what might have happened. Twice, I nearly ran out the door, jumped in the car, and drove the three hours to London. Then I could see her with my own eyes. I would know she was fine. Only the crippling horror of "what if she's not" kept me from walking out the door. If something happened, am I prepared to see the woman I can't live without bleeding out on the floor?

Helplessness keeps me rooted in this uncomfortable high-back chair, my fingers gripping the arms so tightly the wood beneath may splinter. I hate that I'm not there to watch out for her. To protect her. To help her hide with my interventions.

My body had already been vibrating with the anxiety of knowing I wasn't there in case something went wrong. Valen's recap of her response to the ghouls only sent me into a full-blown panic attack. No one can find out what she is. It's not just her safety. It's all of us.

Although he assured me she has been fine since, I can't seem to fucking breathe. My lungs won't expand. The air won't pass from my lips down my throat to inflate them. It's just a constant searing burn as I fight to suck in precious air, all while attempting to appear focused in front of Vincent and Jorddan.

Though he probably meant well, keeping me informed, it only made me feel like I had failed my fellow Grisym. Not that I ever tried to protect our kind before Bri. I certainly didn't. I kept my head down, pretending I was anything but the Grisym I am.

I pretended I couldn't do anything a normal dark wielder couldn't because that's how I survived. That's how I kept the threats both inside and outside my home from finding me and taking me out of this world.

Jorddan insisted there are at least a hundred members of the New Order at Integretew. Most are wielders Bri has never interacted with. She wouldn't know them from Adam. Other than her possibly being able to sense their tattoos, she wouldn't know unless told. Yet another security measure implemented by Jorddan. A way to keep attention away from his daughter.

"They will care for my daughter should she need anything. Not you," he'd reminded me after Valen's call.

Her father and brother overruled me there as well. Our girl has lived so much of her life in the dark, and look where it has gotten her, *gotten us.* It's only fair that she has transparency regarding her allies. It will be easier not to make mistakes and not to trust the wrong person. My argument was shut down the way Jorddan puts Jannell in her place. His point is clear. Bryony is his and his alone to protect. No matter our connection, in his eyes, she is not mine to care for. Not if it goes against his law.

No doubt Roman knows she's attending school there by now. Whether it's because Geneva revealed she was staying here, or because he checked the registrar, doesn't matter. He could be gathering intel just as we are, implanting those sympathetic to his grab for power. Integretew has been an institution that prided itself on inclusion for almost a century. It would be easy to hide light wielders there, regardless of our current educational climate. They've always been welcome.

My phone finally rings, my body lurching across the room to answer it.

"Hello," I pant.

"Hey, are you okay?" Bri asks, and I can almost see her brow furrowing as she sits up in bed, concerned that something else happened and we haven't told her.

A ragged breath leaves me, my chest sagging at the sound of her voice. "I've just been waiting for your call."

"I know. I'm sorry. My service is shit in the administrative wing. I met with Professor Perrue after my classes."

"Rosaleen Perrue?" I croak, my spine snapping straight.

Why would she be there? She retired maybe ten years ago.

"Yeah. Apparently, Dad asked her to return for the semester so she could help me. The professor she replaced miraculously needed a sabbatical," she snorts as if she can't believe it, but I can. Jorddan would do anything to protect his children, especially Bri.

"I'm glad she's there. If I can't be, she is the best option for you to stay hidden. Listen to what she says." With every word, my heart rate slows. The beat turns to an even *bum-bum,* knowing there is someone there to help her. And not just anyone, but one of the most proficient essence manipulators in the world at that.

A soft sigh filters through the line. Shuffling sounds in the background, as if Bri is nuzzling down into her pillow. "I will. I met her as a kid and thought she was the most amazing person. She was the reason I had any hope that someday I would be embraced for who I am."

My heart aches. I understand what she means. Perrue forged a path that many didn't follow, but she was always vocal about her views of segregation between the light and the dark, as well as a persistent advocate for no longer killing off Grisym babies. I can't imagine many of us didn't idolize her.

If only her views had become the majority. If only those in power had listened, we wouldn't be here. But would I have ever met Bri if we weren't?

"Were the rest of your classes okay? No mishaps?"

I can imagine her shaking her head, with laughter in her eyes. Not because there's anything funny about the situation, but with the pure joy of knowing something went right. "Nope, my essence didn't try to kill anyone today, though it was a struggle to keep it from snatching any essence within twenty feet. Rosaleen said we're going to work on that, too. At least until I can get more time with Tosch." Shuffling sounds crackle in the background before Bri groans loudly. "How is Tosch, by the way? Has she found out anything? Did you tell her what you think we are?"

Gemminai Animyrum.

A concept that comes from ghoul breeding. It's where I'd initially learned of it. Uttering those words felt absurd until Vincent's eyes burned with unbridled fury. It wasn't impossible, not with Bri maturing with the use of ghoul magic, and since taking in their essences.

Her deep siphoning pulls, drawing power from Keres, Warrick, and Tarak, play on repeat in my mind. The images fixed within memory as if determined to remain a part of me. She'd barely been coherent, cradled in Aziel's arms, but her essence was alive. It knew what it wanted—a piece of her ghouls.

Like the four of us men, those ghouls belong to her now. More so than the others.

Especially after witnessing what happened that afternoon, I knew I needed to speak with Lionel. Unlike most young wielders still living their "human" lives, he took the time to immerse himself in ghoul studies. I venture to believe no wielder knows ghouls and their nature the way he does. His cooperation is vital if we're to find any clarity for Bri and me. As far as he knows, Bri can command ghouls, and that's it, but it's time we gave him more of the truth. Our existence might depend on it.

He'd been silent as I gave him a summary of the truth. *"With whatever witchcraft Jorddan did to make Bryony mature early, using ghoul power, anything is possible. As far as I know, it hasn't been done. Although that power has been part of her since she was fifteen, and with her being what she is, it would make sense that the ghoul nature is now part of her,"* he'd grunted through the phone, the hum of intrigue present in his tone. *"We have to assume Bryony will continue to take on additional traits of the ghoul race."*

It occurred to me after the fact that I should have shared what happens with our eyes. The change first to their milky white and then the removal of our sense of sight altogether, but I didn't. I became frozen in place. Ghouls are slow to mature; the process is a gradual merge into their adult characteristics. It makes sense that Bri is slowly following that same trajectory.

We can't know for sure. According to detailed accounts, this is a first-time occurrence. We build our notions on nothing but paper-thin speculation. The ability to understand our true capabilities is nearly impossible. It's unclear how connected Bri is to the ghouls. Is it simply that her maturing using their magic allows her to control them, or that her dark side allows her to siphon? Or does it run deeper, into their very cells? Did a part of her evolve into pieces of them?

"Nothing concrete yet," I sigh, wishing I had better news.

We're all shooting in the dark, hoping to hit a bullseye that will lead us to salvation. There's no way around it. When there are no solid sources to rely on, we're forced to face a situation that shouldn't be navigated blindly.

"Okay. One more thing..." Her words trail off as if she's nervous to voice whatever else she wants to tell me. That shift of her eyes would have had me gripping her chin and forcing her gaze to me if I were there. A soft kiss pressed to her pillowy lips, encouraging her to trust me with whatever she needs to say.

Bri has always been safe with me, and I want her to remember that. I need her to live in that truth. To find solace in it, because she is the one with whom I have found complete safety.

"What is it?"

"We haven't found William yet. It's odd no one seems to actually know him, but they still interact with him. I'm worried he changed his appearance again, or he was never really here." I can almost see her biting the inside of her lip, that one brow scrunching low in frustration, and I wish I were there with her.

My ass sinks into the window seat, the chill of the glass at my back keeping me in the present.

"Keep looking," I mumble, unsure if it will do any good. "I'll do more digging on my end, too."

The shuffling resumes, Bri's voice muffled as she speaks to someone in the room with her. "Hey, Knox," Graham comes on the line. "I think Bri might be on to something. We hadn't talked to you yet. I believe you knew the Danvers line is known for being Amovea, but perhaps you were unaware of their blood-line's potency. From what I've found, gifts like that don't skip generations. If that's true, he's a pro. We're not dealing with spellcasting, which will only make this harder."

"Fuck. The other families no longer exist to anyone's knowledge. It was easy to pretend that the Danvers line hadn't retained their gift so easily," I breathe.

"Knox, we need to go. Bri's roommate is coming. We'll be in touch and see you on Friday."

"Midnight. Meet me on the side street."

When the call ends, I only stare into space. My body won't move, and my mind won't travel past the conversation we just had. I'm too old for this shit. Too old to be diving headfirst into problems I may never have had if I had just kept to myself. A reality that would have never existed once I met Bri. But wishful thinking and all.

This should provide us clarity, but it builds on this unending puzzle. The pieces refusing to fit into the bigger picture.

Fuck, if we all survive this, it will be a miracle.

In my heart, I know we won't.

51

VALEN

RAGE IS A CURIOUS emotion. Many describe it as a range of colors. Red. White and hot. Black as night. That's mine. A storm that destroys anything in its path as you blindly reach for your escape. There isn't one. The nothingness of my black rage will consume us both until only I emerge from it.

Not today.

Today it's red as the blood moon. Fury sparks in my veins, knowing some motherfucker was looking for my girlfriend, and whatever bullshit he spewed to Graham was a lie.

My boy had done the logical thing—butter up the secretary in the administrative office. Integretew doesn't assign fucking liaisons or whatever this Percy guy spewed this morning. There's nothing remotely close to it for peers or professors.

"The inclusiveness of our institution has allowed us to refrain from needing such measures. Our students and faculty happily interact on their own," the secretary had recited when I approached her. She'd spoken the words in a rote recitation, as if she'd said them a thousand times.

The moment Graham said his name, I knew exactly who our soon-to-be-dead man was. He'd been out with us at the bars and the Cavea de Mors, his hands and stare finding Bri a few too many times for my liking. A boisterous guy who couldn't help but brag about achievements no one gave a shit about. Most ignored the details of his internship with the Bureau. Still, he continued blabbing, tossing out minute details that opportunists like him would snatch up and store for later.

His voice grated on my nerves. Every word caused my tongue to click over my teeth in annoyance. *Shut the fuck up,* shouted in my head so many times, I'm surprised it never spewed past my lips as I pounded shot after shot.

My essence danced at my fingertips the entire night. Ready to lay him out with every hand he placed on Bri's shoulder. But I couldn't. We're not supposed to make a scene about our relationship. Rules I was willing to abide by until another fucker poked around my forbidden fruit.

We haven't seen Carter since the night we were out in the city. It would be best if it stayed that way unless he, too, wants to be on the other end of my dagger or essence's desire to decay living tissue. He's at the top of my ever-growing list of who can't be trusted. The thought tugging at the corner of my mouth as I stalk down an empty hallway.

"Where are you going?" Bri questioned with a raised brow, her arms folded across her juicy tits. The sight was almost enough to make me turn around and suck those hardened nipples I could see through her shirt into my mouth.

But I didn't, warning Peirce and Graham that I'd slit their throats if they left her side tonight. Who knows how many are watching, tasked with following Bri. If someone notices I took this motherfucker, I don't want our girl to be an easy target while I'm gone.

When she'd grabbed hold of my shirt, kissing me fiercely, that heated threat blossoming in her eyes, I'd wanted nothing more than to fuck her there on the floor just outside her door. *"Don't do anything stupid,"* she'd warned.

I only smirked. I'm definitely about to do something stupid. My woman knows me too well.

That piece of shit has a date with my dagger. It doesn't matter that I swore we would focus on being students, not vigilantes. I'm going to send a message loud and clear. Bryony Guthrie is off limits to anyone but us. Fuck with her, and you die. Simple as that.

Whoever sent him to do gods knows what with Bri will think twice about sending another spy.

Should another man so much as glance her way outside of me, Pierce, Knox, and Graham, I will gouge their motherfucking eyes out. That level of unbridled fury rages through me. Waving flames growing hotter and higher with every step forward.

Percy's survival depends on the motive for deception. An answer such as Roman's head on a spike might be the only admission that spares him. An excuse I can allow, though he'll need to provide adequate proof. Proof Jorddan will judge, not me. Even then, I don't appreciate being lied to. He may have spoken the words to Graham's face, but he is an extension of me. In my mind, deceiving one of us is deceiving all of us.

Flipping a dagger blade to nestle between my fingers, I slam the handle into the guy's door. I hadn't bothered to check his schedule before coming to find him. If he's not here, there's always a Plan B: a minor spell I learned in my first year to mimic the signatures of my classmates in case I ever needed entry into their rooms.

It was easy enough to learn his room number. A quick smile and sob story to the secretary about having an assignment and not being able to communicate properly made it easy. She'd sympathized, stating that these professors work us too hard in the first week.

The old hag immediately took pity on me. Her grandmotherly voice whispering that if I ever needed anything, come to her. She'd be happy to help a sweet soul like me.

The woman knows nothing if she thinks I'm some nice guy who has good intentions.

Good intentions are for the weak. They are just intentions.

The intent to kill.

To dominate.

The desire to live.

Every intention has two sides. A mix of right and wrong, good and bad, moral and immoral.

"Coming," a voice calls from beyond the door. Shuffling and banging are making me think the guy is attempting to tidy up for someone. The question is who?

The door swings open, Percy's eyes going wide as he notices me there. He wears low-slung gray sweatpants and no shirt, his frame about as thin as mine. *Fuck,* I hope I look better than that. Bri has never complained, so I guess I shouldn't give a fuck.

"Hi, Percy. I heard you were looking for my girlfriend." My dagger flips through my fingers, the bite of the blade against my flesh familiar. Welcomed. Necessary.

"I'm not sure who your girlfriend is," he gives a nervous laugh, partially hiding his body behind the door—my invitation to enter. I stalk past him, still twirling my dagger the way I do, my bun loosening at the top of my head when I quickly spin back to face him, glad his room is empty of any witnesses.

"Close the door." He only stares at me, eyes widening, pulse thrumming. I can practically smell the fear on him. He should be fucking terrified. I'm in the mood to remind someone just who the fuck I am. "Percy, I said, close the door."

He still doesn't move, so I swipe my hand to the side, his door slamming shut with a deafening bang. His thin frame jolting as if shocked.

"Look, I don't know who you are or why you think you can charge in here," he sweeps his arm out to the side as if presenting his room. With every word, the volume of his voice rises higher, while unpredicated fear still laces the confidence behind his words.

That's it, pretty boy. Show me every ounce of fear. I like them scared.

Stepping closer, I slip the point of my dagger beneath his chin. "Put some clothes on. We're going for a walk."

"I—"

"No." My dagger waves in front of his eyes, those wide saucers tracking the movement with his audible swallow. "Don't say another fucking word unless it's yes, sir. Put some fucking clothes on. We are going for a walk."

My grin stretches as I watch his Adam's apple bob and his chest quiver. Clumsily shrugging on a shirt and then a heavy coat, he slips his feet into sneakers, and I can't help but vibrate with giddy anticipation. They didn't include me in Yorgan's murder. But today I get to have all the fun.

Tense silence lingers between us as we move through the residence and then out onto the street. A shiver works its way through his body, his gaze shifting left and then right as if he hopes someone will be there to save him. They won't.

It's just you and me, buddy.

Large snowflakes stick to my hair and coat as we weave through the city toward the Cavea de Mors. It's too frigid for this lengthy walk. Still, it's a sacrifice I am willing to make. It wouldn't serve me well to flag a taxi whose driver could then serve as a potential witness. The people on the street will be too cold to recollect. They're too preoccupied with shouldering their way through the dense snow, which is falling harder by the minute.

When I considered where to take care of Percy, our place of rest popped into my mind like a flash of lightning. What better place to make my point than where he'll end up if he fucks with us again? Should I end his life, the body will already be there for the cave diggers. A simple spell will get me into the storage room where they keep the bodies waiting for their crypts.

The temperature seems to have dropped twenty degrees in the past few days, while the wind whips at my face and hair. Flexing my fingers against the cold, I grimace through the pain, tucking away my dagger. Hands tucked into my leather jacket, I debate calling on a heating spell. Only refraining so I don't waste my stores in case Percy puts up a bigger fight than I think he's capable of.

"Where are we going?" Percy asks, teeth chattering. The quiver in his words is so close to a whimper, I nearly bark out a laugh. I love it when they're sniveling and terrified. We're more likely to get answers that way.

"Stop. Talking. I'm tired of hearing your voice."

He sniffs next to me, but doesn't stay quiet. "I know who you are. Lionel Greer's son. What would he say if he knew you kidnapped me?"

"He wouldn't say a damn thing because I didn't kidnap you. I didn't force you to walk out here with me. I didn't compel or threaten you. You chose to follow me because you're smart enough to know I'm not the only one who will fuck up your world if you mess with Bryony. Am I right?"

I wait for his answer, though I don't need one. His silence is enough.

As we near the locked gate of the Cavea de Mors, Percy's body quivers, his gaze narrowing on our destination. "It's locked."

"I'm aware." With another swipe of my hand, the lock clicks open, the gates creaking just wide enough for us to enter. "Go," I order him, exasperated.

Percy shuffles past me, turning sideways to move through the gate's opening. I follow once again, closing and locking it behind us. That sharp click causes Percy to jump, his wide pale blue eyes darting from the skull at the center to my face.

I don't have to tell him to follow me through the dank space; the clapping of my boots and the soft thud of his sneakers echoing off the walls confirm he's still damn-near jogging behind me.

The cavernous space, made of carved stone and with walls lined with actual torches, makes me feel at home. A place curated for death. A place Vincent loathes, while I revel in the power that still creeps behind the walls. Every spell meant to keep this place as it is, prickles against my skin. Magic, I'm not free to take, though I feel it as if it were mine.

I've always said my gifts of necrotizing flesh don't directly kill. Truth is, they don't. The body can survive even as it eats itself. The organs must choose to stop working. The body must find itself in total failure before a wielder takes their last breath. Most times, there's still flesh to consume before the heart stops. When I'm here in a place like this, curated for the dead, with a snap of my fingers, I can believe I solely caused his death. I can believe that in an instant, I can erase anyone from existence.

We stop in the open area the group had partied in, Percy immediately sitting on the closest stone bench as if he knew I would tell him to. Maybe he is finally catching on, realizing he's not getting away from me until I say so.

"Why were you looking for my girlfriend?"

"I told Graham, I am her student liaison," he mumbles as he knots his hands in his lap.

"You're full of shit," I growl, my face dropping close to his before I pull back and sit on the stone across from him. "Try again."

Percy only stares straight ahead. Right over my shoulder, avoiding all eye contact. His silence stretches so long that it seems like he's curating a new lie. "I was assigned to her." There's an unevenness to his words as if he carefully chose his phrasing while still eluding the whole truth.

"By. Who?" A dagger materializes in my hand, the blade slung past his cheek an instant later. His breath hitches. The closeness of that toss was a hair's breadth away from drawing first blood.

"Don't. Do that!" he whines. "Her father! Her father asked me to get close to her." He cries out as my elbow strikes his nose, blood gushing to spray his shirt and the floor. Each drop soaks into the stone, absorbed entirely as if the structure needs the living to survive. "Fuck! You wanker. That hurt," he whines.

I snort, nodding to him. "That was the point, dumbass. What else?"

Another pathetic whimper escapes him as he cowers away from me. "Just to follow her. I-I, uh, was supposed to report back on everything she does. Like... everything."

His eyes cast down, and I know he was ordered to watch her with us. *Sick motherfucker.*

Watching this grown man quiver in front of me, I feel nothing but disgust. I don't have to ask to know which father gave him such fucked-up orders. It can only be Roman. Jorddan wouldn't have made it so obvious. He believes it's safer for her that way. Nor would he want details of his daughter and what happens when she fucks her boyfriends.

I drop in front of him, squatting low, a dagger pointed at the center of his throat. "His name?"

He scrunches his brow as if questioning my sanity. A sign he knows none of the most important details: her true identity, her father, and what she is. For that alone, I can let him live.

"Roman Avalon?" he squeaks as if confused by my question and his answer.

"Were there any other orders?"

"Report back to him weekly. That's it. I-I-I swear," Percy snivels.

Dropping my hand to his shoulder, he flinches so wildly he nearly launches himself backward off the bench. A vision of his skull cracking on the stone floors making me chuckle. "Good man. Change of plans, though." His eyes saucer in his head as my fingers curl tighter around his flesh. "You work for me now."

He swipes at the blood still flowing from his nostrils. "Wh-wha-what do I have to do?"

A wicked grin stretches across my face, and Percy leans as far away from me as his balance will allow. I may be willing to let this leech live, but that doesn't mean he walks out of here without bleeding a little more.

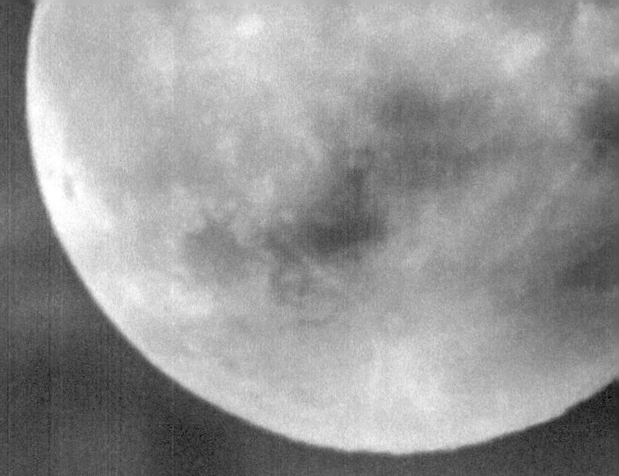

52

BRYONY

ASK ANYONE WHO KNEW me in my life before or has become a friend since, and they'll tell you ghoul studies are the courses I've been waiting for. Previously, it was my hidden obsession with the dark. Each Red Moon, I crawled out onto my balcony, eager to understand a part of my world that my parents had kept from me. My thoughts wandered into a land of make-believe, dying to see a ghoul with my own eyes, itching to touch one and feel its breath on me.

Not that I ever thought I'd sleep with a ghoul, then. I wasn't sure I could as a Grisym. It was just another one of my fascinations I needed to experience in real life.

Nobody from my prior life knew me. They couldn't when they only saw a fabricated half of who I am.

No one knew how deep my obsession with the dark ran. How that history burrowed under my skin and swirled through me, pushing me toward a life I would never lead. I wanted to understand dark wielders and their process of siphoning from ghouls. I wanted to study our differences, but also find out similarities, so I could understand how I fit into my two-sided coin.

Ghouls are now vital parts of my existence. We are bound. I command them.

Before choosing to stay in the UK, I'd resigned myself to not taking a course until my third year. You can't choose electives outside of your wielding class for a general innate studies curriculum until your final year. Even then, it's only if you haven't developed a gift that requires additional coursework to complete your studies. Regardless, I was determined to squeeze in at least one ghoul studies course, though Roman would have blown a gasket when he found out.

Unless you plan on working as a ghoul hunter or in a more scientific position like Lionel, light wielders wouldn't take such courses. My last name could have allowed me to be accepted into any class. Yet again, my light facade stood in the way. My emphasis on the dark arts curriculum would raise questions. Inquiries directed at Roman would only irritate him. The exact opposite of what I was supposed to do.

Who knows how many already noticed I had things to hide? That I was different. That my essence performed differently. A dangerous wielder to any and everyone, especially the light. The wielders who give.

They possess power, though they seldom wield it destructively.

Settling into my chair, my gaze rakes over my classmates. The composition is similar to every other. We, as a student body, are truly mixed. Professor Perrue assured me that integrating education has always been at the forefront of this institution's mission, and I'm seeing that. It's at the core of every word spoken, course taught, and detail hanging on every wall. Integretew bleeds that purpose. And I want more.

Beauxgraton opened the floodgates, allowing me to come into my own. I could ask my curious questions, rooted in self-exploration, with no one so much as blinking *an eye*. I could pretend as if these weren't nuances I learned traveling the world with my father. That I was more sheltered than most might think due to his status within the Council. It was the most freeing experience I had until I came to Integretew. A place that feels like coming home. Here, it's not just about asking questions; I'm required to immerse myself in it all.

A truth that could only be destiny. The home I should have grown up in is only a few hours away. A home where I could have always lived as a Grisym unapologetically. I choose to believe fate brought me here. This was inevitable.

Our professor enters, his features painting him younger than I would have expected. His age is possibly similar to Knox's. He doesn't introduce himself or give any preamble before slinging question after question about ghouls around the room. He calls us each by name, demanding we spew the answers quicker than it takes you to compute he called on us. That thick brow knitting, frown deepening the longer it takes a student to answer. Agitation oozes out of his pores when we don't know the answer, forcing him to move on to the next victim.

"Bryony Avalon. What gift category is the Nigeros most compatible with?"

I shift in my seat as every eye in the room lands on me. Some are anxiously waiting to see if I'll rise to the occasion. Am I as *intelligent* and well-rounded as the director of education's daughter should be? Will I choke? Am I just another light wielder who doesn't know shit about the dark half of our world?

Avoiding my classmates, I lock eyes with our professor before clearing my throat. "Destruction of living material." Confidence drapes my words in an arrogant tone. One I wish I could have softened.

"Meaning?" he presses.

Silently, I'm thanking Valen for being such a cruel man. He'd made sure I understood the extent of his power before I took him as mine. "Meaning gifts that cater to the breakdown of living tissues. Raising internal temperatures, forcing organs to die or eat themselves, cessation of bodily functions."

I don't elaborate further. There's no need. The memory of exactly what I could do with Valen's power still haunts my nightmares; that truth is surely etched into the features on my face. The sounds and scents are alive in my mind, deflation of what had been a whole, solid body, caving in like a wet paper towel. Yorgan's groans still boom through my mind as he'd become nothing but putrified flesh only to re-inflate and begin the process once more.

It gets easier after the first. Valen's promise. Words I don't believe for a second.

Does it?

Do I want it to?

We assumed Yorgan barely suffered because of the combination of essences under my skin. I'd been fighting to channel Valen, but I wasn't in control.

Janelle's amplification took every active gift and made it that much more potent.

My swallow gets stuck in my throat as the images continue to assault me. Dropping me back in those moments I never want to live again. I may often persuade myself that the decision was justified, and I shouldn't let the shame consume me, but it matters. That first kill will live with me forever. It will eat me alive little by little for the rest of my life.

"Acceptable enough," he huffs, continuing on with the next question.

I do my best to scribble down notes throughout class, my hand cramping from trying to keep up with the material. A note to myself: spell a pen or quill next time. I don't want to miss a single bit of information from this class.

Not when it could be the difference between understanding and a mistake.

"Carter James," our professor calls out. "Explain the dynamic between wielder and ghoul."

He nods confidently as I spin around in my seat just in time to catch him winking at me. I haven't seen him since our night out, but there's something different about his appearance now. A difference easy enough to blame on our uniforms or a slight adjustment in the coif of his blond hair.

Tiny details I know in my gut aren't what I'm sensing. My essence stirs as if patting me on the back. It's not that simple. He's changed. If only I could figure out how.

"Ghouls will choose their wielder. Their eyes allow them the ability to sense the essence within the wielder and determine compatibility. If deemed acceptable, the ghoul will allow the channel to open and siphon power to said wielder. The ghoul chooses when to stop." The hair at the nape of my neck prickles. Carter's presence behind me is unsettling. My essence hisses beneath my skin, threatened by his boring gaze at the back of my skull. "Ghouls do not answer to anyone but their kind. They do not obey humans or wielders. We are considered inferior to their race. They do not bow to us, nor will they kneel."

Our professor crosses his arms over his chest. His mouth relaxing as if finally pleased with one of our answers. "And what does it mean if they do?"

Carter's wicked blue stare meets mine, my body once again painfully twisted toward the back of the room where his seat sits against the wall. "It's not possible," he answers. His eyes are locked with mine. Neither of us is blinking. Neither of us will flinch away from the awkward tension that has been pulled taut between us. Our staring contest only ends when my stomach churns, the corner of his mouth quirking high.

"Humor me, Mr. James. What does a ghoul kneeling before a wielder indicate?" Professor No Name presses.

Though I hadn't faced forward again, my gaze remained averted from Carter's face until he spoke. The grin spreads slow and sinister as he leans his elbows on his desk, as if trying to get closer to me, as he relays his words. "It would mean a very greedy wielder took what isn't theirs."

My eyes widen as I quickly shift around in my seat, doing my best to slow my racing heart. The urge to bolt from the room and hide has my pulse bounding at my throat. The stares and whispers that will surely follow whatever that interaction was will chase me through these halls. No doubt, everyone noticed there was a silent battle between Carter and me. Those words were meant to rattle me, I'm sure of it.

My mind whirs, ready to over-analyze everything Carter said. Ready to dissect the nuances and the moments when his facial expressions changed until the next question booms from our professor.

"Describe the connection between ghouls while carrying young."

In theory, I knew ghouls reproduced, but it's never something anyone talks about. Their numbers swell each year. They *reproduce* like any other animal on Earth.

I know their young are slow to mature. They cannot exit the Hell Gates until they have fully matured, but I'd never really thought about the rest. Conception. Pregnancy. Which ghouls carry?

It's a phenomenon we never see. Their underground pits house the young and, presumably, the pregnant ghouls.

"Ghouls can embody either sex—male or female. If a ghoul is in its 'female' form during their couplings and becomes pregnant, it shares its soul, for lack of a better term, with the ghoul who impregnated it for the duration of the pregnancy. Their essences will combine and respond to one another. Their bodily reactions will become bound." Our professor nods as if asking for more. "Essentially, they can feel what the other feels," my classmate adds.

"Very good, and what is the term used for that bond?"

"Gemminai Animyrum," he answers with a grin, leaning back in his seat as if he has something to be smug about.

Fuck he does because what he described…

The term he'd used.

It was the same as Knox had spoken a few days ago.

I intended to dig further on my own, but time hasn't been on our side. The term had seemingly exited my mind until now. Its meaning and use floating in the ether until this class shot it back to me.

Does my ghoul power, given to me during my youth, define what I am now?

Or was it the sliver that Aziel took from me months ago?

It can't be the power I have siphoned from them. Most extrinsic dark wielders get their power from ghouls without shame. It's the light wielders who hold their chins high and refuse to take from anything living. If only they acknowledged it's no different when the power they channel from inanimate objects comes from those living creatures they refuse to touch.

My molars grind, realizing how backward a world we've been living in and how naïve I was to fall in line until I had a choice to do otherwise. I ought to have fought for change earlier. At the age I could grasp the disparities, I could have voiced my opinions. I didn't. My parents shaped me into the person they meant me to be. And I did it to perfection.

The rest of the class trickles by at a glacial pace. My mind fixates on how I'm essentially becoming a ghoul with uncontrollable power. The poster child for exactly why they've been killing off Grisyms for centuries. We're unpredictable. Too different.

Each time I'm called on, I answer the question like a robot. The words are a drone as they pass my lips with just enough information provided to appease our professor, so he moved on to his next victim. No other notes are taken; my heel tapping repeatedly, eager to get out of this room and call Knox.

I'm working on the assumption that he was speculating when he spoke about what he thought we were a few days ago. Did he possess more knowledge and keep it from me?

Our professor claps, signaling the end of class, and my mind already misses the bells that chime at Beauxgraton. My body became conditioned to their pitch—a signal of an ending and beginning for the many chapters of my days.

Stopping at our professor's desk, I wait for him to look up at me. "Hi, Bryony." I give an awkward wave.

"I know your name. How can I help you?"

"Uh, well, I enjoyed class today. Is there any additional material you would recommend reading so I will be better prepared for future classes?" It's an honest request. I have always found the Red Moon and ghouls fascinating. That was merely the mind's youthful infatuation. Preoccupation with the exact thing my parents told me I couldn't have. Yet, now that information is absolutely crucial to the continuation of my existence. How am I supposed to command a world of creatures I don't understand?

Not that I aim to control or rule them. I just can't afford to rely on partial truths. Not anymore.

He pulls out a sheet of paper, scribbling across it with his left hand. The ink only smudges slightly as he drifts over the last line. "These have been the most helpful for me over the years." He hands me the sheet, with seven titles scrawled in neat cursive handwriting.

"Are they in the library?"

"No. I would suggest you go to Kensington's a few blocks from here. Ask for Edmond; he'll give you what you need." A softness melts away the harsh tone he'd used for the past hour and a half.

"Thank you, professor..." I trail off, still clueless about his name. Integretew differs from Beauxgraton. Where we'd been spoon-fed syllabi and professor profiles, I've seen nothing of the sort here.

"Oscar Balfour," he says, shaking my hand.

"Thank you again, Professor Balfour." I wave the sheet as I drop his hand. "I'll be sure to pick these up today."

"You do that, Bryony. Some of us need all the help we can get."

I'm not sure how to take his words as his stony, bluish-gray eyes fix on my face. Studying his features, I can almost convince myself he's like me. It's hard to tell with the shade of his eyes and that close-cropped tiger-orange hair and beard. His eyes are darker than they should be; his hair lighter.

"Don't you have another class?" he deadpans, flipping through a book on his desk.

I hadn't noticed how long I'd been standing there, staring.

"Thank you, Professor Balfour." I turn on my heel, hand on the doorway, when he responds once more.

"Oscar. My friends can call me Oscar." A gust of wind seems to shove me across the threshold into the hall then, the door slamming behind me just as I clear it.

Friend, huh?

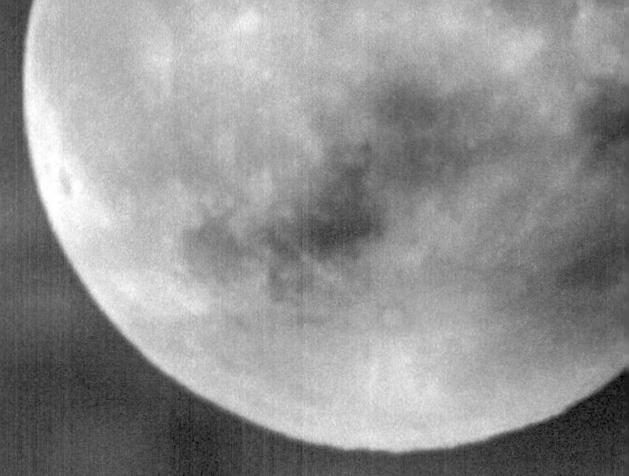

53

BRYONY

PIERCE HADN'T HESITATED TO join me on the short walk to Kensington's. His entire demeanor lit up as if I'd given him the world with the simple question. With the chaos our lives have become, it's easy to forget how we used to be.

Pierce has been obsessed from day one. He latched onto me and never let go. At first, it had been terrifying. Allowing someone to get so close, to sink under my skin, was a risk I wasn't sure I was willing to take. But I'm glad he did.

Pierce held on and never let go, no matter how much distance I put between us. It's been too long since we've been us. I'd forgotten how much he needs this alone time with me. Something this simple made my guy so happy.

It's not just him; I've neglected my relationship with them all. The romance that was budding with Pierce, my friendship with Graham, and well, not killing each other with Valen. There hasn't been time to nurture what we started last semester, and I need it back.

Slipping my fingers through his, I let my cheek rest on his arm. "I miss us." The words are nearly above a whisper, but I know he heard them. Pierce always hears everything I say—even the words communicated in silence.

My former exes are no comparison to my men now. Our relationship wasn't something they cherished or saw a future in. Not the way Pierce does. He has poured so much of himself into us, and it's only fair I do the same.

"Me too," he sighs, kissing the top of my head, giving my hand a soft squeeze. "But we're here together, in this beautiful city. It's you and me. Always."

With each passing day, I feel more grounded here. I love the sounds of London: the architecture and the history all around me. Maybe there's a reason Roman brought me here so often as a child; he knew it, too. Perhaps that was when a small piece of him still loved me.

But no more. For the cameras, he'll continue to pretend to be the doting father. He'll make them all believe how much he cares while hunting me down without prejudice. He finally revealed his true nature to my mother, who didn't even try to protect her other child standing in that driveway.

"What are you thinking about?" Pierce kisses my cheek as we turn the corner.

I hadn't noticed I'd gone quiet, my fingers squeezing his tighter than before. "My mother."

That pitying stare fills his eyes. They've all had it since the day we took Harley home. I can act like my mother not choosing me doesn't hurt. Like I don't care, but I do.

Her actions gutted me when she restricted the freedom I needed to embrace who I was as I grew up. Yet, she comforted me when Harley broke my heart over and over again. She encouraged me when I struggled to control my essence at a young age. Her version of love was subtle, but it was there.

My mother also lied to me. She kept me from my father, which was never part of the agreement they made. Jorddan and I have had long conversations about the existence we could have had together. Rather than cause me any unnecessary issues, he kept quiet. Once I was away at school, he saw the open door to bridge the years he lost with me.

Part of me wishes he'd just taken the risk when I was younger. Those were years I could have avoided Harley's cruelty and Sicily's indifference. I needed guidance and proper artifacts to manage my power. It could have been a lifetime of not feeling so alone.

Though I wish my upbringing were different, easier, I respect Jorddan's choice. It would be simpler if I didn't understand his motives and thought process. But I do, and somehow that's a tougher pill to swallow. Life with or without my father both came with their challenges. There was no straightforward route for any of us.

"Bri..."

"Pierce, please don't. Between you and Graham trying to convince me I'll be fine, and maybe it wasn't what I thought, it just hurts more. Even if she was acting for my sake, she had a chance to tell me that at the manor. She could have laid herself bare, but she only begged for the asshole who made my childhood miserable."

Shaking my hand free, Pierce wraps an arm around my shoulders and once again kisses my temple. "I wasn't going to say any of those things."

"Then what were you going to say?" I sniff, my nose beginning to run from the cold.

"I was going to say, let that pain focus you. Let it remind you of everything we are fighting for, but also remember you're not fighting alone. There are people who love you loudly and without strings."

"Yeah, I know." I roll my eyes. "My dad, Vincent, and Janelle."

"And me. I love you, too." My feet stop, neither refusing to move as if anchored to the ground, but Pierce shifts in front of me, his hands cupping my frozen cheeks. "Bri, families are messy and things don't always go as we plan, but Valen, of all people, taught me there is always someone in your corner who loves you unconditionally. I love you." He presses his mouth to mine, soft and sweet, conveying so much more than should be possible. "No matter what happens, you are not alone here. Whether you want me here or not, I'm not going anywhere. I will be your strength when you're tired. I will be your bravery when you're scared. I will be your heartbeat when it feels like yours has stalled."

Denim blue eyes hold mine. We all knew Pierce felt deeply. Intensely. He gave himself to me without a second thought. No safety net, not a single care, just trust that I would want him too. He had uttered those three words before. But he hadn't repeated them since that day. The feeling may have been there, but I'd forgotten how much I loved hearing the words on his lips. How much I needed that confirmation from him.

Hearing them again has a single tear trickling down my cheek. Emotion swelling in my chest, not realizing I needed this.

I kiss him again. Hard and deep, not caring who's watching us on the cold sidewalk. His arms loop across my back, flattening our bodies against each other as much as the thick coats allow.

When I pull away, ice-cold fingers wipe away my tears. I brace for the chill against my skin, but there's only the warmth Pierce has always given to me so freely. It's his love. That smile. "Thank you. I'm not going to say it back because I know you, and you will tell yourself it was a knee-jerk response instead of my genuine feelings. But thank you for being here today. Thank you for always being here."

He places one more chaste kiss on my mouth, smiling widely. "No place I'd rather be. Now let's go, your brother and Jorddan will skin me alive if I let you freeze to death."

"Don't forget Valen," I chuckle, slipping my fingers back through his.

An exaggerated groan leaves him. "Don't remind me."

We both laugh, covering the last stretch of sidewalk before Pierce tugs open the door to Kensington's Antiques and Books.

Immediate warmth envelops me, a shiver running through my body at the sudden temperature change. The hazy edges of a memory I can't quite grasp resurface with the familiar scent.

"I'll be out in a moment," an accented female voice calls from a room at the back of the store. She sounds miles away, but from the exterior, the place had appeared relatively cozy. Perhaps one day I'll realize there's more magic in this world than I grew up with. More freedom among those who don't live for appearances.

It's almost overstimulating, raking my gaze over every surface. A dream world brought to life before my eyes, just within reach if I dare to grab hold. Old clocks, knick-knacks, and sculptures. Chairs, tables, and odd decor that must be UK fashion.

A woman rounds the corner, wiping her hands on an apron. Her face speaks of an age closer to mine, but the way she carries herself tells me she's older. There's a maturity in her I won't find for at least another decade. An aura that draws me to her.

"How can I help ya?" Her strong Scottish accent takes me aback. I'd expected her to sound like every other Londoner, but she doesn't.

It's disorienting how few seem to be from this fantastic city.

"Oscar Balfour sent me to get some books. Is Edmond here?"

Her brow rises high, her eyes scrutinizing me before flicking to Pierce. "Dark wielder. Extrinsic." Then she turns to me again, circling me as if she'll learn my every secret by doing so. "Grisym. Innate. Powerful. Unique."

My eyes go wide as I back into Pierce. "No. I'm a light wielder."

She only chuckles, resting an elbow on the counter behind her. "Look, deary, you need not lie to me. I'm no threat to you." Her dark brown eyes focus on me, her near-black hair, thickly braided over her shoulder, telling me one thing, but the essence released from her fingers telling me another. Stark white, like frost.

"You're..." I breathe.

"I am. Me mum was dark and me dad light," she only smiles, flagging us behind her. "This way. I keep the books back there."

The space is larger than it appears from the street. There's no free wall space. The floor only allows for narrow paths leading you through the store. Every nook and cranny is filled with someone else's memories. It's how I always viewed antiques, especially when my mother would recount the origins of those she allowed me to watch her reconstruct. They were always someone else's untold stories waiting to be heard.

We enter a small back room. The space is cramped, with the walls covered in shelves. She's quick to pull from each one, not even bothering to look at the sheet of paper I'd handed her, now hanging out of her back jeans pocket.

"This should do for now. I added a personal favorite for ya."

Pierce takes the stack from her, pulling the bag he'd shoved into his pocket in a neat square free.

The woman wipes her hands on her apron as if filth had covered them, her smile never wavering.

"Thank you," I smile back.

"What's your name, deary?" She guides us toward the front, her pace so glacial you'd think she had all the time in the world.

Envy swirls through my stomach. When was the last time I moved as if the world was on my side? "Bryony." I croak, coughing loudly.

"No," she spins to face me. "Bryony Guthrie?"

My mouth goes dry. Why does it seem like everyone here knows who the hell I am?

"No, I'm—" I swallow, unsure if I should answer truthfully.

"I told ya, I'm no enemy of yours. My name is Eilish Fisher. Ya might know my cousin."

"Who?" Pierce slightly angles his body in front of mine.

She chuckles. "Conrad Milgren."

54

PIERSON

THIS WEEK HAS SHAKEN me to my core.

Besides professing my love to a woman who may never love me as much as I love her, the hits keep coming. My nights should be punctuated with cuddles and laughter, snacks and movies, not new secrets and revelations that will only destroy the person who owns my heart.

It never seems to end. There are too many connections. Too many open puzzle pieces at play, we can't seem to fit.

Percy Carden works for Roman.

Carter James is just creepy and fucking weird, as far as we know. It took everything in me not to pack our stuff and run when Bri recapped how her ghoul studies class had gone. The pointed comments and even the questions her professor had asked were too close to the truth for comfort. They set me too far on edge.

It couldn't be a coincidence that they revolved around our current situation. Bri's connection to the ghouls and what we fear she is becoming were suspicions we've only passed amongst ourselves thus far.

Though we've kept quiet, we question Oscar Balfour's motives. He'd been the one driving the line of questioning in class and encouraging his students to dive deeper. His most pointed questions bounced between Bri and Carter, making the hairs stand at the nape of my neck. The goosebumps shooting up my arms, sending a shiver through my body, terrified that Bri will remain stuck in that class all semester with two Roman spies.

So, I lie to myself. It's paranoia. Coincidence. Expected because of the content of the class. We're looking so hard for red flags that we're creating them.

Keep lying to yourself, Pierson.

But it was Eilish Fisher who nearly knocked me on my ass. Conrad fucking Milgren's cousin? Coincidences are beginning to look more like purposeful jabs. It's too odd that a professor who all but exposed Bri in class, then sent her to a bookstore run by Milgren's fucking cousin. The wielding world is small, that is true, but that sickening nausea still sits in my stomach.

Too many coincidences. Too many connections.

Conrad had rarely crossed my mind since we fled Beauxgraton. A man, Valen, and I knew as Jonathan Tillerman—Headmistress Milgren's father. Yet another Grisym hiding in plain sight. Our lives are increasingly beginning to resemble those small television towns where you can't throw a coin without hitting a relative.

I'd wanted to ask how Eilish knew Oscar. She'd revealed Edmond was a family friend and she'd been working with him for almost seven years, but that didn't answer my question. Though Bri fell into a comfortable conversation with the woman, accepting when Eilish refused to let us pay for the books, my suspicions grew. It's strange to want to do a favor for someone you don't know. Perhaps it's a typical enough gesture of kindness, and I've just become so cynical about the world that my mind refuses to accept it.

My temples throb, trying to put it all together. How are Roman or Jorddan tied to all of this? Where does William Danvers fit in? We know he's someone Bri used to interact with, and that Roman used him to advance his career, but that's it.

Fucking Danvers. The guy is like a ghost. There's no sign of him, just the whispers of his rumored existence within the school walls. Everyone knows the name and confirms they've seen him.

"Oh yeah, he's in my history class."

"Yeah, I just saw him in the dining hall."

"He's probably in the lounge. That's where he studies at night."

Even with the countless tips and the timed attacks, we cannot fucking find him.

He seems to be everyone's friend. His return to school at his age especially impressed the first years. His roommate says he's great, and his professors rave about his performance. No one has made a less-than-stellar comment about the guy. A man we cannot find.

Admitting my nerves are fried would be an understatement—likely because my knee is bouncing uncontrollably as Knox drives us back to the manor. My mind whirs, attempting to process every detail Bri and Knox share back and forth. Neither is asking for our input as we sulk in the back.

Tonight, we'll eliminate another name from Bri's list. I've never killed anyone, and I'm not sure I am ready to, but if it means we're all safer, it might be time I lay aside my fears. Perhaps it's time I embraced the destruction my dark power can bring.

Freezing rain pelts the outside of the car, the heat barrier I put up around the windows keeping the windshield clear. Each droplet that strikes my window is just a reminder of how my blood will run cold tonight. I'll no longer be the same after taking a life. However, Jorddan will likely spare us from doing the dirty work. He always has.

He needs us to be sympathetic. Loyal. Not traumatized.

Though I was spared from watching Yorgan rot, Bri showed firsthand the toll that taking a life can have on you. She puts on her brave face, talks herself into believing murder was the only way, but I've held her through the nightmares. No amount of soothing circles rubbed into her bare back or whispered words could keep them away. That night will continue to haunt her no matter what she tells herself.

The SUV skids as we turn onto the gravel drive, Knox grunting in annoyance.

"Try not to kill us on the property," Valen quips. Graham groans as Valen shifts his narrow frame as if that will create more room in the backseat between us. I swear Knox purposely brought the smallest SUV in the Guthrie fleet, knowing Bri would choose the front beside him. Their days together are fewer, she'd crave his touch. Their essences need the connection to exist in a satisfied state.

Bri chuckles as Knox mumbles under his breath. His gaze cuts to her, softening his mood. Unsurprisingly, Bri affects all of us the same way. One look, one smile, one soft laugh, and we're putty in her palms.

The short walk to the front door is enough to soak my hair, tiny icicles clinging to our ends as if we'd spent our evening letting it pour down on our heads.

I'm busy shaking out my coat when squeals make me flinch, the heels of my hands clapping over my ears as my body crouches involuntarily.

Bri has her arms wrapped around Tosch's neck, as Damian's wife squeezes her palms against our girl's back. The two sway side to side as if they haven't seen each other in decades. It's been just under two weeks. They'd grown close. It was obvious from their first encounter.

They pull back, regarding one another the way a grandmother would be stunned that their grandchild has grown. Yet it's Bri's expression that holds my attention. There's no tension in her laugh lines or forehead. Her smile arches high, touching the corners of those captivating eyes. We're witnessing genuine happiness, and it soothes something inside me.

"I'm so glad you're back," Bri breathes. "And I promise I've been working on my control. I have a professor who's been working with me every day."

"Who?" Tosch questions, her golden orange brow arching high.

A wide grin pulls at the corners of Bri's pouty mouth. Her cheeks still pink from the cold. "Rosaleen Perrue. Dad nudged her out of retirement to keep an eye on me."

"Rosaleen is the best of the best. If she's working with you, you don't need me."

Bri rolls her eyes, hooking her arm around Tosch's waist. "I'll always need you. Who else would be my favorite dom?" Tosch cackles loudly, the back of her hand pressing to her mouth as if it will stifle the sound. Bri only continues, "All of you, but please tell me you found something good." Desperation coats Bri's words only for the disappointment to filter into her eyes.

"I wish I could. Other very powerful wielders have used others as vessels, the way you use Knox, but it's unclear how that connection is made. We can only assume it has to do with the power imbalance between the two."

Bri nods. "Our working theory is that it has something to do with the ghouls. We think Knox and I might be Gemminai Animyrum."

"Twin souls?" Tosch gasps before her knowing grin stretches wide. "I'm not sure why I didn't think of that. It makes so much sense. At least we might have one puzzle figured out. However, the way it works with ghouls is through pregnancy, and then the bond breaks, so what breaks you and Knox?"

Knox's eyes go wide with the questions, Bri's pressing shut as if blocking the thought. I doubt any of us wants the answer. We can feel it in our guts. The inevitable. The fate that had always been destined for them. Those two need each other. Their Grisym connection depends on it.

Jorddan and Vincent suddenly enter the foyer, and our group goes awkwardly quiet.

"Sweetheart, welcome home." He pulls Bri into his arms, hugging her close as if he, too, hasn't seen her for a long stretch of time—a potential side-effect of all the years Geneva forced him to live without his daughter. I remember a time when I was younger and my father would hold me like that. That was before. Before I became a disappointment. I harbor no regrets, choosing not to be the villain so many painted dark wielders as.

I miss my parents. We talk occasionally, but seeing Bri so happy with her brother and father makes it hard for me, knowing I've mended nothing with them. It was easier to let them hold on to their opinions about me than fight for understanding. I had Val. He understood me, even if he didn't agree.

My parents shoved me away, not the reverse. There was nothing to do but accept their choice, though they despised mine. I took it for what it was at the time. Perhaps we all should have tried harder to find common ground. Maybe one day we will. Family is precious.

The pure edge I had aimed for all these years has become muddled. The jagged distinction between the pull of darkness and the push of light is nothing but a blur. All this time, I thought I knew who I was and wanted to be. This life has taught me it's not that simple.

We can aim to be the idealistic versions of a wielder. No matter how hard we try to fight it, life will force us to be more. More of what we despise, more than we thought we were capable of, more of what the people we love need. Our existence will never be black and white, so it's time I stop fighting it.

The question is, how do I live with the parts I wish weren't part of me?

"What's the plan?" Graham steps forward, Valen at his side as if tied to his hip.

The two claim they've been working together to solve our many issues, but their new friendship runs deeper. In a way, not constantly dragging me into Valen's shit is refreshing. Graham is a nice guy, but there's a hard edge to him. There's a layer hidden beneath the surface that could have been born of the dark. Character traits deemed unacceptable because they would be against how he "should" act.

"Pierce and Tosch, you will go to Mikhail's office at the bureau building. We will not be able to access her property without persuasion. The spells she has securing her home are signature and blood-sealed," Jorddan announces, his tone flat, almost uninterested.

"If I take her essence, couldn't I get us in?" Bri questions.

Tosch clears her throat. "No. You have too many signatures that aren't hers, nor do you have her blood."

Bri nods, going silent, clearly disappointed she can't do more.

"So you need my... control to force her to let us enter her property?" I ask, though the words knot in my throat. My ability to articulate what my genuine gifts are always seems to die on my tongue. It is despicable to deprive someone of their free will.

I've always hated what I could do until that fight at Beauxgraton. That night, my ability to force action on that group that came for Bri was necessary, and tonight, if it means she's safe, I'll happily do it again. It doesn't matter if I hate myself afterward.

"Precisely. Tosch will be with you should she try to go against you with her magic," Jorddan continues. "Bryony, Valen, Knox, Graham, Oscar, and I will teleport to her property line."

"Oscar? As in Balfour?" Bri gasps. "My professor?"

He stalks into the foyer, appearing from around the corner as if by magic. The familiar blonde in tow, babbling the way she always does. The high-pitched voice and petite stature settling me just a fraction more. *Our friend is safe.*

Yet another squeal fills the foyer as Camilla and Bri run toward each other and hug tightly. "What are you doing here?" Bri gasps. "Dad, what is she doing here?"

"Well, hello to you, too," Camilla clicks her tongue, swatting Bri's arm. "Can I tell her, Mr. Guthrie?"

Jorddan only nods, a humorous grin pulling at the corners of his mouth. An expression reserved only for the things that make his daughter happy.

"I'm sorry I never told ya. I mean it. But I can make portals, so I get to shuffle y'all off to Buffalo. Or wherever!" Camilla beams.

"Portals? As in, like, send us to another place portals?" Graham squeaks.

"You betcha. I never told y'all 'cause I didn't really know I could make them go to other places." Camilla waves her hands through the air. The woman appears radiant. This moment must mean everything to her. Bri's grin wavers, knowing she is the one who first ordered Camilla to be left out of the war. Bri sent her friend away, a task that left a small scar on her soul.

As if to demonstrate, her essence streams from her fingers, a rose-pink hole forming in front of her. She sticks her hand through the cloudy mass, giggling when we all suddenly look up. A similar pink cloud cuts a space through the ceiling, her fingers wiggling as if waving hello.

"I'll be here to hold her portal," Oscar adds.

Clearing my throat, I hesitate to speak up. "Isn't it too dangerous to have us all there? We're kind of a large group." The words come out mumbled. The lack of confidence is noticeable, drawing Jorddan's chin high. Once again, I'm proving I'm not cut out for this life.

Like Valen, the list of those I'd give my life for is small. My parents and those in this room are it. My friends. The family I've made. The people I will defend with everything I have, knowing they would do the same for me.

It seems unnecessary to put us all at risk.

"If you do your job properly, then we'll be just fine," Jorddan retorts, just before Camilla slashes an enormous hole through the foyer, the cloud of smoke so thick you can't see through it.

A portal. The portal that Tosch and I will walk through in a matter of minutes.

You can trust Camilla. She would never intentionally harm you.

There's no choice. Not anymore. Not for me, nor for Bri.

This is all for the mission. For a future that surpasses our wildest imagination.

A sharp inhale expands my chest, my body trembling uncontrollably. Stepping into the cloudy haze, I'm eager to get this night over with. The faster we're done, the faster I can hold my woman in my arms tonight—the woman I love.

There's nothing but a soft cloud of smoke around me. A tremor causes my hand to shake so violently *that* I grab hold of *it*, ignoring the thunderous beat of my heart. I know what we're supposed to find on the other side, but what if we're wrong?

Blinking repeatedly, the street comes into view. The night is silent, with no sounds, or people or cars.

Sharp pain erupts at the back of my skull. Stars burst into my vision, blurring the world around me. Excruciating pain radiates through my body as I crash onto the hard pavement at my feet. Then nothing.

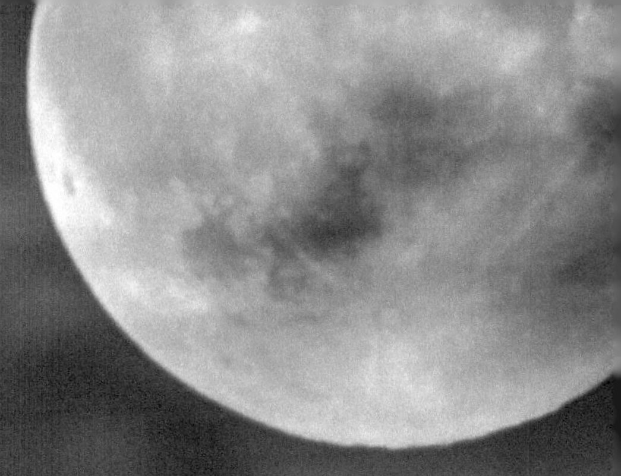

55

BRYONY

PAIN SUDDENLY EXPLODES THROUGH my body, fading as quickly as it hit me. A scream cuts through the foyer. My mind does not realize it was mine until my hand cups the back of my head.

"You okay?" Vincent whispers, placing a hand on my shoulder.

Casting my gaze at the floor, my eyes dart back and forth. My thoughts jumble as I work to parse through them and make sense of what just happened. It wasn't from me. I know that much, but who? "Uh, yeah. Fine." I blink repeatedly, flashing a weak smile.

Dread nestles in my gut. Apprehension nearly buckles my knees. Indecision muddies my mind. A dump of emotions that I somehow avoided before. Their intensity levels are eons above what I experienced heading to my first kill. Perhaps the inability to predict the unknown had kept these feelings from swarming me with Yorgan.

Tonight, an overwhelming voice barrels through my head, telling us to turn back, warning us that something has gone terribly wrong. Shouting for me to stop this before we go too far. A foreshadowing of the end we'll all meet if we're not prepared.

423

My chest tightens. Every breath is a struggle. My mind is convinced we're walking blind into a pit of vipers, and with one strike of a snake's fangs, we're done. The venom will surge through our veins, seeping into our organs, killing us in minutes.

Those precious years, which we all assured ourselves we would have, will be gone. We'll be nothing but the memories of the change we tried to bring to the wielding community.

Tosch stepped through the portal less than a minute behind Pierce, and I wish I had hugged them both before they did. This knot is tightening my insides as whispers dart through my head that it may be the last time I see them.

It's just the risk of what we're doing, I tell myself. Anything to keep from hyperventilating as the portal fades away, blanketing us in silence. My mouth opens, ready to spew a million questions. Did they make it? Are they okay? Should we have been able to hear them while the portal was still open? How will we know if they're in trouble?

Camilla shakes out her hands as if they're physically exhausted. "They got through. I felt it." She nods enthusiastically before blowing out an exaggerated breath.

I can't tell whether she's tired or if she's just as nervous as we are. Either way, my best friend isn't acting normal. A discussion for later, hopefully.

A cloud double the size of the last streams from Camilla's fingers. The coloring is the pale green of moss. It's intriguing how each portal has hosted a unique hue. A detail that sparks my essence's curiosity. It behaves as if it hadn't sensed what Camilla could do before. We spent months together, and other than in class, I can't recall a single instance of Camilla using her essence.

I'm grateful she'll be staying behind here with Vincent. Someone should protect her innocence. Camilla may want to help, but I need her safe.

If anything happened to that tiny nut, I wouldn't forgive myself. Hell, I won't forgive myself if anything happens to anyone here.

I know my father has told me countless times that this isn't just because of me. It's the actions of Roman and the love they both have for my mother. It was their choice to have a family together, despite knowing there would never be a future between them. Another half-truth I have yet to learn all the details of.

No one will tell me what Roman had over Geneva to force her into that blood bond, and why my father killed the wielder who sealed it and erased his memory. Their only chance of finding happiness vanished with a single decision.

What secret could be worth that?

For once, I know it wasn't me. I wouldn't be born for another twelve years.

Valen stops in front of me, gripping my face between his fingers and kissing me hard. "See you on the other side, Forbidden Fruit." Then he walks through.

Graham quickly follows after kissing my forehead, then Oscar.

My hands shake at my sides. Something isn't right. I can feel it inside me. A piece of my essence is bouncing around my insides as if trying to warn me. I wish I knew its origin. The longer I've held an essence, the harder it is to differentiate between my own and "other." I know it's not originally from me, but the signature that makes it distinct seems to fade away, leaving just another swirl working through my body and its abilities ingrained in the fibers of my being.

"What's wrong?" Knox whispers, grabbing hold of my hand.

My head shakes, the words slipping past my lips though I don't mean them. "Nothing. Nothing. Let's go."

Knox and my father walk through the portal seconds ahead of me.

"See ya on the flip side," Camilla winks before I step through the portal, too.

I hadn't even known portals of this magnitude were possible by a single wielder. All I can see are the green clouds around me. They're so soft as they whisper sweet nothings in my ear. The words are so smooth that it's a struggle to make out each one. Intuition is encouraging me to move forward. To follow them. To allow the pillowy softness of the clouds around me to caress my skin.

One foot in front of the other, they seem to say. *Keep going. You're almost there.*

My steps are slow as I strain to hear their actual words. A small tendril breaks free to loop around my wrist. The stream stroking the surface of my skin like a lover, the slower my steps become.

"No," I say. "I can't have you."

It only stays where it is. An essence I don't yet have inside me, but I very much want. Yet I hold back. I fight against it, forcing my feet to move quicker. My ability to resist growing weaker the further I walk. The tendrils lengthen as they wrap around me in earnest. Dense clouds cover my hands and throat before I finally pop out the other side, sucking in the fresh, chilled night air.

Knox pulls me into his chest. "What took you so long?"

I look down at my hands. There's nothing there. Rotating toward the direction we came, there's only a void. The portal had vanished in a matter of seconds. Gone as if it was never there, but I still feel it. That power still calls to me. My skin prickles as if those tendrils are still twirling along my arms and kissing my exposed neck.

"I thought you were supposed to be holding the portal?" I snap at Oscar. "Where is it?"

He waves his hand, and it reappears. The gaping green hole is calling to me, begging me to take it inside me.

"I—What—"

"It's cloaked. I am the only one who can see it while I'm holding it open, unless I will it visible," he says.

I only nod, unsure what else to say as that feeling of dread grows inside me. Dark and dangerous. Gloomy and gruesome.

The surrounding neighborhood is silent. It may be dark out, but it's too quiet for this early in the evening. *Something is wrong.*

A collection of houses and manicured lawns surrounds us. Their appearance is so similar to the one I grew up in. Neighborhoods just like this one span this side of the country. The streets lined with houses cloned after the previous, boasting wealth and well-connected families.

"Which one is hers?" Graham asks.

A heaviness pushes against me as I raise my arm, pointing directly across the street. My eyelashes flutter against my cheeks, shock anchoring me in place, eyeing the house that is right within view. Jorddan warned me I would have to teleport us to the house, but Camilla had taken us straight here.

A hand rests between my shoulder blades. "It seems your friend has better precision than we expected. We'll discuss it later," my father whispers.

"Are you a mind-reader?" I mutter, keeping my voice low.

"No, you're my daughter." He kisses my temple, Graham still watching me before quickly averting his gaze.

A sleek, modern, black and white Tudor stands tall against the dark. I'd been to Mikhail's house a few times as a little girl. It looks as it always did. Pristine. A gem among the older-style modern homes surrounding it. Inside those walls, I'd allowed her to learn my secrets. An awareness I stumbled on too late when I matured at fifteen.

Roman always coached me before I'd perform for the wielders he hired to assist me. The list of what I could and couldn't reveal is specific. I did my best to obey him, to make him proud. Yet, Mikhail was the only one he never gave restrictions to. I was free to let every bit of power course through me and barrel free.

The only exception was in continuing to hide my dark side. They all saw me only as an experimental rabbit, kept in the cage constructed by the man who was supposed to be my dad. I was a specimen to be observed and gawked at with each fresh development in my evolution.

Neither Mikhail nor Roman ever told me what happened with all that she gathered on me. There must be hundreds of those faded brown leather journals in which she recorded every detail. Details I could never see for myself.

A wild exhale would always pass her parted lips as she swept her bangs back with each filled journal. It was a ritual that never changed, as if superstition kept her grounded in the act. A milestone I would look forward to until she would pull another from her satchel, waving her hand through the air, signaling me to continue as I was. That's when the hope melted away.

I once took solace in the silence. I reveled in it. Craved it because it meant I wasn't the focus. No one was asking me to be their showgirl, and I had no chance of making a mistake. It was my only opportunity to lose myself in my thoughts.

Tonight, it unnerves me. Cars should be creeping down the street. We should bear witness to the bustle of families in their homes, their silhouettes visible behind their sheer curtains. Yet, the windows are all dark. There are no barking dogs or overly loud televisions.

The deathly silence sends shivers down my spine. My essence caresses me from within, infusing me with a boost of bravery and encouraging me to disregard those sensations of unease. They won't serve us tonight.

Mikhail's front door lights are the only ones shining bright, illuminating the old snow still littering her lawn in random patches.

I assume we timed Pierce and Tosch's arrival according to Mikhail's work schedule. They'll either mind-control her there or once she arrives here. Whichever is safer.

Please be careful.

But as the minutes tick by, the heat from Knox's spell and Valen's body isn't touching my fraying nerves. That sliver of fear is expanding inside me. The tiny sparks that had lit up my spine are now bursting through my body.

My patience has finally run out when headlights creep down the street before turning into Mikhail's driveway. The sedan idles for a moment before her hand extends out the window, palm resting on what looks like a keypad. The entire box illuminates, casting an eerie glow over the car's interior. In an instant, the scene turns into a horror movie as the gates groan open.

Squinting, Pierce and Tosch's heads are just visible through the rear windshield. Their forms are deathly still, focused straight ahead. We wait several minutes as the car pulls up the semi-short drive before easing inside the garage. My stomach knots as the door winds down, sealing them inside, all while striking them from our view.

My lungs are burning, waiting for the gate to close, our only chance of gaining entrance to her home undetected. The seconds tick by, my intestines knotting all over again. But it remains open.

My gaze flicks up to the Tudor, watching for lights. That will be our roadmap of her movements through the house. A house I've never seen more than the first floor of.

Hours seem to pass before the first light flicks on. The sheer cream curtains revealing the shadow of a person moving before disappearing. Next, the office light blinks on—the space opposite the living area. Soon, light spreads across the yard's side edge. "She's in the kitchen," I drone mindlessly, recalling the layout of her home.

"Let's go," Jorddan whispers, waving us behind him.

We follow his lead, Oscar staying behind to man the portal with Valen.

It's an even-paced trek across the flat expanse of the driveway. We're fully visible from where we stand. The lack of shrubbery and large trees provides us with no cover.

Uncomfortable familiarity hits me in the stomach as we clear the two steps leading to the front door. My father grabs the knob, pushing the door open as if he were entering his own home. He makes no effort to keep quiet or conceal us; he simply walks inside as if he owns the place.

My breaths turn shallow, searching for a sign of Mikhail, Pierce, or Tosch. I want to call out, but my gut tells me not to. That unwavering anxiety continues to grow. A feeling that hasn't left me since we walked into the manor. *Something isn't right.*

Quietly, Knox uses magic to close the door when a voice croons to our left. "So it is true?"

56

BRYONY

IT'S BEEN ALMOST SIX months since I last saw Mikhail. Her final visit was a few weeks before I left for school.

It seemed odd at the time. There was tension between her and my father that day, especially after I mentioned Janelle. Most of our sessions lasted hours, but that day was barely thirty minutes long.

I was thankful she was quick to leave. It was time to move on. Relief flooded my insides, knowing I would never have to see her again. I would never have to hide my dark tendencies as she pushed me to reveal all of myself. It was time to live in the real world. It didn't matter that I'd have to hide there, too. I was no longer a puppet performing for my dad's friends.

It's odd knowing I understood exactly what he was doing then. I respected it, even. Lied to myself that he was only trying to help me and maybe help other wielders. I'd hoped the data they gathered on me might be used to assist others, though he never said so. Still, until Roman turned his back on me, I never resented him for what he put me through. I accepted that there was a price to pay for my life. Too bad, I paid a higher price than I would have ever agreed to if I had known the stakes.

The room is silent except for the pounding of my heart. My pulse thrumming in my ears so loudly my eardrums might burst.

That voice.

Her voice.

Per my memories, there was never any reason to fear her. Not once do I recall her voice causing my body to seize up. Yet, my essence remembers a different experience. It coils inside me, winding tightly around itself, ready to strike in defense. Its war armor clanks into place, teeth bared, while snarling like an animal.

Whatever she did to me, the memories are gone, stolen with the purpose of keeping me ignorant, no doubt. *Fuck. You. Roman Avalon.*

My subconscious remembers terror and betrayal, my essence rioting and screaming to fight while we can. We tried to run before and failed. This time we won't cower. We'll protect.

I stomp it all down, allowing my anger and determination to rage beneath the surface. Each emotion that won't propel me forward in my quest for revenge is squashed with the heel of my boots. Inhaling deeply through my nostrils, I let my dark side billow to the surface. I let it roll and writhe inside me, eager to commit the most heinous acts.

Do your worst, I tell it. *Make her pay.*

Still, I hold the reins, warning the dark that it may only break free when I say. My essence fights against me. Eager to do as it pleases.

You will obey.

As my head tilts to the side, I feel it bend to my will. Both of us are studying the woman I've known my whole life, deciding what we're going to do to her. Just how we're going to make her pay.

"What's true?" I ask, the voice not my own, but familiar.

She cocks her chin in amusement, a slight grin spreading. My tattoo tingling as my father moves in behind me.

"I'm not a mind-reader, Mikhail. But I'm sure you know that from years of studying me." I maintain an even, non-combative tone. Matter-of-fact. Anything to keep her from knowing I'm more rattled than I'll ever admit.

Though murder is the purpose of our visit tonight, immediate aggression won't yield the answers I need. Torture could be fun should she resist, though it could be a potentially messy endeavor. Visions of her blood spraying the walls and her scream shattering the windows are making the corner of my mouth twitch.

I'm definitely spending too much time with Valen these days.

Her eyes bore into mine as if attempting to read the questions zipping through them. Who has she told? What does she really know about me? Where are the journals?

Despite my dark side dancing with the excitement of death at its hands, a sobering desire to find another way burrows in my chest. If I could ensure my safety and save her life, I would. My humanity still battles within me; I hope it always will. I'd rather lock them all away in the dungeon at Guthrie Manor. Trap them in blood curses only I can break. But history has proven that's not an option. Those who run our world don't hesitate to kill. To eliminate any Grisym and everyone who stands with them.

If I allow them to live, they will come after all of us. No one is dying for me. And frankly, I don't want to die either. I've barely lived.

The future is now wide open without Roman reminding me that my studies don't matter, that they are only for appearance. He always had big plans for me. Plans that lacked any meaningful specifics despite how frequently I pleaded for insight.

"Hi Jorddan," Mikhail waves around me. "It's been a long time. It was lovely spending so much time with your daughter." She wears that same tight-lipped grin she's always walked around with. Those thin lips are painted in nude shades that nearly match her complexion.

My molars grind. I'm pissed she chose to ignore my comment but acknowledged my father.

Jorddan inhales deeply before releasing it. The warmth of his breath is harsh against my still-chilled skin. "That it has. I appreciate the years you *may* have helped my daughter, but I'm sure you are aware we are not here for that tonight."

"I couldn't tell with the child army at your back," Mikhail smirks.

"I would hardly say Bryony's friends count as an army," Jorddan responds deadpan. "Speaking of which, where are Pierson and Tosch?"

Mikhail flicks her hand nonchalantly. A dismissal of the two we sent to subdue her. "Safe. Sleeping, we'll say."

It takes everything in me not to charge her. If she hurt them, I won't just murder her. I'll make her suffer. I'll make her beg and plead for mercy, but there won't be any. Not with the way my dark side is pushing to the surface, eager to use its most violent acquired gifts.

The purpose of tonight means nothing if my family is in danger. My friends, my blood, they come first, always.

My neck rolls as my essence rages inside me. That big, heavy fist *bang, bang, banging* against the barrier of my skin. Eager for escape. Eager for vengeance and blood.

A salacious grin pulls at the corner of my mouth. The shift from my grayish-green eyes to pits of black is the door to my power gaining momentum, ready to tear our enemies to ribbons. My eyelids flutter shut, allowing the transition to complete.

Mikhail's audible gasp makes me chuckle darkly. The laugh of a villain rumbling up from my stomach, vibrating through my chest, and bursting out into the room, causing the very foundation to shake. *She didn't know.* My head cocks to the side, studying her reaction, my eyes narrowing to slits. *She does now.*

Cackling laughter builds inside me. My essence elated that we held the upper hand until the bitter end.

My lips part, the first sliver of my essence slipping free, jet-black and menacing. Every star is absent, as if refusing to bring any hope of light to the act against humanity we'll do tonight. A drape meant to blanket tonight in ultimate darkness. Pitch black, so endless, all you can do is beg for the tiniest spark to guide you free.

Mikhail's blonde waves shift as she takes a step back. That cavalier smirk she'd greeted us with melting into a twitching grimace.

"My word. How?" she gasps, another step leaving her stumbling into the arm of the sofa.

Though my essence continues to spill free, filling the room, working its way up into a frenzy, I can speak with complete clarity. "Knox. Graham. Get outside. Now."

"Bri, no!" Graham protests.

"Now." My voice seems to boom through the space, amplified by the magic flowing through me at such a rapid pace I'm unsure how my body isn't spinning itself.

My feet move forward of their own volition. My Grisym stalking its prey. "Mikhail, as far as I know, you never betrayed me. But maybe you have. I will know soon enough." The words escape my lips with the control of tranquil calm, while drenched in the venom of the most delicious villain. "This could have been easy, but I feel it now. You hurt my friends, and I have no choice but to return the favor. Sit."

Mikhail's body flails backward into the seat of the chair with the force of my command. I press my eyes shut, inhaling deeply, feeling for Knox and Graham. My essence hisses, signaling they've all retreated outside. Only then do I allow my eyes to peel open, focusing on the terror etched into Mikhail's features.

Their presence isn't required for the deeds I am about to commit. They don't need to see this. Neither do I, but my essence reminds me I do. The rasp of its words reminds me that this is the way it has to be.

Her life or mine.

Hers.

"Bryony, if anything happens to me, they'll know it was you." Widening eyes meet mine before darting back and forth. The plea unanswered as there's no one left in the room to save her. I won't, nor will my father.

"I. Don't. Care. Where are Pierce and Tosch?"

"Why do your eyes look like that?" Mikhail cowers, leaning back in her chair.

"You might think you know so much about me, and maybe you do. Let's recap, shall we? I will tell you what you're *dying* to know, and you will tell me what I *want* to know. Do you agree?"

Mikhail's eyes go wide, tracking behind me, my father taking several steps back, allowing me to do as I am being led to. Jorddan has never kept me from embracing who I am. On the contrary, he has encouraged it at every turn, giving me the confidence to live in my truth regardless of the consequences. I don't need to be afraid because he will be there to catch me. A parent who understands my essence now forever at my side, leading me. No judgment. Just the freedom to express what I am becoming as a Grisym and Eistiab.

Perhaps I am becoming the villain. The precise image dark wielders have been painted as by their closed-minded light-wielding counterparts. The corner of my mouth twitches again, a wolfish grin itching to break free.

I am no villain. Vigilante sounds more appropriate. *Yes,* my essence rasps in my head. *Yes, that's what we are. Serve her justice, Bryony. Make her pay.*

"Vigilante," I whisper to no one, testing the word on my tongue. Punishing those who would ruin wielders like me. Eradicating those who would eliminate anyone they considered too different. Not right. Abomination.

That word booms through my head, recalling the many times Harley has called me that exact insult. *Abomination.* Every bit of hatred lived in his eyes. The very same emotion flashing in mine convinced this woman wronged me beyond forgiveness. She hasn't confessed yet, but she will. I will know every dirty little secret before I snap her pathetic neck.

We always do.

"Speak," I command in a low snarl.

Mikhail's eyes blink slowly. Her lips parting, ready to spill her confessions. "Roman asked me to monitor your changes as you grew up. I kept my notes in my journals. They are sealed here in the house. Upstairs in the vault in my bedroom," Mikhail stares straight ahead, the words droning out of her as if she has somehow become a robot. "I did not know you were a Grisym until you were a teenager. When I brought my concerns to Roman about your unique abilities, he confessed what you were."

"And who have you told that information to? Have you shared your journals?"

"Yes," she breathes, the first set of tears streaking down her cheeks as she tries to fight against my control.

Struggle all you'd like. We're not letting you go.

"Explain."

"Yes. The Council has copies of every journal entry I have made about you. They know everything." Another tear breaks free, carrying a trail of brown mascara.

"You told them what she is?" Jorddan booms racing across the room, a rope of his essence snapping out and around her throat, squeezing.

"Yes," Mikhail chokes.

"Dad, release her. I can handle this."

Jorddan doesn't release his essence from around her neck but loosens the hold.

"You. How are you..." Mikhail begins.

"Oh, right? I promised to tell you about myself as well. Where to begin? Jorddan Guthrie is my father. He forced me to mature at fifteen using ghoul power. The color change you're witnessing now is because of my connection to them." With a single blink, the onyx shifts to that milky white. "I can command the ghouls, too."

Mikhail's eyes bulge as she tries to sit back further in her chair. Nothing but terror flashes back at me in her big doe eyes.

Good. You should be terrified. You're not walking out of here tonight. Not alive.

Mikhail swallows hard. "That's not possible."

"It is. How do I get into your vault, and where are my friends?" I sneer.

"My blood. You need my blood," she whimpers. "Your friends are still in the garage in the car. You won't get away with this, Bryony. They will find you. If anything happens to me, they will come after you."

Taking several steps back toward the front door, my grin spreads again.

"Good," I reply before throwing one last command over my shoulder. "Choke."

I ignore the gagging sounds behind me. I ignore the lamps and decor crashing to the floor as Mikhail writhes around her living room.

A cold resolve settles in my chest. I'm killing again.

Remorse nearly crippled me last time. Countless nights and self-talks were needed to pull me out of that pit of devastation. I killed someone. Ending a man's existence threatened to break me. Not this time. Not with the truth sucking every bit of air out of the room.

I wait for the self-hatred to bring me back to the Bri I've always known; it doesn't come.

There's nothing but the cold, hard edge of revenge.

She hurt my friends and my family. And she exposed me.

She threatened everything.

She can choke on every one of my secrets she spilled.

I won't lose a wink of sleep.

57

GRAHAM

THE FRONT DOOR SWINGS open silently. Jorddan hovers in the entryway, hands clasped in front of his body, staring ahead. His expression gives nothing away. His every feature is void of emotion. There are no indications of what took place in here after Bri forced us to leave written in his stare or posture. The scene sends rivulets of sweat down my spine with just a single glimpse of his stoic demeanor. There's just nothing.

My body hesitates to move across the threshold and back into the house. My essence is aware that something terrible happened in there. *No, is* happening. Still. Currently.

I'm anchored in place as Knox races past me and then Valen.

"What happened?" Valen pants as he darts through the front door.

Faint gagging noises filter in from the living room, my pulse spiking, worried it's Bri. Yet knowing it can't be. She's there in front of me, sitting on the steps, her elbows resting on her knees, head bowed between her shoulders.

"What the hell happened?" Knox barks.

"I killed her or am killing her," Bri responds, her white eyes meeting ours as she looks up. "She's been telling the Council everything. Every. Thing. You all need to distance yourselves from me."

"Fuck that!" Valen pushes through us, squatting in front of her. "Are you okay?"

"I killed her," Bri sighs.

"How do you feel?" he presses.

She takes a moment to answer, her fingers twisting around one another. "Good," she whimpers, a single tear slipping down her cheek. "I feel like I stood up for myself. For my safety."

Valen's mouth crashes into Bri's. The kiss is indecent as he pulls her to her feet, their mouths refusing to break contact. His tongue sweeps into her mouth with a groan, her palms gripping his mid-back. They break with a heavy breath, Valen cupping her chin harshly. "Don't you ever regret removing filth from this world. Do you hear me?"

She nods, their foreheads touching.

"We can do this later," Knox growls. "Where are Pierce and Tosch?"

"She said they were in the garage," Bri supplies, pulling away from Valen. "You guys go help them, and I'll grab what we need from the vault."

She turns toward the stairs, ready to climb and handle yet another thing on her own, but I lurch forward and grab her wrist. "You're not going anywhere alone."

She only nods, her eyes distant. Bri isn't here with us. Our girl is lost somewhere in her head and needs our support.

Bri will take this upon herself. Her eyes will betray her as she claims this was all about protecting her life and chances for a future. Her actions stopped being about her a long time ago. Everything she does is for us. Those she values most. No way in hell we're letting her do any of this alone again. She sacrificed for us; we can do the same.

The second floor is just as immaculately decorated as the downstairs area. Meticulous thought went into the placement of every art print on the walls, the bushel of flowers in a vase, and the bowls showcased on the tables. Pieces that are unique but not gaudy. Pieces that likely held significance for the deceased wielder downstairs.

I'm not sure what happened to Yorgan's body after our first murder, or what they will do with Mikhail's body now. Something is unsettling about rifling through her house while she's a fresh corpse downstairs. As if we don't have respect for our dead, when they are one of our greatest treasures. Even those who disgust us.

"Did she say where this vault is?" I ask as we wander down the hallway. Each door we pass is closed. Each was painted in the same bland cream as the last. A contrast to the warm, earthy taupe covering the walls.

"No. She didn't have to." There's a pregnant pause as if Bri is gathering her thoughts. Or perhaps the aftermath of tonight's events is finally taking its toll. Then she continues as if her words flowed without a stop. "Anyone who has a blood-sealed vault would only keep it in one of two places: hidden in an office or the basement. Her house doesn't have a basement."

"How do you know that?"

"I remember asking when I was a child. Harley used to lock me down in ours, and I wasn't a fan of small spaces for a long time. I-I," a cleansing breath funnels in through her nose and out past her parted lips. "That's what my essence remembered. Mikhail tried to take me down there, but I didn't want to go." There's no inflection in her tone, but it's as if I can feel the sadness floating inside her.

Another piece of my heart shatters knowing how cruel Harley had been to her. "Bri, that's... that's fucking awful."

"It doesn't matter. What's done is done."

"It *does* matter. How could you give him back to Roman after he treated you like that?" I snap, my jaw clenching with fury.

She spins toward me, tears building behind her moss-green and gray eyes. "Because keeping all of you alive is more important than what happens to me. What don't you get about that?"

I recoil as if she physically slapped me. Emotions are high right now, but she hasn't taken that tone with me since earlier this year when she caught me creeping on her and Knox. In truth, it seems she's been softer with me since I found out she's a Grisym, as if she believes that one wrong word or phrase will send me running for the hills.

I'm dumbfounded, failing to understand how she still believes I won't choose her when I have chosen her every day. What will convince her if my actions as of late haven't?

Still, I won't stand here and let her project her anger onto me. I won't let her isolate herself and continue to face the world alone. She is still my best friend. I still want her to share her burdens with me. "I do get it, but you're too busy pretending like none of us chose to stand here with you. We did. I did, so knock off whatever this attitude is."

Her eyes are wide, staring back at me. As if preparing to speak, her lips roll inward before parting. Yet, not a sound breaks free. Her gaze tracks down to my mouth before finding my eyes again. My cue to steal this moment with her. Closing the distance between us, my hand cups the back of her head, pulling her mouth to mine. Shaking fingers grip the front of my jacket, our mouths moving together as if they've been apart for eons. Hungry and wanting and needy.

I can't help but breathe her in, holding her close to me. When I finally pull away, she licks her lips, her eyes focused downward. "You are not alone in any of this." My knees bend, head ducking so we're eye-level, a tiny smirk playing at the corner of my mouth. "Even if everything I've ever told myself is against this new rebellious streak." I mean every word, even if she doesn't believe it yet.

She releases a watery laugh, tugging at my coat. "Thank you. I'm just tired of endangering everyone I care about because I'm the one they're after."

"It's our choice, not yours. Let's go find what we're looking for so we can get home. We have studying to get done this weekend."

She only rolls her eyes, but that soft smile pulls at her lips. Enough to make me believe she's okay. Enough to make me think we might find normalcy again one day.

I follow her down the upstairs hallway. With a flick of her wrist, each door we pass flies open, only for her clenched fist to force it to slam shut again. She continues onward, abruptly halting when she reaches a door near the end of the hall. It looks no different from the others, but Bri senses something.

Instead of using her power, Bri cautiously wraps her fingers around the knob before twisting and slowly edging the door open. Where the other rooms had clearly been guestrooms or storage, this one sends my jaw to the floor. I assume it's an office, but the walls appear more like a murder board. Pictures, articles, and strings connecting one to another cover the majority of the space.

"Holy hell," she breathes, taking in the walls.

News articles, clippings, photos, handwritten notes, and photocopied pages line the walls. Every bit of information is about Grisyms and how Bri correlated as a child. The strings connecting her to known facts about her kind were labeled with more details than I thought anyone knew.

But there are others, too. Photos of wielders I've known throughout my life and others whom I've never seen.

"What is this?" Knox breathes, his steps coming to a halt just inside the door. I'd been so focused on scanning the walls, I hadn't heard him and Jorddan enter behind me.

"She's been... hunting us. Reporting everyone she suspected to the Council. That woman there, I remember seeing that her husband reported her as missing a few years ago, then he supposedly committed suicide. What if they took her and killed him?" Bri whispers.

My mind whirs with the possibilities.

We're living in a world we always knew to be true. But it's easy to deceive ourselves and pretend there's nothing beneath the surface. There is. A realm full of dirty dealings, betrayal, and lies.

"Take it. All of it," Bri orders.

Knox's essence seeps from his fingertips, the tendrils spreading to blanket all the walls, only to come away, leaving them bare with nothing but the pins and hanging string. Every sheet of paper that lined the walls now rests in his palm, stacked in a neat pile as if someone had taken ample time to ensure the edges were in line.

"Where is the vault?" I ask, spinning to check where it might be.

Bri only moves to a smooth area of the wall, pressing her hand to it, breathing in and releasing her essence out. "It's here." She presses in closer to the wall, her palm flattening against the surface. "Cadere," she whispers.

The house shakes around us. Bits of sheetrock breaking free and crumbling to the ground. The foundation quakes, and we reach out to steady our balance. Eyes glued to the wall, we watch it fall away, revealing the vault beyond it.

Nothing else is disturbed despite the quake that just shook the house on its foundation; not a single crack mars the walls, the items scattered across the surface of the desk exactly where they'd been when we entered.

A heavy metal door glares back at us now. Bri only stares at the studded charcoal surface, head cocked to the side. The same stance she takes when her eyes change on their own. The other parts of her storming to the surface, taking hold of the reins. A sign of one of her many essences succeeded in fighting its way to the forefront. A new co-ruler beside her own for whatever the moment brings.

"Come," she whispers. "Come."

We all stand in silence, my heart racing, as I contemplate what she has summoned this time. Only when a stream of bright red fluid floats between us and into her waiting palm, do I understand. *Holy fuck*, she just summoned that woman's blood out of her body to open the door. I've never known a wielder to do that.

On its own, Bri's essence can do amazing things. Unspeakable things. Combined with the other magic that lives in her veins, she's miraculous. Bri is a unique creature who equally intrigues and terrifies me. Not because I actually fear my best friend anymore. I don't. But I fear what might happen if she continues to take and evolve. I fear what another loss of control might result in.

The small stream settles in her palm, the profile of her face revealing those black pits. The minuscule amount of blood gracefully morphs into the shape of a key, levitating away from her skin to enter a small hole at the right side of the door. It's not an actual keyhole, but the blood enters just the same.

And we wait.

Long moments of nothing stretch before a heavy lock unlatches and the door cracks open.

Bri pulls it open all the way, revealing a room of shelves. Each one is full of the journals Bri described. Every shelf stretches the length of its wall and is labeled with a name. Three hold Bri's while the others showcase other names. Other wielders.

"Take them all," Jorddan orders.

This time, he does the task himself, mumbling an incoherent spell before every volume disappears from sight.

"Where did you send them?" I ask, staring at the blank shelves.

"Somewhere safe."

58

BRYONY

THE HIGH OF AN adrenaline spike, shoving against the numbness weighing down my limbs, detaches me from the present. Only films portray an existence as convoluted as mine has become. It can't be real. This cannot be my life.

But it is. *Accept it, Bri.*

The others are speaking, but I don't hear their words. Their words muffled like the rush of the ocean plowing over my head. Wave after wave crashing, only allowing me brief seconds to suck in another breath before I'm pulled under again.

There were so many of us. Hundreds of wielders lined Mikhail's walls. Wielders she either knew were Grisyms or suspected to be. If she were reporting me, I have no doubt she also reported them. It's been quite some time since that information about me was first handed over to the Council. I can only assume I'm not the only one, which means they've had this vault of ammunition they've just been sitting on. *Why?*

Sure, they may have been eliminating some of those other Griysms, and I'm unaware, but why not me?

How many of those faces that were hanging on the wall aren't as lucky as I've been? Why protect me? Why spare me?

Stifling a sob, tears burn behind my eyes, devastated that so many lives have been or will be lost because we're seen as a threat. And maybe we are. Maybe we are too dangerous or unpredictable. Maybe we are more powerful.

We are still living beings. We deserve life as much as anyone else.

My chin dips close to my chest, my gaze once again focused on my palms. They're spotless to the naked eye. There's not a speck of dirt on them. But I see the blood. All of it. Mine, my family, my friends. The crimson of the two I've killed and the countless others who never got a chance glares back at me. The volume seems to grow as I carry the weight of the Grisym race on my shoulders. Too many of them could be lost, too.

My feet are barely moving as we shuffle back across the street. Glancing over my shoulder, the house appears just as it had been before we entered. Though lit, with the entry locked up tight, there's no forgetting what we left behind: the corpse of a wielder crumpled on the living room floor.

Pierce and Tosch haven't woken up yet. The two slung over Knox and my father's shoulders. Their bodies are as limp as I imagine Mikhail's is.

Bile creeps up my throat, knowing I was the reason they were hurt. Logically, the blame originates with Roman. I know that. Yet the guilt threatens to drown me. It was my kill list, my enemies, my identity we were trying to protect.

Not only had that bitch physically hit them, she'd cursed them, too. Not the kind you hear about in fairytales, where it passes down generations and only a kiss can break it. That sort of nonsense is bullshit in our world.

Curses exist in varying degrees of strength and destructiveness. A governing truth that exists for all magic in the veins of every wielder and the spells we cast. Mikhail had used a relatively mild version. One just strong enough to ensure her safety. A paralysis curse that will leave them immobilized for at least twelve hours.

They can hear, see, and feel, but they are helpless. There's nothing to do but wait for it to wear off. I question which is worse: witnessing everything around you with no way to respond, or missing it all under the cold blanket of unconsciousness.

I'd still kissed Pierce's mouth, whispering how I made her pay, and hugged Tosch to my chest, apologizing but promising I would update Damian.

Fuck, he is going to be livid. His wife is everything to him. A love story that might never have happened if Tosch's parents hadn't thought to protect her in such an unconventional way. He won't blame me, but I blame myself.

With the swipe of his hand, Oscar brought the portal back into focus. One by one, we stepped through with him bringing up the rear. Our somber mood hung heavy in the air, filling the foyer as we reentered my family's home.

Even Camilla kept her gaze down and lips pressed shut—an unusual feat for her. My best friend only took my hand and walked with me upstairs. There was no objection as she led me to my room, held me close, and then shuffled off to hers. Jorddan insisted that she and Oscar stay the night. The somberness of the evening was better to be slept on, even if daylight was already streaming through the massive windows.

Only I never slept. I've been lying here for hours, running it all back in my head. Were there signs I should have seen?

This isn't the first time I've contemplated how much easier my life would be if I fell in line. Had I just behaved as a good little light wielder, perhaps we could have avoided all of this. An existence that may have eventually suffocated me, smothered under the enormous weight of expectation.

No matter which way I spin the shoulda, woulda, couldas, I arrive at the same answer.

No matter the starting point or the turns taken, we'd be right here. We'd still be drowning in our secrets. We'd still be hiding and constantly looking over our shoulders. Grisym designation still ends in death. None of that would have changed had I taken the coward's way out.

Anyone I've ever known would still be in danger. It doesn't matter if they knew my truth. The Council doesn't care.

A humorless laugh escapes me. "Roman, this is all your fault," I whisper to no one.

His choices would still have put me in danger. He let others into our home. He let them know what I am. All it would take is one person to betray us. To no longer care about his influence or the threats he delivered so kindly, they seemed like compliments.

Mikhail and countless others have made choices, too. The decisions of the few often dictate the consequences forced on the masses. A path that leads to killing or being killed rather than putting aside unfounded prejudices and living in acceptance.

A groan rumbles through my chest as I log roll onto my back. My muscles aching as if I had engaged in novel strenuous activity. With a whisper, the curtains part, revealing the burning glow of the sun finally setting on yet another day. Our limbo stretches through the days, chasing the cycle of the beginning and end of another twenty-four hours.

It's not long before I convince myself to climb out of bed and shower. A jolt, I hope, jump-starts my momentum for what's left of the day. That might motivate me to leave this damn room instead of hiding away with my feelings.

Solitude was what I needed before, but now I'm not sure. Still, they all respected it. Not a single knock, text, or call came through. It was just me and my endless racing thoughts. My ability to overthink at every turn holds me prisoner, tucked under the weighted duvet.

Exhaustion could just as easily have kept them all away. Between the time difference and our never-ending plate of shit, it's messing with my head. Tilting me further off balance than I already was. I can't be the only one.

The warm spray of the shower eases the tension in my muscles. My thoughts slow to a more manageable pace as I let the soapsuds and water coat my body. There will be nothing additional. No washing my hair or shaving. It would take more energy than I have to spare.

The contents of those journals will require everything I have left. My focus, my emotions, my energy. First, food and an exorbitant amount of it. Perhaps endless calories will fill the hole that seems to be expanding inside me. I also want to review everything Knox gathered. Hopefully, I'll be able to enlist Graham to help. His research reveals tiny details others miss. The minutiae that give us an edge.

Cutting the water, my essence streams from my fingers, splitting in two through the bathroom. One tendril snatches my towel, and the other my robe.

My stars are back, twinkling brighter than ever. A reminder that there's still light inside me, despite the most heinous act I committed a day ago. Normally,

I wouldn't use my essence for something so frivolous, but I was so tired that I didn't even think to hang it on the hook before stepping into the shower.

It's a stumble through the motions. Each task is more laborious than the last. Brushing my teeth, adding moisturizer to my hair and oil to my roots, applying serum to my face, and even inspecting my smattering of freckles to check for more.

It's something I've done since I was a kid. I enjoyed having so many, but my siblings didn't. That was before I realized how different I really was from them. For years, I scrutinized my face, hunting for new chocolate-colored dots. Hope soared when there were no fresh freckles, and then quickly faded, realizing the old ones hadn't blended in with my complexion. I understood that I couldn't change internally to become more similar to my siblings, so I had to rely on external physical features.

Beauxgraton reversed that mindset, too. The catalyst that launched me into this brave, proud version of Bri. My freckles became a part of my identity that I once again loved, just as I did when I was a little girl. They were beautiful. They made me unique. Special.

Dropping my towel on the floor, I saunter back into my bedroom feeling a little lighter, a little more Bri.

"Morning, gorgeous," a voice croons from the bed. My hand flies to my chest, my body lurching back several feet.

My men are all seated on the bed, each with his legs crossed at the ankles, side by side. If their appearances weren't so starkly different, I'd call them clones with their matching grins and arms folded over their chests.

I rake my gaze over each of them one by one. My stare catches on Valen with that damn dagger flipping between his fingers, and my skin heats. Then there's Knox on the end, so close to the edge, I wonder if he's ready to bolt.

"Why are you all in here?"

"To check on you," Graham replies.

I can only stare at the sight before me. It's not the first time I've had them all in my bed. Memories of the night we planned to run away over winter break and movie nights filter to the forefront of my mind. Even with my bed here being a massive California King, they seem to take up every inch, filling the space in my bed and my heart. The spot at the center of my sternum aches for them, causing me to run the heel of my palm over it as a soft smile pulls at my lips.

"And no Camilla?" I quirk a brow.

"She's with Oscar. They've been talking portals for hours," Valen snorts as if annoyed, but there's no missing the slight upward tug at the corner of his mouth. A soft chuckle escapes me, knowing Valen would have done just about anything not to like Camilla. She's loud, cheerful, and doesn't have a sinister bone in her body. They embody perfect opposites. He'll never admit it, but he loves her too, in his own way. She's one of us.

"I should go find her," I mumble, turning toward the dresser to find some clothing.

"No," Pierce's voice stops me. "You should come get into this bed and let us hold you."

I take a steadying breath, my head bowed. He must think I'm shaken by what I did last night. Who knows what the others told him. "I'm fine. I promise."

"I don't care. Come here, Bryony."

There's no denying him, especially after Mikhail viciously attacked him because of me. Abandoning the clothing I was going to grab, I crawl up the center of the bed.

Once upon a time, I would have hidden my nakedness. Covering my body in clothing that smoothed my soft belly and thick thighs. I would have attempted to make my body more palatable for others, though I loved it. Sometimes it doesn't matter how much you love yourself when the person you love constantly reminds you they don't like what they see. You work to appease them. You hide because being loved is more important than your internal feelings.

Pierce and Graham shift slightly, but there's not enough room for me to sit between them. My ass is too big, and they didn't design this bed for a full-figured woman and four decently sized men.

I'm ready to stay at their feet when Pierce leans forward, grabbing my wrist. "My lap."

My throat goes dry knowing I am naked beneath my robe and about to straddle one of my boyfriends while sitting here with all the others. It's not like we haven't had fun as a group before. I've taken them all in pairs.

This moment is different, though. My heart is racing at the intensity of having the four of them watch me.

But as I look into their eyes, I'm not the only one with lust brewing inside me. So I let Pierce pull me forward, his hands finding my hips as I straddle his lap. I'd been so drawn to their faces, I hadn't noticed he was already hard.

His length presses against my bare core. The cotton of his pajama pants does nothing to staunch the heat radiating off him. Or maybe it's me.

Knox's hand immediately finds my bare thigh. Warm fingers trail over my skin, every nerve firing at the minimal contact. A shiver runs down my spine as the tip of one finger traces along the crease between my hip and pelvis.

The bed groans as Graham leans over, kissing my mouth, his tongue sweeping inside to dance with mine. My fingers sink into his hair, pulling him closer to me, our mouths slanting at an odd angle. Still, I give him everything.

They deserve all of me, and I want to give them that.

Only Valen isn't touching me physically. My body craves the sting of his dagger and the roughness of his palms. Still, there's no missing his dark eyes glinting as he attempts to restrain himself.

Pierce had made this sound so innocent. But my body knew differently. The lust burning in their gazes as they raked their eyes down my robe-covered body gave them away. My essence is stirring beneath the surface, eager to absorb the power of my men as they bury themselves inside me. I swear my essence is hornier than I've ever been.

Graham finally pulls away, grinning like a fool. "That's how I would have said good morning had we been awake."

A flush creeps over my skin, but I stamp down the feelings brewing in my lower belly. Turning my focus back to Pierce, I run my hand over his stubbled cheek. I've always seen him clean-shaven, not even with a five o'clock shadow, until now. "How are you feeling?"

"Like I got my skull cracked, but I'm more worried about you."

"I told you—"

"We know what you said," Knox interjects. "But you forget I know exactly how you feel." He hadn't meant the words sexually, but my core pulses as his fingers drift over that crease again, those pine green eyes studying my features.

"You're right. I feel a lot of things, but *I am fine*. I don't care that I killed her, especially after seeing that room. More than anything, I grapple with why I don't care. Am I a bad person, or have circumstances pushed me so far that all I can see is the justice I'm serving for the people I love?" My fingers brush back Knox's unruly waves from his forehead, the length a little longer, the curls a bit more coiled. My fingers knot in his hair, pulling his face to me, kissing him hard and deep, only to quickly pull away. "What you're feeling is what I feel for all of you and our friends. The anger and pain that comes with knowing your association with me could be catastrophic for you."

The bed shifts again, Valen's scent enveloping me from behind as his hands sneak into the part of my robe, each palm squeezing my full breasts. "I. Will. Kill. Anyone who so much as looks at you the wrong way." His teeth lightly scratch along my earlobe. "Don't worry about us."

"What are you doing?" I breathe, my chest rising and falling in exaggerated pumps.

My oversensitized skin burns under their touch. Every nerve is firing and yearning for more. A hiss sneaking past my teeth when Valen pinches both peaked nipples between his fingers, chuckling in my ear.

Pierce's mouth crashes to mine as Graham peppers kisses along my right thigh while Knox still teases along the left.

"There was a time you said all of us or none of us," Valen whispers my declaration back to me against the side of my throat, his fingers tweaking my nipples harder, causing my moan to vibrate into Pierce's mouth. "It's time to make good on your ultimatum."

59

WYNSTON

Our plan was simple: check on our woman, get her what she needs, and cuddle—though I was determined to skip that part. It wasn't to seduce her or get wrapped up in another fucking orgy. It wasn't some plot we hatched as a group, but maybe more of a silent understanding.

Other than that single occasion with the ghoul, I vowed I would only ever take Bri alone. The morning after we arrived here at the manor was an exception after we'd nearly lost our lives. Somehow, fucking Bri didn't bother me, but having the guys in bed with us made me shift uncomfortably. It shouldn't. Dark wielders are very open about sex, especially extrinsics and charters, because the ghoul pits are practically one massive monster orgy. But my conscience told me I shouldn't be fucking a student with another joining in.

Thinking back, does it matter?

It felt wrong, as if I was purposely aiming to cross every line. A barrier that no longer exists. Not since I resigned from my position.

Professor of Essence Manipulation. The career I'd worked so hard for. Janelle believes I'll be back; my job is still mine next semester. That prestigious position is just waiting for me on a silver platter. A post I'm convinced I have no intention of returning to. When I told Janelle I wouldn't be back, I was resolute in

455

that decision. There was no hesitation or contemplation about whether I was making a mistake. In my gut, I knew I wasn't. Deep down, I knew there was more I needed to do with what I'd been given. Shaping young minds was just the start. A beginning that originated with Professor Opperman.

Yet as we stood there recapping what we were facing as a race, a calm settled over me. I'd done more than I'd set out to do. I repaid and honored the promises I made to the professor who made me.

Our infrastructure as a wielding community is archaic. We all know it, yet those in power refuse to change it because it means they lose their iron grip on us. I'd watched the effect this had on Bri and me this year. I witnessed Tillerman, Janelle, and Jorddan step out of the shadows so they no longer bore the weight alone. It was time to do more. Give more.

Countless times, people have told me that my talents and intelligence would serve me better elsewhere. And as my fingers slip through Bri's wet pussy, I know I've found it with her and her family.

It was a silent understanding as the four of us filed into the dining room for dinner, only to find Bri's chair empty. No one had seen her all day, but I'd felt her. Those slow-rolling waves of emotion had remained at a consistent low churn from the moment she shuffled up to her room this morning until she locked eyes with us as she exited her bathroom. An even sway that made me believe she was still fast asleep or staring at the ceiling, lost in her obsessive thoughts.

Graham and Pierce immediately jumped to the worst-case scenario. That she'd fallen into that bottomless pit of despair from which she never fully climbed out after Yorgan. I focused on how her essence moved inside me. It's whispered words and needs.

Us. It needed us.

We meant only a quick visit. Kiss her and hold her for a few minutes. Assure her we're all here for her, however, whenever. Simple. Innocent.

Sharing the space with them sparked that same stomach-churning discomfort as if we're still doing something wrong. Not as her professor, but as an older man in her father's house. Vincent and Jorddan tolerate me at best. The olive branch was likely extended only because of what I am to Bri. Imagining what I desire to do to his daughter, in this bed, feels disrespectful.

Yet, it's not stopping me. Our essences won't allow us to hold back, and who am I to deny magic what it needs?

We all crave her all day, every minute. It doesn't matter who is around or the societal norms we're plowing over.

Yet I crossed the line as soon as I ran my palm up her thigh and grazed my finger over the edge of her pelvis. And now, as my fingers press soft circles into her clit, I no longer give a fuck.

I want her, and I need her. It doesn't matter if they do too.

Bri's legs spread a little wider, welcoming my touch as Pierce devours her mouth and Valen kneads at her heavy breasts. So full, with her dark nipples peaked and waiting to be licked. Shoving Valen's hand away, I take one into my mouth. Licking and sucking around the swollen nub as she grinds in my hand and Pierce's crotch, hissing through their kiss.

The connection of their mouths breaks with a loud smack. "Who's first?" she breathes.

Her grayish-green eyes are bright. Hooded with lust, but focused.

I hadn't expected this to escalate so fast. We thought she'd want to talk, or we'd have to force our comfort on her. Bri will act tough until she hits a point where she's too overwhelmed to do so. We prepared for that, but not this.

We hadn't expected her to welcome us all into her bed at once. Her desire to take us one after another only makes my cock throb painfully, my length so hard that only an orgasm or two might bring it down. Shit like this doesn't happen in real life. It's the twisted fantasies men have all their lives. Yet, how many get to live it?

Fuck, am I ready for that?

The ghoul was one thing. That was about a power exchange. About determining her ability to siphon from a ghoul. The sex had been out of this world. It has been like that from the very first time I had her, as if that greedy, tight pussy was made just for me.

Even that morning with Valen and her weeks ago was different. Emotions were high. Bri and I had been so connected that it was like Valen didn't even exist. It was just the two of us, seamlessly blending into one another.

My cock swells in my sweats. The fucker is so eager to sink inside her, I groan out loud. I need to feel her walls wrap around us and squeeze until she pulls my release out of me. Until every drop of my cum fills her while I continue to drive into her, forcing her to release her essence and moan my name. And when I'm done, I'll fuck every last drop of us back inside her with my tongue, exactly where it belongs.

Another audible groan leaves me imagining her heated flesh moving against me as she rides my cock, this one more strained than the last as my brows scrunch together. Our essences are swirling around the room, knocking shit over as they often do. And the bite of her nails raking over my bare chest as her head falls back, leaves me begging for more.

The fantasy ends as her body is torn out of my hold. Blinking several times, my mind is slow to process Graham flipping Bri onto her back, pinning her to the bed. He kisses her hard, tugging the robe down her arms, exposing the expanse of her chest and torso to him.

I swear, a shudder runs through his body as his fingers trail over her bare skin.

Reality leaves me frozen. Graham is a rule-follower. He's tough on Bri because he wants the best for her, but he has an ingrained kindness in him. No part of me would have ever expected dominance.

Confidence, sure. Graham's family taught him to walk around with his chin held high. To put his best foot forward. Let no one see you rattled. Be the best.

I just always thought of him as passive. Arrogant. A know-it-all. But not the type to snatch his woman, throw her down, and then ravage her body.

We watch as he trails kisses down her stomach, her body writhing beneath him. Her groan reverberates off the walls as his lips graze her seam, her legs falling open impossibly wider.

"Why am I the only one naked?" she pants.

Graham laps at her, her fingers sinking into his hair, pulling hard the way she always does mine. Pain, I've always welcomed if it means I get to taste her. Move inside her.

As if we coordinated a routine, Pierce, Valen, and I strip off our shirts, tossing our pants somewhere in the room to follow. Thank fuck Pierce had the decency to wear some fucking underwear, but not Valen. His cock is standing proud as he strokes himself.

With a grin, he moves up the center of the bed before straddling Bri's face. Her eyes narrow on him as he taps her lips with the swollen head. Rubbing himself back and forth across her lips, smearing his pre-cum. "Open up for me, Forbidden Fruit. Suck my cock."

Her lips part slowly, allowing him to inch his way into her mouth. Her cheeks immediately hollow as he sinks in deeper. The muscles in his thighs flex with the scrape of her nails down their length, his hips pumping at a furious pace.

She takes him all, swallowing him down, but never breaking eye contact, while Graham continues to lick, suck, and fuck her with his tongue. With every gagging noise, Valen's grin only grows wider, dark and wolfish, enjoying forcing Bri to take all of him.

My dick only grows harder watching her, and I can't wait anymore. I need to be inside her.

Grabbing Graham's shoulder, I pull him away, his face coated in her arousal.

I don't even have the patience to take off my boxer briefs, yanking myself free before I sink into her. That wet warmth that feels like fucking home surrounds me. Her walls pulse around me, tightening to the point I can barely pull back.

My pace is slow. The even roll of my hips forward and back, keeping time with Valen's dip into her mouth. Keeping my torso as straight as possible, the muscles strain. It's uncomfortable as hell, but I refuse to get that close to Valen's naked ass.

But fuck, I've never been harder watching another man fuck my woman's mouth while I claim her pussy.

Bri writhes beneath us, her essence releasing from her fingers to fill the room. Mine follows eagerly, mixing with hers. It's been too long. We went from moments like this every day to almost nothing at all. Our magic isn't happy. Neither am I. It's not the sex I crave necessarily, but the undeniable connection we share. My Gemminai Animyrum. A term I recite in my mind as if it were of endearment. Our souls and life forces are connected.

How?

Who the fuck cares?

She's mine.

"Move," Pierce orders Valen, but he only pistons his hips into her mouth faster, his movements becoming a frantic, uneven pace before he comes undone. He roars her name, his palm slamming into the headboard so forcefully I swear the wood cracks. A black cloud bursts from him, the wave mixing with Bri and me as the three dance through the space above us.

I only quicken my pace, determined to make our girl come first. There's no pulling out until she coats my cock and her inner thighs in our releases. The combination leaking out around us, soaking the sheets, only for us to fuck her again. Only for me to fuck every last drop back inside her. A reminder that she's mine. Always.

When Valen finally collapses at her side, Pierce eyes me as if demanding I do the same, but I can't. Her walls are spasming around me, tightening on my hardening length, ready to milk me dry when her own release rips through her. It's all hers, every drop. "Make me come," I groan, pumping harder and faster.

Bryony can take everything from me. My essence. My cum. My heart. It's all fucking hers.

My lower back spasms as I unload into her wet pussy. Her walls are squeezing me tight while ropes of my cum fill her. Every ragged breath is nothing more than a wheeze as my hips continue to slowly roll into her, drawing out her release until her limbs begin to go limp.

There's nothing but the feel of her fluttering walls and our ragged breaths. Just Bri and me in this moment.

Valen's face dipping back into my line of sight reminds me we're not alone. It's not just us tucked away in the cabin. The one place on school property that became ours. Valen bends low, gripping her chin between his long fingers. "That's our good girl. Now, you're going to ride Pierce." She nods, but doesn't move. "Don't you want to be filled with all of our cum, Forbidden Fruit?"

She nods again, accepting his kiss. A kiss that could only taste like him on her lips.

This shit isn't supposed to be this hot. I'm not supposed to want to be in this bed, with these young people, fucking this woman I have no business wanting but couldn't let go of. This is all so fucking messy.

Pierce shifts forward, linking his fingers through hers, helping her sit up. Bri's body sags as if she's too tired even to hold up her head, a lazy grin playing at her swollen lips. "I've missed you," he whispers, settling on his back.

Bri grips him, a slow stroke of his shaft, before Graham helps lift her hips, notching Pierce at her entrance. "I love you, too," she grins, then she drops, impaling herself on him.

Pierce's barked curse bounces off the walls, our released essences swirling into a storm to match the emotions flowing through her. I can feel every single one. Ecstasy. Love. Passion. Desire. Fear. The sweet and sour tang of addiction. A feeling I'm all too familiar with.

We all might be. Bryony Guthrie is our drug, and we will always need another hit.

They move together, slow and sensual. A rhythm I would expect from her and Graham—at least I would have before I watched him eat her pussy like a starved man. Then again, both he and Pierce are softer souls.

Allowing my mind to wander, I realize I've witnessed the shadow of ruthlessness that lives beneath Graham's skin. The reason he and Valen have finally bonded, more than likely.

"Fuck, Bri," Pierce groans, his fingers digging into her full hips.

Those long curls trail down her back as she exposes the column of her throat. Sweat glistens on her brown skin, my lips latching onto the spot just below her jaw. The taste of salt explodes on my tongue as I suck harder. That pain prickles at my scalp as she reaches back, her fingers sinking into my hair and curling into a fist.

"More," she moans. "Yes, just like that." She bites her bottom lip, her eyes pressing shut as Pierce dictates the pace and nibbles at her flesh.

Knotting her hair around my fist, I pull her head back further, my mouth capturing hers in a bruising kiss. She immediately opens up to me, our tongues dancing to a tantalizing beat. I should care that another man's release is on her tongue, but I don't. My Grisym still tastes as delicious as always.

"You're doing so good," Valen praises. "You like taking all our cocks, don't you?"

Bri only groans into my mouth, her body bouncing as Pierce bucks up into her from below. The clap of their skin is thunderous in my ears, inviting me to pull away from her so my hooded eyes latch onto where he sinks into her over and over again.

"I thought so," Valen chuckles. The sound is dark, a type of laugh that evokes thoughts of mischief. "Graham, have you ever fucked a woman's ass before?"

There's too much happening to focus, until Bri's fingers wrap around my shaft, squeezing tight. The feel of her skin on mine drops me back into the present, back into focus. I can only watch her face. Study her reaction. Get lost in the feel of our shared essence moving through me.

Graham's body goes straight, his eyes darting between Valen's and mine before he croaks his answer. "No."

Valen only grins wider. "Well, it's your lucky day; our girl is just begging for it."

Fuck! My cock springs back to life, imagining him plunging into her juicy ass, filling her the way I had months ago. A groan vibrates up my chest and throat as she fists my dick, my body coiling tight, ready to come all over again.

I am too fucking old for this shit.

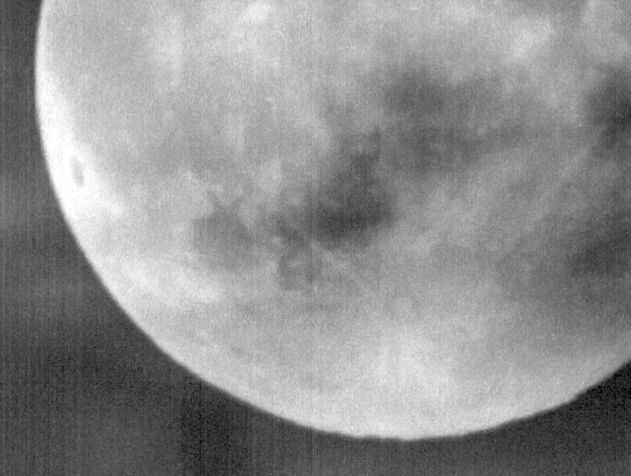

60

BRYONY

MY BODY WRITHES, MY internal temperature so high that the sweat seems to pour out of me. Every inch of my skin responds to the slightest touch, as if my nerve endings have multiplied and ramped up their sensitivity.

It's too much.

It's not enough.

Having all four of my men at once is everything. It's the most delicious high, leaving me sated until the next brush of their fingers over my heated flesh.

My magic rolls through me, basking in every emotion one could imagine. Each one fluttering through my belly as if it's the first time they've had the chance to enjoy Club Bri.

It's overwhelming, exciting, terrifying, the biggest fucking turn-on.

Euphoria flows through me, experiencing it all at once, while accepting that I want it all. I need it. All of them. Just like this.

I'm lost in the sensations until a hand runs over my ass, the cold kiss of lube circling my tight hole. My hips shift, attempting to pull away from the icy touch.

No!

I've only done that once with Knox and Aziel.

"I can't," I pant, my tits bouncing with the force of Pierce fucking me. His cock driving deeper and deeper into my core with every pump of his hips.

"Are you my girl?" Valen purrs, flicking the tip of his tongue along the ridge of my ear, before loudly sucking the lobe between his lips.

I only nod, unable to form words as yet another orgasm crescendos through me.

"That's what I thought. Lean forward."

I do as he says, Pierce stretching me while a finger plays at my puckered hole, slowly dipping in, swirling, and then slipping out. The discomfort of a second finger added causes me to arch my back, the pressure making me gasp as my release finally tears through me. My body quivers, shaking so violently I lose my rhythm with Pierce, but he doesn't stop, his arm hooked under my knee, opening me up for him as he rolls up into me. Long, punishing strokes that keep me riding the high of yet another release.

"Gods above, y'all are going to kill me," I breathe.

"Not a chance," Valen says, running his teeth along the curves of my jaw. The added sensation sends a shiver down my spine; my walls still fluttering, wanting more, needing more. My pussy is such a greedy whore. She never gets enough of them, even when I'm wrung out with exhaustion.

I fight for breath as Pierce thickens, stretching me more. A few more thrusts before he, too, spills free inside me. The mix of me, him, and Knox filling my pussy draws out my sated grin. *Fuck,* is being filled with multiple men's cum supposed to feel this good?

Weaving my hand between our bodies, I run my fingers through the mess between my legs, my digits coated in the evidence of our orgasms. Rubbing my thumb and pointer finger together, my head tilts watching our thick arousal move, before I suck them clean, moaning loudly.

"Fuck. Me," Pierce groans, his eyes rolling back into his head as his body falls onto the pillow.

"Move her," Valen orders Knox, his arms wrapping around my middle to yank me off Pierce, Valen taking his place.

His cock stands tall at his hips, his tattoos dark and antagonistic against his skin. I'd forgotten how sexy they all were. Maybe because I've never taken the time to explore them all. Valen and I are quick to fuck and then move on with our time. When we sleep, we sleep. There was no purpose in exploring the ink that marks his skin.

But I crawl to him, straddling his hips the way I'd done with Pierce. My body is so keyed up, I don't take my time sliding down his shaft, his barked curses only making me grin.

My fingers curl around Valen's throat, my body leaning forward, flicking my tongue over his lips. "Looks like I'm in charge now."

Valen's arm loops around my back, holding me to his chest when I try to sit up straight. But I don't miss his nod, Graham once again lining up behind me.

His swollen head notches at my puckered hole, the muscles clenching tight, not ready to let someone in again. It had been amazing with Knox and Aziel, but it won't be the same when the cock entering me can't adjust to my insides.

A gasped breath leaves me as Graham presses forward. The pain is the same. That burn accompanied by the stretching of my flesh. His hips pulsing in the tiniest flexes, trying to gain ground, only causing me to hiss through my clenched teeth. "Shit. I—"

My fingers curl around the wrinkled sheets. "Keep going," I pant.

So he presses in further, my body so full I can barely tolerate it. Every breath is a ragged fight for air. Valen is already moving inside me, not bothering to allow Graham a moment to settle himself, too.

"Just breathe, baby. Relax. You've done this before, right?" Pierce's voice is soothing in my ear, his palm rubbing circles into my lower back, only making me want to arch for him, craving his touch to roam over the curve of my ass and squeeze.

I nod, struggling to find calm. The fight against my essence and body proves to be my most brutal battle as I try to hold back my release. The fullness of my men inside me is hurrying me toward the precipice of pleasure. A cliff I shouldn't be so close to so quickly again.

"I can't—" I gasp.

"You can," Pierce encourages me, kissing my forehead. "You're doing so well, and you look so pretty taking all of us."

My nod is barely perceptible, yet the curls that aren't soaked in sweat and already plastered to my skin sway. The weight making my head feel heavier than it should.

Breathe, Bri. Just breathe.

"Valen. Grah—" I don't get his name out before he seats himself in my ass, a glass-shattering scream tearing up my throat. "Fuck!" My shout turns to a groan.

"Look at you taking them both," Pierce praises. "We're going to take care of you because we love you."

The room goes silent, but Pierce doesn't stop stroking my hair, his denim blue eyes locked with mine. He'd spoken the words, and today I'd finally said them back, but the rest of the guys... well, they haven't.

How can he speak for them?

Why does his saying those words open me up?

My body relaxes, allowing my men to move inside me.

The rhythm is an awkward push-pull between the three of us. Graham and Valen work together to find a beat. Regardless of the distance that may weasel its way between us, they'll always feel like heaven. A drug too good to quit. No, they're stuck with me now—*I hope.*

My body is too full, and my essence is begging to burst free. Only tiny tendrils had leaked free before. They tentatively poke and prod, curious how far I'll let them wander before allowing every bit of magic to burst free. The moment my lips part again, it fills the room, blanketing us in a darkness so pure that the black pits my eyes are becoming seem bright.

As if our souls lock into place, we find our rhythm. The three of us move in tandem while Pierce and Knox run their hands over my body.

This is what we all needed. Though they all pledged themselves to me, this moment thrusts us into an unbreakable bond. *We chose* each other, forming a support system. *They chose* to tolerate one another because of me, but tonight, in this bed, the commitment stretches beyond a surface-level moment in the Vault as if we are pledging our lives to one another.

Our bodies move, noises, grunts, and curses filling the void. Their essences leak free of them, too. Our individual streams holding their colors as they wind and slither past each other. They weave as if this existence was meant for them together.

They were.

I am not ordinary, and with them bound to me, neither are they.

Yet another storm builds inside me, my body wrung out from the multiple orgasms but ready to give one more to the two men inside me. Prepared to give them everything, just as they have given me tonight.

"Harder," I moan. "Fuck me harder."

Valen only cackles into the dark, pumping into me, our bodies suddenly flipping as if weightless. The caress of his malicious essence wraps around our limbs to move us. My ass slaps into Graham's pelvis as he lands beneath me.

Our rhythm never loses a beat, my legs held wider to allow Valen better access as my heels dig into the mattress.

The press of an essence against my slit sends me spiraling—Knox's essence. The swirl of magic pressing against my swollen bud, sending me hurdling toward the edge faster and faster. At times, it seems my body knows the touch of his power better than my own.

I chant their names one by one, Valen's release filling me seconds later.

He's quick to pull away, my and Graham's bodies once again shifting so I'm the one on my back, his body pressing into mine as he slides back inside my cum-filled pussy.

"Don't pull out this time," I whisper.

Our cloud of darkness thickens, snuffing out every bit of light. Graham's face is now visibly hidden, yet I can sense the contortion of his features. I can feel his warm breath on my skin and his essence's agreement with my demand. But I sense his apprehension, my palm finding his bare chest, allowing him to find comfort in my touch.

We should all be more careful. Although there are nuances that elevate a wielder's body function above that of the human race, pregnancy isn't one of them. With that category, there's no difference between them and us. Still, I need them. I need their cum to fill my core.

Graham grinds into me harder, spilling inside me several thrusts later, my core too full to hold the remnants of my orgasms and all three of them.

The mixture of us soaks my thighs, dripping down onto the sweat-soaked sheets. We're all a mess.

"Open your mouths," I rasp, sucking down gulps of air greedily.

My ghoul senses push back to the forefront. My vision is gone, but the others are elevated. The nearly silent draw of their mouths opening causes my grin to spread. Our essences float back to each of us, with a tiny sliver of mine hitching a ride alongside theirs. Only a few minutes pass before the room clears. As I have taken a piece of them, their shells now hold me too. How odd it is to think both my father and I live beneath our skin.

"That was amazing," Graham exhales loudly, bending forward to kiss my mouth.

"It was, but I think you all should have a taste. It's only fair you clean up the mess you made." My voice escapes as a sultry purr, though I can barely catch my breath.

I don't recognize this woman. Prior to them, I lacked sexual boldness. I enjoyed it fine, but these four bring out the feral goddess in me. She's eager to please. Eager to take. Ecstatic to receive.

My men stare back at me with lust, further darkening their gazes. Valen's the first to shrug his shoulders, his mouth clamping over my center. His tongue laps at me for a few long strokes before rolling to the side, shoving Knox's shoulder. He, too, dips between my legs, moaning as he sucks at my sensitive flesh, with Graham and Pierce following.

I'm spent, thoroughly fucked, and exhausted. Needing restful sleep, I'll be of no use to anyone for quite some time.

Just when I think they're done, Knox once again pushes inside me, his cock seemingly harder than it had been. He leans his body over me, his lips brushing my ear. "Just in case there's any left. It's best I fuck it back inside you."

Gods above, save me.

61

BRYONY

THE AFTERMATH OF OUR foursome should have taken longer than thirty minutes to restructure. Yet somehow we showered, dressed, and tidied the room in that short time before leaving to go our separate ways.

Our essences wreaked havoc in my room. Broken vases and picture frames litter the floor; the chairs are overturned, and somehow, our essences have shredded the carpet.

Knox had snapped his fingers and miraculously cleaned the sheets while Pierce had tended to the room, and Valen had taken care of our clothing.

"I'm going to go find Camilla," I say as we all filter out into the hallway. "I want to see her before she heads back to Beauxgraton."

One by one, they press indecent kisses to my lips, wandering off down the hallway to their respective rooms. I suspect we all need a little alone time after our fuckfest. A good way to keep them distracted so I can handle my own investigation.

My core is sore, and my thighs shake as I walk, but I try to put it out of my mind. Still, moisture pools between my thighs, soaking the fresh panties I just put on. My skin ignites as if my men are still moving inside me, my core throbbing, replaying Knox's words in my mind.

Fuck. I cover my mouth, unsure if I'd barked that single word aloud. *"Just in case there's any left. It's best I fuck it back inside you."*

Who the fuck says things like that?

My hips shift as I turn the corner toward the staircase, my fingertips trailing over the wallpaper. The custom rugs that have lined these floors for who knows how long scrape along the bottom of my bare feet. My family history lives within these walls. History I want to know and be a part of.

The plan was to speak with my father about staying here after graduation before classes started. Our last bit of time alone focused elsewhere. For once, courage failed me. A side effect of years of my mother and Roman shutting down my questions and desires for myself. I learned to accept the life that my parents handed me.

I chickened out before, but today, bravery forces my chin a little higher. My shoulders roll back a little more, a posture so straight my spine aches.

"You summoned me." My father appears out of nowhere, my heart rate spiking so quickly I nearly tumble over.

With my hand on my chest, I fight to slow my breathing. "I, uh. Well, I was thinking about you," I mumble.

"That's enough, my dear. I will always come when you call." A soft smile pulls at his mouth, his goatee shifting with the movement.

"Since you're here, I want to ask you something."

He nods, gesturing for me to continue. We're silent for a moment, weaving through the hallways of the manor. Our pace is glacial, while I dig deep for that bravery once more.

It was almost too easy to learn the layout of the manor. As if the halls whispered to me, guiding each step, I've always seemed to know exactly where to go. It can't be from memory; I wasn't even walking when my mother and I left. I was too young to remember anything then, and I don't believe I've been back since, unless someone wiped my memories.

The thought makes me chuckle. Stolen memories would explain so many things. Filling the gaps in my memory that I only realized were oddly missing once I learned of my parentage. With a slight shake of my head, I refocus my thoughts. Once again, searching for a morsel of bravery to ask my father what's really on my heart.

"I was wondering if I could stay here once I graduate? The manor already feels like home. And well, I wouldn't have anywhere else to go." The words tumble past my lips in a nervous rush.

I'm almost thrown off balance as my father pulls me into his side. "Bryony, this is your home. You're true home. You never have to ask to stay here."

"I, well... we're new. You've always known me, but I've only just learned who you are. It felt like something I should ask about instead of assuming."

"I understand, but you are my daughter, are you not?"

A snorted laugh leaves me, rolling my eyes. A moment that seems so natural. Like we've always been this way together. "I've always been your daughter, Dad."

A wide, closed-mouth grin stretches across his face. "Then anything that is mine is also yours. The manor is your home, even when you choose to strike out on your own. Everything in it is also yours."

"Did you know this was going to happen?" I ask. "Not necessarily the whole Grisyms rise thing," I roll my eyes, waving my hands through the air as if it's some ridiculous statement. "But my getting to see you again, and us having a relationship?"

"We were always supposed to have one," he deadpans as we begin our descent down the curved staircase. "We had a deal, your mother and I. Once you were old enough to understand, we—" He points a finger between his chest and mine. "—were always supposed to have a relationship. When they called on me just after your fifteenth birthday, explaining what was happening to you and how you often slipped into these fugue states, I remained hopeful that it would be the gateway to them allowing me into your life. So, I infused your essence with the ghoul magic and waited. Still," he sighs wearily, "they kept you away."

"What happened the night you, uh, made me mature?" I question, rolling my hands in front of my stomach. I deserve to know, but it makes me no less nervous to ask.

"They brought you to me in the middle of the night after putting you under a sleeping curse. I did what I needed to help you, and then they ordered me to leave." His dark eyes bore into mine. "I'm sorry, sweetheart. I didn't fight to stay that night. It could have been ammunition for Roman to alter the terms of our agreement. I would not accept that risk. Do you understand?"

A weak smile pulls at the corner of my mouth before I nod. We're silent for a few moments before I break it. "Why would Mom do that?" Tears spring to my eyes, knowing we missed so much time together. "I should have been working with you instead of the strangers Roman brought into our home," I sniffle. It may have helped me hide, though inside I'd still be dying.

A sad smile pulls at the corners of his mouth, something dulling behind his eyes. "It's still a conversation I must have with her. As you know, I am not happy with the betrayal, but I also believe she was doing what she thought was best to keep you safe. She's never outright said so, but I believe she knew more about Roman's intentions than she has ever let on."

"It's not fair." I hate that my voice sounds like I'm whining, but it's the truth.

The way they sheltered me didn't benefit me at all. Did it help any of us in the end? They all would have been safer leaving me with Jorddan, but I guess they couldn't. They had already perpetuated the lie that I was Roman's youngest. How would it look if my mother didn't return home with me?

"Believe me, my dear, I am furious with your mother. If she weren't the owner of my heart, I would eradicate her from this earth faster than you took your next breath for keeping you from me." My father sighs heavily, releasing me. "Ultimately, I believe she did what she thought was right." My father stops suddenly, running a thumb over my cheek. "She did what she thought was best to protect you. For that, I can let go of some of the anger."

"That makes one of us," I huff, continuing down the last section of the steps. "Thank you. For everything. I mean helping me and my friends and…"

"I would give my life for you. There is no ask too large; however, the next time you and your lovers decide to engage in… group activities, soundproof the room."

My hand covers my mouth, my eyes wide. "You heard us?"

"Sweetheart, multiple universes heard you all," he scoffs.

"Heard what?" Camilla chirps, stopping at the bottom of the steps.

"Nothing!" I croak. "Uh, nothing."

My father only gives a slight grin before disappearing down the hall to the left, likely returning to his office.

"Bryony Guthrie, you better share your secrets or I swear on all that is unholy I will pull them free like a flippin' exorcism." Camilla's expression is so serious. I miss this. I miss us. All our friends, our laughter, and our quirks. We had a lot of fun, despite the mishaps we experienced last semester.

"Will you keep quiet?" I shush her, grabbing her by the wrist and stalking through the parlor doors, shutting them behind us.

"Well, I ain't gettin' any younger waitin'," Camilla crosses her arms once we're standing dead center of the room. Far enough away from the entry point, no one passing by should be able to hear us.

"My dad heard me having sex. It's one thing for him to know about it, but another for him to hear it. In his house." Embarrassment flushes my cheeks. My palms slap into my face as I release a guttural groan. "It's not that I'm ashamed of my exploits with the guys," I continue, dropping my arms to my side. "It's more so that Dad and I are new, and in a way, those old habits die hard. I want him to like me. To love me. I want him to keep looking at me like he has been given the greatest gift of his life. I've never had that from a parent."

My confession is like succumbing to oozing knife wounds. Each word is a sharp slice across my skin. Those deep-seated feelings were ones I kept to myself. No one knew.

"Oh, you hussy, we all heard that," Camilla waves me off. My eyes snap to hers as she grins like a Cheshire cat. I just poured my heart out, and she's laughing about my sex life?

There are words on my tongue, but my mouth just opens and closes several times as I search for the right words, eventually giving up and letting them spill free. "Gods, does the whole house know I just had a fucking orgy?" I groan.

"Well, hot diggity dog! It's about time you put all that fine meat to use at once. Want to tell me about it?" A grin spreads on her face, that white-blonde brow arching high.

"Not here, but if you want to know, I'll tell you." I lean closer, eyeing the door before whispering, "Just later."

"I'm holdin' you to that, roomie."

I don't hesitate to pull her into my arms. When we first met, Camilla's constant hugs had been overstimulating. The cheeriness and high-pitched voice grated on my nerves, but now I miss them. My days are boring without her weird phrases and how nosy she is. I miss how much she only wants to be part of her friends' worlds so she can share those moments with us.

"Can't. Breathe," she gasps before I finally let her go. "You never liked my hugs before," she cocks her chin, narrowing her eyes at me.

"I—What—Yes..."

"Don't lie to me, you butt monkey. But that's the past. You like them now." That grin spreads again, gratitude swelling inside my chest. Fortune has finally shone down on me, having a friend like Camilla. I'll never take that for granted again.

I only laugh, shaking my head. "How is everyone back at Beauxgraton?"

"Askin' about y'all, but we don't say anything. Collin and I spend a lot of time together. Damian eats with us sometimes. Valen and Cute Boy's friends are still bum-holes," she whispers the last word as if there's anyone else here to hear it.

"No whispers?" I ask.

She shakes her head, those straight blonde strands swaying as if they are the star of the show. "That imposter even showed up on the first day of classes to welcome everyone back and rave about how great our institution was. *Blah blah blah*," her hand mimicking the sound, "but my daughter will be studying abroad at Integretew for the semester to achieve the most well-rounded education."

"He? What?" I nearly choke on my words.

My heart pounds. Why would he do that when he had already publicly announced that he was pulling me from school altogether?

"Oh, it gets better. Harley has taken over Knox's job." Camilla nods wildly, proud of the gossip she shared with me.

Rumors circulated that Harley planned to secure a position at the school. However, I didn't know he'd been successful. I can only hope it wasn't one more thing everyone was keeping from me.

Hearing that he's allowed inside those walls, near my people, makes my pulse race. My mind whirring with the possibilities of everything that could go wrong.

"You all need to be careful. Make sure the twins and Sean know, too. Don't do anything stupid." I grab her hands, staring into her blue eyes. "If anything happens because of me…"

"You stop that right now. We chose to stand by you. Your daddy said I can have one of his fancy tattoos when I come back next time, an' everything."

"Jesus, Cammie."

"We are with you. We all deserve to live as who we are." Those tiny arms wrap around me again, her fingers digging into my back as she holds me close. I swear I've hugged this girl more in the past two days than I did all last semester.

"Thank you. Now, how much longer do I have with you before you leave?"

Matching grins spread across our faces, only to drop as someone shoves the twin parlor doors open; Damian and Tosch enter moments later, hand in hand. They're so fucking cute it makes me sick sometimes. Or maybe that's just envy sitting at the base of my belly.

"Of course, y'all are done tussling the sheets just when we were about to have fun," Camilla rolls her eyes.

Damian groans, rolling his eyes too, before his large palm claps his face. "Cammie, what have I told you about saying stuff like that?"

My head snaps to the side, eyeing Damian. Not once have I ever heard him call Camilla anything but her name, but he used her nickname. The nickname *I* gave her.

"If you're gonna be my friend, you gotta deal with the spice," she cocks a hip, snapping her arms up like a flamingo dancer, and we all laugh, except Damian.

"Whatever. Time to go."

Tosch kisses Damian indecently, while Camilla showcases her palm, a new portal forming in front of her. This one shimmers in a captivating blue hue. Damian reluctantly lets go of Tosch's hand, walking through first, blowing her a kiss just before he disappears.

"See ya soon, floozy," Camilla waves as she steps forward, the smoke swirling into a smaller and smaller circle until it disappears.

"Floozy?" Tosch questions, standing beside me.

"Apparently, the whole house heard us having an orgy," I groan.

A soft snort leaves her. "Looks like our next lesson is soundproofing a room. Dame and I didn't hear a thing, and neither did you."

Fuck my whole entire life.

62

VALEN

THE PAST FEW MONTHS have flown by like a silent sandstorm. The haze swep*t* in, only to clear the old, leaving a new, layered ground beneath our feet. Life at Integretew requires consistent participation from the student body, unlike Beauxgraton. The founders created their program as it stands to unite all wielders, while fostering appreciation for similarities and differences.

Fuck that.

I don't have time for the Kumbaya bullshit.

Jorddan has remained adamant about keeping us out of the dirty work. His new mandate *is* putting a real damper on my parade. Our fearless leader put us in the corner and expects us to sit down and take it.

We have, but I fucking hate it. If that man weren't Bri's father, I'd raise hell over underutilizing our gifts and talents.

No New Order member still enrolled as a student at a wielding institution may take part in missions involving travel outside of the country and/or state. Nor may they take part in any activities or missions dictated by the New Order that involve harm, potential physical harm, or murder.

It hasn't stopped the "adults" from handling business. More captures and kills are added to the tally weekly. The unveiled secrets are piling up. Determining who deserves our trust becomes harder with each passing day. My own fucking brother included.

No matter how many times Sean has tried to corner him into a sit-down, Dustin has another fucking excuse.

I'm working.

There's a fire to put out.

My mother isn't doing well.

That last one was fucking news to me. Not like they'd tell me anyhow. Dad is still pissed off because I've chosen to stand beside Jorddan despite losing my life for it. Yet, I know Jorddan has been consulting with him. They've been having covert conversations that my father didn't think would get back to me. I'm unsure if it's his version of a truce or if maybe he just better understands our purpose. It doesn't matter. Help like his could be invaluable.

With every wielder no longer breathing, it should be easier to release the breaths we continue to hold, but it's not. More than ever, we're looking over our shoulders.

Jorddan, Vincent, and Knox tried to hide the incoming threats from us. And they did until Knox called me back to the manor alone about a month ago.

"You better tell me the fucking truth," he'd spat in my face. *"Did you send these threats? Did you fucking write these?"* The veins at his temple were throbbing, protruding so much I swore one would pop.

He'd shown them all to me. There were dozens of letters in handwriting so similar to mine that, without careful scrutiny, it would be easy to say they were the same. Each detailed more gruesome threats than the last. Things that even made my stomach churn in response.

"Why do you assume it's me?" I'd shoved them back at him, my anger boiling to the point of no control at the things they said they would do to Bri and her family.

"Because you sent that letter to Bri's brother last semester," he roared. I almost denied it. I don't know how he knew. *"On my life, I swear, it wasn't me,"* I'd promised. It was all I could offer. Thankfully, it was enough for Knox to get off my ass about it.

Finding my focus after that was nearly impossible. Classes became nothing more than a nuisance. Studying was an afterthought. Every piece of my brain's functioning revolved around discovering who the fuck was sending detailed letters about dismembering bodies using their essence or curses that could inflict what felt like endless pain.

Another month has passed, and we're no closer to finding the sender of those letters. Unfortunately, I've once again had to split my attention. I have my own shit I've been working on. We'll call it preparation for the Red Moon Festival.

Bri's link to the ghouls has us all on edge. The last Red Moon, we hadn't known. She didn't have her horde of four, and the others hadn't felt her. She has called on her quartet of ghouls several times, siphoning their power, drinking them down to the point she's out of it for days.

We've all fucked our respective ghouls while they fucked her, Graham only standing there staring at the debauchery. It's only been a benefit for Pierce and me. Jorddan *is* allowing us to take additional artifacts to store our essences in, should we run into trouble. We keep our collection sealed in Bri's closet. With her roommate barely stepping foot in their room more than twice a week, rifling around to grab new clothing or replacement toiletries, it's the safest place we could think of.

The most terrifying pit in our stomachs is the wait. We all believe the Council is coming. How or when remains a mystery. They know what Bri is. They have for years. What the hell are they waiting for?

It took weeks to sift through Mikhail's files. Fortunately, those we keep closest to us weren't even on her suspect list. No Knox, Vincent, Janelle, or Jorddan.

One name continues to stand out. The same fucking name that keeps taunting us. His fucking shadow seems to lurk around every corner, but is gone the moment we turn it. Carter James is like an apparition that likes to fuck with you, but then disappears when the weird shit happens.

Bri finally admitted her essence loses its shit when he's around or looks her way. It's why she curls into herself or suddenly bolts from the room. We got pissed because she waited over a month to tell us. A fucking month! Apparently,

Tosch knew; her only explanation is what Bri has experienced when she went to Yorgan and Mikhail's—either her essence remembers him or another does.

He's unusual. Something we can't quite figure out niggling at the base of our skulls. He's just wrong.

A crackling noise fills the room. "Students, please report to the gardens for an announcement." Our secretary never attended a human school—an experience she loves to remind us she wishes she'd had. So recreating those years, she always prefers to amplify her announcements to sound like they're coming from a microphone. It's weird as hell and disruptive, especially first thing in the morning.

Groaning, I shrug on my leather jacket, finger-combing my hair into a fresh bun, before making my way outside.

It's only been a few days since the freezing cold temperatures shifted to almost pleasant spring weather. A small mercy. There are fewer questions about us venturing out when a blizzard isn't raging outside with temperatures low enough to leave us with frostbite.

When that last class lets out on a Friday, the four of us usually already have our bags packed, ready to disappear for the weekend. We *typically* spend them at the manor. Occasionally, Jorddan sends us to check on the other Grisyms at the closed light schools around the world. My crew earned Jorddan's trust early on. We showed him we wouldn't question orders or balk at the hard tasks. It's why he sends us to liaise with the leaders of the Grisym harbor sites.

Bri is always at the manor. Either getting to know her father and brother, or being tortured by Tosch. It's better that way. Safer.

It's that same reminder that repeats in my head. All it would take is one sighting. Just one glimpse for someone to report back to Roman where she's traveled to, whether with ill intent or accidentally. Then I would have to gut them, leaving yet another dead body for the New Order to dispose of.

Fortunately, there's only so much Roman can do while she attends Integretew. He won't make a scene if it preserves his image to the world.

At first, we didn't try to keep our weekend disappearing act inconspicuous. We ignored the wandering eyes of our classmates and their questions. Avoiding them proved simple for a while. Then, people started digging.

Professors started to question our dedication to our studies. Bri's excuse that she has a luxurious family home close by covered her, but made no sense for us.

We made a point of avoiding being seen together as much as possible, our staggered meeting times for Fridays helping us dodge our classmates as we snuck to designated meeting spots away from the main building.

None of us sought to form outside relationships here, but we're glad Bri did. She and that bookshop owner might as well be tied at the fucking hip. The pair often meets to examine ancient texts, gossip, and enjoy tea at various cafes. When tucked away with their books their fingers scroll line by line as they absorb every word. She's even been helpful to Graham in finding more creative ways to harness power. As a charter herself, she had to get creative.

Bri and Pierce come into view across the path with their fingers linked. My molars grind. I wasn't above outing us, but Pierce *is* once again the only one who *receives* her affection like that in front of everyone. Occasionally, she'll slip one of us a kiss or allow me to fuck her until she can barely walk in a random room, but that's it. That's all we get. Strangely, it gave Graham and me an additional bonding point.

The rumors about her dating all three of us surfaced rather quickly. My big mouth chose not to hide us anymore. We confirmed each one. Still, her behavior hasn't changed. *Perhaps* it's because we haven't pushed for it. We've accepted Bri giving herself to us the way she chose, but it's not enough anymore.

Not when the proverbial hammer is hanging over our heads. Our situation constantly rides a fine line that could shift at any moment. A truth that has changed me more than I care to admit. I've never wanted to claim a woman publicly before. I didn't have time. Fucking them was one thing. Even casual relationships were no bother, but there is nothing casual about our relationship with Bryony Guthrie.

Graham is rambling on about something beside me. Our paths crossed as I made my way here. My focus remains divided between his words, her face, and fucking Carter and Percy approaching Pierce and Bri from behind. It's the first time we've seen the two of them together outside of class.

The similarities between the two roll through my head. A list tallied and stored for me to analyze later. Or not. I could just gut them both and be done with it. Percy has proved increasingly worthless, anyhow. Problem solved.

Percy had been smart enough to steer clear of Bri after our little chat. An encounter I wish I had fucking chopped the bastard into bite-sized pieces as he pathetically sniveled and pleaded for me to stop.

Roman isn't the only one who has people watching. So does Jorddan. So do I.

Jorddan explicitly stated Bri is never to be alone. Unfortunately, I only trust myself with her, but I can't always be there. I needed to ensure her protection, especially at school. So what if I had Pierce coerce them into doing my bidding?

Percy has continued reporting back to Roman. The details are insignificant, except for the ones about our group often being gone on the weekends. Fortunately, the bastard has no idea where we go, though I suspect he knows it has something to do with Jorddan and our pledge to him.

A smirk pulls at the corner of my mouth, stopping in front of them. "Are you lost?" The hint of sarcasm in my voice draws Carter's blond brows low, causing my lip to curl as I fight against a grin.

"We're just being friendly. You should try it sometime," he quips.

"I have enough friends." Bri gives a tight smile. "If you'll excuse us, we were in the middle of a conversation that had nothing to do with you."

I want to howl at my girl's sass. Then, fuck her senseless for making me so damn proud.

Carter *tsks*, running his fingers through his golden locks. "I don't think Daddy would like you being so rude. Now would he?"

"Feel free to ask him," she grins widely, turning toward the two men, with the three of us at her back. A reenactment of how we all once stood behind her last semester. *No*, we stood at her side. That's what Bri has always demanded of us.

The chatter of our classmates fills the garden as the student body spills out into the courtyard. Why the headmaster insists on doing our group assemblies out here, even when it was snowing and bitterly cold, is beyond me. I suspect it's due to the sheer volume of us here.

Having us packed in here so tightly puts me on edge. My hackles shoot sky-high, waiting for the worst. Shifting us to the edge of the garden, we arrange ourselves in front of a massive tree. The best we'll be able to do to keep away a sneak attack.

My jaw works, wishing this bullshit would get underway. I have somewhere to be today, and this impromptu assembly is wasting my fucking time.

"Thank you all for joining us," Headmaster Hawthorne booms over the student body. "We have fabulous news to share. As part of the initiative to continue integrating our light students into our dark institutions, this upcoming Red Moon Ball will open its doors to any wielding student and staff worldwide who would like to attend."

The dull roar of conversation, which had been alive as the headmaster started his announcements, snaps into silence. Everyone's gaze fixes on the petite man levitating in front of us, his salt and pepper beard and bald head revealing his age.

The first time I saw him, I almost mistook him for a child based solely on his size. Had I not gotten a good look at his weathered skin and the harsh wrinkles across his forehead and at the corners of his eyes, I wouldn't have known. His small hands and short limbs only make him appear disproportionate. Nevertheless, he is an ally. One I took advantage of thanks to my father's name.

We had never met before, but he and my father used to conduct research together. Their published work on ghoul breeding brought new and insightful information to the variations in hues and temperaments we were seeing. Similar to light and dark wielders, the ghouls were mixing. They, too, were born anew.

"We will welcome our guests with grace and openness," Headmaster Hawthorne continues. "We have been able to revitalize Smithshire to use as quarters for our guests."

"But isn't it closed?" a voice calls out in the crowd.

I fight to hold back my grin, knowing Hawthorne would have had to go through Jorddan to use the former light school. It was one of the few we'd yet to inhabit with refugee Grisyms. It's another old institution that needed upgrades, and rather than worry about those then, we just left it abandoned.

"Yes, it is." Sadness coats Hawthorne's words. A genuine emotion. He's always been sympathetic to the fight for equality among all wielders. "Though it is a shame to lose such a fine institution, we have done some remodeling specifically for this occasion."

"When will they arrive?" another voice calls out.

"Our guests will begin arriving next Friday. They will be free to engage in the Red Moon Festival, which is open to all light and dark wielders to attend, and then for the ball Saturday night."

A roar of cheers booms around us at the announcement. The clapping and whistles are making me bristle. Hundreds of voices chattering all at once around us, drawing out my scowl. I hate this shit.

"You are all dismissed," Hawthorne announces, his slight frame floating over the student body, carrying him upward to land on a small balcony.

"Graham, let's go," I grunt.

"Where are you going?" Bri grabs my hand, forcing me to stop my retreat.

Squeezing her hand slightly, I toss her a wink. "I have something to take care of. Graham is coming with me."

"And Pierce and I weren't included, why?" Her mouth presses into an angry pout. One that only makes me chuckle as I pull her curvy body into mine. Her gasp widens my grin as I envision all the things I would like to do to her. But not now.

Later.

Licking across her lips, the taste of her Chapstick almost makes me groan. Fucking sour apple. Just like my Forbidden Fruit. I kiss her indecently, not caring who's watching or what they might think of us. Bryony is mine, and anyone else can fuck off if they have a problem with it.

"You'll see later tonight," I whisper against her mouth. "Leave that pretty cunt for when I get back, okay?" Her eyes go wide, but lust is building behind them.

"I swear if you go do something stupid, you're never touching me with another dagger," she shoves away from me, that glint still shining in her green and gray eyes.

A snort leaves me. "At least I can still touch you."

Then I pull Graham behind me and disappear into the crowd. "Uh, you never actually told me where we're going," he mutters, stumbling to keep up with me.

"Time for some new ink," I say as we exit the front of the main building, the bustle of traffic zooming by past us.

Graham doesn't say another word until we enter the tattoo parlor, my hand clasping with an artist I've been following for some time. A wielder like us.

All of my tattoos, except for Jorddan's, are basic, nothing more than human ink on skin. There's no magic infused into them, but today's will be different.

I took Jorddan under my skin by choice, intending to serve a purpose. Today I'll take Bri in too because that's where she's always lived.

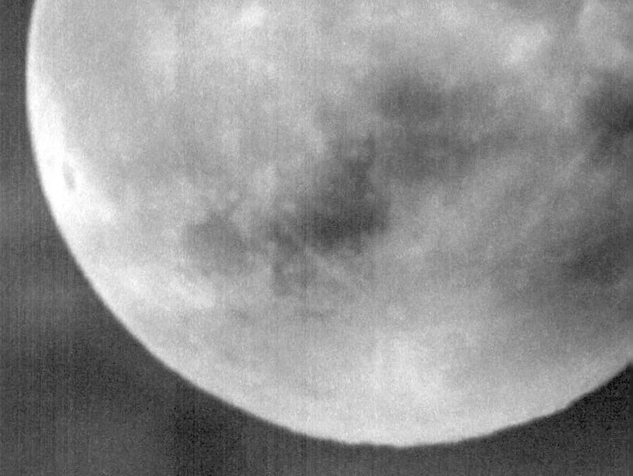

63

BRYONY

Not even the gods themselves could have kept me from racing out of the courtyard and straight to my room. We haven't seen our friends in months, so hearing that announcement sparked new life in me. Hope that I'll get to see them and hold them. This chaotic life has taught me the value of precious relationships, and I can only hope the upcoming Red Moon Ball will be an opportunity for us to breathe and laugh together.

Valen and Graham can go off and do whatever weird shit they're into together these days. The lot of us have grown so used to it we've stopped questioning. There are more pressing matters than those two finally getting along.

But I needed to call my best friend. Glancing at my screen, absent of messages from anyone, I'm guessing they don't know yet.

Then it hits me. Roman's approval would have proved vital in this decision. At least I would assume so. To my knowledge, nobody has ever executed or even proposed anything like this. Light wielders were never invited to dark celebrations until the institutions merged this year.

My breath turns heavy as I turn the corner into my hallway, my door within view. Roman could set us all up for a devastating fall. The bastard is vile enough to do so, even if he wasn't the one who proposed the event.

It doesn't matter, Bri. We can be ready for him no matter what.

Clutching my phone to my chest, pressing my opposite palm to my door, I slip into my room. That man can plot and plan all he wants. I'm not missing my chance to have my friends here for the Red Moon Festival. They'd be safer here with us than there, anyway.

At least, I'll tell myself that until the world comes crashing down on us and I'm responsible for it.

Stop it, Bri.

Launching myself onto the bed, I prop my pillows under my head. Now is not the time for worst-case-scenario-pit-of-despair thoughts.

The phone rings as I wait for Camilla to answer, not caring about the time difference. The little princess will be fast asleep, but this is huge. It can't wait.

"Hello," she groans.

My body bolts upright, my grin wide. "Have you heard?"

"Bryony, you'd better be havin' a mid-life crisis or be drownin' in a sinkhole to be callin' me at this hour."

I only roll my eyes. It's just after five in the morning her time. Plenty of time for a few more hours of sleep.

"Integretew has opened its doors to any student in the world for the upcoming Red Moon Festival," I shout with excitement.

"Lower your voice, you cockatoo," she groans. "I'm a light wielder."

I groan too. It's no use trying to talk to her until she's good and awake. Only then will I get the level of excitement I'd hoped for. "I'll call you later," I sigh, resigned that I'll have to sit with this good news alone for a few more hours.

"Love you, floozy."

"Love you too, Cammie," I chuckle before the line goes dead.

A knock sounds at my door, pulling my attention away from my phone. With a wave of my hand, the door swings open. Pierce nearly tumbles over the threshold as if he'd been leaning on the door waiting, mumbling a curse as he regains his balance.

"Sorry. I didn't mean to leave you behind. Just really wanted to call Cammie." I lift my phone as if to prove I called her, before letting my hand fall back to my lap.

"Bri, I think you should calm down about this." Pierce sits beside me, the bed groaning beneath our weight.

"Why?"

"You're still being watched. We all are. What if this is just to get to you?"

"Pierce—" But the words fail me. I was thrilled to see our friends again—my first genuine friends.

I had forgotten those same thoughts had just played through my mind. It's a consideration I won't ignore, nor will I miss out on the opportunity to see everyone if the threat isn't immediate. I didn't need him to remind me; I can harbor those fears all on my own. But for just a minute, I'd rather not focus on them. I'd rather live in the bliss of this moment, eager to believe perhaps something bright is coming our way. I hadn't forgotten that those fears had just streamed through my head, but I also didn't want to focus on them.

There's no forgetting that the Council has detailed intel on me. The Bureau likely does, too. Nightmares of them experimenting on me and draining my power haunt me too many nights to forget. In my dreams, every wielder who has witnessed what I can do constructs stages to showcase me to their peers. Their puppet strings are attached to my elbows and knees, forcing me to perform magic and spells I shouldn't. Reminders aside, it's impossible to forget I went from being one man's pawn to a target for our entire race.

I can only thank the gods that Harley hasn't given any of my friends or Janelle a hard time. I imagine Roman sent him there just to spy, not to intervene. His task is likely to gather information that puts them ahead of us, but there's nothing for them to find. Except for the one time Camilla came out here to hold the portal, we've kept them out. We've kept them as safe as we can, given they're associated with me.

"I know the past few months have seemed quiet, but that's what worries me most. I care about you too much to let us get comfortable." Pierce's tone pulls my gaze back to his. The strain of his syllables woven with the weariness of the drawn-out letters knots my insides.

My hand finds his cheek. The short beard he's allowed himself to grow in is rough beneath my fingers, making me giggle as the short strands tickle my skin. "You can't spend so much time worrying about me that you don't enjoy yourself."

I've told them this countless times, especially Pierce. Valen somehow manages to amp up his asshole behavior and find a balance, while Graham focuses on his studies. However, sometimes it seems like Pierce only has me. I know he pledged himself to Jorddan a long time ago, but that doesn't mean he has to stop living because I'm supposed to play it safe and don't always choose to.

I took not a single risk for twenty-five years. It's an existence that drags you down and suffocates you. Always waiting for the other shoe to drop doesn't mean it eventually will.

In truth, I'm terrified every second of every day. I have nightmares that wake me in a cold sweat at night, my men wrapping me in their arms to calm me. I am constantly scrutinizing every person I come across, while my head remains permanently turned over my shoulder. But I wouldn't trade this life to go back to my old one.

At least this is living. It doesn't matter if it's not quite the life from my fantasies. It's life on my terms.

Eilish gave me a piece of essence so I can at least sense the nuances of a wielder; however, her power doesn't extend to intent.

It's impossible to tell who's on our side and who isn't, but if I sit here and wait for everyone to reveal themselves as friend or foe, I'll only drown myself and everyone around me.

One day, my luck will run out. At some point, I'll no longer have the advantage of hiding as a light wielder and Roman's daughter. Someone will find out the truth and share it, or someone who already knows will betray us.

There's freedom in knowing that one day my enemies will come for me. I could hide or pretend all I want, but they will come. Nothing I do can stop that. Acceptance broke the chains I'd allowed everyone else to put on me. Fear keeps me vigilant.

That's how you live through an existence like mine. But Pierce and I aren't the same. I only wish Pierce could find the same peace I have. Though I do love how he's become as fierce a protector as Valen.

Luck doesn't begin to describe my fortune in Pierce finding and picking me. He's been so many firsts for me, but I never told him. Above all, he's the first boyfriend who loved me for who I am and has only ever asked for more.

Those rich, denim blue eyes meet mine, his palm cupping my jaw. "You. Are. My entire world. I've told you that. I don't care if it's pathetic."

"It's not pathetic," I roll my eyes. "We're just so young to stop living when so much of this is out of our control."

Pierce's lips press to mine, soft and searching. His deliberate movements convey so much more than spoken words could. "I want to see our friends too, but not at your expense."

And I know what he's saying; he has stood beside me and become what he never wanted to be. Though he is very wrong about that.

Pierce tapped into the dark power within him that he loathes so much. He did it for us. For me. Every time he dips into the side of him he hates most, he also loses a piece of himself. A piece of the man he wishes he were born as. If only he could see that he is precisely the man he wants to be. The power he wields doesn't change that. "If anything happens, it's not on you to save us. I won't ask you to do that." His hand drops from my face, but I won't let him look away, gripping his cheeks between my palms.

He turns his face, kissing my palm. "You have a potions exam to study for, and you need some work." He bares his teeth, hardly containing his laughter. That sparkle returns to his dark blue eyes, the hue no longer resembling the tumultuous deep sea.

My jaw flexes as a small laugh drifts out of me. He isn't wrong, yet the scholar within despises being reminded that my performance is anything less than the best. I've excelled almost everywhere, especially in essence manipulation, which is a class I do my best to participate in as little as possible.

The mishaps keep happening. Just last week, I accidentally snatched another essence, and when a classmate called it out, I had to bring my own to my palm, willing it to be pitch black so I could pretend I'd trapped it there the whole time.

Thankfully, Professor Perrue quickly snatched it away, just as Knox did for me many times. She used it as a lesson in the illusion of manipulation.

Mastering the subtle practice takes decades, though nobody reacted when a first-year student succeeded. Or rather, *this* first year. I'd heard the whispers at Beauxgraton. Their assumptions about my abilities caused me to duck my head instead of lean into my skill. I wasn't supposed to be as gifted as I already was, not as a newly matured wielder. Still, my classmates expected the world out of the director of education's youngest daughter. Where I was often met with declarations and stares of contention at Beauxgraton, here that prowess is applauded—due to my abilities, not my identity. It's an equally calming and uncomfortable feeling I am slowly coming to terms with.

Pierce leads us to the law library, one we christened the same as Beauxgraton. The cozy niche libraries seem to be abandoned most days. Occasionally, you'll see a student in their last year wandering through the door or faculty; otherwise, they remain empty. The guys and I have taken advantage of that. They've become our meeting spots at times, or where we study and can freely assist one another.

With a roll of my palm, two light orbs appear, shooting to the ceiling, providing us additional light. Though this is my preferred library, it's darker than the rest: all stained wood shelves and umber couches. The gilded sconces lining the walls provide only dim light, casting eerie shadows that I welcome as if they were my own.

Slumping onto the same couch Pierce and I had sex on just a few weeks ago, I sigh heavily, waiting for him to voice the topic of my demise.

Thus far, my assignments have involved crafting the simplest concoctions. Potions that infants should be able to perfect. Yet I have only succeeded in nearly blowing up the entire main building, burning off my classmates' eyebrows, turning my skin red for forty-eight hours, and enlarging the frogs kept in the classroom to the size of humans.

No single outcome has ever been the intended result of the mixtures.

Needless to say, I have finally found something I absolutely do not excel at. If I don't pass this class, there's no way I'll be able to move on to elixirs, serums, or creating my own recipes—all things I'm expected to be well-versed in by graduation.

Good luck!

"Okay, which one are you struggling with the most?" Pierce turns to face me, the table lined with beakers and miniature cauldrons, mortars and pestles, ingredients, and a fucking helmet.

"A helmet?" I squawk.

"Oh, yeah. That's for me," he winces. I only groan, leaning further into the couch. "Let's start with a love potion," he grins.

"Seriously?" His grin only grows wider. "I already love you, so how is that helpful?"

He only shrugs. "Maybe I just wanted to hear you say those words."

64

BRYONY

WELL, POTION PRACTICE COULD have gone worse.

Neither of us was harmed. Furthermore, the school still stands. However, the couch is now missing a few pillows. I'd made a decent casting potion that allowed me to project my body *two whole feet* away from where I actually was, but it likely wouldn't earn me a passing score.

There is no one with more patience than Pierce. He'd talked me through every step, allowed me to make mistakes, and then explained where I detoured. For hours, we worked on every potion covered this semester, over and over. Not once did he let me quit.

Just like Beauxgraton, we're constantly asked to do practical demonstrations of our skills. That fear that things will go awry clings to my insides. There were so many mishaps when I started attending school, ones I couldn't control or understand. Somehow, I anticipated a less bumpy journey when I engaged with more advanced wielders before Beauxgraton. I didn't think I'd struggle or have a single faux pas.

I clearly misjudged how complicated existence could become for a Grisym in hiding.

Now it's different. I've embraced what lives under the surface. I've allowed it to take form and work its way free. In that way, I've made my abilities even harder to control. My essence wants to permanently dismantle the cage I was trapped in my whole life. It aims to explore and showcase its own unique perspective—a bit of flash I can't afford.

I hate that I have to continue to be a light wielder. If only there were a scenario where no one knew me. I wish Roman had never publicly claimed me as his own. I wish I'd had a choice to live as a dark wielder the way Knox did. Then I could at least explore my Grisym tendencies with less trepidation.

"Whatcha thinkin' 'bout?" Camilla questions, nuzzling down into her pillows.

Now that she has revealed her secret about portals, we take advantage of it. A few times a week, she builds one between us. It beats having to talk over video. It also means she's thrown a few pillows my way; the girl has an arm.

Fortunately, my roommate cares more about spending every waking moment with her boyfriend than ever coming back to our room. At this point, I'm one more night away from living completely alone. Most of her dresser doesn't even hold her clothes anymore, and her toiletries haven't been in the bathroom since the second week of classes.

It's a small blessing. It gives the guys and me a place to meet privately. But just as importantly, I get this time alone with my best friend. And because students are not permitted to use portals inside institutions outside of class, an empty room helps.

"Nothing," I mumble, running my fingers through my hair. My mind has been running a mile a minute these past few hours. I needed it to slow down. Oddly enough, detangling my wet, curly hair with my fingers has always been the method.

It takes patience and care. Each small chunk is handled with slow strokes, allowing every knot to work its way free. Each curl feels a mile long as I work my fingers through. Its length now extends six inches past my mid-back, while the curls corkscrew more than ever.

My shoulders burn as I get to the last section, my bangs. Bangs I cut a few weeks into the semester in an effort to pretend I could be someone different.

Just one more way to widen the gap between the Bryony I was raised as and who I am now.

Shaking out my arms, Camilla eyes me with skepticism. "I'm gonna braid it," I roll my eyes. From her expression, I was seconds away from getting a lecture. She'd witnessed too many mornings of near breakdowns as I navigated attempting to tame a newly tangled and frizzy mess because I chose to sleep with wet hair.

"You're a dirty, dirty liar, Bryony... Guthrie." The pause before she says my real last name is typical. It's her way of ensuring the coast is clear before voicing it aloud.

It takes a moment to realize she wasn't talking about something as superficial as my hair, but the brush-off response I'd just given her a few minutes ago. When we met, I might have been able to hide my crippling worries, but I can no longer do so.

"I have another potions practical tomorrow," I mutter, my chin dropping to my chest.

Her exasperated sigh pulls my gaze back up to meet hers. "Look here, Missy, you are a bad b-i-t-c-h." A barking laugh leaves me listening to Camilla spell out bitch. The woman still won't say a single crude word, but now and again, she'll be brave enough to spell it. These are some of my favorite moments with her. Those instances when she wears her quirks proudly, no matter how others respond, make me proud. "You hush now. Listen to me. If it all goes down the crapper, so what? We're supposed to make mistakes, ya know, bust our faces a little." I can only laugh again.

"Camilla Van Buren, you are the love of my life," I snort, covering my mouth as tears leak from the corners of my eyes.

Her pert nose wrinkles, those blue eyes narrowing. "I already told ya, you're not my type. Stop tryin' to get frisky with me."

The laughter barrels out of me once more. I miss my friend so much. I need these moments more than I care to admit. This tiny slice of normalcy serves as a reminder that I'm more than my troubles. "Sorry," I wheeze, my stomach aching painfully from my non-stop laughter.

"Speaking of such private matters, where's all your man meat? No one taking a ride on the Bri train tonight?" She bellows out a *whoo-whoo* sound before *chugga, chugga* fills the room.

"You might think you're not vulgar, my friend, but your mouth is just as filthy as the rest of us."

"That didn't answer my question. I know you've been doin' the git down on every flat surface."

"Gods, it's not like that. Okay, it is. My poor vagina needs a minute sometimes, but between the four of them and the ghouls..."

"The ghouls?" Camilla sits up in bed, staring at me with wide, curious eyes.

Only Knox and the guys know about my personal entourage of ghouls. Though I say I am the one summoning them, it almost feels like they call out to me. We meet on the manor grounds, usually after dark, regularly. I fuck them and the guys in tandem, siphoning more power than should be possible.

Perception is a funny thing. Assumptions can be deadly. Yet I have both when it comes to my "relationship" with my ghouls. The more times I take them, the more power it seems I can siphon. My body has rebelled less with consistency and time, though I am often exhausted for days after. The need to funnel power to Knox or my vessels is more of a random occurrence than the norm. A change I'd mentioned to Tosch and Eilish. They both agreed it's in my head.

There is finite space, especially as an innate wielder. It's our only "weakness," per se. Generally, our shells hold less essence, though we can self-replenish, unlike extrinsics and sometimes charters. It means we can get tired while burning through our stores faster.

But I am different. I feel different. I won't say it to their faces, but I think they are both wrong. There's just no way for me to prove it when I still have to use Knox and my collection of urns as vessels at times.

"I, uh..."

"Don't you dare lie to me," Camilla warns, her little leg lifted as if ready to march right through the portal, which is only big enough for our upper bodies—well, hers, not mine. A single boob might fit through, but that might be it.

"The guys have been taking me out to see my ghouls. You know the four I named? I don't know how to describe it. It's almost as if I can feel them reaching out for me or something, so I teleport us to the manor, screw them all, and then just come back."

"Only I would have a best friend who not only horizontal tangos with four men but four ghouls, too. Hot damn, girl," Camilla fans herself before realizing what she said, her hand clapping over her mouth while I roll with laughter.

The ache that had been thrumming in my stomach muscles shifts. My insides are rolling in anticipation. *Valen.* I can feel him as if he's right here with me. The sliver of essence that has fused with mine, swirling through my body.

With a swipe of my fingers, my door flies open, and there he is in those slim-fit faded black jeans and a t-shirt. His signature leather jacket fits him perfectly, molding to his lean frame. His entire wardrobe marks him as dark and dangerous.

The dark hue of his hair shines under the hallway torch lights. His bun is artfully messy as usual. I have never been attracted to men with long hair, but Valen's wild curls make my core tighten. The moisture building between my legs enough to leave my panties soaked. Panties, I skipped slipping on after my shower.

"Speaking of..." I glare at Valen, warning him to stay silent. "Cammie, Valen is here. I'll talk to you later."

"No ma'am. Not until my least favorite boyfriend of yours says hello."

I can only laugh again. Camilla makes no secret that she still has issues with Valen. Mainly for the way he first treated me and his lack of romantic gestures to "keep me."

"Hi, Camilla," he deadpans, settling next to me on the bed, running the tip of his nose along my cheek.

He doesn't hesitate to take the skin at the side of my neck between his lips, my hiss drawing Camilla's eyes wide.

"Cammie, I—"

"Camilla, you'd better go unless you're into watching me fuck my girlfriend. I don't give a fuck. You wouldn't be the first," Valen smirks.

"Floozy," Camilla chirps, and then the portal closes, Valen's mouth instantly closing over mine.

"Hello to you, too," I chuckle, pulling away. "Where have you and Graham been this whole time? Actually, where is he?" My eyes dart around the room as if he'll magically appear. "Have you been pretending to like him so you could murder him and make it look like an accident?" I voice the words with a laugh, but secretly, my chest seizes. When I met Valen, it wouldn't have seemed far-fetched at all. Even now, that same skepticism makes me question from time to time.

"He has an exam to study for, and I have something for you."

"Your dick doesn't count," I snicker as he climbs over me.

"You can have that too, but that's not what I have for you."

Crawling backward, he allows me to sit up, yanking off his jacket and then his shirt.

I can only stare at the many tattoos covering his arms and torso. Some of which I've traced and know the stories of now, but there are more that I don't. Somehow, the ones on his chest look different. Scooting forward, I focus on the spot right about where his heart would be.

There's a new tattoo there. A dagger that's a replica of his favorite—a gift from his father. The blade appears as if it's piercing his skin, bright red blood oozing out around the wound. I turn my head to the side, my eyes scanning over the writing.

"Forbidden Fruit," I whisper as I trace the words on the blade.

My eyes find his, those dark pools exposed for once. Nothing is guarding them, keeping me from knowing how much he's feeling in this moment.

Sucking in a short breath, my lungs burn as if I can't breathe properly. "Valen, why did you get this?"

"Bri, there are plenty of days I still think about killing you. About how easy life would be without you in it, but like our friends, I can't live without you either. I'm not going to do some romantic shit for you, but I did this so that I could feel you all the time. This tattoo and Jorddan's are the only ones infused with an essence. It's the only way I knew how to show you."

"Show me what?" I ask, butterflies floating through my stomach, waiting for his response.

"You're mine."

My body jerks forward, crushing my lips to his. Pierce told me Valen was a better man than he appeared. He has proven that to me so many times.

The kiss deepens as our mouths slant, his groan vibrating up his throat and into my chest before he pulls away.

"Calm down, my Little Forbidden Fruit. I still have something to give you."

Dropping my hands, I lean back. "The tattoo wasn't it?"

"No, baby," he coos against my cheek. "That was for me, but this is for you."

The tattoo was modeled after the very dagger he pulls out. The same one his father had given him to ensure he'd always be protected. He flips the knife in the air, his fingertips catching the blade as he points the handle in my direction.

"Valen."

"It's yours. Take it." I hesitate until he speaks again. "Please." That single word crashes through every bit of apprehension.

"Why are you—"

"It's spelled to answer to you now. It's currently full of my signature, but as you use it, you'll be able to add your own. Always keep a little of me in there; your essence should be able to amplify it that way," he says so monotone, I'm not sure how to take it.

Emotion swells in my chest as I let the dagger rest in my palms. The metal is warm against my skin as if it had been resting against his for some time. "Valen, why are you giving this to me?"

He leans in close, his lips brushing mine, his hands cupping the back of my head. "Because no one hurts you but me."

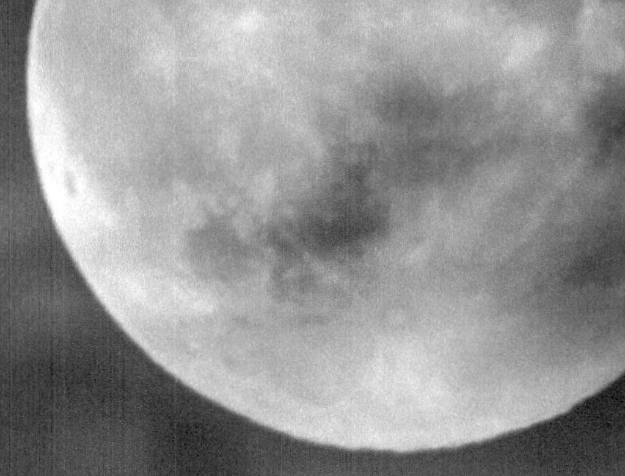

65

BRYONY

JUST WHEN I THOUGHT the semester was going smoothly, my phone pinged with an email from the Headmaster's office.

Not once, growing up in human schools, was I ever called to the principal's or dean's office. It felt like a significant accomplishment, especially since so many of my classmates had spent ample time there. Then I had Janelle at Beauxgraton, who called on me and allowed her private space to become a sanctuary.

Here, that email feels like I'm walking into the dungeons of hell.

"Baby, it's fine," Valen nuzzled my neck, holding me against his chest. *"You can trust him. I know him."*

"Maybe you can trust him," I'd scoffed, climbing out of bed. *"But can I? Can my father?"*

I'd showered, dressed, and promptly left the room. That was twenty minutes ago, and now it feels like I can't breathe.

Like I'm seconds away from my world shattering.

Valen's words play over and over in my head. The conviction behind them and the way he'd held me tighter, making me feel safe.

My trust is my most precious asset. Value, I can't afford to lose. It's better to only leave it in the hands I've already placed it in.

The wooden frame of the chair digs into my back as my body shifts against the narrow seat. A seat made for someone with smaller hips and ass than I've ever had. Discomfort I've learned to live with.

The soft tap of my heel against the floor only makes my heart race faster. My swallow is painful as I force each one.

Countless students and staff wander past me, not a single one acknowledging me as I wait outside the headmaster's office. Whether it be out of disinterest or fear of why I may have been called here, it doesn't matter.

The door finally creaks open, Headmaster Hawthorne appearing just beside me. His petite frame still gives me pause, though his presence dominates any room he enters. You take notice of his aura, your shoulders rolling back, eager to respect the honor of being near the man.

"Bryony, please come in." His voice almost has a lyrical quality to it. One that a father may use when soothing his child, but there's an edge there, too. One that reminds you he is the one in charge, and it's best not to make him shift from his kind demeanor.

I can sense it in him. Many host a temper or short fuses, but the Headmaster has a fire-breathing dragon within—not literally. With one breath, he could set the entire world ablaze.

A weak smile pulls at the corner of my mouth. The type that would reveal the knots forming in my stomach. Nervousness washes over me in a crashing wave as too many possibilities circle in my mind for me to know which part worries me most.

"Thank you, Headmaster," I mumble, settling into the chair on the other side of his desk.

The same wood frames the upholstered back and seat. My fingers grab hold of the arms, squeezing them tightly. The effort to keep my essence from bursting free in defense forcing my molars to grind. "Why am I here?"

"The Red Moon Festival is coming up this weekend."

"Yes. Are students still permitted to attend? Only to observe, of course...for me," I quickly add.

His close-lipped smile makes his salt-and-pepper beard twitch. "Unfortunately, Ms. Avalon, I have orders to keep you from the ghoul pits."

My heart sinks. I believed I could finally embrace this tradition, free from judgment regarding my attendance. Once again, someone has taken it from me. "May I ask who gave you the order?" My voice is small, though disappointment and fury race through me.

"Your father. He explained that you are not always in control of your essence around ghouls or others releasing their essences. He asked that I keep you away for the night."

I'm on my feet, ready to tell this man where he can shove it. Roman can no longer dictate what I do anymore, even if we're all keeping up this charade for everyone's safety.

But then I pause, replaying his words in my mind. Roman doesn't know about my inability to control my essence with the ghouls that I know of. Lowering myself back into my seat, my gaze remains locked on Headmaster Hawthorne. "You said my father..."

"I did." He gives nothing else away, but something sparks behind his eyes. Something that tells me he knows.

Sweat trickles down my spine as I lean slightly forward in my chair. "Headmaster, what am I?"

That's when he grins widely, his thin lips finally parting. "My dear, you are the future we all need. Grisym. Eistiab. Gemminai Animyrum. You will save us all."

My breath hitches. He'd said it all so plainly. As if he intimately knows me and my secrets. That hope I've seen in the stare of so many other New Order members shines bright in his stare. Hope is just as dangerous as assumptions. And I shouldn't be the one they put it in. "Headmaster..."

"It's okay. I am a close friend of Lionel Greer. He is the one who connected Jorddan and me. I've never been a supporter of your father, but I do agree with what he is trying to do. For all of us. Including me."

"You're a...?"

"I am—a light father and dark mother. Because of wielders like your father, I have lived a full life. Though it's one in the shadows, I will do what I can to support the cause distantly." His smile is weak, but somehow reassures me that he is yet another person I can trust.

"Did you know when I transferred here?"

"No. I found out everything only a few weeks ago; otherwise, I would have done more. I am thankful you've at least had Oscar and Rosaleen. You now have me, too."

"Thank you, Headmaster." I go to stand, ready to thank the gods for yet another someone in my corner.

"Bryony," I spin back to face him as he too stands. "All of your friends will be here for the ball. It's best you all keep your wits about you. There are too many spies within these walls, and I can only see so far."

My head tilts, attempting to decipher what he means. The wording reminds me of the riddles Grandma Avalon used to tease me with. My mouth opens to ask if he knew—knows—her, but I once again shut it down, nodding. Vincent never said anyone beyond him, my father, Knox, Pierce, and Valen know she is still alive, hidden away. Nor have they told me when or if I'll ever see her again.

I'm lost in my thoughts, wandering the halls, when the weight of an arm settles across my shoulders. The scent isn't one of my men. Whoever this is should feel lucky Valen isn't around to rot his arm off his body.

"Are you excited for the ball?" Carter croons, his broad smile making my stomach churn.

My essence violently swirls through my stomach and up my throat, threatening to break free yet again. I wait for the pain to lance through me, but it remains a dull ache. There are warning sirens blaring in my head, urging me to run, but I refuse to give the asshole the satisfaction.

Against what? Why is he so dangerous? I plead with my essence to give me answers. Any clue that might explain this reaction. It's clear I don't recall everything from my sessions with these wielders growing up, but Carter has by far produced the most exaggerated response thus far. I need to know why.

"Thrilled," sarcasm coats the single word. "Now remove your arm."

He only grips me tighter, unbalancing me as he pulls me to this side. "You should be nicer to me," he whispers.

"Not interested."

"You will be." Then he releases me, taking two steps backward.

I should walk away.

I shouldn't poke the bear, but I do, staring him down with a scowl. "The next time you touch me, Carter, I will show you exactly what I am."

He *tsks*, winking. "What makes you think I don't already know?"

Turning away from me with the smoothest rotation, his shoes clapping against the stone floors, he struts down the hall as if he were the king of the world. He certainly carries himself as such. *No kings*, my essence hisses. I absolutely agree.

The man rubs me every wrong way. His random moments of showing up unannounced and his comfort with touching me are a bit more than I can continue to tolerate. My patience only runs so far, and that distance is pretty damn short.

Everything inside me screams Carter is the most dangerous type. The type that leaves you at someone else's mercy. The kind that leaves you pleading for death.

Glancing down at my watch, my heart rate spikes. *Five minutes.*

My potions practical is waiting. I can only pray to every god who will listen that I don't burn the place to ash.

66

PIERSON

I LIE AWAKE IN bed, counting the seconds until I can move.

Graham and Valen are both sleeping with Bri tonight. Those two are a team of their own now. I keep waiting for the jealousy to hit, but it stays oddly absent. My world should feel off balance, but it doesn't. Valen has always been my best friend, but in truth, nothing has actually changed between us.

The time he would spend with the others or alone at Beauxgraton is now divided between Bri and Graham. Perhaps that's why it seems as though nothing has changed.

My roommate snores beside me, deep drags that sound like a stalled truck every few seconds. It's much worse on the nights he drinks to the point of blackout. My need for soundproof barriers has become increasingly necessary. The guy went from partying only on the weekends to drinking every night. A habit that begins at sunrise most days, and then continues until he's stumbling into the room, barely able to keep his balance.

The only reason I don't care is that he's often too drunk to ask where I disappear off to or about my relationship with Bri. It makes it easier to hide all of my secrets, too.

One. Two. Three. Four. My recount of the seconds begins again. Each recitation of *one* kicks off a new minute. Each minute is another reminder that I can hardly breathe, stuck here waiting.

I have no need to consult a clock to know when it's time to climb out of bed for another late-night excursion. The exact hour and minutes are ingrained in me now. Months of creeping off alone, coupled with the paranoia of being caught, drive that internal clock.

Seven additional sixty-second cycles pass before I leave the bed, donning sneakers and a hoodie. My roommate snores into his pillow, the trash can beside his bed lined with a containment spell. If the guy pukes while I'm gone, I do not want to come back to that putrid scent or chunks all over the floor.

Pulling my hood over my unruly hair, I step out of the room, ready for a night of peace.

The halls are mostly empty. Every student who passes me moves as if I'm not even there. The fascination with the Americans doesn't exist here. For centuries, we have frequented these and similar institutions worldwide. It's nothing new.

We're nothing special.

The cool air of the night slides against my skin as I step outside, glancing right then left. All appears as it should be. There are no indications spies are watching me, but there are no signs of the New Order soldiers either. They excel at disappearing into the shadows; humans don't notice them, and wielders keep their distance.

Tucking my hands in my pockets, I duck my head and start down the street. It's the same path I've taken so many nights alone that it doesn't take a single thought for my feet to guide me through the city.

A necessary solitude for the assignment I've been given. Only Jorddan and Vincent know about it. Vincent threatened to take Bri away if I so much as breathed a word about it to anyone. It makes me feel privileged, as if I finally serve some purpose for the cause.

Jorddan was the one who pulled me aside and asked me why being part of the New Order was important to me. It was a trip down memory lane that forced me to focus on myself for once. We all knew I joined because of Valen. But taking a moment to think about it, he's not why I stayed, *I am.*

The New Order developed into more than just a group of rebels seeking change and resorting to crime to achieve their goals. They're smart and calculating. Many of us are just ordinary wielders running toward an existence removed from the one we were told to live in.

Living for the cause gave me the freedom to explore being a mix between the light and the dark. An opportunity to dance in the haze of gray that too many are terrified to embrace.

The best part is I don't have to use my gifts as intended. When I arrive at my destination tonight, I get to be exactly who I've always wanted to be. I get to give and not take.

My heart used to feel heavy knowing that I would never be like my fellow dark wielders. I didn't fit in with my friends at home, nor when I was left with no choice but to attend Beauxgraton. Birth should have switched Graham and me. He has enjoyed becoming a subdued version of the villain Valen has always played up.

That's what I used to believe with everything that I am.

I once tried to convince myself that Valen was putting on an act. A rugged exterior, curated so no one would fuck with him. Over the years, I've come to realize who he truly is. He is that shadowy figure who shows no remorse for his actions, harboring neither regrets nor hesitation. Valen would readily destroy the world for the ones he loves. He won't look back or shed a single tear, but that's why we need him. It's why Bri needs him. Valen won't hesitate.

I do a quick check of my surroundings again before turning another corner, slipping down a dark alleyway.

The dank scent of dirty water fills my nostrils. Each city holds these elements. Alleys and corners exist where expectations don't align with the fabricated view of perfection we present. We all have dirt we would rather no one saw. But it's there. It's part of us and does nothing to detract from the beauty of the bigger picture.

Stopping halfway down the alley, I look left, then right again, removing my hands from my hoodie before I press them against the brick wall. The ground seems to shake beneath me as I channel the earth magic that lives here. Sucking what I need from below up through the wall and into my palms, my body vibrates with power.

"I am the one who may enter. You will open your doors for me. For I am here to protect the gem which hides inside." I recite the words three times. Once Jorddan gave my essence as an approved signature, I had to craft a spell that allowed entrance.

The wall shakes beneath my palms, tiny pieces of rock falling to the ground at my feet—each chunk shooting shocks of water high as they strike the puddle's surface.

"Enter," the wall seems to whisper to me. Pressing harder, the solid brick allows me to pass through it. My body shifts from one side to the other in four quick steps.

Rolling out my neck, I breathe as the earth magic I'd taken once again leaves my body. It wasn't mine to hold to begin with. Like the earth magic anywhere, the power here has its own properties, its own rules. Here, you use what you need and give it right back.

A labyrinth of hallways lies before me. They are never the same. A safety feature of the in-between place we're in.

The same brick that lines the exterior of the building lines the walls. Each one is colored a unique shade of rusty-brown.

Pressing my eyes shut, I release a sliver of my essence, allowing it to move through the hallways. It will guide me. It always does. On my own, it would take too long to reach my target.

Moments later, it returns, humming and vibrating with excitement. It used to seem as though my essence resented me the same way my family did. It behaved as if it despised my refusal to accept the devastation it could inflict.

But now, since Jorddan gave me this assignment, the way it simmers beneath the surface has changed. It has experienced the power of manipulating my essence into submission of a different kind. The power we hold is both to give and to take. The power of dichotomy. Absentmindedly, I wonder if Bri often feels the same.

Does her essence delight in its capacity to shift form whenever it chooses?

That is true power. Power that wins wars and brings peace. That is why I continue to stand with the New Order.

We, together, can shift this reality, which many among us didn't intend for. An existence that predated the birth of my friends and me. A mess we are now tasked with washing clean.

Following my essence, as it waves back and forth before me, we swiftly move through the brick tunnels. Only dim lighting from sconces illuminates the way. Their positions are so disparate, one nearly falls into shadow before bounding back into the faint glow. The tiny circle of pure gold dimmed at the edges, as if ready to be consumed by the surrounding ebony brushing along its curves.

My essence stops at another wall. I once again recite those words, my voice and essence signature allowing me entrance.

This time, instead of a labyrinth of hallways, it's floating platforms with doors. I must enter only one. Its hue matches the drab brown of all the others, but my signature beckons. A piece of me was woven in the wood's magic, so I could always find my way.

"Levare," I whisper, my feet suddenly hovering off the floor. Keeping my tendril of essence touching my skin, it guides us toward a lone door hovering near the ceiling this time. The location is never the same. This room has a unique configuration each time, serving as another means of safeguarding those here. Sometimes the doors are metal, wood, or even glass. The colors change, as do the size and shape, but the magic does not.

My feet find the short lip at the edge of the door, my palm finding the center, as I recite my entrance spell. An invisible latch releases, the door creaking open only a sliver. My mouth pulls into a wide grin as I enter, spotting one of my favorite people.

"It's about time," an elderly female's voice cackles, her white hair fanning out over her shoulders and down her back as she stares out of spellbound windows. The rotating illusion exists solely for her to view. The scene ranges from nature to sea storms, transporting her to anywhere but here.

"You and your granddaughter have no patience," I chuckle, closing the door behind me.

"And yet you love us both," she retorts, turning to face me.

"How could I not?"

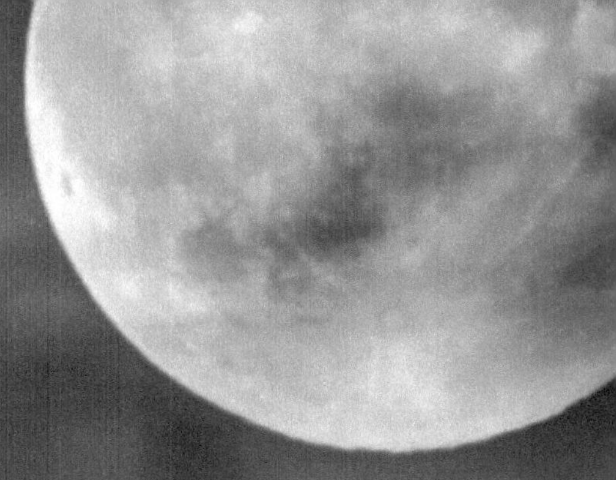

67

WYNSTON

EXHAUSTION PULLS AT MY limbs as I enter the main gate onto Beauxgraton's campus. It's been some time since I've traveled like a human. A red eye from the UK and then the car ride here has my body aching like I actually did physical activity other than having sex with my girlfriend.

I used to. It's how I maintained my slowly aging body, but the habit has become few and far between since relocating.

Rather than sit around the manor waiting for Bri's friends to show, I volunteered to retrieve them. My face might make them feel more at ease than a member of the New Order. A plan, Jorddan thought, was brilliant on our part, especially since I'm still tied to the institution.

Even though I'm on sabbatical, my appearance would face fewer questions compared to that of strangers or new arrivals at the school. Beauxgraton has been my home since I graduated from Kellerman. A place I never thought I'd leave until we did. Others will remember that too.

Plenty of others are traveling to Integretew as well, but I'm not here for them. I'm here for Camilla, Mailee, Collin, Sean, Kaia, Kormoran, Damian, and Whitney—their crew.

The ones they care about most—names Bri requested.

Janelle arranged for me to gather them from the foyer of the main building and then escort them to the outskirts of the grounds. Camilla will then portal us back to the manor. A safe landing spot instead of going straight to London. Besides the garden, there isn't a large enough space.

Who attends this weekend will remain unknown until we see their faces with our own eyes. There are too many what-ifs. Too many possibilities. Fortunately, the open invitation was extended to current students and staff. Though it could give plenty of enemies access to this weekend's festivities, I can be there too.

Either way, Jorddan has an army of students at his disposal. Loyal supporters who would follow him to the ends of the earth, many without knowing the exact reason, but we need them.

Everyone's support is crucial for whatever is on the horizon. There can't be just one hero. Collectively is the only way we have a chance of survival.

None of us knows precisely what is coming. But we feel it. It's the pit that lingers in our guts. The anxiety that keeps our minds racing day and night.

Only Davora Avalon can see our future. Yet, none of us can see her.

Only Vincent and Jorddan know her location. They've confirmed that much. They know she is safe and well, but how remains a mystery. There are a million questions I wish I could ask her. How extensive will the repairs be after the destruction? How many of us will die for a better future?

With Davora, how many could we save?

Tugging my jacket closer around my body, the wind from the mountains whips with unforgiving force. The UK weather isn't much better, but I do not miss this wind. Here, the heavy gusts appear to blow with equal force during spring and winter. There's no reprieve from its punishing violence.

My gaze roves over the main building. Each stone and imperfection is just as it was when we all fled into the night. I haven't been back since. In truth, part of me didn't think I ever would.

I accepted that. Excitement began to grow inside me, believing this was the journey I needed. An adventure and purpose beyond what I would have chosen for myself. But that pang still hits me in the chest. My past exists here, with a future I can still envision within its walls.

With a heavy sigh, I climb the front steps. All seems to be the same as my eyes roam over the grounds. And it finally occurs to me I'm the one who's different now.

The door seems heavier beneath my palm than before. The prolonged groan of the hinges makes me wince as my muscles push against the weight. Was it always this heavy? Or have I already forgotten? Perhaps I've just grown used to using standard doors for months now.

"Wynston," Janelle greets me. "Right on time."

I force a smile, marching over to Janelle, pulling her into a tight hug. My collar hides the movement of my lips near her ear, though my eyes still scan the periphery to ensure no one is watching suspiciously. "Any problems?"

The single squeeze of her fingers on my shoulder blades tells me everything I need to know.

"Look who is back," Kormoran leans against the wall, his ankles crossed, with that demented yet dead look in his eyes.

"Good to see you too."

"Hi, Professor," Kaia rounds from behind me. "Too bad you can't party with the students this time," she croons.

A shiver works its way through my body. The twins always seemed off. But Kaia, she's... creepy. Unhinged. Evil reincarnate. She and her brother are vicious, but there's a level of crazy that lives behind her stare that unnerves me.

She circles me again, like a shark closing in on prey. Those dark eyes rake over my frame. Head to toe. Then, head to toe again, before she struts over to her brother.

Their stances match. A display that says it's them against the world. They are not a pair to be fucked with.

"Where are the others?" I've barely gotten the question out when the sharp crack of a trunk against stone pulls my attention from Janelle.

It's a sound that never leaves your memory. When I started school, we had to carry our own luggage to our rooms. It was a few years after I graduated that they stopped. There were too many injuries with newly matured wielders maiming each other. The spells were thrown around as we attempted to move our things the "easy" way.

My gaze tracks Camilla tugging a trunk double her size, the monstrosity hitting each step on the way down. The noise causes Kaia to sigh loudly, rolling her eyes as if her time is being wasted. "Why didn't you magic it down the stairs?" I ask Camilla, dodging Kaia to assist.

"'Cause," she breathes heavily, her blonde hair clinging to her damp cheeks and forehead, "steering a trunk the size of a walrus's butt is not my bread and butter."

"Uh, right?" With a roll of my wrist, my essence streams free, wrapping itself around the case, effortlessly lifting it several feet off the floor.

"Professor," Camilla pants heavily, "you are by far the hero of the day."

My mouth opens to respond. Yet, I'm unsure whether to correct her in that I am no longer a professor or thank her for the unnecessary compliment. But once again, my focus darts to the four-pronged grand staircase. Boisterous laughter funnels from the top of the closest flight, Mailee, Whitney, and Collin coming into view moments later. They at least have the decency to have bags they can actually carry.

"Where's Damian and Sean?" I ask Kormoran.

The quicker we're gone, the better.

"What's the rush? Tryna get back to your student?" Kaia taunts.

Anger rockets through me. The Twins don't care for Bri, and I don't care for them. That twisted pair couldn't graduate soon enough. Having them in class was a constant strain on my ability not to lose my shit with my students.

Arrogance doesn't make for a good wielder in training, but a dangerous one.

Dialing Damian's number on my phone, it rings several times before he answers. "We're coming."

"Hurry up. There's a strict timeline." I grit the words already itching with irritation.

Damian goes silent, but grunts before hanging up.

A source tipped us off that council members may be watching the schools to see who travels to London this weekend. A joint celebration of this magnitude has never been executed before. Depending on whom they're watching, it could be an opportunity to act on the information Mikhail handed them.

Fucking traitorous wench.

I've poured over every journal, every digital document on her laptop, and even records from her office that a soldier was able to confiscate. There are no clues as to why she gave them the information. Who she was handing it off to, or even what she gained.

We have her research, but we lack a motive to work from.

A sense of helplessness has set in. They advise being cautious in your search for answers. You'll either find exactly what you're looking for or nothing at all. The crushing weight of the secrets hidden in that dead woman's mind sits heavily on my chest. I can't protect us from something I don't understand.

It's the ultimate worst feeling. That bone-deep heaviness of knowing you're completely worthless destroys me.

We've been working tirelessly, locating every name that has ever come up in Mikhail's journals. The first third was easy enough. They were Grisyms, either part of the New Order, in prominent positions, or dead.

The living are the challenge. Hiding in plain sight, or the ones who may not know their origins.

Without Eilish, it would be nearly impossible. It doesn't take much to be considered a Grisym. One drop involving Grisym or opposing blood could entirely change you. It's a matter of how potent the drop is. The power that your bloodline holds can dictate all. Many pass their gifts down through the generations. The gifts that are unimaginable and devastating. Just as many others share zero correlation with their relatives.

Hiking his bag higher on his shoulder, Damian is the first out the front doors, with me bringing up the rear behind Camilla's trunk.

A brush of fingers over my shoulder blade makes me pause. "Wynston, please be careful," Janelle all but whispers. Pain and desperation coat her words. The fear she is trying to keep hidden is peeking through the cracks she pretends don't exist.

"We are. That's why I'm here." A weak smile barely moves my lips before they sink back into neutrality.

Janelle's stare softens, her mouth opening as if she has more to say. Her questions about Bryony are on the tip of her tongue. Jorddan has all but iced her out, so I've been her gateway. It's not my place to keep her out of Bri's life. Not when she's been a fixture since birth.

Janelle served as Bri's sole connection to what she considered a stolen existence until she discovered her grandmother was alive again. *"I was supposed to have more time with her,"* she'd often whispered into my chest as I held her.

"She's okay. Safe. The guys are looking out for her at school, as are Rosaleen and Oscar Balfour. And she spends a lot of time with Eilish." Janelle's eyes soften at the mention of her relative, a fondness causing her mouth to twitch. "No major issues." I keep my tone soft. Placating. Hoping it will help curb the worry swirling in her creased eyes. She truly loves Bri, just like the rest of us, but Jorddan is determined to limit the risks he is willing to take.

He hasn't forgotten that Janelle helped convince Roman to send Bri to Beauxgraton. Their partnership functioned well until Roman's true nature became clear. A collaboration turned betrayal.

Janelle did what she thought was right. She was protecting a woman she always viewed as her own granddaughter.

Roman thought Janelle was another pawn he could use to get his way. He was wrong. But so were we.

"I—"

Reaching for her hands, I cup hers in mine. "Bri knows you care, and when the time is right, Jorddan will, too. Just be patient. Our girl is okay..." There's no need to add *for now*. It's always "for now." There are no guarantees in the pit of hell we've been dropped into. There's no promise of tomorrow or the peace of security. "I'll see you in a few days."

Janelle is reluctant to release my hands, and I refuse to yank them from her grasp. Fear lives in both of our hearts. All our hearts. Even if we're not brave enough to release those words into the universe.

Her secrets cast dark shadows over her features. Hers and Tillerman's. How many others inside these walls cower under their shadows, too?

How many shuffle through their days, hoping no one will discover what hides beneath the surface and carefully curated words?

"Take care of her," Janelle whispers as I disappear through the front door, the heavy slab slamming behind me as if a gust of wind shut me out.

"Let's go," I grumble, pushing ahead of the group.

Shaking my thoughts clear of the heartfelt moment with Janelle, my focus falls into place. It's my job to protect the students at my back. The promise of danger prickles along my skin, forcing me to be as alert as possible. Every sound, every minuscule thing that moves, and every breath less than even at my back spikes my already racing pulse.

The tension we all carry is palpable as we angle past the lake and through the treeline. The acrid stench of fear and anxiety mixes through the air, wafting up my nostrils with each gust of wind. But something else finds us as we come to a small clearing bordering the edge of a cliff.

Typically, Camilla is full of chatter. The words tumbling past her lips so freely, it's a wonder she ever held them in. Yet, she remains silent. The lack of her high-pitched voice echoing off the trees, amplifying every noise around us, sends unease vaulting through my gut. *Something's wrong.*

The skyline looms ahead of us. Gray and filled with the same gloom that sits at the base of my stomach most days.

"Camilla," I call.

She steps through our group, taking a deep breath before whispering into her palm. Her crystalline essence twirls around her delicate fingers in the most elegant wave, forming that familiar cloud. I'm not sure what the colors mean. Most who form portals maintain the color of their essence, but not Camilla's. It's as if the colors represent a mood or her emotional connection to the location she is forming the portal to.

Each one she has formed has been a different shade. This one is a soft mauve. "Alright, hustle on through, yah whippersnappers," she chirps.

One by one, I watch each of them disappear through the portal, knowing I have to go before Camilla does. Her one limitation: she can only sustain portal openings briefly, should she also plan to travel through. Seconds that barely permitted her to reach the far side.

"Right behind me," I remind her.

"You betcha," she grins. She sing-songs with that thick Southern inflection in her words. Her voice faltering, though she attempts to hide it.

Camilla feels the weight of this moment. It's a burden she is carrying for her friend. Weight, I wish I could bear for both of them.

Stepping through to the other side, pitch black darkness surrounds us. The manor property is seemingly darker than usual. Calling a ball of light to my palm, the surrounding area illuminates. Nothing seems out of the norm. From here, the manor's lights appear tiny and faint, almost impossible to focus on, though they are what guide us through the dark.

I realize we're on a different piece of land. An area of the property I'm not sure I've been on before.

It's only moments later that Camilla tumbles through, her face pale and hands trembling.

"Camilla, what happened?"

"Harley," she breathes. "He's coming."

68

BRYONY

I'D BEEN PACING MY room like an anxious panther, waiting to hear that our friends had arrived safely, when Graham barged in.

I've never seen his features so hard. So unforgiving. So much like Valen's violent stare or the twins' wicked grimace.

Not bothering to ask him what was going on, I took his hand and followed him through the door. My ragged breaths were all I could hear outside of my heart pounding in my ears.

Something happened.

Something went wrong.

I should have been there.

If anyone gets hurt because of me... I'll fucking kill them.

My thoughts continue to spiral as Pierce and Valen relay information while they guide me through the halls. I hear them. Every word funnels in through one ear and out of the other, not a single one computing for me to process and respond to.

All I can focus on is putting one foot in front of the other, slowing my breaths, and willing my essence to stay beneath my skin. If it bursts free now, everyone will see what I am. There will be no more hiding. No more pretending I am the well-behaved youngest child of Roman and Geneva Avalon.

For once, I question whether I care.

I ignore it. My refusal to acknowledge the answer feels like a choice. Even if it's one I can't afford.

I barely notice when we've tumbled out onto the street, Graham continuing to pull me toward the spot I always teleport us from. As the spring weather creeps in, the trees have become fuller and more vibrant. An area that had always hidden us, providing even more coverage. The sounds of the city are alive. I'd prefer to be part of the hustle and bustle instead of racing off to more dire news.

Horns honk as we dash across the street, a car narrowly missing barreling into us as Graham yanks me out of the way.

Still, I can't ask what's going on.

I can't face the truth that I might have lost someone.

Everyone who died that night at Beauxgraton wasn't a person I knew. We didn't have a past or a relationship. It was easier to see them as casualties of war. A heartbreaking incident, yet it served a purpose. It was for the greater good.

I won't feel the same if I lose my friends.

Not if, but when.

Eventually, the consequences of this war we didn't start, but are determined to finish, will catch us. It can only end one of two ways, with us panting to victory or pulverized in the mud.

"Bryony! Bryony!" Graham shakes me by the arms.

My gaze snaps to his as if thrown out of a trance, my eyes struggling to focus on the gold in his hypnotic, bluish-green eyes. "I—hold on."

We all grab hands the way we've done so many times. I don't have a minute to waste asking questions they themselves might not even have answers to. I can only focus on the emotions warring behind their eyes. Fury. Worry. Pain.

My essence swirls around us, forming an illusion shield. A barrier that turns us invisible to anyone within fifty feet until I can teleport us away. Eilish taught me how to project it predictably, insisting we should use that extra layer of protection.

We don't know who's watching us. The prying eyes that seem to lurk around every corner could be anywhere. London, like any major city, leaves plenty of places to hide. My gifts are still a secret to those close to me. Both the Eistiab and the teleportation. If someone were to latch onto the lingering signature following my departure, it could be disastrous.

The search for internal peace that allows me to teleport is slow to find me. An inconvenience that follows me like a dark plague anytime there is a rush. As if the universe knows time is the one thing I can't afford to lose, but it steals those precious seconds anyhow with a wicked cackle and saccharine grin.

The particles that make up our beings split apart. Drifting from point A to point B at the most glacial of paces. This moment progresses as if in slow motion. My eyes peeling open for once, watching us move through time and space.

My mother always warned me to keep my eyes closed. The experience of watching teleporting happen in real time would disorient me. My mind would warp. Our primitive nature is incapable of understanding how I could watch the molecules float through the gray haze and not be whole.

Today is the first time I've disobeyed her. The first time I've allowed my consciousness and vision to merge.

Maybe this was the missing clue. As if I only needed to see what we were, beautiful when broken into a million pieces, only for our bodies to reform in the damp grass.

We don't dictate how the magic chooses to tear us apart and put us back together; it does. The time can vary based on location or even my emotions. It's as if my essence knows I'm tumbling over myself searching for the truth. It's holding me back, protecting me, maybe from the answers I may not want to hear.

The balmy spring air caresses my cheeks, my breathing just as ragged as it had been racing through the hallways of Integretew.

My newfound love for running carries me to the manor faster than I can process that I'd moved. My arms are pumping, and the flaps of my jacket are billowing out behind me. Unsure if the guys are on my heels, I charge ahead. I don't care. I need to know why the rush.

My heart fractures. Tiny pieces falling to the floor at my feet as I recall the list of those I love. Each name is a new punch to the gut as I claw for the courage to say goodbye.

Who must I mourn tonight when this weekend should be one of celebration?

I've barely made it up the front steps when the door flies open, Knox catching me as I barrel into his arms. His hand runs down the back of my head, trying to soothe me. His whispered "shh" does nothing to calm my nerves.

"What happened?" I pant.

"Come inside. I'll explain." Warm fingers snake through mine, leading me inside with a soft tug. The panting breaths of my guys on my neck confirming they were right there with me.

We head to the parlor, our usual meeting spot. Everyone who should be is here. All of us accounted for.

My heart stops then, thinking it might be Merrick and his family or Janelle or my mother. "Someone tell me what the hell is going on?"

Camilla's eyes meet mine, her skin paler than usual. There's something so haunted in her stare. My stomach is knotting as panic surges through me.

"When we were leaving, Harley found us just before Camilla stepped into the portal. We never heard or saw him following us. Per the Council, the rules have changed for this weekend. The Red Moon ball isn't just open to students and staff around the world. They, uh, are allowing anyone related to those individuals. Though Harley could have come before, he had been adamant he wouldn't, according to Janelle," Knox relays.

"So...." I draw out the word, not understanding why we're still talking about my asshole half-brother.

"Harley is coming here, and he's bringing... reinforcements," Camilla chokes out as a shudder works through her petite frame.

"Fuck!" I bark. "I hate him." Harley, predictably, would spoil the weekend for me. Driven to prevent what should be a joyous celebration of my other half because it would kill him to let me have one damn thing.

I've never said those words and meant them. I always reserved a piece of myself for him. Yet, for the first time, I do. Years spent waiting and wishing for my brother to love me have hardened me. Everything that has happened since I became a wielding student has proved to me we will never be the same. He will never accept me, no matter how much I lie to myself that someday he will.

"Bryony," Vincent cups my shoulders. "It will be fine."

"No. It won't. Harley has had it out for me my whole life. If he comes here and has access to me, there's no telling what he'll do." A shiver runs down my spine, my intrusive thoughts fighting to take hold.

Delusion is a kiss of death. I slowly came to terms with never having his love. I accepted it. Still, I never believed he would physically harm me. My bleeding heart convinced a sliver of love lived inside him. Those foolish notions no longer linger with me.

Given the chance, that monster wouldn't hesitate to eliminate me.

Vincent gives another soft squeeze, pulling me out of my spiral. "You won't be there alone. Your friends will all be there, and Knox too."

"What?" I gasp, my eyes darting between my brother and Knox.

"Technically, I am still a professor at Beauxgraton. Although I had told Janelle I was quitting, she still put me down for a research sabbatical for the semester. I'll be there."

"Why didn't you tell me that?" I grit through my teeth, holding back a whimper of relief.

I'm not angry; I'm just hurt he didn't think he could tell me. Knox knows I plan to stay here even after the semester. I've already started my transfer paperwork. I would understand if he wanted to return to his previous career. It changes nothing between us.

"I only found out about an hour ago when I called Janelle," Knox says, running a hand over my hair once again.

"Dammit," I bark.

"Bryony, calm down," my father warns. I only eye him with a narrowing gaze. We'd had months of relative calm. I should have known it would unravel in time. We were bound to fall.

My essence thrums beneath the surface, the hammering against my skin finally breaking free. Bursts of smoky tendrils rip from me, swirling through the room as I scream. I've held it in for so long, maintaining my calm and my trust in my father and brother, but I can't anymore. I can't pretend I'm not losing it constantly, worried about everyone and how to keep myself alive long enough to protect them, too.

I'm exhausted. My knees are weak, and my heart is heavy. I can endure only so much. How much longer can I maintain this image I've curated to keep myself alive?

Still, I know I have to fight this overwhelming feeling to let myself give in and break.

If I do, people die.

If I fail them, it will all be for nothing.

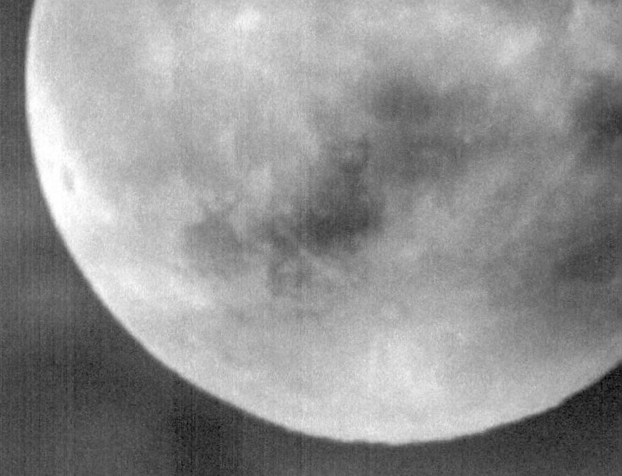

69

BRYONY

New Moon Fridays are a breath of fresh air. The administration has suspended class sessions due to the arrival of students and faculty from around the world, which began this morning. We're their hosts, their tour guides. We're meant to be available and hospitable.

Rather than trapping us inside the school walls, they sent us out on adventures around the city. Everything from structured tours to pub crawls and aimless wandering.

It's been a whirlwind. Our two groups of friends are running wild through the city together. Even the twins seem to be enjoying themselves. Then again, it could be the beers they've chugged from every pub we've passed.

It's almost enough for me to forget my brother is somewhere in this city. My thoughts endlessly swirl with a list of individuals who may or may not be aware of my true nature. They could be here, too. I won't know until they make themselves known. A reality that steals my breath the way a punch to the gut would.

I recognized so many faculty faces from years of traveling the world with Roman. Not a single one treated me differently. It was the same excitement they've always met me with, coupled with "We haven't seen you in years," or "You've grown up so beautifully." *Blah. Blah. Blah.*

I want to believe them.

I also wish I were slathered in a truth serum so that the simplest touch would automatically make every truth spill past their lips. Their secrets would fall into the palm of my hand. They'd be mine. Too bad, Oscar and Knox warned me against my diabolical plan.

The two are currently meeting with Rosaleen. Knox had arrived at the main building this morning, questioning where he could find her office. It was part of the plan for him to arrive fresh-faced and eager to meet his idol. The image was safer than having him trek through London with a bunch of students.

Perception is everything. My father reminded us of that before we were shuttled into the city. We're here to bond with others from around the world. For that reason alone, we allowed others from our classes and their friends to tag along. We move as a group, but there's no merging of the two sides.

They are outsiders to our whispered words and inside jokes. Several with noses turned up, witnessing my open affection with Valen, Pierce, and Graham. Actions we will no longer apologize for. Not when time is precious and slipping away.

"We should head back soon," Whitney yawns. "It's going to take forever for all of us to get ready in your room, Bri."

Ready for what? They can literally wear anything to go out to the ghoul pit. "Don't you guys have private rooms at Smithshire?" I quirk a brow.

Ordinarily, I would not object to their presence, but I was hoping for some time alone with my men before they leave for the Red Moon Festival. An event that my father banned me from attending for my safety.

Graham volunteered to stay behind with me, but once again, we worried about how others might perceive it. Considering we expect every other light wielder to venture to the ghoul pit, how would it look for him to bow out?

Maybe we're overthinking it. Perhaps no one would notice. There are countless light wielders appalled by the Red Moon Festival. It's assumed they are not the ones in attendance this weekend, though. Those who opposed wouldn't come within a foot of the celebration.

It's a perpetual cycle of "what ifs" and maybes. Will they perceive us this way or that? It's exhausting and often leaves us with a damned if you do, damned if you don't decision.

"We do," Camilla loops an arm through mine. "But we miss our favorite lady of the night." She and Whitney burst into laughter. Laughter, I can't help but join them in. It feels too good to let it free. A release I needed as badly as I need my men inside me.

"Fine. My room it is. I guess at least your stuff will already be there for movie night when you get back," I sigh, letting my cheek fall to the top of Camilla's head.

Valen's arm drops over my shoulders, flanking my other side, his short facial hair and lips brushing the shell of my ear. "Don't worry, Forbidden Fruit, we'll fuck you the moment everyone leaves."

My insides heat, my core throbbing at the purr of his words. The base of my spine tightening in anticipation of being ravaged by my men. It feels like it's been too long since I've had them. All of them. There's no counting the number of threesomes we've had. My guys love pairing off to have their way with me. But we've never fucked as a group again. Though my body hums with excitement at the prospect, we can't. We don't have the proper security here to allow ourselves to be that free.

Hell, Knox being anywhere near my room will look odd.

Like Beauxgraton, there are strict rules here about faculty fraternizing with the students. Unless the headmaster first receives a report about a dire emergency, they aren't even allowed on student floors and wings.

The mischief we pulled off at Beauxgraton would be a shitstorm here.

My face turns slightly, Valen's mouth finding mine. "Maybe," I whisper, brushing my lips against his once more before shoving him away.

"Fuck," Sean chortles. "It's still so weird thinking about you being with all three of them."

"I would assume so since you only found out," Whitney rebuts, squeezing his side where her arm wraps around his waist. It's not true. Sean has known since the first night we came to Guthrie Manor after fleeing. I assume he just kept it to himself.

It had been interesting witnessing a new romance blossom between the two last semester. Warmth fills me now, knowing it has not only continued but thrived. Those lines between the light and dark continue to dissolve into nothing but blurred lines.

"You say it like you've known forever," he grumbles.

"Maybe I have." Whitney flashes him a coy smile, winking.

She hasn't. I told her before they arrived to avoid surprising her. Not that we lied to our friends last year; we just didn't advertise the extent of it. Until my father led everyone to the manor a few months back, Camilla was our only friend who knew it all. Thankfully, Whitney was spared the horror of that night. Sean had convinced her to stay in her room when he felt Jorddan's call.

Our group only laughs at the two bickering over something so inconsequential. But it feels good. We needed today to breathe. That hit of joy soars through us, enjoying our friends' company. Today, we're just a group of young people living through similar chapters in life. For the next forty-eight hours, none of our worries matter.

It seems so odd that we start so much later than our human counterparts. They're already settled into careers with families and adult responsibilities. As wielders, our adult lives don't honestly begin until after our wielding education. Our sole path to flourish in our fucked-up world.

"Bri!"

"Hmm," I jerk to attention, lost in my thoughts. A common occurrence for me these days. "Sorry, what did you ask me?"

"Are we all coming back to your room tonight?" Sean quirks a brow, leaning around Whitney to look at me.

"Um. Yeah. My roommate is always gone, so we should have the place to ourselves."

"I've missed our movie nights," Collin drapes an arm over Camilla's shoulder, completely ignoring Mailee, Camilla's girlfriend, who was happy to take my place at her side when Valen stole me away.

"Stop touching my girlfriend before you become a quadriplegic," Mailee deadpans. Her monotonous demeanor hasn't changed. From the day we met her, she seldom expressed emotion. I can only imagine that's what drew Camilla to her. They are polar opposites in every sense of the word.

Collin only chuckles, rubbing his fingers along Mailee's arm. "You know, you two might actually like it if you gave it a try."

"Ugh, drop it, Collin. No one is having a threesome with you," I snicker.

"Worth trying. It's not fair you're the only one who gets to have regular orgies," he snorts, suggestively waggling his dark brows.

Graham's cheeks flush. The color is so bright it would be impossible to miss or explain away. "It's not always like that."

The confidence he's been walking around with seems to fade away. Graham is the last one to talk about our relationship out loud. It's been that way since it started, but witnessing the emotions he wears on his sleeve now makes my heart ache.

"We should head back. You guys don't want to miss the portals," I sigh, grabbing hold of Graham's hand, turning our group around.

The return trip feels quicker than it ought to. Precious minutes slipping away, pilfering the hours shared amongst my friends.

With a bit of persuasion, we'd gotten them to agree to get ready in their rooms and then meet in mine. For the weekend, students possess complete access to Integretew structures, as if they were attendees here too. A convenience not only for my friends but also for our enemies.

"Graham, come with me," I whisper, keeping hold of his hand as we move in the opposite direction from Pierce and Valen. One of them mumbles a protest at our backs, but I can't quite make out the words.

We weave through loitering bodies; some are schoolmates, with the majority visiting from other global institutions. Glimpses of the faces reveal some I recognize, but we don't acknowledge each other. For once, I feel invisible, and that feels amazing.

There has been no tension, fighting, or discrimination between the two sides. Each resident has welcomed visitors with openness, each side embracing the other regardless of where we came from. It's a beautiful thing to witness. It's my father and Rosaleen's life's work coming to fruition, even if it's only for a few days.

As we clear the staircase at the end of my hall, my name stops me in my tracks. "Bryony?"

I turn, recognizing the lilt, but unable to place it. Then I spot her, Jade Morgan, one of my closest friends from Seela. She left without so much as a goodbye. Until now, I hadn't seen or spoken to her. There were no responses to my comments on social media or texts. I hate to admit that it hurt. We were the closest in our group. So, her radio silence was a new knife to the heart for months.

The pain of abandonment still lingers. I hadn't known it until I just peered into her honey-almond eyes and saw what we lost.

Her slender arms wrap around me, pulling me into a hug. The long, straight, jet-black hair that used to sit at her hips now barely grazes her collarbones. The color is as natural as her breast implants. Born with fiery auburn hair that never suited her complexion, she was quick to dye it in her teens and has ever since. "Have you lost weight?" she gasps.

"I don't know. Maybe." The question makes me uncomfortable. In my old life, I would have had an exact answer. I'd know the number on the scale and the exact measurements I needed for a custom gown. Not because I cared anymore, but because my mother and my siblings did. My size was always a reminder of how different I was from the rest.

I haven't paid a lick of attention since I left for Beauxgraton. I didn't have to.

Her face settles into an expression revealing her every regret. "I've missed you. I wanted to call you so many times, but I didn't want to risk it."

There's genuine sincerity in her tone, forcing me to pause and replay her words in my head. "Risk what?"

Her narrow, dark brows furrow, but her skin remains wrinkle-free. "My education and my parents' jobs."

"Jade, I have no idea what you're talking about." I suck in a long breath. She did not play games, nor did she mince words, so I'm rattled by her actions now.

She tilts her head to the side, studying my face. "You really don't, do you?"

"No, she doesn't," Graham pipes in. Jade's gaze rakes down the length of his body before settling back on his face.

"Good work."

"Jade."

"Right," she rolls her eyes. "Your dad threatened us all. If we kept in touch with you, we'd be banned from ever attending any wielding school, and our parents wouldn't work another day in the wielding world." She reaches for me before dropping her hand.

"Come again?" I take a step closer to her, my mouth set in an unforgiving line.

"Bri, I'm sorry. We would never intentionally leave you behind." Her warm, trembling palms grip mine. "You have to understand, we did what we had to do. I can't comprehend why your dad would work so hard to alienate you. But we were…" Her gaze tracks down to our feet before meeting mine again, tears clouding the soft amber hue. "We were scared."

She'd never be able to comprehend the truth. The reason wouldn't make sense to her. But the pieces fall into place with her confession.

Should I encounter that asshole again, he will regret every word directed toward someone I care about, just like his buddy, Mikhail.

70

GRAHAM

THAT PINPRICK OF DOOM travels down my spine, listening to Bri's conversation with her friend. Initially, the confession, then their shared sorrow and joy concerning lost experiences together. It was equally heartwarming and soul-crushing to witness.

Roman did that to her.

His list of grievances grows longer by the second. How could he treat her so poorly? How could anyone disrespect a child they raised in an effort to alienate them from the world, so you're all they have? So, the lies you told them about no one else wanting a relationship with that child would appear to be true. Was there never an ounce of genuine caring in his heart for her?

My fingers twitch as Bri's smile spreads, but never touches her eyes. Her response is genuine. She's missed her friend. Bri is happy for her former friend's good fortune, but her mind is elsewhere. Distracted by her brilliant mind reweaving the threads, adding this new information on Roman.

Bri's emotions stir beneath the surface as she aggressively rubs her thumb and pointer together. They're raw, tearing open old wounds that threaten to overwhelm her. Fighting for composure, she tries to be pleasant while being cautious to conceal information that could hurt us. Her fist clenches at her side as she fights for calm, the quiver of her arm revealing that she's on the verge of losing control.

Our lack of Grisym blood could save many of us. Plausible deniability. Artificial distance. There's plenty, especially we light wielders with strong upbringings, could do to save ourselves. It's that ever-present distinction between the individuals our community praises and those it prefers to punish.

I'm not sure how her half-siblings, mother, and Roman would claim the same. No matter how loudly Harley shouts his opposition regarding Grisyms, he wouldn't be able to make any reasonable claim. How could they trust a person dwelling within the same home as a Grisym for years? He would have seen something, heard something.

The nail in the Avalon coffin is Mikhail's journals. She documented every correspondence and session. Later, we found embedded recordings of her conversations with Roman. The most damaging proof concerning that bastard now rests with us.

It might be that Bri's abilities were more obvious to me because I've known what she is, but I don't understand how someone could miss them. Especially not when they're searching for it. The clues were presented to them on a silver platter.

The bedroom door slams, and my body involuntarily flinches at the sharp crack. Only the occupants assigned to the room can "transport" through the door. Visitors must enter the old-fashioned way.

Bri's marching footsteps carry her across the room in seconds, her eyes trained on the window, watching the sun set. The heart of who she is calls out to the Red Moon she won't get to experience tonight.

None of us has said it to her face, but we couldn't be happier that her father banned her from joining us at the pit. It's just one less disaster we may have had to cover up.

Bri may command the ghouls, but there's no telling how they would respond. Would they actually do her bidding, or, better yet, pretend like she is nothing but a light wielder? Do they have that type of control outside of their carnal and power urges? Would they care or understand that, to the rest of the world, she can't be theirs?

The worst-case scenario would be if they appeared at the ghoul pit and demanded to fuck her. If Aziel, Warrick, Tarak, and Keres spoke in front of everyone, claiming her, and then they obeyed. How would she explain that?

Gods if they kneeled. I swallow past the lump in my throat just imagining the scene that has no chance of happening since Bri is banned from the pit.

An audible groan escapes me as I scrub my hands over my face, the endless possibilities causing my temples to ache. Possibilities we believe we've ruled out, but could still happen. Those ghouls recognize us. They could still demand their queen.

The ghouls bow to no one. They are their own masters. At least they were until Bri.

Sliding up behind her, my fingers curl around her biceps, gripping her lightly. As if my touch alone was all she needed, every bit of tension bleeds from her body. "Go ahead," I whisper, lowering my mouth to her ear.

The round curve of her ass presses against my pelvis, my cock swelling just from the contact. An audible swallow makes me pull her in closer, softly pressing my lips to the side of her throat. "That fucking bastard!" she bellows. "How could he do that to me? Who would do that to their child? Oh wait, I was never his, so of course he wouldn't care."

I say nothing as Bri continues her rant. I only hold her, throwing up a soundproof barrier around the room. Right now, I am the safe place she needs to release her frustrations. From the start, we shared everything. Her only omission, forgiven. She couldn't trust anyone who didn't need to know she was a Grisym.

I am still the one she comes to when she needs to clear her mind and free herself of the thoughts and what-ifs that torment her. A release from the frustrations burdening her, and the oppression granted by the Council to anyone they considered inferior.

"Graham, could you imagine if he succeeded in completely alienating me from everyone? I wouldn't stand a chance against whatever he and Harley have planned."

"Bri, listen to me," I spin her in my arms, my hands rising to cup her warm cheeks. Looking at her hard now, I realize her friend had been right. The cut of her jaw is sharper, her waist and stomach trimmer. Not that I would care if it weren't. Bryony is the sexiest woman I've ever laid eyes on. A statement that remains true without including her looks at all. "You would have never been alone. We were meant to find each other. Me, you, Pierce, and Valen. Knox, too. Your father would never have abandoned you. From what we've learned, he never did."

"You know what I mean." She rolls her eyes, shifting to pull out of my hold, but I only adjust my grip, my palms cupping her jaw tightly, my thumbs brushing over her cheeks. The sight of her flush creeping up her throat makes my dick twitch.

"I do, but it would have never happened." My mouth presses to hers. Firm. Confident. The single taste of her shooting through my body, my cock swelling in my slacks. I'd only meant to kiss her to reassure her, but my body has other plans.

Plans that involve her bare skin on mine. I intend to have her moan my name as I move inside her. This one time, I'd take her slow. Our movements would be unhurried, like we have all the time in the world. We don't. It won't be long before our friends are knocking at her door, a few ready to have their first Red Moon Festival experience—me included.

"Thank you," she breathes against my mouth.

"Let me have you," I plead. Her bright eyes find mine, the answer there without her needing words. "Just me and you."

She only grins, her palms finding my chest. It's a slow, torturous drag of her fingers down my torso, before her knees meet the rug beneath my feet. Her eyes never leave mine as she teases me, running a palm over my swollen dick over my pants, while unbuckling my belt with the other hand. The whip of the leather pulled through my belt loops fills the room before the length of it clanks to the floor by the door. Her essence whipping back toward her as if waiting for the next task.

Heat licks through my body. The flames scorch my insides as I burn for her.

"Bri, let me have you," I achingly groan, running my fingers beneath her chin. When I'd said the words before, I'd wanted to be the one to bring her pleasure. The one to make her knees weak as she clung to my bare back, silently begging for more. But I know that look. The one that shines with gratitude and wicked repayment. She's going to thank me first, whether I like it or not.

If we're lucky, there will be time for more. Enough time to get lost in the best person I have ever known.

The buzz of my zipper lowering causes my gaze to shoot down to her face again. Those eyes are still smiling up at me. In seconds, she has my pants and boxer briefs around my ankles, her essence swirling around my legs, paralyzing me. "Stay still," she smirks, fisting my length in her palm.

A hiss leaves me with her squeeze, my back wanting to bow, but her essence only allows me to tip so far. She wants me at her mercy. She wants to worship me the way we all do her.

She wastes no time, swirling her tongue around the head, shuffling closer on her knees. Her moans and hums vibrating up her throat and to the tip of her tongue, making the base of my spine tingle.

Every muscle tightens and strains.

"I like it when you save this for me," she grins.

I watch as she makes a show of swiping her tongue over the opening, licking up my pre-cum. The feel of her mouth on me and the lust in her multicolored eyes set me on edge. My fingers sink into her hair, and I try to pump my hips forward, ready to sink into her mouth, but I can't. Her magic holds me still. This is her game. Her show. I am the only contestant who will wind up busting down her throat when she's done with me.

"Shit. Bri. Just like that," I groan, my eyes pressing closed as she takes me to the back of her throat. "You look gorgeous on your knees."

She smiles around me, sucking harder. Faster. She takes me to the back of her throat, only to gag, lick me like a lollipop, and swallow my length again.

I was afraid to tell Bri I enjoy having my dick sucked. Women I'd been with before didn't like it, and I wasn't going to force them. But Valen encouraged me to be honest. So I was. The words had barely fumbled past my lips before she yanked my pants down my thighs and sucked me in deep. It's a match for what she does to me now, working me hard. That tingle intensifying, my body warning me it's on the verge of release.

But Bri notices. She knows my body. The sounds I make and the way my forearm shakes when I twist the length of her hair around my fist when I'm about to come. Her change in pace eases me away from the edge. Those soft fingers caressing my shaft with the softness of her tongue, only to swallow me down like it's nothing.

She'd told me she'd never wanted to suck a cock so bad until she met us. For us, she wanted to taste the saltiness of our skin and our cum on her tongue. To feel that vein pulse alongside every long pull of her mouth.

Her lips spread wide over my cock. Pretty, swollen, and dusky pink. "Gods, I'm so fucking in love with you," I groan, tightening my hold on her curls.

Her essence finally releases me, my hips pumping forward, as I fuck her mouth. The bite of her nails into my thighs only makes me flex into her face harder. I'd been nervous about this, too. On the outside, I'm a well-put-together man who presents himself with the utmost decorum, but in bed, I'm different. I dislike people questioning or disobeying me. Bri quickly fell in line, just another sign we were meant for each other.

Her hum vibrates along my shaft. That tingle shooting down my spine. Bri will want to swallow my cum, but I want to be inside her when I blow. It's become some unspoken rule within our group. The place we all prefer to finish. Only Knox is adamant about fucking every last drop back inside her, though. We've never asked about the compulsion, nor will we. He's not the warm and fuzzy type. He doesn't share his feelings with us or what he's thinking, except for his concern for Bri's safety.

"Let go," I growl. She only grips me tighter, her magic once again holding me in place. "Let me come inside you."

She shakes her head, sucking me harder. Her cheeks are hollowing so much, I wonder how she continues at the pace we're setting together.

"Bryony, I'm warning you."

She only swipes her hand, sealing my lips tight. That tingle turns to sparks of lightning, my balls drawing up and length thickening inside her warm, wet mouth. I want to scream out. I like her name on my lips, but she won't let me speak. Not when the first shot of my release slithers down her throat, or when I keep coming. Every last drop swallowed down like a savory treat.

Only when my breaths are no longer quivering does her mouth pop free of my semi-hard length. She swipes a finger through the air, and my lips break apart with enough force that my body jerks forward.

"Whoops," she giggles. "Still working on that counterspell."

I suck in a gasping breath before pulling her to me and kissing her hard.

"Try that again, Bri and I will fuck you so hard you won't be able to walk or sit for a week."

Her arms loop around my neck, smiling up at me. "Sounds like fun."

71

WYNSTON

Before Bri, the last time I stepped foot in a ghoul pit with students was my first year at Kellerman.

It only took one near mistake for me to learn. A single instance of a nosy bastard calling out my innate abilities for too many to ask questions about why I was out there fucking ghouls alongside them, siphoning enough power to turn a county to ash.

It took months to explain it away. Countless rebuttals dancing around curiosity and inconsistency with my essence. Multiple classes where I made intentional errors to prove it before my classmates moved on to another topic of interest.

From that day on, I went to the ghoul pits alone. I would time it so that the last faculty members would leave for the night, get in, and then rush back to campus. To my knowledge, no one ever saw me. No one knew.

When I came to Beauxgraton and the faculty made a big deal of visiting the pit together, I froze. I'd become a bit of a loner in my younger years, so it was easy to be the arrogant, new, broody asshole with a chip on his shoulder who kept to himself. The individual unwilling to join the others. They labeled me grouchy, pretentious, and snobby; I clung to that misconception like a lifeline. It was everything I had to protect myself from anyone learning the truth.

I'm jittery as hell moving alongside Bri's friends toward the ghoul pit. The presence of others spikes my heart rate more than the identities of the people beside me do. Wielders, I need to keep safe at any cost.

We're too exposed. There are too many on opposing sides, and we don't know who they are. Not all of them. Not yet.

If anything happens to anyone Bri cares about, that's something I will carry on my conscience. A sword that will twist deeper and deeper into my gut, even with her forgiveness.

My greatest fear, though, is her. Bri takes impulsivity to the extreme. Her inability to care about the risk comes up far too often.

I would do anything for her. I'd willingly die protecting her, destroying anyone who would harm her; nonetheless, this does not alter the fear that has plagued me for decades. The fear of discovery. The fear of death.

How is it possible to love someone with every fiber of your being and still not want to die for them?

Willing is not wanting. A reminder I often give myself.

If she exposes herself to protect all of us, it could have the opposite effect than she believes. All it takes is one determined elite on the Council or Bureau to dig and dig until they find the truth. They'll latch onto the false personas we've lived under for years. They'll learn that not everyone is what they seem.

I don't want to die.

I don't want any of us to die.

"Professor Knox," Camilla chirps. "Will you siphon power tonight?"

I quirk a brow at her. Her performance holds up, posing pertinent questions like the inquisitive light wielder experiencing this novel moment. With every "Professor Knox" out of her mouth, my body jerks involuntarily. Like tiny shocks of electricity are poking at my ass. No doubt making me look jumpy as hell, definitely not as relaxed as I should be.

No matter how Janelle tries to spin it, I quit my job. I am no longer a professor of anything. Frustratingly, I remain unsure if I desire to be again.

I am just a Grisym, living as a dark wielder, in a relationship with another Grisym, posing as a light wielder, who is the daughter of the most wanted dark wielder and leader of the New Order. No big fucking deal, right?

My hands run through my hair for the millionth time. The waves that I had perfectly styled probably now stand at odd angles. The same way they do when Bri tugs at the stands when I'm buried deep inside her.

I adjust myself in my khakis. Now is not the fucking time to sport an erection thinking about our girlfriend.

"It'll depend on how crowded it is," I answer.

It's the truth. I've grown so used to keeping myself hidden while siphoning. Not because I react poorly. It's just simply who I've become now.

And no matter what I am, innates don't need to siphon. So they don't.

Nerves twist my stomach in knots. My palms are clammy as I wipe them against my pants. The mixture of Bri and me writhes beneath the surface. The combination eager for a taste of that decadent ghoul power.

Her essence can sense them nearby, sniffing them out and salivating like a dog starving for a T-bone steak. That's why they banned her from coming here tonight. At least if they seek me out, we can manage the situation. There would be no explaining that away for Bri.

"But Professor, aren't you innate?" My eyes press shut at Mailee's question. The woman was always too perceptive for her own good. It's a wonder she knew nothing about the group before she got here.

There's no retort or explanation. She is the most uninformed individual at present. We told her only enough to keep suspicion at bay. My identity wasn't on the need-to-know list.

Mailee only knows Bri is with Pierce, Graham, and Valen. Beyond that, she knows nothing, and we'd like to keep it that way.

I wish Whitney were the same, but Sean told her everything after Bri revealed our relationship. She remains ignorant that we're Grisyms. It was the one thing he had to keep to himself. There were already too many who knew. Too many of whom we don't believe will turn on us, but could, or worse, be taken into custody and forced to answer truthfully.

It had been a stretch coming up with a story of why we were at Guthrie Manor. A distant, long-dead familial connection had seemed enough to appease Whitney and Mailee, but it was like ash on Bri's tongue, denying that Jorddan was her father. Fortunately, Vincent stayed out of sight, so they never got the chance to see the siblings side by side.

"Just because we're innate doesn't mean we can't take in more," I answer, hoping neither of them will ask me another damn thing.

It's the truth. Weaker innate wielders will, at times, siphon to help them regulate how they use their stores. An exception to the rule rather than the norm.

It's a clusterfuck of wielders and ghouls before us. Still, the roar of moans, panting, and grunts does not hit our ears until we cross the invisible barrier, causing Whitney, Camilla, and Graham to gasp loudly. More ghouls than I've seen in one place fill the expanse of open land. Even Bri hadn't summoned this many the night we escaped.

"Shit," Pierce breathes next to me.

My gaze rakes over the hundreds of ghouls gathered in the open field. All present except Bri's four. "Yeah. They must have sensed there would be more dark wielders here than normal."

Valen and Kormoran only cackle like hyenas charging forward. I'd expected those two to act like fools. Die-hards like them wouldn't change their behavior just because a million threats are breathing down our necks.

I expect Kaia to join them, eager to fuck the night away like the power-hungry woman she is, but she stays put. Her body is still, while her eyes roam over the crowd as if expecting someone.

It's impossible to read her expression or body language.

The shift in her usual demeanor sends my hackles high, as I wonder who has her behaving more reserved than I've ever seen her. Her narrow eyes squint into the distance, lips rolling over one another with impatience and... nerves?

Kaia Vue, nervous?

"You're wasting time," I grunt in her direction. As if pulled from a stupor, she jolts away from me.

"Fuck off, Knox. No one needed you here as a motherfucking babysitter. Go fuck your girlfriend and leave the rest of us alone."

"Kaia, knock it off," Sean snaps. "You can be such a fucking bitch. Go get fucked so you can stop ruining everyone's mood."

A thick rope of tension surrounds us all, Kaia and Sean staring each other down with wicked resentment. I've never seen them at odds before. That crew skulked around at Valen's back and said nothing, except the twins. They'd snap at everyone and everything, Kormoran throwing around his muscles and Kaia her cursed words—literally.

A dark stream seeps out of Sean's fingertips, his eyes turning that same deadly black. Kaia flinches as if preparing to attack. Her movements are too slow before Sean's essence twists up her legs and then presses in at her temples. His head falls back, and he inhales deeply as the sliver of blue memory tears free, slithering through the few feet between them, before the thin strip funnels past his lips.

I've never seen Sean consume a memory, but, *fuck*, it's terrifying. His eyes roll back into his head, and his body goes rigid.

"What's happening?" Whitney whines, reaching for him, only for Camilla to yank her back against her chest.

"He's taken her memory."

Whitney exhales with the most exaggerated breath, watching her boyfriend become what she was always told to stay clear of. *Here's why light and dark shouldn't combine.* Every lie she has ever been told about the dark flashes in her pale eyes, but she doesn't flinch away. She steps closer, eyes wide with awe and the unknown.

Kaia fights against the restraint of Sean's essence, his head finally righting itself before he flashes her a murderous grin.

"You fucking bitch," he growls.

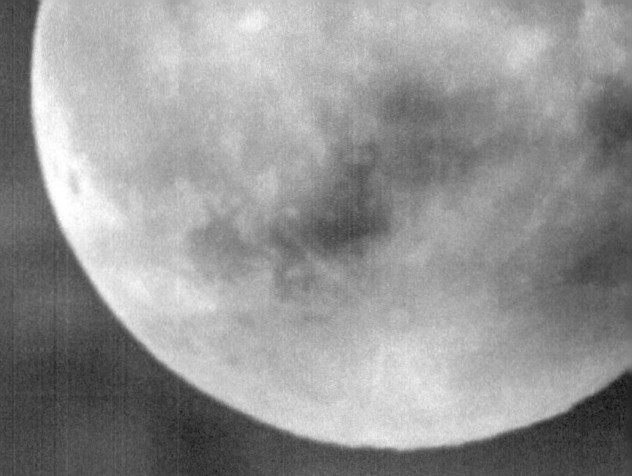

72

BRYONY

I'D BEEN CONTENT TO spend the night alone, eager to have a few moments to myself to parse through every detail repeatedly. It's all I do when it's just me. The journey back to the beginning is always the same, as I venture over the jagged rocks lining my path. Each restart becomes less complicated until reaching the fork, where new insights insert themselves, forcing my exploration of novel territory. The pain and unknowns cut into me unforgivingly, but I move forward. Then I begin again.

It's draining. Exhausting. Soul-sucking.

Occasionally, I'll find some minute correlation that propels us forward.

Mostly, I allow myself to drown in the past. The pain and the lies swirling to the surface, inflicting their damage until I cast them away. I let it consume me until every misstep is nothing more than bitter poison on my tongue. The taste is so putrid it refocuses me.

It reminds me of everything there is to lose.

The saying that hindsight is twenty-twenty is bullshit. There's truth to it, but it does nothing to change the past or inform your decisions moving forward. It's a saying that leaves many of us feeling comfortable as victims, making the excuse that what happened is done and there's nothing I can do about it.

I don't believe that.

Not anymore.

There's no changing the past, but by brushing it under the rug, it ingrains itself in your DNA. It becomes a part of you that you can never carve out. It defines you.

Frankly, I have no plans. There's no concept of how I'll manage this and move forward. But I refuse to be a victim. Not anymore. So I'll don my battle armor and charge into the unknown with my war cry roaring through the skies.

I had a "father" who manipulated me and everyone around me. He alienated me and showered me with a fake love that nearly suffocated me in a protective blanket that was just the noose around my neck. The rope tightening with each obeyed order and "yes, sir."

Meeting Knox loosened the knot. It allowed my vision to once again become clear. Embracing my dark side tore the thing to shreds. The fibers clung to my clothes and lined the floor at my feet. Recurring images of each difficulty I continue to struggle against, together with remnants from past events that continue to linger, shadow me. They'll dirty who I have become, no matter how hard I work to brush them away.

The only thing to do is strip. Tear off the outer layer to reveal the clean flesh beneath. Then I can be free. Truly free. I tell myself that's what this endless cycle is. It's shedding that skin with each recitation. I'm letting the past burn away the old flesh.

Then we can move forward.

Maybe then the possibility of a safe future might be within reach. A future of equality, respect, and freedom.

Determined to avoid anyone who might have skipped the Red Moon Festival or been quick to return, I sequestered myself in my room.

A space I consider only mine most days.

My essence loops through the space, drifting up, then down, and then to both the left and right, mimicking my thoughts. The stars twinkle, lighting the way. As if reminding me, in the dark, a dim light can still shine beautifully, shimmering as small glimmers meant to enhance, rather than overpower.

A knock suddenly pulls me out of my pacing. It's too early for my friends to be back. I doubt Valen has even had his fill yet.

Pulling my curls up in a messy bun, I shuffle over to the door, opening it wide, expecting my friends to burst through, but it's Vincent.

"What are you doing here?"

"I can't want to see my sister?" He pulls the crooked grin he seems to save only for me and Damian.

"Of course," I agree, shaking my head and ushering him inside. He likely wanted to monitor me while everyone was out at the ghoul pits. There are wielders from all over the world here. Anyone could be out to get us. Not to mention, William Danvers continues to elude us. A fact that leaves me wanting to tear my hair out.

"No one stayed with you tonight?" Vincent questions. I turn to face him, my eyes narrowing.

A prickle tingles at the nape of my neck, a pit forming in my stomach. He knows the plan was for all of them to go together. Why would he think we would deviate?

My eyes search his, but something is off. The way he asked the question sounded like my brother, but he didn't speak like him. The inflection was a little more proper. Each word was a bit more clipped. A cadence that doesn't match the relaxed flow in which we usually chat.

Shaking off the ridiculous thought, I flash my brother a smirk. "You knew everyone was going to be out at the ghoul pit. You probably helped convince Dad to keep me away."

Vincent only shakes his head, running his palms down his thighs as he slides into the wooden chair in front of my desk. His fingers run over the notebooks and textbooks I threw there yesterday. My rush to prepare to see everyone has allowed me to ignore my studies for the weekend, and it shows. A fact that would usually make me cringe.

"Different from when you attended here?" I cock my head toward the ghoul history textbooks he's fingering along the spine.

"Excuse me?" A hint of indignation leaks into his tone. My brow arching high in response, confused by the added bass in his voice.

"You were a student here too, or did you forget?" I snort.

His brow furrows before he lets out a laugh that isn't quite his. "Yes, I remember. I was reminiscing and missed your question."

"Sure." The single word is drawn out before I sink onto my bed. "How did you get up here?" I ask, that pinprick of warning becoming stronger. More urgent.

"You have a lot of questions tonight," he snickers, with a dark undertone he's never used before.

My magic somersaults beneath my skin. My essence is telling me something is wrong. Vincent is wrong.

"How did you get up here?" I ask again. The words were delivered more slowly. More deliberate. Panic seizes my insides as this stranger continues to grin at me with a smile that is all wrong.

He only laughs, shaking his head again. The cackle of it is not my brother's. *This. Man. Is. Not. My. Brother.*

He casually stalks across the room, sitting beside me on the bed. My essence bangs at the door I'm keeping it trapped behind. A constant *crack, crack, crack* with its massive fist demanding I let it free, but I won't.

I don't know who this is impersonating my brother. He looks just like him. He sounds like him, even smells like him, but the eyes are wrong. The tone of voice and avoidance of my questions are wrong. There's no telling whether this stranger knows I am onto him. I can't tell, but if he thinks he's still fooling me, I will keep up the charade to ensure my safety.

Part of that is not letting my essence free. When it releases in defense, it isn't easy to shift the color before it explodes around me. Control, Tosch says, is improving, but not nearly fast enough to keep me hidden.

The imposter drops his arm around my shoulder, a gesture Vincent does all the time. "I was a student here, too. There's still a way to get these old walls to recognize my signature."

It's a perfectly reasonable explanation. One that could be possible, but I trust my magic. I trust the power roaring through my veins. My focus calls on the piece of Vincent that lives inside me to confirm my suspicions.

Not me. Not me. Not me. Not me. Not me. Not me.

The essence hisses through my mind. It's that same voice that boomed and confirmed my long-dead grandmother wasn't buried in the Cavea de Mors as I believed.

Leaning into his touch, I let my head rest on his shoulder. "Big brother, I'm okay. Shouldn't you be off in Seela, taking care of business?"

The man stiffens beneath me, dropping his arm before he clears his throat. "You seem like you're trying to get rid of me."

"Never," I giggle, putting on my best act. "We just know Father has given us all specific assignments. We don't have room for any missteps."

His eyes narrow on mine as if assessing my words. The skepticism flashes across his irises, clouding them. The colors shifting before settling back to that deep brown and crystalline gray.

I blink several times, convinced I imagined what I saw, but knowing I didn't. I'd seen another set of eyes. Eyes that look so familiar, but I can't place.

"You're right. But maybe I should stay here with you until one of your boyfriends returns."

My heart rate spikes. Vincent never calls the guys my boyfriends. He never calls them anything other than their names, and the men he's allowing to live as long as I'm still happy.

If I wasn't sure before, I am now, this man isn't my brother. Embarrassment, anger, and paranoia course through me. I don't give a fuck who he is, but he needs to go.

"It's fine. Really. I am going to get some studying done before all my friends get here for movie night." A playful shove at his shoulder causes him to grimace at me—another tell. Vincent would never.

"Movie night?" he questions as if he's never heard the words before.

"Yes, get out of here," I chuckle, shoving at his shoulder again. "I'll see you next weekend."

His jaw only works as I push him toward the door, a flick of my fingers throwing it open to reveal my friends coming down the hall.

Valen's eyes immediately meet mine, his steps quickening. "Didn't expect to see you here, Vincent," he says cooly.

"Just taking care of my sister." Then fake Vincent moves along the hall, toward the left rather than straight forward, which would have been his exit. *He's headed the wrong way.*

My friends file into the room, Valen spinning me to face him. "Who the fuck was that?"

"I don't know, but he sure as hell wasn't my brother."

73

VALEN

THE PUREST FORM OF anger rolls through me. White. Hot. Uncontrollable. This is not how the night was supposed to go.

A Nigeros made an appearance. A rarity. It wasn't the one Bri had claimed as hers. The frame was different. Its demeanor was more menacing. And that dark creature was exactly what I needed.

A night with those wicked ghouls can give me enough power to last me a year. Just one fuck and I am prepared to level everything around me.

I'd been seconds from roaring my release, my insides burning from the overflow of magic, when I'd heard Kaia scream. Her body crashed to the ground under Sean's power, his body straddling her middle as he restrained her with bands of his essence.

Kaia has a mouth as filthy as the rest of us, but even I winced at the level of profanity she'd thrown at the group staring down at her.

Kor ran for her first, and I accepted that the night was done. Jogging after him, I could only curse under my breath. His sister has always been trouble. We should have ditched her a long time ago.

It was only after Sean revealed Kaia's betrayal that I understood. The taut restraint on my temper snapped so quickly that it cracked through me. If not for Pierce and Graham holding me back and Knox binding me with his essence, I may have killed her. I would have enjoyed watching that traitorous bitch rot.

That bitch fought the entire way up here to Bri's room. Camilla eventually sealed her lips because all the profanity was making her uncomfortable.

I wasn't prepared to come face-to-face with another disaster before crossing the threshold into my girlfriend's room. This was supposed to be a good fucking weekend. Sure, we prepared for the worst. Every damn scenario you could think of. But, fuck, for once I was ready to enjoy the best.

Some motherfucker was in here, impersonating her brother. Who the fuck would be brave enough to test us like that? Who the fuck has the ability or the knowledge to know she'd be here alone?

That red rage returns. My daggers were poised and ready to sink into the heart of whoever betrayed us. Ready to tear through the spine of whoever had the fucking backbone to oppose Jorddan.

I could barely control myself as an audible growl escaped me. The urge to burn the place to ash until someone tells me exactly what I fucking want to know, causing my breath to be nothing more than short pants through my nostrils as my fists shake at my sides.

Every detail about the stranger ran through my mind. It was like I could smell it on him as he tried to weasel his way through our group.

No one had the answer. A reality that only drove my frustration higher.

Knox was the one to challenge me; both of us were seconds from wrapping our fingers around the other's throat.

The one name Sean uttered freed us from the sea of fury.

William Danvers.

And not just that fucking ghost's name. He'd only said that Kaia was playing both sides outside. Not that she was fucking meeting with the wielder we have been searching high and low for all semester.

She's been with him. Talking to him. Fucking him!

She knew the list. We made sure my crew did before going back to school to protect themselves.

Sean had only pulled an immediate memory; the information wasn't enough to give the whole picture, though. However, Kaia had better hope Jorddan chooses Sean to extract her secrets when he arrives. Sean will take what he needs and move on. Not Jorddan; he'll make you beg for mercy. He'll make it hurt as your knees buckle and you cower at his feet.

Thinking back, Kaia's hatred of Bryony started before the semester began. We'd heard rumors that the director's daughter would be attending Beauxgraton. Those were the first signs of Kaia's true feelings. It was nothing more than hearsay. The topic dropped and was forgotten as quickly as it had come up.

There was a time I hated Forbidden Fruit, too. I wanted her dead. Sometimes I still do. In my mind, she was a threat. Now we all know the truth. Bryony is our greatest asset.

One could argue our asses wouldn't be on the line if we weren't so fucking obsessed with her. I don't think that's true, though. Regardless, I need her alive more than I need her dead. I need her attention and that sweet pussy. I need her lips on mine, and that snarl she gives me when I piss her off, and a dagger inevitably ends up at her throat until she can calm down.

I. Fucking. Need. Her.

"Sit the fuck down," I snarl at Kaia.

The bitch dares to sneer at me. She's gone against not only Bri but also her loyalty to Jorddan. He is unforgiving. Bri might disregard some bullshit given a suitable explanation, but Jorddan won't. Once he has the answers he wants, it's not likely Kaia will still be breathing.

Which likely means Kormoran will be next. He'll throw himself into a rage over his twin sister. Their bond is one only a twin could understand. But I don't give a fuck.

Those tattoos, infused with Jorddan's essence, were a choice. We chose him and the mission over everything else. Go against it and you're asking for your death sentence.

"Val, you don't understand." Kormoran grabs my arm, his eyes pleading with me.

His one weakness shines in his dark eyes. He's a bastard tougher than a ghoul when it comes to his twin. His other half by birth. This weakness is one I never felt shame about exploiting, and that remains true now. Especially now.

My gaze tracks down to where he holds me. With a flick of my focus to his free hand, my essence draws a dagger from my side that slams into his palm. The blade twists with the tilt of my head, only sinking deep enough to wedge between his bones and tissues.

"Don't fucking touch me if you're going to side with her. I don't give a fuck what you or she has to say anymore." Another dagger points at Kaia's face, hovering a hair's breadth from the space between her slanted eyes. "You'd better hope Jorddan does, though. He's your only chance of making it out of here alive."

"I can't believe you!" Kaia shouts just as Knox soundproofs the room. "We've been friends for years. We are loyal to each other, and no matter what, you're once again picking that fucking mixed-blood cunt who has ruined everything. You want to throw threats at me and Kor about our death sentences?" Kaia releases a humorless laugh, sneering at me. "Wake up, Valen. She is yours."

I lower my face close to Kaia's, avoiding the dagger. "Shut. Your. Mouth."

Kaia only grins wickedly. "For years, I thought Pierson was your only weakness, but now..." Her eyes darken as if she's calling to her essence, but it stays hidden. "That piece of ass is. Isn't she? How does it feel to have someone in your life you'll beg and barter for, Valen? How does it feel to know you can't survive without her?"

Kaia's words purr through the room, my hand shaking, ready to grab hold of the dagger handle, driving it forward into the hard bone of her skull. Better yet, into her heart. One forceful jab into the chest. That's all I need. Her lesson for daring to continue to disrespect Bri.

Fuck Kaia and her ability to see right through me. In truth, I can't say I've worked hard to hide what Bri means to me. I would kill for her. I would die for her. Fuck everyone who came before her.

My hand darts out, fingers curling around Kaia's throat. "I thought Jorddan, and I made ourselves clear. One more less than rainbow injected word about that woman over there, and I will eviscerate you, wait for Vincent to bring you back to life, watch every memory, and then I'll laugh while I watch you slowly eat yourself all over again." I squeeze a little more, Kaia's chin jutting upward.

"Or maybe I'll let Bri do it herself. She's done it once. You remember that, don't you?"

A shudder works through Kaia's body as she tries to pull out of my hold.

Camilla's eyes are the first ones I find when I finally look up. I'd expected her to be terrified, but she's expressionless, staring at Kaia, her lips suddenly parting. "And I'll throw your stinky hindquarters through a portal to purgatory!" I almost want to laugh at the gravity of her words. Our little fairy is tough; I'll give her that.

The woman is fuming, too. She won't stand by while someone repeatedly threatens her first friend who accepted her. I've never seen Camilla angry, but the she-devil is right there beneath the surface. Vicious. Calculating. Not sunshine and daisies like we assumed.

She might curse before the year finishes at this rate. Maybe, *damn* or *hell*. *Shit*, if she's extra feisty that day.

"Dad's here," Bri interjects, a hand on my shoulder meant to draw me away. My mind says to go with her, to regain my composure and let Jorddan deal with Kaia, but my body won't obey. My fingers only tighten around her throat, her near-black eyes shifting to the side as Jorddan walks through the door.

Only then do I release her, my essence dancing at my fingertips, waiting to squeeze once more.

He says nothing as he hugs his daughter, pressing a soft kiss to her forehead and then pulling up a chair in front of where we'd had Kaia sit. "You, my dear, are a disappointment."

"Jorddan, I did what you told me to do."

I jolt back as if slapped. What the fuck is going on here?

"No. You didn't. What were your orders?" Jorddan casually leans back in his chair, his hands resting in his lap as if he's attending a royal tea, not interrogating a traitor.

"Find Danvers," her voice lowers. "Gather information."

"And were you successful?" Jorddan shifts, running his fingers over his goatee, eyes laser-focused on Kaia's face.

"Yes. No. I mean..." I've never seen Kaia truly sweat, but she is now, her body trembling under Jorddan's pointed stare. "I know he's been working with

Roman, and they are planning something big. Something that will rock the entire wielding world."

Jorddan's jaw ticks. The only giveaway that he's losing his patience. "But that's not all you did, is it?"

"No," she whispers, letting her chin fall to her chest. "I... I grew infatuated."

Jorddan *tsks*, pulling Kaia's gaze back up to him. "No, Kaia. You betrayed us. You fucked the enemy and then pledged yourself to him."

"Jorddan, you have to understand..." I've never heard Kaia beg or that quivering plea in her voice. My eyes narrow, wondering how much of this is genuine or fake.

"No. I don't. I understand you can't be trusted. Neither can your brother. What should I do with you?"

"Jorddan, I haven't told him anything!" Kaia squeals.

"Maybe not, but you are playing both sides. Are you not?" Her head bows with a sniffle. "I can't allow that. Stand," he flicks two fingers upward.

Kaia shakily gets to her feet. Kormoran slides in beside her.

Jorddan is showing them mercy, but will deliver something so much worse.

When we first took Jorddan's name, we knew there was no removing it. We would forever be tied to him. A bond that benefits us, but never harms him. The bond prevents betrayal. There's only one way out. *Death.* We knew and still made that choice.

Yet, what soon will transpire proves considerably worse than dying. A fate that will leave them pleading for their lives to end.

"Show me," Jorddan orders.

The twins slowly reveal their tattoos of his name. The letters seem to ripple over their skin. Their elevation stretches so high that it's as if they are trying to break free.

"What's happening?" Whitney pants, Sean pulling her into his chest.

His palm brushes over her hair, kissing the crown of her head before whispering to his girlfriend. "Shhh, baby. Just close your eyes and hold on to me."

I hadn't witnessed Sean like that with a female. He doesn't fall into deep, heartfelt relationships or pledge everything he is to anyone. He fucks them and moves on. The same applied to us, excluding Pierce. Watching his tender side toward Whitney prompts the belief that I can improve with Bri. Maybe I can be more like Pierce or Graham, but do I want to be? Would she still want me without my threats, our banter, and the daggers dragging over her soft skin?

Jorddan's eyes shift, the black even darker than I've ever seen before. A wave works through the room, his essence billowing out around us with a violent wave. He then centers his palm on each of their chests.

Kaia's ragged breathing fills the room, Kormoran grabbing her hand and squeezing it tightly. Their already fair skin turns ghostly white as they hold each other tighter. Grips so tight the bones could snap.

Kormoran grits his teeth, a single tear slipping down Kaia's cheek before her blood-curdling scream fills the room.

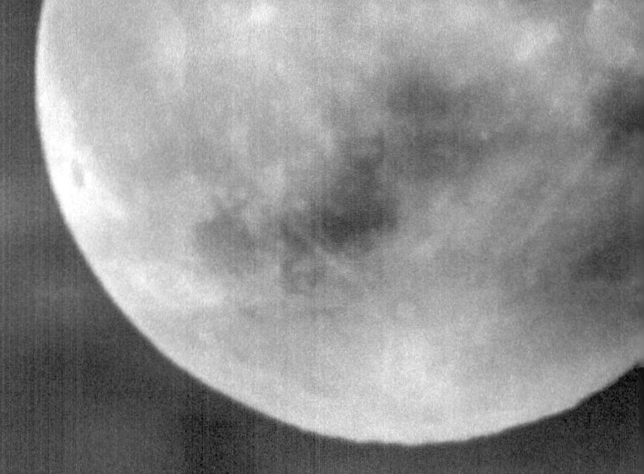

74

Bryony

I'm not sure what I'm seeing?

Is he cleaving himself from them or just igniting their bodies with the worst kind of pain? I wish I knew. I wish I understood.

Part of me even wishes I cared enough to stop it. Since Roman's attack, it's as if pieces of my humanity have been crumbling away. My former empathy transformed into a sharp edge that strikes before inquiring about answers.

I've become this detached person who can simply watch the consequences of one's actions without so much as flinching. There's not an ounce of reaction as my father punishes two of his own, not from him or from me.

What have I become?

As Kaia's scream tears through my room, Whitney sobs into Sean's chest while he presses his palms against her ears, and Camilla covers her own. I'm aware of everyone's responses as I clock their micro-movements or extreme flinches, but my eyes never shift away from the twins' tattoos. I'm mesmerized as they wave and ignite with color against their pale olive skin.

The letters move as a unit. Undulating in an urgent wave as the black magic-infused ink glows an iridescent onyx. The musky but refined sensation of ancient power moves through me, my tattoo tingling just over my heart.

I can feel it. All of it. Every bit of torment he casts on them plays inside me. Horrible pain that would bring me to my knees, but somehow isn't affecting me the same. It's like a shadowy imitation experiencing their anguish.

Gods, their suffering is worse compared to the punishment my mind could create. It's all-consuming and endless.

Valen frequently reminds me that there are things worse than death. This is. This would leave me on my knees, kissing my tormentors' boots, pleading for the mercy of death.

When we took on my father's name, his essence became infused with our tissues. Every delicate structure now tears itself apart from the inside, punishing them for dishonoring the bond he gave them. The oath they took has been broken, but the bond will remain.

The connection will not be as it was before. This is a new configuration. Painful and bruising. A constant reminder of what Kaia's betrayal felt like to Jorddan.

It's unclear how I know exactly what's happening. I feel his intent and their pain. My essence waving as if ready to take over should my father give us the go-ahead.

It's inside me. My essence pleading to add to the torment they will live with for life.

I suspect Jorddan could bring this to an end with a snap of his fingers. He could undo the curse he's placed on them. Remove the pain, which will serve as a reminder of Kaia's betrayal. Could, but won't.

He is not a man of second chances. A trait I admire. He's taught me what being too forgiving can do. He reminded me of how much harm that can cause. I don't foresee myself becoming quite as cold as him, but no longer the invertebrate Roman raised me to be either.

It's as if the minutes stretch into years, Kaia's screams and Kormoran's grunts filling the space until they don't. Until they are quiet, their chests heaving.

"I have shown you a mercy today," Jorddan deadpans, straightening his sports coat. "Keep my daughter out of your thoughts, and you shall only feel this low-level pain. That infuriating ache that persists until it drives you mad." In my mind, my father has constantly reminded me of a fairytale villain. That voice. The dark hair and goatee. The dark clothing and the way he speaks. It oozes from him. "So it would be best if you thought only of my darling daughter in the brightest of lights. Should one more threat pass your lips or any of our plans find their way to the ears of that scum, I will not hesitate to kill you. Are we clear?"

I've never seen Kaia show humility. There's no remorse or apology within her, but now her eyes lower to the floor, her lips rolling, forcing the single dimple in her left upper cheek to pop.

When her eyes meet my father's again, they're different. "I'm sorry I disappointed you."

"Sean," Jorddan calls him forward. "Extract."

Waves of glittery blue tendrils seep from Kaia and Kormoran's temples. The two scrunching their features against the intrusion, yet the room stays silent.

We watch.

We wait.

Knox's hand finds the back of my neck, his fingers pressing against the knots that have formed from holding my muscles tense all night. I involuntarily lean into his touch, letting it draw the poison and worry from my bones.

Once Sean is done, we'll know what Kaia has been hiding. We'll know how deep her betrayal runs.

The thought causes the knots in my stomach to tighten. Unforgiving and twisting ropes that leave me wanting to whimper in pain. How much more danger will we face because Kaia may have told our secrets?

I hope she didn't. I hope that despite her hatred of me, her loyalty to my father kept her lips shut tight.

My heart softens a fraction. She's not the only one who fell for the enemy. Valen is proof of how easily that can happen. The heart and soul will draw whatever attachments they want.

In this instance, Kaia's dishonesty has affected more than just her. Her actions impact us all, and we're the ones left to elbow through the consequences. My family is on the line because she made a choice—a selfish one.

The worst part is that, with those choices, she failed to pick a side. She has been riding the fine line between them and us, dipping her toe in one territory or the other as it suited her interests. A line once uncrossed cannot be recrossed. Contamination happens the moment someone breaches that border.

The consequences of your actions then become your new trajectory. Those repercussions remain part of your existence. The wounds and scars linger, festering until the day you die.

The lines of memories between Sean and the twins continue to flow freely. Sean's body remains stiff as if possessed by some spirit he can't fight against. His body spasms and twitches uncontrollably.

Whitney's whimpers fill the room, her arms looping around his middle, careful to avoid those two connections.

"Hmm," my father hums when Sean's body stops convulsing under her touch. He remains stiff, eyes still rolled back, but there's a calmness as he continues to extract everything he needs from them.

The trio collapses to the floor within minutes. Their limbs tangled as their chests rise and fall in exaggerated pumps. *Not dead then.*

The twins rub their temples awkwardly, climbing back to their feet while Whitney and Collin help Sean back to his.

"Tell us," my father commands.

"Kormoran is completely innocent, other than knowing his sister fell in love with Danvers. He's spilled none of our secrets, nor has he compromised his loyalty."

Kormoran's eyes meet Jorddan's, but my father barely acknowledges him. "Continue," he prompts.

"Kaia hasn't shared any of our secrets either. She has fallen for Danvers and knows the many faces he wears. She knows his secrets, but once she slept with him, she was never going to give him up to us."

"And what plans do we need to be aware of?" Jorddan questions, folding his hands in front of him.

Sean swallows loudly, the room thick with the sourness of sweaty skin and anxious thoughts. "Roman sold her for use to the Council."

"Sold me?" I question.

"Yes."

"For what?"

Kaia's eyes meet mine, this time without an ounce of disdain. "You should run."

75

BRYONY

Kaia's words echo in my mind as I stare at her. The room melts away. Everything from the bodies and their warmth to the mess on my desk. To the rumpled pillows at the head of my bed and the tumbler on my nightstand. It all just fades away.

"You should run."

No.

Not anymore.

I am the light.

I am the dark.

You are Grisym, my essence hisses.

I have spent my years hiding. I have spent the past few months running.

I am the blanket of gray.

I am the only thing standing between them and destruction.

There will be no more running.

No more hiding.

"No, Kaia." My shoulders square before the woman who disgraced her bond to my father. "You should."

76

BRYONY

My first Red Moon Ball had been fantastic.

That evening inspired belief in fresh starts that included friendship, dancing, and amusement. It was all there at my fingertips if I was willing to grab hold. And I did. I latched onto it all. The regal attire and glittering diamonds. The man who ravaged me in a historical library. It was perfect.

Memories of Pierce's hands and mouth on me draw heat into my body. My core is clenching and pulsing, hoping for more of that tonight, craving anything to release the muscles coiled tight in my shoulders and back. A night of fun and fucking under the Red Moon would be the perfect nightcap.

I've been here on this balcony a while, the crimson jeweled A-line strapless gown flowing around me. The bodice cinches my waist as the immaculate detailing catches the light of the setting sun. This dress had fit me perfectly at the beginning of last semester. Between the stress and the running, my figure has slimmed. The curves are still there. My frame is still full; there's just more tone to it.

I'd been trying on the dress this morning, ready to experiment with hairstyles, only for the damn thing to nearly fall to my ankles. Whitney had to alter it with a reformation spell for me so that I didn't flash everyone my tits tonight.

With a gentle nudge, I prompted everyone toward the grand ballroom, fabricating an explanation about a summons to the headmaster's office. I'd waved them off with a forced chuckle. *"I'm sure it's just my dad laying down the law again. Go. I'll see you in a few."* My guys questioned it, but I held firm, throwing in some made-up order from my father for good measure.

We haven't seen the twins since last night. I assume they returned to Beauxgraton, but none of us is sure, and I refuse to ask my father to locate them. We can only thank the gods above that he didn't kill them both last night.

Perhaps a Kaia-less existence would be enjoyable, I shrug to no one, telling myself not to grin at the thought. What I mind, though, is pointless bloodshed. She could disappear, but I don't want her dead. I don't want that on my conscience.

Though Kormoran is a fucking ass to anyone but his sister, I wanted my father to free him of his torment. He'd omitted information, but there was no actual harm that came from it. He'd remained loyal to us. To the cause. To the future only my father can see.

A soft breeze blows my loose curls off my face, the warmer air brushing my shoulders. London is such a beautiful place. A place that has quickly become home.

I've thought about staying countless times now. The grapple between the pros and cons always leaves me in the same place. *You're damned if you do, damned if you don't.* I've tried to ignore the pang that settles in my chest, considering not returning to Beauxgraton. Though it's responsible for how far I've come, it's not a place I chose for myself. But London is.

Glancing down at my watch, I've been gone long enough. It's only a matter of time before the guys come searching for me. Worse, they may call my father. Now is not the time for me to disappear, just so I can have a moment alone with my thoughts. I cannot indulge in such selfishness.

Kaia warned me I should run, but I won't. I'm tired of hiding. Tired of running. Tired of pretending.

And in a moment of clarity, I'd given her the same warning. Perhaps she and her brother took that as their clean break from the New Order.

Whatever is coming for me, I'll face.

With one more deep breath, I turn my back on the outside world. Chin held high and shoulders back, my heels click over the stone floors as I make my way to my friends. The hallways of history on either side of me remind me that there's more story to write. There's more to the pictures than the moments captured in the frames and the decor mounted on the walls. We are the future.

Every corridor is empty, filled with music instead of bodies. My shoulders shimmying the closer I draw to the ball. Happiness and excitement bloom in my chest; my heart is convinced tonight will be yet another occasion we'll never forget.

Everyone is down in the main hall, light and dark wielders alike. Similar to Beauxgraton, they've blended the dress traditions; here, if you wear white, black, or red from either side, you are dressed appropriately—gowns for the women and tuxedos for the men.

I'd seen so many with dresses of mixed colors. Skirts the color of crimson or black with crystalline details. The men in their white and black tuxes with red bow ties are a most delicious view.

Witnessing my father's vision is beautiful. There's only acceptance. A blending of the sides. A united community.

However, I'm not delusional enough to believe that everyone here possesses that open mindset. No group of people ever completely sees eye to eye. Disagreements and exceptions will exist on both sides. But peace and equality can exist if we let them. The ball before me is proof.

Blaring music grows louder as I descend the main staircase, the amplified bass thrumming through my chest. The grand ballroom's ground floor rests on the main level, similar to Beauxgraton. However, here there's a second story with a mezzanine.

I enter via the second level, tables lining the edge with wielders and food and drinks.

Below, a massive dance floor takes up most of the space. Graham and our group of friends from school have stolen the center, dancing away. Even Sean has joined them, his hands on Whitney's hips as they move to the beat.

This feels like my first Red Moon ball. Surely a good omen for what's coming for the remainder of the evening. Our moment to breathe and enjoy the people we love.

"If you ever feel like walking down those steps, I'd love to dance with you." Pierce's voice fills my ear, making me jump before he kisses my bare shoulder. His chuckle only drawing the narrowing of my eyes as I glance back at him.

Heat settles in my lower belly as the memories of our first kiss assault me. The confident pressure of his lips and hands in my hair as he held me against those cold stones are alive in my mind. It wasn't long after that his face was buried between my thighs, his tongue flicking over my soaked flesh before sinking inside me.

My panties are wet, eager to recreate the moment.

Later, Bri. Get a grip.

Gazing up at Pierce's handsome face, he's so at ease. Happy even. When was the last time he smiled so freely? When was the last time we all lived?

It could all collapse tonight, though I doubt it. The presumption rests on shaky ground. Only a gut feeling, which hasn't led me astray for some time, guides me.

This evening is about tradition, revered even amongst the most despicable light wielders. Tradition is one value every wielder clings to like a life jacket.

Extending my hand to him, he takes it, kissing my knuckles. But then he releases me, bending low to scoop up the train of my dress. "Hang on to my arm. I don't want you to trip."

Holy fuck does my heart explode. Pierce cared for me with a tenderness no one has ever matched, despite the gesture being so small. Valen and their friends may have called him weak, but there's a quiet strength to him. One that speaks volumes more than he can imagine.

He leads us to our friends, the group welcoming us with a round of cheers. Graham's warm palms find my already flushed cheeks, his lips pressing a long kiss to mine. They taste of salt and liquor. A delicious combination.

"What was that for?" I giggle.

"Because I missed you." Graham takes my hand, spinning me into the center of the circle, Pierce joining in as we all swivel side to side, singing every word of the eighties song booming through the space.

Time seems to pass at a dull roar; the sweat turns our skin sticky, and our throats are sore from laughing and yelling over the music. Our men keep our glasses full and our circle of ladies guarded from those looking to dance with anyone.

It took a while, but we finally found Valen slumped at the bar and dragged him out there with us. He'd been reluctant, barely moving, when we shoved him into the circle. My essence called to my fingers, enchanting him to move along with me, which actually made him crack half a smile.

Fanning my face, a slower beat finally filters through the room.

Following the guys off the floor, leaving Camilla, Mailee, Whitney, and Sean out there, I'm desperate to take off these stilettos. Letting loose a tendril of essence, it swirls around my feet, cooling them. The chill soothes the ache before a finger taps my shoulder. "Dance with me."

The voice sounds familiar to my foggy mind. But when I spin around, the face isn't one I know. I've never seen this man before, but I could have met him anywhere. He could be anyone.

Here in London, it's easier to forget I am supposed to be the daughter of a prominent figure. At Beauxgraton, it was the salacious whisper on everyone's lips. But not here. Here, I am just another student. Not a single classmate has brought up my lineage with me directly—a small mercy.

I've seen so many faces over the years. Some I remember. Many, I don't.

They never seem to forget me, though. It doesn't matter what age they met me or how my appearance may have changed since then. They recognize my face, and their smiles widen, as though they've perpetually been part of my existence.

"Sure," I smile, slipping out of my shoes and handing them to Pierce.

"Keep your hands to yourself..." Valen growls, his eyes raking down the man's form before returning to his face. "If you want to keep them."

"Valen," I run my hand along his short beard before curling my fingers around his chin so his eyes meet mine. "Behave, baby. It's okay." My voice oozes confidence, even though I don't quite feel it. The slight purr to my words, as if I were some sort of vixen, is nothing more than a show.

I'm not scared, per se, but we've been on high alert for anyone who has approached us, even Jade. Thus far, suspicion of these unfamiliar individuals proves unwarranted. Many have known me because of Roman, and others, Valen, because of his father. No one has hinted at knowing the truth of the lives we've been living for the past six months. They're nothing more than meaningless blasts from the past.

Following the man to the dance floor, I can't help but analyze the way he moves. Broad shoulders, narrow waist, long, powerful legs, thick with muscle. He moves like a predator on the prowl. He's clearly a light wielder with his sandy-colored hair. A shade that's a near match for Roman and my half-siblings. Eyes of clear blue water catch mine when he turns to face me again, smiling widely, extending a hand to me. I take it, placing my other hand on his upper arm. The space between our bodies is cavernous. A necessity to keep Valen from storming over here.

The current ballad shifts into another, this stranger pressing his fingers into my lower back, pulling me closer. My gasp is unavoidable when I almost lose my balance, stumbling into his chest. My pulse quickens as I peer up at his face, studying his eyes locked on mine. There's nothing there. Not a single emotion at all.

Shifting my gaze, I keep it level, knowing we're turning and soon I'll catch sight of my guys.

As if none of them are willing to sit, they stand at the edge of the dance floor, my red jeweled heels still hanging from Pierce's fingers while Valen twirls daggers at his sides.

Warm breath breezes over the shell of my ear, the stranger's face lowering. "I hear you've been looking for me."

My body flinches away at his words, the adrenaline of my fight-or-flight response shooting through my veins. His hold only tightens, bringing our fronts flush. My stomach is rolling at having another man so close to me. "Let me go."

His tongue clicks, *tsk, tsk, tsk*. "I can't do that. It's been a long time. You were barely a teenager back then."

"William, let. Me. Go," I grit, while fighting to keep my features neutral.

"Tell me, Bryony, has it been frustrating trying to find me in a crowd? Trying to decide which student I was the whole time?" A devious chuckle sounds in my ear, his lips so close they brush the shell.

My head jerks back, searching his features for any bit of familiarity. I've never seen him before. This man could be anyone. But then I watch as his features shift. Within seconds, his features transform into the William Danvers I once knew. Then, Carter James. Then so many others I've seen since I've been here.

I'd been suspicious he was Carter, but now I'm sure. William has been ingratiating himself into our lives every day. Wearing the many faces of our classmates as if it's nothing. Just a fresh change of appearance to start the day.

"Why did you give my father his position as director of education? What did you have to gain?" I ask, cocking my chin higher, my nails digging into his biceps.

He smiles widely, flashing teeth that are large and white. Too white. Too unnatural. "This," he waves a hand out to the side. "Power. He became director, so I could work for him inside our schools to... make changes as he sees fit."

"What does that even mean?" Confusion bleeds into my tone, as frustration burns inside me.

"Not every death is a magical accident," he whispers, that wolfish grin sending a shiver down my spine. "Some are on purpose." The lilt of his words almost sounds sweet. So coated in sugar, it takes me a moment to grasp their meaning.

My stomach drops.

"You've been killing Grisyms."

"Not all of them, we've kept a few," he winks. "Maybe we'll keep you, too."

77

BRYONY

EVERY BREATH BURNS LIKE the fire of a million suns in my lungs. The fight for survival is imminent as William licks his lips, grinning down at me. Those long fingers still dig into my lower back, pressing so hard they'll bruise.

Memories of the years I would accompany my father to the wielding institutions filter to the forefront of my mind. There were a number of reasons he might visit a school, but post-student deaths are the occasions I remember the most. My heart broke knowing we'd lost another young wielder in an accident. There isn't a single instance I can recall of my father not traveling for those losses. It was always "good practice" or "protocol" according to him.

Those were the visits when I was under no circumstances allowed in his meetings. He wouldn't even bring me to the offices with him and ordered me to sit outside. I'd be sent on an adventure on the school grounds: a scavenger hunt or a tour given by a staff member whom he trusted, while I waited.

No conversation ever reached my ears beyond those office doors. Those talks weren't intended for children. Specifically, not meant for me. I would have discovered what Roman was then. That would have been unacceptable.

I would've done anything to see the pride shining in Roman's blue eyes. Obedience was a driving force for me until I left home. I never desired to act contrary to his wishes, for fear of losing his acceptance. I was so desperate for the unconditional love that was anything but.

I wish I had been disobedient, pressing my ear to the cool wood, hoping to catch a confession. The spells were there in my head. My essence could have performed them. But I obeyed because Daddy's love and acceptance meant everything.

There was no reason to suspect anything about those meetings. Being Roman's daughter didn't make me privy to his conversations. Sure, there were certain privileges, but his business matters weren't among them.

The image I had of Roman continues to shatter. Not that there was much positivity left to cling to regarding him. His character and how he had changed toward me were enough. Knowing the truth of those deaths now obliterates any fondness that might have lingered. Roman didn't give a fuck about those people. As Harley always claimed, my kind was always something to be eliminated.

Initially, I wavered on the matter of Roman's fate. He still raised me. He still took care of me, even if the motivation wasn't noble. Death is so final. There's no reversing it. I'm no longer conflicted, not after this. Let the asshole burn.

I want his blood soaking into my clothes and his heart in my hands, still beating outside his body. A shiver works through me at my violent thoughts. Thoughts I used to shake free, but now I embrace them. I let them flow through me and take shape, so my essence learns the image. Then, should I choose to bring them to life, we can strike with as little as a single thought.

"Thank you for the dance," I step out of William's hold.

"Not so fast, Bryony." Cool fingers wrap around my wrist, my gaze tracking down to where he holds me.

"William, I don't care who you think you are. I don't care if you can shift or if you have my father's protection. You heard what will happen if you don't let me go." I snatch my arm away, the pleasant woman I'd been washing away as if a tsunami had struck.

"Put that fucking smile back on your face," he growls, leaning in close. "Or the next dead bodies we hear about at an institution will be the professor you're fucking and your father. Maybe even your brother. It was so fun wearing his face."

I draw back as if slapped, my eyes searching his face, and I see it. That same dead stare lived behind fake Vincent's eyes last night, but I let a wolfish grin spread across my face instead of cowering. "Well then, if you know who my father, my brother, and I are, then you know you don't have the power to kill us."

Something shifts behind William's stare, his jaw working. One moment of vulnerability is all I require to allow a single command to flit through my mind. *Kneel.*

His knees hit the floor, the crack of bone on solid wood tugging the corner of my mouth up in the slightest. "That's what I thought. Come to me," I coo.

A sliver of his essence streams past his parted lips, a shade of frost that dances as if this were some whimsical moment. Holding out my palm, it settles, stretching and poking at the barrier of my skin.

"What are you doing?" he growls.

"Stand." In a single jerky motion, he's back on his feet, but I hold him where he is. "I thought you knew what I am." His magic dances around my fingers, my essence eager to take him in.

"I—" his words stop abruptly as he watches me absorb his essence.

"Let me be clear, William. I won't kill you because I'm not in the mood tonight, but now you are part of me."

"What do you mean, part of you?"

"Oh, so you don't know who you fucked with?" I cackle softly. *Come close.* "I have one word for you. Eistiab."

His gasp is louder than I would have expected. The music does nothing to hide his reaction when our faces are so close. "You're lying."

I only shrug. "You just watched me take your essence. Do you need further demonstration?" He only stares, so I dig within me, searching for the piece of him, allowing my essence to become what he can do. Like when my eyes change, I feel my features shift, pinching and stretching and shrinking until he can see his own face staring back at him. His actual face. "See." Then I will it away, my smile stretching wider. "If I find out you've murdered another of my kind, our next encounter won't be this pleasant. After all, your gift isn't the only one I've stolen."

William stands there staring after me as I beeline for my guys. Our group of friends is close by, gathered with Knox on the outskirts. Their attempt to remain engaged with another professor's ramblings about the importance of mixed education fails when they spot me marching their way.

"What was that?" Camilla whisper-yells as I reach them.

"That was William Danvers. He's been impersonating different students the whole time. That's why we couldn't find him. I need all of you to stay here, except you four." I point out my four men.

"What are you going to do?" Collin questions.

"Nothing. I just need you all to stay here. It's safer that way. Please, just... stay here." They all nod, concern flashing in their eyes.

Pierce once again bundles my dress, still holding my shoes, moving to my side. The others fan out behind us as if blocking me from any danger. I appreciate them and all they do. Their presence allows me to lie to myself. Just false beliefs that no one can see the emotions splashed across my face.

No one says a word as we ascend the stairs to the second-story mezzanine and then disappear through the double doors held open and trimmed in blood-red flowers. My men follow me toward the hallway of balconies as I lead us to the exact spot I'd lingered before the ball. A place I often visit to find solace and quiet.

I can already feel my body rebelling, sharp jolts jabbing me in the stomach with every step I take forward.

"Bri, we can't do this here," Knox hisses.

"I'm fine. I can hold it." The words easily pass my lips, though I don't believe them. My body revolts more severely when I accept light gifts. Our suspicion revolves around the fact that Jorddan's dark bloodlines are stronger. The magic is more potent.

We cannot be sure why I react the way I do. Tosch hasn't been able to solve the conundrum that I am, and it unsettles us all. Bryony Guthrie remains a mystery. An unknown. The ultimate threat.

Understanding what I am, coupled with my abilities, is equally pressing as eliminating our opposition. Prior to knowing my father, I believed tranquility held more merit than teaching lessons. I now grasp the truth. Peace isn't mine to cuddle with at night. That's not a luxury I'll be able to afford anytime soon. These wielders aren't changing. They will not put their prejudices aside.

It becomes a justice scale always out of balance. Are our lives worth theirs? Is the elimination of a handful of wielders who only care for power worth the weight our consciences will carry? The blood that will always coat our hands and live in our hearts won't disappear, no matter our justification.

"Bri!" Knox barks my name.

I'm barely stumbling onto the balcony, struggling to keep control, my body convulsing as I fight to keep my essence trapped behind my tightly pressed lips. The swipe of my hand forces the doors to slam with enough force that I swear the concrete balcony floor quakes beneath our feet. Each is a slab of heavy wood adorned with intricate metal weavings of swirls and abstract patterns, reminiscent of the appearance of our essences.

Turning my back to the ledge, I lean hard on it, gagging against the magic pounding to get out. My essence beats at the seam, my hands barely gripping the back of Knox's head, pulling his mouth to mine before it breaks free. Our essences mix between our mouths, as he does his best to suck as much of us down as he can.

My vessel. My safe place when my magic goes wrong.

He deepens the kiss, devouring my mouth, inhaling us both.

I hadn't brought them out here for anything but a private place to speak and think, but as my body rages, I know it won't settle without taking Knox inside me.

My fingers fumble with his belt buckle, barely popping the button on his tux pants open and releasing his zipper before my essence bursts free of my fingertips. Our usual vortex surrounds us, Valen cursing as his and Pierce's essences release, too, caging us in, shielding us from the outside world so they don't see the debauchery.

Anyone looking up would get a scene they weren't prepared for. Me fucking Knox, while my essence rages, too many shades darker than what I pretend to be. It's storm ripping and roaring uncontrollably until my man pulls an orgasm out of me. The exact shit I cannot allow anyone to witness.

Knox's hands bundle up my dress, Graham spewing an endless stream of curses as if unsure what the hell is happening.

In seconds, my feet are off the floor, my body levitating as our essences hold me high. Knox's fingers are icy as they shift my thong aside, only to slip those fingers inside me first. He works them fast, swiping and curling inside my soaked core, my walls fluttering as heat licks up my spine. My mouth falls open, moaning loudly, riding his fingers, hungry for his cock to replace them.

"Bri, I need you to control it. Calm down," he grits.

"I... can't."

My head falls back, more of my essence pouring out of me as Pierce and Valen fight to keep it behind the wall they've built. The power coursing out of my dark lover caresses my skin, reminding me it will protect. Valen hadn't offloaded what he had siphoned last night. It's the kiss of a Nigeros, but not mine. The signature is slightly different. Still, I crave it. It's rawer. Darker. Pure.

"Knox," I breathe as his fingers move inside me, curling to hit the spot that makes my body writhe beneath him. My whole being lights up, more of my essence pouring free. Its massive fists bang against the wall my guys built. It wants out. *They shouldn't try to cage someone like us*, it hisses.

"Shhh, just focus on me. Focus on controlling your power. You can do it," Knox grits through clenched teeth.

His voice is a soothing song, but the way his fingers move inside me riles me up.

We wanted this. We needed this. We always do.

"More," I moan. "Please. More."

His fingers retreat before he grabs behind my thighs. Our essences still hold me up, but he grips me hard as if afraid to let me go. Reaching between us, I run my fingers through my arousal, coating them before I grab hold of his shaft. I paint him in me, notching him at my entrance. "No mercy," I whisper before he slams home.

A guttural scream bursts from me as the storm finally settles, and Knox retreats only to drive forward with enough force that the stone at my back cracks.

My hands fumble to hold on to him, my nails digging into his arm and the rear of his neck as he sets a punishing pace. Each pump of his hips settles my essence while heating my insides. A dichotomy I've never questioned but only embraced, drinking it down like the water I need to survive.

"Yes. There. Just like that," I moan, biting into my lower lip, my body finally done expelling my essence. That beautiful pewter surrounds us as I moan and Knox grunts.

I can feel the guys run their fingers through the combination of us. They've never witnessed the storm's center. It's the peace that follows with that soft caress of ecstasy along your skin that they know.

"Let go, Bri. Let. Go," Knox orders, and I do.

My belly tightens, walls clenching him tight. My body unravels around him, my release barreling through me like a freight train. But I hold on tight. Keeping his body against mine as he continues to move inside me. He shows no signs of stopping, but I want his release too. I need to feel him come undone.

Whispering in his ear, his body melts against me. "Thank you. I love you."

He fills me seconds later. Those last three uneven thrusts remind me he is mine. Divine intervention linked our destinies, but we still choose one another.

With an open kiss to the side of my throat, he finally stops moving, my body still held in the air. "I'm keeping you, so you'll keep every drop."

78

Pierson

My body won't stop shaking, a low-level, consistent vibration working through my bones relentlessly. The adrenaline spike is making my pulse bound at my throat and wrist, making it hard to take in precious air.

With every deep breath we're gifted, we're struck in the gut with a new hit. There's no true peace. Not a single pinpoint of light at the end of the tunnel.

An imposter Vincent, Kaia's betrayal, this guy clearly threatening Bri, and now her magic rebelling in the open. Anyone could have seen her. They could have seen us.

We seem to always be on the verge of getting caught. Just a step from turning a corner that will lead to our downfall.

It's constantly something.

I'm tired.

It's too much some days, but it's the life we chose. *She* is the life we chose.

Still, there are times I contemplate whether I'd be here if not for my friendship with Valen. Bri believes our fates were bound. That there's nothing we could have done to avoid each other, regardless of the path. But do I?

It's a silent trek back to Bri's room, the hallways nearly empty. The ball will continue through the evening, concluding at dawn as the sun replaces our precious Red Moon. That's tradition.

Thank goodness she and Knox aren't still wearing those freaky white eyes. A match for the ghouls, I've continued to fuck out of necessity. After channeling from the earth a few months ago, their magic feels wrong to me. My body is taking longer than expected to acclimatize. The transfer of my specially curated objects is more unpredictable.

Integretew, fortunately, does not have restrictions on channeling from the earth, unlike Beauxgraton. It has allowed me to have more stable stores for class, while utilizing the raw ghoul power for other purposes.

Checking my phone, it's not even midnight. How the fuck can so much happen in a night without us tumbling into the next day?

The moment we're shut in Bri's room, Knox forms our soundproof barrier that glows a soft blue, and my frustration boils over.

"What the fuck was that, Bri?" I haven't lost my temper like this since the night I found out Valen threatened her. A time when we were still new. Before we were all hers and she was ours.

"You've seen me react that way before." She brushes past me, tossing herself onto her bed, falling onto her back. Her cleavage presses against the top edge of her gown. Her breasts threatening to spill free with just one more heavy breath.

"That's not what I'm talking about," I charge toward her. Valen's arm shoots out in front of me, keeping me from getting closer.

"You need to watch your fucking tone." Valen's voice is low, a violent threat glimmering in his dark eyes.

"Fuck off. You have some fucking nerve when you still think about killing your own girlfriend," I retort.

"Enough," Bri all but whispers.

"Upset, she prefers my daggers to your puppy-dog bullshit? Grow some fucking balls for once," Valen sneers in my face.

"I said enough!" I'd missed Bri moving to sit at the edge of the mattress, her fingers curling over the edge, head bowed. The room seems to shake beneath us, her essence dancing at her feet as sharp points. "If you two want to argue over stupid shit, get out. I have enough on my mind without you four at each other's throats."

"Why am I being included here?" Graham questions, with his hands held high. Always a fucking suck-up to her until she does something he disagrees with.

"I told you, it was all of you or none. Keep acting like children when nooses are tightening around our throats, and it will be none."

My heart drops. Every word from her lips was delivered with intent. With a warning, not just some empty threat. If I know Bri, I know she means what she says. If we become the wrong kind of distraction or get in the way, she won't hesitate to move on without us.

Clearing my throat, I take a step toward her, ready to apologize, but she holds up her hand, stopping me. "I'm not in the mood," she snaps.

"Tell us what Danvers said." Knox keeps his voice level, but he's barely hanging on to his composure by a thread. It's clear from the way his jaw muscles twitch and his darkening glare. Still, he sits across from her, waiting for her eyes to meet his.

"Since he became director of education, my father has been murdering and maybe capturing Grisyms. Danvers is his flunky. He has been shifting his appearance, walking into institutions, and taking or killing them. That's why he was on no one's radar until he came here. I'm guessing ISW has a higher Grisym population than most institutions since it's always opened its doors to everyone."

"Damn," Graham groans, shaking his head as he sinks onto the bed beside Knox. "How many?"

"I-I don't know," Bri shakes her head, her hands tangling in her lap. It's as if her profound sadness settles in my chest. I can feel it moving inside me, weeping for wielders she has never known. Wielders who are just like her. Killed for being nothing more than a product of their parents.

She didn't ask to be a Grisym, and neither did they. A sentiment I relate to. I never requested power born of the shadows, either. Only my prison isn't a death sentence.

Uncomfortable silence falls over the room. They've been murdering innocent wielders for years. How did they know? Most light and dark wielders who have sexual relationships don't stay together for the long term. There's no future. No chance of having that happy family. Their children would be illegal and murdered, and they could be too.

"There were so many times growing up that I traveled with Roman, I would hear him and my mom talking about another tragic, magical death, and the ways he intended to make schools safer. Ultimately, magic proved to be what it is. Accidents were inevitable, especially as we pushed the boundaries of nurturing young wielders and making them better. Stronger." She shakes her head in disbelief as she chews the inside of her lip. It's the first sign she's beating herself up for missing this all these years.

How could she have known? She grew up believing one thing, but only recently did she find out it was all wrong. A lie. An injustice.

"That doesn't matter now." Sliding in beside her, she melts into my hold, my fingers rubbing along her arm. Goosebumps rise beneath my lazy touch, causing her to nuzzle in closer. "What do you want to do about it?"

She releases a deep breath, catching each of our stares. "I'll talk to my dad."

"That's not what I asked you." I force her gaze to mine. We shielded her and followed protocol, yet what appears before me is someone ready to take control, making her own decisions. She never had the freedom to make her own choices. I'll be damned if we don't give her that now.

Sitting up, she inhales a deep breath. As she stands tall, calling her shoes to her, the ruby red heels land right side up. One foot and then the other, she steps into them, her eyes slow to rise from the floor to a spot of nothingness ahead.

That resolve is back—the hard edge she has been slowly developing. Her shoulders roll back as her confidence bubbles to the surface. A glimmer finding its way back into her uniquely gray and sage eyes.

There she is.

"We're going back to the ball. We're going to enjoy our friends and pretend as if nothing happened tonight. Tomorrow we hunt."

Bri marches past us, clearing Knox's barrier with a swipe of her arm. For as often as she loses control of her essence, it's amazing how easily she can do simple things. Without a second thought, she overrides another's spells or powers as if it's as easy as breathing. Maybe that's because we all live inside her now. It takes her no effort to become any wielder she wants to be.

I'm last in line when my phone vibrates in my pocket.

"What's wrong?" I breathe into the line.

The telephone I gave her should have been used only for emergencies. Even with it, she'd have to risk lowering the protection spells we have on her cell to use it.

"They raided every cell. I knew they were coming and escaped."

My heart stops beating. It literally ceases to pump blood through my body. *Fuck. Fuck. Fuck.*

"What's happening?" Bri turns to face me. "Pierce, what is going on? Who is that?"

My mouth opens and closes, but the words won't come. They ordered me not to tell her. We were all given assignments, and this was mine.

Bri snatches the phone from my hand, looking at the caller ID before bringing the device to her ear. "Who is this?"

"My baby," I hear Davora sigh, just before the phone falls to the floor.

"How?" Bri breathes. "Why?"

"Bryony, I'm sorry. I can't right now. I have to go."

Then I'm gone, off to find the one person my girl never thought she'd see again.

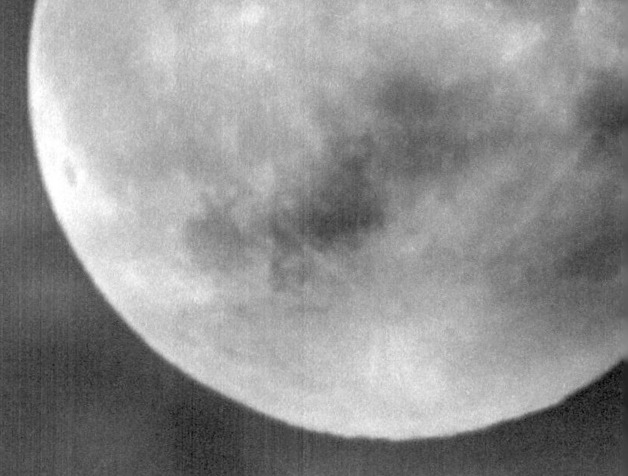

79

GRAHAM

The reset Bri ordered not even ten minutes ago faded away with that call to Pierce. His absence as we entered the grand ballroom is an unexpected burden. The weight of the world is stomping on my chest as my anxiety skyrockets.

No one here knows. They only see Bri's smile as she spots Camilla flailing on the dance floor. Valen's strut at our woman's side. Knox shaking hands with a former colleague, laughing loudly at some joke he finds no humor in. My finger flexes against Bri's hip, tightening my hold across the small of her back. Natural. Normal. A gesture any doting boyfriend would do.

They don't realize we're down by one. Or that our hearts are racing, wondering what trouble he's just run off to all alone.

Pierce bolted so fast that there was no chance for questions. Not a spare second of opportunity to plan.

All we could do was speculate as he warded the hall, keeping us from following for a solid fifteen minutes. There were no assurances as Bri fell to the floor, tucking her knees into her chest. Valen nor Knox had a clue why Pierce had been talking to Davora. Apart from Vincent and Jorddan, she should've received no communication from anyone.

It makes no sense.

Our friends crowd around us as we join them on the dance floor. Their stares are filled with silent questions and scrutiny. They can sense that something is amiss. How long before they ask where Pierce is? The lies and the truth are both nestled on the tips of our tongues, waiting to see which we'll choose.

They, too, do their best to act normal. Our crew stumbling over to the dessert table, their laughter unnaturally loud in my ears.

This is all wrong.

It's all so messed up.

Attempting to think of anything but our current hellscape, I allow my gaze to rake over the grand ballroom. My mind is getting lost in the culture and history that is the Integretew School of Wielding. It seems odd to be in school halfway across the world, but I'd be a liar if I said I didn't appreciate the forward-thinking approach to education here. It eliminates the need for competition, instead relying on collaboration, which fosters strength and understanding, elevating us all.

It has not erased my desire to be the best. They still grade us. Our techniques and abilities are constantly scrutinized and then criticized or praised. The desire to finish top of the class hasn't just melted away. If anything, it burns stronger. My education could be the pathway to change in our world. Instead of crooked wielders like Roman sitting in power, I could. That's my version of actual power.

Eyeing Bri, I fight those old feelings. The doubt of inferiority that crushed me when I first met her swirls at the base of my stomach. My girlfriend is still my toughest competition.

Determination courses through me. A steadfast resolve to suppress those prior insecurities. A decision made to stray from the path of bitterness, embracing the fact that Bri only makes me stronger. Work harder. Strive for more; reach for everything.

Not that it's been easy for any of us to focus on our studies this semester. The hits just keep on coming. Every gut punch is a fresh distraction we've left scrambling to recover from. The pull away from the life I'd known and envisioned is carrying me further out to sea. A distance that my parents are beginning to notice.

They still don't understand my choice to study abroad here. Nor my choice to become a professor of history. That career choice may shift with time. It's too soon to tell, but the seed has been planted. This year has taught me I can manage more "different" than I would have believed.

It's all Roman's doing, really. He showed us what abuse of power can do.

Education always seemed like the noblest field. Molding young intellectual minds, hoping to improve the future ahead. Perhaps that heartless dick harbored those sentiments once upon a time. When his intentions were genuine and he cared for someone other than himself. Maybe.

It's a "what if" I will probably never know the answer to. A reality I'm surprisingly content with.

Now, I'm unsure if educating young wielders is enough.

Those whom the elite deem unworthy inhabit a dark, horrible domain. They'll be oppressed, forgotten, beaten down, and bruised, and our ruling bodies won't care. In their minds, they are creating the existence we should be proud of. Innate light wielders will always sit on the throne; anyone else is a peasant.

We're in the middle of a war. This struggle against small-minded wielders will bury too many in the Cavea de Mors. The gravediggers will be working overtime to give our kind a resting place. Unless they lived on the opposing side, they'll be buried there in a show of appreciation for their sacrifice to the cause. The others will be sent to Hollimore in Prague and Vale da Morte in South America.

"Who wants to dance?" I ask.

I need to move. Sitting here at this table has me in my head. I'm overthinking, worrying about every potential detail, all of which I can do nothing about tonight. A debate rages within me: would I do anything differently?

It's the same debate I've had every day, knowing I wouldn't. These are the first friends who have made me feel accepted and like I am worth more than an image my parents curated for me and grades on paper.

I hold real value.

"Me!" Whitney's hands shoot up in the air, Mailee and Camilla both groaning in unison. If Whitney is getting out there, then she's dragging the girls along.

There's no point in waiting for her to drag them to their feet; we stand as one, a united front, shuffling out to the dance floor.

The DJ has an eclectic taste. Every genre blares through the speakers in a random pattern. It keeps everyone happy and the dance floor full.

A teenage dance anthem fills the speakers, every word shouted by all in attendance. A group of girls shimmies next to me, trying to draw my attention. Two blondes and one with honey brown hair. Their features hint at their light origins, but can I even be sure these days?

The taller blonde turns her back to me so her ass rubs against my side. My salute of a wave does nothing to warn her off. Bri doesn't need yet another reason to lose her shit tonight. Our Grisym is by far the most territorial woman I've ever met. You don't touch what's hers.

"You hang out with a lot of dark wielders," she smiles up at me. Shimmering pools of soft amber stare back at me, flooded with heat.

"I attend Beauxgraton, but I'm studying abroad here this semester. Makes sense that I would have dark-wielding friends." Every word is the truth. The sentences are purposely strung together to remain as vague as possible.

"Maybe." She spins around in a circle beside me. "But maybe not."

"Have fun tonight," I salute-wave again, signaling to our crew I'm leaving the dance floor.

Few occupy the bar as I lean against its edge. Solitude's tranquility soothes me until a male's deep baritone startles me, my elbow nearly slipping from the edge and landing me on my ass.

"What can I getcha?" The man wipes down the counter, his thick Irish accent catching my attention. Quickly casting my gaze down the length of the bar, he's the only soul present. Even the others who had been nursing their drinks when I first walked up have disappeared.

He hadn't been here earlier. It's been the same worker all night until now. Short with mocha skin and soft green eyes that seem to twinkle with silent jokes. The memory of the original bartender and Bri comparing their eye colors is vivid in my mind. The two cackling at nothing as it filled my heart with everything. That laugh is the reason for waking up in the morning. The reason I fight to be the best version of myself.

Ignoring the prickle down my spine, I tell myself they switched out. Standard practice for a twelve-hour-long celebration, right? With thousands of attendees tonight, the staff would need a break or backup. The booze and food never stop at these gatherings. We will party from seven o'clock sharp until sunrise.

"Old Fashioned, please."

The guy taps the bar, disappearing to do what he does best. My gaze tracks back to Bri, watching her and Camilla hold hands while whipping their heads side to side, cackling like a pair of fools. They look so happy.

"Why'd you run off?" The blonde slides up next to me. "Naomi," she holds out her hand. Her accent is slight, making it very hard to place.

"Graham." I shake her hand. My parents taught me to be a gentleman. The least I can do is suffer through this interaction with this woman, obviously trying to hit on me.

"You've been looking at her all night." She nods in Bri's direction. Her gaze rakes down the length of my woman's body, unimpressed.

"Well, she is my girlfriend."

Noami only snorts, snatching my drink from the counter before my fingers can wrap around the glass. She takes a sip, her throat bobbing with her smile. She's not shy about raking her gaze down my frame, rolling her shoulders side to side as if in invitation.

Before Bri, distractions from women were rare. And now, except for Bri, Camilla, and the few other female friends I've made, I don't even notice the others. My studies always came first. If I dated someone or slept with them, it was so superficial a connection that you could argue it wasn't one at all.

"Interesting choice," she cocks a brow, placing my drink in my hand, intentionally running her fingers over mine.

"Where do you go to school?" I ask.

"Just transferred to Erobus this semester. With no light schools left, we've been forced to mix with...them." She says *them* with such disdain, I almost want to wipe the grimace off her face.

"Then why attend a Red Moon Ball at a historically dark school if you don't like dark wielders?" I smirk. My fingers tighten around the glass, my grip so firm my hand shakes. The glass is only mere seconds from shattering in my palm as my essence stirs.

"We heard something big was going down tonight. A hit to the dark world, if you will. Figured it was here only to find out it's close by." She shrugs, pouting with disappointment. "I was going to invite you to find out what it might be with me tonight, but it seems you're already occupied."

"Something like what?" I question, taking a step back as the woman advances on me.

A wicked gleam flashes in her eyes. The amber darkening before flashing bright again. "Have you ever heard of Hendyre Reformatory?"

My brow lowers. Of course, I've heard of it. They keep some of the most dangerous wielders there. Not the criminals, as humans suspect. Instead, it's for those who have lost their minds to the magic and need to be detained. There's a version of one in every country.

Hendyre is the most famous because no one has ever escaped from its labyrinth.

"Yes," I swallow hard, already hyperaware that my body is responding poorly to the words the woman has yet to voice.

"Someone is being kept there. A woman the Bureau has been after."

"Okay..."

I'm not sure where she's going with this. It's not unusual for the Bureau or the Council to break people out of prisons or even mental institutions. It doesn't seem like anything worth traveling from Greece for.

"Supposedly, the Council got word that there are hordes of Grisyms being hidden around the world, and she knows where," Naomi giggles as if she's sharing the juiciest gossip. That coy grin flashes my way again, nausea causing me to gag at her continued advances.

And my blood runs cold.

Until now, I hadn't known where Pierce had run off to.

But now... now the air burns in my lungs. Our boy may have run straight into their trap.

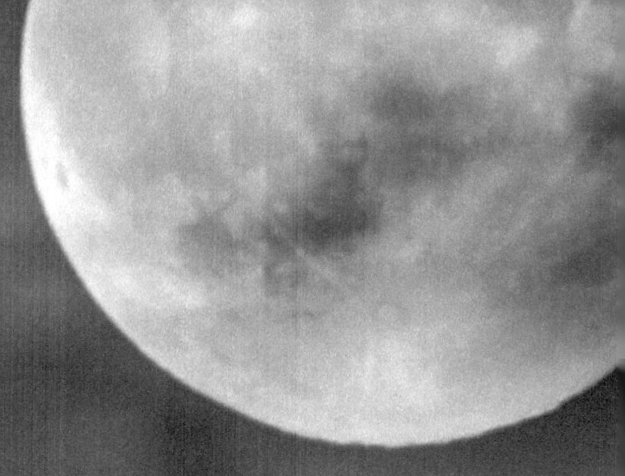

80

BRYONY

CHANGE CAN BE SOMETHING we embrace or run from. This year has been nothing but staggering spikes and dips from the baseline I'd always known. Some good. Some bad. Even more beyond categorization. There's been pain and laughter. Sadness and unimaginable joy. I've lost and found.

Missing a Red Moon sunrise and the peace it brings guts me. I don't recall ever missing that stunning sphere melt behind the horizon, shifting into the colors of a peaceful sunrise. That seamless blend from the harsh beauty of crimson to the pinks and soft robin egg blue has always been a reset. Like maybe the next cycle between then and the next Red Moon would be filled with endless possibilities. Ones that allowed me to embrace the Grisym.

This was a first I never expected to experience.

With Graham's return came our departure. The night was over. No more laughter. No more dancing. We split to our respective rooms, grabbing overnight bags before we all met back in my room, still dressed in our formal attire. Altering or removing the makeup consumed time we didn't have to waste.

Disregarding the rules or potential indoor portal failure, Camilla waved her petite hands through the air. We wasted no time running through it as a group instead of one by one. Camilla's fingers looped through mine as I tugged her through the portal behind me.

My body swayed as we exited the other side. Portals are like any other transport magic. Your body needs time to acclimate to the change in space and time. We hadn't given it a thought as we sprinted through, eager to reach the manor.

Our exit point is dead center in the foyer, every light shining bright as if welcoming me back home.

We'd worried tonight was a setup, but it turned out to be the best distraction.

My grandmother. They were hunting for my grandmother, but who told them where she was? There's only one reasonable explanation. We have a rat among us. Someone running their mouth and telling our secrets about her and the Grisyms my father has been harboring.

This is becoming a witch hunt.

The hours have passed at an agonizing pace. My body is refusing to calm, and my mind is racing with every possibility of what has gone wrong. With every glance at my watch, the vice around my heart tightens, or my stomach drops. Pierce and Grandma Avalon still aren't here.

My bodily reactions refuse to settle, no matter how much Vincent and my father tell me to calm down. They didn't see Pierce's face. They hadn't heard her voice.

"Bryony, sweetheart, please sit down. They are capable of taking care of themselves," my father urges.

"But what if they're not? We have no idea what that raid was like. There's nothing on the news or in our media outlets. It's like it didn't happen at all," I shout. "How could you keep this from me?"

My father's mouth twitches, his composure waning. He has always let me rant, but I'm not the only one on edge tonight. "Because I needed to keep her safe and Pierce needed someone to learn from."

"I don't even know what that last part means," I groan, running my fingers through my hair, every knot forcing me to tug, only to yank my fingers from the curly mop angrily. It's an infuriating process on repeat, only driving my raging emotions through the roof before I slump in defeat.

"Wynston," my father ignores me. "Please take the others back to Beauxgraton. Damian will return later. He's busy with Tosch."

I release a heavy breath, trying to calm myself enough to hug my friends. My father is right. They need to get back to school, hopefully, back to safety.

"Missy, you don't go doin' anything I'm gonna have to spank you for," Camilla warns. That same childish seriousness marks her face as I pull her in for a tight hug.

"I'm going to miss you, too. Thank you."

"Don't go findin' some other dirty-talking Southern belle to replace me." Another warning, but I catch the watery quality of her words. Camilla never had friends who accepted her for who she was. She may not believe it, but I always have. Even when she drove me crazy, I liked her that way.

My cheek rests on the top of her head. "Cammie, I could never. There's no replacing you."

We break from our embrace, my goodbyes much shorter with everyone else. Especially with the twins and Damian missing in action, it doesn't take long.

"I promise once the semester is over, we're all going on a much-needed beach vacation," I sniffle, trying to put on my best happy smile. But it never reaches my eyes. My nose only burns as I fight back tears.

Please *keep them safe.*

I have no idea who I am praying to—anyone who will listen, maybe.

My father only groans behind me, forcing the roll of my eyes.

Though Knox will be back, he steps forward, kissing my mouth hard. "Please stay out of trouble until I get back." The warmth of his forehead presses into mine, our eyes fluttering closed. "Please, Bri."

The crack in his voice nearly breaks my heart, my hands finding his chest. "I promise."

A promise I will do everything in my power not to break. Everyone in this room has done so much for me since we met. They've sacrificed their relationships, time, and lives for me. The least I can do is keep a simple promise.

We watch them leave in silence. There's nothing else to say as the portal swirls into nothing but thin air.

Slumping down onto the couch, I'm not sure how much time passes before my eyes drift shut. It was easier to let exhaustion win.

I shift awake only when a hand lands on my forearm, my eyes peeling open to weathered pale skin and the gold woven ring my grandmother always wore on her left middle finger.

"Hello, Bryony." My eyes meet hers, a sob breaking free as my hand cups my mouth.

It's just the two of us here in the parlor. My tears tumble freely down my cheeks. The sting of holding them in finally releases without everyone here to see me fall apart. But it's the smile of my favorite person in the world that grounds me. That makes me feel safe enough to let it all out. For sixty seconds, I don't have to be brave.

"Where have you been?"

"Safe." She runs her hand over my hair. "You don't wear it straight anymore." It's not a question. From the day I can remember, I'd always had my hair straightened. My mother insisted on it even when I was a toddler.

"Yeah. I like it better this way."

"Me too." Her fingers grip my chin, bringing my eyes back to meet hers. "You have grown up to be such an amazing woman. I worried that when I left you, that son of mine and your lousy brother would stifle who you were meant to be."

Her voice is exactly as I remember it. It's as if I'm a little girl again, and no time has passed.

"You know, they told me you died naturally for the longest time. They lied to me."

Her hands cup mine. I expect them to be cold, but they warm me from the outside in. "Bryony, I'm very sorry, but I did it to protect you. To protect your father."

"Roman is not my father. He never was." I hate that my words are nearly growled. My grandmother was always good to me. She doesn't deserve such disrespect, but I will not allow another person on this earth to call Roman my father.

"Sweetie, I mean Jorddan. You know I wanted him and your mother to be together, right?" She sighs longingly, her gaze drifting toward the windows at the far end of the room. The drapes parted just enough to catch a glimpse of the darkness beyond. "But," her eyes find mine once more. "Sometimes the grudges of men are hard to break."

"What do you mean?"

She sighs heavily, tugging my arm softly so my head falls into her lap. Just like she always used to, her fingers lightly brush over my hair.

"Roman and your mother were a business transaction, for lack of better terms. She was a promised gift to him for the betrayal between their fathers. Please don't ask me for the details. They're not important."

"They are to me," I argue.

"Your mother was already in love with Jorddan. The two met when she was fifteen. They were smitten. Soul mates, if those really existed. Though she'd been engaged to my son for years, she was still Jorddan's. He knew, and he hated it, but he was too busy climbing the political ranks to let what he called a fling detract from his desire for power. When she got pregnant with Vincent, he was furious, but again, he made no effort to stand between them. In public, she was his fiancée, and there was nothing to it."

My grandmother pauses, her fingers continuing to stroke my hair lightly. Gods, I've missed her.

"Well, when Geneva told Roman she wasn't coming back, he lost it. That's when they had the blood oath performed. Roman wasn't losing someone as powerful as your mother. Not to a dark wielder," my grandmother chuckles. "Jorddan knew the only way to protect your mother and Vincent was to ensure the oath could never be undone. He had the wielder killed, his memories stolen, and her body stashed somewhere he could never find it."

"He told me," I whisper.

"Then, your mother and Roman had your half-siblings. Roman was so thrilled with them and their abilities, along with his climb to director of education, that he hadn't noticed Geneva sneaking back to Jorddan. She could see them only a few times a year because of Vincent, but she found other ways to meet him. Then you came along. Geneva did nothing to hide that you weren't

Roman's. She even boasted that you were Jorddan's. For a year, the four of you lived as a happy family here in this manor. I did what I could to protect that, but with the blood oath, when Roman demanded she return to him and bring you along, there was nothing she could do. You were the prize he then presented to the world."

"He's been killing us. All this time," I say.

"I know. I think part of him loved you, but another part of him hated what your kind represented, too. You were always a chess piece to play, and so was I. It's why I killed myself. I safeguarded what I knew when it was clear no one was going to listen to me."

Another tear slips free, remembering the pain of losing my grandmother. I almost didn't survive it, and knowing she has been alive for years now, I know I couldn't bear to lose her again.

"I asked Dad if I could stay here after graduation." The words release quietly, averting my gaze, unsure how she'll respond. Unsure how I want her to respond.

"I'm glad. This has always been your home, sweet girl."

"Did you always know what I am?" I ask after a beat of silence.

"I did. You often tried to snatch my essence, but I never let you. It's not a curse I wanted you to have to live with."

"It's not a curse, Grandma."

"But it is. When you can see the future at will, the way I can, it means you hold every advantage in this life. Even those with the best intentions will use it for their own interests. It's dangerous."

I understand exactly what she's saying. She'd said so many times she would rather lose her ability than live another day with it.

"Grandma, I need to ask you something else." She nods. "You always talked about rogue ghouls. You said we'd see them more and more, and of course, that is true. There were tons of sightings after you passed. The statistics show that they've increased exponentially over the past decade. Why?" I'd almost forgotten about the sightings until now. We had too many other things to worry about.

But hearing the question leave my lips, I realize I knew the answer all along. I just didn't know how to interpret it.

She stares at me quizzically. "You haven't figured it out yet?"

I shake my head. "No. Maybe. Tell me why."

"Your soul was reckless. After you matured early, you felt it. The turmoil inside you."

I only nod. I had. It was easy to assume it was nothing more than the effects of maturing early. Inside, I was crying out for help to control my power. I was pleading for someone to save me from the magic that rolled inside me at a furious pace sometimes. "Yes," I breathe.

"Sweetheart, you called them."

I should have known.

81

BRYONY

For once, bright sunlight shines through the windows of my bedroom. Rolling to my side, tucking my hands under my cheek, my eyes flutter shut. The warmth washes over my cheeks. Warmth that reminds me of love and family.

My empty bed and silence are a welcome peace this morning. I can't remember the last time I slept alone. It's a constant revolution of bodies around me. There's minimal opportunity to sit in the quiet of a blank mind and just breathe.

My grandmother and I were up for hours talking, while I caught her up on life. She apologized for Pierce keeping her secret and told me how she had been working with him to "reroute" his gifts.

Though our magic has roots we can't disrupt, there are ways to build new systems off of them. To force your magic in a different direction, in a way.

I knew how much Pierce wished he had been born different. His desire to reside on the opposite end of the wielding spectrum is no secret. It breaks my heart that it's not something I can change for him. From the way Davora spoke about him, her kindness and inquisitive nature shining through, he must have told her, too. Perhaps sharing lessened his burden. Especially knowing the type of woman she was. Davora Avalon grabs hold of your hands, guiding you toward your desired destination, no questions asked.

Jorddan wanted someone to be a companion for her while we were in London. So many things pulled us in different directions with this war raging all around us, but he strove to give us all a constant when he could. My father is a perceptive man. He notices everything, including Pierce's struggle with the power he had to use. Naturally, my clairvoyant grandmother was the answer.

Grandma Avalon gushed about him. My cheeks flush with her compliments of his talent and respectful demeanor. *"He's my favorite,"* she shouldered me with a knowing grin.

"Of whom?" I'd squeaked.

"Your many boyfriends." Her wink had made me flush all over again. My heart raced as I told her how we met. Pierce was the first of my men to steal my heart.

There was no need to tell her. She'd seen it and heard Pierce's version of how he fell in love seemingly overnight. She declined to share whether happiness awaited us. That's how she'd always been. Despite my persistence, she directed me to focus on the present. To cling to those moments and commit them to memory. To breathe them in and make them home.

"Life is better lived when you don't know what to expect. When the answers are there, you wait with expectations that will inevitably let you down when they don't live up to the illusion you've built in your mind."

Rolling onto my back, something like hope fills my chest. I have my grandmother back, and for now, we're all safe. Knox confirmed it when he arrived just before we shuffled up to bed.

Our Integretew visitors will all be gone by the time we return to campus. The raid had been a failure. The Bureau troops sent in, returning home with their tails tucked between their legs.

For once, there are no overt threats on the horizon. Perhaps that's nothing more than an illusion, but for now, we'll accept it as such. We'll bask in the ignorance of our enemies.

Maybe we'll end this school year without fighting for our lives.

Slipping out of bed, I take a quick shower before shooting off a quick text to Tosch.

Me: *Will you be back today?*

There's no immediate response, so I dress in comfy sweats and a loose off-the-shoulder shirt to wander downstairs for some breakfast.

Laughter sounds from the dining room as I draw closer. Grandma Avalon leads the charge, telling stories of me as a child while the guys sit around the table digging into their plates.

There are several others here, too. Our New Order soldiers are gathered around the table like family. Eilish and Oscar are huddled and whispering to one another as my friend attempts to stifle her cackling laughter.

"Good afternoon, sweetheart," my grandmother coos, standing to pull me into a hug. "We tried to wake you, but you were gone like the wind."

I hold her close, inhaling her scent. It's the same perfume as when I was younger. Those irritating tears burn behind my eyes once again, reminding me of how much time we missed, but hoping the years we have left together will be even better.

She releases me, guiding me to my open seat. "Thanks for letting me sleep. There hasn't been much of that lately."

"Well, that's normal when you're shaggin' four blokes and ghouls," Eilish snickers, popping a piece of sausage into her mouth.

"Eilish," I groan. "Why?"

She shrugs, Oscar's face going pale. "We all know about it."

"Just the same, I would rather not talk about my sex life in front of my brother, father, grandmother, and professor." I bury my face in my hands. There's a lot I can become accustomed to. Freely talking about who I am sleeping with in front of my family may never be one of them.

"Fine. I won't say another word." She mimes sealing her lips with a key before giggling softly.

I only glare at her, knowing my new friend is so full of shit it makes my stomach hurt.

It's easy enough to fall into the conversation around the table. The topic quickly forgotten as we all fall back under Grandma Avalon's spell. Her storytelling is like listening to a ballad play. The elements are so fantastical you'd think they were lore, but every word is the absolute truth. Our truth. Mine and hers.

As many stories as she has of me, there are equal shares for Vincent. A boy she never quite said she knew personally, as we spoke last night. She speaks as if she saw him often. As if she had spent countless hours with him.

My lips part, encouraging me to voice my question. To ask for the specifics. The how, why, and when. But I hold back, rolling my lips into my mouth, attempting to hold the words in.

I feel like an intruder, prying into the life they shared. They'd have told me if they'd wanted to. Those memories are theirs to hold, not mine.

Still, jealousy swirls in my stomach. Grandma Avalon had always been mine. I never had to share her. Not even with my half-siblings. They thought she was a crazy old kook, too, so they avoided her. Even Merrick, who was kind to me.

I'm fascinated by the life she led. She revealed plenty during her youth, yet presently, as an adult, she offers complete transparency regarding her complicated history. I've felt every emotion flow through me as I listened to her words. Life seems richer now that I understand her better.

"Grandma, how would you know that?" I ask while she cackles over the first time Vincent accidentally brought a human back to life.

"I was there," she answers matter-of-factly. She reaches for Vincent, his smile spreading as she takes his hand.

"I hadn't really had a chance to have this conversation with you yet," Vincent places a hand on my shoulder. "But Grandma Avalon has been the only grandmother I've ever known. Our mother was always close to her, despite not wanting Roman. Your grandmother has been in my life since I was born."

Tears burn behind my eyes and nose. This family is so full of secrets. Although this one does not induce an instant desire to vanish into a black hole, their shared history simultaneously crushes my heart, then mends the broken pieces.

Vincent and I, due to Grandma Avalon's meddling, were often closer than I ever knew. Though Vincent benefited from additional years with her post-revival, I don't resent him for it. In contrast, I'm glad they had each other. Glad she wasn't brought back just to be alone.

"It makes me happy you had her," I whisper, pulling him into a side hug. It's the truth. Vincent also warrants the boundless love I experienced from the woman seated across from me.

"This may not be obvious to you, but my son is a disappointment," she pats my hand. "He was the only one I produced, so I needed something better to look forward to. Jorddan first filled that void, then Vincent came along, and of course, you. The people in this room are my family, regardless of blood."

A single tear slips free. "Fuck, I'm such an emotional mess lately," I let out a wet laugh. "Can we just talk about fun stuff?"

"Like that vacation you promised us?" Pierce chuckles from the other end of the table.

"We do have a few months to kill," I chuckle, popping a potato square into my mouth, the herbs melting on my tongue with the butter. Just the way I like them. My father nods my way with a crooked grin. "As much as I love the manor, I'm more than happy to lounge on a beach for a few weeks."

"I'm not sitting out on some sandy beach in the hot ass sun," Valen grunts, leaning back in his chair and crossing his arms.

"Then stay here I shrug. Graham, Pierce, Knox, and I will have the time of our lives. Maybe Tosch and Camilla, too."

"The hell you are..."

My grandmother's hand rises, her pointer angled toward the ceiling in warning. "I would advise you not to finish that statement right now." There's a glint in her eye. Valen was about to blurt out some filthy comment, and she saw it.

"I will take a vacation anywhere," Knox groans. "You young wielders wear me out."

Eilish coughs, Oscar rolling his eyes, knowing where her wayward thoughts went. She's like a teenage boy sometimes, but I love her all the more for it. There's never a dull moment. No holding back. Just pure, crude Eilish at all times.

"If the conditions are right, you're free to go where you choose," my father nods, before wiping his mouth and pushing away from the head of the table. "But if you'll excuse Davora and me, we have a few things we need to tend to."

My grandmother follows his lead, wiping her mouth, while Knox pulls out her chair and helps her stand. "Bryony, please stay until we are done with...business. I'd like to see you off before you return to school."

"Of course," I smile after her.

My reluctance to return only worsens with my grandmother's presence here. I want to live in this blissful bubble where nothing bad can touch us. Within the walls of this manor, we are safe. We can be happy and pretend that every demon hunting us isn't lurking just around the corner.

I'm so lost in the fantasy, I hadn't realized I'd moved to the large two-story floor-to-ceiling windows at the back end of the dining room.

The lake shimmers under the setting sun. In the distance, the tall grass dances softly.

Something shifts inside me, Knox's hand landing on the small of my back.

"I think someone is here to see you."

82

VALEN

Bri has been many things to me since we met. The enemy. A pain in my ass. Sexy as fuck. A ball buster. But never has she looked as beautiful as the moment Knox whispered that her beloved ghouls were here.

That instant where her light gleamed like the sun was worth every second. I'm a man who hates the sun as much as I loathe the light. Except when it's her. Bri is the only light this world needs. The only light I need.

He hadn't even confirmed they were on the property before I felt them.

I couldn't tear my gaze from the glimmer in her gray and green eyes. Or those fawn freckles that seem brighter against her warm tawny skin. But, fuck, that smile. That smile could bring a man to his knees and force his cock into the stiffest rod.

Her long curly hair is wild as she races through the field. Hair that I love to pull and twist around my fist. Curls that I twirl around my finger when I watch her sleep.

It takes everything in me to ignore the jiggle of her ass with her pounding steps. Those loose-fitting sweatpants do nothing to hide her curves. Even if they did, I know exactly what's underneath.

We all follow her, Knox on her heels, while the rest of us sprint behind her.

Curiosity drove Eilish and Oscar to their feet, the pair chasing behind us, too. Bri is an anomaly. No one has ever commanded ghouls or any other magical creature in our history. They are from earth magic. They are the second purest form of power. The pair weren't going to miss witnessing this firsthand.

Bri comes to a halt as her four ghouls stand in a line with several others at their backs. Outside of the Red Moon weekends, it's rare to see ghouls in broad daylight. The rogues often roam during the hours of darkness.

"Bryony, safe," Aziel growls, cupping his clawed hand behind her head and pulling her to him.

"I'm safe." Her palms find his stomach, her gaze locked with his. With a single blink, her eyes shift to that glowing milky white. In the past few months, she has learned she can change them at will. She's learned that there are two versions of the white she can mimic: the original version, where she retains her sight, and the enhanced version, where she adopts the ghouls' senses.

There's never been a creature as amazing as Bryony Guthrie, and I get to call her mine.

Bri pushes up on her toes, placing a kiss at the center of Aziel's chest before stepping out of his hold. She moves to the Nigeros next; her gaze finding mine before tracking back down to her. "Keres," she nods. Its dick only grows in response, but it says nothing in return.

She'd said Aziel is the only one who regularly speaks; its words are so much clearer than the first time I'd encountered it with her.

It's fucking insane witnessing what has happened between her and these creatures made to give us power. I've studied these creatures my whole life with my father. Bri allowed me to share updates with my father on her progress with them, including how the four align with our magical preferences. It didn't take a genius to understand why those three ghouls came to her. Our girl took our essences inside her, making her compatible with them. Yet, others have come too. Pure breeds and mixes my father and his colleagues are still working to classify. Bri taking us inside her has made her a match for these ghouls, but other varieties have come to her, too. Different breeds that match the other essences she's taken under her skin.

Yet, she has only named these four. Only fucked these four.

Bryony is their keeper. Their queen.

We watch as she repeats the process with Warrick and Tarak. Warrick running its forked tongue over her mouth before lifting her off the ground to bring their mouths together. "War, I've told you that's fucking gross. Stop licking me like that."

It grunts, places her back on her feet, and instead stretches its tongue long to run over her cheek.

"You're lucky you're one of my favorites," she points a finger at it, and I swear it smiles at her. Those sharp teeth glinting in the setting sun, the thin lips stretching wide.

"Fuck. That's..." Eilish gasps. The woman acts as if she's never been near those deadly teeth.

"You all can come closer," Bri flags Eilish and Oscar with a welcoming grin. We all move forward as a group, Graham tense as he comes within a few feet of Aziel. Despite his being with us when we sneak out here to fuck the ghouls, he keeps his distance. He has an ingrained fear because of every story he's heard about light wielders coming into contact with the beasts.

Each ghoul focuses its stare on Bri. Watching and waiting. "Bryony is mine," Aziel growls.

"Yes," she nods. "And you are all mine."

As one, they roar, cross their arms over their chests in an X, and kneel. Their heads bow. Their bodies so still you'd think they were no longer breathing. The muscles of their backs roll as they wait.

With a wave of Bri's hand, they stand in unison, the ground quaking beneath our feet with their heavy steps. Glowing eyes lock on her face, waiting for her instruction.

"They kneeled for you," Oscar breathes.

"Did you think she made that up?" Knox questions.

"Well... No... I—fuck! This is crazy."

Bri seems to ignore us, moving through the throng of ghouls, placing a kiss at the center of each chest. I'm not sure where the gesture came from or what it means. None of us knows what the crossed arms mean either, but right where their forearms meet matches the spot she kisses each one.

We watch in silence, not out of fear but awe. We are witnessing one of the most miraculous sights. Bri could teach us so much about the ghouls. Her deeper connection to them could save lives. Not only wielders but the ghouls themselves.

As the rogue ghouls continue to break into our world more frequently, they've seemed to rage more. The ghoul hunters, in turn, have developed stronger tranquilizers and death darts. Ones infused with none other than dark magic that brings instant death to the most unruly ghouls.

"Why are you here?" Bri asks, stopping in front of Aziel again.

But it is Warrick who responds, his words almost too clear to be true. "Here." He points to the center of his chest. "Inside here, Bryony called us to come."

"I'm sorry," she sighs. "Last night… there was a lot that happened. But I'm okay. I'm safe."

"Our Bryony not safe," Warrick roars, baring his teeth. The points seemingly extend the longer they're in view. Lengthening daggers ready to tear into supple flesh.

It's amazing that so many ghouls have spoken to Bri, even if the words are barely intelligible. It's so rare. This is a once-in-a-lifetime miracle. We may never witness something this earth-shattering again.

"Warrick, I am fine. I'm here at home. It's safe. Later, I will go back to school. It's safe there too."

"No!" Warrick roars.

"Stop!" Bri orders him, her tone unforgiving. It immediately kneels at her feet, the solid, hard cock that had been bobbing at its pelvis sinking back inside. "You will all return home. Thank you for coming, but I am safe. If I need you, I will call."

Once again, they kneel as one, their arms crossing their chests before they stand, turn, and race off into the trees. The ground shakes beneath us with the retreat, each thunderous step a reminder that Bri has an entire army of ghouls at her beck and call. There's nothing to worry about. We're all safe.

"Uh, so… does that happen often?" Oscar questions.

"Do you want to tell him or should I?" Vincent quirks a grin at his sister, dropping an arm across her shoulders.

"If you wanted to know who's responsible for all the rogue ghouls, their elevated magic levels, and that..." she points behind her. "Exhibit A: Bryony Guthrie, and her intense emotions."

"Come again?" Eilish quirks a brow.

"Pretty much if I'm in any sort of distress, no matter how minor, my magic calls out to them," Bri bares her teeth as if in apology.

"Bloody hell," Eilish breathes. "You're either going to save or destroy us all."

She has never been more right.

83

BRYONY

Professor Perrue is going to eat me alive if I keep her waiting. She's a brilliant woman. As patient as they come, but she does not tolerate tardiness.

It's not like I was even doing anything fun.

The more time I've spent at wielding school, the more the morning person I used to be fades away. Where I could start my days with a pep in my step, most days it's an endless struggle just to swing my legs over the edge of the bed. My body seems to ache, and that groggy fog refuses to leave until that first sip of liquid caffeine. Coffee, I didn't have time to chug this morning after Graham and I had been up half the night studying for our spellcasting exam.

Yet another practical I can't afford to lose focus on. My mind is operating under the fear of not exposing myself. It's essential that I know these spells inside and out. The pronunciation of the spoken spells must be perfect. The clarity of enunciation in my mind and on my lips crystal clear.

We'd practiced until I thought my head would explode. Until I was convinced, I was on the precipice of depletion. Yet, we never reached the bottom of the well. As my body has its own reservoir to pull from, within seconds, I'd be full again.

Graham had channeled from one of my vessels, so he wouldn't have to worry about wasting his own stores, which are more compatible with his power. His mending ability, which had come to light by accident in class, earned him an additional course. Headmaster Hawthorne refuses to allow him to let the gift remain unrefined.

Graham was bitter about the whole ordeal for days. Unwilling or wanting to expose his ability more than it had been. He hasn't used it since bringing Valen back.

My guy was shaken after he saved Valen's life. An inanimate object was one thing; a person was another. It was a talent he used to cure his boredom or fix little things that had broken. Not the bodies of wielders. We have discussed this topic several times, but the replies remain consistent. *"I just need time, Bryony."*

My breaths are ragged as I slip into Professor Purrue's office, her back to me while she replaces a book on the far shelf. The rich wood shines as if newly polished.

"Just on time." Her words are clipped, but there seems to be something else beneath them.

Humor maybe.

As always, I can't help but rake my gaze over the walls of her office. Where most professors have windows, she'd happily taken a space with none. Books cover every wall. Some for pleasure, others harboring every bit of information on our world. Behind her desk is a massive revolving shelf, locked by a spell only she can undo. Along the backside, which remains hidden behind the wall, are texts on forbidden topics of our world. It's how I've learned more about Grisyms and what it means to be an Eistiab. It hasn't helped me control the outbursts when they happen, but it feels good to have someone who allows me to understand what I am on my own terms.

I've spent hours locked in the tiny closet behind the wall just reading. Learning. Absorbing.

"I was up late studying." My words sound sheepish. The excuse, as stupid as it is, passes my lips, but I voice it anyhow. Perrue commends honesty, even when it's not what she wants to hear.

"Are you ready?" She purses her lips, leaning on the edge of her desk as I drop my bag in the leather armchair closest to me.

"I think so. We practiced so much, I think I could do every spell we've covered in death."

"Then you should have practiced a little longer." My eyes meet hers at her words. Humor flashes behind them before she gives a little one-shoulder shrug. "Even the dead can mess up a simple spell."

I can only chuckle. Despite her stern nature, humor dances inside her, too. Never taking things too seriously, but ensuring you understand the dire nature of the world we live in.

Those yellow eyes bore into mine, and I can only wonder what she sees in me. Her help has gone beyond what they ordered from her. Yet she, too, has become someone I can wholeheartedly trust.

Though maybe I shouldn't.

I shouldn't trust anyone. Not fully.

Anyone could betray me at any moment.

"We'll be doing manipulation of earth magic today. Have you ever handled it before?"

"I don't... I'm not sure," I admit. I may have Pierce's essence and that of the ghouls, but I've never channeled from the earth.

Her lips purse harder, the nude shade painted over them darkening. She stands, moving to a small chest on one of her shelves, pulling out an Emari Orb. It glows bright green. It reminds me of the leaves and grass in summer with its softer metallic shade, and tendrils moving beneath the surface. They seem to poke at the glass as if calling to me, the closer she gets.

"Can you control your essence if you take in new power yet?"

"Sometimes. It's unpredictable, but usually it's worse when it's light magic."

Professor Perrue only grunts, running her hand over the curve of the globe. The glass fades away, but the swirls stay put, rotating in her palm. "Do you trust me?"

"Yes." I stand a little straighter as she stops right in front of me.

"Here's what we are going to do. I will act as your anchor. You are going to take this earth magic. Do not hold back or resist it. Take it all. Let it become you. Simultaneously, I am going to anchor my essence to you. You do not need to focus on me. I can resist your essence taking mine. Focus all your energy on calmly absorbing this new power. Breathe it in and let it settle. I will stay anchored to you until we are sure your body will not react, and if it does, I will be here to help control it."

I nod, but sweat trickles down my spine. There's never been a reason to attempt something like this. Tosch and I discussed it, but she and my father agreed it wasn't a good idea to try, given the volatility of my magic.

"What if..." I can't voice the question. I know how hungry my power can be. Eager to consume everything in its path. To devour any magical gift within reach. Unwilling to be denied.

They are right to want someone like me dead. We are clueless regarding any absolute limits. Does there come a point when my essence decides it's consumed enough and refuses to take any more?

If so, when?

If not, what type of super-wielder will I become? Will I, too, end up in a place like Hendyre?

"Bryony, you need to focus. Are you ready?" I nod again. "I am going to anchor to you first. The moment you feel my essence touch yours, take it." She raises her hand, holding the Earth magic slightly. For the last time, I nod before we begin.

My heart races as I watch the tendrils of my professor's essence reach for me. It moves with a calm smoothness. I can feel it. No fear. No hesitation. It's not scared of being taken. It welcomes the challenge of rejecting me.

Her magic feels like the cool brush of river water over my skin, slithering over my open palm and curling around my wrist, its tail extended and still connected to Professor Perrue a foot away. A leash. A white waving leash. The anchor.

Come.

The earth magic rolls toward my other open palm like a boulder down a hill. Wild and untamed. Raw. So raw. So pure. So much more addictive than the ancient dark power of the ghouls.

I want it.

I need it.

Every bit of it is mine.

My eyes shift as I inhale every drop. This new power makes my insides sing. My light side fades, cowering behind the dark—the dominant side. That's clear now. Hard around the edges, smooth and shimmering with gold, the earth power infuses into my tissues.

"Calm, Bryony. Control it."

As if shaken back into myself, my bounding pulse slows.

You will comply. Settle. Heel.

It's a fight as I grit my teeth against the push and pull, forcing the new magic to comply.

Several long moments pass, but it finally blends into my essence, becoming part of me. New power never incorporates itself so fast. It remains separate, fighting for that spot on the throne until I either calm or my body rebels.

"I think... I think you can let go," I breathe.

Professor Perrue is slow to pull her rope of essence back; those yellow eyes never leave mine, even once we're no longer connected. "How do you feel?" she asks.

My eyes trace the floor, enjoying the new feel of my enhanced essence flowing through my body. I feel different, but not in a negative way. Not in a way that makes me believe I am going to lose control.

When my eyes finally meet hers again, my lips part while I still question what I'm going to say. Then, the corner of my mouth twitches. "Better than ever."

84

BRYONY

My session with Professor Perrue was the perfect start to my day. Her help left me in a state of steadfast positivity. I feel untouchable for once. Even when Carter found me and attempted to threaten me, I felt nothing but the bliss in my veins. All it took was a simple tug on the piece of him inside me, and his attitude changed. He became a pleasant fool, apologizing for bothering me, promising I wouldn't see him again for the day. Though we both know I'll be stuck with him in history this afternoon.

For once, I wasn't nervous about a practical. Without even thinking, my essence complied. There was no fight for control or compliance.

It's been interesting watching my classmates attempting to manipulate earth magic. My recent addition seems to giggle inside me, watching others struggle to force the most raw and oldest magic to do as they say.

"Be gentle with it," Professor Perrue guides us.

Graham expertly coaches the ball of magic to do his bidding. His focus is intense, his grin confident. "You might do better than me for once," I chuckle, nudging his shoulder.

He throws me a wry grin but says nothing as I allow the magic to roll over my fingers in a lazy pattern. His eyes narrow on my face, likely noticing I'm not even paying attention to it as I effortlessly play with the glowing green tendrils as if they were my own. "Did you?" He lowers his face close to mine. "Did you take some?" His chin cocks toward the tendrils dancing over my fingers.

"Yes, earlier."

He nods, but I see that flash of disappointment behind his eyes. I am only doing so well because my essence isn't working so hard to consume power I've already allowed in. In his mind, I've outmatched him, and he didn't even have a fighting chance to outperform me.

I'm looking for something to say. Anything to convince him his merits have nothing to do with mine, but this academic rivalry has always existed between us. I fear it always will.

I can only hope it doesn't tear us apart.

A classmate screams as their ball of magic clings to their face. The chatter and shouts in response masked the sound of the classroom door being thrown open, followed by the clomping footsteps of someone entering the room.

Booted feet march forward, the clicks of guns being cocked finally drawing Professor Perrue's attention from my classmate's mishap. "What's the meaning of this?"

A man hands Professor Perrue a sheet of parchment without a word while four others surround my desk, a fifth pointing a dart gun at me. The same type they use to put down rogue ghouls.

"Bri?" Graham questions, trying to peek through the bodies surrounding me.

"This is preposterous!" Professor Perrue shouts. "You have no..."

"We have every authority to be here and take Miss Avalon. Don't cause a scene, Rosaleen," Archibald Daniels, William's uncle and one of the council chairs, announces as he halts his steps right behind the soldier holding the gun pointed directly at my heart.

Without a word, I absorb the magic in my palm. Soon, everyone will know exactly what I am. What's the point in hiding it anymore?

We knew this time would come. We knew they would find me. Everyone warned me time and time again, but I stayed. I allowed myself to get comfortable and pretend that we could live this happy ending.

Standing from my seat, my fingertips press into the surface of the desk.

"Hands behind your back," one soldier orders.

Without a word, keeping my focus trained ahead, I ignore the whispers sounding around the room. I ignore Graham launching himself from his seat, and the soldier in his jet black tactical gear, now holding him back and away from me.

It's as if everything moves in slow motion.

The cold stone cuff materializes around my wrists, weighing down my arms. My shoulders pull uncomfortably at the sockets. I fight to call upon my essence. To demand that it soothe the ache, but it doesn't answer. I feel... empty.

It shouldn't surprise me that they put me in suppression cuffs. If they're here for me, they know exactly what I am. There's no question about it. They would want to be prepared, ensuring I was void of any means to fight back.

"Bryony Avalon," Archibald begins.

"If you are going to arrest me, Council Daniels, then please use my proper name." I keep my chin high, emotions hidden behind my eyes. I refuse to give them anything. They charged into my school and class, making a spectacle in front of everyone. So, I will make sure my account is accurately conveyed. I've let too many people tell my story for me in the past. No more.

"Fine. You want to do this here?" With that smug pout, Council Daniels tugs at the lapels of his suit jacket as if that will further remind us he's in power. He's the one in charge here. He has nothing to lose.

"Sir, with all due respect, you chose to arrest me publicly. You could have kept this quiet, but then who would be here to watch your show?" There's a taunt in my words. An intentional jab at his buttons for airing my secrets this way. "How would they know who saved our community if there was no audience?" I snort, my words remaining light, but draped in sarcasm.

"Watch your tone, girl," Archibald snaps. "Bryony Guthrie." Gasps sound around the room, the whisper growing louder with each passing second. "Are you aware of the reasons you are under arrest today?"

"I am."

Help me.

There's no answer. Not from my father or Knox or the ghouls. There's just... silence.

"And do you dispute the reasoning?"

"Archibald, enough!" Professor Perrue barks behind him. "Stop this. Now!"

"Rosaleen, I will arrest you, too, if you don't stop interfering. This... thing," he waves his hand in my direction, "is a threat to our laws, safety, and community. This is Council and Bureau business now, so unless you want to share a cell with your student... Be. Quiet."

"Council Daniels," I draw his attention back to me. This has gone on long enough. There's no need to involve everyone else further than we already have. "I have no dispute."

His eyes narrow as the dart-holding soldier moves slightly to the side, putting the councilman in full view, the man William impersonated to give my father the power to kill my kind. Rage soars through my insides. These people are all the same. Only the light should prevail, but not with me here. Not while I'm still alive. I've already dimmed the lights. They'd better hope I never master the dark.

"No dispute," he says the words slowly as if they hold a funky taste on his tongue.

"No. You clearly wanted everyone to know what a danger I am. So let them. I, Bryony Guthrie, am being arrested today because I am a Grisym." My chin lifts higher. There's nothing they can hold over me now.

Archibald sneers, his hands balling into fists at his side. "Take her away."

The soldier at my back tugs at my arm, my thigh painfully smacking into the edge of the desk as they force me out of the room.

This time I'm on my own. I can't call on my father. I can't summon my ghouls.

It's just me.

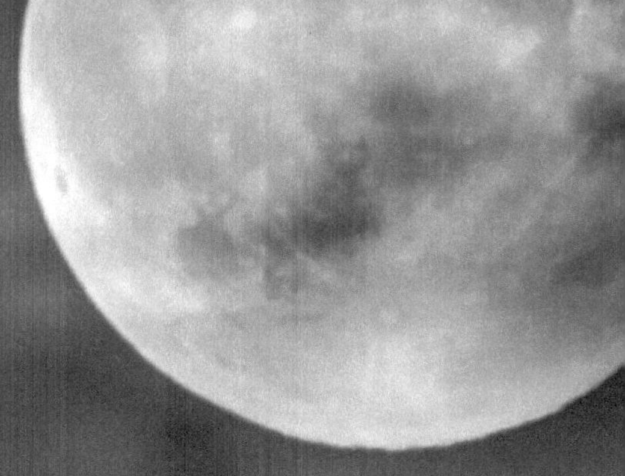

85

PIERSON

My heart races as we run through the hallways of Integretew. Graham pants heavily at my side, while Valen doesn't make a single sound.

This is everything we feared. Everything we worked so hard to prevent.

But there was no stopping it, was there?

Graham barged into my classroom in the middle of my presentation, my mouth open, ready to speak, when we locked eyes. Sweat dripped from his flushed face as he told me they'd arrested Bri. His gaping eyes were bloodshot, darting in varying directions like a scared, wounded animal. I've never seen him move so fast, bolting back through the door without even waiting to see if I would follow him. Not another word passed my lips, my belongings left behind, stumbling after him.

Together, we raced up a side stairwell in search of Valen. We didn't pause to take a breath or speak a word as we launched ourselves up those two flights of stairs. We'd found him slouched in his seat, twirling his dagger. Without speaking, he rose from his seat, slinging his bag over his shoulder and chasing us down the hall.

Our feet pound against the stone floors, our essences shoving our classmates out of our way before we push through the front doors.

I've been calling out to Jorddan this entire time. I can only hope he is listening to me and will feel the urgency, then notify Knox. That he'll understand the worst has happened by the sound of my internal pleas.

The Council or the Bureau—I'm not sure which—took his daughter. They marched in here and snatched her in plain sight. If we'd known, there would not have been a thing we could have done. If we had interfered, they would have led us out in cuffs, too.

"How are we going to get to the manor?" Graham pants, his hands falling to his knees as my gaze darts back and forth down the street.

"Fuck! I don't know. I called out to Jorddan, but—"

The funk of helplessness oozes out of our pores. My fingers sink into my hair and tug at the roots. I have no idea what to do. No idea how to fix this. How do I save her?

An SUV slows, stopping just in front of us. "Get in," Knox shouts.

The three of us immediately toss ourselves into the backseat, next to Grandma Avalon. Her chuckle is unexpected as Graham scrunches himself in, his ass landing in my lap.

"How did you know?" I wheeze. My lungs burn, and my head is pounding.

"I saw it," Grandma Avalon answers as Knox floors it through the streets of London.

I should have known. The woman sees any and everything. Both at will and involuntarily.

"So, what do we do?" Graham groans as his head hits the roof of the car for the umpteenth time.

Jorddan's eyes meet mine in the rearview mirror, his eyes haunted but filled with fury. "We're going back to the manor, and then to the Council Chamber." He pulls his focus back to the road ahead. "I heard you, Pierson. I'm proud."

His compliment settles in my chest, but now isn't the time for sentimental shit. "Is that where they'll take her?" I ask.

"It's the only place they have suppression cells that I know of. It's the only place they could keep her and not risk her being able to fight back."

"Fuck!" Valen barks. "I will kill every fucking one of them," he growls.

"I'll help," Graham adds.

We stay silent in the back seat for the remainder of the car ride. The three hours are filled with Knox and Jorddan hosting their own low-level conversation between themselves.

Entering the manor, our feet thunder like a herd of lumbering elephants. Jorddan's icy calm remains locked in place. There doesn't seem to be any urgency to retrieve his daughter as he moves through the foyer and slowly lowers himself into an armchair. Crossing his legs, his gaze drifts off into the distance. Each nonchalant movement causes my blood to boil.

Why isn't he moving faster? Why aren't we doing more?

If the Council has Bri, they will kill her. They know what she is. We've known that for so long, but we did nothing.

We. Did. Nothing.

"Why the fuck are we just standing here?" I shout. "You all preach about Bryony being so important to you, and we're all just standing here!" My temper flares, the darkest parts of my power rising to the surface. There's fresh earth magic in my veins. Here, I'm free to channel it whenever I want, as much as I want, so I've been taking advantage. With earth magic, I don't have to store it. I can hold it.

And now it bursts free, a violent wave as every emotion and every fear and my breaking heart crash through the barrier of my skin. Shards of glass fly, decor and windows shattering around us, while the very foundation rattles beneath our feet, but I don't stop. I can't. I've kept the real me trapped inside for so long, and now it can no longer be contained.

When my screams finally subside, I open my eyes, viewing the destruction I caused to the manor.

"Pierce, listen to me," Jorddan places a hand on my shoulder. "We all love her. We will get her back, but it does us no good to dash in unprepared. It could be a trap for all of us."

My chest heaves as my chin falls to it. My hands hang limp at my sides. Shame washing through me for not keeping my composure. For destroying my heart's home.

"I will say, though, son. It's about time you saw what you are capable of." My eyes meet Jorddan's, a grin pulling at the corners of his mouth, that goatee stretching wide. He's never smiled at me before. Not once.

"Jorddan, if I may," Graham interrupts the moment.

Jorddan only nods as Graham raises his hands, letting his essence fill the room. It seeps into every crevice. The dense cloud is stealing our vision as it drapes the entryway in a frosty haze. But it's clear what he's doing. The clinking of glass reassembling and wood splintering itself back together fills our ears.

Only a handful of minutes pass before the cloud clears, and the manor returns to the exact state it had been in before.

"I haven't used my mending since that night," Graham breathes. "But I couldn't let Bri come home to a ruined house."

"Let's all take a moment to compose ourselves. Janelle, Damian, and Camilla will be here shortly."

I'm surprised Sean will not be coming too, but it could just as easily mean Jorddan gave him a different job. Hopefully, assembling every follower we have to march on the Council offices. They can't keep her. They can't have Bri, not for their personal use or for her life.

I won't allow it.

The streets are quiet as we step through the portal in front of the Council headquarters. Though it seems abandoned for the night, I know better. Like any other wielder-commissioned business or official government building, protocol requires the exterior to be spelled. A safeguard for us, not merely just against the humans who might discover our activities, but our own kind, too.

Structures dedicated to official wielding policy and procedure host business day and night. We are a race that never sleeps.

Our crew huddles together: me, Jorddan, Valen, Graham, Damian, Tosch, Vincent, Knox, Headmistress Milgren, Grandma Avalon, and Camilla. Twenty of the New Order stand at our backs. Our tiny army ready to charge the Council chambers and take our girl back.

I suck in a deep breath, trying to settle myself before we walk in there. There's no time for a repeat of what I'd done at the manor. No time for me to make mistakes that could cost all of us our lives.

There's no telling what we'll find. Whether it be pseudo-kindness, gaslighting, or resistance, we need to keep our heads level.

Those of us who are extrinsic and charters powered up before we left. The antique vault supplied us with everything we needed to fight back.

We hope we won't need to. We hope it was nothing more than a precaution, but my gut tells me it was necessary.

"We're going to get her back," Graham clasps my shoulder.

"We have to. I can't live without her," I whisper into the night.

"None of us can," Valen adds, twirling a dagger. I've noticed I haven't seen him with his favorite in a while.

Nodding toward his hands, my eyes narrow on the two bronze metal trophies. "Where is the one your dad gave you?"

"Our girl has it, and I intend to show her how to use it." With that, Valen breaks formation and marches to the council doors. He blows them wide open, overriding the simple spell that had been there.

Too simple.

It shouldn't have been that easy.

But that doesn't stop us, our group marching forward through the main entryway and down the center toward the massive double doors that lead to the chamber. A room outfitted with tiered seats to host Council and Bureau meetings. The incline reminiscent of one of those medical theaters pictured in history books.

Jorddan swipes his hand, the door swinging open to reveal a full room. Every pair of eyes shifts toward us as we fill the entryway. "Where is my daughter?" Jorddan's voice booms.

Every step is calculated as he moves forward. Slow and methodical until he reaches the edge of the steeply inclined stairs.

Archibald Daniels stands in the center of the chamber, down on the main floor. So far below us, he almost appears to be a toy. Just a trinket I could flick into oblivion with my fingers.

Rows of seating stretch upwards from the chamber's center. A perfect sphere large enough to fit half a football field. There is one long table with enough seats for the council chairs. Each body fills a seat that matches the name on the placard in front of it.

Only there's an additional wielder standing with them. Carter James. No, not Carter. That had been a facade. This is William Danvers, and he's wearing his proper face.

It takes everything in me not to charge down the stairs.

He'd better pray none of us make it through this because I will force him to tear his own body apart while he screams for mercy.

"Jorddan, welcome," Archibald grins. "She's here. Alive," he sniffs. "If that's what you're worried about."

"Hi Jorddan. Mother." Roman suddenly appears in the crowd, his suit perfectly pressed, though it's the middle of the night. "My daughter claimed you, as did my wife, so here's the product of those consequences."

Jorddan begins to move down the steps. The four of us guys following close on his heels. He keeps his composure, not biting back at Roman's taunt. Roman knows that no matter how this ends, he has lost the most precious treasure here. The woman he called his daughter, and the one he could never make his wife, want nothing to do with him.

"As I just stated, I am only here for my daughter. Keep Geneva if you'd like." Jorddan's eye twitches with his words. He'd said them, but didn't mean them. Despite his rage, he would move heaven and earth for her return. He'd give everything to have his family back, whole and happy.

"She's right here," William grins wickedly. A soldier guarding a side door snaps his fingers, and Bri appears.

She jolts into the center of the room, her knees nearly buckling under her, teeth gritted as she barely maintains her balance. Her grimace is pronounced as she adjusts her arms, still cuffed behind her, with a suppression stone.

"Now that we're all here," Archibald announces. "This trial can begin."

86

BRYONY

RADIATING PAIN SEARS THROUGH my shoulders. These soldiers have been tugging me around by my cuffs and my upper arms with no regard. Cuffs that were specially made for someone as powerful as me.

They could have transported me where I needed to go. But it was Archibald fucking Daniels who insisted they take no chances with me. *"Keep that thing in line,"* he'd snarled as they hauled me out of the school and into a waiting armored truck, lined with the same suppression stone. From there, they took me to the International Wielding Administration building, where we all portaled here. Then Soldier Douche literally threw me into an empty cell, leaving me with nothing more than my thoughts and memories.

Why would they care?

To them, I am as good as dead. I am a problem that needs to be eradicated.

My life will change forever if I survive this. I outed myself in front of everyone. This time, Pierce wasn't there to erase their memories. No doubt the rumors have already stretched through half of the wielding world by now. By morning, every news outlet and social media platform will have its version of my story plastered everywhere for everyone to see.

My eyes rake over the individuals filling the seats, my glare locking with that of my mother, seated in the front row.

She tries hard to hide her tears, but they shine so bright behind her light eyes. Her mouthed, "I'm so sorry," only causes my lip to curl in disgust. She could have saved us from this. My mother has held so much power in the center of her palm for a lifetime, and she did nothing.

No matter what, she could have defended her child, but no, she chose the path of least resistance. I love my mother, but I don't want her apology. It means nothing. For once, I don't want a damn thing from her. Not her love, or her time, or her promises. She can disappear with all the others I've stopped giving a shit about.

Her negligence and avoidance are part of what led us to this point. She is as responsible as the assholes hosting this bogus show.

"Council members, tonight we are putting Bryony Guthrie on trial," Archibald announces, projecting his voice with an amplification spell. The tenor grates on my nerves, my teeth once again gritting against the pain slicing through my shoulders from my restraints.

A rush of murmurs fills the room. I'd wondered if Archibald had come in here making a scene and prancing around bragging that he'd caught the most prized Grisym the world has ever seen—Grandma Avalon's description, not mine.

A hand shoots high, a woman I don't recognize. "Excuse me, Council Daniels, but did you just say Guthrie? As in the Jorddan Guthrie standing over there?" She points at my father. Her arm quivering as if terrified he'll strike her down for so much as looking his way. Had this woman not been listening when my father marched in here demanding my release?

His eyes remain trained on me. He pays her no mind. Jorddan's presence has nothing to do with her. He isn't here for her or any of them. Just me. I pity the ones who stand in his way. He'll destroy them without a second thought. Those that survive will have firsthand proof that my father committed every cruelty they've ever blamed on him.

"Yes!" I answer, attempting to control some of the narrative. "My mother, Geneva Avalon or Guthrie, depending on which man she is siding with that day, is in love with my father, Jorddan Guthrie. I am their only child. A Grisym."

"But you..." she continues.

"That's not important!" Archibald snaps.

"Council Daniels," another member argues, "it is. How has this woman managed to stay hidden for twenty-five years? Roman, did you know?" He sucks in a sharp breath, his fingertips pressing to his chest as if in offense.

Roman stands tall, his mouth open, ready to reply. But once again, I blurt out my answer. "Yes. He's the one who has kept me hidden all these years. You might want to bring him down here and put him on trial, too. While we're at it, add William to the list. He's the one who made Roman the director of education."

"Enough!" Archibald bellows. "You will shut your mouth and stop telling these lies." His face turns beet red, veins popping along his narrow throat and temple.

"Give me a truth serum, or a spell. I assure you, everything I've said tonight is the truth." I'm hoping my taunt will be enough for them to think I'm not bluffing. Most of what I've said is true. Everything except being an only child. Vincent doesn't need to be involved in this.

But if I'm going down, I'm taking Roman with me. Everyone I love will be safer that way.

"I said enough. You are on trial. You don't speak unless I tell you to," Archibald sneers, once again straightening his lapels.

Winking, I toss my head to the side as if giving a salute. "Aye aye, Captain."

I realize I'm walking a fine line here, causing mischief. Poking the bear in all the wrong places. It's nothing more than an attention grab. An attempt at keeping the focus fixed on me, redirecting it from the standing group atop the stairs. My people. My heart.

They deserve safety and happy lives.

"Roman," another voice calls from the crowd. "Is this true? Did your wife cheat on you? Did you raise a dark wielder's Grisym child?"

Roman spins to face the room, his back pressed against the rail lining the front row of seats. "Esteemed members of this council, I did raise a Grisym. I did protect her. Believe me, I was unaware of what she was until she matured. I feared for my life and the safety of my children, so I kept quiet, shipping her off to school. It was then that I learned who her biological father is. We all know what Jorddan has done to light wielders over the years. How could I not protect my other three children, two of whom have their own?"

He's good. So good I almost believe him, but every word is a lie.

Roman suddenly begins coughing, choking, and pounding on his chest. His face turns blue, and others rush to help him until he passes out on the floor.

"That ought to keep him from telling more lies for a while," my grandmother quips, wiping her hands together loudly. "Such a disappointment."

"No more outbursts!" Archibald shouts. "This thing beside me is an abomination, a violation of our laws. With her abilities, she is a danger to our society and every wielder in existence."

"What abilities?" a voice calls.

Taking two shuffling steps forward, I lift my chin in the direction the voice came from. "I'm an Eistiab. I can also command ghouls. That about covers the high points," I snort, attempting to readjust my arms once more.

"You've heard it, everyone," Council Etherman adds. "She's bragging about controlling those beasts."

"If she's an Eistiab, she's rare," a member hesitantly says. "There hasn't been one in centuries." Skepticism coats her words. My pulse ratcheting higher, praying they won't ask for a demonstration.

"She's a Grisym," Archibald snarls. "This thing shouldn't have made it past birth."

"Call my daughter a thing one more time, and this meeting will no longer be civil, Archibald. As you know, you have your own secrets that could destroy you. Please do not make me use them. Continue your sham of a trial, then I'll be taking my daughter home." My gaze bores into my father's, wishing he would take just one moment to look at me. But he remains focused, fury blazing in his steely eyes.

Council Daniel scoffs once again, pulling at his suit lapels. "You will not. Take a good look, Jorddan. This is the last time you will ever see her."

Something flashes behind my father's eyes. "Dad, please don't. Please…" I beg.

The Council chairs only laugh at my plea. I've revealed a weakness. Something they can exploit. Gone is the sarcastic swagger I'd just met them with. I can't let anything happen to the people I love.

My gaze sweeps over those present within the chamber once more, lingering when meeting those of my men, brother, and grandmother. I hope they all know I love them.

This is for you. I'm sorry.

"This has to stop," I all but whisper. The words are scratchy in my throat. Terror wrapping itself around my heart. Many claim they aren't of mortality in the face of inevitability, but I am. I've always been terrified to pass from this life to the next. We understood beforehand that being a Grisym guaranteed execution. *I'm not ready. I'm scared.* My nose burns as I cock my chin a fraction higher. "You wanted to present me as a dangerous Grisym. You did that. Just give me my sentence and get this over with."

Archibald smiles, wicked and full of mirth, as if he's thrilled I gave in so easily. With a wave of his hand, two soldiers come forward, each one placing a hand on my shoulders, forcing me to my knees. They hit the hard ground with a crack. The pain explodes through my kneecaps and up my thighs to the base of my spine. Every nerve ending firing, shooting out through my limbs, my whimper breaking free despite fighting to hold it in.

My eyes press shut. *Breathe, Bri. Breathe through it.*

I refuse to shed a tear. I refuse to make another sound. Not for these bastards.

"Do you dispute any of the charges against you, Bryony Guthrie?" Archibald's voice reverberates off the walls, my head slowly lifting to meet his unforgiving stare.

"No."

"Do you yield to this Council's decision, whatever it may be?" he continues.

"Yes, but under one condition."

"You're not in a position to make demands."

"One condition," I repeat.

"Speak it," Council Etherman agrees.

"Everyone on those steps walks free. They are never punished for having any association with me." It's the last thing I can do for them. This is the last bit of peace I may ever give them. The only way my death can protect them.

"And you will yield?" Archibald questions.

"Yes."

"Then let that stand on the record. Bryony Guthrie, the sentence for being found to have mixed blood is death. However, as a council, we will give you a choice, as you are a rare breed."

My chin lifts, eyes finding Archibald's once more. That wolfish, cocky grin still stretches across his face. He has solidified his victory. He won.

"A choice?" I whisper.

"You can work for the Council, operating as we order you to, or die. What will it be?"

The room goes deathly silent. Every pair of eyes is on me. The ones from the people I love standing on those stairs are the ones I avoid. I can't bear to witness their expressions when I answer.

I accepted my fate a long time ago. Before this semester. Before Beauxgraton and my early maturity. I think I knew from the day I understood what I was that termination was always my end of the line.

I will never have a long, prosperous life. There will be no graduation, career, or children. My life will end because of fear and hatred.

My nose burns with unshed tears as I settle on my mother's face. Tears stream down her cheeks. Tears I've never seen her shed until last semester at Beauxgraton. I wish she had been better to me. I wish she had prioritized Vincent and me the same as Harley, Merrick, and Sicily instead of taking the path of least resistance.

I wish I'd had more time with my guys. I wish I'd told them all how much they mean to me, how they saved me.

I wish I could hug my friends one more time.

"Choose, Bryony."

With a slow, inhaled breath, I keep my eyes trained on my mother's face. "Death."

THANK YOU FOR
READING!
YOUR NEXT READ IS
JUST A PAGE AWAY…

Also by Britton Brinkley

<u>Misfits Trilogy (with L.A. Scott)</u>
Misunderstood
Misfortune
Accepted

<u>Night Life Duology</u>
Night Life
Night Life 2: Will to Fight

<u>The Company Series</u>
The Tournament
The Target (COMING 1-19-26)

<u>Disavowed Birthright Trilogy</u>
Rise of the Grisym
Dimmer of the Light

Master of the Dark (COMING 2026)

<u>Fall of the Phoenix Trilogy</u>
Feathers of Truth
Feathers of Destruction
Feathers of Change (COMING 12-19-25)

<u>Scarlet Hearts</u>
Scarlet Hearts
Broken Promises (COMING 2026)

<u>Boulder Ranch</u>
Ride Me
Buck Me (by Ashley Willow)
Want Me (COMING 11-15-25)
Love Me (by Ashley Willow – COMING 11-15-25)
Save Me (COMING 4-20-26)
Hunt Me (by Ashley Willow – COMING 4-20-26)

<u>Dagger & Sword</u>
The Shadows That Shackle (COMING 10-25-25)

<u>Baudelaire Blood</u>
Venetia (COMING 10-13-25)

<u>The Loyals</u>
The Loyals (COMING 11-1-25)

About the Author

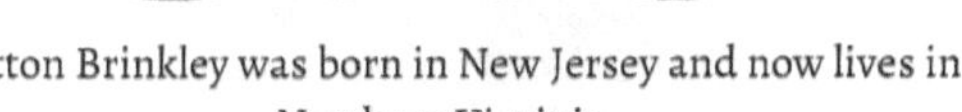

Britton Brinkley was born in New Jersey and now lives in Northern Virginia.

Growing up an avid reader, the sciences and ancient civilizations mesmerized her. She has always loved immersing herself in new worlds. Britton now enjoys creating her own with her writing buddies Jay Gatsby and the little psycho Artemis Prime (the cats).

When she isn't writing, she's likely either reading, watching Criminal Minds, or some other true crime show on Investigation Discovery.

Learn More at BrittonBrinkley.com